'50
Aug
10-19

Peacock Alley

Dorothy Horn

譚娟
娟印

Peacock Alley

A novel *by*
Dorothy Hom

ABOOKS
Alive Book Publishing

This is a work of fiction. Names, characters, places and incidents either are
products of the author's imagination or are used fictitiously. While the broader
setting is based upon documented accounts of the times, any resemblence to
actual events, locales or persons, living or dead, is entirely coincidental.

Additional copies may be ordered from the publisher for
educational, business, promotional or premium use.
For information, contact ALIVE Book Publishing at:
alivebookpublishing.com, or call (925) 837-7303.

Book Design by Eli Sedaghatinia

ISBN 13
978-1-63132-001-9

ISBN 10
1631320017

Library of Congress Control Number: 2014900184

Library of Congress Cataloging-in-Publication Data
is available upon request.

First Edition

Published in the United States of America by ALIVE Book Publishing
and ALIVE Publishing Group, imprints of Advanced Publishing LLC
3200 A Danville Blvd., Suite 204, Alamo, California 94507
alivebookpublishing.com

PRINTED IN THE UNITED STATES OF AMERICA

10 9 8 7 6 5 4 3 2 1

dedicated

To all the grandmothers
of the world

Foreword

This book was fifty years in the making. Over this extremely long stretch of time many people have had a hand in shaping it; starting with my creative writing mentor, Ms. Maren Elwood, whose book, Characters Make Your Story, is still available some sixty-five years after its first printing. The many others who contributed their time and energy to get this work finally published are far too numerous to mention by name; however, to all of you I offer my sincere thanks. May Kwan Yin shower her blessings upon you and may Kwan Koong watch over you.

Cast of characters

Aileen: Eldest Daughter's first child; Liah's first grandchild

Joe Banyon: Reporter for the Los Angeles Daily News

Brad Barkley: Sallie's boyfriend; Elton Barkley's son

Elton Barkley: Los Angeles district attorney

Hoh Chan: Liah's gardener

Sallie Chang: Switchboard operator used by Lee Tzo to tip off the police

Charlie: The Dragon's Den bartender

Chelo: Bartender at Selah's

Cook: Tam Loong, becomes like a father to Liah's children and a spouse to her

Ted Crosset: Children's schoolteacher on the Dobney estates

Edward Dobney: Owner of the Dobney estates

Lucille Dobney: Edward Dobney's wife who gave the peacock and peahen to Liah

Soong Hee: Family friend who helps family on their trip from Dai Faw to Loo Sahng

Elder Hua: Elder of the Four Families Association

Elder Lee Ti: Elder of the House of Lee in Dai Faw

Elder Lee Ting: Elder of the House of Lee in Dai Faw

Elder Lew Yet Hai: Elder of the Six Companies Association

Emmi: Sui Sin, Second Daughter, Liah's seventh and last child

Fatt On: Close family friend

Sen Fei: Elderly homeless actress and friend of Liah

Florence: Lan Gil, Eldest Daughter, Liah's third child and Aileen's mother

Kam Fong: Council member

Lee Gan: Sen's brother

Hubert: Emmi's boyfriend and eventual husband

Jui Jinn: Veteran of WWI and owner of a café in Chinatown and Council Member

Lalo: Bartender at Selah's

Lim Tao: Chinese banker and Member of the Council

Lin Fah: Liah's name before it is changed via a typographical error by immigration officials in Dai Faw

Little John: L.A. police officer and The Cat's partner

Mahtineh/Martinez: Farmer and friend of Sen

Mark Marchesson: Owner of Chinatown real estate including most of Peacock Alley

Mei Gem: The wife William brings home from Hong Kong

Mei-Tai: Tzo's concubine replacing Mei-Mei

Mert: Ming Chu, Fifth Son, Liah's sixth child

Professor: Chang On Wei, Liah's closest ally in the formation of the Council and a good friend

Cousin Quock: Sen's cousin and a fisherman in Northern California

Madam Quock: Liah's friend from Dai Faw, mother of Yook Lan

Renee: Chef who works for Selah

Wong Sang: Member of the Council and co-owner of gambling house with Liah

Selah: Chinese and Mexican American brothel owner and Liah's best friend

Cousin Shah: Sen's cousin who lives in Loo Sahng near rail yards and an early member of the Council

Shelley: Sui Loon, Second Son, Liah's second child

Tom Soo: Junior Council member who becomes a lawyer

Stuckey: Bert Stuhson, convicted with Trouble of Sam Yin's murder

Dr. Sung: Shares an office with Tom, treats patients in Chinatown

The Cat: An L.A. police detective who knew Liah in Dai Faw

Theo: Sam Gem, Third Son, Liah's fourth child

Thomas: Gan Hing, First Son, Liah's first child

Mah Ting: Family friend who they stay with on trip to Loo Sahng

Toh: Eldest Daughter's husband and Aileen's adoring father

Trouble: James McKinnon, convicted of Sam Yin's murder with Stuckey

Lee Sen: Liah's husband

Lee Tzu Tzo: Brothel owner, Council member always at odds with Liah

Cousin Shan Suey Wah: Worked aboard ships that cruised the Orient; supplied Liah with Apinyin

Lee Wah: Importer and Council Member

William: Wai Ng, Fourth Son, Liah's fifth child

Chon Woo: Owner of Dragon's Den Bar and Council Member

Wong Foon: Proprietor of Wong's Café

Sam Yin: Man murdered in Chinatown whose killers Tom Soo aides in prosecuting

Sui Yin: Sam Yin's widow

Yook Lan: Madam Quock's daughter, an aspiring opera singer as a teen

Prologue

NIGHT OF TERROR

In 1904, employment in Californ (California), especially in the cities of Loo Sahng (Los Angeles) and Dai Faw (San Francisco), was scarce. Hunger gnawed and desperation for a place to sleep spared none of the common folk.

The rail workers who had swamped California during the building of the railways were used to fat paychecks. Now they found themselves destitute.

Those immigrant Chinese coolies who had worked on the railroad migrated early on to menial jobs in shoe and cigar factories, and many went to work on farms. A good many who did not want to leave their city homes did "dirty work"– mopping floors and cleaning toilets and outhouses. A few of the more prosperous Chinese managed to open laundries and bathhouses.

To make ends meet, many Chinese lived fifteen to twenty people in a room. Some labored by day and others by night and shared their beds in shifts. They were all determined to ride out the bad times, managing to save a few dollars each month to bring their families to Gem Sahn (America, or "the Golden Mountain"). Many of the men brought their sons or nephews to the new land so they could labor side by side or help with the family business, adding their monies to the family till. A few farsighted Chinese sent their sons to the schools of the Fahn Gwai (white man or "White Devil") in hopes that the next generation of Chinese might cope better with life on the White Devil's level.

As the economic crush became worse, the idle White Devils began to notice the industrious yellow men ("Chinks") seemingly doing well. In reaction they took up the cudgel against the Chinks for usurping their jobs. Fueled by the whites' uneducated frustration, hatred grew by the day, and soon a cry went out to exterminate the Chinese. The White Devils had found their scapegoat!

Mob violence grew with each jobless day, and anger grew to senseless proportions with the burning, shooting, looting, and killing of Chinese wherever and whenever they were encountered. So common was the murder of Chinese that there arose a phrase among the whites: "A Chinaman's life is beneath that of his mule."

A politician running for office seized upon the widespread hatred of the Chinese, building his platform on the cause of the white working man and attacking the "unfair" labor practices of businesses that hired Chinese who were willing to work for lower pay. Thus was planted the unfounded belief that Chinese undercut the white man's chances of fair wages, thereby robbing him of jobs that would give him the means to retain his dignity and self-respect.

The white businesses for which the Chinese worked fought back, saying the men of their own race refused to do the work the Chinese were doing. They claimed the politician was using the emotional unrest of the white populace to get himself elected. But it was too late; many came to believe that the Chinks were to blame for the Depression.

Thus, in the wee hours before dawn on June 1, 1904, a group of masked white men stealthily crept up the slopes to the terraced farms in an area called the Peninsula on the outskirts of Dai Faw.

They stopped at the top, looked around and, seeing the area deserted, raced into the group of buildings housing Chinese farm workers. Those carrying clubs shattered windows: others threw in blazing torches made of rags soaked in oil. Once the tinder-dry buildings were burning furiously, the men darted back down the slopes, jumped onto their waiting horses, and fled into the darkness.

It was during this turbulent time in history that we begin our story.

1904

YEAR OF THE DRAGON

On June 6 in the Fahn Gwai's year of 1904, five days after the senseless raids upon the Chinese farmers high in the terraced lands of San Francisco, the frightened and bewildered tenants crept back at dawn to survey the damage, some to retrieve anything not consumed by the fires set by the Fahn Gwai devils. One tiny, wizened man furtively looked about him for several moments, then raced to the base of a pine tree and hastily dug up a tin of hoarded money. Without a backward glance, he then disappeared down a back road.

Lee Sen sat atop his wagon, gazing brokenheartedly at the still-smoldering vegetables. His glance came to rest on his prized strawberry patch. His strawberries, four inches in diameter, were so succulent and sweet, the Fahn Gwai hotels paid him premium prices for them. It was his strawberry patch that had kept Sen from believing he was a total failure in Gem Sahn.

He stared at the charred skeleton of what had been a three-room house and was gripped with terror at the knowledge that he, his wife and their seven children had almost perished in the flames. Only the cellar bedroom, with its crudely shored-up tunnel, had allowed them to escape to an unused firebreak overgrown with shrubs. They had huddled in the underbrush, then made their way up higher to a deserted dirt back road. Hours later, they arrived at the Lee Family Association House. Once again Sen gratefully thanked his predecessors for their farsightedness in building cellar rooms and escape passageways. Those wretched immigrants had learned the hard way how the Fahn

Gwai mobs set fire to their houses to drive them outside, where they waited to shoot them down in cold blood.

A cold anger drove out his fear, and Sen shook his head. Why, throughout his sojourn in Gem Sahn, did the Fahn Gwai so persecute him and his people? Surely it was untrue that Chinese immigrants stole jobs from them. Why couldn't the Fahn Gwai work in the cigar factories or the shoe factories, and if no jobs were available, why couldn't they do the dirty work of slopping out the garbage cans or cleaning the toilets? Silently he cursed the white man.

It was decided by the elders of the Tong, the House of Lee, to send Sen and his family to Loo Sahng the City of Angels, Los Angeles. There Sen would look for his cousin Shah, who lived somewhere near the train yards of the Southern Pacific and Union Pacific railroads. Perhaps if Sen was lucky his cousin could secure him a job washing the locomotives. However, Sen hoped that perhaps his cousin Shah could find him a farm to work on, for he was a farmer and knew no other trade.

Uncertainty plagued Sen despite his agreement to leave Dai Faw. As the horses pulling his wagon moved forward, he felt the sweat on his palms dampening the reins as he gripped them for tangible support. Out of habit he reached into his vest pocket, touching a gold pocket watch, round and smooth, a gift from his mother and relatives when he had left his home in the small village in China to travel to Hong Kong, where he boarded the clipper for Gem Sahn. He fingered the shiny smoothness much like a man might finger a pebble.

The gold watch awakened memories of his mother as he drew it from his pocket, transporting Sen back to his village in Kwangtung and to the night before he departed for Hong Kong. As he remembered the painful farewells, his mother's pathetic face flashed before him, and Sen could hear the echoes of her plaint.

"My son, the Gods have no pity to wrest you from me like this! Yet I know my tears are futile. We mortals toil and fight to change the course of our life's waters but fight in vain. Our lot in life (*Meng-Sui*) is irrevocably written on heavenly tablets. Neither your lot nor those of your ancestors (*Feng-Sui*) can be altered one degree!"

Sen winced; he felt again her farewell embrace and heard his own sobs as he pleaded with his mother to cancel his voyage. Abruptly his mother pushed him away.

Her voice trembled bravely: "Don't squander your strength or your tears, son. The waters of life flow through time, carrying you where they will. If your Meng-Sui is good, you'll live in felicity's garden; if not, be prepared to fight the icy waters that threaten to extinguish your life's fire. Expect to be carried by life's currents, thrust upon unknown shores to live out your days until the waters again carry you to your destined Feng-Sui and your final rest and peace. For as long as the winds blow and the rains fall upon the earth and upon men, both good and the evil will descend from the heavens."

With a sob she stepped back to wave Sen off. "My son, you can only fight to survive, and when your span of life is done, know that you are then closer to your eternal life, free from strife. It is not known how you will fare in Gem Sahn, but however the life, it is already written. Now go, before my tears rise to drown us both. May Kwan Yin bestow her mercy on you and Kwan Koong (*the Warrior God*) provide you strength."

Sen's hands were trembling, his breath rapid, as he clutched the watch tightly. The memories awakened a deep yearning. His mother's words, handed down from her mother and her mother's mother through generations of matriarchs, rang hollow in his ear. He sighed; the farewells were so long ago yet still so vivid.

A sudden thought hit him as he replaced the watch in his pocket. He was now thirty-nine years old! He shook his head; no closer to his dreams of wealth, which his older brother, Gan, had promised! In fact, his older brother was no longer alive. Even now it was hard for Sen to acknowledge his brother's murder. Tears of hatred threatened to flood his eyes, for the white hoodlum murderers had been set free by the judge, who had solemnly declared that the men had held no forethought of malice and had merely intended to harass Gan! How cheaply the Fahn Gwai held a life, at least the life of a Chinaman! Sen shook his head again. Where had the time gone? Gan's murder had happened fifteen years earlier.

Memories, which Sen had kept locked in for the past fifteen years, tumbled forth. It was a bright June day in 1884, a day much like this one, when Sen had first set foot on Fahn Gwai soil and suffered a traumatic reunion with Gan. His brother had been angered by Sen's remark about how much Gan had aged. Although only twenty-four, four years older than Sen, Gan appeared forty. Now Sen knew why. He wiped his eyes as if to brush away his brother's image.

A soft cough jolted Sen from his reveries. He glanced quickly at his wife, Liah, then turned his head. She should not see his pain. Poor woman, if life for him were hard, how much more so for Liah, who had given birth seven times!

Sen recalled Liah's porcelain skin as he had first seen her as she came through the gates of the immigration detention center. He winced seeing her skin, now sunburned; Liah no longer possessed her youthful beauty. His anger swelled—anger at himself and at the Gods for forcing his wife to endure such rigors and privations. And if all that were not bad enough, now they faced a journey filled with unknowns.

Sen almost wished he could return to the elders. It was not yet too late to ask that they find another farm, that the family be allowed to remain in Dai Faw. But even as his fears cried out for them to remain, an inner voice cried, no, go to Loo Sahng!

And wouldn't that be better? In the fourteen years he'd farmed on the Peninsula, he'd been evicted five times. This last raid on his farm almost cost his family their lives. How many more times must he place his family in jeopardy? He moaned softly and reached into his vest pocket and withdrew a crumpled piece of paper, a map drawn by his cousin Qui, who had made several trips to Loo Sahng. The lines made no sense to Sen; they looked rather like chicken scratches. Sen shoved the paper back into his vest pocket, stopped the wagon, and turned to his wife.

"My mind is clouded, Liah. We are embarking on a journey without knowledge of where we are going, with only the directions of Cousin Qui, who is not certain of his map. What if misfortune befalls us? There would be no one to help us. Even if a Fahn Gwai were willing to help, I could not understand his words. You must decide for us. Do we go or do we stay? Another thing I must tell you: there is no certainty we will be able to find my cousin Shah once we reach Loo Sahng."

Liah caught her breath and quickly lowered her head. Never before had she been asked for her opinion, let alone on such a weighty decision. She clutched her tiny infant girl tightly to her breast. The sheer terror of their escape from the deadly flames prompted her to reply softly, "I do not know what Loo Sahng holds for us, my husband, but I know I cannot face another time like this last raid. Surely the ill winds that brought us to this day are a sign for a change. But only you can say whether we go or stay. You must choose for us."

Liah's blind faith in him only made Sen feel a deeper guilt, as if their current plight were his fault. Yet he had toiled long and hard to take care of this family. Fighting the impulse to blurt out a decision to stay, Sen turned to stare at his first born, a son, birthed on the tenth day of June, 1893. It seemed impossible, but Eldest Son, Gan Hing, was almost twelve. Born only two years after Liah's arrival from Kwangtung, Gan Hing was stocky with a dark complexion like his father's, but the boy's obdurate spirit and fearlessness were unlike Sen. With such a will, his eldest child would fare better than he had.

Number Two son, Sui Loon squatted beside his older brother. Catching his father's eye, the eleven-year-old son smiled shyly at his father, then lowered his eyes. Like his mother, Sui Loon had a smoother, lighter complexion. Although he was small-boned, the boy was tall for his age, almost as tall as his older brother.

Number Three Child, a daughter, Lan Gil, sitting in the wagon and tiring of the wait, squirmed and pushed against her older brother Gan. He scowled and shoved her back. A glare from Sen abruptly ended the scuffle. Eldest Daughter, thought Sen, was headstrong and brash; no man would ever desire her for a wife. He would have to speak to Liah about curbing her spirit.

Like all Chinese parents, Sen and Liah seldom called their children by their names. The children were called by number according to the order of their birth. Lan Gil, the first girl, born on the twelfth of July in the Fahn Gwai's year of 1895, was called Eldest Daughter. If Sen's memory served him well, both Sui Loon and Lan Gil were born on their second farm on the San Francisco Peninsula. It wasn't long after Lan Gil's birth that the Fahn Gwai ran them off that farm.

Once opened, the floodgates damming Sen's memories swung wide. His fourth child, a son, San Gem, was born on the eleventh day of January in 1897, followed two years later on the twelfth of May, 1899, by his fifth child, also a son, whom he named Wai Ng after his favorite cousin. His sixth child, another son, this one named Ming Chu, was birthed in the fruit orchards of Selma in the Fahn Gwai year of 1900 on the twentieth day of January.

They had hardly lived there a year before Fahn Gwai pressures caused Sen to move again. Although this move was not caused by raids or fire, Sen had sensed the ill will, through the snickering and name calling whenever he went to town for supplies. Rather than wait to be chased from his home again, Sen asked the elders at the House of Lee to locate another farm for him.

When his family had settled onto the tiny farm on the terraced lands of Dai Faw, Sen had believed his dream was at last coming true. The first year he dared not hope that here they had found a permanent home. After the second year had passed, Sen allowed himself to make plans for their future. Because of the premium prices he received for his strawberries, they now had a bit of money saved. At the beginning of their fourth year, in 1904, his seventh child was born. This daughter, Sui Sin, was only four months old when again the Fahn Gwai struck again.

Suddenly he realized that each time he had become a father, disaster had struck. Quickly, he discarded the thought. The Gods couldn't be that heartless!

To push the idea from his mind, Sen thought of his anger on the night of the last raid and how he wanted to stand and fight the Fahn Gwai, despite the possibility that he might lose his life. He was sick to death of running!

It was his wife who had begged him to leave. Did he want her left alone with seven fatherless children? Think of them! Nevertheless, Sen relived that one short moment, gloriously free from fear of harm or death, when he wanted to challenge the enemy. His shoulders slumped as he recalled that fleeting moment.

His eyes caught sight of the huge boxes of foodstuffs that his friend Fatt On had pressed upon him. His eyes misted at the thought of that generous and compassionate man. Would he ever be able to repay him for his constant assistance? In spite of his sorrow, Sen smiled as he recalled when he and Fatt On had traded store for farm. Fatt On, who was no farmer, was happy to trade his farm for the store that had belonged to Sen's dead brother.

Sen's thoughts wandered from Fatt On to the House of Lee and Elder Lee Ti, and to the House of Wong and Elder Wong Ting. Without the two elders, Sen would have perished long ago. Whatever was he going to do without his three friends?

At last, with the resignation born of the realization of their desperate circumstances, Sen turned forward and shouted, "All right, we will go to Loo Sahng! We can't be any worse off than if we stayed." As a fatherly afterthought, he added, "Does anyone have to go to the toilet? If so, you'd better go now!"

Sen's command to the children jolted Liah from her lethargy. "Children, put on your shoes before you go! Take them off before climbing onto the *minhois*. I don't want them soiled. These quilts will have to serve as bedding until we get to Loo Sahng."

Sen spied a slack rope securing a water keg and jumped off to retie it. At the same time, he tightened the ropes holding down the wagon bed's canvas cover. He jiggled the heavy poles lashed to the side of the wagon to ensure they were secure. In case of severe wind or rain, wooden boards could enclose the sides of the wagon.

They had six kegs of water and four boxes of food to last them until they reached their destination. Sen sighed. He had filled the water kegs even though Cousin Qui had guaranteed that there was a wide river flowing by the towns of *Flesinoh* (Fresno) and *Bakafeh* (Bakersfield) where he could refill the kegs. Sen was still doubtful; he was expecting the worst.

Sen quickly filled a bucket from a water trough and offered it to the horses. He grinned foolishly at his wife and said, "Just in case they're thirsty." He then refilled the bucket and placed it carefully into the bed of the wagon. "I'll use this to water my strawberry plants."

Liah complained that the bucket might spill and spoil her minhois. Her husband's retort that they could always buy new ones was of little comfort. These minhois were special. She had brought them from home. She wondered, was there ever again going to be a place they could call "home," a permanent place for the next generation to put down roots? Liah recalled that first time she had cried for Sen to go to the authorities for restitution, but he had sneered, "Justice for me, against the Fahn Gwai? Woman, stop your dreaming!"

Liah, being the obedient wife, remained silent, but she was vexed by her husband's temerity. Yet she knew he was right. If she'd heard a few tales from Sen, she'd heard a thousand from fellow countrymen, tales of unfair taxation of her people in the mining camps, of the Fahn Gwai's attempts to prohibit them from using long bamboo poles with baskets on each end to carry their wares, even of legislation forcing them to cut off their queues! The last outrage left Liah in a cold sweat each time she recalled it. Didn't the barbarians know that to cut off their queues meant that they would be exiled from their homeland?

Liah squirmed on the wooden wagon seat. She tried to ignore a small voice at the back of her mind prodding her to remember there were also good Fahn Gwai. Like the woman who had given her blankets and food when they were ousted from their first farm. And how about the kind woman who had given her children books, pencils and paper each time she came to buy produce at the woman's roadside stand? Didn't she teach Eldest Daughter the alphabet? And what about the Fahn Gwai on their third farm who braved death by coming in the middle of the night to warn them of the impending morning raid? She shook her head thinking less than a handful of good Fahn Gwai in the face of thousands. The wagon started off. As it rumbled down the dirt road, Liah pursed her lips as the small voice reminded her of the Fahn Gwai who was so good that the emperor had bestowed a position of trust on him. Yet even this esteemed Fahn Gwai could not secure a lasting document of peace with the Fahn Gwai government. Wasn't it so that the Fahn Gwai had broken their promises and usurped China's territories?

If Liah had attended Fahn Gwai school, she would have known that the Fahn Gwai's name was Anson Burlingame, U.S. minister to China's Qing Empire during the Lincoln administration. When his tour of duty ended, the emperor had asked Burlingame to represent his kingdom in affairs of government with the outside world.

The bouncing of the wagon brought Liah out of her musing. For now, she sought a more comfortable position on the hard seat, dreading the long journey to Loo Sahng.

The journey dragged on for almost four weeks. The family traveled during the coolest and safer hours of night and rested during the day. Sen cursed their snail's pace, but he knew the horses could not sustain a faster pace over the great distance with their heavy load. Oftentimes, Sen was irritated by the children' demands to stop along the roadway. Liah, fatigued and frightened, sat silently during her husband's tirades. She prayed for endurance and murmured several times half-aloud to Kwan Yin, the Goddess of Mercy, to sustain her.

Each time they stopped for water or supplies, Sen would venture out alone. He turned a deaf ear to his wife's pleas that he take Eldest Son in case there was trouble. Sen retorted, "If there is difficulty, I don't want to be hindered by a child!"

Years later Liah would grin at the memories of this journey to Loo Sahng, their blind man's tour. They met their own countrymen only three times along their entire journey. The first encounter was in the small hamlet of *Dahleno* (Delano). Woo Sang, an aged solitary man, had welcomed them, telling them that he was a miner.

"Alas," the old man moaned, "There was a time when the diggings were good. Not as good as when the Fahn Gwai dug here, but I made money."

When asked why he was yet here, the old man laughed. "I was a fool! I went to Dai Faw to celebrate and nearly lost all my money on *paikil* (dominoes). I lost almost a thousand dollars, fool that I was! When I looked at my remaining two hundred-odd dollars, I ran out of the place! I wanted to kill myself for being so foolish! I didn't though," smiled the old man wistfully. "I thought of my wife and the hardships of her village and on the next day I sent her a hundred dollars. I returned here with the rest of my money and opened up a grocery store."

The man invited them to stay at his house. Liah cooked supper and the old man grinned as he smelled the salt fish steaming in the hot rice. After supper, Liah and the children bedded down in the front of the man's home while Sen and Woo Sang sat on the front stoop and chatted. The old man leaned against the back of his cane chair and pulled contently on his water pipe.

"Not all of my life has been a failure," he murmured while he relit the pipe. "I did manage to bring my nephew to Gem Sahn. He took himself a half-breed woman and now runs my store. Every week he stops in to see to my needs. I'm not really alone," he nodded. "At the moment there are three other elders here, all waiting to pass on. We play dominoes and checkers and share our meals and, once in a while, we get drunk."

Sen related his own miseries, particularly that of their long journey to Loo Sahng and of their need to find his cousin Shah.

Much later, feeling relaxed from his conversation with the old man, Sen untethered his horses and led them to the water trough. Once they had drunk their fill, he retraced his steps and tethered them under a spreading oak tree. In the darkness of the house, Sen listened beyond the quiet sounds of his sleeping family to the soft chirping of crickets before finally falling asleep.

The next day Woo Sang's nephew came by with his three children. Sen patted the heads of the three unruly half-breed boys while Liah gave each a red packet of money.

When all was repacked into their wagon, Sen smilingly pressed several dollars into Woo Sang's hand saying, "For your next drunk." Woo Sang grinned and pointed to several boxes. "Not much, but it will take the hunger away: just bread, ham, cookies and a crate of apples, oranges and bananas."

Woo Sang's last words to Sen instilled some confidence: he gave Sen directions to a side road they could travel with little risk of meeting any Fahn Gwai.

The second time they happened upon their countrymen was at a fruit stand in *Flesinoh*, where they met Lew Wing. Lew Wing and his wife ran a sizable grocery store in the poor section of town. They shared two days of rest and joyful hot meals with them. They caught up on the news from Dai Faw and Loo Sahng while the children ran in the meadows, screeching and working off long pent-up energy.

The night before they took their leave, Sen showed Lew Wing his hand-drawn map. "Unfortunately," murmured Lew Wing, "I have not been to Loo Sahng, so I cannot help you. But at your next town, Bakafeh you will be able to ask directions. Bakafeh has a larger settlement of our countrymen and I'm sure you will be able to find help there."

As they were boarding their wagon, Lew Wing handed Sen a large box and a shopping bag filled with provisions. "We have made sandwiches for you. And hopefully the oranges and apples will slake your thirst. Be sure to drink the bottles of milk before the heat of the day, or else they will sour."

Mrs. Lew took Liah's hands in hers. The older woman's face was as wistful as her voice as she spoke. "May Kwan Yin lead your footsteps and, perhaps when we finally get the chance to go to Loo Sahng, you can show us around Chinatown."

In Bakersfield they had their third encounter with their countrymen. As Mr. Lew had promised, the Bakersfield Chinatown was twice the size of the Fresno settlement and more densely populated and cohesive. There Sen met his next acquaintance in a Chinese grocery store.

Soong Hee took Sen and his family to the café where he worked as a cook. As a part of his meager pay, the café owners provided him with a room at the back of the property. Their new friend invited Sen and his family to share a hot meal of rice, salt fish, Chinese sausages and mixed greens; Liah was delighted with the tureen of pork and melon soup.

After supper Liah, asked if she and the family could bathe, as she had asked of the earlier countrymen they'd met. While they did so, Soong Hee and Sen sat outside and examined Sen's crude map of Loo

Sahng. Soong Hee explained, "This long wide line is the main street." He drew another shorter line running parallel to the main street but gently arcing around the main road. This, he explained, was where the railroad tracks veered off the main road for a mile or so before reappearing.

"I've been to Loo Sahng quite a few times and it is so. Pay no heed to the many cross streets or forks in the road. Just follow the railroad tracks to the end and it will take you to China Street. You'll know you're close to China Street when the tracks begin to curve like an 'S'. There, just before the 'S,' will be the beginning of China Street."

Although Sen felt a new surge of confidence with this information, he was not yet clear about finding China Street. So Soon Hee patiently retraced the line on the map, explaining that there was a huge feed store on the left side of the road, with a grove of orange trees on the right.

"In fact, when you come to the grove of trees, China Street is only a little more than a mile off. The name of the street is *Ahlamedah* (Alameda) North."

Once again, they were ready to resume their journey. Liah sat upon the wagon's hard wooden bench clutching sacks of sandwiches and doughnuts. She handed two sacks of fruit to Eldest Son.

"Remember," Soong Hee reminded them, "be patient. It is a long way before the end of the tracks. May Kwan Koong guide your footsteps on this journey."

Sen reached down to shake Soong Hee's hand but such gratitude was superfluous, as Soong Hee shouted to the children, "Eat the apples and oranges; they will slake your thirst better than water."

The children quit their playful romping to lean out of the side of the wagon, waving and shouting their goodbyes.

The last leg of their journey was the most difficult. The three eldest children fought constantly. Hot and tired, the children were disgruntled. The family's possessions took up a large space in the wagon and there was little room to move about. Sen's impatience to reach Loo

Sahng made him irritable each time they had to stop for the children. Sen's strength was depleted and Liah was beside herself as she groped for self-control.

Liah pleaded, "Could we not stop to spend the night? The children are exhausted and I am faint. Soong Hee warned it was a good deal farther before we come to China Street."

She cast about for a suitable spot to rest for the evening as she spoke. Under the fading rays of the July sun, the landscape appeared fiercely alien. "See?" She cried, pointing to a cluster of trees on the far side of the road. "Why not spend the night and start out early tomorrow, refreshed and in daylight?"

"Very well," grumbled Sen, drawing the reins up as he guided the horses off the road. "I had hoped to be with Cousin Shah tonight, but I suppose it is getting dark."

He drove the horses into a field and stopped under an ancient oak tree and its canopy of shade-giving branches. The children scrambled off the wagon, shouting and pushing. Curious about their new surroundings, their energy was instantly revitalized, sending them scampering hither and yon as they explored.

Sen unhitched the horses, tethered them to a low branch, and tended to their water and feed. He ran his hands up and down their hot bodies, searching for strained or injured muscles. He examined their legs and hooves with particular care. Slightly heavier than plow horses, their broad backs and stocky legs were impressive. Without horses a farmer might as well have no hands. Satisfied, Sen turned his attention to the landscape.

That night they ate the last of their bread and meat for supper. While Sen smoked a cigarette, Liah bedded down the children, warning them to go to sleep as she was too tired to tolerate any noise or horseplay. Calling out to her husband, Liah urged him to get his sleep, too. Curled into a corner of the wagon, Liah moaned as her body ached but soon her weariness overcame her pain and she fell fast asleep. By the time, Sen at last climbed into the wagon, a velvety soft darkness had enveloped the landscape.

Sen was the first to awaken. He gazed about the wilderness of tall grasses flush with the small, clustered yellow blossoms of wild mustard and a profusion of wild orange poppies. He felt as if he were at the edge of the world with not another living soul around. It was a pristine land, untrodden by human feet.

He wondered where he was. From a distance he spied a strange, waxy clustered white flower atop a trunk-like stem. It was growing out of what appeared to be a base of spiny leaves with needles at each tip. The wonderment of seeing a yucca excited Sen and he leaned over to nudge Liah awake. Liah was hard to rouse, so great was her need for sleep, but Eldest Son awoke, demanding something to eat. Second Son, roused by the voices of his brother and father, sat up and muttered that he too was hungry.

Sen stared at his two sons and marveled at the marked differences in their physical appearance. Eldest Son, Gan Hing, was stocky and with a dark complexion, while Second Son, Sui Loon, was lanky and with a light complexion. Both were of the same parents, why was there such a striking difference?

Where had time gone? Now with seven children, he could not remember all their birth dates, although he vividly recalled Second Daughter's day, for that had just occurred. He sighed feeling a vague sadness.

Liah, slowly stirring, stared a moment at the three of them, then quickly roused. She muttered that there was no more food. "The bread crusts are for the two youngest, but you may each have an apple."

Sen, seeing his sons' crestfallen faces, quickly comforted them. "When we get to Cousin Shah's you may both eat to your heart's content. For now, I'll hitch up the horses and we'll be on our way."

Three hours later, at eleven o'clock, Sen breathed a sigh of relief as he spied the expected train tracks. "We're here just as Soong Hee said.

Look at the train tracks. Now all we have to do is go to the end of these tracks and look for Cousin Shah."

An hour later Sen ecstatically pointed to the 'S' curve of the tracks and shouted that they had arrived! He drove the wagon up to an acacia tree and stopped. "Rest here, I'll go look for Cousin Shah. There is not much shade, but it's better than nothing."

Liah nodded wordlessly. Pale and faint, it was still her task to manage the children, now excited, adventurous, and energetic. The journey had not been easy at the start, but now at the end, with everyone hot, tired, and hungry, the task was almost impossible.

Sen returned twenty minutes later accompanied by Cousin Shah, a short, lean and very tiny sun burnt man, his queue as long as he was tall. Cousin Shah recoiled from the noisy onslaught of children who scrambled down from the wagon to crowd around him. Sen roared, "Wild Indians, be quiet! Cousin Shah is not used to such a racket!"

Cousin Shah lived in a one-room shack just inside the train yards where the trains first entered. He apologized to Liah, "I live alone and don't pay much attention to things." As he spoke, he hastily snatched up soiled clothing and bedding, and tossed them into a laundry bag on the other side of the room. "You folks can sleep here tonight, I'll stay with a friend." He picked up a broom and began sweeping. "Once I mop the floor, you can place the minhois down for the children."

While the children and Liah napped, Cousin Shah and Sen stabled the horses and went to get food at a café. At the dinner table that night, Sen admonished the children for their manners. Sen ordered the children to thank Cousin Shah, but the tiny man snapped. "It isn't necessary! Just slake your hunger."

That evening Liah and the children bedded down early. Sen and Cousin Shah returned to the café, which was filled with farmers, laborers, and businessmen returning from their jobs. Sen recanted his tale of woe and narrow escapes in Dai Faw. Tearfully he murmured half-aloud to himself, "Ah, that Gan's Meng-Sui demanded such a violent death!"

"Don't grieve for the dead," advised Cousin Shah, his hand upon Sen's. "Gan is far better off than any of us. As for his family, who will never see him again, it is so decreed. We cannot change that. For his fulfillment of having brought you and your wife to Gem Sahn, he's earned his eternal rest." Cousin Shah dropped his voice, softly reassuring Sen that neither he nor his family would live in want so long as he lived.

When asked what Sen hoped to do in Loo Sahng, Sen replied, "I will work in the train yards with you. I never intend for a Fahn Gwai to run me off my farm again!"

"Be not in such haste, Sen, I've already left word for Mah Ting to contact me. He is a prosperous farmer. He'll be in town tomorrow night. If it is permissible, my idea is that he will drive all of you to his farm. There you will have a chance to see what farms are available. I know Mah Ting makes a lot of money. He sells his entire crop to the wholesale produce markets. Perhaps he can make arrangements for you to do the same. He said he could make more money if he sold retail, but that takes too much time and effort. So why not wait and see."

Sen and Cousin Shah shared another drink. By nine o'clock that evening the café was filled to capacity. Men in their loose-fitting trousers and sleeveless undershirts drank cold tea and *Ng Ga Pei* (rice wine) to cool off. As usual, the discussions centered on Fahn Gwai stupidity and the current drought. As the evening wore on, the discussions turned into shouting matches. Some of the men shouted that the Fahn Gwai had just voted on a water bond of twenty-eight million dollars to bring water from two hundred and fifty miles away. In a smug tone, one man confided that a Fahn Gwai had already approached him to work on the Owens River Project.

"Hey, Shah," he shouted, "perhaps your cousin wouldn't mind going to work digging ditches and post holes. The pay is not that good but better than he can get working here in China Street."

Another man, Lew Lung, filled Sen in on the history of the struggle between the city of Los Angeles and a group of farmers over water rights. The farmers had demanded that Los Angeles stop diverting so much water from the river used to irrigate their fields. "The Loo Sahng government went to court to force the farmers to remove their dam on the river so water could flow to the city. The court declared that the water did not belong to landowners, but to all the people."

A voice from the back of the room guffawed. "Well, it seems nobody is going to get the water because there isn't any and there won't be any until it rains!"

Sen felt a sense of confusion, for he had spied numerous water kegs in the kitchen of the café. When he asked Cousin Shah about it, Cousin Shah quietly warned Sen never to mention water outside of Chinatown. "We do not want the Fahn Gwai to learn of our water source. Old Tong and Lew Sam drive their wagons every week in the late hours of the night to Mah Ting's farm. He has a spring on his place and we pay the men twenty-five cents for each keg of water they haul. Even when they go for the water, they make certain the kegs are covered with bamboo matting in case the Fahn Gwai should stop them. We must be careful not to waste any water, for Mah Ting's well may dry up."

With a small twinge of guilt, Sen remembered how he had previously watered down the two-dozen strawberry plants he'd potted in two large bamboo planters. He resolved then to use their overnight cold tea to water his plants.

—

Mah Ting arrived on the second day of July at six o'clock in the evening. He urged Sen to ready his family for the trip to his farm. Then he made a slight motion with his hand. Several men who had accompanied him scanned the area to make sure no one was around and then rushed to the wagon and unloaded several kegs of water.

"Use them sparingly," he warned Cousin Shah. "I will have to cut back on the water supply for the well is not as full as before. We'll forego the water for the rest of this week and hopefully the water level will rise. Tell the others and tell the old men not to come tomorrow night. I will let them know when to return."

After supper that evening, they set out for his farm. Eldest Son and Second Son rode with Mah Ting in his wagon.

"About Mah Ting," Sen muttered to Liah, "He's a celery farmer and does well."

"Is he married?" inquired Liah.

"Not that I know of, but should you see a female on the premises, I don't want you to ask any questions. Understand?"

For the remainder of the long ride, Liah sat silently contemplating Mah Ting's life. If there were a woman there, would she be Chinese or some other race? Suddenly Liah was impatient to arrive. She smiled, thinking how females could be such curious creatures. The children romping and shouting boisterously in the wagon caught her attention. She clapped her hands, shouting for silence.

"Leave them be!" growled Sen. "There's so short a time to be children."

Dusk was setting in when finally they arrived at Mah Ting's farm. In the low light Sen could only make out the sea of furrows spreading as far as the eye could see. They rumbled off the main road onto a smaller dirt road for another hundred yards before pulling up to a large wooden barn located on the right side of the farm. Mah Ting's house was set back farther from the barn. Mah Ting led them to the back door of the house and pushed open the door. He explained that he never locked it, for people all around knew him and besides they were honest. Liah gaped at the man as though he had lost his senses. Fahn Gwai, honest? But she said nothing. Weariness was overtaking her and she longed for sleep.

They walked through the kitchen into the front room where Mah Ting pointed to the floor. The oldest children could sleep on their min-hois here. He took Sen and Liah into a hallway, and pointed to the first door to the right and explained, "You two and the baby can sleep in there. That bedroom belongs to my cousin who is now in China. He is bringing his wife and son to Gem Sahn. My room is the second room down. The third room will be for my nephew when it is completed."

The next morning Sen was awakened by a rooster's crow. He crept carefully from bed, dressed quickly, then walked out the back door. Above him, the sky was tinged pink and the air was yet cool on his face. In the field, Mah Ting was hunched over, culling young celery plants. On the far side of the field, three workers were performing the same task. Although his body yet ached from the arduous journey, Sen could not resist the farmer's call. He knelt down to feel the soil between his fingers, smelling the moist pungent earth. The heady aroma filled him with the sense that he'd come home. Work in the city? Never! Sen shook his head. Not even without the promise of personal safety. He was a farmer and could never be anything else!

Mah Ting grinned and asked if Sen had slept well. The look on Sen's face answered his question.

Five and a half ours later, Mah Ting signaled to Sen that it was time to stop for the noon meal. As they walked toward the house, he explained that the three Mexican workers were seasonal. Ordinarily he and his cousin worked the land by themselves. "My cousin, as I said before, is now in China making preparations to bring his family to Gem Sahn."

Liah had prepared lunch and was waiting at the door when they walked up. Mah Ting took in a long breath and grinning exclaimed, "It's a long time since I had a hot meal at noon and salt fish steamed in rice at that!"

That night after work, and every night thereafter, Mah Ting drove Sen around the farmlands. Once or twice he pointed out a piece of land he thought might have underground water. "Of course it will take time and money to dig for wells, but the drought being what it is, we cannot wait in hope of rain."

Two weeks later, as the men headed back to Mah Ting's farm, Sen pointed to some land beyond a narrow dirt road. He asked Mah Ting about it. Mah Ting dismissed Sen's questions. "Only Mexican laborers and crop pickers live there. Here, we'll drive down and you will see it is useless land."

As they drove past it, Sen stared at the crude wooden shacks, each with sagging clotheslines of laundry flapping in the breeze. Colorful little garden plots of tall corn, pepper vines and chili peppers filled the yards. A dusty rooster, followed by a brood of squawking hens and yellow chicks pecking at the dried dirt, flapped his wings angrily as they rattled by in their wagon.

A half-mile down the road Mah Ting was dismayed at Sen's interest, which mounted with each mile. "You," he shook his head as he spoke, "don't want anything here, Sen! You're an experienced farmer, this outcropping is too rocky and it will take money to clear away these huge boulders. Let me show you another place."

What had attracted Sen was a stretch of rubble land, five miles outside the fertile farmlands of Lankershim, called Tijuana Flats. Twenty-one miles to the south was the sprawling city of Los Angeles.

Seeing tall hills and a dry riverbank, Mah Ting pointed to the desolate landscape. "It's cheap enough rent, but only the Mexicans live here. It is not for the kind of farming we do. This land is useless!" Nevertheless, the following Sunday afternoon Sen asked Mah Ting to drive him back to Tijuana Flats. Sen walked around, digging into the dirt, feeling the soil deep down, and stopping now and then to survey the land. Mah Ting, sprawled atop his wagon, which he'd parked under a lacy pepper tree, raised himself from time to time only to shake his head before slumping back into his seat.

The fierce sunshine beat down on Sen. He wiped the sweat from his face and trudged to the northern boundary and looked up at the tall hills rising toward the heavens. Yes, he thought, this piece of land, cradled by the hills and mountains on one side and a now empty riverbed running by the western border, was it. The wild panorama was comforting. Despite the vivid memory of the raid on his last farm in Dai Faw, Sen strode up to Mah Ting and told him that he'd found his farm and asked if Mah Ting could help him make inquiries as to the owner and the amount of the rent.

Mah Ting jerked himself upright and raised his hands in horror as he gazed at Sen. "You are mad! It will take at least twenty men to move those boulders. Think, Sen! Why not consider the land up a ways from my place? At least that land is cleared and plowed. Besides, there is no water here!" However, Sen shook his head and replied, "Not even you and your underground water will survive if the rains don't come soon. I must have this land! Will you help me get it?"

—

Sen and his family remained with Mah Ting during the months of July, August, and September while Cousin Shah, Mah Ting and their friends helped him clear the land of rubble and rocks. In the beginning, all the men thought Sen either mad or stupid or both, but once they cleared away the center of the land, they began to see Sen's vision. From the outside, the land appeared hostile and useless, but beneath the boulders, shrubs, trees and cacti lay rich soil. Nutrients carried by previous floods had enriched the soil trapped within the rocky crevices.

During the ensuing building of the house and the raising of the barn's framework the men jested about Sen's wisdom or lack thereof. They doubted his logistics when Sen kept insisting rain was on its way. It was only a matter of the atmospheric pressure coinciding with the clouds, he would explain. But behind his back, most of the men shook their heads as they worked.

By October the house was done and Mah Ting suggested a week of rest. "It isn't as though you need the barn completed immediately. You don't have any poultry or livestock, except the horses. We'll put up the walls of the barn when we're rested. By working on Saturdays and Sundays, it should only take us a week or two to complete."

Sen heaved a big sigh but nodded and thanked all the men who had helped with the work. He asked Mah Ting how he could ever repay him.

Mah Ting snapped, "You can't, Sen. We all do what is necessary to help each other. Isn't that the way our ancestors survived in the past? Your children will be the beneficiaries of our toil. You ought to know that by now!"

Cousin Shah nodded. "I suggest we go back to Mah Ting's. I'm sure Liah will have cooked supper by now. I can almost smell the salt fish steaming in the rice."

Mah Ting guffawed, "You know, each time I eat your wife's cooking I am tempted to get a wife of my own! Then I recall my mother nagging my father and I change my mind just as quickly. I'd just as soon forego the hot meals as put up with that."

All the men snickered and laughed. Climbing aboard the two wagons, they shouted that they were famished.

—

The night before Sen was to move into his new house, he felt the same mix of reticence and elation that he had felt the night before he left home for Gem Sahn. Sen had been filled with hope then but now, almost twenty years later, he despaired of his future. A sadness colored his thoughts and Sen closed his eyes tightly as if by doing so he could banish his pessimism. He felt Liah's warmth against him and slowly fatigue overtook him and Sen fell into a fitful sleep.

He dreamed of the moment when at last the clipper, Bald Eagle, had moored in Gem Sahn. Sen had joined the excited, chattering men surging toward the opening in the side of the vessel. Everyone was pressing to get off and the exodus was disorderly to say the least. Slung across each man's shoulders were cumbersome baskets hanging from poles containing all of their worldly possessions. The baskets kept colliding and tangling and the men, their hands clutching bedrolls and boxes, were unable to control them.

Sen felt a rush of fresh air and caught sight of the blinding June sunshine flooding into the dark hold of the ship. This was the first light he had seen since boarding the vessel sixty-nine days earlier. Throughout the trip he had reminded himself that the year was 1884 and the month was June. The calculations meant nothing to him, for the Chinese lunar calendar was the only way he could calculate time. He hung onto that date, for Cousin Qui and Brother Gan had told him that during the immigration cross examination, all of his answers had to correlate with the Fahn Gwai's calendar.

For the moment, as he awaited his turn to disembark, homesickness painfully nagged at him. He yearned for his young bride of seven and a half months. He recalled how terrified he had been when he descended into the ship's dark, dank bowels. He had shuddered when entering; now, fool that he was, he was afraid to leave the darkness to face the unknown. Sen held back, observing how the other men fared before inching his own way toward the open hatch. Sen felt a push from behind and suddenly found himself standing in the dazzling sunshine. He stepped onto the narrow gangplank and walked gingerly across, high above the murky water, onto the wharf. Carried along with the impatient throng, he found himself in front of a long row of tables manned by impassive, disinterested Fahn Gwai officers.

Confusion overwhelmed Sen as each consecutive immigration officer grabbed his entry papers. He followed the long line, and his papers were scanned, then stamped and passed along, each officer curtly nodding in turn for Sen to move on. Sen caught sight of the immigration detention area, a long rectangular shed with high walls and windows at the very top. A tremor ran through Sen as he recalled his older brother's warning: "Be absolutely correct with your answers. Detainment is not pleasant and oftentimes prolonged and perilous."

However, his papers were found to be acceptable. His health was hastily checked and he was declared disease free. Baggage was then examined and found to be free of contraband. Outside the detention area at last, Sen watched a group of new arrivals being greeted by a Chinese, whom he would later learn was a representative of the Six Companies Association. The Chinese man's manner was confident, almost with a hint of swagger, and he wore Fahn Gwai clothes as he called to the men, "Come, let us leave at once! You will go from here to meet the Elders. Then you will sign your debts of contract. We don't want hoodlums to congregate and throw rocks at us. Hurry up now with your stuff. Later, we will have a feast in your honor."

Sen was shocked at what he had just heard: Who and why would anyone want to throw rocks at them?

Hearing loud voices, Sen turned around just in time to see several Fahn Gwai waving their arms and herding a group of his countrymen through the immigration line. Unbeknownst to Sen, these Fahn Gwai were agents from Western Woolen Mills and the Cubanos Cigar Factory and the group of Chinese were indentured workers. If Sen could have understood the Fahn Gwai, he would have been furious, for the three agents were laughing and deriding what they called "a motley crew of Chinks. Pigtails! Ugh!"

Sen cast about an anxious eye, scanning the crowd for his older brother, Gan. He hung onto his heavy valise with his right hand and with his left, gripped the cords tied around his bedroll. Sen was not clad in the usual long blue cotton coat and matching baggy trousers of his fellow countrymen. As Brother Gan had suggested, he wore dark blue woolen suit pants with matching coat and vest and a creamy white silk shirt. On his feet was his first pair of store-bought Fahn Gwai shoes. Around his neck, he wore a foreigner's long necktie. A foreigner's hat concealed his queue, neatly tucked beneath it.

Sen's anxieties mounted as he waited for Gan. Suppose his older brother couldn't come dockside? What would he do? Ignorant of the Fahn Gwai's language, whom could he turn to for help? Sen felt a mounting panic as he stood watching strangers pushing past him. Through his befuddled fright, Sen heard a faintly familiar voice shouting his name. At last he caught sight of his older brother.

With a flood of relief, Sen dropped his belongings and greeted his brother. For a brief moment of uninhibited joy, the two brothers embraced. They laughed and cried at the joy of their reunion, then, as if prodded by an unseen signal, Gan picked up Sen's valise and motioned for Sen to take his bedroll. "We must be on our way, otherwise hoodlums will harass or even stone us," Gan said.

They quickly loaded Sen's things into Gan's wagon and Gan urged the horses to leave Portsmouth Square. Sen tensely watched as Gan kept looking behind him, from left to right, as he whipped the horses.

"What's the hurry, Brother?" asked Sen. He pointed to a majestic building. "Is that a Fahn Gwai palace?"

Gan chuckled. "Never mind, Sen, that place is not for us. It's the Fahn Gwai's finest hotel. I hear tell from a cousin of ours who works in the hotel laundry that there are separate carpeted rooms with a toilet, bath, and basin for each bedroom."

Gan didn't know the name (it was the Grand Hotel) nor did Gan know the names of the gambling halls they passed (the Bella Union, the El Dorado and the High Stakes). What he did know and told Sen was that none of these places were safe places for Chinese.

They drove a few blocks in silence, then Sen asked about the two groups of Chinese he'd seen dockside and asked about the Fahn Gwai's behavior. He also asked about the warning the Chinese agent had issued to the men about hoodlums who might stone them, which Gan himself had repeated. "Is that so, my older brother?"

Gan sighed. "I hate to start right in telling you of the evil here, but what the agent was saying is true... and then some. But we'll speak of these things later."

Sen's fears, aroused by his older brother's acknowledgement, filled him with apprehension. He, too, began to glance from side to side and look behind him, not knowing exactly what he was looking for.

"Brother," muttered Gan, "One more thing. Be sure you keep your queue tucked up like you have it now. The Fahn Gwai hoodlums derive great pleasure from pulling us by our hair. In the past, they have tied two of our countrymen back to back by their queues then taken shots at them just to see them dance."

"What have we done to deserve such disfavor?" asked Sen. He was shocked at Gan's reaction to his question, for Sen had never seen his older brother be so belligerent.

"What have we done? The Fahn Gwai's life has been bettered because of us. We clean his house, wash his clothes, cook his meals and tend to his children, besides catering to the silly whims of his wife! Surely as the sun rises and sets each day, he'd not have his railroad if it weren't for the sweat and toil of our people, yes, even at the expense of many of our lives. Even his reclaimed land is the result of backbreaking efforts by our people. Ours is the misfortune of having a different skin color, and of doing our work too well for too reasonable a sum of money."

Gan turned and pointed back toward Portsmouth Square. "The waters of the bay used to lap where the square is now. Our people sweated in summer and were chilled in winter working to fill in that land. In time you, too will know of what I speak."

Seeing his brother's trepidation, Gan paused and laughed good-naturedly. "My newly arrived relative, have no fear. Our earlier countrymen have taught us how to survive the Fahn Gwai's persecutions. You will learn the precautions to take when in the Fahn Gwai's presence... even at a distance. Now, no more unpleasant talk. I would not have brought these things up if you hadn't asked about the indentured men."

After a few more blocks, Gan pointed ahead. "Two more blocks and we'll be home. My store is off an alley just off Du Pon Gai."

Sen would have been confused had he been able to read the street signs, for Du Pon Gai was actually Grant Avenue. Unable to read the Fahn Gwai's history books, Gan didn't know that before the United States wrested California from Mexico, the street was named Calle de la Fundacion, later becoming Dupont Street before finally being re-named Grant Avenue.

Du Pon Gai was the lifeline of Gan's life. With its many cross streets and sunless, narrow alleyways running like tributaries, Du Pon Gai was indeed the river of life for many in San Francisco's Chinatown.

Sen muttered, "Why did you not tell me of these dangers before I left home? If I had known, I would not have come!"

Gan's reply was terse, "Never mind. Despite the situation, life is better here. Now keep alert, for I will name the streets for you. These streets make up our town and it is wise not to stray."

When they came to a narrow alley, Gan reined in the horses. "That's my store, the third one... the red one on the left hand side of the alley. Here, this is your key. Be sure you unlock all three locks, or else you'll not be able to open the door. I will return the wagon to the stables. Your bedroom is the second one down the hall. Take a rest. Later we will pay our respects to the Elders at the House of Lee."

Hours later a sound from the kitchen woke Sen from a fitful slumber. Completely disoriented, he bolted upright, clutching the sides of the wooden cot to keep from falling off. It was a few moments before Sen realized he was in his brother's home, ashore in Gem Sahn. Still groggy, he got to his feet and stumbled to the kitchen where Gan was preparing tea.

Later, on their way to the House of Lee, Gan again tried to acquaint Sen with the street names, but Sen was too engrossed gawking at his new surroundings. It was a comfort to Sen to find the environment of Gem Sahn so akin to Hong Kong, with little brightly painted red and green stalls selling fruit, vegetables, candles and all the dried and pre-served fruits and salted plums from China. Red banners with bold, black-inked Chinese characters billowed in the gentle breezes so re-minded him of home. But most of all, it was the voices of men chatting in a language Sen understood; it was like coming home again!

The House of Lee was situated in a narrow, cluttered alley off Clay Gai. Gan and Sen entered through a gloomy doorway and climbed the stairs to the third floor. Gan paused to give Sen last minute instructions.

"To remain alive in the Fahn Gwai's land you'll need the wisdom of our Elders. Their survival in the early days has endowed them with strength and experience. Your problem-free entry is greatly due to their endeavors. Pay your due respects."

The stairway corridor reeked with the mustiness of sunless years and stale odors from unventilated kitchens. At the top of the stairs Gan took a key from his pocket and unlocked three locks.

Sen, assailed with uneasiness, asked why there were three locks. He did not hear his brother's reply, for Gan pushed him inside the door. Sen found himself in a huge front room with a row of windows across high walls and chairs lining the length of both sides of the room. There were three large round tables in the center each surrounded by chairs. At the middle table sat six wizened old men, chatting amiably and shar-ing jasmine tea and pastries. The patriarchs, dressed in padded long robes, appeared lost in their warm, cumbersome garb. Gan walked up to a white-haired man with a long flowing beard covering his face and chin. Gan bowed low, then introduced Sen to Elder Lee Ti. Elder Lee Ti, in turn, introduced Sen to his five companions.

Elder Lee Ti set his long bamboo water pipe into a wooden tub and motioned for Sen to be seated. "I am glad to meet the younger brother of Gan. Did you have an arduous journey? If it was anything like mine, you must be utterly exhausted. Twenty-odd years ago, the journey took ninety miserable days. Did you get seasick?"

"No, sir, but I could not eat much. The food tasted slightly rancid and the air was so stale I could hardly breathe. Indeed, in my cramped space, I couldn't eat or sleep. I felt at times I would not survive to see Gem Sahn. But I will be fine in a few days."

The old man on Elder Lee Ti's right chuckled. "You're fortunate, my son, for having had meals! When I came over, the captain would not allow our cook to go topside, not even to heat water for tea. The weather was foul and I recall hot meals only a few dozen times. Half the time we starved. If it hadn't been for our tinned foods, I would have died for certain!"

Elder Lee Ti sighed then said, "Please indulge an old man's desire for news from home. How are your mother and father? And is Great Aunt still suffering from her many aches and pains?"

Sen dutifully and patiently answered all Elder Lee Ti's questions, and those the other elders asked as well. He told of recent changes in the village. "The old well collapsed after last year's floods and we now have a new well and four rice paddies north of the old one. Oh, yes, Fourth Uncle ran off to the city with a young dancer. When he tried to return, Fourth Aunt refused to take him back. She says since he found a younger girl more desirable, she no longer has to fulfill her wifely duties. Nothing the family does or threatens can make her change her mind. Up to the time of my departure, Fourth Uncle had been living at Second Uncle's house.

The old men laughed. Elder Lee Ti wiped the tears from his bushy-browed eyes, "I think Fourth Uncle's lost a home. If I remember correctly, Fourth Aunt is a shrew! Ah, how easily one forgets the faults of our loved ones when one is far away. I'd forgotten what a nag she is!"

Elder Lee Ti motioned toward the back of the room. "Gan, why don't you take Sen back to the kitchen to meet the others? Be sure you stay for supper so Sen can meet the men who are now working."

Sen found himself carefully following Gan through a dimly lit room filled with rows of cots. In the semi-darkness, as he and Gan tiptoed through to the kitchen, he could discern the vague shapes of sleeping men.

Gan whispered that many of the men worked odd hours. "Many of the men work during the night, hence they sleep during the day."

There were eighteen at dinner that evening. Again, Sen spoke of home and informed each man of how his family was doing. Sen could not help seeing their expressions of anxiety and guilt and he thought, why was it that he sensed such hopelessness in their glances?

Gan finally glanced up at the wall clock: it was eight-thirty, time to leave for home.

Elder Lee Ti warned Sen of the violence of the times. "The economic times here are bad. The Fahn Gwai blame us, 'the yellow scourge', for the monetary slump. Their accusations, of course, are unfounded, but the Fahn Gwai persist in their persecution. Be wary. Keep your queue out of sight and be as inconspicuous as you can. Keep your distance. When you see a crowd of Fahn Gwai, go the other way. If you stay within China Gai your chances of safety are one hundred fold better. Again, I welcome you to Gem Sahn. May the Gods lead you to good fortune."

On his first night in Gem Sahn, Sen found sleep out of reach. Tossing and turning on his narrow cot, he yearned for his wife, Lin Fah, and ached for the familiarity of home. In his agony, Sen turned his face to the wall and wiped away his tears, silently beseeching the Gods for blessed sleep.

As the hours of the night dragged on, Sen felt the rolling sensation of the vessel and several times he was wrested from the brink of sleep as he imagined his cot was tipping over. In the darkness of his room, Sen cursed his feelings of hopelessness and his decision to come to Gem Sahn.

Toward dawn, as Sen continued tossing and turning, he finally opened his eyes and sat up abruptly, gaping at the room as he emerged from his dream. Feeling Liah beside him, he relaxed as he realized he'd been dreaming! Sen leaned over Liah and whispered, "Lin Fah, wake up it's time to move into our new home. Wake up!"

Sen was relieved when Liah did not awaken immediately, for it would have distressed her to hear her real name. Sen still felt anger at the immigration people whose typographical error had changed Lin Fah's name to "Liah". Sen patted Liah's backside as he again whispered for her to awaken. "Time to get the children ready; wake up, Liah."

TIJUANA FLATS

Sen moved his family into their new home on the twenty-third day of November in the Fahn Gwai's year of 1904, the Chinese Year of the Dragon.

Liah fearfully lamented, "If only our parents were here to advise us. We do not know if this day is astrologically auspicious!" Almost in tears, Liah faced her husband, "Are you certain our house is facing the right direction? We can't expect the ancestral winds of good fortune to envelope us unless it is."

Sen impatiently replied, "Light your incense and beseech the Gods for their indulgence. They can't expect us to know everything."

Liah retorted, "I will, I will. How can we hope to live without Kwan Koong's protection or the Kwan Yin's blessings? Will you and the children unload our belongings while I light the incense?"

Incense smoke filled the house with the heavy scent of jasmine. When their few belongings were unloaded, Liah went outside. She stared at a small wooden outbuilding. Cousin Shah came up beside her and pointed to a path of newly laid stepping-stones.

"That way no one needs to muddy their shoes during the rains. We also allowed for a bathing area inside. When the well is dug, it won't be difficult to get water for bathing."

Sen placed the four water kegs they'd brought from Dai Faw just outside the back door. He pointed sternly at his eldest and second sons. "You two will have the job of keeping the water kegs filled and I don't want to hear from your mother that you are remiss." Sen's eyes flickered with doubt as he added, "if there is ever water in the river."

Mah Ting was quick to reassure Sen that each night after work he would bring the water needed. "This drought can't go on forever!"

It was almost impossible for Liah to sleep that first night. Their bedroom was built in the cellar of the house. The bedroom floor, though covered with bamboo matting, was unyielding. Even atop her minhois, Liah felt the discomfort of the hard floor. She lay awake, fearing that perhaps the unpaneled walls of this underground room might collapse, burying them below ground.

Liah awakened the next morning relieved they were not buried inside their underground bedroom. She began to prepare their breakfast of rice and her fears disappeared, as the aggravating chore of cooking on an open-air fire required all her attention. The wind that swept over the lowlands made it difficult to regulate the fire. Liah needed to bring the water in the rice pot to a boil, then in order to quickly diminish the flame to keep the rice from burning, she reached into the flames to pull out some of the burning logs. She lost patience and shouted for the children to leave her alone. She was relieved she only had to reheat the pork and greens Cousin Shah had provided, realizing Liah would have enough trouble cooking the rice.

When they were finished with the meal, Sen took the boys with him to scout along the riverbank for wood and, hopefully, water.

Liah hung curtains and two embroidered pictures she'd brought from her home in Kwangtung: one a silk embroidered peacock and the other the God of Longevity. They were both thirty inches wide and forty inches long, with smooth black teakwood dowels attached to each end. Red silk tassels hung from both sides of each picture. Very gently she placed a hand-carved cherry wood Buddha atop an orange crate. She promised Kwan Koong that as soon as she could, she would have a fitting altar for him as well as another one for Kwan Yin.

When finished, she stepped back to inspect their meager furnishings. Then she turned her mind to the noon meal. Perhaps if she busied herself, her morbid feelings would dissipate.

In the weeks that followed, Mah Ting, Cousin Shah and their friends came each Sunday to help complete the barn and to panel their secret underground room walls. On the day the walls were finally secured, Liah felt a heaviness disappear. She would sleep better now without the fear of the walls collapsing on her. Sen, on the other hand, worried about the exposure of the underground tunnel's opening.

Cousin Shah instructed them to lug large boulders to the opening and to pile them in a natural, inconspicuous, array, with a large slab hiding the opening. "When the shrubs grow around it, no one will dream such a tunnel exists!! Just be sure the children never leave the slab lying on the ground."

Sen replied, "I'll make certain the slab is leaning against the opening with only enough room to enter and leave. Only at night will I make certain it is flush with the boulders. I thank you, sir, for now I feel safe."

A month later, Cousin Shah, Mah Ting and their friends arrived with a wagonload of used bricks. Cousin Shah explained, "I couldn't find a wood burning stove, but a brick one is even better." He grinned. "They were either over-priced or not the right size." He pointed to a far corner of the kitchen. "We'll have to put in a vent through the ceiling."

At the supper table that night, Sen announced, "Now that our home is done, I want all of you to come for supper this coming Sunday. It will be a celebration for all of your hard and generous labors."

Mah Ting chuckled. "Just so you won't think the barn is useless, I've made arrangements for some hens and a rooster. They are my gifts for the children."

Liah smiled shyly, "We thank you, sirs. It is fitting the first feast in our home should be in your honor."

Liah's gratitude embarrassed Cousin Shah. "Harrumph! Just be certain you do not use the stove before the week is out. Next time I come I will bring some sacks of coal. On these cold nights you can put several pieces into the pit and they will keep the room warm. You won't have to build a new fire each morning."

One of the men, Wai Fook, lamented the backbreaking labor of digging the irrigation ditches. Mah Ting laughed, "Sen and I have inspected the river banks. We've calculated that if we dig where the river is the deepest it will be necessary only to dig deep trenches to the mouth of the river. Once the water is conducted onto the land, the irrigation ditches need only be a foot deep."

Sen grinned, ""If we ever get any rain it will only be necessary to dig the trenches three feet deep and five feet wide. With a sluice gate at the mouth of the ditches, we can control the flow and we will have as much water as we need." He looked at his children. "Mah Ting and I have also decided to dig a pool near the house. The children will then not have to walk a long distance for water."

The men all groaned, "Yes… if the rains ever come!"

The morning of the celebration on the second day of December, Liah warned her brood, "I will not tolerate anyone crying or fighting and ruining this auspicious event! Is that clear, especially my Eldest Daughter?"

Liah eyed her, "While you cannot do the heavy work, I expect you to do the lighter work and you can begin by sweeping the floors and raking the twigs and branches from around the house."

Liah felt a tugging on her skirt and looked down at her four-year-old son clamoring to help, too. "Yes, my Fifth Son, you may help fill the hens' nests with straw to make them comfortable so the boxes will be ready when the chickens arrive. Make them soft enough so that the eggs will not break."

She picked up her baby daughter, changed her diaper, strapped her into a sling and tied her onto her back. It was ten o'clock when Liah finished with the housework and she began preparations for their afternoon meal. Elation crowded out all other emotions as Liah carefully placed wood into the new stove and lit the fire. As instructed by Cousin Shah, she placed only enough wood to start the flames, then she added the coal. Quickly she washed the rice and emptied the rinse water into one of the kegs. With the water shortage, she could not be wasteful.

When the rice was ready to steam, she quickly added a generous portion of sausages and a large hunk of salt fish to the pot. She clamped on the cover and inhaled the heady aroma. For a few minutes, she watched the laboring flames, waiting to see that the rice did not burn. Next, she assembled celery, onions, chard and black mushrooms for the compote. Suddenly, Sen began shouting excitedly outside. She rushed out to see what was the matter. She stared dumbfounded for a moment, then burst into laughter.

Cousin Shah and Fong Wan had arrived. They were seated atop the front seat of the wagon, but the rest of the men sat on chairs around a table in the bed of the wagon. Cousin Shah grinned, "How else can we transport the table and chairs with room left over for the men?"

Cousin Shah reached under his seat and extracted several large boxes and handed them to Liah. "I thought it might be difficult for you to cook for the first time on the new stove, so I brought barbecued pork and roast ducks."

All through the day, Liah felt the joy of shared laughter. With great pride, she listened to the ring of laughter in her husband's voice as he explained to one man the reason he chose this desolate spot. "If you'd lived through as many raids and evictions as I, you would have chosen the same spot. I've made my last mistake of making my place attractive to the Fahn Gwai. Who would ever want this place?"

Later that night, alone with Liah at the kitchen table, Sen gently caressed his wife's arm. "Moving to Loo Sahng has changed my lot in life.

I feel in my heart that the Gods are finally smiling on me. My wife, you were right."

Liah lowered her eyes as she returned her husband's touch. "It was your decision, my husband. I am grateful for your wisdom. Your Meng-Sui indeed has changed for the better."

Sen stifled a yawn as he rubbed an aching shoulder. "The labor of making this place livable has left me with bruised muscles."

"Wait, my husband," Liah cried as she ran to the cupboard and grabbed a jug of herb-alcohol. "Let me apply this potion to your sore muscles. It will ease the pain and relax you." As Liah massaged Sen's shoulders she was thankful for her mother's wisdom. "I am indeed grateful for my mother's insistence that I bring this jug of Het-A-Dew to Gem Sahn. You should have seen my displeasure when she insisted. I've come to learn how smart my mother is!"

Enjoying his massage, Sen sighed, "I also recall my mother's insistence about the jug. I gave mine to Elder Lee Ti because he was all out. With his rheumatism he said the medicinal brew was a gift from heaven. What will you do when this jug is empty?"

"Never fear, my husband, I am already aging another jug. Remember when I asked you to buy the supply of herbs? Part of it went into the other jug of alcohol to age."

Sen flexed his arms and shoulders and declared his wife was right; his arms and shoulders did feel more relaxed and now only slightly sore.

"Well, let us go to bed, my husband. In the morning you will find the pain gone. You go ahead. I want to light a taper to Kwan Yin for her bounties today."

On the eighteenth of December, the men put the finishing touches on the walls around the well. Cousin Shah grinned as he lowered a bucket into its depths. "I know it's foolish to try for water, but I want to know how much underground water there is. It will take a long time for the water to settle, but if it rains the water table will be higher."

Sen chuckled. "The rains will come! When they do, my two eldest sons will be the benefactors of the well."

"I hope you are prophetic Sen. Unless the rains come soon, even my well is going to be dry," Mah Ting added.

Cousin Shah grimaced. "The Fahn Gwai say that if it doesn't rain this year, all our lives will be in jeopardy. Lucky for us that Mah Ting and Quan Soon have wells. Otherwise our people in town would be suffering. Do you know that water is almost a dollar for a bucketful? Can you imagine the Fahn Gwai making money off their people because of a drought?"

Sen frowned, slightly embarrassed when Liah offered to light extra tapers to Kwan Yin. "She will send rain."

Mah Ting smiled. "Yes, light the tapers, Liah, for what does it matter who sends the rain as long as it rains! Well, I must leave now." He stretched and said he was going home to bed.

Sen and Liah watched as Cousin Shah drove his wagon filled with their good friends over the rocky terrain and onto the dirt road. Sen felt somewhat doubtful about the rains he had said would come. "Come, my wife, let us also go to bed. Tomorrow comes early."

—

Sen was up the next morning and every morning thereafter at dawn, scanning the heavens for some sign of rain. Without precipitation, nothing was possible.

Liah philosophically urged him to finish the interior of the house, for when it did rain Sen would be too busy planting his crops. With reluctance, Sen set about his chores in the house; he contrived a pole along one side of their cellar bedroom for their clothing and he built two shelves the length of the room for their other belongings. He built cupboards in the kitchen for the cookware and dishes, another for their foodstuffs, and a long sturdy chopping board that would double as a worktable. Tired, Sen was ready to quit his labors and to wait for the rains when Liah nagged him to begin work on the chicken coops so they would be ready when the chickens arrived. "Not for me will you build them. Mah Ting says as soon as the coops are made, he will send us a rooster and hens. You do want them, don't you? Besides, Cousin Shah said he is giving you three braces of ducks and geese. They also have to have some place to lay eggs and nest."

Sen flexed his muscles. "I'll think about it tomorrow. Besides, I have yet to put a second coat of paint on the barn doors."

In the following months, Liah became increasingly alarmed; there were no signs of rain. She lit tapers to Kwan Yin, beseeching her for assistance. She recalled Cousin Shah's warning regarding the peril to their lives if the drought was prolonged. Impulsively, Liah lit another taper and a coil of incense as well to the Goddess of Mercy, Kwan Yin.

1905

YEAR OF THE SNAKE

The Fahn Gwai's New Year of nineteen hundred and five, the Chinese Year of the Snake, found Sen with time on his hands. His restless mood deepened with the dim prospect of rain and the abortive end to his dream of a bountiful crop. He despaired of the efforts of Mah Ting, Cousin Shah and all their friends who came each Sunday to dig the irrigation ditches. In his head, he heard echoes of Wei Wong's lament, "Why are we building moats, when everyone knows that rain is not going to fall?" This lament only increased Liah's feeling of indebtedness to the men. Only Liah was confident that the Goddess would send rain.

On the night of April seventh, Liah was awakened. Had she heard a faint rumble overhead? She slipped from bed and went outside, but even before she held her hand out she knew the rains had finally come! For a long moment, she allowed the gentle rain to touch her hands, then she raced indoors to awaken Sen.

Together they watched the heavy mist grow into a gentle shower and they prayed for the rain to continue. Sen grinned as Liah embraced him, crying happily that Kwan Yin never failed. When she cried that she must light a taper in thanks to Kwan Yin, Sen said, "I'll come with you. I can't believe it is really raining. I almost gave up the idea that I could ever plant my crops!"

The rain fell throughout the night and into the early hours of dawn. At times it seemed as if the sky had opened its portals, releasing all of its moisture. By mid-morning the sun weakly glimmered through the drizzle and by afternoon the parched earth had absorbed all the moisture that had fallen. It appeared as if it had never rained. A puddle here and there under trees was the only evidence of the night's rains. The pool of water, trapped halfway back from the river, was a disappointing mire of gooey mud.

In town, they thought about how the Loo Sahng city fathers had discussed building a reservoir, but no one believed the plan would go further than talk. The city fathers hadn't even repaired the essential bridge linking Pueblo Town to the rest of the city. Consequently, the news of the Fahn Gwai Council's proposed plan for water conservation was pessimistically accepted in Chinatown. The Fahn Gwai were always speaking of dams and flood basins. lived here for twenty years and I haven't seen anything started. If the rains do not continue we might as well move from Loo Sahng."

Mah Ting and Liah were silent. Mah Ting did not want to bring up the issue that only three of them had wells on their land: himself, Sen and Quan Soon. But Soon's well was almost dry and Mah Ting feared if the drought lasted much longer, he'd be forced to withhold water from his countrymen. "For these many years I've allocated water to Chinatown, but if more rain doesn't come, I am afraid I will have to think of my crops," he said with reluctance.

Sen shook his head. "I hope your premonitions are wrong for I'd hate to move again!"

Mah Ting smiled, "Well, let us pray that the drought is done. Surely there is nothing we can do to alter the conditions, so we might as well have faith."

There were two days of cool, sunny weather followed by another downpour; this one harder and lasting for two days. Even the river seemed wider and deeper. Liah set out buckets to catch the water, which she planned to use for washing their clothes. In town, Cousin Shah and all the residents of Chinatown set out buckets, tubs and barrels, not believing the drought was broken. While the Los Angeles River swelled, so much water at once meant runoff to the sea.

The rains continued. Even the Fahn Gwai's newspaper jubilantly declared the long drought was over! In Liah's house, and throughout Chinatown, there was rejoicing and thanksgiving offered to the Gods.

On the twenty-seventh day of April, Mah Ting came to Liah's farm to plow the ground. Sen's happiness overflowed at the supper table. "Just think, in another week I will be able to seed. Oh, Liah, I feel my life renewed! If we have a good crop, Mah Ting will take me to the wholesale market. From the money I will get he said he'd help me purchase a plow. While Mah Ting is generous, I cannot expect him to give me help each season. Is that not so, my wife? We should not be dependent on others."

Liah lowered her eyes to hide the reflection of love in her eyes. Her husband's restive moods had frightened her, but now everything was right again. She murmured, "In the beginning I thought Cousin Shah was wrong, but now I know our home is facing the right direction. All the tears that flowed in our earlier years were for this time. My husband, I am joyful for our good fortune."

Sen scanned his wife's face and he thought how simple her life was, with her faith in the Gods. If only he could place his life in the hands of the Gods. Poor woman, living all these years in constant need and fear. Sen felt guilty for the times he'd berated her. Weren't her requests always for the children? Who, if not he, was to provide for his family? Sen impulsively decided to allow Liah to keep the egg money once they began to sell their eggs. Magically, his guilt disappeared, as if this decision would cancel out all her earlier suffering.

Liah also had guilt feelings. Poor Sen, so many mouths to feed and so many feet to keep in shoes. He did his utmost, but the Fahn Gwai always seemed to shatter his plans. In her womanly way, Liah heaped all their ills on the Fahn Gwai. It was unforgivable how the barbarians had destroyed her husband's spirit and his courage. Liah whispered, "Believe in your newfound promise. Tonight I shall plead with Kwan Yin for a good harvest."

At the end of the day's sowing, Sen stood at the edge of the field, rubbing his aching shoulders as he viewed the results of his toil. Liah ran out to the clearing and declared her admiration for the straight furrows. She giggled, "Do you remember the first time we saw Fatt On's farm? Oh, such a disaster! Indeed, he was no farmer!"

Sen chuckled. "I do indeed." Suddenly his mind flashed back to his farm in Dai Faw. "So many things have happened since then!"

Liah sensed Sen's sadness and knew he was thinking of Dai Faw. "Come into the house, Sen. I have a good meal waiting."

The worry lines on Sen's face deepened. "Liah, it's just that so much depends on this first planting."

"Oh, do not worry, my husband. You are a seasoned farmer."

Throughout the next six weeks, Sen was up at dawn and worked until long after the sun disappeared behind the tall hills. Sen was culling strawberries when Mah Ting came to inform him of the wholesaler's promise to take his crop.

Mah Ting reached out for one of the bright red strawberries. "These are the largest, sweetest berries I've ever eaten. And, Sen, your tomatoes! How do you get them so red and large? I wouldn't allow the children to harvest them, lest they bruise them. You'll get premium prices for these two items."

Mah Ting sauntered around the compound, inspecting the boxes of lettuce, carrots, radishes and bell peppers. "It's a good thing you didn't allow the carrots to get too large; these look tender enough to eat raw! Say, does Liah know how to pickle the chard? If so, you can bring in more money on the pickled greens. Our grocery stores will buy all she can pickle."

Sen muttered, "She's from the old country, isn't she? Of course! What about salted duck eggs? Will they bring in a better price if they're salted?"

Mah Ting nodded and said, I'll be by next week to pick up your produce. It shouldn't sit long after picking. The fresher it is, the better the prices."

Emotions ran high in Sen's house on the eleventh day of June when Mah Ting came to take their first harvest to market. Twelve lugs of red, firm, large tomatoes; several crates of tender carrots, peppers, Chinese chard and mustard greens; and seven crates of lettuce were ready. Mah Ting nodded his approval at the two bushel baskets of new peas. "Did you measure them, Sen? They're so uniform in size! I still do not believe the size and taste of your strawberries! They will bring in the most money. Let us load up and I will see you this afternoon."

Liah stepped timidly forward and asked Mah Ting if he'd like to take a tub of pickled chard to town. "I made it for the family, but if it brings in money, I'd like to sell it. I also have ten dozen duck eggs that are ready and twenty dozen chicken eggs, if you would market them for me."

"Fine, Liah, I'll take them with me," he replied. "I'll see you folks sometime this afternoon. I have a few errands to do in Chinatown. If you'd like anything at the store, I'd be happy to pick it up for you."

Sen thanked Mah Ting. "No, thanks, there is nothing we need in town."

After Mah Ting drove off, Sen worked furiously in the field, preparing the ground for their second crop. His brain whirled with visions of success and failure: one moment he had plenty of money and the next he was turned down because his crops were not good enough. Sen panicked. What if the men at the produce house turned down his produce? How would he survive the coming year? How could he face Mah Ting, who already considered his choice of land for a farm a folly? How could he face all the men who had labored so long and hard for him? Sen was almost beside himself. He worked even harder at clearing the debris in the fields.

At two-thirty in the afternoon, Sen heard wagon wheels approaching. He felt like running away. He would not be able to face Liah if Mah Ting had returned with his produce unsold. Liah's insistent, excited voice cut through his befuddlement. He ran toward the house.

"Forty-five dollars!" shouted Liah, her face wreathed in a smile.

"Not all of that is for the produce, Sen," explained Mah Ting. "Nine dollars and fifteen cents came from the sale of the pickled chard and the eggs."

Sen fingered the money, then finally broke into a broad grin. "Oh, you must stay for supper, Mah Ting."

Liah smiled, "We are having steamed salt fish and sausages. I know you have a fondness for them!"

"Of course I'll stay," replied Ma Ting, "Salt fish and liver sausages steamed in rice is my favorite meal."

Early the next morning Sen was back in his fields, picking up rocks and rubble unearthed by the plow. One more plowing and the ground would be ready for the manure. It was a week before seeding and his heart almost burst with anticipation. He smiled at his over-zealous precaution in adding a bit of manure. The soil was fertile enough from the years of rich nutrients deposited by the overflowing river.

—

It was late September when Sen again awaited Mah Ting's return from the market. Sen calculated that with his produce almost double in quantity, plus the salted duck eggs and five tubs of pickled mustard greens and chard, the profit ought to be higher than that of the first trip to the market with their initial crop. A quiver of excitement tore through his spine as Sen thought of the three new chicken coops and two duck yards they had built. Yes, the Gods were indeed smiling upon him!

The second crop brought in fifty-eight dollars, twelve dollars and forty-eight cents of which was for Liah's eggs and pickled vegetables. That night, before bed, Sen reached into a drawer and withdrew a box, which he handed to his wife.

Liah asked, "What is this, my husband?"

Sen grinned proudly and urged her to open it. As Liah lifted the lid, her eyes sparkled as they fell upon many coins and paper money. "Oh, Sen, how much?"

"One hundred fifteen dollars and forty-eight cents. Of course, not all of that is from produce; a portion of it is from the eggs and pickled vegetables." Sen paused, then murmured matter-of-factly, "Thirty-five dollars and sixty cents is what your efforts have brought in and you shall have it to do with as you want."

Liah gasped and stared at her husband for a long moment. Never in her entire life had she had so much wealth! Liah shook her head; she couldn't accept it, at least not until the plow was paid for. Sen smiled tenderly as he counted out the exact amount and pressed the monies into her hand. "Take it, Liah. Don't worry about the plow. Mah Ting said there is a company that deals in farm tools. With his recommendation, I could buy a new one with a bit of money down and then make small monthly payments. Please take the money, my wife."

Liah's face lit up. She was flushed with pleasure as she anticipated all the things she would do for the children. It had been so long since they'd had any pleasures. And it had only been during the recent short span of their lives that they had been free from worries and strife. "My husband, if you are certain I should have this money, I will take it gratefully," she said. A moment later, she asked Sen if he would take them to China Street on Sunday. "The children need shoes and they haven't had an outing for a long time. I will need yarn to knit our winter clothing and get flannel to make sleeping clothes. Perhaps we'll even have supper at a café and invite Cousin Shah and Mah Ting to join us."

Sen smiled, "Let us wait and see how my work goes. If I am done early enough, we'll all go to China Street."

—

Summer dragged on and Indian summer was intolerable for Liah. She hated the sticky perspiration and the larger loads of laundry. Most of all, she despaired of the inroads the sun made on her skin. Surely, in the entire world, there was no sun as ruthless as the one in Loo Sahng! At least Dai Faw, being near the sea, was blessed with afternoon respites from the summer's heat. She, for one, would welcome autumn. As swiftly as she yearned for autumn, Liah also thought of the inconvenience of the rains that accompanied it: the muddy feet, the cold and the children's confinement indoors. Sometimes, she reasoned, the Gods didn't understand a human's needs.

By the end of September, Sen was restless. Without crops to occupy his mind, he found time heavy on his hands. Only the family vegetables, which required little care, remained and with all the buildings newly painted, there was little repair work for him to do. Liah felt Sen was underfoot and one day she suggested he visit Cousin Shah in China Street. "While you're there, why not lay in some supplies? We need rice, taro root flour, salt fish and, oh, yes, be sure to get some liver sausages and tinned fish plus two pounds of black mushrooms. Buy some of the dried noodles and wafers for the children, too."

Sen, who had been sitting around lethargically, jumped atop his wagon seat immediately and started out on the bumpy trip to China Street. A few miles down the road, he was startled when a swarthy, overall-clad man suddenly came into view, standing in the middle of the road waving. A terror gripped him, but as Sen neared the man, he saw his stricken face. Sen drew up on the reins. The man's look of desperation was one Sen understood well.

The Mexican pantomimed that he needed a ride into town. His *madre* was ill! He pointed to his "casa," a shack nearly obscured by a billowing, lacy pepper tree. Sen didn't comprehend much of what the man said; nevertheless, he motioned for the stranger to climb aboard.

When they reached the Plaza, Sen pantomimed that if the man would meet him in the same spot, he'd give him a ride home. Sen pointed to the clock on the steeple wall, six o'clock. Martinez, which Sen pronounced "Mahtineh," nodded gratefully.

A few minutes after six o'clock, Sen drove his wagon alongside the grassy Plaza and looked about for Martinez. Sen thought that he could wait a few more minutes, for the man lived such a distance away. Ten minutes later, Sen spied Martinez accompanied by an old woman, her shoulders stooped, shuffling in the manner of the aged. Martinez's face was flooded with a look of utter relief and gratitude when he saw Sen and the wagon. Sen brushed aside the man's profuse apologies and helped the old woman onto the wagon seat.

Their trip home was silent. Sen glanced several times at Martinez but words would not come. Once Martinez's mother looked up at Sen with a faint sad smile, such sadness that Sen winced. Sen drew up the reins when he reached the same spot in the road where he'd first seen Martinez.

Martinez motioned for Sen to wait as he raced toward his house. A few minutes later, followed by a woman clad in a colorful skirt and white blouse surrounded by a swarm of noisy children, Martinez handed Sen a huge bottle. Sen refused, but Martinez's gratitude was not to be denied. As he drove off, Sen turned his head and saw the entire family waving and shouting "Adios!"

On Tuesday afternoon, two days after their meeting, Martinez appeared at Sen's farm. Liah was half-frightened by the stranger until Sen explained how he had met Martinez. Martinez handed Liah a bag of dried corn and pantomimed feeding the chickens. Liah bowed and accepted the sack full of corn. Martinez also pantomimed the making of corn meal, but Liah was unable to understand.

Sen took Martinez out to his fields, then showed him around the barn. In sign language and pidgin English, Martinez pantomimed that he wanted to help Sen with his work. Sen shook his head, saying there wasn't enough work for wages, but if he was willing, they'd work together and Martinez could take home what vegetables, fruit and eggs that Sen could spare.

The children of both Sen and Martinez became the great benefactors of their parents' meeting. After that, they spent their playtime in each other's homes, even sharing meals. When Sen's eldest daughter informed her father that Martinez was Mexican and that his name was pronounced *Mar-tee-nez*, Sen retorted haughtily, "Mahtineh is what I've called him and whatever his nationality, Mahtineh is a very good man."

One evening, as Sen counted heads around their supper table, he jested, "If it were not enough to feed seven mouths of our own, we now have six more!"

Liah chided, "Oh, Sen, how can you say that? The children do not eat that much and, besides, I think it is fine for our children to know others of their age. I suspect they're learning to speak the Mexican language, for the sounds they speak do not sound like Fahn Gwai."

Sen guffawed, "Our children do not speak Fahn Gwai, but now they're speaking Mexican? I wonder if Mahtineh's children are speaking Chinese."

Eldest Daughter contradicted her father. "We do too speak Fahn Gwai! Remember when we lived in Dai Faw, when elder brothers and I helped sell vegetables on our farm? A nice Fahn Gwai lady came each week and brought us books and helped us to read and talk. We speak some Fahn Gwai, but we just don't read or write it too well." Sen nodded, "You are right, Eldest Daughter, your Ba Ba had forgotten."

The days felt cooler and the sun shone more briefly each day as October faded and autumn came to the farm. Sen did not take his children as often to visit Mahtineh's home. Thoughts of winter reminded him that the Fahn Gwai's New Year was approaching and, following it, their

Chinese New Year. Liah checked their Chinese calendar and confirmed that 1906 was to be the Year of the Horse.

Unlike the previous years, the approaching New Year of the Horse filled Liah with warmth and anticipation. For wasn't it so, she now had ample money to celebrate the feast day? Liah closed her eyes, seeing her egg money tucked safely in a leather pouch amid the clutter of clothing in her drawer. How important was money! With it everything was possible; without it, not even the necessities of life were within reach. She vowed that the upcoming New Year would be lavishly celebrated. She would make up for earlier years. Visions of all of her favorite foods, the rice wine, incense, tapers, pyramids of fresh shiny fruits and the sounds of laughter whirled through Liah's mind. For the first time, she was both joyous and content, now secure and financially able to make possible a few more luxuries in their daily lives.

1906

YEAR OF THE HORSE

Nineteen hundred and six began to unfold for Liah much the same as the fifteen months before had, except this year, the Year of the Horse, they were to have their own celebration in their new home.

Liah was in a frenzy, preparing the traditional Chinese pyramid-shaped *doong*, a symbol of the Chinese New Year, which required a tremendous amount of intricate cooking and an inordinate amount of time. Ti leaves needed to be washed and boiled clean. A ball of string with which to keep the *doong* from falling apart had to be found and made ready. All the component ingredients needed to be assembled: Chinese liver sausages, salt fat pork, salted fish, Chinese black mushrooms and salted duck eggs. Liah also had to gather and measure out the culled sweet rice, lotus seeds, dried shrimp and raw peanuts. Moreover, these very special *doong* required all the ingredients be diced, quartered, sliced or hulled. As she worked, Liah's heart was light and the cares that had dogged her life seemed to have vanished. Her thoughts turned to the happiness she had seen on her husband's face as Sen informed her of his decision to purchase his plow the following week. Seeing his face shining with hope, she marveled at how much younger than his thirty-eight years he now appeared. Ah, indeed the Year of the Horse bode nothing but happiness, thought Liah as she happily readied the *doong* for the celebration feast.

Sen munched on an apple as he watched Liah carefully arrange Ti leaves in the palm of her hand, forming the first of the four sides of the pyramid. He wondered at how the Ti leaves retained their position. Each time Liah reached out for an ingredient, adding a bit more rice to the pockets, Sen was amazed at her patience. The *doong* was ingeniously pleated as she built the pyramid. She then strategically tied and knotted cotton string around each *doong*, ensuring the ingredients would not spill out in the steaming process. "What a tedious process," thought Sen. A twinge of guilt invaded his thoughts as he considered that, if Liah were home in the village, the preparation of the New Year's *doong* would be a time for all the women in the village to congregate and have a competition to see who could make the tastiest and shapeliest *doong*. This would have helped to relieve the tedium of the task. To think he had wrested her from a sheltered life and thrust her into the midst of insecurity and hostility. He silently promised himself that after he'd purchased his plow, he would buy her a sewing machine. He grinned; perhaps if Liah did not have to sew their clothes by hand, he'd have a decent shirt and pair of pants. Sen cleared his throat, "I was thinking that once I buy my plow, I'd save money to buy you a sewing machine. What do you say to that?"

Liah, taken by surprise, felt her heart pound. She glanced up and their eyes caught, locking in a rare instant of loving contentment. She murmured, "I will be done with the *doong* by tomorrow night. For a while I was not certain I'd finish in time."

Sen grunted contentedly. Although Liah did not thank him, Sen knew she was grateful. Such was the way of marriage, he sighed. Thoughts were so much more important than words.

Besides the cooking, Liah tended to the house and sewed the family's New Year's clothes. "Why couldn't her family make an effort to be more careful with their clothing?" she thought as she resentfully scrubbed a large pile of dirty laundry.

The Year of the Horse was celebrated for two days and nights. Mah Ting, Cousin Shah and many of the men who had helped in the building of their home were invited. The feast was even more elaborate with Cousin Shah's offering of roast ducks and barbequed ribs and pork. Mah Ting's generous gifts of the Chinese liquor Ng Ga Pei for the adults and soda water for the children livened up the festivities.

The Ng Ga Pei flowed freely and, for the first time since being in Gem Sahn, Sen got drunk. As he looked down at Sen, Cousin Shah remarked wryly, "I believe this kind of drinking is good for him. He's too intense and somber. Well, Sen, may the New Year bring you and your family health, wealth and happiness!"

After two days, Liah was loath to end the celebration. It was not only the gaiety, the eating, drinking, and laughter, but also the aromas of the New Year's celebration that she did not want to end. The fragrance of the symmetrical mounds of oranges, tangerines, Chinese pears and persimmons mingled with that of the Chinese lilies and taro roots. The spicy aromas of anise, garlic, ginger and Ng Ga Pei vied for a place with the crisp smell of fried noodles, roast duck, roast pork, spiced chicken and moon cakes. Their home was overwhelmed with the smells and the sounds of the New Year.

Liah knew that for the remainder of her life she would always hold this celebration keenly in her heart and mind. Wistfully, like a child, she wanted the joy to last forever, but knew in her heart that that was impossible. Ah, well, two days of festivities were better than nothing. Once more, Liah turned her mind to daily life.

On the fourteenth of February, Mah Ting arrived to take Sen to Fahn Gwai town to purchase his plow. "I know you won't be using the implement for a while, but by planting time I won't have the time to take you to purchase it."

Sen replied, "Don't worry, Mah Ting, today suits me fine. Let's go!"

It was late afternoon before Liah heard the wagon wheels returning. Anxious to see the new plow, she went out on the front porch to wait for the men.

Sen leaped from the wagon and shouted that now he was a real farmer! "We'll pick it up next week, Liah."

"Why next week, Sen? Why not today? I don't understand."

Mah Ting, his arms loaded with packages, hurried to explain that it was the way the company did business. "They do not keep heavy farm equipment on hand. Only when it is ordered does the warehouse ship the implement to the store. This large company is well known throughout the United States. You should see their catalogue of merchandise! You can even buy clothing and bedding or household goods by simply sending in an order with the right numbers!"

Mah Ting declined Sen's invitation for supper despite being tempted by liver sausage and salt fish. "My cousin's wife will be annoyed if I don't have supper at home. You know how women from the old country are. They are sometimes unreasonably irritable. But thank you anyway."

Sen trotted around the kitchen while Liah finished preparing supper, showing her the various items in the catalogue. "You can look through the book when you have time. There is even a sewing machine you may want."

After supper, the discussion continued. Liah turned with exasperation to her husband and declared that it was out of the question for her to buy a sewing machine; they did not have the money. "You don't need money, Liah. I've been trying to tell you, I only put down twenty dollars on the plow and I signed a paper guaranteeing I'd make the monthly payments."

"Sen, this is foolishness. How can you sign such a paper? You can't write Fahn Gwai. I don't understand!"

Sen, with a feeling of superiority, retorted that he didn't expect her to understand the ways of business, but that he would appreciate it if she realized that he did. "I made an 'X' on a piece of paper and Mah Ting signed his name, too. Now we can buy anything we want."

Liah shook her head. "No. We shall buy nothing except with money. Now, shall we prepare for bed?"

—

In the days following Sen's trip to the Fahn Gwai's store to order his plow, Liah's mind turned to the future of her children. Without a formal education in the Fahn Gwai's school they would grow up to follow in their father's footsteps, becoming shadows in the Fahn Gwai's world, taking whatever the barbarians deemed good enough. But Liah's main concern was that her children not fear the White Devils, as their father did! Each time Liah had broached the subject of schooling, however, Sen had refused without discussion.

One afternoon, as Sen teased Eldest Son about his grasp of what Señora Mahtineh had told him about corn being good for the chickens, Liah again brought up the subject of school. Perhaps this time Sen would not forbid her children to have an education.

"Sen," she murmured, "It's been on my mind that the children should be going to school. Unlike you or me, they ought to be able to face life with something more than the role of a persecuted slave. If they understood, spoke and wrote the Fahn Gwai's language they would be able to earn a better living. The Mexicans have a school and Mahtineh said the teachers would teach our children."

Abruptly, Sen's mood changed, his voice became stern and somewhat angry. "What need do they have of Fahn Gwai education, my wife? How many times, woman, do I have to tell you that the Fahn Gwai will not hire our children. Not when they have the opportunity to hire a Fahn Gwai. You're dreaming foolish dreams and I will have no more of it!"

Liah quickly lowered her head. Her husband was too pessimistic. Did he not believe that things would change for the better? If not a great deal, surely their children's lives would be less desperate. She could not go on if she did not believe such an improvement would occur. She must intercede for Sen with the Goddess.

On the morning of the twenty-fourth day of the Fahn Gwai's month of February, Liah and Sen's house stirred with tension and anticipation. For today Sen was to pick up his new plow.

Mah Ting entered the front door, wondering if anything ever happened in Sen's house that was anything less than a banner day. Envy engulfed Mah Ting fleetingly, for it was a fortunate man who was surrounded by a loving family. Perhaps he, too, should bring his family from the old country. But immediately Mah Ting vetoed the thought. With his luck, his wife would turn out just like his cousin's. Two such females under one roof would be a disaster!

Liah's heart pounded and her pride soared when Sen told her she would not need to prepare supper. He announced that she need only cook the rice, for he would bring home some special foods from China Street. He grinned foolishly as he added, "To celebrate my new plow!"

Eldest Son cried for his father not to forget the liver sausages. Eldest Daughter inquired as to whether her father was bringing home some fried squab. Sen smiled indulgently, "Yes, I'll not only bring home the sausages and squab, but perhaps also a slab of barbequed pig!"

That afternoon Liah and the children were waiting at the front of the house when Mah Ting's wagon rumbled down the road. Liah was puzzled to see Mahtineh with them. Sen explained that he needed the man's assistance to unload the heavy implement.

The children swarmed around the wagon in an attempt to see the new plow as Sen shouted at them to get back. Handing Liah several large, heavy boxes he leaped off the wagon and began to untie the ropes. The three men pulled, tugged and pushed the heavy implement toward the edge of the wagon. Gasping for breath, they grunted and cursed.

"You'd think they'd place the damn plow closer to the edge. Then we'd not be struggling," complained Sen.

Mah Ting urged patience. "Any closer to the edge and the plow could be jarred off. Now when I count to three, we'll all push at one time."

With that, they finally lowered the plow to the ground. Sen turned proudly to Liah. "Doesn't it make you feel good? It's beautiful, don't you think?"

Mah Ting retorted cryptically, "Enjoy the newness, Sen, for in a few months it will be just like any other plow, just an implement to break your back on!"

Mahtineh ran his worn, work-calloused hands over the plow's handle and softly marveled half-aloud at how much easier it would now be to plow. Sen smiled and offered the use of the plow to Mahtineh, enjoying the grin the offer evoked on Mahtineh's face.

The next morning, before the sun had appeared above the tall hills, Sen crept carefully out of bed. He quickly dressed and went out to the barn where in the dim predawn light he gazed at his shiny plowshare. He touched it much as a lover, and ran his hands along its smooth, cold surface. How sturdy, he thought, as he admired its gleaming blades. For a split second, he entertained the idea of taking it out for a trial run, but then he shook his head. Liah might think him mad! But only a moment more had passed before Sen reached for the horses' reins and led the horses from the stall.

A glorious exultation flowed through him as Sen followed the turn of the plow. The give of earth turning beneath the blades and the pungent fragrance of the upturned soil, moist with the promise of life, filled Sen with joy. In the stillness of the first light, Sen heard Liah's voice. He turned to see her signaling him to return to the house.

With his face glowing with a slightly foolish grin, Sen stopped the horses and clapped like a child. "Oh, it feels so good. My own plow! The earth is so pungent and it can only mean rich soil. It seems the promise of life was never so vital."

"It is wonderful to see you so vibrant, my husband."

"Then you don't think me mad for doing this foolish thing?"

"No," answered Liah, with a faint indulgent smile on her face.

—

On April twentieth, Sen drove his wagon into China Street for supplies. He stopped at Cousin Shah's place as was his habit. When he rapped on the door, no one answered, but Sen heard noises inside. Sen tried the knob and was surprised to find the door unlocked. He said to himself, "What's this, unlocked so early in the day?" As he entered Cousin Shah's house, he saw a group of men gathered around a table speaking rapidly with concern evident in their voices. Sen sensed something was terribly wrong, for no one paid him heed. The men were huddled over a newspaper laid out on the table. Sen rushed over and demanded to know what was the matter. Cousin Shah's face was pale and drawn as he stared dully at Sen.

Sen cried again, "What is it, Cousin?"

"Aiyah!" moaned Cousin Shah, covering his face with his hands. "The Gods have cursed us! All is lost!"

"I do not understand, Shah. Please explain!"

One man raised his head and in a dull, shocked tone muttered, "An earthquake and fire has taken all of Dai Faw!"

Sen recoiled, thunderstruck. When he was able to gather his wits, he gasped, "When?"

Someone muttered, "The eighteenth day of this month."

The faces of Elder Lee Ti and of Elder Wong Ting flashed before Sen. And what about Fatt On, his generous and loyal friend? Half-aloud Sen moaned, "Oh, no, not them!"

Sen pushed himself in for a better look at the newspaper. He peered at the photographs of the earthquake's aftermath. He could not believe it, for destruction was everywhere. Sen gasped, "I won't accept that all is gone." He leaned over and pointed. "Is that all that's left of China Street, Du Pon Gai and Fish Alley? Where is Deadman's Corner? Look, even the big Fahn Gwai church is nothing but a gutted skeleton!"

His legs felt weak as Sen fell into a chair, his body heavy and his mind disoriented. Even as he recalled the photographs, his mind fought to discount them. "Not Elder Lee Ti, nor Elder Wong Ting and certainly not Fatt On! They must be alive!" Sen turned and shouted, "Doesn't the Fahn Gwai newspaper say anything about our people?"

Lew Loong looked up and sneered, "About us? The 'Yellow Peril'? Has the calamity erased your senses? They're probably ecstatic our people were wiped out!"

Cousin Shah raised his head and shouted as he pointed an accusing finger at Loong. "Spit and speak again! Our people are yet alive. We'll just have to wait for word. It will be hard to do, but the Gods have made us sturdy, or else we'd have perished long ago!"

Sen shook his head, trying desperately not to sob, for the possibility of the deaths of three of the most important friends in his life revived memories of his murdered older brother. Sen gestured helplessly and mumbled half-aloud that he had to get home. "I must tell Liah!"

Liah heard the returning wagon and waited in the house for Sen. When he did not enter, she rushed outside to see what was keeping him. "What's happened, Sen? You look as if the end of the world has come."

Sen dropped the reins and shook his head slowly. "It might as well be! Two days ago, on the eighteenth, an earthquake leveled Dai Faw. The entire city went up in smoke. They say the town is now under martial law and that a search is being launched for the bodies." He hunched back in his seat on the wagon and moaned, "I saw the photographs, Liah, and all is destruction. I know no one is alive. Not under all that rubble! Oh, Liah, what am I going to do without Elders Li and Wong? And what about Fatt On? I shouldn't want to go on if they are dead."

Liah motioned for her first-born son to unload the wagon and unhitch the horses, then she urged her husband off the wagon and led him into the house where he slumped into a chair and buried his face in his arms.

"Get hold of yourself, Sen," pleaded Liah. She prepared to reheat his supper. "There is nothing we can do at this time. I feel it in my heart that your three companions are yet alive, especially Fatt On. His Meng-Sui was strong and good. Wait and see! You'll know I'm right. Meanwhile have supper to reinforce your body and spirit. Keep faith with Kwan Koong for their safety. The Gods have eyes!"

Even as she spoke, Liah's courage faltered. She, too, despaired of the demise of the generous, gluttonous Fatt On who had done so much to ensure their comfort.

"Meng-Sui, life-water," muttered Sen. "Yes, Fatt On was always a lucky man."

Liah left her husband to himself. She frowned as he pushed aside his rice bowl and leaned forward on his elbows, his mind eons away. It was not until Liah saw him wince that she knew Sen was re-living the murder of his older brother, Gan. It was always that way with Sen; whenever misfortune struck. Would Sen never forget and let Gan become a citizen of the heavenly world?

Deep in thought, Sen remembered his brother as his thoughts went back in time and he could vividly recall the events.

"I'm going to the bank to send another money draft back to the family," Gan had announced. "Sen, you watch the store."

Sen nodded. "Do not hurry, Gan, there is not much to do today. I'll finish the sweeping and restock the shelves."

An hour lapsed. Sen, finished with his work, sat at the window looking out into the alley. He saw his brother approaching. Suddenly, as Gan was about to cross the alley, three Fahn Gwai hoodlums came from out of nowhere. One jumped Gan while the other two youths pummeled and beat their fists into his face. They roared with laughter as

Gan tried to break free. Like a cat with a mouse, they allowed Gan to get free, only to reach out and grab him by his queue.

Sen cowered behind the counter, watching in horror, wanting to go out to help, but too frightened to move. One man raised his arm and Sen saw the glint of steel. Panic overwhelmed his immobility and Sen dashed out to aid his older brother.

Too late! Sen winced as he saw the ruffian's hand plunge downward. Overcome with terror, Sen darted back into the store, ran to the rear door and raced to the House of Lee where he poured out his story to the Elders before falling into a faint.

The Elders administered to the stricken Sen while four young men quickly and quietly left. Ten minutes later they returned carrying Gan's body covered in a sheet. Sen stared uncomprehendingly at the body for a full ten minutes then he broke into paroxysms of sobs.

The Elders whispered to each other and decided Sen was in no condition to make funeral arrangements. They would do it. Afterwards the Elders sent Sen to stay with a cousin who farmed on the Peninsula, just outside the city.

Six weeks later, on the twentieth of April, in the Fahn Gwai year of 1890, the Elders sent Cousin Qui to fetch Sen.

Elder Lee Ti gently informed Sen of the arrival of his wife, Lin Fah, in Dai Faw. Sen stared dully at the old man without reaction. Elder Ti, after three attempts, assigned Cousin Qui to accompany Sen to the dock. "He is in no condition to go alone."

As they headed there, Cousin Qui glanced nervously at the rigid Sen beside him and wished the episode at dockside were done. Unknown to the Elders, Qui was apprehensive about leaving China Street. He muttered tersely, "Sen, do you know Lin Fah is arriving today? Do you?"

Sen nodded silently. Qui continued, "Well, then, when we get there you must go to the immigration building to wait for her. I'll stay outside with the horse and wagon. Do you understand?"

Again, Sen nodded without a word.

Cousin Qui, agitated, thought to reprimand Sen, but shook his head. What could one expect from a man so stricken with guilt? If only Sen would realize that there was nothing he could have done for Gan. Gan's Meng-Sui demanded such a demise.

Cousin Qui stopped just outside the wharf area and pulled the wagon up among the odiferous fishing nets. He nudged Sen roughly to push him off the wagon seat. He pointed, "There! That's the place! I'll wait for you here. Now, Sen, you must go to your wife."

Sen gaped for a moment, then climbed down off the wagon. Suddenly, he felt tense. Looking up, he heard Cousin Qui urging him to go. Sen darted toward a building at the water's edge. He was relieved to see the first and second waves of passengers disembarking from a ship, for he knew that only once they had left the ship would the steerage passengers be allowed to leave. He skirted the crowds of Fahn Gwai, feeling the sweat in his palms, the wetness of terror. Each shove, each shout, sent dread down his spine. His fear of a possible Fahn Gwai attack was overwhelming.

His terror gave way to anxiety as his thoughts finally turned to Lin Fah. As he entered the building, the memory of his own arduous journey reminded Sen that Lin Fah would be weak as she would not have eaten well during her long journey. He hoped that the noxious bilge odors and the enervating steam of the closed quarters would not have made his wife too ill, for if she were to faint in the immigration building, it would mean detention.

The disembarkation of passengers was a long process. Almost an hour later, Sen, peering out a window, saw the first Chinese Coolie at the ship's rail. At the first appearance of Lin Fah he forgot his fears and rushed out of the building. At the fence separating passengers from the land, he shouted excitedly to his wife. Lin Fah did not recognize the stranger calling to her, but she turned to move toward him. Sen quickly dissuaded her, "Hurry, get back to the head of the line or you'll be all day getting out."

Although her husband's appearance seemed strange, Lin Fah recognized Sen's voice. She nodded and rejoined the group of immigrants making their way out. She was shocked at Sen's appearance; he looked so different from how she remembered him. He was so much taller and bigger, especially in the shoulders. He was no longer the boy-groom, with his smooth, light skin. He was now so dark and rough looking. She wondered what he'd been doing. He looked like a sun burnt farmer! She wondered what had happened to his queue. She didn't know that he had hidden it beneath his hat.

Suddenly, recalling Sen's brusque command to get back into the line, she began to fret. What if he didn't like her anymore? Whatever would she do? But Lin Fah had no time for further fretting, for as she entered the building she had to turn her attention to the ordeal of the immigration interrogation.

In the outer waiting room, Sen was also having misgivings about their reunion. Lin Fah was as tiny as when he had last seen her, but even with the resurgence of his memories, Sen was startled at her miniscule appearance. Perhaps he had grown accustomed to seeing the well-developed women of Gold Mountain. He marveled at her tiny, oval face, her high cheekbones and smooth, porcelain complexion.

Sen suddenly felt cheated. Eight-odd years of separation! He vowed that he and Lin Fah would make up for all those lost years. Sen felt tears rising to the back of his eyes as he thought of his brother. Gan was never to know his sister-in-law; he was not to be a part of this happy reunion. He must tell Lin Fah of the anguish in his heart. In his desire to share his innermost emotions with someone close, time became insufferably slow.

Sen became more restless as the hour hand on the wall clock touched three. Two hours had inched by. His own anticipation was heightened by other families reuniting around him, laughing and sobbing in joy. Still another hour passed and Sen was becoming alarmed, for Lin Fah's clearance was taking much longer than his own. He prayed to Kwan Koong that nothing was wrong. Just as he had finally worked up enough courage to inquire if anything was wrong, the gate opened and Lin Fah came through.

Sen dashed across the huge expanse of waiting room with all the intention of grabbing Lin Fah into his arms. He wanted to kiss her and tell her all the things in his heart. But as he approached her, Sen became reserved. When finally they faced each other, all Sen could do was to smile. He bowed his head slightly and took her by the arm to lead her outside. Lin Fah was also shy. She had bowed low before Sen took her arm. Even though their first meeting after the long years apart was silent and restrained, each sensed the other's joy.

Outside, the impact of their reunion dissipated as they faced each other shyly. Sen roused to attend to Lin Fah's luggage. "I will need to ask for Cousin Qui's help with your trunk," he explained to Lin Fah.

Sen moaned as he hoisted Lin Fah's steamer trunk onto its side so he and Cousin Qui could load it onto the wagon. "What," he huffed, "did you do? Bring all the village's possessions?" Cousin Qui chuckled as he lifted one end of the trunk and slipped it onto the wagon.

Lin Fah cried out for careful handling as Sen and Cousin Qui roughly shoved and pulled at another huge crate. "That one contains the jugs of herbal alcohol and medicinal brews my mother insisted I bring!"

The trip back to Gan's store was uncomfortable for both of them, as they sought but could not find any words.

Sen sighed. Even if he could speak, he wouldn't in the presence of Cousin Qui. Sen smiled and saw Lin Fah drop her eyes. Lin Fah, seeing her husband's face filled with longing and desire, felt inadequate.

Some distance farther, Lin Fah timidly asked, "Do you know the helpful Fahn Gwai woman who helped me in the questioning? I was surprised to hear her speak our language. If it had not been for her immeasurable assistance, I'd never have survived the ordeal."

Sen shrugged, "I don't know her name, but she's a church lady. In China Street she is known as a tigress. I hear tell she enters our Tong rooms to rescue slave girls." Having offered this explanation, Sen lapsed into silence for the remainder of the ride home.

When Sen and Lin Fah were finally alone in Gan's store, Sen turned to his wife and broke into tears. Lin Fah went to him at once. Bewildered, she held him close as she inquired as what was the matter. Between Sen's sobs, Lin Fah learned of the violent death of her brother-in-law.

Sen sobbed inconsolably, "I ran away! I didn't even go to my brother's aid! My own brother... I was a coward!" Lin Fah gripped Sen even closer. "But you said it was so sudden an attack, over so quickly. You did not have time to help. Do not blame yourself, Sen. Gan's Meng-Sui declared it so."

Lin Fah's eyes roved around the room as she held her husband. She was crestfallen at what she saw. She'd had visions of riches and luxuries, but looking about her, she found neither. All at once she felt trapped. "What," she silently asked, "is my new life to be? What is expected of me?"

That evening in the darkness of their bedroom, Sen and Lin Fah bridged the span of their long separation.

When finally Sen unclasped her, Lin Fah, drowsy and depleted, felt a sense of desolation. She asked herself, was she expecting too much? Could it be his grief? Somehow she was disappointed in their reunion. All at once, she blushed. Such unwomanly contemplations! Exhausted from her journey and the stress of the reunion, Lin Fah cuddled closer to her husband with the thought of tomorrow. Tomorrow would be better.

—

Three months later Sen received Lin Fah's entry documents. He was horrified when the immigration interpreter informed him of a discrepancy in his wife's name. The officials in Hong Kong had entered her name phonetically. Ignorant of the Chinese pronunciation, they had written her name as "Liah".

Lin Fah, when told, was furious! She demanded the young man correct the misspelling.

The young college student, who earned his tuition money working as an immigration interpreter, curtly retorted, "Madam, there is too much government process to go through to do that! As far as you are concerned, be thankful you were admitted! Use your real name for practical purposes, but legally when you have to sign papers, you must use 'Liah'. I am sorry, there is nothing I can do. Good day to you both."

Sen nervously tried to calm his wife. Motioning to the young man to leave, Sen whispered to him, "You know how Chinese women are about their names. My wife is no different." She was as lovely as her name—Lin Fah, Lotus Blossom.

Two weeks following the young interpreter's visit, Lin Fah went to her husband with an apology. "I am ashamed of my tirade. It is just that I feel the Fahn Gwai have stripped me of the one thing that is truly mine–my name. I've decided that if the government has changed my name to Liah, then Liah is what you may call me. Still, my heart is sad and my mind is angered at the callousness of the Fahn Gwai. How would they like it if we did that to them?"

During the next few months, Sen found that he was not a businessman. He lamented not having learned from his older brother. Sen's frustration came to a climax one day after a series of mishaps. In total frustration, he locked the front door of the store and declared angrily that he was not a shopkeeper but a farmer.

Liah allowed her husband to rant and afterwards in a timid voice she tried to soothe him. "I've noted your discontent of late but did not know the cause. I feared I was to blame. Why not appeal to the House of Lee? They might be able to locate a farm for you. All that is important is your happiness, my husband."

His wife's concern left Sen with a sense of guilt. Poor woman, alone in Gem Sahn with only an irritable, angry husband. Calmed by his sense of guilt, Sen agreed to Liah's suggestion; he'd go immediately.

Soon Sen returned home in high spirits. The Elders had promised to act on his behalf.

"When they told me to be patient, and to do my best until they find the right place, I smiled indulgently. My wife, I beg forgiveness for my sullen nature of late. Have no fear, I will not give in to my temper again."

—

It was the first week in August when Fatt On happened to drop in at the Six Companies House. He deplored the rigors of farming and he told the Elders as much. He was a city man unused to the strenuous labors of a farm. A store, even a small café, was better than pitting his body and mind against the seasons.

Two weeks later, on the twentieth day of August in 1892, Fatt On and Sen traded places. Fatt On took over Sen's store and Sen took over Fatt On's farm.

Fatt On pressed Sen to take whatever supplies he needed to sustain them for the coming months as he hadn't put in any crops.

Liah watched as the fat, smiling man loaded Sen's wagon with boxes of tinned salted fish, mullet, pickled turnips, and preserved fruits. He then added baskets filled with black mushrooms, Chinese peas, mustard greens, chard and fresh fruits. Sen protested when Fatt On started to load sacks of flour, rice, sugar, salt and noodles. "You've already given us too much!" Sen said.

However, Fatt On was insistent. He continued to press upon them several sacks of shrimp, squid and scallops. "You'll need every bit of this. There is no food at the farm." He smiled sheepishly, "As you will soon find, I am no farmer! Oh, I almost forgot, take this keg of salted duck eggs and some fresh chicken eggs. I will come to see you in a few weeks and if there are things you need, I will be happy to bring them out to you. You do not know how happy you have made me. Life on the farm was slowly killing me. Now I can live again."

Liah pressed her palms together in a gesture of gratitude, smiling shyly as she lowered her eyes.

Fatt On waved aside her thanks, muttering that he was the one who should thank them.

Sen turned impulsively to Liah to say that he wished to see Elders Lee and Wong once again to thank them for their help. "The two Elders have done so much for me, I cannot leave without showing my gratitude one more time. You wait here, I will be back soon."

An hour later Sen returned with an armful of clothing. "Elder Wong gave these to me. He said they belonged to Dak. Look, Liah, woolen shirts, sweaters, and a raincoat and rain hat. Even a couple of pairs of leather boots! Now I will be outfitted for a long time. I am fortunate that Dak wore the same size clothing. These two pairs of leather shoes fit me like they were my own."

Liah smiled. "Who is this Dak? He must be rich to have left so many expensive clothes. It seems it was for your good fortune, Sen."

Sen laughed. "No, Dak is a young man who went back to China to find himself a wife. I think Dak expected to return to Gem Sahn. It was his older brother's idea for him to return to China. As Dak is a pleasure-seeking youth, of course, Elder Wong has no intention of allowing Dak to return. Poor Dak!"

Sen shook hands with Fatt On, took a last look at the store, then turned away. Fatt On shouted goodbye and, with a last wish for their good fortune, he watched as Sen and Liah's wagon rumbled away.

—

Their new farm was a few miles from Dai Faw out on the Peninsula. Sen pointed to a row of pine trees. "There! A ways back from that clump of trees is our new home!"

Sen drove the team of horses up to the barn, then helped Liah off the wagon. Turning, he ran like an anxious schoolboy out to the fields.

Liah, clutching a metal box containing her jewels and the little money they had earned at Gan's store, followed her husband.

Sen was appalled at what he was seeing, for Fatt On indeed was not a farmer! The furrows were all uneven, crooked and much too shallow. Sen cried, "Just look at those furrows, too shallow in spots and too deep in others! Well, my wife, just wait, things will change and we'll have a good farm."

He motioned for Liah to follow as he darted toward the barn. Opening the doors he expected to find livestock. Disappointment clouded his face as he looked around the barn and found only a few scrawny chickens and ducks scrambling noisily out of his way.

"Oh, well, we will buy some pigs, maybe even a cow, with the money we have left. Come, let's inspect our house."

Liah gasped as Sen pushed open the door to the two-room farmhouse. The house reeked of various odors; the smells of human, animal and food were heavy and suffocating. Liah cried, "Fatt On was no housekeeper either! Ugh, what filth; it will take years to clean out all this mess and smell!"

"No hurry, my wife," sighed Sen, "we'll do what we can each day. It will get done."

They left their belongings on the ground near the wagon. Liah refused to enter what she called the "pig sty" with her belongings.

Sen unhitched the horses and led them to the tiny pasture, then returned to Liah. "Where are we to sleep this night if you refuse to enter the house?"

Liah pointed to the barn. "At least it smells better than that house!"

The next day they began working from sun up until the sun had gone down. Liah worked on readying the house as Sen labored in the fields. Liah scrubbed and rescrubbed the walls and floors. She washed and rewashed the grimy windows. The front door was left open night and day in of the hope that it would diminish the unpleasant odors that still clung stubbornly to the air. Liah lit incense sticks constantly to purify the atmosphere. It was two weeks before the house was ready for them to move in.

The results of Sen's labors in the fields were immediately evident. Symmetrical furrows appeared. Surely the drainage was improved, mused Sen. Life was hard, but Sen felt alive and much happier.

One evening Sen felt his joy was complete when Liah shyly confided that she was with child.

Sen gaped disbelievingly. He reached out and embraced her, whispering, "Why did you not tell me sooner? Oh, my wife, I am the happiest man on earth! If your date of conception is right...." Sen thought a moment. "The baby should be birthed in June of next year."

Five months later, on the tenth day of June in the year of eighteen hundred and ninety-three, their son, Gan Hing was born. Following the earth-shattering experience of childbirth, Sen and Liah found themselves drawn closer together by the shock of such a momentous event. For Liah, it was the closest she had felt to Sen since her arrival from China. She was ready to believe things would be better. Sen's delight over their first-born son filled Liah with gratitude. She whispered, "A first-born son is a good omen, my husband."

—

Sen felt someone shaking him. Opening his eyes he was surprised to see Liah peering anxiously down at him.

"Sen, come to bed. There is nothing you can do until we get more news from Dai Faw. Do not worry, I am certain Fatt On and Elders Lee Ti and Wong are safe."

Sen heaved himself out of the chair at the table and followed his wife to their bedroom. As he bent to untie his shoelaces, he murmured, "You know, I was dreaming of Fatt On and how we traded places. I also

dreamed of the birth of our eldest son. You know, Liah, I've been think-
ing so often of that man. Just the other day my thoughts were of Fatt
On and his generosity. We would never have survived without his help.
Now, this cursed earthquake! I fear for his life."

Liah had a devout belief in the destiny of the heavens. She believed
that the Gods fated each person to a prearranged plan for life, desig-
nating each person's time and manner of death. She sighed, "Do not
waste your energies, Sen. If Fatt On's Meng-Sui is decreed for a long
life, he will survive. It is the same for the Elders. We cannot fight against
Meng-Sui, my husband, any more than we can change Feng-Sui."

Sen could not sleep, tossing and turning as he moaned his worry. At
one point during the night he bolted upright in bed. Reaching for Liah,
he clung to her, sobbing anew.

Liah comforted him, much in the way she had so many years earlier.
She was chagrined to find Sen had not grown up one bit, at least not
emotionally.

Sen's voice was muffled in the folds of Liah's gown, but she understood that he wanted to go to Dai Faw to search for his three benefactors.

Liah cradled Sen as if he were a child, explaining, "If things are as
bad as the newspapers say, you had better wait a while. Your presence
will only add one more person to feed amid the shortages."

Sen's eyelids began to feel heavy as he muttered, "I must see for myself... I cannot accept the judgment of the Gods... must know... one
way or another." Then he drifted off to sleep.

Sen, in his private grief had not noticed Liah's agony. She recalled
Fatt On's tender understanding of things. Liah wiped an errant tear
from her eye. Since learning of the earthquake and fire, she too had been
constantly plagued by images of his jovial and cherubic face. Mostly
Liah recalled how Fatt On was always there when help was needed.

The incident that kept returning to her mind was when they had
been run off their land on the Peninsula. Fatt On had taken them all in

and, with his usual generosity, he had fed and boarded them. He even bought toys, canned milk and clothes for their son. Liah's tears overflowed as she thought of how Fatt On had wheedled the truth from her regarding why she was so morose and frightened at the time and had roared with laughter when she confessed that she was again with child. He said he would be happy to tell Sen the blessed news.

Liah slipped out of bed and went to the kitchen to light another taper to Kwan Yin for the safety of Sen's three friends. Especially fervent were her prayers for Fatt On's safety. It seemed to Liah that Fatt On's presence lurked in her mind, urging her to keep the faith. Like Sen, she too yearned to know for certain the fate of their friends. For the first time in her life, she found herself faltering in her firm beliefs. She did not, *could not*, rely entirely upon the whims of the Gods. Climbing back into bed, Liah sought solace in slumber.

Over the succeeding days, Liah became increasingly alarmed as Sen became more and more distant and withdrawn. One night she beseeched his return to reality. "Put aside your grief. Turn your mind to the living. We need you, Sen. Sen, do you hear me? Leave death in the hands of the Gods. Fatt On, the Elders, even your brother Gan are out of your reach now. If they perished in the disaster, you are unable to change their destiny."

Sen heaved a deep sigh. Silently gazing at his wife, he wondered at her stoic attitude about death.

Liah, as if divining her husband's accusation of callousness, crept from their bed and went into the kitchen. She wiped tears from her eyes, fighting back her wild desire to scream. Her grief was even sharper because she could not vent, not without frightening Sen or their son. She opened the back door and stared out into the darkness to another time when she had repressed her need for vocalizing her grief. It was the day the immigration interpreter had informed her of the typographical error in her name. Liah had bitten her lips to keep from screaming "I have nothing that's truly my own, not even a name!"

The helpless frustration that plagued her then nettled her now even more. Somehow, Liah vowed, one of her children must learn to negotiate the Fahn Gwai's world and become educated in the Fahn Gwai's law! Then no other person need be helpless as their one true possession is stripped from them, that of their name. Hearing her husband's call, Liah returned to bed.

The next morning, with the first rays of dawn, Sen was out in the fields. He painstakingly broke off the suckers from the main stems of each of the plants in the rows of different crops. There were tomatoes, bell peppers and bitter melon. Nearby he'd planted peach trees. Wearing a pointed hat made of straw tied under his chin, his queue falling over one shoulder, he appeared much as would a farmer of his native Kwangtung working in the rice paddies. His private peaceful world was suddenly shattered when he heard Liah's cry. Looking up in alarm, he saw her waving her arms in excitement for him to come. He dropped his trowel and raced toward her. Huffing and panting, he gasped, "What is it? What has happened?"

Liah pointed toward the house. He wrenched open the door and bounded inside.

Cousin Quock roared his greeting, embracing Sen with an affectionate bear hug. Pandemonium and laughter resounded throughout the house. Cousin Quock bellowed, "I would never have found your place if Cousin Shah had not been along! Loo Sahng, bah! I could never have found my way around town!"

"Cousin Quock, you are the best fisherman in Dai Faw! You would not have gotten lost!"

"Out on the ocean with the sun, moon and stars, it is impossible to get lost. But on land, now that's a different story," roared Cousin Quock. "Oh, I forgot, I've got several sacks in the wagon."

Sen grinned, "Cousin Quock, did you bring crabs and shrimps? I haven't eaten a decent crab since leaving Dai Faw! Oh, where are you fishing these days?"

Cousin Quock was silent a moment, then with a sneer he replied, "Not in Dai Faw if that's what you're asking! I'm still down the coast in Montaleh (*Monterey*). Damn Fahn Gwai fishermen! This new breed of Fahn Gwai is vicious and greedy, not like the men who fished in Dai Faw when I first came."

The children, listening and watching, found the six-foot, bald-headed fisherman with his black bushy moustache, formidable. They huddled at the far end of the room, watching his every move, not daring to speak above hushed whispers. It was as if the devil, Tsao Tsao, whom their mother summoned whenever they were naughty had suddenly come to life. Cousin Quock's voice bounced off the walls and filled every nook of the tiny house.

Eldest Son, the most daring of the seven children, recovered his courage enough to nudge his younger brother. "A giant! Looks like he could eat us up in a single gulp."

Second Son whispered back, his tone was filled with envy, "Yeah, and no queue either. Lucky devil."

Fourth Son nodded silently in agreement, while Third Son gave his queue a disrespectful flip, with a muttered, "Yeah."

Cousin Quock suddenly remembered that he had some letters for Sen. He stopped talking and stuck his hands into his pants pocket. "One is from Elder Ti and here is one from Elder Wong and Cousin Qui. You will be glad to hear that Elder Ti suffered only a few bruises and a sprained wrist when he stumbled. Oh, and Fatt On is fine. He was away visiting a cousin in Second Town (*Sacramento*) when the earthquake happened. I hear tell the city wants to move our people when they re-build, but our people have refused to be relocated." Cousin Quock's voice softened, "Oh, yes, Fatt On said to tell you that he will visit you one of these days, but your store is no more."

Sen heaved a big sigh. "You do not know how you've given me back my life. For these many weeks I've been sick about the quake and fire, not knowing whether our people were alive."

Sen caught a glance of his children huddled against the wall. He beckoned, "Come and meet Cousin Quock. Your father used to work for him on his fishing boat."

Sen looked fondly at his first-born son. "This is Gan Hing, he's almost fourteen. Say, Cousin Quock, could Gan work for you? That will make a man of him! I remember in the beginning I couldn't seem to move fast enough to suit you!" Sen chuckled. "In fact, now that I think about it, I was afraid of you, sir."

Cousin Quock's arm shot out and hauled Eldest Son to his side. The big man gripped Gan Hing's arm. "Hmmm, pretty strong muscles! Sure, he can come work for me, but not before he's fifteen. I'll make a man of him!" Cousin Quock looked down at Gan and asked, "Would you like to work for me, son?"

Eldest Son nodded wordlessly and quickly fled back to the other side of the room.

Second Son whispered that the idea sounded like good fun. Did brother think the giant would let him come along, too? Could older brother ask permission for him, too?

"Ask him yourself. He's scary with that bald head and black moustache! Anyways, what's the rush? *I* can't even go until I'm fifteen years old." Gan Hing flexed his arm, complaining that the big man sure had a strong grip.

"Say, how about cooking the crabs and shrimps?" roared Cousin Quock as he spun around to face Liah. "I'll help you make my marinade. Come on, children, we are going to cook the crabs. Want to watch?"

Cousin Quock supervised as Liah dropped the crabs into a large pot of boiling water. He hovered over her as she prepared his secret marinade of vinegar, ginger root, soy sauce, peanut oil and sesame oil.

"Be certain you mince the ginger fine, Liah. And mix the marinade thoroughly."

Sen peeled the shrimps, showing his children how to make certain the shells and legs were removed; then he dropped them into the marinade.

After they had eaten Sen sighed, "I haven't tasted the likes of this since I quit working for you, Cousin Quock. It especially reminds me of our nightly meals of salt fish steamed in rice."

Cousin Quock leaned back in his chair. Wiping off his fingers, he said, "Do you know it's almost fifteen years since that first day you and your lazy friend came to ask me for a job? Speaking of your lazy friend, his older brother, Dak, Elder Wong tells me, is now married and recently became a father for the fourth time."

The big man's bombastic humor kept the family in jovial spirits. Liah's gratitude was immense for the big fisherman, for she had not heard Sen laugh so much since they had left Dai Faw.

"Dak, a father! Impossible!" cried Sen, "Dak said he was going to remain a bachelor his entire life!"

Cousin Quock bellowed, "Well, he's not only married, but he's a father of four! What's more, he's a hard working merchant. It seems Elder Wong made a wise move when he sent Dak home."

"I believe you, Cousin, women have a cunning way of enslaving a man and Dak's no different. How many sons does he have, sir?"

"I believe Elder Wong said Dak has three sons and one daughter."

Liah heaped a platter of fried noodles and set it in front of Cousin Quock who quickly declined saying that he'd had enough. "What about you children? Take this platter of noodles and there's a lot more shrimp and crabs. Eat up! Growing children need a lot of nourishment!"

Two hours later, the children groaned that they could not eat another bite.

The next morning Liah saw a marked improvement in Sen. He was so full of life, bounding about in high spirits.

"Liah, wouldn't it be fine if Fatt On should visit us this next year? Strange, just a few days ago I spoke of independence when we, in truth, never are. I recall Mah Ting's irritation when I bemoaned the fact that I could never repay his generosities. Nor could I repay any of them for their labors. Now I understand it is for the children we all do for one another. I now understand what Mah Ting meant. Even now, as I speak, I can't help wanting to tell Fatt On what he means to me. Do you think me foolish, or too humble?"

"No, my husband. Fatt On is very special to the both of us. However, don't overburden yourself with too much gratitude. As long as you help someone else who is in need, you will have repaid the debt. When you gave Mahtineh a ride, even though you were terrified, you indirectly repaid your debt to Cousin Shah, Mah Ting and all the others. If you must be grateful, then thank Kwan Koong as I shall thank Kwan Yin."

With the knowledge that Elders Lee and Wong and Fatt On were safe, Sen was able to turn his mind to the farm again. All through the hot summer, Sen arduously tended his crops. This year Liah was even busier than the previous year. She sun-dried trays of sweet potatoes, pickled white peaches and preserved and pickled hot spicy peppers for the winter. Sen exhorted his wife to spend more time pickling chard and mustard greens.

When Mah Ting arrived on the nineteenth day of September for Sen's crop, Liah was disturbed to discover that Sen had not gotten over his distrust and fright of the Fahn Gwai.

Mah Ting had suggested Sen go along to meet the Fahn Gwai and to learn the business procedure. "It isn't that I do not want to go for you, but in case something happens to me, you will be able to carry on."

Sen shook his head vehemently and declared, "I will not face a Fahn Gwai. Not even to sell my crops!"

"But Sen," cried Liah, "you went to buy your plow. What is different about meeting this Fahn Gwai?"

Sen whirled around and snarled at this wife. "Enough woman. You do not tell me what to do! You don't know how I quavered in that man's presence. Only because of my fierce desire to own the implement did I face up to him."

Suddenly embarrassed by his outburst, his voice became apologetic as he promised a future meeting. "Someday, but not now."

"I understand, Sen," replied Mah Ting as he quickly changed the subject, "I will be by this afternoon to drop off your money. Liah, do you need anything from China Street? I will gladly pick it up for you."

Liah shook her head. Still upset by her husband's outburst, she quietly replied, "No, thank you, sir. Sen bought me supplies last week. Would you take supper with us tonight? I know how much you favor salt fish steamed in rice."

"Yes, off course I will, Liah. I'll be back around five-thirty or six." Mah Ting winked at Eldest Son. "Perhaps I'll bring you some liver sausages. Now I'm off to the market."

Turning to Liah, Sen remarked somewhat apologetically that he shouldn't have spoken so sharply to her.

Liah shook her head. "No need for that, my husband. I was out of place in my remarks. You have a right to be cautious. Now, let us have a snack. Then you can begin clearing the ground for our winter crops."

The money from the sale of his produce was more than expected and Sen proudly took his family to China Street on the following Sunday for shopping and supper. As they walked around, men in the cafés smiled and commented on his good fortune in having so many healthy and smart children, which always pleased Sen.

Liah asked Sen to take her to the Mexican store, saying she wanted to buy more yarn to make their winter sweaters. In her heart, she also wanted to purchase more books for her children. Shyly, she mentioned that she wanted to knit herself a new sweater for her birthday. Hopefully, thought Liah, she had prodded her husband's memory. Her special feast day was approaching on the twenty-ninth day of September. Such a tiny thing to wish for, a gift to remember one's day of birth.

LIAH'S FEAST DAY

Liah fretted all during the next few days, hoping to see some sign of a gift. She watched out of the corner of her eye for the slightest sign of secrecy, but, alas, there were none. It couldn't be that Sen refused to acknowledge her feast day. Perhaps Sen meant to buy the gift on the day before. It couldn't be that he could not afford a gift, for the plow was nearly paid off.

The twenty-ninth day of September arrived with a gloom enveloping Liah. Not only had Sen not presented her with a gift, but he hadn't even wished her a happy feast day. The fact that she was thirty-nine years old lay heavy on her heart. She felt cheated. In her village back home, there would have been a festive celebration for the mother of seven children.

When, at the end of the day, Liah glanced up at the setting sun, she gave up any hope of her birthday being celebrated. Sen was too engrossed with daily survival to give any thought or importance to such things as education and the future, much less birthdays.

It was clear to her that if the children were to have anything more than the roof over their heads, shoes on their feet and food in their stomachs, the burden was to be on her shoulders. Oh, she winced, but how was she going to do it all?

They were seated around the supper table when Sen leaned over and petted Liah's arm and wished her a happy feast day. Liah groaned silently as he continued, "You are indeed a fortunate woman, seven healthy children for your old age! Not to mention the grandsons you will have in the future."

Liah's eyes were lowered as she rebelled silently. How in Kwan

Koong's scheme were her sons to meet suitable wives, hidden away in this desolation? She clenched her fists, her fingernails digging into her palms.

During the long night, Liah's self-pity and anxieties turned to fury. Her husband's hopeless outlook on life was the result of the Fahn Gwai's punishing cruelties. But, oh, why couldn't Sen lift his head despite the circumstances? Didn't he realize he owed an obligation to his children to improve their lots in life? Late that night, she clung to Sen as if pleading for his strength, but his only response was heavy snoring.

SILENT TERROR

Around midnight, loud, wild voices jarred the stillness. Liah awakened with a start. Sen, already alert, clapped his hand over her mouth as he pointed upward at the ceiling of their cellar bedroom.

Liah trembled and winced at the sound of pots crashing and dishes shattering against the walls. Fahn Gwai laughter, demonical and violent, accompanied each act of destruction.

After several moments of silent terror, Liah's fright turned into a burning fury! "Barbarians! May Kwan Koong and lightning strike them dead."

Sen scowled for silence. He whispered, "Quickly, wake the children and keep them quiet. We must flee!"

Liah, spurred to action, sprang from her bed and gently shook Eldest and Second Sons, who were already partly aroused. She whispered, "No noise! It is the Fahn Gwai. We must flee! Quickly, help your younger brothers with their shoes and clothing. Mother will awaken the girls. Quietly now."

Eldest and Second Sons needed no prodding; they understood the danger as they heard the crashing of furniture being broken. The noises frightened the baby and she began to whimper. Sen softly cursed as

Liah held the baby close to her breast, trying to muffle the infant's cries.

Sen's heart pounded; he could hardly breathe. He'd been evicted five different times from his previous homes, but this was the first time that he had found himself and his family caught unaware. There had been no early warnings from friendly neighbors, he thought, as he cursed their isolation.

Visions of earlier massacres flashed before him. Images of slain men, women and even children, were seared into his memory. He recalled the exceptionally brutal Truckee raid in which more than thirty-eight of his people's lives had been lost. They had been burned within their homes or shot to death as they sought to escape. That, vowed Sen, would not be the fate of his family.

He herded his family together, warning them of the need for silence, then he slowly raised the cellar door. Sen heard the loud voices of the Fahn Gwai. Dropping the door back down gently, he found his hands were wet and his forehead beaded with perspiration as he fought his mounting terror.

The children were stumbling around in the darkness searching for last minute possessions. Sen ordered them to be silent. Once more he timidly lifted the heavy door, cursing to himself for not oiling the hinges. When the opening was large enough for them to exit, Sen helped each of them through. He ordered them to seek the shelter of the heavy bushes next to the house.

Outside, Sen pointed to the thicket of trees dotting the western perimeter of their land. Eldest and Second Sons dragged their younger brothers and sister while Sen carried Fifth Son and Liah carried the baby. Liah stopped only once, to rearrange a leather pouch filled with the family jewels and monies as it poked painfully into her ribs.

They crept along the open ground, darting into the shadows, first of the wagon and plow, then a clump of berry bushes, then finally the cover of the trees. Only then did Sen allow the children to stop a moment to finish dressing. "Button up your sweaters, it is cold where we are going. Liah, dress the baby later. I don't want her to bawl."

Sen pointed to a spot halfway up the hillside. "See that clump of bushes next to the two huge boulders near the oak? Right behind them is a cave where you can hide while I go to Cousin Shah for help."

Liah nodded wordlessly. She was too breathless and fatigued to speak.

Once inside the dark cave, Liah shuddered at the dampness.

Sen addressed the children, "Stay here and be quiet. No matter what you hear outside, do not investigate! Your very lives depend upon obedience. Understand?"

Sen gathered the family around him and kissed each child, admonishing his two eldest sons that they were now in charge of the family. "Take good care of your mother, brothers and sisters. Be brave, Father will be back soon."

Sen enveloped his wife in his arms for a few brief moments, then abruptly left.

Liah heard Sen rolling boulders up to the cave's opening and heard the snap of branches as he used limbs to brush away his footprints. She cried out for her husband's safety, for him to take care and return to them.

Sen looked up at the full bright moon and cursed. He remained crouched in the shrubbery until he was certain no one was about, then he made his way to the top of the hill toward the road. He peered up and down the road before coming out of the shadows and darting toward town. Once or twice, he scrambled into the cover of bushes as a wagon rattled by. A few miles away, he heard a wagonload of boisterous men approaching and recognized the voices of the terrorists who had been in his home. Sen's fury flared. His first impulse was to leap out and club the men, but he knew he was outnumbered. Besides, what would happen to his family if he were killed? After his first spike of anger, his terror returned and shamefacedly Sen raced toward town.

It took Sen four hours to reach Loo Sahng. He plodded along the dirt road leading to the stables along *Mah Loo* unable to move any faster. His adrenaline depleted, Sen could hardly duck down to make his way between the logs of a fence behind the stables. The last few yards to Cousin Shah's shack were the most difficult. Sen staggered up to the door and pounded noisily. Hysteria began to mount in Sen as he shouted, "It is me, Sen! Cousin Shah, open the door quick!"

There was a thump and a rustling and shuffling as Cousin Shah fumbled sleepily in the darkness. Moments later, Sen heard the bolts slide back. Sen pushed himself into the room, his voice shrill and his words incoherent.

Cousin Shah turned up the kerosene lamp and saw Sen slumped in a chair, shaking uncontrollably. From the few confused words and phrases Sen uttered, Cousin Shah ascertained that the Fahn Gwai had raided Sen's home. Shamelessly, Sen tearfully begged for his cousin's help.

Cousin Shah extended a glass of whiskey to Sen and ordered him to drink it. "Your family is safe for the time. We will return with food and water after you have rested. Now sleep. You will need your strength. Take my cot, I've already had enough rest."

Leaning wearily back into the chair, Cousin Shah watched Sen's sleeping face. Drugged by the stiff shot of whiskey, Sen appeared to be resting peacefully. Cousin Shah sat, his mind busy with a plan for salvaging Sen's family possessions and relocating his family. Throughout the long night, he dozed off, waking repeatedly to look at the clock. He knew that until eight o'clock, there was no way to reach his foreman or to notify Mah Ting of the night's events.

—

Sen slept for ten fitful hours and upon waking felt drugged and fatigued.

Cousin Shah was aghast when Sen declared that he was glad that if the Gods meant for him to lose his farm, it was best that the raid had occurred in the middle of the night.

Alarmed, Cousin Shah gasped, "Glad? Did the night's events rob you of your sanity? Sen, you'd better rest a bit longer. The strain has been too much for you!"

"No, Cousin Shah," insisted Sen, "You do not understand. All of my life I have dreaded a face-to-face confrontation with the Fahn Gwai. I've been bedeviled with the fear of who would take care of my family should I be killed. This fear made me a coward. I know now that Meng-Sui prevails. I know a confrontation with the White Devils does not necessarily mean death. Do you know what I mean?"

—

The children were finally asleep. In the peaceful quiet, Liah leaned against the dirt wall of the cave. She closed her eyes, trying to rest, to think, but her mind was filled with concern and anxiety for her children's welfare. She was hoping for Sen's safe return with food and drink. She dreaded the moment of the children's awakening again and their cries for food. The younger ones did not understand why they were in a dark, damp cave.

Liah became restive as the hours dragged on. It wasn't her precarious situation that bothered her but the helpless feeling of being caged. She turned and scratched a line on the wall. She knew it was Saturday night. Bitterly, she knew it to be so because of her uncelebrated feast day.

Silently and urgently, she prayed to Kwan Yin to deliver her family safely from this cave and to allow her husband's safe return. "If you do these things, I'll not ask another of you."

Her prayers said, Liah realized ruefully that she had just alienated herself from any future assistance from the Goddess. Philosophically, she excused herself from the promise she'd just made. The Gods would understand the circumstances that had wrested such a ridiculous promise. However, if the Gods held her to a promise made in a moment of terror, then she would have to resign herself to unfulfilled dreams. Sorrow welled up within her, for the Gods' denial would mean her children would be the ones to suffer.

The sun had been shining all day, but its warmth did not penetrate the dense cover of foliage at the mouth of the cave. Liah rubbed her hands together until they warmed, then stuck them back inside her vest pockets. She looked down wistfully at her huddled children. They had awakened, but she had urged them back to sleep, promising to awaken them as soon as their father returned. Besides, she explained to them, the time would pass faster in sleep.

A tenderness flooded her body as Liah looked down at her two eldest sons. She thought about how their efforts to be men only made them seem more helpless to her. Liah held her youngest child tightly and cajoled her to sleep. She rocked the infant until she fell asleep, then she placed her among the other sleeping children.

Liah dozed. When she awakened, it was dark. She rose to make another mark on the wall beside the first one, but suddenly heard a rustling noise outside the cave. She leaped to her feet and ran to the entrance of the cave, straining to identify the sounds. Silently she prayed, "Most revered Kwan Yin, do not let it be the Fahn Gwai." She darted back to her children. If they were all to die, let them die as a family.

It wasn't until she heard someone dragging away the boulders that she recognized Sen's voice. Liah sprang back to her feet and ran to Sen, clutching him in relief. Then she saw Cousin Shah in the shadows and immediately stepped away from Sen to bow low.

Cousin Shah handed Liah a blanket roll and cautioned her to unwrap it carefully, for there was food inside. Sen also had a blanket roll; he laid it on the ground, unrolled it and handed Liah a package of meat buns and sweet rolls. Then he and Cousin Shah each pulled oranges from their pockets.

"Oh, yes!" murmured Cousin Shah. "I brought a bucket of water and a jug of milk. I'll bring them inside."

The children, awakened by the adults' voices, clamored noisily with their hands outstretched for food.

"You should ration the food and water in case we can't get back tomorrow," Cousin Shah warned. "Hopefully we can find a new home for you soon, for my little place will not be comfortable for a lengthy stay. Be patient, Liah."

Showing his impatience to get going, Cousin Shah left the cave.

Sen turned to his children. "Obey your mother! Eat only when she allows, for the food must be rationed. Understand?" He looked at his two eldest sons and urged them to be men, then he turned to Liah. He let his eyes express what he was unable to say with words. Then he too was gone.

Liah settled herself down for another long vigil. She amused the children during the day with stories of her childhood in her native village. When she tired, she asked Eldest Daughter to tell her brothers the stories she had read in her reader. When evening fell, she rose and moved to the mouth of the cave. She felt shivers run down her spine as she groped in the darkness as if wiping way cobwebs. At the entrance, she peered out into the darkness. When the children were once again asleep, Liah picked up a blanket, wrapped it about her and tried to settle into sleep. Holding her infant daughter in her lap, Liah leaned against the wall and closed her eyes. Throughout the night, Liah was constantly jolted awake at sudden noises. The sound of creaking branches, the terrible hooting of owls and the yapping of coyotes made her fear the cave was being invaded. Once, when Liah heard something sniffing at the cave's entrance, she searched for a weapon to ward off the beasts she was certain would break through their barricade at any moment. Liah prayed silently for her husband to return and take them from this damp prison.

The curtain of night hung motionless for many hours, then slowly began to waver as it gave way to the shadows before dawn. The rising sun slowly dissipated the darkness as a new day dawned. Liah fretted as she realized there were only five more buns and very little water remaining. She prayed that the men would return soon.

—

It was on Tuesday, a half-our after midnight, when Sen finally returned.

Liah, sleeping the drugged sleep of the exhausted, was slow to awaken. Not until she heard Sen and Cousin Shah pulling away the branches at the mouth of the cave did she open her eyes. With her heart beating fast, sheer relief flooded her and an almost tearful Liah rushed to the entrance.

It took some moments before Sen's words announcing that Cousin Shah had already found them a new home sunk in. When she finally understood, she silently gave thanks to Kwan Yin that their frightful nightmare was at an end.

Cousin Shah explained that Sen had been hired by a wealthy oilman who not only would pay Sen a wage but also provide living quarters for his wife and children. There were others of their kind already working on the man's estate.

Tears of relief streamed down her face. She wiped them away furtively and quickly turned to awaken the children, so as not to allow Cousin Shah to see her tears.

The children quickly rushed about, gathering up their belongings, wanting only to be free of the dank, dark cave. Once outside, Sen growled at the children to quiet their noisy voices as they scrambled down the hill and ran toward the waiting wagon. "Be quiet! Do you want the Fahn Gwai to hear us?"

The wagon wheels complained noisily as Cousin Shah urged the horse to go faster. When Sen fearfully questioned the wisdom of making so much noise, Cousin Shah shook his head. "No need for alarm! This is an access road the farmers use to drive their wagons to market. Hopefully we will not meet a wagon full of Fahn Gwai revelers on their way home. That's the reason for our haste; another two hours and the Fahn Gwai will be returning home from the saloons."

Sen handed Liah a handkerchief knotted at one corner. "I went back with Cousin Shah to the farm. We salvaged what we could and sold the horses, plow and livestock to Mahtineh."

With a quick, incredulous glance at her husband, Liah's emotion turned to anger. "What? You were so close to us and you didn't even stop to bring food or drink?"

"We could not do that, Liah," answered Cousin Shah. "We might have given away your hiding place. Besides, we knew we would be here tonight. No matter now, the children will have plenty of food at my place."

For the remainder of the ride to Cousin Shah's home, Liah was silent. Morose and bitter, she thought of the thirty-five dollars knotted up in her husband's handkerchief. Such a paltry sum for two years of toil. Fatalistic, as Liah was, she had to admit the Gods had been generous with them. Fortunately, she had been frugal with her own egg monies, and if someone had to profit from their misfortunes, she was glad it was Mahtineh.

Her thoughts then shifted to their new home. Was their new master a generous man? What kind of a house would they have? Would they be paid enough money to live on? Liah lamented to herself that while the Gods doled out goodness with one hand, they took back with the other.

Heaving a sigh, Liah mused to herself, "Surely on the face of the earth there must be a place where she and her family, as well as her countrymen, could live in peace without fear of being evicted." A faint stirring at the back of her mind irritated Liah. Whatever the Gods were trying to tell her, why couldn't they be more explicit? Why this annoying veil of mystery?

—

While Liah and the children slept, Cousin Shah and Sen talked in low tones.

"My advice to you, Sen, is to remain as long as you can with this Fahn Gwai. I hear tell he has an affinity for our people. He has even traveled in our homeland. At least stay there until the children are older and can help support the family."

Sen nodded in agreement.

An urgent rapping on the door caused Sen to leap from his chair with a frightened expression.

Cousin Shah motioned Sen to sit down, as he opened the door to Mah Ting.

Upon entering, Mah Ting glanced a moment at Sen, then told them that the rancher, whose men had demolished Sen's farm, had forced the men to pay for all Sen's damages and to restore his place. "He said it wouldn't happen again and to accept his apologies. The men were out on a Saturday night binge. He hoped you'd understand!"

"A night on the town!" snorted Cousin Shah angrily. "They frightened his family half to death, besides demolishing his house and crops. The men ought to be horse-whipped or shot!"

Mah Ting replied gently, "Sen liked his farm so much, I thought he might consider going back. The Fahn Gwai will pay for all damages and even rebuild the house into a finer place. What do you say, Sen?"

Cousin Shah was about to refuse on Sen's behalf, but Mah Ting shook his head and said, "It is Sen's farm; the answer should be Sen's."

Sen shook his head. "Even if I wanted to, I could not return. I've sold my implements and my animals and, besides, my wife is so terrified I do not think she would consent to return. However, I thank you for all you have done for us. Perhaps I will see you when I come to China

Street on my days off. Good-bye my friend. May Kwan Koong's shadow ever be with you."

THE DOBNEY ESTATES

A few minutes before ten o'clock on the morning of October first in the Fahn Gwai's year of 1906, the foreman from the Dobney estates, Seragio, rapped noisily on the door. Seragio and Cousin Shah exchanged jovial greetings and Cousin Shah introduced Sen. Seragio peered at the seven children and winked mischievously, "Ah, I see you poor man like me! I, too, have big family... nine ninos and ninas. What is there for poor people except to make babies?"

Seragio roared, gesturing obscenely. Sen frowned until his cousin explained; then he guffawed. Liah scowled at the men and hurried to ready the children.

Liah sat on the front seat of the wagon with her young baby in her arms while their youngest son, Fifth Son, sat beside her. Sen and the other five children sat in the bed of the wagon. Cousin Shah hoisted a hundred-pound sack of rice up to Sen along with several cartons of spices and foodstuffs. "These will hold you until you come to China Street. Good-bye, may Kwan Koong be by your side. Good-bye, Liah; good-bye, children!"

Cousin Shah then gazed at Liah with a serious expression. "I hope your new home is to your liking. I suggest you stay there at least until your children are grown. Until Kwan Yin shows you a better road, stay on the one you're now traveling, Liah."

The children kept their faces turned toward Cousin Shah, waving and shouting good-byes, until they turned the corner onto Alameda South, then they settled down for the ride.

Liah, not quite recovered from her imprisonment in the hillside cave, clutched her infant daughter close, huddling close to her fifth son. Neither Sen's reassurances that their new home was a haven against the Fahn Gwai nor their master's generosity and love of the Chinese had any effect. Liah huddled silently.

The children, so terrified three nights earlier, seemed to have forgotten their ordeal as they listened to Seragio's running commentary about Los Angeles. Liah emerged from her dark fear when she saw the neat rows of stores with their fancy decorated, shiny windows and she enviously noted that even the streets were clean. Seragio's voice penetrated Liah's concentration. "Mama, Main Street! See, trolley cars!" The foreman then turned to Sen, "Belasco Theater! You know, girlee show?" The foreman's lewd grin left no doubt what he meant.

The children crowded at the side of the wagon, enthralled with the new sights. Liah cried for them to sit back; did they want to tip the vehicle? Her warnings fell upon deaf ears as Eldest Son leaped to his feet, asking if a particularly huge building belonged to the government.

The foreman shook a menacing finger at Eldest Son and warned him that if he behaved badly, he'd have to go to court. "That courthouse of Los Angeles. Big place, eh? Four blocks big. See, Main Street. That is street we are on now and that one on the left is Court Street, then Market Street and over there is Spring Street. Four blocks big!"

A few miles farther on the Pacific Electric Railroad was installing new tracks. With debris and piles of freshly dug up earth everywhere, it appeared as if an earthquake or war had ravaged the land. Twelve-year old Eldest Daughter, Gil Lan, screamed in fright! "Was big fight?"

Seragio howled in mirth at Gan Hing and Sui Loon pantomiming "Bang, Bang!" "No, No!" shouted Seragio. "Gonna be big red cars, mebbe someday go twenty-five miles an hour, mebbe someday run two thousand miles all over city. Cars go pretty fast, too, forty miles hour."

When they approached the strip bordering downtown Los Angeles on Glendale Boulevard, Seragio drew up the reins, pointing rather proudly. "See, I show you boss man's business. Savvy? Oilman!" He waved his hand in a broad sweep to indicate the entire area belonged to their boss man. "Oil derrick, Mama! Savvy?"

Liah shrugged her shoulders as if the information was of little importance. She wrinkled up her nose to indicate the unpleasant odor.

Eldest Son watched the moving arms of the pumps and asked, "Where's the oil?"

"No oil on top, son. Pipes go way down to get. Boss man make much money, very rich!"

Liah screwed up her face again and asked Sen how people could live in the area with that awful smell. She grimaced at the pools of sludge around the platforms. Ugh!

A few miles out the oilfields with their tall, skeletal derricks gave way to gentle green hillsides and neatly furrowed earth behind wire or wooden fences. Sen breathed in the heady aroma of oranges and lemons and sighed.

Liah intuitively knew he was thinking of home in Kwangtung. "Never mind, Sen," she said. "Someday we will have a home of our own, maybe even in our homeland. A permanent place to raise a generation of grandsons."

Soon the gently sloping hills and small farms gave way to larger mansions with high walls. Sen could see the tops of citrus trees as they drove along the dirt road. All at once, the dirt road was bisected by a wide, black driveway leading up to iron double gates set about three hundred yards back from the road. A uniformed guard with a German shepherd walked back and forth.

Second Son shouted that the place looked like a palace. To their shock, Seragio turned off the dirt road onto the paved driveway. The uniformed guard unlocked the gates, pulling them back for Seragio to pass. The two men exchanged friendly greetings as the family drove by.

Liah glanced about as they rumbled up the wide, winding driveway banked by groves of lemon and orange trees on the right, a hill rising

on the left. It was as if Liah had entered a place primeval, serene, with
the air so fresh. The clouds were so low, she felt she could reach out
and gather an armful. At a fork in the driveway, Seragio turned left
down the narrower road. The children sat subdued in the wagon, as if
the tranquility demanded their silence. Suddenly the wagon lurched to
a halt as Seragio cursed. A peacock and peahen were in the middle of
the road. The foreman explained to Liah that the birds belonged to the
boss lady. Liah was wide-eyed! Such omens of good joss!

Several blocks farther on, Seragio turned off the paved road onto a
dirt one which curved behind a grove of eucalyptus trees. "Mama, pretty
soon your casa," he said. Just around the bend, the wagon came to a stop
and Seragio pointed to a white wooden bungalow. "See? Your casa."

Liah stared at the white bungalow set against the foot of a hill, nestled
among several tall eucalyptus trees and the most massive oak tree she'd
ever seen! Bitterly she thought: In exchange for their security against the
Fahn Gwai, she'd be held voluntary prisoner behind the high walls and
Sen would labor for a paltry twenty dollars a month. She vowed that
someday she would live among her own people, safe from Fahn Gwai
persecutions. Again, she felt the faint stirring at the back of her head;
however, she had no time to ponder the rustling of the Gods as Sen
shouted for her to get down and help with the unloading.

Seragio clambered down and motioned that he wanted to teach Liah
how to use the wood- and coal-burning stove: how much wood to feed
into the stove and then how much coal to add. He pointed to the
Franklin stove in the front room. "Savvy, Mama? Same thing, first put
wood, then put coal. We go now get coal and wood."

Seragio took a wheelbarrow and motioned Sen to follow him; he'd
show him where the wood and coal were stored. The children ran
around like deer newly released from captivity as they explored their
new surroundings. Eldest Son, now aged 14, led his sister and brothers
up the hill, darting on and off the secluded pathway behind the house,
only to be called back.

Liah glared, "How do you know what is lurking in the bushes? Now go with your father."

The children cavorted around their father as they went. "Each of you carry an armload of wood. Might as well make yourselves useful," Liah said after their second trip. When they returned, Sen glared at his wife. "This is their third trip! The last time! We have already four sacks of coal and where are you going to put all that wood?"

"Behind the house. I do not want to run short of fuel when you're working. Eldest Son and the children can bring more wood tomorrow. Now, clean up and we'll have supper. It was thoughtful of Cousin Shah to have given us spiced ribs, rice and chard. It would have been difficult for me to use the stove for the first time to cook a decent supper."

Eldest Son and Second Son slept in the screened porch while the four other younger children slept on minhois in the smaller bedroom. Liah and Sen, with their infant daughter, slept in the larger room.

Ten days later Sen was assigned to work in the orchards while the two eldest sons did odd chores. Twenty dollars a month was Sen's stipend, fifteen dollars more for the two sons. Liah moaned over the meager wages and Sen wrathfully chided, "Woman! Will you never be satisfied? After all, what meaningful work can our two sons do but odd jobs?"

Sen returned home from his first week's work and proudly announced to Liah that the Chinese workers did none of the backbreaking, dirty work. Rather, the master said theirs were the artistic, creative hands and assigned them the planting and cultivation of the crops and gardens. "The Mexicans do the cleanup and maintenance work," Sen said.

Sen's master, Mr. Edward James Dobney, was a shrewd, hard-working hard-fighting oilman whose education had come at the end of a shovel. He had sweated under broiling sun, toiling with the troublesome drilling machinery, gambling that the poison gas pockets in the earth's bowels wouldn't kill him. His wealth, Seragio pointed out, was well deserved. Sen learned from the foreman that his master had dug on ten sites before his first oil well came in. Seragio laughed as he also confided, "For long time, master one rough man until his wife make 'im genteel. His wife named Lucille. Master still no likee high-tone music, high-tone people, but him do what he wife says... Mo better, peaceful, master said. But him don't like high-tone females, he like 'um real female. Master wife say she divorce him."

One evening, Sen returned home and informed Liah that if she'd like to, she could work in the big house. Liah shook her head at first then, tempted by the money, agreed to try it. On Thanksgiving night Liah followed Seragio to the big house and timidly entered the kitchen. There she came face-to-face with a buxom blonde known as Cook.

Liah was ill at ease at first, for she felt the other help were making fun of her. She recoiled when the upstairs maid stuck out her leg to trip Liah as she carried a platter of green onions, radishes and carrots to the table. Liah's fright vanished as anger took over, but it was unnecessary for Cook intervened, waving a spoon menacingly at the smirking maid.

As the night wore on it was evident to Liah that Cook was the boss of the kitchen. As the staff came to get their own supper, Liah knew why: The level of esteem the Cook held the person in dictated the quality and quantity of supper each staff member received. But why should the woman be so kind to her?

The answer came at the end of the night's work when Cook pantomimed she wanted Liah to stop by Mr. Louie's house. Mr. Louie was one of the eldest and most senior of the Chinese workers on the Dobney estates and the Cook was clearly enamored with him. "Gib him cakes, savvy?"

Liah nodded dumbly and saw a flush on the Cook's face and understood. Liah was weary by the time she reached Mr. Louie's cottage. Mr. Louie shook his head, "Aiyah, that female would have me fat as a pig! Come, come, see all the pastries she sends. Why don't you take some home for your children! I'll only give it away to the Mexican girls who come by."

Liah's eyebrows rose. Quickly she selected several cakes and a bag of chocolate cookies as Mr. Louie continued, "Liah, send one of your children tomorrow and I'll be glad to give them some more pastries and, oh, yes, here's a platter of ham and turkey for you."

Liah returned often to work at the mansion because Cook requested her services. Liah did not mind when she had to drop off pastries for Mr. Louie. It was a small favor for the monies she earned.

Liah obediently gave Sen the three to five dollars she earned at the mansion, but kept the tips for herself. To her this was not dishonest, for did not the master say the money was for her? Besides, it was not as if she was keeping the money for herself; rather it was a nest egg for their growing family. Now and then a nagging fear clutched at her. Suppose one of her sons became involved with a Fahn Gwai? She decided she must speak with Sen soon about a suitable match for their two eldest sons.

On New Year's Eve Liah worked until dawn. As she left, tired, she clutched the large bag of turkey, chicken and roast beef Cook had given her. "Seven children," Cook declared, "and for such a tiny body! You take for children, savvy?"

The gray dawn lightened as she walked up the curved driveway and she saw Sen walking toward her. His voice was more fearful than irritated. "Where have you been all night? I was afraid something might have happened to you."

Mildly angered, Liah retorted, "Where but slaving in the kitchen!" She thrust the heavy bag into her husband's arms. "Take this, my arms are half-broken from lugging the food. I had to walk so far along the driveway."

Sen gaped a moment, then shook his head. "You didn't take the short cut through the orchard? It would save you a half-hour's walk! Never mind. Tomorrow I'll show you the way."

The next day at dawn, Sen took Liah through the garage area and orchard to show her the way. He took a detour to show her the master's huge patio garden. In the daylight, the eerie shapes that seemed so threatening during the night now took on beautiful forms. Enviously, Liah marveled at the tall, wide French windows opening upon the flag-stone terrace. Looking at the massive iron furniture surrounded by huge pots of foliage, roses and gardenias and the long, wide expanse of rolling, manicured lawn, Liah felt an almost visceral pleasure. She imagined her master and mistress enjoying their meals among these lovely surroundings. It only magnified how utilitarian was her cottage.

Sen pointed to a pathway leading away from the patio. "Mr. Louie tells me there is another secluded spot with a lily pond, golden carp and a thirty-foot fountain. I hear the entire area is surrounded with blos-soms and trees from our country."

"Oh, Sen," pleaded Liah. "Do you suppose they might have some lily bulbs? Also if there is a peony tree, perhaps I could get a cutting?"

Sen pulled away. "Do you suppose I'd jeopardize my job for some paltry bulbs and a cutting? I'll ask Mr. Louie and see if the gardener can get them. Come on, I don't want to run into the master."

On their way back to the garage area, Sen pointed to grounds sur-rounded by hedges, telling Liah that it was where the tennis and bad-minton courts were located. "And on the other side is their swimming pool. It's even bigger than our house."

Liah said nothing, only sighing as she plodded along behind her husband. In her mind she gently reminded the Gods it was nothing so lavish she wanted for her family, only a permanent place to put down their roots.

1907

YEAR OF THE RAM

L iah's morale dipped after the Fahn Gwai's New Year. She recalled her own celebration the year before, the Year of the Horse.
Now, she sadly pondered, they no longer had a home of their
own, not even the freedom to come and go. It was now the Year of the
Ram. Liah sighed. Perhaps Sen might allow her to ride into town with
the foreman to buy some liver sausages, moon cakes and even some
black mushrooms. If only he would. Anything to escape her seemingly
imprisonment on the estate!

However, the Year of the Ram was barely celebrated in Liah's home.
Mr. Louie stopped by with packets of lucky money, moon cakes for the
children and a jar of candied ginger for Liah. Wong Wei stopped by to
give the children their packets of lucky money and a bag of coconut
candies, and to give Liah a gift box of lychee nuts. Liah wailed that she
felt like a pauper with nothing to give the men. Wong Wei quickly
shook his head. "Do not feel that way, Liah. Your children afford us a
chance to celebrate our New Year. That gives us great pleasure!"

In the following months Liah looked forward to working in the big
house. The diversion was the only thing that prevented a total collapse
of her sanity. One day, an argument ensued between the upstairs and
downstairs maids as to whose job was the most difficult. In their hostile
mood, the girls sought release from their frustrations and picked on
Liah. Cook pantomimed the girls' argument. Olivia, the upstairs maid,
scoffed and said Cook was wasting her time. "She ain't gonna understand in a million years!"

"Oh, yeah?" glared Cook. "I wouldn't be surprised if the little lady didn't understand most everything you say! What do you say to that, my darlin's?"

The two maids glared at Liah. Olivia muttered, "I'd say that was nervy. I don't like eavesdroppers, especially if they pretend to be stupid."

"Oh, don't get your dander up, dearie," scowled Cook. "Liah's okay. And one more thing, don't let me catch either of you picking on her either."

—

Spring of 1907 came early to the Dobney estates. Good omen, thought Edward Dobney, as he gazed from his third-story aerie and study out over his domain; it was the swiftest way he could assure himself that his employees were doing their jobs according to his instructions.

He could see that the sombreroed Mexicans were trimming the trees along the winding driveway; along the side of the mansion another two or three were sweeping and raking leaves. There were five or six more workers repairing and painting the bungalows at the rear of the estate. He frowned, would maintenance never end? He noticed the garage was ready for another coat of paint and the housing for his private auto needed repairs.

Edward saw from a distance that the chauffeur was washing his sports car. Good, he'd drive the red speedster to his oil wells this afternoon. He saw his wife's town coupe and his daughter's Aston sitting to one side, waiting their turns to be washed, waxed and polished.

He glanced at his watch: eleven o'clock and his errant son had not yet arrived. To Edward, tardiness was unforgivable.

"Damn kid! For two cents I'd shove a spade in his worthless hands and push him into the oilfields. Bet that would teach him how to act like a man." Edward turned his focus to the driveway, overlooking the treetops to the gate. No sign of either his son or his streamlined racer. He turned, telephoned the gateman, and left orders that his son come directly to his office. Edward slammed down the telephone receiver and walked over to the heavy sliding door; he yanked it open and stalked out to the roof garden. He felt pleasure at the sound of water cascading from the lily-pond into the pool below. He leaned over the rail and inspected the rare, multicolored carp swimming in the pond, and frowned at the scraggly water lilies. He strode back into his study immediately and telephoned Seragio. "See to it that the lily pots are re-planted. And in the future, make certain the pots are kept in a healthy condition. Not only do I admire their beauty, but the Koi fish like to nibble on the leaves."

The next day Seragio led Sen through the kitchen into the spacious, luxuriantly carpeted dining room, through the salon and into the vestibule with its marble floors. Sen was filled with awe yet somehow fearful. He was careful as he walked over the thick Persian rugs, glanc-ing backward o make certain he was leaving no muddy footprints. The last thing he needed was to be fired because of that. As they climbed the stairs to Edward's study, Sen could not resist running his hands over the polished mahogany paneling.

The foreman rapped smartly on the door several times before he tried turning the knob. Seragio grinned. "Boss man not here."

Sen gaped at the wide, floor-to-ceiling glass room, the heavy drapes, and the oversized desk with its matching oversized leather chair. And so many telephones! So many books! Did the master read them all? And the thick, cocoa-colored carpet, like walking on air. Sen admired the rich, dark mahogany paneling and shelves, both of the same wood that lined the stairway.

Outside on the roof garden, Sen frowned when he saw the entire panorama of the estate, including his own tiny bungalow. The master could see his every move, even when he was at home. Sen was shocked.

The master could see him no matter where he was! Sen's face registered displeasure as well as concern. The foreman grinned at Sen's consternation. "Yeah, boss man sees everything. Everything, my good friend."

Sen made a mental note to warn his co-workers that when they had to relieve themselves, they should do it on the other side of the trees where the boss man couldn't see them. Sen turned his attention to the lilies in the pond. He was so engrossed in repotting them, he did not hear Edward Dobney enter the study. It was not until the big man startled him by thanking him in Chinese that he realized he was there: "Dor geh, dor jeh."

Edward's face broke into a broad smile, but Sen continued reworking the soil in the square wooden pots, making certain the soil was properly leached out so that the soil wouldn't give up its fertilizers to harm the carp or muddy the water. Sen listened uncomfortably as Edward spoke at length of the high value he placed on his Chinese help, on their diligence and their honesty. Edward pantomimed that their pointed straw hats and their loose-fitting coats and trousers reminded him of his stay in Hong Kong and Macao. Edward pointed to the long, winding driveway, saying that it reminded him of the wide, flowing waters of the Yangtze River. Edward sensed Sen's perplexity and cursed his own stupidity for not having learned the language when in China.

Edward walked to the edge of the roof garden, shaking his head at the whirling pace of time. Mentally, he calculated the age of his first hired Chinese, old Soong Hee's age. God, that was over twenty years ago! Soong must be over seventy now. Time caught up with Edward as he recalled Soong's severe illness. Edward had summoned his personal physician, who diagnosed the malady as pneumonia. Edward sent a Mexican woman to tend Soong, who long thereafter brought Soong rich broths and roasted meats to aid his recovery.

When Soong recovered, Edward kept in mind his loyal service before his illness. "Let him care for the birds in the aviary and whatever work he wants to do. I'd retire the old man, but he's proud and wouldn't take to charity. God knows Soong has earned his rest."

Soong reminded Edward of the Pied Piper; recalling this made Edward smile. The children would swarm about Soong as he visited the aviary every day. Most of all, he felt warm at the memory of the wide smile on Soong's face as he plodded down the long driveway: the children gave Soong a feeling of belonging.

Edward's mind wandered from old Soong to the aviary garden, his favorite spot on the entire estate, with the exception of his study. A square block and a half surrounded by a six-and-a-half-foot concrete wall with a chain-link cover rising thirty feet into the air kept his birds from flying off. Game ducks, pheasants, quail, canaries, parrots, cockatoos, toucans and swans all shared the beautiful aviary. Most dramatically the peacocks and peahens drew the delight of people who came each weekend with their children to peer into the fern-foliaged Eden. Edward paused in his reflections, deciding pheasant would be nice for supper. He returned to the study, picked up the telephone and dialed his kitchen.

Long afterwards, Edward lounged in his oversized leather swivel chair, his anger against his son assuaged by the prospect of supper. In the back of his mind though there still remained a burning desire to chastise his son for being tardy. It occurred to Edward that he could cut his son off without a dime. That, he knew, would force him to act like a man! Even as he contemplated that plan, however, Edward knew it was hopeless, for Lucille would keep Edward Jr. in money. And once again, Edward lashed out mentally at his wife for her weakness.

He leaned back in his chair, closing his eyes. Edward recalled Seragio on their first meeting. The foreman was nineteen years old when he came for an interview. Edward, at the time, was walking his pet lioness, Suggie, which he had shipped home when he was on safari in Kenya. Edward's frown turned to a grin as he recalled how Seragio saw Suggie and shimmied up an orange tree, refusing to come down. Metzgar, his Rhodesian ridgeback, did not help the situation with his low growling as he hugged his master's side. Edward chuckled as he drifted off, remembering that Seragio never did come down from that tree that day.

Liah held a more practical view of the aviary garden than Edward. Each time her children went along with old Soong, she was spared the ordeal of bathing them. Old Soong roared with laughter as Eldest Son, Second Son and the rest of the children scrambled among the moist grass trying to catch the quail or splash in the pond and under the waterfall while trying to snare the trout with their oversized nets. One rule in Liah's household was that the children were never to enter the aviary garden without old Soong and never to set foot in the master's zoo without an adult. But for growing boys, rules were made to be broken.

As Edward continued to doze, Liah's Third and Fourth Sons invaded his dreams. The two boys were feeding the monkeys when Mr. Louie and Edward surprised them. Edward had never seen such tongue-tied youngsters. They cowered under Mr. Louie's glare—a silent threat to tell their mother. Nothing Edward offered could alter their stony glances, not even offers to pet Suggie or ride the camel.

Even in his dreams Edward involuntarily shook his head. Not money, certainly not his power could stay the hands of time. The camel, Alice, was a gift from Sheikh Ali Jaber when he had visited Jordan. My God, that was fourteen years ago! His Japanese bear, Mr. Goto San, was a gift from an industrialist when he visited Tokyo—and that was eight years ago.

The lioness, Suggie, evoked the greatest emotions; Edward, believer in the code of the hunter and the hunted, couldn't walk away from the limping lioness. It cost him eight hundred dollars to trap and ship her to his estate. But it had been worth every damn cent!

Edward stirred in his sleep and suddenly jolted wide awake. Did he or didn't he do Suggie a favor? Was she fortunate to have her sheltered life or would she have fared better with a harder, shorter life of freedom? Freedom Edward understood and prized above all things. Wasn't it so that the freedom he craved was destroying his marriage? In his drowsy state Edward knew that should marriage interfere with his freedom, it would be freedom he'd choose.

With his admission that he valued freedom over marriage, Edward's mind again focused on the two youngsters. Damned gutsy kids and they looked smart, too. He made a mental note to keep track of them, perhaps even help them financially with their education. His practical mind argued the wisdom of such a move. Perhaps they, too, might be better off in their own world and his philanthropic motivations were nothing but meddling. "Damn, if only my son would knuckle down with his studies, I'd not feel so frustrated. Bet those two kids would make my financial help worthwhile!"

He let his feet plop to the floor and reached for the phone. Perhaps he and his mistress could do the town. He sure as hell didn't want to keep thinking about those two Chink kids and his worthless son.

A week later, Edward could avoid his son's laziness no longer. Since his son's expulsion from college, he'd refused to meet with his father. One morning, at breakfast, in one of his rare moments of rage, Edward demanded to know his intent. "I'll not have an idler for a son! Either you enter another institution or I'll have you at the end of a shovel. It might do you some good if you were to do an honest day's work. I'll give you two days to make up your mind."

Edward stormed out of the dining room, into his study and slumped into his upholstered swivel chair. If only his wife would allow him to make a man of their son. A man who'd someday inherit his millions must know how to work and think. Besides, too many people's lives depended upon his being successful. Damn! Edward leaped to his feet and marched into his roof garden.

Like an enraged, restless animal, he paced back and forth on the bricked terrace. Suddenly, he stopped and stood watching several children playing on the winding driveway. They were too young to work, but by God not too young to study!

He summoned Seragio. The foreman listened to Edward's plan of initiating a school for the children of his employees. The hothouse his wife had once used to cultivate her orchids, long ago abandoned for other interests, would be the ideal place for a classroom. "Have the place cleaned out immediately," said Edward. "When that's done, let me know and I'll have furniture and equipment set up."

Seragio nodded, inquiring which children his boss wanted to attend classes. Edward paused, then with a generous sweep of his hand, replied, "All the youngsters, including the older ones who'll have more need for education–the seventeen-, eighteen- and nineteen-year-olds. As soon as I've found an instructor, school will begin."

Liah's spirits had lifted with the warmth of the May sunshine. Her disappointment over a largely uncelebrated New Year of the Ram diminished. No longer did she turn to her bamboo pipe, no longer was she forced to burn incense to cloak the odor of the opiate. She entertained the suspicion that perhaps her husband knew she'd gone back to smoking Ap*inyin* (opium), but to date he had said nothing.

Glancing out her window she had been astonished to see the master's long, black limousine pull up, but she was prudent to hide her elation when Sen gruffly informed her of the upcoming classes. Silently she breathed a prayer of thanks to Kwan Yin. Now her children need never be enslaved to the Fahn Gwai for lack of proficiency in their language. To her children, especially to her third son, she warned, "The master is generous, but one doesn't know if the Gods will always smile on him. So exert all of your concentration upon your studies. Do you hear me, my Third Son?"

On the fifth day of June in the Fahn Gwai's year of 1907, Liah was as excited as her children on their first day of school. Third Son, still resisting, received a scathing glare from his mother. Reluctantly he followed his older brothers out the front door.

The younger children returned home from class exuberant with their impressions of the teacher Ted Crosset. Eldest Daughter bubbled that their teacher was the smartest man in the whole world—and so handsome.

Liah listened, thinking that for such a young man to be a teacher, he indeed had to be brilliant. In fact Ted Crosset was a middle-aged, frustrated writer who had yet to be published. Until he had received the offer to teach on the Dobney estates, he had been on the bitter side of disappointment and had accepted the teaching job planning only to stay until something better came along. Each time his manuscripts were rejected, his self-esteem dropped a humiliating degree, almost driving him to give up his career as a writer. Ted Crosset's youthful appearance was the result of his athletic interests, especially hiking, swimming and tennis—three activities he hoped to continue while on the Dobney estates. His blond hair, cropped very short, and his clear blue eyes magnified by his eyeglasses, lent an air of youthfulness and intellect. When he raised his eyebrow cynically, he did appear very wise. Whatever Ted could teach the children, he would be Liah's children's first contact with the outside world.

On that first morning, Ted Crosset was plagued by the thought that he'd made a big mistake, that he could do nothing with these motley-looking children. However, challenged by failure, Ted set his mind to educating theses students: either educate them or else!

He divided the children into two groups. The younger children, too young to learn academically, would be taught visually and by oral instruction. The second group, the older children, was divided again, those with a smattering of English into one group and those who were totally illiterate into the other group.

The first week was cumbersome, especially roll call. Ted was frustrated by his inability to remember Liah's children's names. It was so confusing to him that the children addressed each other by different positions of hierarchy within their family. For instance, First-born Son was sometimes called Elder Brother, Second-born Son was also known as Second Brother and so on down the line. Ted thought they all should have English names.

When Ted suggested giving them names, Eldest Daughter shook her head vehemently. Ted frowned, resenting the young girl's supercilious air. His first impulse was to chide her, but then he wondered how he would act if he were in the same position.

"Well," he retorted, "let me try again. Each of you will tell me your Chinese name."

Eldest Daughter promptly and proudly announced, "Me Lan Gil, me Numbah One fehlo." She pointed, "Her Lee Sui Sin. She Numbah Two!"

It was on the tip of Ted's tongue to correct the young girl's pronunciation, but he dimly recalled that it was difficult for Chinese to pronounce the 'r' sounds.

Eldest Son, somewhat proud of being the first-born of the family, informed Ted that he was Lee Gan Hing, then Ted listened as each of the other children recited not only his or her Chinese name, but also the position he or she occupied on the family ladder. Ted knew he'd definitely never master the names, nor was he going to stop and do arithmetic each time he wanted a child's attention.

"I do not like this any better than you, but it is mandatory that you have English names. Therefore, I'll give you one week to come up with a name or else I will give you one," he said.

Afterward, Ted asked Eldest Son how he and his sisters and brothers had learned to speak English. Eldest Son stammered, "Er, ah, Mah-Mah sell tings in Dai Faw. Me hep sell too. Me no speakee too good, no can lead, no can lite."

Eldest Daughter chimed in proudly, "Me lead, me lite too. Malican ladee gib me book, hep me ebbry time she come by."

Ted glanced down at Liah's youngest child, a shy, half-frightened toddler about three years old who looked more like two. While he felt that she was probably too young to learn, Ted didn't have the heart to bar her from the class. Perhaps she'd assimilate a few rudiments.

Ted nodded. "Good. While you two do not speak well, at least you speak more than the Mexican children. But do not worry, we shall remedy that deficiency with daily grammar lessons and reading."

Ted glanced at Eldest Son. "I hope you children also speak Chinese. The more languages you speak, the better. Never turn your back on your culture and certainly never forget how to speak Chinese. The Chinese people are the most honorable and smartest people in the world."

Third Son pantomimed that perhaps teacher was making funny. "Mah-Mah no like Fahn Gwai." he muttered. "Mah-Mah chop-chop hand."

Ted smiled at the young boy's gesture, as if hitting his fingers with a chopstick, and laughed, "Now, tell me what is Fahn Gwai?"

"Fahn Gwai," snickered Third Son. "You, Fahn Gwai. Bok Gwai!"

Eldest Daughter glared at her younger brother, threatening to tell Mah-Mah. Ted Crosset silenced Third Son. "Your anger toward your sister leads me to believe what you said was not polite. Well, you can stop making fun of me right now. You do not like it when the white man makes fun of you? Well, I don't like it either."

He turned his attention back to the group. "Now," he demanded, "what is Fahn Gwai?"

Eldest Son replied lamely, "Bok Gwai is Fahn Gwai! All same Amelican!"

Eldest Daughter, now subdued, quietly explained, "Bok Gwai same as Fahn Gwai. You Fahn Gwai."

It took a few moments of reasoning before Ted Crosset could unravel the logic of the children's explanation. "You mean Bok Gwai or Fahn Gwai means white man?"

Eldest Son nodded, "Debbil, Bok Debbil!"

Ted was silent for a while, then broke into laughter. "So that's it!

White devil?" He turned, pointing a finger at Third Son. "I do not ever want to hear you make fun of me! Understand? Savvy?"

Eldest Daughter muttered something in Chinese. Third Son pursed his lips and angrily answered back in Chinese.

Ted cut short their argument. "And savvy this, all of you. No more speaking Chinese in class. I shall see that the Mexican children also speak only English in class. That's the only way any of you will ever learn the Fahn Gwai's language!" Ted's eyes twinkled as he used the Chinese word for White Devil.

—

Monday morning a week later, Ted asked Liah's children for their Fahn Gwai names. Eldest Son proudly informed him that he wanted to be called Thomas.

"Good choice." exclaimed Ted. "Thomas Jefferson was one of our outstanding presidents, our third president. George Washington was our first president."

Eldest Son shook his head. "No, me likes man makee 'lectric! Me Thomas A. Addison."

"Edison, eh?" corrected Ted. "That's also a good name and a hero to follow. Very well, Thomas."

"Mister?" asked Second Son timidly. "Me likee name with S."

Ted was taken aback by the youngster's request. "How come S and not another letter in the alphabet, son?"

Second Son smirked as he shot a glance toward his older brother. "Me alla times Numbah Two. If me name start with S, me come Numbah One. Thomas come Numbah Two!"

For a moment Ted Crosset stared wordlessly. He smiled gently down at the youngster, thinking how wise for one so young. If only he'd accepted life with the same kind of humorous grace perhaps then he'd have evaded the pain of the past six years. Aloud Ted began to list the names, "Sam, Saul, Seth, Stanley, Socrates, Simpson, Sherman, Shelley...."

"What, Shelley?" interrupted Second Son, "I like!"

"He was a British poet. Do you think you would like to use his name?"

Eldest Son snickered in Chinese. "Why not a general's name or even a president's name?"

Ted narrowed his eyes at Eldest Son. "That will do, Thomas. I said no more speaking in Chinese and I mean it!"

Eldest Daughter was eager to reveal her choice of names. "Me likee Flolenz. Me hep doctor, me big."

Third Son hollered derisively in Chinese, "A nurse? You don't have the kindness or the patience. Patients would die in your care."

Ted's patience had reached its limit. He picked up a ruler and declared that though it wasn't a chopstick, it would work just as well. He flicked it smartly across Third Son's hand. "Just like your mother when you disobey! Now, no more speaking in Chinese."

Ted pronounced Florence several times and had Eldest Daughter repeat it after him. The children giggled as Eldest Daughter tried to pronounce her R's. After many attempts, her face was radiant as she slowly enunciated "Florrr-ence".

Third Son, spurred by his sister's earlier story about Theodore Roosevelt and the Rough Riders, informed Ted his choice was "Theodoh".

It was several minutes before Ted grasped what he was saying and only when Third Son said he liked to "ride hoss".

Ted nodded, "Theodore Roosevelt was one of our dynamic men."

Fourth Son chose William. Fifth Son liked the name Merton. Second Daughter gazed uncomprehendingly at her teacher. Ted squatted beside her, tousling her hair. "You're too young to think of a name, so I'll give you one. Because your eyes always seem to asking 'Who am I?' I'll call you Emmi."

Third Son roared with laughter, but Ted silenced him.

"Now I want each of you to practice writing your names and you should practice saying them aloud so the sound will become natural to your ears as well.

—

A month later, Ted Crosset came to dinner at Liah's cottage. Liah thought that indeed the teacher was as scholarly as Eldest Daughter had said and as handsome. His clothes, she noticed, were elegant but not as formal as the master's; she didn't feel uncomfortable as she did in her master's presence. She was puzzled by the deep sadness in Ted's eyes. If only Sen would be a bit more friendly toward him.

Ted was amazed at Liah's diminutive stature. Such a tiny woman to have given birth to seven children. As supper progressed, it amused him to see that Liah was the undisputed boss of the home. Where then was the myth that Chinese women were subjugated nonentities in life? He smiled as he drew from the deep recesses of memory a story he'd read many years before. The favorite wife of a wealthy Chinese lord not only received whatever her heart desired, but ruled his entire household by her feminine charms and well-timed tirades and tears. Such was the unseen, silken cord that strangled!

At school most of Liah's children enjoyed their education, each for different reasons. To Thomas and Shelley, school was a respite from work for four hours; for Florence and William it quenched their thirst for knowledge; for Emmi, her crayons, coloring books and Ted Crosset's stories were sheer joy. Theo, however, cared not at all for school and spent his time cutting up in class, as much as Ted would allow.

As the weeks passed, Thomas, Shelley, Florence and William began losing their pidgin English accents and showing interest in the outside world. Mert and Theo struggled with grammar, but Ted encouraged both boys, saying that by speaking and writing more, they too would become fluent. Mert's interests were piqued when he discovered an automotive mechanics magazine on Ted's desk. Much to Ted's pleasure, the young boy began not only reading but asking what certain sentences and words meant, and Ted showed him how to use the dictionary. Still Ted anguished over how he could reach Theo. Of all of Liah's children, Theo had the sharpest mind, but for some unknown reason, the boy continued to alternate between pidgin English and flawless English depending on which suited his mood. Ted was pleased, however, that all of the children had become Americanized enough to shorten their names. Thomas A. became Thomas, Shelley Shel, Theodore Theo, Merton Mert. Strangely enough, William was always called William. Perhaps, reasoned Ted, it was the boy's dignity, which unconsciously prevented his brothers and sisters from calling him Will. Another discovery Ted made was that beneath William's passive nature lay a core of strength, which sometimes made itself known, especially when Theo tried to bully him.

With their close daily contact as students and teacher, Ted became their confidante as well as mentor. It was during one of their evening chats that Thomas voiced his desire to become a truck driver, someday owning his own truck. Ted smiled, asking Thomas his age.

"Almost sixteen, sir."

Ted nodded sympathetically, recalling his own impatience to grow up. He asked Thomas to be patient and meanwhile, to study and train. When asked what training, Ted replied, "Study some of the mechanics' manuals Mert reads, and you will know it takes strength as well as skill to handle a big rig. Why don't you and Shel come jogging with me in the evening? It'll pass the time and build up your endurance and physical strength." The teacher paused. "One more thing–don't be surprised if you and Shel change your minds about what you want to do many times before you grow up."

Ted looked down at the young, stubborn face as Thomas shook his head, murmuring that he was certain he'd not change his mind. In an attempt to be practical, Ted reassured Thomas it was admirable to have perseverance, but life did not always award a man his dreams.

"Have you," he asked, "ever thought that a truck owner may not want a young Chinese lad to drive for him? You can't blame the man, for a truck costs a great deal of money and there is always the chance of the driver being in an accident. Just be patient and if it is meant for you to drive, or even own a truck, it will come about."

Thomas frowned. "You sound just like my mother. Meng-Sui and all that junk!"

Ted shook his head. "No, Thomas. It is dangerous for you to reject her philosophy, founded or not. Your mother has lived through many more harrowing years than you and maybe she knows something you don't. Anyway, you have a ways to go before you come face-to-face with your aspirations. You have many years of growing up to do yet."

—

Through his involvement with Liah's children, Ted was aghast one morning as he thought of the children not by name but by their number in the hierarchy of the family! For a brief second, he was shocked how Chinese he'd become, smiling as he recalled his admission earlier that he could never learn their number-names. In a moment of truth, he realized that how much better the world would be to live in if people could make an effort to know each other better. Filed in the back of his mind were countless anecdotes he did not consider writing material at the time, but one day would discover were a fount of saleable stories.

For the moment, however, in his desperate search for literary success, Ted was blinded to the commonplace themes and instead grasped at nobler subjects. He was concerned and perplexed about Thomas, Shel and

William, mostly William. Liah's two eldest sons were quickly growing into men; but Ted wondered how long Liah could hold them prisoner behind tall walls. William was so sensitive and so eager for knowledge, but so filled with temerity, much of it from his earlier days of fleeing the Fahn Gwai. Ted wondered if he could ever free the young boy from his inferiority complex. Ah, well, Ted sighed, it was in the laps of the Gods, as Liah would say. All he could do was endow them with as much knowledge and secondhand information about life on the outside as he could. He smiled; if he'd been Chinese, like Liah he'd say "life-waters".

Ted continued to ponder how he could at least convince William that college was within his grasp, that teaching could be his vocation. He became filled with anger at his own people. To use cruelty and force on a people was bad enough, but to rob a youngster of his right to dream was unspeakable! Suddenly Ted saw a solution: Why couldn't he acquaint his countrymen with the Chinese? Immediately he went to his desk, grabbed a pen and a piece of foolscap paper. For a long moment, he wavered, then took up his pen and began to write.

After that, Ted's time became precious. There were not enough hours in the day to teach, to write, and do for Liah's children. On Saturdays, he borrowed Seragio's truck and took them to the museum, the library and even to a movie once. It amused Ted to see Florence agog over the movie stars. In these intimate moments with the children, Ted was struck by how little he knew about the Chinese people. Perhaps that same ignorance was what fomented such fierce rejection by his countrymen.

Ted felt a guilty twinge as he took Liah's children on picnics, teaching them etiquette and the correct use of fork and knife. To assuage the guilt that he did not do the same thing for the rest of his students, Ted told himself that there were simply too many.

—

On the ninth day of September, Sen was summoned to the front gate to meet a visitor. When Sen asked who the visitor was, Seragio said he didn't know the man but had offered him a ride. From a distance, Sen recognized Cousin Wah's oddly shaped green and white striped cap and duffle bag.

Cousin Shan Suey Wah, Liah's first cousin, worked as galley help on the Dollar Steamship Line, which cruised the Orient. Every four months he made port in Loo Sahng and Dai Faw. He was Liah's communications link with her family and, more importantly, her source of the poppy opiate, Apinyin.

On their long trudge back to the cottage Sen noticed the tiny man matched his long strides with no apparent effort. And carrying the heavy duffle bag, too! Cousin Wah certainly will live a long time, Sen thought. At that instant Sen stopped, turning as he exclaimed, "I am not only a fool, but a rude fool! Here, let me carry the bag. I was so occupied with my tale of woe, I forgot my manners."

As Sen hoisted the heavy bag onto his shoulders, he remarked, "This weighs as much as you!"

The tiny curmudgeon snarled as he spat, "I can carry twice the load and not tire. Now, enough about your travails in Dai Faw. Be grateful to Kwan Koong you are now in Loo Sahng. In Dai Faw our people are suffering the Fahn Gwai's wrath because of the slump in the economy. The pale-faced idiots blame us for their evil days. Be content to live here in such beautiful surroundings."

Liah, waiting at the doorway, rushed outside to greet Cousin Wah. Her children noisily pushed forward and crowded around the tiny man. Cousin Wah stared hard at Liah, then nodded slightly. A rush of relief surged through Liah as she realized that he had brought her supply of Apinyin. The old sailor grinned a fleeting moment at the children, abruptly answering Liah's inquiry about his health.

"My health? How do you expect? Strong! I have no bad habits to warp my bodily strength. Now let me go inside the house, or else the children will burst with curiosity."

Liah cried loudly for manners, as the children and Cousin Wah pushed through the front door. He said, "Let me take off my jacket, children. Then we'll see what's inside the bag."

Once seated, Cousin Wah crooked his finger at Eldest Son. "You seem to have grown four inches since I last saw you. When you get meat on those bones, then perhaps you might do a day's work."

Shelley grinned as the old man muttered, somewhat proudly, that Second Son was not far behind his older brother. "Who knows but that I will have two boys working with me in the galley." He looked hard at Second Son then nodded his approval. In a gruff tone, he said, "From what I see now, you will be lots taller than your older brother but not as hefty. But that's fine. Size is not everything. Learn to use your head, learn Kung Fu and languages and you'll be all right."

The tiny man untied the duffle bag and reached into the canvas depths for the gifts, at times almost crawling inside. Eldest Son and Second Son saw carved handles sticking out of their ornately carved sheaths and reached out eagerly. Cousin Wah drew them back. "I know your mother thinks you're too young for weapons, but the truth is that you must learn self-defense. Know that these blades are weapons of death, so respect their use!"

Sen nodded. "Cousin Wah, allow the two boys to examine them, then they'll give them to me for safekeeping." Sen eyed his two sons. "You may learn to use them while at work. Now you will not have to borrow other people's knives. Thank your cousin."

Third, Fourth and Fifth Sons reached out for their gifts, shiny lacquered boxes. Cousin Wah roared disapproval when Third Son asked what they were. "Where's your curiosity? Open them and figure them out for yourselves. Now, let me give your sisters and mother their gifts."

Eldest Daughter pushed closer at Cousin Wah's mention of presents and peered over his shoulder. She accepted her tissue wrapped package while Liah accepted her gift and that of her youngest daughter.

Eldest Daughter squealed in delight as she held up a cheongsam of blue brocade and exclaimed, "There's also a matching pair of slippers, Mah-Mah."

Liah smiled, at the same time chiding her cousin for squandering his money. "You ought to be saving for your old age. The heat in the galley is not good for your health."

Cousin Wah scornfully scolded her, saying that he was as healthy and strong as the first day he stepped onto Gem Sahn soil. "Look who is giving advice. I'd say you are too thin, Liah, and pale, too. Besides, if it brings me joy to spend on the children, it is my prerogative. Now, let me give Sen his gift."

Sen's eyes lit up when he tried on the long, padded jacket with dark blue matching thick-soled slippers. "You're an astute man, Cousin Wah, to have given me exactly the thing I need and in the right size. I do thank you, sir."

The tiny man grinned at Sen, then faced Liah. He handed her several packages from her mother and warned, "I'd advise you to sparingly use the medicine your mother sent you. It is not good for your health."

Liah exchanged knowing glances with her cousin, then accepted the gifts of preserved fruit, spices, ginger and tea sent by her mother. Afterwards, she eagerly reached out for the tins of Apinyin, quickly hiding them under the tissues.

Cousin Wah turned to the children, teasing, "I see you are no longer interested in the jars of *mok-matong*." In a flash, each child grabbed a clay jar of the sticky, viscous molasses-like candy and ran for a chopstick to dig it out. "Mok-matong!" cried Eldest Son. "It's my favorite candy!"

Liah was animated and a festive air presided over the supper table. The black mushrooms sent to her by her grandmother helped make the meager dinner a feast. Mushrooms stuffed with pork hash was the most delicious dish in the entire spectrum of food, thought Liah, as she dished the sautéed chicken, pork and vegetable compote into a dish.

Just before nine o'clock, Cousin Wah jumped to his feet. "I must be at the front gate by a quarter of ten, or else the man will not wait."

Sen ducked into the bedroom, and reappeared a moment later with two gold coins. "Cousin Wah, if I can ask your generosity, I would like my mother to have one of these twenty dollar coins, and the other one is for Liah's mother. Please do not tell them of our misfortunes; rather tell them we are all fine and happy. And, sir, it is not necessary for all the gifts. We will welcome you without them, sir."

Liah's eyes filled with warmth at her husband's generosity toward her mother. Sen nodded quick acknowledgement of her gratitude. Even before Cousin Wah, he did not want any intimacy displayed.

Liah turned to her children after Cousin Wah's departure, ordering them to put away the Mok-matong. "There's always tomorrow and what would you do for sweets then if you consumed all of it today?"

When Sen returned, he smiled at Liah. "Cousin Wah said you were not to worry about your medicine. He said if we ever move, he'd always contact Cousin Shah. He also said he didn't like you being so thin, that you ought to eat more, worry less and not fight your circumstances. Meng-Sui being what it is, it doesn't change things." Sen appraised his wife and agreed with Cousin Wah.

Liah, reinforced with the four tins of Apinyin, spent a good night's rest. Just before falling to sleep she thought of the cheongsam Cousin Wah had given her, wondering where on earth on the estates she would wear it.

—

Liah's children, growing adept in the Fahn Gwai's language, spoke it constantly, even forgetting to speak Chinese at the supper table. Liah's chopsticks smartly cracked across their knuckles, accompanied with a warning glare. Their father would not tolerate Fahn Gwai being spoken. One night after a chopstick chastisement, Sen scowled. "I told you no good would come from their education in Fahn Gwai ways. What good is their knowledge of outside affairs when we are living within these safe walls?"

Liah lowered her eyes, her entire body tensing with desperation. Her husband's reference to the uselessness of a Fahn Gwai education was his way of saying they'd remain behind the walls. She was in exile! Suddenly the monies she hoarded for the outside meant nothing at all.

In the following weeks Liah fell into a deep depression, dark and hopeless, turning once more to the forgetfulness of her bamboo pipe. This time she neither tried to cloak the pungent fumes nor cared if Sen found out she'd gone back to her filthy habit—that was Sen's opinion of Apinyin.

The first Sunday of each month the families of the Chinese and Mexican workers on the Dobney estates shared a picnic. Although Sen knew of these picnics, he'd never mentioned them. But now, to divert his wife's sullen silences, he suggested the family attend. "Of course, this means you'll have to prepare a bit of food. Everyone contributes to the feast," he said.

In the backyard of Garcia, one of the other workers, Liah discovered a familiar plant while admiring a phalanx of Chinese lilies and roses. She asked if she could have some lily bulbs and perhaps a few cuttings from the roses. Then she pivoted and pointed to the poppy plants, asking if she could have some of them, too. Neither Liah nor Garcia could speak each other's language, and Liah could not understand Fahn Gwai, but in the expanse of their illiteracy, their eyes and their hands pantomimed lucid thoughts.

Garcia, at first reluctant, scanned Liah's face. Instinctively he knew she was experienced with the use of the flowers. Garcia grinned back at Liah. He plucked a number of plants, pantomiming she was to plant them out of sight, perhaps in her backyard. At the end of the day, Liah happily had several rose cuttings, lily bulbs and, more importantly, poppy plants!

In the silent serenity of her small room, Liah's mind churned, wandering thousands of miles back to her home, recalling how her mother and the villagers rendered the potent Apinyin in her opium supply from the poppy pods. She prayed to Kwan Koong that Cousin Wah would never fail her, that she'd not be forced to the intricate, tedious chore of rendering the resin herself.

Liah involuntarily smiled as she remembered the semi-sweet bitter Apinyin tea her mother had forced upon her whenever she had stomach cramps or intestinal disorders. She tenderly remembered how her younger brothers fought and cried when forced to drink the brew. She fell asleep with a fierce dream that Cousin Wah would always be there to supply her Apinyin. The persistent stirring at the back of her mind pushed forward, but in her semi-drowsy mind, Liah could not link the thought to her life. Perhaps the Goddess would reveal the entire truth at another time.

—

In the time that followed, Ted Crossett enjoyed a position of honor in Liah's home, diminishing his feelings of loneliness, almost setting aside the resentments brought about by his failures. Unencumbered by fear of another failure, Ted began to write, this time drawing upon his experiences on the Dobney estates. His first story, "Hired Children," sold on its first time out. Ted stared at the check, consumed with boundless jubilation, knowing the feeling of success to be exactly as he had so often imagined it.

Shelley was an added source of amusement for Ted, swaggering as he reminded his peers that the teacher's story was about his wanting a name beginning with an S, so that for once he'd come before his older brother, Thomas.

Liah insisted they celebrate the auspicious event with a dinner. At the supper table several nights later, Ted presented Liah with a jeweled teakwood box, decoratively hinged in brass. "Tell your mother, Thomas, this gift in no way expresses all that is in my heart. It was she who reminded me of my own childhood which I'd forgotten."

Ted's face was slightly guilty as he informed the children that he'd ordered a set of reference books for them. "As a token of my affection and with the hope you will make good use of them." He turned to Mert, "I also ordered you an encyclopedia of auto mechanics."

—

On Thanksgiving, Liah's children had their first taste of turkey, with all the trimmings. Edward Dobney, in response to Ted's request, had sent the class a Thanksgiving feast. During the supper, Ted noticed William slipping slices of turkey onto a napkin and said, "There is no need for that, William. I've already planned to make up a plate for your parents." A gentle expression crossed Ted's face, for it would have been William who'd be the one to think of his mother.

Christmas of 1907 was a revelation for Liah's children, it being their first celebration of the holiday. The celebration was held in the school-room, with a candlelit tree decorated with shiny baubles. Red and green-ribboned gifts lay around the tree. The children were wide-eyed at the artificial fireplace with the racks of red stockings crammed full of apples, chewing gum and candy canes. There was a table covered with a cloth decorated with red poinsettias and sparkling green, red and gold spangles on which were sitting platters of cookies shaped like stars, Christmas trees and Santa Claus.

When Seragio entered the classroom wearing a bushy white beard and a red Santa suit trimmed in white, Liah's children sat with their mouths agape, not knowing what was happening. The Mexican children, however, knew that Santa meant gifts and began clamoring for the breaking of the piñata tied with multi-colored ribbons that was hanging from the ceiling.

Ted chose Thomas and another older Mexican boy to break the papier-mâché donkey piñata. After three or four whacks, the donkey burst, spilling brightly wrapped candies all over the floor. Pandemonium ensued as the children scrambled on their knees to retrieve the sweets, some of the girls using their skirts to hold the candies.

In the midst of the shouting, laughing and occasional bickering, Mr. Dobney entered; his chauffeur following close behind laden with brightly decorated boxes. Ted felt a surging elation that the boss would come in person to wish his students a merry Christmas and to bring gifts, too. Mr. Dobney whispered to Ted, "They're only Santa candy boxes... and here's a gift for you, too."

Ted had it on his tongue to remind Mr. Dobney that he'd already received his cash bonus, but the look on Edward's face made him keep his silence. It wasn't often his employer was so youthfully happy. Like the proverbial Santa Claus, Edward shouted "Merry Christmas to all!" Then Mr. Dobney disappeared through the front door.

1908

YEAR OF THE MONKEY

With the approaching New Year of 1908, Sen steeled himself against his wife's onslaught regarding moving onto China Street. It was always like that when the Fahn Gwai's New Year came, for their Chinese New Year followed.

During a shopping trip to China Street to purchase staples for their feast, Liah complained to Cousin Shah. Shah's retort was terse. "Stay where you are, Liah. This is Gem Sahn. The boys will find their own wives. As for Sen, it is good to be sheltered behind the estate walls. At least wait until the children are grown."

It was not only Cousin Shah's advice that depressed Liah, but when he challenged her belief in Meng-Sui, she felt anger. With a heavy heart Liah prepared for the Year of the Monkey.

Ted Crosset was invited to the feast and was enthralled with the new and exotic foods. He met Wong Wei, Mr. Louie and Soong Hee and was amazed that their usual sedate faces could crease into so many laugh lines. As Ted sipped the Ng Ga Pei, he thought that this rice wine would put the cowboy's red-eye to shame. In honor of the New Year, not wanting to cast a shadow on the gaiety and superstitious anticipatory happiness of the Year of the Monkey, Ted managed to down a thimble-sized cup of the heady rice wine. As the evening progressed, Ted discovered another facet of the Chinese character: They surely can drink! Though they frequently became red in the face, they exhibited few signs of drunkenness. Liah, usually quiet, was animated, without her usual inhibitions, drinking alongside the men, seeming to feel little effect from the heady brew. With Liah allowing him entry into her family circle and insight into their daily lives, Ted once again realized how little he knew about the Chinese. There was so much ignorance among his countrymen about the pleasures of their intimate, meaningful lives. Ted, humbled and touched by the depth Liah was allowing him into the inner circle of her life, decided he'd write about the Chinese Year of the Monkey and he'd research the basis of their calculations of the year. However, there was much he had to learn before he could even begin the story.

At the end of the evening. Liah, loosened by her intake of Ng Ga Pei, mischievously patted her cheek, pantomiming that the teacher should drink more often, that a rosy complexion complimented his appearance. Thomas, embarrassed, explained his mother's meaning, at which Ted grinned.

"No need to be embarrassed, Thomas. I thoroughly agree with her, but I'm afraid my stomach is not like hers. I couldn't begin to drink as much," Ted said. "Good night and thank your mother for a wonderful evening."

—

One April morning Liah was cultivating the flowerbed in the front yard when a shiny yellow coupe drove up. An attractive, expensively dressed lady stepped out and approached her. Wong Wei, the beekeeper, was passing by. He immediately stopped in his tracks to bow low and Liah knew the elegant lady was her mistress.

Such a sadness in her eyes, thought Liah. Why? She lived in luxury and had all the money she could spend. Then a flash of recollection: Cook had chuckled once, saying, "Boss man and boss lady no sleep in one bed, not even in same room. Boss man has sweet lady outside."

The woman asked if Liah would like to pose for her. She sculpted, she said, but Lucille Dobney saw that Liah did not understand. She took Liah by the hand and led her to the car, motioning for her to enter. As they drove up the driveway, Liah's mind was whirling. She stole a furtive glance at the woman, hoping that perhaps boss lady's face would reveal the purpose of the ride, but no.

Liah followed her mistress through the columned verandah, through the impressive carved doorway held open by a tall uniformed man and stood in awe in the circular, marble-floored vestibule. Lucille smiled, again reaching for Liah's hand, and led her up the wide, carpeted spiral staircase. Liah followed, her thin-soled slippers gingerly treading the deep carpet cushioning the steps.

Lucille felt foolish telling the tiny woman the marble was imported from Italy, the carpets from Persia, but somehow she needed to speak. Liah's eyes missed not a thing, not the oversized jardinières filled with sweet-smelling plants nor the marble statue at the first landing, and she certainly didn't miss the airy fragrances.

At the end of the long, carpeted expanse, Lucille flung open the door to her studio. Liah took in the glass-walled room, marveling at the work involved in keeping it glistening. Lucille led her to a long table and showed Liah several busts so life-like Liah gasped in fascination. Lucille pantomimed she wanted Liah to sit for her, that she wanted to sculpt a likeness of her. She sighed at the uncomprehending look on Liah's face, then reached into her purse and took out a five-dollar bill, which she pressed in Liah's hand. Liah got the point.

Over the next several months Liah went to the studio three times a week. She and her mistress developed a unique friendship and after each session, Liah brought home tales for Sen. The first time Liah used the bathroom was a trip to fantasyland. The room was almost as large as Liah's entire house; the huge, gleaming sunken bathtub was almost like a miniature swimming pool. The door to the dressing room was ajar and Liah saw rows of dresses and wondered when her mistress ever wore so many. When she used the basin, Liah's eyed bulged with wonderment. The handles were plated twenty-four carat gold! Lucille peeked inside the room and Liah, grinning, pantomimed what a clever way to hoard money.

Four months later, on the second day of August, Lucille showed Liah the bust. Liah gaped at the unfamiliar face for a long time. The deep anxiety lines, the eyes sunken in their sockets and the high protruding cheek bones accentuating the hollow cheeks. It was the face of an old woman!

Liah shook her head. Unbelievable that twelve years of marriage and seven children could alter the flesh so. No, that couldn't be her image.

Lucille stood by helplessly, watching Liah's incredulous reaction and wished she could ease the reality. Somehow Lucille identified with Liah. Not even her wealth could change the bleakness Lucille felt. Lucille reached gently for Liah's hand. "Do not fret, my dear, you are yet a beautiful woman. Savvy? Life will work out for the both of us!"

The tone of Lucille's voice and the pained eyes, gave Liah to know her mistress sympathized and somehow her distress eased. In the loneliness of Liah's plight, it was comforting to have another female understand.

That Lucille was not all emotion and softness, Liah learned later, however, when the master burst into the studio, waving his arms about and shouting wrathfully. Although Liah could not understand the quarrel, she saw Lucille's warmth freeze, and saw her softness harden into a blazing fury. Liah flinched as Edward raised his hand, but Lucille stood motionless, gazing placidly at her husband. He immediately dropped his hand and flung himself from the room.

As she left for home, Liah realized that she must change her attitude and adopt her mistress's manner of resistance. She crossed the concrete drive and walked into the orchard, smiling as she recalled her mother's words, "The silken cord," advised her mother, "my daughter, can strangle even more certainly than a thick rope."

At the time, Liah had neither comprehended the meaning nor made any effort to decipher it but rather accepted the advice as so much prating from an overanxious mother. Liah suddenly realized she'd never heard an argument between her parents yet her mother seemed to live her life as she ordered.

By the time Liah reached their bungalow, the conviction and courage had left her. How she wished she could just once stand up to Sen and say what was on her mind. Always Sen's upraised eyebrow, his disapproving eyes, made her back down. Liah opened the door and murmured, "When will I ever be like my mistress?" The reality of standing up to Sen seemed so remote. Before Liah knew it, she was preparing the Apinyin and dreamily contemplating the escape of the bamboo pipe.

1911

YEAR OF THE BOAR

Life for Liah in 1909 and 1910 had sped by, thanks to her relationship with her mistress and the extra monies she earned. As 1911 dawned, she continued to obediently give Sen four dollars each time she worked, but retained any monies above that. To Liah, retention of that money was not dishonest, for wasn't it so that she was saving for the family's future on the outside?

Only one nagging fear marred an otherwise bearable sojourn behind the estate walls—that her children were leaning too much toward the Fahn Gwai's way of thinking. Trying to prevent any Fahn Gwai spoken at their dinner table was a losing battle with her chopsticks. Eldest Son most often disturbed her tranquility with his constant bursts of temper and threats to run off in the middle of the night. How can a mother expect him to learn about the trucking business if he were kept in captivity? Yes, captivity! Now, with the numerous jobs offered to the Chinese to help in the reclamation and canal work, he and Shelley were missing the opportunity of their lifetimes to earn and save money toward their truck.

Liah scowled but said nothing. Inside, she seethed with anger, more so as she was filled with fear that Eldest and Second Sons might indeed run away. They might even take unto themselves Fahn Gwai wives! In her fearful state of mind, she made a rash promise to them to speak once more to Sen about moving, but please, would her sons promise never to run off?

Ted Crosset became uneasy when he learned about Thomas's vehemence against being locked behind the estate walls, and brought in even more information about the trucking business for Thomas to study.

"It is not only about operating your vehicle and keeping it in running condition, but you will also need to find companies who would be willing to entrust their goods for you to transport. After all, you are a bit young and inexperienced," Ted explained. "Then there are the routes to learn and the examinations to pass in order to obtain a trucking license. So, Thomas, do not go off half-cocked and suffer disaster."

He had it in mind to remind Thomas that as a Chinese there would be prejudices, which would lose him contracts to Fahn Gwai drivers, but he held his tongue. The young man had enough emotional dilemmas without burdening him with an unjust, unchangeable problem.

He turned his mind to Florence and William, the two most promising of his students. It was too bad, he thought. The chances of them going to college were bleak. If only Meng-Sui would allow it. Ted smiled to himself, thinking how much of Liah's philosophy had rubbed off on him.

—

Tensions grew between Sen and Liah. During one of their wrath-filled arguments, he realized how his wife had changed, that his was the power usurped and hers newly attained. A shocking blow to his male pride overwhelmed his anger: a mere female now held the power in his life.

Sen suspected Liah had been withholding part of her earnings, but he couldn't confront her about it, not without a disgusting quarrel. The bungalow walls were so thin, Sen didn't want his children to be burdened with more of their bickering. It was not the money, but the demoralizing disobedience that Sen felt was a slap to his maleness. Mostly he deplored his wife's independence.

In the following days, Sen became silent and at night turned away from his wife's body as her punishment, but his fury mounted when his own physical cravings were denied and Liah's penance became his own.

During these three years, Lucille Dobney was frustrated by her inability to fathom the tiny woman's quicksand emotions, sparkling one moment, then lapsing into an abyss evident in the opaque depths of Liah's eyes. Surely, thought Lucille, Liah's earlier years of persecution and peril must by now be softened by life within the estate walls. In her desire to help Liah, Lucille did the only thing she knew how to do–generously giving her money each time Liah came to pose for her. But one afternoon, purely by chance, Lucille discovered how to bring a smile to Liah's face. Offhandedly, she asked if Liah could mend a tiny rip on the sleeve of her mandarin coat, saying she did not trust such a lovely brocade to American seamstresses.

Liah was thrilled. She took the coat in her hands to examine the tear. It was a pleasure to feel the rich brocade. Since it was no longer necessary to sew for her children, it had been such a long time since Liah had need of her sewing skills. Lucille watched the tedious work as Liah extracted a sliver of thread from the hem of the coat, then meticulously wove the thread into the tear. As she sewed, Liah wondered why a Fahn Gwai woman owned a wedding coat.

Lucille sighed. Over the years, she'd probed and observed, hoping to discover what things delighted the tiny woman only to find it was such a trivial thing as a silk brocade. Somewhere in the back of her mind, Lucille weighed Liah's needs against her own, finding her own a bit ludicrous. In the big mansion with all of its amenities and luxuries, happiness eluded her. For a second, Lucille found herself envious of Liah.

What had happened to her idyllic marriage? The first several years with Edward had been heaven-made, but somewhere it had gone wrong. She peered through her unhappiness and felt again the pain she'd suffered when she had first discovered her husband's philandering. An affair Lucille could understand, but riotous nights with cheap bar girls? No, she had not wronged Edward; he was to blame for their marital problems. Lucille sighed again as she pushed away the thought of divorce. The future frightened her. Could she continue to endure the countless incidents that degraded her position as Edward's wife? On the other hand, didn't her son and daughter deserve a clean slate to begin their lives? As for herself, didn't she deserve to grow old in a serene and dignified manner?

—

Liah returned home from the big house one day, exuberant with the lovely brocades her mistress had given her. When she handed Sen the four dollars, she smiled. "Wouldn't it be nice when we go to the outside and have all these fabrics to make cheongsams?"

Sen bitingly chided, "No more talk of leaving! And do not think for a moment I am as stupid as you think. I know you make more money than you give me."

Liah recoiled, "I am not being dishonest. Mistress said the extra three dollars I am keeping were my tip for mending her coat without a trace of the tear."

Sen's voice was threatening and filled with sarcasm, "Oh, so now you understand the Fahn Gwai's tongue!"

Liah lowered her head, muttering, "No, I do not speak Fahn Gwai, but my mistress pantomimes very well."

Sen heaved a weary sigh. It was useless to press Liah any further, not without an ugly argument, and he did not want to subject himself to the shame of his children hearing yet another fight between their parents.

—

The beginning of each year was a time of distressingly taut nerves, and the new Fahn Gwai year of 1911 was no exception. The eleventh day of January was Third Son Theo's fourteenth year on earth and on the twentieth day was Fifth Son Mert's feast day–his eleventh year on earth.

The family, fearing Liah's nervous wrath, behaved and gave their mother a wide berth. Thomas, because he was the eldest and as yet unmarried, suffered the most. Usually it was on the celebration of her youngest child Emmi's feast day, on the tenth day in February, when Liah erupted into a fiery lamentation. Had the Gods forsaken her? Was she to be deprived of grandsons? How, behind these walls, could she find suitable wives for Eldest and Second Sons?

Somehow Fourth Son escaped his mother's anger. Perhaps she recognized the youngster's deep love for books or perhaps she saw in William the lawyer who would champion the cause of his people. Whatever the reason, Liah did not rail at William as she did the others.

Ted Crosset often listened to Thomas's heated bitterness, looking on helplessly. In a desperate attempt to comfort him, Ted mentioned Meng-Sui. "If it is for you to leave for the outside, your fate will make it possible."

Thomas's desperate desire to leave the estates was overtaken by the announcement in the papers about the Owens River Project, a monumental engineering feat which involved a tunnel being built under Lake Elizabeth in the north to funnel water to the city, water that had started its journey via thirty-five miles of open canals into Owens Lake where another canal of 900-feet-per-second capacity would carry it through twenty-three miles of open canals and another thirty-seven miles of cemented canals winding their way through the Owens Valley to the Haiwee Reservoir 200 feet above the lake. From there, the water would flow to Little Lake through thirty-four more miles of covered cement conduits, flumes and siphons. Finally, the water would travel nineteen miles through the desolate stretches of Jawbone Canyon in the Mojave Desert and sixty more miles to Antelope Valley where it would reach Lake Elizabeth.

The Chinese were pouring in from Dai Faw and Noo Yok to work on the reclamation and canals, which had been underway since 1908.

Thomas moaned. "All that work with good pay and we're locked behind these walls! For two cents I'd sneak off in the middle of the night. There's no use arguing with Mah-Mah!"

It was on Ted's mind to speak of Meng-Sui again, but Thomas's expression was stubborn and fierce, so Ted remained silent. As Thomas barged out the door, Ted said quietly, "Thomas, the future belongs to he who labors and has faith and patience. The choice is yours."

Ted watched the stocky figure go down the path, without a backward glance. It appeared Thomas was on his way to speak with his mother once more.

Two weeks later, Sen went to China Street with the foreman. Upon his return home, he informed Liah about the River Project, saying that many of their people were now being recruited by the Fahn Gwai. "Wong Dak and Soong Sing have signed up as cooks on the railroad. Work is seven days a week and confined to a wild terrain, but they say they don't mind. They'll be able to save the entire hundred dollars a month and return to our homeland."

Sen paused, then reiterated their two sons' desire to move to the outside. Liah's shock lapsed into fury! "To break up a family for the sake of money? Never! We shall move as a family if and when you get the courage to face the Fahn Gwai."

At Liah's accusation of cowardice, Sen lashed out at her filthy Apinyin habit. Liah, uncowed, fought back. She accused Sen of being the cause of her return to the opiate: If he'd move the family to China Street instead of imprisoning her behind the estate walls, she'd have no need for it.

Sen challenged, "Oh, and leave your mistress? Surely you would not give up the lucrative job and all its monies." His eyes narrowed as he continued, "And remember that I am aware of the money you withhold each time. Not that I care for the few dollars, but your disobedience and dishonesty galls me! I am not blind, nor am I stupid, Liah!"

In their sleeping porch, Thomas and Shelley huddled in misery as their parents' angry voices filled the small house. Thomas, caught up in the controversy between his parents, felt his mother had no business accusing his father of cowardice. If only his father would stop accusing Mama of withholding monies. His father couldn't help his fear, not if stories of Fahn Gwai persecutions were even half-true. In the back of his mind lurked the misty shadow of the terror he felt as a young child when they were dragged off into the black cave to escape the Fahn Gwai. Still, his father ought to try and see his mother's view: not all Fahn Gwai were evil. Not all desired to see him dead. Why couldn't his father make an effort to live beside the Fahn Gwai?

In the abyss of his torment, Thomas heard his brother's voice. "God, I want out, but not at the expense of Mah and Pah quarreling. I'm going in to stop it." Thomas's face darkened as he spoke sharply. "No, I'm the oldest, I'll do it."

He went in, pulled up a chair and tried to speak with them but Sen only stalked out of the bedroom, charged through the front room and out the front door, slamming it viciously as he went. Balefully, Thomas glared at his penitent mother who'd promised she'd give up the Apinyin habit, but both knew it was an empty promise. Her habit was too deeply rooted to be eradicated and certainly not under these tense circumstances. In the silence of the house, Thomas ruefully realized that despite the quarrels, neither he nor Shelley had obtained their freedom. Suddenly he rose from his chair, pushed it roughly aside and went to find Ted Crosset.

1912

YEAR OF THE RAT

On the twentieth day of June, in the Fahn Gwai's year of nineteen hundred and twelve, Sen went to see Cousin Shah in China Street. Seragio dropped him off at the train yard, telling him to be there at seven that night if he wanted to ride back.

Sen rapped on Cousin Shah's door, thinking it strange as he tried the knob and found it unlocked. The laughter within gave Sen to believe Cousin Shah was having a celebration. So early in the day?

A moment later Sen stared and gasped at his cousin's shorn hair. "Are you mad, Cousin Shah? What did you do to your queue?"

There was a roar of laughter as the others turned to reveal their own haircuts. Wang Sang had a mirror in his hand trying to see the back of his neck. Chon Woo turned to Sen. "You look terrible with that pony tail of yours. Come on, let's take him to the barber!"

Sen half-angrily pushed Chon aside as the bar owner grabbed for his queue. "Cousin Shah," Sen said. "I demand to know the reason behind this madness!"

A thoughtful silence suddenly hung in the room, Reality thrust itself forward as Cousin Shah sighed; he hated to break the exalted mood which gripped them all. Nevertheless Cousin Shah found himself back in the drab world ruled by the Fahn Gwai. Wearily he murmured, "So you want to know the cause of our madness?"

Shah took Sen's arm and led him to the table. "Look at those newspaper photographs, Sen. That's Granduncle and his son. Do you notice their shorn hair? Oh, and here's a picture of our first cousins, too. Now do you understand? Our countrymen have overthrown the Emperor! The Emperor and his army are vanquished and our people have cut off their queues as a symbol of independence!"

"Here, Sen," Sang handed him a letter. It read in part, "On the twelfth day of February of this year, the Emperor signed a declaration of abdication." Sang said, "My cousin goes on to tell how Sun Yat-Sen and his men fought the Emperor and were victorious!"

Still dubious, Sen wondered aloud how it was that they had had no inkling of such a revolution before.

Wong Sang impatiently shouted, "Sen, take our word for it, we really are liberated! Did you know that Sun Yat-Sen was in Gem Sahn many times for conferences and to raise monies among his intellectual friends? In fact, I hear he was in Dai Faw and Loo Sahng planning and training his men. They say that once he was smuggled into Loo Sahng on a potato barge. If you don't believe me, ask Professor. He knows everything."

Cousin Shah nodded. "I think Professor was actually in on the planning. He's hinted several times to me that there were fresh winds blowing abroad and not to be surprised if by this year we saw changes in our country. Now, what about cutting off your queue?"

Chon Woo pulled Sen by his arm. "Come on, Sen, let's get that pigtail of yours cut off!"

Sen accompanied the four men to the barbershop. When they arrived, Sen peeked nervously into the window and saw the conservative scholar, the one they called Professor. Whatever doubts Sen had now vanished as Professor's queue fell to the floor in long, heavy flurries.

Professor smiled at Sen. "I feel my head is pounds lighter already, not to mention that the yoke of submission is now cast from our backs."

Sen smiled at Professor. A rush of emotions clutched Sen's body as he sat down in the barber's chair. His hands were moist with nervous excitement, for the idea of short hair had never occurred to him. Cousin

Quock flashed into his mind. The lusty, loud fisherman predicted over twelve years ago that his countrymen would one day cut off their queues. Sen smiled as he recalled the huge fisherman's ridicule of his queue.

Cousin Quock wasn't a political genius or a fortuneteller. When Sen first met him and gaped at his bald head, the big man roared. "What's the matter with you? Haven't you ever seen a bald head? Of course I've cut off my queue! Why not? I do not plan to go home; besides it's much more comfortable to work without that mane of hair. Someday, you too will cut it off. Mark my words. Then maybe the Fahn Gwai will leave us alone!"

Sen winced as the shears hacked off its first hank. Liah's face flashed before him and he felt a measure of importance. He imagined her incredulous look, her distressed cries, then heard himself superciliously explaining the facts. His children, too, would be dismayed. Sen was lost in these thoughts until he felt a gentle tap. The barber was handing him a mirror.

At his first glance at the back of his head and neck, he quickly ran his hand over the naked expanse. After a few minutes of reflection, Sen gave the mirror back to the barber, turning and grinning foolishly at his companions. "I still find it hard to believe. Never would I have dreamed of being without a queue. Wait until my family sees me! They'll think me drunk or mad."

"No more talk!" Chon Woo cried. "Let's go to my place and we'll drink a toast to our freedom—1912, the year we really became men! You come, too, Professor. All of you!"

—

Seragio gawked wordlessly at Sen, then mumbled, "My friend, you got no more tail! Aiyah, you drunk! Come, I take you home. Man, your wife she be one mad woman. Come on!"

The foreman halted the wagon in front of Sen's bungalow, reaching out a hand to steady Sen as he lumbered down and reeled toward the door. "Hey, man, you get good sleep. Tomorrow, you have one big head!"

Sen paid no heed to the foreman, as he stumbled to the door. He rapped and shouted for Liah. Thomas was first to peer out the front room window. He gaped uncomprehendingly at his father's efforts to show off his shorn queue. Then he screamed for his mother.

Liah led her husband into the bedroom. At first she was too occupied to notice his haircut, then suddenly she stopped rigid, gasped and screamed, "Your queue, Sen! What have you done? Aiyah, you've gone mad in your drunkenness!"

Sen waved her distress aside, muttering for her not to worry. The other children poured into the bedroom and, seeing their father half-slumped on the bed, gaped silently. Liah became alarmed when her husband began to laugh, waving his arms wildly as he muttered something about subservience and wearing the queue.

Incoherently he smirked, "Now we are free!" He sat upright, suddenly pointing a finger at his sons. "Tomorrow morning, cut off your queues! Liah, do you hear me? Our emperor was dethroned!"

As instantly as he thought of his sons, Sen lapsed back into recalling the night's frivolity, chuckling as he tried to recount the events for Liah. "You should have seen them. Each man with a mirror, gaping at his naked neck. Me, too! A strange feeling not to have the weight of the queue on my neck."

Liah, silent and apprehensive, thought she'd ask Sen again in the morning; he was too drunk now to know of what he spoke.

Sen stood and waved at Eldest Son, demanding a pencil. "I want to circle this auspicious date when the Chings were deposed!"

Thomas gingerly approached his father with the pencil. "Are you sure of what you speak, Father?"

Sen whirled around and almost fell. Second Son quickly caught him and held him up. "No, I'm not sure of the details, but of cutting off our queues, I'm positive. I saw pictures of our family in China; all the men had shorn hair. Cousin Shah told me the tenth day of the tenth month was when the Emperor fled."

Liah signaled her two eldest sons to put their father to bed. Sen feebly pushed them aside, declaring himself sober enough to know of what he spoke. "I only got drunk afterwards, when Chon Woo took us all to his bar to celebrate!"

The family left Sen to sleep off his drunkenness. Tomorrow Liah would again ask for the truth.

—

Ted Crosset stared a long moment at Liah's sons, but said nothing about their short hair. At the end of class, Ted pulled Thomas aside and whispered that he had thought it was a royal edict that all male subjects wore queues "Isn't it dangerous that you've cut them off? Does your father know about this?"

Thomas smiled and related his father's drunken state on Saturday night and how his mother was aghast at his father's shorn hair. Ted roared with laughter and all the children joined in. Theo said, "And you know what, sir? My mother still does not know whether to believe Father or not. She asked that the foreman drive her to China Street this weekend to make certain."

Ted wiped off his eyeglasses, inquiring if the boys missed their queues.

Theo shook his head vigorously. "Naw, it was a pain in the neck. Now I can look like any other guy!"

"No, sir," Shelley concurred. "I was sick and tired of being different and having to fight about the long queue. Besides, I was tired of explaining."

Theo began to laugh again. "You should have seen my mother, sir. She didn't know whether to be mad or glad. Boy, was Father stinko!"

"Well, sir," murmured Thomas, "I guess my brothers said all there is to say. I, too am happy about my short hair, although for the first few minutes it felt strange not to have so much hair on the back of my neck. It feels so much lighter."

William said timidly, "I only hope our father is right!"

Ted smiled at William. The young boy was so serious and Ted silently hoped William had no need to worry.

William suddenly turned to face Ted. "Sir, it doesn't really matter whether my father is right or wrong. None of us intend to visit China, so what's the difference?"

Ted's voice was gentle. "You know, William, I hope each of you will have the opportunity to visit the land of your origin. China is a very old country, full of beautiful traditions and, despite her bloody history, it is the most civilized country in the world. However, if I were you boys, I'd invest more time and interest in your lessons. I believe that is the only way you will become fully integrated with the Fahn Gwai."

Liah's sons gaped a long moment at their teacher, then burst into laughter at Ted's usage of the Chinese names for Americans and America.

—

Seragio met Sen at work and, chiding him for his drunkenness, asked if his wife had chastised him. The foreman pantomimed Sen's drunken reeling and pitching about. Sen reddened and chuckled.

In the months that followed, Sen's personality began to change by degrees. In the first few weeks, he was constantly looking out the corner of his eye to see if any Fahn Gwai were staring at him; only then could he relax. A few of his countrymen who had not yet been to China Street and had not cut off their queues, looked enviously at Sen's short hair, yet were afraid to be caught up in a fiasco of misinformation.

As the strangeness of short hair wore off, Sen realized his fright of the Fahn Gwai had also diminished. In his mind, Sen ignored the fact that while he allowed some Fahn Gwai to come close, he still maintained enough distance to escape if violence threatened.

Liah, now more lucid as a result of using her bamboo pipe less, began to notice the change in her husband as well. Sensing Sen was less afraid of the Fahn Gwai, she began a more forceful campaign to move to the outside. "We need a better place for our children, a place where our sons and their families can live without fear and our grandchildren can flourish, a place where we will be able to find wives for our sons and husbands for our daughters."

Sen felt despair return. Why, if he had gained the courage to be among the Fahn Gwai, did he still cringe when arguing with his wife? Sen snapped back wrathfully, "Bah! We are not in China, woman! Our children will select their own spouses. I will hear no more talk of moving!"

—

The summer of 1912 was a period of rapid growth for Liah's children, but for her it was painful. She felt her children slipping beyond the reach of her authority. If only they were in China Street, they would naturally adopt the tradition of filial piety. For the first time she cursed their Fahn Gwai education.

In desperation she confronted her husband to move yet again. "Do you want your sons to visit prostitutes or, worse yet, marry a Fahn Gwai female? Here, locked behind the estate walls, how can they meet a girl of our race? We must move, my husband, for the children's sake!"

Sen irately challenged, "What makes you think our sons will agree to marry the girls of our choice? Besides, they have no desire for the bonds of marriage."

"They have no choice!" snapped Liah. "Our parents never asked our pleasure! That is one reason I want to live in China Street. I will be able to put out the word for a suitable match. Will you at least ask Cousin

Shah to keep his eyes open for a desirable girl? Eldest Son is now nineteen years old! Too old to be without a wife. And while you're at it, look around for a girl for our Second Son, too."

Sen nodded wearily. Whenever his wife wore that grim look on her face, it was impossible to change her mind. Sen scowled, "All right, but I'll brook no interference from you!"

Sen strode away. Inside the bedroom, he flopped on the bed and covered his face with his arm. The recurring rumors of his master's divorce had already shattered his serenity. Sen didn't want to return to the outside. If only the Gods would allow him another two years here, his children would be old enough to take care of themselves. Too tired to curse the Gods, Sen's mind was nevertheless full of anger against them. Instead he cursed his Meng-Sui, which had brought him to this day. Sen turned on his side, seeking solace in sleep.

—

Toward autumn, Sen found additional reasons to curse the Gods. The rumors of the master's divorce became a reality. He gaped fearfully as Seragio pantomimed the details of the divorce. Sen wanted to know if he and the others would be allowed to continue to work on the estate. Seragio shrugged and indicated maybe, but he had heard that the new owners were not the same kind of people as their current master and mistress.

Liah was stunned when Sen gave her the news. While she'd wanted to move to the outside, she'd made no arrangements. Where would they live? They'd certainly need a large place what with their future sons-in-law and daughters-in-law, not to mention the grandchildren. Liah cried out in frustration.

That night Liah took stock of what she would leave should they move to the outside. Without her mistress, life behind the tall walls would be impossible. A rush of tears stung her eyes at the thought that she'd see her mistress no more. Meng-Sui could be so cruel! Another fear assailed her: what about her children's education? She knew in her heart Sen would not allow them to go to school if it meant money out of his own pocket. Liah vowed that no matter the cost, she'd see to it that her children went to school. They must not grow up to be like her and Sen, illiterate slaves of the Fahn Gwai.

A stirring at the back of her head tensed her body. This time she cried out for the Gods to make themselves heard, to indicate what they wanted of her. Did they not see the gravity of her situation? She muttered, "I need no more riddles now."

Liah's thoughts reverted to her earlier years in Dai Faw. Such a long time since her arrest. It had been a strange turn of fate when the judge sent her to a rehabilitation program to break her Apinyin habit instead of prison. At the time, she was too frightened to be grateful for the small daily portion of Apinyin given to her there to alleviate the agony of withdrawal. Now as she looked back on the event, Liah remembered how her seafaring cousin had brought her the drug and she had sold it to many of her countrymen.

In a blinding revelation, Liah gasped. Yes, that was it! Why not do the same thing in Loo Sahng? Surely there must be others who needed Apinyin. At least that huge Fahn Gwai police vice officer from Dai Faw wouldn't dog her footsteps. She grinned, recalling how she had dubbed him 'The Cat'. A sense of accomplishment came over Liah as she recalled the big officer's constant attempts to catch her in the act of peddling Apinyin.

Cousin Suey Wah surely would not object to bringing larger amounts of the opiate. He must know a large family needed outside income. She decided to speak with him if she could before they moved to the outside.

Liah shook her head. She couldn't help but wonder about the Fahn Gwai's aversion to Apinyin. What was so different about their cigarettes or alcohol? Users of Apinyin did not go out into the streets and commit drunken mayhem. If the Gods meant for her to sell Apinyin, the way would be free of obstacles. Well, first things first: They must move to the outside.

Several days later Liah delivered another cake to Mr. Louie. At the last moment, she timidly inquired if he'd heard any news about the master's divorce.

"Yes, but the foreman said those of us who wish to may remain and work for the new owners. Perhaps with your large family you and Sen ought to consider this."

Liah shook her head and cried, "No, I hear the new owners are not a bit like our master. Besides, without my mistress, life on the estate will be dreary. No, we must move."

"What about Sen? He led me to believe he will remain here."

Liah shook her head. "No, if we are to move, it's my responsibility to find a place. Could you tell me if you know of any vacancies suitable for my large family?"

Mr. Louie paused for he wanted no part in an argument between a husband and wife. Liah, sensing his hesitancy, told him not to worry. "I will give Sen the information and if he wills it, and if the Gods mean for us to move, we will."

Mr. Louie nodded. "There are several places, but your best option would be the alley beside the railroad tracks. I don't know if you will like the place, for the alley is dirty, sooty and noisy. If I were you, I'd give this more thought."

Liah replied that she had to think of her unmarried sons. They must marry their own kind and where could she find a suitable match for her sons on this estate? And later she'd have to marry off her eldest daughter.

Mr. Louie laughed heartily at Liah's lamentations. "Liah, in Gem Sahn children pick their own spouses. Your sons are yet young; do not worry. If it is their Meng-Sui to be married, neither you nor I can deter it. Well, I have things to do if I am to leave this next week. I'll say good-bye now, for I may not have the chance later."

Liah nodded, persisting with one more question. "Surely you will have to work on the outside, sir. Are there jobs for us there? Perhaps jobs for Sen and our two eldest sons?"

"Ask your Cousin Shah, Liah. He knows all there is to know of China Street; besides that, he knows the landlord of that row of buildings along the alley. One thing I'd advise, because of your large family think carefully before you leave this place. Room and wages for an entire family are hard to come by."

Liah shook her head. "I thank you, sir, for the information. I'll speak with Cousin Shah. I am determined to move. May the Gods follow your footsteps. I hope we shall meet in China Street soon."

—

When Sen returned from the fields that evening, Liah asked if he wouldn't ask the foreman to take her into town. "While I am there to buy shoes for the children, I might as well look around for a suitable place. Mr. Louie told me there is a row of places along the alley next to the train yard. They are large enough for us. He said for me to speak to Cousin Shah."

Sen's first reaction was to silence his wife, to say that they were re-maining on the estate, that he was the head of their family and would decide when and where they'd move. The grim expression on Liah's face forced Sen to back down. Sen felt despair, for in the last two years his wife had become a distressingly stubborn and disobedient female. He was tempted to strike her, punish her for her insolence; instead he angrily retorted, "I think you're premature in your plans. These divorce rumors have been around for some time. Even if the master gets di-vorced, he told the foreman those of us who wanted to could stay on."

"Oh, no," cried Liah. "The rumors are true! Cook told me she was quitting in ten days; that she has a new job. She even asked me to go with her. Of course I told her no. She said the mistress had introduced her and the butler to the new owners and she didn't like them. She thought they were too haughty and uncouth. Please, Sen, please let us move to the outside."

Her husband's silence chilled Liah's heart. Somehow she had to convince him. Liah's heart was racing, her palms were moist and with great effort she pleaded for them to move. "Our sons will never amount to much if imprisoned behind these walls. I am certain this chain of events is a sign for us to change the place of our abode."

After the words tumbled out, Liah paused, waiting for Sen's argument, but there was not the slightest indication he'd even heard her. Her fear then turned to anger. Why did Sen always turn a deaf ear to her appeals?

Liah made her last attempt. "Sen, I've never complained, never asked for a thing. I am asking now that we move to China Street. We must not remain! Our sons must have a chance to make a place for themselves and for our grandchildren. Our daughters soon must wed. Do you not think of their future? Do you not care to have grandsons? We need a permanent place where we can put down roots instead of running from place to place? I cannot live like this! I am getting older, less strong and less brave, less able to withstand the unknown!"

Sen glowered, then without a word he strode out of the house. Liah watched him disappear down the road. She sighed; at least he didn't say no. With a heavy heart she turned her attention to supper.

—

There were mixed emotions amongst Liah's children about moving from the estate. Thomas and Shelley hid their enthusiasm, hoping their mother would be able to convince Father that they had to leave. When Theo cried to be included in his brothers' plan for a trucking line, Thomas growled, "You're still young, Theo. Go to school for a few more years, then join us. Besides, trucking is tough work. Who knows? You might want to do something else. Wouldn't it be a terrible thing if at that time you found out you should have stayed in school?"

"Who cares about tough work? I want to drive a truck with you guys. With three of us, we ought to own two or three trucks!"

Thomas growled, "Okay, but promise you'll stay in school, at least through graduation from high school?"

Theo bit his lip in sheer disappointment, but he nodded.

William and Flo were crestfallen; of all the children, they were the ones who were fearful their education would be over once on the outside. William despaired of the fact that he wouldn't have the chance to become a teacher. When Flo cried that her world had come to an end, William tried to comfort her. "Mr. Crosset told me there are public schools on the outside and that they are free."

"So what?" wailed Flo. "Baba won't let us go!"

—

The final day of school on the estate was held on the twenty-ninth of June. The closing session was quiet, orderly and solemn. At the end of the short class, Ted Crosset wrote his name on the blackboard. "My address is also here for you in case you'd like to write to me. I promise I will answer each and every letter." He turned and grinned at the class. "In fact, I'll correct the letters and mail them back to you."

Ted's voice was husky as he informed the class he'd never forget them. "In the future, if you have any questions or problems, you know where to find me. The address I gave you is my parents' home."

He turned to Flo with his last remark. The girl's face was so tragic it was almost unbearable to look at. "Flo, you have such drive and eager-ness for knowledge, I sincerely hope you will have the opportunity to continue your education. If not, please make use of the public libraries. President Lincoln was self-taught and you, too, can learn if you want to badly enough." Ted paused. "Do not hesitate to write to me. It will be good practice for your language. And one more thing, Flo, if you'll sheath your tongue, you will find life will be softer on you. I want you to promise me you will try."

Flo nodded wordlessly, her head bent, for she didn't want the teacher to see her tears. Ted turned immediately to the class. "Mr. Dobney in-formed me you may take whatever books, pencils or supplies you want."

The classroom exploded into bedlam as the students made a grab for books, papers, pencils, colors pens and inkpots. Flo screamed for Thomas to help the younger kids, as she stacked reference books, read-ers and spellers. William quietly selected history, arithmetic and science manuals as well as a useful assortment of school supplies.

"Theo," shouted Flo. "I know you don't care for books and stuff, but help Mert gather the automotive manuals. Get us some rulers, erasers and maps, and ask Mr. Crosset if we can have the globe."

Flo shrieked in anger at a Mexican child struggling with Emmi over a box of crayons and paints. "Shelley, help Emmi! That kid is trying to take away her Crayolas!"

Thomas and Ted Crosset talked at the far corner of the greenhouse. Ted murmured as they shook hands. "Take good care of your family, Thomas. You are fortunate to have such a wonderful group, especially your mother. She's priceless." He gazed thoughtfully and then added, "Do not resent your mother's wisdom and love. Tell her I'll be by some-time this week to say my good-byes. Please write; I want to keep in touch. Good luck to you. Your family is very special to me."

Ted turned, took a long last look at the students, then hurried out the door.

1913

Year of the Ox

The day before her departure, Lucille Dobney sent for Liah. Their sorrow was pantomimed, etched on their faces as Lucille shook hands, then impulsively took Liah in her arms. Both women cried, each for her own reasons. When they broke from their embrace, Liah spied the peacock and ran to say good-bye.

Lucille smiled, pantomiming that she wanted Liah to have the peacock and his mate. Liah was at a loss to comprehend what she meant until Lucille snapped leashes around the birds' necks and handed the leashes to Liah. Liah gaped, for never would she have thought her mistress would part with her omens of good luck. Liah quickly, shyly murmured, "Tankee velly muchee."

For a moment, Lucille turned her face to hide her emotions, then she patted Liah on the shoulder. "I shall miss you, my dear. Go with God."

Liah did not comprehend her mistress's farewell, but had she done so, she would have replied, "May your Meng Sui be kind. May Kwan Yin guide your footsteps and may health, wealth and happiness follow wherever you go." All Liah could say was said with a nod of her head, her tear-misted eyes and her sad smile.

Liah's heart was light as she made her way home with her peacock and peahen. The idea of continuing to live on the estate was appalling, for without her mistress life here would be without meaning. She must force Sen to allow her to go to China Street this very Sunday! It was then that Liah knew she was more like her mistress than she had realized.

Wasn't it true that for the past year and a half she'd kept all the monies her mistress gave her? She blushed as she acknowledged she did give her husband three or four dollars, but any money above that she'd kept. Not even when Sen hinted that she'd earned more than what she'd given him had she given him more.

Wasn't it so that she no longer went to bed when Sen did, but stayed up to do as she wanted? Liah smiled as she touched the bright green and yellow scarf around her neck, thinking of the bits of color she'd added to her wardrobe, something she'd never have dared to do if she had lived in her native village, at least not without the disdain of her women friends, especially her mother-in-law. And Sen, he would have ordered her to quit her colorful garb, for he would have obeyed his mother.

Liah's assessment of her independent attitude was correct, for Sen had also noticed the subtle changes in her behavior. No longer did Liah ask his pleasure before uttering her own opinions. Although he'd taken her to task several times, Sen could not sway Liah from her newfound freedom. It shamed Sen to argue or fight with his wife, for he was embarrassed by his loss of face each time Liah triumphed. The walls of their bedroom were so thin that all their conversations could be overheard. In order to keep tranquility, Sen had become withdrawn while Liah had grown stronger.

Liah, too occupied with her plans of moving, had not noticed a change in her husband until he no longer came to her with his physical needs. Even this did not become apparent until Sen refused her own physical longings. By the time Liah reached home, she knew without a doubt they had to move. This time she must win the argument.

Sen was resting in the front room. Proudly she pointed to the peacock and peahen. "My mistress gave them to me. She also said we could take whatever furniture we wanted from our house. Of course, we'll take everything. Isn't it wonderful to have our very own symbols of good joss? Oh, this Sunday when I go to China Street I will look around for a suitable abode."

Sen grunted and walked into the bedroom. He wanted to stop his wife's talk of moving, wanted to tell her they were staying and that he'd no longer stand for anymore of her disobedience, but he could not. He threw himself on top of the bed, stared up at the ceiling, and fought the impulse to go shake some sense into his wife. Sen dreaded moving. He had vowed never to live among the Fahn Gwai. Surely Liah must remember the terror of their eviction from Tijuana Flats? Behind the estate walls they'd be safe until the children grew up. Why couldn't she see that?

In the back of his mind, Sen wrestled with the future of his children. Imprisoned behind the walls he hated to admit they'd never find themselves, no matter how safe. In that respect he begrudgingly admitted his wife was correct, but why did she not allow him the decision? He scowled, muttering half-aloud, "Just wait until she finds out how difficult employment is on the outside. Just wait until she's confronted by strange Fahn Gwai."

Sen threw his arm across his eyes as if to blot out the past five years which had robbed him of a dutiful wife. He muttered to himself that he would regain his position as head of his family again some day soon.

—

The next day the chauffeur came to the house with a huge box, saying his mistress had indicated it was for Liah. The children crowded around and Sen gazed from across the room as Liah untied the cords. She burst with excitement as she saw the mandarin wedding coat together with several coats and sweaters. On top there was a small jewelry box. "Oh, Sen, just look! My mistress gave me her twenty-dollar gold piece and the solid gold chain. Oh, what good joss, this gift!"

Sen said nothing, but Eldest Daughter began to try on a luxurious cashmere sweater until Liah scowled, ordering her to put it down.

When Sen returned home from work that day, his face was wreathed in smiles. "The master was most generous today! He gave all his employees a sizeable bonus. Mr. Louie said it was to tide us over until we found employment. I got a hundred and fifty dollars!"

Liah listened as her two sons also waved their hundred dollar bills. Shelley grinned, "I've never had so much money in my life!"

Liah silently held out her hands and obediently Thomas and Shelley handed over their money. Sen murmured that Soong Hee was the luckiest. "The master found him a room in China Street and paid his rent for a year. On top of that, he gave him one hundred dollars and said he'd receive the same amount each month until he no longer needed it. The master must have an endless source of monies."

"It is sad to leave, even when my heart demands we move to China Street." Liah's eyes misted and she quickly looked at Sen. "But the Gods dictate that we must rejoin our people."

Sen silently scowled and went directly to their bedroom and closed the door.

Liah, in her curiosity about the other men, asked if Mr. Louie had received monies. Thomas impatiently replied, "Mah, it is not our business; but if you must know, Mr. Louie got three hundred dollars because he is the eldest employee after Soong Hee."

—

Liah watched Lucille's limousine as it slowly drove past their bungalow. Lucille turned a somber face to the window as she gently waved farewell. Liah's eyes misted and she felt a shock of pain, for the realization finally hit her that she'd never see her mistress again. This bitter separation strengthened her determination to leave the estate as soon as possible. If they waited, perhaps Sen would change his mind and remain to work for the new owners.

A week after her mistress departed, on the ninth day of July, Liah and the children went to China Street without Sen. The ride in Seragio's wagon was noisy, exuberant, and plagued with unleashed energies. Unlike five years earlier, now as Seragio pointed out the master's oil wells, Thomas and Shelley were impressed.

Seragio halted the wagon in front of Cousin Shah's shack. He pointed to his wrist watch and said, "Mama, five o'clock, you be here. Savvy?" The foreman held up his hand showing five fingers.

Thomas, somewhat peeved at the foreman's condescending attitude toward his mother, retorted curtly, "I understand, sir, and we'll be here sharply at five."

Cousin Shah was flabbergasted when he saw Liah and the children. Already alerted by Sen, Cousin Shah was piqued by Liah's determination to move onto China Street. Sensing his displeasure, Liah nevertheless inquired about the buildings near the train yards.

Cousin Shah curtly pointed to a spot, nodding toward an area on the far side of the train yard. "Over there. Mr. Louie is right. There are twelve huge places, several already rented. I won't go with you to see the landlord, but his office is in the middle of Marchesson Gai, named after the landlord. You can't miss it; it's the only three story building on the street. However, have lunch first."

They ate at Wong's Café on Dragon Den Road. Afterwards Cousin Shah led them down Pig Alley, through a short cut to Marchesson Street and pointed down the block. "There, that tall building is where the landlord is. Eldest Son can interpret for you. I bid you good day."

Mark Marchesson was busy at his desk when Liah walked in. He was taken aback at the sight of the children, but mostly at the tiny woman. Thomas introduced his mother, explaining that they wanted to see the stores along the side of the alley by the train yards. Marchesson shook hands, quickly smiling at Liah. "Please," he instructed Thomas, "ask your mother to forgive me for staring, but it is unusual to see an unaccompanied woman in China Street. As a matter of fact, I haven't seen too many Chinese ladies at all, come to think of it."

Thomas was quick to explain that his father was working and could not come. Besides it would be his mother's decision as to which store, for she alone knew what was necessary. Many storefronts in Chinatown had private rooms in the back and above the premises and Liah planned to convert a commercial store for residential use. Mr. Marchesson nodded. "Would she like to see the stores now?"

While they made their way down dusty, unpaved Marchesson Street, Mark, as he was known, spoke of his early days in Los Angeles, using its Chinese name, Loo Sahng. He admired the Chinese people for their industry and frugality. Thomas bristled, disliking the man's patronizing attitude. Self-preservation and poverty were more like it! Thomas's voice was edged with rancor as he explained why his mother wanted to live on China Street. "Not since we were evicted from our last farm in Lankershim has she felt secure among the Fahn Gwai. She hasn't forgotten the harrowing times we had in Dai Faw, which was our reason for having to move to Loo Sahng."

"Distressing," murmured Mr. Marchesson, "however, we haven't had any violence here since the horrible massacre many years ago." He then chuckled, "You know, I was the first to rent to your people. I suppose it doesn't matter much to you, son, but this street is named after me. Probably because I own so much of the property here. I am proud of my intimate association with your people. I've been around them so much, I almost speak Chinese. That is, I understand most conversations and speak some badly pronounced words." He grinned as he said, "However, I speak good pidgin English."

Liah, plodding silently beside the Fahn Gwai, found the heat and dust suffocating, made worse by the children's cavorting, which stirred up even more dust. Abruptly she issued a command for obedience.

Liah followed Mr. Marchesson as he stepped off the dirt street onto a cobblestone walk. She paused, wiping the perspiration from her face, as she looked up at a sagging trellis heavy with honeysuckle and wisteria. She stared at the chain-link fence along the train yard lined by weary foliage. Seared by many summer suns and lack of water, the ivy, hibiscus and oleanders were barely alive. If only there was a suitable store, she'd revive the greenery once she moved in.

Mark observed Liah's facial expressions and found himself smiling at her and she at him. He sighed. Too bad she did not have more to smile about. Together, they walked up and down the cobblestone walk, Liah scrutinizing each doorway as if looking for an omen. To Mark it seemed as if the tiny woman saw the dreary alley as something other than it was. Something stirred within him that he couldn't define, but he felt attracted to the little lady.

Thomas explained to Mr. Marchesson that his mother planned to change the ugly alley into a beautiful garden. It would become the most beautiful spot in China Street. "Your mother," smiled Mark, "is a pioneer as my mother was. Both have the same strong character and lofty dreams."

On their third turn through the alley, Liah marched up to a red doorway and pointed. The tall landlord, with slightly graying hair, searched his huge ring of keys. "Ah, here, the key to Number Three."

Mr. Marchesson pulled open the double screen doors, revealing a pair of stout wooden doors with glass panels on the upper halves. Liah marveled! The doors were almost four inches thick! She thought that once reinforced with wood to cover the glass and barred within, entry would be impossible.

She glanced up and down the cobblestones in the hope of seeing another tenant but there was no one about. Suddenly a vision of a full-fledged Chinatown entered her head, but just as quickly Liah scoffed at the notion. She wasn't even moved in yet! Foolish woman, the time was not yet to be thinking of a Chinatown.

The rent for the store was twenty dollars a month, payable in advance, explained Mark, but if the store was too large for her, he had other smaller places. "Of course, they're not located by the train yards, but on Dragon's Den Road and on the dirt road beside the stock yards."

Liah shook her head at Thomas. "Tell the landlord I'll take this place, but first I'd like to measure and draw up a few simple plans for your father. We will have to partition off bedrooms, build cupboards and shelves before we move in. The store will be divided into three parts. The first is to be the public room where we can visit and do business; the second part—the largest section—will be bedrooms, with a hallway on the left which will lead to the rear and to the kitchen. There'll be another door on the right side, which will be Fifth Son's bedroom. There will be two bedrooms opening into the hallway, one for the two girls and the other for Third and Fourth Sons. Your father and I will have a room on the right side of the hall. Your brother and you will have a bedroom off the kitchen."

Thomas asked anxiously if his mother was not premature in planning. She didn't have to pay the rent until they were sure of moving. "Father said he was the head of our family and I think you ought to ask his opinion."

Liah frowned. "If he allows us to move to China Street, I do not care if he is the head of the house or I am!" Distracted, Liah glanced toward the rear of the store, on the far left, and moved over to inspect a stove and wok. "Such a big wok! I wonder why they're here? Well, it doesn't matter; it'll save us the expense of buying both a stove and a wok. Then she pointed to the pair of windows high along the rear of the store. "Do you think the landlord would put up screens for me? That will give us the air circulation we will need."

Mr. Marchesson nodded. "I see your mother also wants to do a lot of partitioning. I have a good deal of used lumber along the side of the railroad yard; she's welcome to take it. It'll save her the expense of buying it."

Liah's broad smile, her humble, low bow, especially when she held her hands up with palms together in a gesture of thanks, embarrassed Mark. "No need for that, little lady. It's my pleasure."

Their conversation was momentarily drowned out when a Southern Pacific freight train rolled into the yard. The landlord gestured that the noise was deafening. Liah pantomimed back that it was all right, they'd just have to get used to the noise. Besides, she smiled weakly, "Once the shrubberies and vines were revived, the noise would be buffered. Now, let's see the upstairs."

They climbed the stairs to the second floor. Liah heard her eldest son as he pointed out the danger of the steep stairs, which had no railings. Liah impatiently agreed, but there were more important things to do first.

She delighted in the three hexagonal windows at either end of the room, but wondered why someone went to the expense of installing stained-glass sections. Again she asked if screens could be installed. Certainly in the heat of summer they'd need the air circulation. Once more Mr. Marchesson nodded.

In her mind's eye, Liah could see three rooms partitioned off for guest bedrooms, each with its own hexagon window. The remainder of the huge room could be used for a meeting room, perhaps even a gambling room. Certainly gambling would bring in some needed income. Once again there was a rustling in the back if her head. Irritably, Liah brushed the annoyance away. If the Gods could not speak in clearer thoughts, she was too busy to speculate what they were trying to tell her.

Liah reached into her purse, taking out the sketch she'd begun downstairs and carefully drew in vents for each bedroom. Thomas watched, then asked what they were for. She sighed. "None of the downstairs bedrooms will have windows. Long vents at the top of the partitions will allow some airflow. I am hoping your father will devise a way to keep the vents open or closed."

She walked over to the windows facing the train yard, looking out at the wide expanse of tracks and then to the idle boxcars and passenger cars at the far right side of the yard. "I wonder how the Fahn Gwai know which engines go with which cars?" she mused. "I wonder where Cousin Shah works."

Thomas wiped the perspiration from his face and muttered half-angrily, "I don't know, Mah-Mah, but if you're through looking, let's get out of here. It's not only hot, but stuffy as well."

As they came down the stairs, Liah heard the noisy racket of her younger children chasing each other around the empty store. Liah shouted a command for silence. Instantly, the children came up sheepishly to stand quietly beside her.

Mr. Marchesson frowned. He thought of how his family always ignored his commands. Always his orders were resented, and his daughter and son followed his wife's example of contradicting him. With sadness, Mark thought about how he'd been divorced from his first wife for nearly fifteen years now and that his children had gone with their mother. Though he was given partial custody of his children, early on Mark had given up his rights. His son and daughter were too willfully spoiled and disobedient for him to handle.

Mr. Marchesson was startled out of his thoughts about his family when Liah gently touched him on the sleeve. She held out a twenty-dollar gold coin. Mr. Marchesson smiled gently as he took it, then turned to Thomas and inquired if his mother would like him to arrange for the utilities to be turned on. Liah's face brightened; she told Thomas yes, and to ask if he could have them turned on by the end of next week. She would be most grateful. "Your father and Cousin Shah can then work during the night."

Once more Thomas tried to persuade his mother to speak with his father before proceeding with the plans, but Liah shook her head vehemently. "If I left it to your father, we'd never move! Besides, what about you and Second Son? I thought the two of you were anxious to leave?"

"Not if it means quarreling between you and Father."

Liah shrugged her shoulders. "If your father will not move, then I'll have to forfeit my monies. Come, let's go to the grocery store. I need a few spices and we'll even buy some barbequed meats for supper."

Thomas smiled weakly at his mother, knowing it was useless to argue. In a way he admired her courage to stand up to his father. It was this admiration that forged such a close tie between him and his mother, forcing Thomas to be obedient, even when he did not want to.

Mr. Marchesson apologized that he had only two front door keys and two back door keys. "I'll have more made for you and will give them to you when you move in." He grinned, "Please tell your mother I do not believe in leases, only the traditional handshake." With that, Mr. Marchesson held out his hand. Liah looked at him for a moment, then, urged by Eldest Son, placed her hand in Mr. Marchesson's hand. Suddenly, Mr. Marchesson turned to the children and asked if they'd ever had a chocolate soda.

No? Well, then, Mr. Marchesson said, would they would like to go with him to the confectionary shop? Thomas turned to his mother, "It's so hot today, perhaps a soda will be good for all of us."

Liah's children found the swiveling stools lots of fun, swinging around and around on them until their mother frowned. She cautioned for less noise. Once more, Mark was deeply impressed with their quick response, remarking to Thomas that he was always touched by the obedience and reverence Chinese children showed their elders.

"We have no choice, sir," retorted Thomas, grinning. "Either we respect and obey or we're punished. Fahn Gwai parents indulge their children and I used to envy them, but now that I'm a little older, I realize that the discipline was good for me."

They said their good-byes on the sidewalk afterward. Mr. Marchesson laughed heartily when Thomas said his mother apologized for not being able to pronounce his name properly. "It's all right."

Mark Marchesson watched as Liah and her children walked down Marchesson Street and only when she turned off at Alameda South toward the apron of the train yard did he walk back to his office. Something in Liah sparked a dormant emotion and he sighed. He stopped to light a cigarette, then muttered, "I'd better turn on the utilities. Liah doesn't look like someone who allows grass to grow under her feet."

By the time he'd reached his office, Mark thought about putting a numeral three on the door of Liah's place, but he decided to wait. His long association with the Chinese taught him that they had a different attitude about things. If Liah wanted a number on her door, she'd have asked.

Sen returned from work that day to find Liah waiting at the door, excited with news about the store she'd rented in China Street. The landlord was a generous and nice man, and he was going to have the utilities turned on for them by the end of the next week. "Now, you and Cousin Shah can work at night to fix the place up."

Liah handed Sen the two sheets of paper she'd used to sketch her tentative plan. Sen frowned as he scanned them, finally remarking gruffly that it would cost a good deal to do what she wanted. "Lumber costs money."

Liah quickly explained. "The landlord told me he had a good deal of lumber stacked along the fence inside the train yard and said I could take whatever I needed without paying."

It was on Sen's mind to chide his wife for acting without consulting him first, but he remained silent. Thomas stood nearby, waiting for the explosion of his father's displeasure, and was relieved when it did not occur.

Sen's voice was stern as he gruffly muttered, "All right. You have disobeyed me and rented a store. But I warn you, if you are impatient, Liah, I'll not allow it. I want no interference from you. Is that understood? Cousin Shah and I will work when time and energy allow. So, no more talk of moving."

Seragio drove into town each Saturday afternoon, taking Sen with him. Sen remained with Cousin Shah overnight, working each Sunday and returning that night with Seragio. When Liah asked whether the foreman minded making so many trips into the city, Sen scoffed. "He likes to drive the master's new horseless wagon into town; besides I buy him several drinks and supper."

"And is the work coming along all right?" inquired Liah.

"In about three more weeks, perhaps we can begin to think of moving. I'll let you know what day. The foreman said we can move all the furniture there first, and then the next day he'll drive us there."

Over the next several weeks, Liah packed their clothing and begged for Sen to bring home more boxes in which to carry their belongings. It was only during the long nights that she worried whether Cousin Suey Wah would remember to go to Cousin Shah's to determine their whereabouts. However, she had faith that the Gods had eyes and would see to it that she was not deprived of her Apinyin. For a second she wished she could give up her habit but too long had she been enslaved.

PEACOCK PROPHECY

Each time Seragio and Sen went to China Street, they moved a few pieces of furniture and some boxes of clothes and dishes. The foreman said it would make the final moving day a lot easier, but the bungalow began to take on a forlorn appearance. Each time Sen returned home, he thought of his life, this bareness. It seemed he had nothing to show for his lifetime of toil. His children, almost grown, seemed not to need him; his wife so headstrong, so stubborn, was disobedient. This sense of failure coupled with the fearful return to the outside world of Fahn Gwai drove Sen into a deep, dark moodiness.

Liah, occupied with packing, did not share her husband's misgivings. The only gnawing dread she had was the possibility Cousin Suey Wah might not know of their whereabouts and she'd be cut off from her source of Apinyin. Liah cursed her stupidity for not having paid more attention to her mother when she had rendered the resin from the poppy pod, but then Liah reasoned: how could a child know the future need of such information? She prayed to Kwan Yin's generosity that Cousin Suey Wah would come to visit before they moved.

Especially when Sen spent the weekends in China Street, Liah found the sleepless hours of night long and frightful. Her mistress had said Cook was enjoying herself on an ocean cruise. Even as Cook was leaving the estates for another job, she had begged Liah to follow. The night Cook left, Liah's mind had run back over the five years she'd been on the estates. A ghastly length of time out of one's life! While life had been good, the reality of her sons and their bachelorhood was unendurable. The only worthwhile portion of their stay was her leather pouch containing the nine hundred-odd dollars and family gems, which would secure their lives on the outside. Ruefully, she bemoaned the scant amount of monies, but the Gods decreed it so.

The morning of the move arrived at last. Seragio appeared at the bungalow proud as a little boy with a new toy. The master had allowed him the use of his new steam wagon. While the men loaded the odds and ends onto the bed of the wagon, Mert busied himself checking out each part of the engine, his manual in hand. Discovering there was a reserve water tank, Mert crawled underneath to examine it and to check out the braking system.

At last, the loading done, Sen herded his children onto the wagon, instructing Liah to sit beside Seragio with their youngest child. Sen ran back inside the bungalow to make certain everything was taken. His eye caught the calendar on the wall. He sighed, wondering if the Fahn Gwai's superstition about the number thirteen was valid, for not only was it the thirteenth day of August, but in the year of 1913. Seragio came to get Sen and saw the calendar. He urged, "No look thirteen, my friend. Let's go."

Back in the driver's seat, Seragio pushed several knobs, pulled others and jiggled the choke, nearly pulling it from the dash. Several times the vehicle stumbled forward, only to hobble to a halt. Liah's confidence in the contraption waned.

Seragio, his face flushed with exertion, muttered to no one in particular, "I not know how she goes, but I already make plenty pressure in garage. This wagon, she use kerosene. See gauge? She show mucho water pressure. When she low, I turn this knob pronto and she go."

Mert's eyes were riveted on each part as Seragio pointed to a burner as he lit it. The wagon vibrated again, the engine sputtered, catching only to die again. On his third try, the engine caught and held a rough, vibrating roar.

Quickly Seragio pushed a lever in the notched wheel on the side of the steering rod and the wagon began to roll forward slowly. The children shouted; Sen and Liah waited silently, half-expecting the vehicle to halt again. As the motor threatened to die again, Liah moaned, "Why couldn't he have used horses?" Sen frowned, admonishing, "Quit your impatience, woman. Leave the man be."

Sen gave his wife a withering look, warning for silence. Thomas kidded Mert as he traced the diagrams in his manual. "By the time you can afford a car, the mechanics will be different."

Mert pursed his lips and hotly contested that Thomas was wrong. "Ted Crosset told me the principles of steam-driven cars will never change. So leave me alone!"

Their trip to China Street was exciting, not only unique because of the horseless wagon, but because the town of Los Angeles seemed even larger, more built up than it had during their trip to China Street to rent the store not so long ago. The outskirts of town already seemed denser with new buildings. Thomas spied a hotel they hadn't noticed on their last trip. Surrounded by spacious gardens and winding driveways, the white edifice peeking from over the treetops was elegant.

"That, kid," drawled the foreman, "is Beverly Hills Hotel, new. Builded mebbe four years ago. High-tone place."

When they reached First Street, Seragio pointed to a two-story building and laughed. "You kids be good or policeman put you in jail. That is Los Angeles Central Police Department."

Theo pointed to the touring cars, "Do policeman ride cars?"

The foreman nodded. Theo proclaimed to his mother that when he grew up he would be a car policeman. Liah pursed her lips. "Third Son, put the idea out of your head. The Fahn Gwai will never allow you to be a policeman."

Just then the engine stalled. Seragio cursed as he climbed out to discover the problem. "Damn. She no got steam. We wait now."

Liah shot an accusing eye at Sen. "I told you we should have used horses."

Sen defiantly retorted, "I told you then and I tell you now: I will tolerate none of your impatience. Besides, what good are horses now? We haven't got them, so sit and wait."

Liah breathed in relief when Seragio got the car re-started and at last they turned off Alameda South onto Marchesson Street. Seragio turned to the left at the jog in the road and rolled to a halt at the entrance of the alley. Many of the residents were in the street. They gawked at the horseless contraption and Sen was not without a sense of pride as he climbed down from it. He and Seragio hoisted the mattresses on their shoulders and shouted for the children to get out of their way and for Liah to open the doors. Liah remained outside to direct the unloading of the crates containing the peacock and the peahen. All the activity sent the birds into a fit of earsplitting screeching. Liah tried to allay their fears by cooing gently, "Just a few more minutes, you'll be free. Do not fret my koong jeks."

Tom and Shelley pushed their crates to the edge of the wagon. Liah warned for gentleness. "We do not want to further frighten them."

Liah was aware of the crowd at the entrance of the alley. She felt a flush of pride when a woman exclaimed, "Look, two koong jeks. How lucky she is to have her own symbols of good joss."

Another woman ran out from the group to get a better view of the peacock and his mate. Liah smiled as the woman complimented her on the possession of good luck. Liah replied, "Their good joss shall bring all of us good luck. I thank you."

Liah finally stepped inside. Her eyes sparkled at the shiny varnished floors. She must thank Cousin Shah. For the moment, she needed to direct the placing of the furniture. While the pieces were old, Liah arranged them as if they were her most precious possessions. When the last piece of furniture was in its exact spot, Sen and Seragio escaped to the alley to cool off and rest. Sen flopped down on a bench while the foreman leaned against a wall. He pointed up and down the alley. "My friend, all places different color. Your place is red. Good thing doors green and light yellow. Red light, you go crazy, man."

Thomas walked by, overheard the foreman's quip. His face reddened with displeasure. "Mah-Mah said red is a lucky color, that's why she chose Number Three."

"Number Three?" answered Seragio as he looked up and down the alley. "I see no number on none of places. How come you tink this is Number Three? No make sense to me."

Sen chuckled. Suddenly the ambiance was shattered by an incoming freight train. When it had passed, Seragio shook his head. "My friend, gonna be lotsa noise. Trains all the time come and go."

Sen frowned, pulling Seragio by the arm and pointed in the direction of Dead Man's Alley. Seragio grinned, "Sure my friend, me ready for drink."

Thomas glared as his father and the foreman sauntered out onto Marchesson Street toward Dead Man's Alley, a shortcut to Dragon's Den Road, the location of The Dragon's Den Bar owned by Chon Woo.

Liah surveyed her kitchen. It would be the most lived-in room in the whole house. Most of the family's activities took place in the kitchen.

In summer, it would be the coolest spot; in winter, the warmest. She was pleased with the floor-to-ceiling shelves along the right side of the room. On the wall to the left just inside the kitchen door were six large bins with two shelves above them. In the corner, to the right of the bins, stood a cooler to store food, with air vents top and bottom. To the right of the cooler was a cupboard for dishes; below that, two shelves for cookware. Liah stared at the giant wok and stove, thinking she'd better look around for a box to stand on or she'd never reach the brazier.

Liah turned to her children. "All right, each of you listen carefully. I will assign you rooms." She turned to Eldest Son and Second Son, pointing to the room off the kitchen. "That is yours. Now unpack your belongings and put them in their proper places." She turned to William and Theo. "You, my Third and Fourth Sons, will share the room in the corridor, the first one as you enter the corridor. Eldest and Second Daughter, you will share the other room off the corridor. Fifth Son, your bedroom is the room off the front room. Now, all of you get your things put away. Cousin Shah is bringing supper in a few moments. This is our first meal in our new house. Let us have no arguments and do everything immediately."

The children scrambled for their boxes. Liah called for Eldest Daughter to make haste. "I want you in the kitchen to help me put away the foodstuffs. One bin is for the rice, one for the noodles and dried foods, and one is for the cookies and pastries. Leave two bins empty for me. I want to sort the mushrooms before putting them away. The other bin is for the dried herbs and the dried seasonings I need for soups."

Liah opened the back door and peered out. She was surprised to see another building to one side at the rear of the alley. She also saw bamboo matting spanning the space between her building and the next. She knew from experience people lived in the area beneath the bamboo matting. She'd seen many of these open-air dwellings in Dai Faw.

A dry, warm breeze enveloped her and she thought of the need for a screen door. The cool night breezes would relieve the day's heat; besides they needed the ventilation. She closed the door, locking all three locks. Many years ago, when she spied triple-locks on doors, she thought them ludicrous, but time had taught her that the locks were vital to their survival; they were insurance against forced entry by the Fahn Gwai. She glanced at a four-by-four length of wood in the corner and nodded her approval. With that obstacle across the door, no one would ever be able to force his way inside.

She climbed the stairs to the mezzanine, feeling a sharp disappointment. The room was exactly as she first saw it. Paint cans, varnish cans and stacks of lumber were neatly stacked in one corner. "Ah well," she murmured, "at least we've moved in."

That evening, Liah's heart was at rest, filled not only with happiness and gratitude, but also with pride that they now resided in China Street. She gazed around the supper table, giving silent thanks to Kwan Yin for their first meal in their new home. Halfway through supper, Liah asked Cousin Shah if she could lean on his generosity a second time, to build a cellar, a secret place to store their foodstuffs and a retreat in time of trouble. "Of course, because of its secrecy, it'll be only you and Sen who could do the work."

Cousin Shah looked over at Sen, then back to Liah, wondering why the secret room? It was Sen who answered Liah. "We are tired, especially Cousin Shah who has to work in the train yard. As soon as we finish the upstairs, I'll see what can be done." He narrowed his eyes, his tone slightly threatening. "But I'll have none of your impatience."

"Another thing Liah hasn't thought of," murmured Cousin Shah. "It will be costly, the lumber and all."

Liah's face brightened, "Oh, well, the lumber will be of no expense. Marchesson said I could use whatever I need."

Liah's fourteen-year-old son, William and thirteen-year-old Mert offered to go and bring home the lumber. Cousin Shah shook his head. "You two boys are not yet men. I'll do it."

A titter went around the table. William and Mert retaliated by pinching and kicking their tormentors under the table. Sen saw the scuffling and glowered. "Behave yourselves, or else you'll go to bed without supper."

Liah eyed Cousin Shah with displeasure. "My two sons are more men than many of our men. Do not underestimate them."

Cousin Shah quickly rephrased his comment. "What I meant was their bodies are not fully developed yet, that the strength required to move the heavy lumber might prove injurious to their future growth. Besides, seeing two young boys, the foreman might stop them. I think I'd better bring the lumber home." Cousin Shah paused, "I think the landlord must think highly of you, Liah. That lumber is new, not used lumber like you said." Liah said nothing as her eyes caught Sen's.

They found it difficult to sleep the first night, with the roar and crashing of the freight trains. Sen grumbled, "How do you expect me to sleep with this constant earsplitting noise?"

Liah cooed, "In time, Sen, when the shrubberies and vines have grown back, the noise will be toned down. Meanwhile, try to make the best of things." To herself, Liah wondered if it were not too late to rejuvenate the shrubberies. Well, Liah argued stubbornly, they'd just have to plant new ones. In the early hours of dawn, Liah fell into an exhausted slumber.

On an errand for his mother not long after they moved in, Theo discovered there was a playground at the end of Marchesson Street. Upon reaching home, he excitedly told his mother of a baseball field and a Chinese-style clubhouse. "And they also have a wading pool and swings and a slide. Emmi should like that."

Liah, inwardly relieved, outwardly warned they'd only go out to play after their chores were done. In her heart, she thanked Kwan Yin for the playground, for then while Sen and Cousin Shah worked on the rooms upstairs, the children would not be underfoot.

Two weeks after moving in, on the twenty-sixth day of August, Liah was working in the garden when she spied a group of children walking down the street with books under their arms. She called out, inquiring if they were coming home from school. To her joy, they told her that there was a school in Fahn Gwai town.

That afternoon Liah shared the news with her children. "School? In Fahn Gwai town?" gasped Florence. She said she and William wanted to chance the Fahn Gwai and go to school. "All of you will go!" replied Liah.

Theo scowled. "I'm sixteen. Why do I have to go? I want to work with my two brothers."

"You will go to school and not only that, Third Son, you will bring home good grades. I'll not have any of my sons slaves of the Fahn Gwai because of language. Now, do your chores. I'll have Eldest Son look into how you may attend school and where it is."

"Mah-Mah, can I go and find out? I can ask around," Florence asked.

"No Eldest Daughter, it is not fitting for you to traipse around town alone. I'll have Eldest Son do it."

Two days later, Thomas informed his mother that school began on the first week in September. "They will have to take tests in order to be placed in the proper grades. I've made arrangements for the kids to take their tests next Monday."

He turned to the kids. "The school is on Macy Street, just six blocks from here. And classes begin at eight-thirty, so be ready to leave at eight o'clock. I'll take you there for the first time."

"What about our tests?" wailed Florence. "We don't know the way."

Thomas scowled, "I said I'd take you, didn't I? After the second time you ought to be able to find your way, or else get lost. Then you'll learn good."

On Monday morning, Florence and William were the only ones eager to take their tests. Emmi, nine years old, sniveling, hung onto her mother's skirt and whined that she was scared. Flo, exasperated, chided, "Oh, come on. Who's going to hurt you, Em? We'll all be there to protect you."

After sending her children off, Liah remained a long time at the entrance of the alley, sending a silent plea to Kwan Yin to protect her children while in Fahn Gwai town. While Eldest Son would accompany them today and on their first day of school, nevertheless it was a worry for Liah for days to come. A half-our on Fahn Gwai streets was such a long time to be exposed to possible harm, she thought.

Once school started, the leisure and peace Liah had looked forward to never materialized. She was up at seven to prepare breakfast for the schoolchildren, then a meal for her two oldest sons at nine-thirty, followed by a noon meal for Sen and Cousin Shah. No sooner than her chores were done and it was time for the return of her schoolchildren, then snacks for them followed by the preparations of their evening meal.

One night, Liah moaned about the long and arduous day while getting ready for bed. Sen gloated, "We could have remained on the estate, but no. You wanted to move to China Street. So be quiet. Besides, all the time you spend on the garden is wasted. Nothing will revive those shrubberies and flowers."

Liah said nothing, but promised herself never to complain to Sen again.

On the seventeenth day of September, Thomas and Shelley returned home exuberantly shouting that they'd been hired at the produce market. "Now we'll have the chance to learn about business and save our money for a truck. We'll have our own business, hauling for the farmers."

Sen smiled, but in his heart he felt shame that his two sons were working and he'd not yet been hired by the train yards.

September came to a close. To Liah's relief, Cousin Shah at last announced that the upstairs was done. "Of course, the floors are not yet completely dry. Keep the children from going upstairs for another two or three days."

Liah nodded. "I am grateful for your efforts, Cousin Shah. Let us have our noon meal."

While Sen and Cousin Shah ate, Liah asked timidly again if it was possible to build a cellar. Sen glowered, "Woman, are you never satisfied? Besides, do you realize the toil involved in digging and hauling out the dirt?"

Cousin Shah shook his head. "I think Liah has good reason to want a secret cellar. You can never tell what the future holds. The cellar might be the difference between life and death if problems arise with the Fahn Gwai. I noticed the vent holes along the side of the building, which means there is a space under the house. It will not be a problem with the dumping of dirt. But give us a few days to rest, then we'll think about it, Liah."

While Cousin Shah and Sen worked on the cellar, Liah redoubled her energies on the garden: cultivating, fertilizing, pruning and planting new seedlings. She gently coaxed the shrubs and flowers to grow. At one point, Liah giggled as if the plants could understand. So engrossed, Liah hardly noticed the passersby who shook their heads as if to silently say the garden was a lost cause, the seared foliage couldn't be brought back to life. But no one dared utter one word of disbelief. The children playing in the alley, accustomed to Liah's presence, no longer came up and plied her with their questions.

THE PROFESSOR

One morning in the garden, Liah lost track of time and not until the sun was directly overhead did she look around in alarm. Sen would surely admonish her if lunch were late. She sprinted over the cobblestones and into the house, racing to the kitchen.

She washed the rice, placed the enameled-iron pot on the stove and turned her attention to slicing the beef she planned to sauté with black mushrooms and chard. As she lightly seared the garlic and ginger, she heard a stirring inside the bedroom.

When Sen entered the kitchen and spied Liah standing atop a box to cook, he exploded. "If only you could see how ridiculous you look. Had you allowed us to remain on the estates, you'd not now be straining to reach the wok. Who, but a six-foot giant could use it?" Without another word, he went into the bathroom and slammed the door.

By the time Sen returned, Liah was dishing up rice and had placed a serving dish of mixed chard, beef and black mushrooms on the table. Sen picked up his chopsticks and grumpily began to eat.

Thomas waited in his bedroom for his father to leave for the day. His life was complicated enough without inheriting a quarrel between his parents. Thomas understood that his father's idleness was eating at his guts, especially now that he and Shelley had jobs; still his mother had been right in wanting to move to China Street.

When he heard the back door slam, he cracked open his bedroom door, then went into the kitchen. Mother and son silently greeted each other. They shared their meal and a sympathetic smile or two. Thomas finished and laid an arm on his mother's. "Mah-Mah, Father does not mean to be angry. It's only that he is not working while we are that makes him ashamed. You'll see, once he gets a job at the train yard, he'll be happy."

Liah smiled weakly at her son's attempt to comfort her: so bold, so forthright and fierce, so much akin to her nature. She recalled advice she'd overheard when Sen spoke privately about his son's carnal overindulgence and a broad smile played on her face. Yes, Liah believed her first-born son was certainly male.

The two shared a cigarette, both lost in silent, private thoughts. Thomas thought that at best the cigarettes were poor substitutes for his mother's Apinyin. Impulsively, he leaned over and patted Liah on the arm. "Thank you for the meal, Mah-Mah. I didn't get much sleep last night, so I'll turn in now." Before she could chide him, Thomas ducked back into his bedroom.

Liah sat alone at the table. The prideful thoughts of her gentle, yet fierce first born turned to her youngest son, Fifth Son. His passiveness alarmed her; being like his father availed him nothing. It crossed her mind that the family's suffering and privations were the result of her husband's inability to stand up to others. Perhaps when Fifth Son matured more, his masculinity would emerge. Well, she wasn't going to leave Fifth Son to chance; she'd find out if there was a man on China Street who taught the art of self-defense.

The room suddenly seemed confining, the walls closing in. Liah fled to her garden. At the entrance of the alley, Liah looked down Marchesson Street. She felt the sun on the back of her neck as she stepped off the cobblestones. She walked over to the shade of an acacia tree, sat on a bench there and gazed down the length of the street. "How dismal," she thought.

The street was three and a half blocks long, springing out of the grimy soot of the train yards to ignominiously die at the end of Mah Loo (Horse Road), having reached nowhere. The street housed so many souls and so many unfulfilled dreams, all with no hope of the future. Liah felt despair as she thought it was the same with Lion's Den Alley and Dragon's Den Road. Surely the Gods meant more for them in life?

Liah had to agree with the Chinese name, Mah Loo for Horse Road. She screwed up her face at the memory of the overwhelming stench of the stockyards and the slaughterhouses there. The strong odor of horse manure mingled with decaying flesh emanating from them assaulted one's senses.

Her own despair was forgotten as she thought of the residents who were forced to live along Mah Loo. The half-dozen or more two- and three-story rooming houses inadequately sheltered twice the number of people they were meant to house; housing was at a premium and doubling up was the only way to accommodate everyone.

She rose, walking back to her garden. She must succeed in making the garden verdant and sweet smelling. She smiled at her own over self-confidence as it occurred to her she might also grow shrubberies and flowers along Mah Loo.

A disturbance caused her to turn her head and she returned to the entrance of the alley once more to investigate. Down the block, a group of Mexican boys were blocking the path of an old Chinese woman. The muscles of Liah's neck stiffened and her legs became taut as she readied herself to race to the old woman's aid. At the last moment, the old crone struck out with her cane and the boys allowed her to pass. Liah cursed silently. Was there no place on the earth where they could live without persecution?

Once again, the idea of unification plagued her. Frustration crept in, for who was she to attempt such a gargantuan project? Could a mere woman on China Gai unify her people against Fahn Gwai? Wasn't it so, even Fahn Gwai children would torment and disrespectfully treat an old woman? Stubbornly, an inner voice chided her: Was it not her intent to move to China Street to live in peace and security? Why then, was it not her duty to raise the cudgel if the men wouldn't? There was no permanence while they lived in fear.

She walked back to her garden, staring down the cobblestone path, thinking how dreary and forlorn everything was. The paint on the eleven stores facing the train yard was weatherworn as were the red bricks peeking from under the peeling paint. At least her building was painted red and red bricks showing through did not seem as noticeable. Ah, that Kwan Yin would show her the way.

Back in her garden, Liah spaded the dirt, weeding half-heartedly, but her mind wouldn't stop spinning. Ideas on how to improve the town popped into and out of her mind and she longed for someone to discuss them with. But who? Most residents would scoff and think her mad. Surely Sen would chastise her for being a fool.

Suddenly, the serenity of the alley was shattered by Liah's peacock and peahen as they shrieked to be let outdoors. Hurriedly, she went inside, snapped on their halter leashes and cooed for their cooperation.

"Now, if you learn to stay within the limits of the alley, then you would-n't have to be penned indoors." The peacock cackled raucously as if he understood his mistress's words, tugging impatiently at his leash. She pushed aside the double screen doors and stepped back into the alley, the sun gathering the day's heat and penetrating the vine-covered arbor.

It was two o'clock in the afternoon, the sun was blazing and the air was becoming humid and uncomfortable. Liah walked her pets up and down the alley, the cobblestones hot under her thin soles. She was so engrossed in thought that she did not notice the approach of a serious, bespectacled man. Only when they were almost abreast did Liah draw back in frightened surprise.

He bowed slightly. "Madam, I am sorry if I startled you, but I've seen you out here daily with your lovely peacocks. The koong jeks are not only beautiful but lend a grace to this ugly alley."

Liah lowered her eyes as she murmured, "I quite agree with you, sir. Besides all that, the koong jeks are an omen of good joss. I was not as startled as I was surprised to see you, sir. You are the first person I've met in China Street since moving here." She pointed to the red door. "We live at Number Three."

"I know. I watched as you folks moved in. Allow me to introduce myself. I am Chang On Wei, but everyone in China Street calls me Pro-fessor. I am a student of calligraphy and philosophy." He turned, point-ing to the blue doorway at the junction of Marchesson Street and the alley, where Marchesson Street doubled in width creating a sharp jog at the alley's entrance. "I live there, the blue doorway, Number Four."

"Oh, now, I remember you, sir. You're the man who convinced my husband to cut off his queue." Liah saw the scholar's perplexity swiftly change to pride as she explained: "When our people were cutting off their queues, Sen was hesitant until he saw you in the barber's chair. It was your presence that gave him the courage to cut his."

Liah happily confided she was very honored to have Professor as a neighbor. She pointed to the garden strip and lamented its sorry state.

"If perhaps you might instruct the neighbors in the alley to pour the cold tea from their teapots, it'll make my job slightly easier. The wisteria and honeysuckle vines overhead seem to be coming back and the oleanders seem to be sending up new shoots, but the other shrubs are slow in their revival, especially the ivy next to the chain-link fence. If we could encourage a healthy growth of vines, it would hide the ugliness of the train yard, not to speak of keeping out the soot and noise."

Professor puffed on his pipe and nodded. "I've seen you here daily working on the foliage. Do not feel too badly if they are beyond help. Too long have they been neglected. Still, I hope your efforts will be successful, for as you say, it'll bring a little beauty to this dreary alley."

Professor walked beside Liah as she made many laps up and down the cobblestones with the peacocks, then finally wiped his face. "Look, it's so very hot today, why not allow the peacocks to have some freedom? Surely with the cluster of rubbish cans at the end of the alley, they can't escape without our knowing."

Liah looked to the rear of the alley, pondered the idea a moment, then nodded. "I suppose I should allow them their freedom. At least then I'll know if they will remain on the cobblestones. We can sit on the bench under the acacia tree and I can keep my eye on them."

The peacock and his mate looked hard at Liah as they felt the weight of the leashes removed. For a moment, they remained beside her, then the peacock moved several feet away as if testing the reality of his freedom. The peahen followed. Together they pecked on the cobblestones and made their way to the rear of the alley.

The first several moments Liah kept an alert eye on her two pets. Each time she called out, they turned and made their way back to her. Professor grinned. "See? I told you they wouldn't run off."

After a while Liah finished explaining her plans for putting in Chinese lilies and irises and daffodils along the border of the garden. She glanced at the scholar's placid face. A flash ignited her mind and she thought why not? Was the man not a scholar who would understand a unified town? She launched in and told him her plans for unifying China Street.

Professor took his pipe from his mouth and gaped a moment at the tiny woman's plans. She defended them as well as her proposal for a governing body and services for the settlement's needy and children. "I am thinking mostly of the children who must be given the chance to remain in one place, to go to Fahn Gwai school *and* to Chinese school. They must not be yoked to slavery in the Fahn Gwai's world."

Professor was taken aback to hear such radical talk from a woman. He remained silent as Liah continued. "A unified Chinatown with a sentry system of protection from danger and to keep the Fahn Gwai, especially the police, from our town."

Professor knocked the ashes from his pipe, cleaned out the stem and said, finally, "It will take monies we do not have to execute such a proposal. Nor is there any cohesion among the people here. How can we hope to unify them?" He paused, then somewhat uncomfortably explained that the men would surely ridicule the efforts of a mere woman.

Liah's chin was stuck out in determination, but she said nothing. At length, Professor said blandly, "You know how passive our people are. While they want safety and seclusion, not one of them would lift a hand to help. Their only wish is to finish out their current lives on this earth and perhaps in their next lives, they will enjoy better times."

Liah's lips protruded petulantly. "Well, if the residents will not help, then my task will be that much harder. All I want in this life is to know my children are free from Fahn Gwai persecution." She turned hopefully to Professor. "Perhaps when our people see the changes, they will help." Before the scholar could reply, Liah muttered, "No matter, sir, I must do what I must do whether the people want to help or not."

Her eyes fell on the scholar as she asked if he would not assist her. "Surely, you must know someone who will help begin the turnaround? If we sit and wait for the Gods to deliver us, we shall perish without hope. I ask you in the name of our children who will inherit our legacy."

Professor didn't answer and Liah became occupied coaxing the peacocks back onto the cobblestones. He got up and walked with her as Liah pushed them toward the cobblestones, first gently then more firmly, all the while cooing, "Tsk, tsk." When finally she swatted at the peacock with the leashes, Professor was amazed to see him raucously scold her. When the peacock's frustrated shrieks subsided, he willingly returned to the cobblestones. Liah giggled, "See, Professor? He is intelligent enough to know he can't win, so he obeys."

The scholar grinned. A few yards farther down the walk, Professor stopped, exclaiming, "I just got a wonderful idea, Liah. Why not name this alley 'Peacock Alley'? I think the name is appropriate."

"How fitting, Professor!" A moment later, Liah wailed, "But how will people know?"

The scholar smiled broadly. "Never fear, Liah. I will make two wooden signs, one for the entrance and one for the rear of the walkway. People will know."

Liah nodded as she looked up at the sun. She drew the leashes around her pets, opened the door to Number Three and pushed them inside. She remained by the door to speak a moment longer. "Professor, I am so pleased you thought of the name 'Peacock Alley'. The sounds are so Chinese, not to speak of the good joss the name evokes. I am sure you and I will become good friends and allies."

Allies? Professor was stunned. What did this tiny lady mean? Oh, well, he thought, women have strange ways of expressing themselves. But somehow this one has many unspoken thoughts. Professor's eyes were speculating as he bowed slightly, then crossed the street.

—

The next day Liah was not surprised to meet Professor in Peacock Alley. He held two pieces of wood and a hammer. Proudly, he extended the wooden pieces and Liah saw they contained characters that were not only inked but also slightly carved to emphasize the words: Peacock Alley.

Liah bowed slightly, gesturing thanks with her tiny hands clasped palms together. "I do not write, but the characters are so strong, so forcefully written. And how do you get the ink so ebony black?"

Professor reached into his vest pockets for nails, walked over to a post and hammered up the first street sign. He stepped back, viewed it and smiled. "If I say so myself, it does look elegantly official. Now, let us go to the rear of the alley and post this one."

"Somehow," murmured Liah when they finished posting the second sign, "Peacock Alley sounds so lovely and is even lovelier when written. I thank you, sir. Shall we sit under the acacia tree? I can watch the peacocks from there."

The peacock and his mate walked around the cobblestone path pecking at seeds and bugs. Professor lit his pipe and leisurely drew in his first puff as he watched the peacocks.

The nutty aroma of tobacco wafted in the air. Pleasant odor, thought Liah. A silence wedged between them. Later the scholar cleared his throat, then smiled. "Last night I did not sleep too well thinking of our conversation. I'd like to hear more about your plans and mostly how you hope to bring them into reality."

Liah felt a surge of warm encouragement. She explained her fervor to fortify, unify and guard China Street. For the first time in her life, she spoke of Sen's older brother, Gan, and how he was violently beaten to death in broad daylight. She spoke of the many times Fahn Gwai raided their farms and of the last time when they barely escaped with their lives and Sen decided to move to Loo Sahng. "You must understand how heartbreaking it was when, again, on our farm on the outskirts of Loo Sahng, we were once more routed by the drunken Fahn Gwai."

Liah's eyes softened as she spoke of their five years on the Dobney estates. "Those five years were the only years of peace and security we've known, the only place where we have lived more than a few years."

She turned to face the scholar, her hands tightly clasped. "Although we lived securely, we were, nevertheless, prisoners behind the high walls. We were so lonely, without many of our countrymen there to share our problems or our joys. I suppose it was because of my insistence that Sen moved to China Street. That is why I want to unify and protect us. I do not think I could survive another attack."

Professor nodded. "I know the feeling, Liah. I also have lived through an attack and lost my uncle and brother. Now, I am alone." He saw the hatred in Liah's eyes and thought, what a wild one this one is. In spite of his personal doubts that Liah would ever succeed, Professor felt a stirring of hope. Who knew what was possible when the Gods smiled? Surely, the Gods seemed to favor Liah.

Through the mists of his meditation, Professor heard Liah's voice. "Please, sir, tell me what happened to your uncle and brother?"

The scholar took in a deep breath and began to speak, slowly at first then, as emotion took hold, his speech quickened. "There was a dispute between two Tongs over the ownership of a female. Things went beyond good sense and the police came. In the noisy confusion of angry Tong members and the policemen's efforts to quell the disturbance, shots were fired and a policeman fell. The police blamed the Chinese for the policeman's death, despite the fact that many of the Fahn Gwai spectators were shooting off their guns. Like fire, wild fire, a mob assembled and the Fahn Gwai tried to avenge the policeman's death. Things like this happen rapidly and people converged on the scene in carts, wagons, horses and on foot."

Liah bit her lips to keep from crying out, for Professor's face was stony, laid bare by the memories. The scholar gulped several breaths of air then continued. "I was only a boy of twelve at the time of the massacre. We lived several doors down from where the police and Tong members were fighting, almost to the top of Fargo Hill. We were having supper when we heard the first shots and then a volley of gunfire. My uncle heard loud voices coming closer and pushed my brother and me toward the bathroom. He then ran back to get the moneybox. My older brother shouted that he didn't have time, then pulled away some boxes concealing a trap door, yanked up the door and shoved me down the stairs. He said he was going to help uncle and that he'd be right back. I tried to resist but he pushed me and I fell down the stairs. When I got back up the stairs, he'd locked the door. Through the floorboards I heard the shattering of glass and the sounds of wanton destruction. Afterward, having done their damage, the Fahn Gwai returned to the street again and silence descended."

Professor sat stonily silent. Finally he muttered, "I never saw my uncle and brother again."

They were quiet for several moments, and then the Professor was startled by Liah's gentle touch on his arm. He blushed, embarrassed. "It has been a long time since that massacre, but the memory is as fresh as if it happened yesterday. The pain I thought was gone is yet present."

His expression was apologetic. "I'd spare you the grisly details, but you wanted to know the truth. The riots did not stop there. The following night mobs again converged on us. A larger, wilder and drunker mob set fire to all the stores that had not already burned down, looting the buildings before they set fire to the structures. Even our temple was defiled—all the trappings, porcelains and monies were taken. Although the city repudiates this, it is rumored that the police played a part in this second riot. Otherwise, how could the rioters have positioned themselves on all four corners of the street and shot our people as they escaped from the fires without the police responding?"

Liah felt the walls of the surrounding buildings closing in on her and silently waited for Professor to continue, as his face gave her to believe there was yet more to tell. "I was one of those returning home when I heard the sounds of gunfire, sirens and the shrieks of our dying. I hid out in the hayloft across the street." He shook his head. "I shall never forget the sounds of the dying, especially that of the men caught inside their burning stores."

Liah sighed, filled with hatred of the Fahn Gwai, especially the police who had imposed such harsh punishment just to avenge the death of one of their men. It did not seem plausible that one of her countrymen would have a gun, let alone have had the courage to take aim at a policeman. She'd have to inquire about more details, but not at this time. The trauma of the memories was too great.

At length, Professor smiled sadly. "Is it clear now why I do understand what you are trying to do? I understand fully your deep need for preparedness. My life today is the result of my uncle's foresight in having a means of escape prepared. The stairs underneath our store led to a dark, narrow tunnel, which led to the sewage tunnels. It was there I spent the night and in the morning worked my way along the drainage pipes to the bridge at the outskirts of Macy Gai. Many of our people also had tunnels leading to that same spot, for I met up with over a dozen people who were as terrified as I was."

The scholar sighed. "The crazy drunks hung seven of our people from the temple eaves and stationed their men to stand guard that we might not retrieve their bodies. I suppose the barbarians knew of our belief that one's eternal rest is denied unless one's remains be returned to our homeland." Professor tapped his pipe against the tree trunk and continued apologetically. "It's a grisly tale, indeed, but you wanted to hear the truth. And things did not end there, for the next day more mobs came to finish up the destruction. Afterwards, they held a parade flaunting their baskets of monies, porcelains, silks and more trappings from our temple. Hideously, the bodies of another seven of our slain countrymen were tied to the sides of the wagons by their queues."

Liah exclaimed, "This sacrilegious crime must never again happen. We must make certain of that!"

Professor, his voice soft and filled with sadness, next told Liah of the daring raid by the relatives of those who were slain. His voice rose in pitch and became somewhat proud as he said, "Our people rescued the bodies of the men on the temple eaves, but the seven men who were tied to the wagons by their queues were never seen again."

"Barbarous infidels. This is the same insane hatred that dogged Sen and that's why he is so afraid of the Fahn Gwai. It was only by my insistence that we moved to China Street. I pray to Kwan Yin it was no mistake."

Professor's face was strained with the effort of remembering, his hands in tight fists. "Thirty-six years ago, yet the ghastliness is still vivid today." He shook his head. "I suppose it was your memories of Dai Faw that awakened my painful past. Now you know why I so understand your need for isolation and protection against the Fahn Gwai."

He reached into his vest pocket for his watch. "I see it is now time for me to go to the newsstand for my copy of the Dai Faw See Bo. I bid you good day. Perhaps tomorrow our conversation will be of a happier nature."

Liah remained seated under the acacia tree, praying earnestly to Kwan Yin for the eternal rest of the seven men whose bodies were never found and for Professor's peace of mind. Her heart ached for the seven men, never to return to their homeland, never to be buried with their ancestors and, most of all, never to enjoy their lives embraced by the harmony of Feng-Sui. Such eternal obliteration was incomprehensible. And Liah's fury was directed at the Fahn Gwai who were responsible.

She reached inside her tunic for a handkerchief and wiped her eyes as she turned her thoughts to Professor again. Such a lifetime of punishment, to have lost his entire family. Liah unclenched her fists, muttering through clenched teeth, "This dastardly occurrence shall never happen again." She turned her eyes skyward. "Please, Kwan Yin, help me. Secure this town and be beside me as I try."

—

Throughout the remainder of the day, Professor's tale haunted Liah. Each time she thought of the people burning inside the buildings, she winced, crying out to Kwan Yin for mercy. If only Professor was wrong. If only the residents would put aside their passiveness and take up the fight against the Fahn Gwai. Surely, the men would help, once they learned why she wanted to unify and guard China Street. Liah knew she faced a gargantuan task. If only the Goddess would stand beside her.

Several nights afterwards, when Professor was on his way to Wong's Café for supper, he ran into Wong Sang. He asked him, "I met Lee Sen's wife the other day and we had a long chat. Have you met her yet, Sang?"

Wong Sang shook his head. "No and I don't want to. They say she is quite headstrong and has a feisty temper. It behooves me to stay away. If there's one thing I don't need, it's a headstrong, tongue-lashing female."

"You're wrong, Sang!" replied Professor. "I've spoken with her twice and did not find Liah either headstrong or feisty. I found her very intelligent, surely farsighted. She's real ambitious too."

Wong Sang sneered. "Ah, an intelligent, ambitious female is another thing I do not need"

Professor frowned, drawing himself up, and retorted, "No need to get huffy, Sang. Sneer if you want, but Liah's vision of a town united, safe from Fahn Gwai intrusion, with a Council to govern and to administer welfare for the aged, sick or needy doesn't seem half-bad."

Wong Sang's raised his eyebrows and burst into laughter. "She must be crazy. We do not have enough people here to make a town, let alone a Council and a guard system. What does she mean by a town impervious to Fahn Gwai and police? Is she referring to her Apinyin habit? Surely you don't believe her, Professor?"

The scholar shrugged. "It isn't as crazy as you think. History records monumental changes wrought from small fissures on the surface. I've never been wrong in my judgment of people. Somehow I have a strong feeling about Liah. As for you thinking there are not enough of us for a town, you are mistaken. There are more than you think. We have over two hundred men living on the apron and around the perimeter of the train yards, perhaps another six or seven hundred in the ten blocks surrounding Marchesson Street, Dragon's Den Road, Lion's Den Alley, not to mention the ones living in Peacock Alley and Fargo Alley on the other side of Alameda South." Professor paused, then asked Wong Sang how he liked the name, 'Peacock Alley'.

Wong Sang shrugged. "An alley is an alley. Still, it does give the place an identity and is a damned sight easier to say than 'the alley next to the train yards'."

They continued along Marchesson Street making their way to the shortcut through Pig Alley. Professor murmured, "You know, I wouldn't be surprised if Liah didn't start doing something about her ideas of unifying the town. She gave me the impression the time for dreaming and planning is over. She was so adamant, I must give her credit. It makes me feel good that someone is going to try to upgrade our town. At least, it wouldn't hurt to attempt it. I, for one, will give her all the help she needs. What about you, Sang?"

Wong Sang sneered again. "Professor, if I were you, I would stop reading all those ideological books. You're getting impractical. Harrumph, a Chinatown indeed! And impervious to Fahn Gwai attack yet. The two of you are daydreaming."

Stabs of jealousy struck Sang several times during their walk when passersby called out to the scholar. If only they knew Professor's fantasies, they'd not be so free with their admiration.

Sang refused Professor's invitation to dinner. "No, got too many things to do. You aren't the only one with obligations. I'll be seeing you around."

Not long after, Liah was returning from the meat market and unexpectedly ran into Wong Sang leaving Peacock Alley. Wong Sang nodded politely, stepping aside to let her pass. "Are you not Wong Sang? I am Liah, wife of Lee Sen, perhaps you might spare me a few moments? I'd like to speak with you."

Wong Sang, taken by surprise, was trapped into listening to Liah's plans for a governed, protected Chinatown. When she was finished, she asked if he was interested in helping, perhaps even joining the Council.

He blurted hastily, "Of course. You let Professor know when you're ready and he'll notify me. For now, I must hurry."

Liah was not to be put off. "I am ready to meet now. Perhaps you and Professor can come for tea. We can discuss the plans then. Will you come?"

Sang thought that Professor was right: this one is tenacious and certainly ambitious. Sang nodded, "Yes, yes, let Professor know the day and the hour and I'll be there."

"We live at Number Three, the red place in Peacock Alley."

Wong nodded and mumbled, "I know," as he was scooting out of the alley.

Liah dumped the packages onto the kitchen table and her spirits soared, her mind whirling with a thousand and one details. The Tenet of Laws must be drafted by Professor. His was the academic mind that could translate her wishes into a legal, written document. But for the moment she'd better have supper on the table or Sen would have something to carp about.

Once supper was done and Sen already in bed, Liah sent Fifth Son to summon Professor. The scholar came reluctantly, positive Liah would press for an early meeting. He was not yet ready to commit himself, needing more time to think. Liah was not only ambitious but also impatient, he thought.

When Liah told him of her plans to make Wong Sang one of the charter members of the Council, Professor was aghast. "I don't think you understand. The man is a scoundrel. Sang is greedy and dishonest and to put Chinatown in his hands would be a breach of security."

"Not only would I name Wong Sang to the Council, but the bar owner, Chon Woo, too," cried Liah. "Don't you see, sir? If we only have ethical people on the Council, we'll spend all of our time policing and enforcing the law. With Chon and Sang on the Council, they'll keep their kind of people in line. Please, sir, I've given this considerable thought. Our panel ought to be an authoritative body and those two will make people sit up and listen."

Professor nodded, shocked that Liah would be so intuitive. However, he was not yet convinced. "Perhaps we ought to wait a little longer before calling a meeting. We cannot expect to build a town on half-truths, with people who are less."

"Oh, sir, trust my judgment. I am a woman and my intuition tells me I am right. I also have a logical brain, at least when it comes to protecting myself. All my life I've had to live with danger. In time of Tong wars, we'll be much better off by having the men the caliber of Chon and Sang."

"Tong wars?" gasped Professor. "Liah, we haven't had so serious an event since that last disastrous price we paid."

The scholar and Liah fell into a lengthy silence. Liah was first to speak. "Sir, I know you're shocked with my choices of Chon and Sang and now with the mention of another Tong war, but we must be realistic. When tempers are flaring or the stakes high enough, men will forget. Yes, even the memories of that last holocaust. I know the possibility of another Tong war is remote, but by having prepared for such an event, we can put it from our minds."

"I must admit you've given more thought to the Council than I. You are right. Preparedness is always good."

Liah smiled, then eagerly asked if Professor couldn't draw up a Tenet of Laws. She had asked Sang to come to a meeting. She had yet to ask Chon. "With the three of us, we can iron out the details of the document before others are asked to meet. Please, if you will select a date which is convenient for you, then we'll tell Sang."

Professor sighed, "I suppose the date must be auspicious," to which Liah nodded. "For such an important beginning, the Gods must smile on us that day. While I hold ideas of what the Council ought to be and what laws are necessary to keep law and order, I must rely heavily on your abilities as a scholar to put them down on paper."

As Professor made his way home, his head whirled with the myriad details he and Liah had discussed. He had to admit that Liah was thorough. The idea of unifying the town and setting up a protective sentry system made a lot of sense, yet he couldn't shake the fear of potential failure. The residents of China Street would never kowtow to Liah's laws, nor pay the levies she meant to initiate. Still, why not a unified town and why not him at its beginnings?

Inside his windowless front room, Professor lit the candle on his writing table. Ah, that he should rely upon kerosene lamps and candles for light to conserve money. Someday, he might not have to be so stingy with his money and he would use the Fahn Gwai's convenient electrical light. It wasn't so much the money for electricity, but the expense of wiring the place for it. Perhaps the city would someday bring in the necessary wires. He thought, how fortunate for Liah she lived where the Fahn Gwai had once had his offices, otherwise she'd not have electrical lighting. He could not help but lament the failure of his people to have warmth and comfort, for was that not the reason they came to labor in Gem Sahn? The outdoor people lived no better than their counterparts did back in the villages of China.

He waited for the flame to settle into a steady light, watching the feeble flickering strengthen into a bright flame. The weird dancing shadows on the wall settled into distorted shapes. The burden of responsibility began to sit heavily on his mind again.

Quickly, he poured a bit of water onto his ink slate and slowly mixed it with his ink stick. He reached over to the jar of brushes, selected one suitable for small print and tested the ink. The texture was right. He poised the brush over the paper then, deep in thought and with a bold wrist stroke, he inked the characters: Tenet of Laws. Such a weighty phrase, he thought. At the same time he smiled, for the two characters were executed flawlessly. Squarely shaped, the texture of strength and emphasis were in the right places, the swoop of brush strokes just right. He was yet an adept calligrapher.

For an instant, Professor pondered his sense of pride in his writing abilities. Was he becoming egotistical in his old age? Or was it a pride that came with years of long hours of practice and inspiration? He hoped the latter.

The flame burned steadily as Professor hunched over his writing table, enrapt with the philosophy of ethics, stopping now and then to rub his aching shoulders. Three hours later, he set down his brush, took off his spectacles and gently rubbed his eyes. The wall clock indicated seven o'clock. Time was so fleeting, he thought, when one was engrossed. He'd stop at Wong's for supper, then finish up the document afterward.

—

The next day, Professor was back at Wong's Café for lunch. As he was preparing to return home, he heard Wong Sang call out to him. "Hey, Professor, you're right. I had the misfortune of running into Sen's wife yesterday. She's not only pushy but also ambitious. Imagine, us a town, a unified town. Isn't that a laugh?"

This angered Professor, but he was not in the mood for an argument. "You're entitled to your thoughts, Sang, but the idea is sound. I do not think the plans are funny. Now, if you'll excuse me, I must be getting home."

Wong Sang followed Professor into the dark recess of Pig Alley, the shortcut to Marchesson Street. The scholar heard Sang's laughter, his derisions of Liah. "She's crazy, that one."

When they emerged from the dark, narrow alley, Professor wiped the perspiration from his brow. "It's too stifling to go home, I'm going to cool off under the acacia tree." There he filled his pipe and Wong Sang, joining him to sit, continued his derogatory tirade against Liah. Suddenly Sang saw the sign, 'Peacock Alley' and pointed. "I suppose Liah had the audacity to name the alley. Peacock Alley indeed. Just because she happens to own the koong jeks."

"You're wrong, Sang, I named the alley. Don't you think the name is appropriate? There was a slight smirk on Professor's face when he saw Sang's embarrassment. Professor lit his pipe, drew several contented puffs, then drawled, "By the way, Sang, there is to be a meeting at Number Three on the second day of October, at three in the afternoon. I told Liah I'd tell you."

"Not me, I'm not going. I only said yes to get rid of her." Sang turned an inquisitive eye on Professor. "Are you going?"

Professor nodded. "It doesn't hurt to listen; besides Liah makes a lot of sense. I think you ought to attend, since you promised."

"You make excuses for me, Professor. I'm not getting mixed up in some female's crazy scheme."

Professor scowled. "Liah's plans make too much sense for me to make light of them. If you don't want to attend, then don't, but do not expect me to lie for you."

Wong Sang's face darkened. "Well, I hope you won't give me away. I may decide to join at a later time."

Professor stood up and glowered. "I'm no stool pigeon, Sang. Besides, Liah is a smart woman. She'll see through your sham."

Wong Sang quickly apologized. It surprised him, Professor's anger. He'd always thought the scholar to be a passive man, but perhaps he was mistaken. "No offense, sir; maybe Liah might be able to unify the town. I hear she has a lucrative trade in Apinyin and has a load of gold. Is that so?"

Professor shrugged. "How should I know? Well, I haven't got all day. Please excuse me, I'm going in to wash up and take a rest before going for the paper."

Sang nodded. Professor watched as Sang made his own way down the street. Professor muttered, "Bet that ferret is going to see Chon at The Dragon's Den Bar. I wonder what he has in mind, asking about Liah's finances."

Professor knew that whatever he had in mind, it was for Sang's benefit. He sighed as he unlocked his door and walked into the stuffy heat of his room. In spite of his dislike of the dust, he left the front door propped open with a chair.

—

On the twenty-ninth day of September, Liah was happy as she prepared dinner–her birthday dinner. It did not matter if Sen would not buy her a gift, for living among her own people was gift enough, not to mention that if Kwan Yin were willing, she'd unite China Street and be able to live in safety and serenity. Liah smiled guiltily, for having seen the gift box in her eldest son's bedroom allowed her to conclude that the children had a surprise for her.

The day following her birthday supper, Liah was separating lily bulbs in the garden when Professor hurried into Peacock Alley. He smiled as he spied his signposts and made a mental note to give them a coat of varnish. It wouldn't do to have the rains erase the black characters. Liah called out to him. "What a coincidence, sir. I would have sent Fifth Son to tell you I wanted to speak with you."

Professor scowled as he informed Liah he'd spoken to Wong Sang and that she'd better forget about him. "He said to tell you that he had a previous engagement and wouldn't be able to attend. We should probably postpone the meeting."

Liah smiled knowingly. "I half-expected that of Sang. Never mind. With him or without him, we shall go ahead with our plans. We must have a document before asking others to become part of the Council."

Professor, caught off guard by her unruffled attitude, almost laughed in relief. He vowed: Never again would he cover for anyone else. The white lie he'd just told made him feel somehow unworthy of Liah. She deserved better.

Unbeknownst to Professor, Liah's expansive mood was a consequence her birthday celebration. Eldest Son and Second Son, along with the other children, had given her a money gift of fifty dollars. It was not the monies, but the pride that made her heart burst, pride in the generous love of her children.

That night, Liah pondered the reasons for Professor's postponement of their first meeting. She hoped it was not because he was reluctant. Without the scholar's help, she would not succeed. Liah needed Professor's education. In her heart, Liah sleepily offered up a prayer to Kwan Yin. The Goddess would understand how tiring her day had been; otherwise she'd get up and light a coil of incense. In her exhausted state, Liah prayed to Kwan Yin to send her someone to help with the household chores, if only to prepare the meals and do the laundry. Tomorrow, thought Liah, was another day and who knew what it would bring.

Just before she dropped off to sleep, Liah became distressed thinking about how she would tell Sen of the Council. It wasn't that she was afraid of confronting him; rather she disliked the energy required to pacify him afterwards, not to mention the patience required to cajole him out of his moodiness. Being the practical woman she was, Liah thought that if the right moment to broach the subject never came, Sen would just have to find out about the meeting afterwards. Surely, it wouldn't affect his outburst one way or the other.

—

The next day Liah was seated in her upholstered chair in the kitchen when Professor entered. He had a sheaf of papers in hand and apologetically asked if she would look at them. "Of course, sir, but you'll have to read them to me. I do not have the benefit of being literate."

It was in the back of Professor's mind to address what he felt was the overpowering authority the Council would be granting its leader, but knowing that certainly Liah would be elected to head the Council, he felt uncomfortable broaching the subject. Several times, as they discussed the duties and authorities that would be granted each of the Council's officers, he almost spoke up, but always lost his courage at the last moment. This inability to discuss what seemed like the near-dictatorship of the chairman, left Professor with a feeling of futility and a certainty the Council would not be formed. However, so much time had he spent on the document, the Council had become a life-giving force in his mind. In the end, Liah leaned back in her chair and smiled. "That is a very thorough, impressive document. It must have taken you a good deal of thought, time and energy, not to mention foresight."

Once again Professor thought to speak of the chairmanship but failed. Liah was puzzled at the man's discomfort, wondering if her praise had insulted him. Scholars, she thought, were a strange breed. Suddenly, she looked up at the wall clock. "Professor, why don't you have supper with us tonight? Dinner will be simple fare, but you might enjoy the company."

"I should be honored, but I must decline. I have spent so much time on the document that I've neglected much of my other business. I should go home and catch up with my letters. People have deadlines when they send their mail home. Another time."

"I understand, sir. Meanwhile, I look forward to seeing you on the second day of October. I hope Wong Sang remembers. Good day, sir."

THE START

Liah was up very early on October second, rushing through her chores to free herself to hold the first meeting with Professor and Wong Sang. As soon as she'd fed Sen, cleaned the house and done some laundry, she prepared the makings for supper. It would save her a great deal of time later. It was only after she'd prepared the minced pork with spiced pickled greens and assembled the ingredients for the sautéed chicken liver, gizzard, black mushrooms and bamboo shoots for the chard, that she sat down to smoke a cigarette. She took several puffs and thought how unsatisfying a cigarette was compared to Apinyin.

She was pleased when at three o'clock sharp Professor walked in. Promptness was something she valued highly. They had shared several cups of tea when Liah looked up at the wall clock. "It's fifteen after the hour, we might as well begin. I do not believe Wong Sang meant to be here."

At four-thirty they heard the screen doors open and slam. Liah ran out, only to be met by Wong Sang with a sheepish look on his face as he made a lame excuse for being late. Wong Sang glanced suspiciously at Professor and then at the sheaves of paper on the table. "What have the two of you been up to?" Even as he asked, Wong Sang was fearful he'd missed out on something.

Professor's displeased expression quickly elicited an apology. "I meant nothing disrespectful; you needn't be so sensitive, Professor."

"I'm not sensitive and you are insulting, Sang."

Wong Sang pointed to the papers. "Perhaps you can give me a few details. I have some time before another appointment with a man who wants to open up a gambling house and who asked if I'd be his partner."

Professor sighed. He explained the map outlined the perimeter of China Street. Sang examined the five-block area including Marchesson Gai, Lion's Den Alley and Dragon's Den Road, all connected by Mah Loo. "What," he demanded, "about Fargo Alley and Allison Gai? Just because they are located on the other side of the tracks, I'm certain they won't like being excluded."

Professor's face darkened. "That's the way it'll have to be until we have enough monies to afford to offer them the same services we'll be offering this area. After all, with the services to the residents, it takes a lot of money, which we hope to raise through taxation."

"Taxes?" echoed Sang with amazement. "From whom?"

"From the business houses and cafés. After all, we give them business, they ought to turn around and do something for the people."

"They won't do it!" declared Sang hotly. "Besides, who are you to set up laws and levy taxes?"

Professor whirled about, pointing his finger angrily. "We have heard nothing from you but criticism. I say the men will pay once they know what the money is for and how it will be administered and, of course, the consequences if they refuse."

Wong Sang lapsed into silence, then spied the diagram of the octagon. "What's that for?"

"Eight men. They will be the Council members who will sit in judgment for disputes and who will guide the government of China Street. A ninth, a deserving young man, will also sit on the panel to see to the affairs of our youth. As a junior member he will not have voting power, at least not until he has matured and knows the Council's aims and its governing policies"

Sang mumbled under his breath. "You and Liah have been very thorough in your schemes."

Liah narrowed her eyes. Professor was taken aback by her stony, fiery expression. "Schemes, Sang?" Liah hissed. "Explain!"

Sang's mouth fell open for a split second, gaping at Liah. Never in his life had Sang been the target of a mere woman's displeasure and he wanted to retaliate, but her wrath, both fiery and icy, was something with which he did not know how to cope. So he remained silent. It was Professor who brokered the impasse. "Sang, we have too much to do, too much to think about, without your negative views. Let us allow the townspeople to accept or reject our plan. It takes a great deal of monies to take care of our aged and destitute, our children's school and, most importantly the sentry system we hope to establish to prevent Fahn Gwai intrusion into China Gai."

"Sentries?" Sang made no more comment lest both Professor and Liah decided to oust him. It might be valuable to him to be a member, he thought, no matter how revolutionary the scheme.

With a slight sneer, Sang asked who was going to lead the august governing body. Like an arrow from a bow, Professor shot back, "Liah, of course."

Wong Sang's mouth fell open again, staring in disbelief. He mumbled, "Er, ah, I didn't mean to stay so long. I do have an appointment. We'll discuss things at another time. I bid you two good day." He swiftly rose and left.

After Sang's departure, Liah's eyes twinkled and she burst into laughter. "I do believe Sang was shocked. It's strange how transparent a man's eyes are when he is lying. He doesn't have an appointment."

The wall clock struck the hour of five and Liah sighed, "There is no more time to discuss our plans, for the children will be home soon. We'll continue tomorrow if that is suitable, sir."

Professor heard the front door open and slam several times followed by the clatter and shouts of children as they burst into the kitchen. In a moment, he was surrounded by noisy children, pushing and shoving and clamoring that they were hungry. Liah held up her hand and the noise eased as they waited. It was too close to suppertime, but if they were hungry, they might each have several cookies and a glass of milk. "And do not annoy me, for I have supper to prepare and, Eldest Daughter, I'll need your help."

"Sir," said Liah, "it would be an honor if you were to take supper with us tonight. That way we can yet speak of the Council as I prepare supper."

Sen returned a few minutes before six and was at first taken aback by the presence of a stranger until he recognized Professor. Immediately he reached out a hand. "How pleasant, sir. Please be welcome in our home."

Dinner was a warm, touching time for Professor. Since he lost his uncle and older brother, he had eaten his meals either alone or at Wong's Café. Sen chuckled at one point during supper. "The children are noisy, aren't they? I suppose the din is deafening when you're not used to it."

Liah shot the children a warning glance and the noise ceased immediately. Professor held up his hand in apology. "No, no, it's all right, Liah. The noise is not disagreeable. Let them be. It's just that I've been alone for such a long time. It's also been a while since I've had a home cooked meal. Living alone, I either eat at Wong's or else I have steamed fish with rice alone at home or open a can of spiced mullet."

"I'm afraid life hasn't tamed them yet, sir," Liah's tone was somewhat somber, but Professor smiled.

"Sen, I think you already know how fortunate you are. Life is bearable when one has family around who care and with whom you belong. Indeed, I do not mind the children's exuberance."

At supper's end, Sen rose and again shook hands with the scholar. "I hope you will come again, sir. I am a creature of habit. When my stomach is full, I am ready to sleep. I bid you a pleasant good night."

The chore of washing dishes was even louder than the noise at the table. At one point Professor was alarmed by the pugilistic-sounding arguments. Theo swore it wasn't his day to help with the dishes, while Mert and William argued he was trying to get out of work. Flo shrieked angrily that she wasn't going to wash or dry because she'd helped with dinner. Flo also argued hotly with William over whose turn it was to sweep the floor and take out the rubbish. Liah whirled about, uttered a blanket warning for good behavior, then resumed her discussion with

Professor. It was the only indication Professor knew she was aware of the discord.

"Shall we go into the front room, sir? It will be more comfortable for you. Pay them no heed, they may fight among themselves, but let an outsider threaten one of them and they band together. There is a deep bond of love among them, despite their bickering."

Once seated in the living room, a comfortable serenity enveloped Professor as he pulled on his pipe. In the kitchen there was yet the noise and clatter, but in the front room, the angry voices sounded muted. Professor warned Liah about Wong Sang and Chon Woo's instability and dishonesty. Liah clung to her belief that it took men of Sang's and Chon's ruthlessness to govern the town. "The Tenet of Laws with provisions for Council member's deportment will prevent either man from stepping out of line without serious punishment. Believe me, sir, I know what I'm doing. You'll thank me someday for having removed the burden of policing the baser elements in town."

The kitchen wall clock had chimed eleven times when Professor jumped up from his chair. "My, how time eludes one when one is pleasantly occupied. I must bid you good night and thank you for sharing your family. It brought back memories of my uncle and older brother."

Liah watched from her doorway as the scholar made his way across the cobblestones to Number Four. When Professor closed his door, Liah felt a quiver of hope dart through her mind. Perhaps now, with Professor's help, she'd see her dream of a fortified China Gai, a place where she and the family could live forever in safety. She prayed for Kwan Koong and Kwan Yin's benevolence on Professor's and her efforts.

Liah closed the door. She had just finished her cup of tea when Fifth Son came home. She heard him closing the green shutters on the two windows in the front room and knew he was boarding up the house for the night. The windows were barred and boarded up and the front doors were secured from inside with a long four-by-four wooden bar,

held in place by two L-shaped, iron brackets, bolted on each side of the
wall, making entry impossible.

"You're a good son," she murmured as he came in and kissed her
cheek. "I know it is a chore to board up each night."

Long afterwards, Liah was focused upon her fifth son and his gentleness and passivity, hoping he wouldn't grow up like his father. While
it was good to be passive, it was also detrimental if the passivity grew
to slavish obedience. A sudden apprehension gripped her when she
wondered if Fifth Son was a homosexual. Her face grim, Liah decided
to engage a Kung Fu instructor for her fifth son and Fourth Son too. It
wouldn't hurt to teach them the art of self-defense. Besides, if Fifth Son
were effeminate, the exposure to manly activities would perhaps diminish the condition. Tomorrow she'd ask Professor.

Two days after his meeting and evening with Liah, Professor was
enjoying lunch at Wong's Café when Wong Sang and Chon Woo entered. "Hey, Professor," shouted Sang. "What did that female dragon
say about me after I left? Nothing good I know."

Wong Sang climbed onto the stool next to Professor as Chon Woo
took an empty seat on the other side. "Professor," Chon nudged, "what
did the two of you scheme? Conspire to hogtie the town and what an
absurd idea of taxes. No businessman will agree to that. I know I won't
pay."

Professor stiffened, his face dark with anger. Chon Woo quickly retracted, "I was only joking, sir. Can't you take a joke? Come on!"

Professor's voice was gruff as he rebuked both men, who then asked
in unison, "Let me buy you lunch, sir."

"No thanks, I'll buy my own meal. I need no bribes to tell you what
Liah and I discussed. The town will know of our plans sooner or later.
I'd have told you without your offer of lunch."

Chon's face reddened. "It's not a bribe, Professor. I just wanted to
treat you, that's all. Now, what did you speak of?"

Wong Sang impatiently brushed aside Chon's questions to demand once again what Liah said of him. "Well," said Professor with a smug smile, "you didn't fool her one bit, Sang. She knew you were lying."

Wong Sang recoiled, his face pink with embarrassment, guffawing to hide his discomfort. "Well, now, since she knows what a scoundrel I am, she won't want me on the Council."

Chon quipped, "I guess I was lucky. Liah hasn't gotten her claws into me and she won't if I have my way."

Professor's voice was gruff as he rebuked both men. "If I were you, I wouldn't make fun of Liah's plans. They hold a good deal of merit and promise. In the beginning I thought Liah was prattling, but upon learning of her harrowing experiences in Dai Faw, I readily understood her need of security. My advice is that if the two of you don't want to be a part of Liah's Council, I wouldn't be an obstacle. I don't think she's one to be trifled with."

Wong Sang smirked, "You of all people to be taken in by Liah's silver tongue. All idle dreams can't succeed."

Professor lashed out. "Wong Sang, you are not only blind, but a blind fool. Liah wants a permanent place to raise her children in safety from the Fahn Gwai. If you'd been through the perils she has, you two would also want security from Fahn Gwai persecution too. What Liah wants will also benefit us. Now, leave me alone to finish my lunch."

"Come on, Professor," cajoled Chon, "don't get sore. Liah exaggerated. It serves our people right for living in Dai Faw. Why don't they move to Loo Sahng?"

"Chon, you make me sick!" Professor's voice was loud and angry. "Just because you've been here eight years and have a bar catering to Fahn Gwai you think you're as good as they are. Well, why don't you ask one of your so-called Fahn Gwai friends to sponsor you for citizenship? Or perhaps ask if one of them would rent you an apartment in their part of town?"

A small group of men jostled about Professor and Sang. Suddenly, Sang wanted the discussion ended. "Professor, do not blame Chon too much. He doesn't understand. He hasn't lived through the perils you and I have."

Professor wiped his spectacles and smiled. "Before I cease this talking, Chon, I want you to know that Liah was attacked over five years ago on her farm on the outskirts of Loo Sahng. What do you have to say about that? That's why Cousin Shah found them a place on an oil millionaire's estate to live. That's the only period of time Liah's been able to live more than a few years in safety."

A man standing nearby who had overheard the conversation shouted that Professor was absolutely correct. "Chon, you were not here when the dastardly Fahn Gwai murdered so many of our people!"

Professor sighed. "Chon, I myself lost my entire family when the Fahn Gwai raided China Street. I'm not going to go into the grisly details. Anyone who's lived here for over ten years can tell you. If Liah's plans work, all of us can walk the streets of our town in total safety."

Professor glanced at the businessmen clustered about them, listening. Why not, he thought? What better time to share with people an idea of what Liah was attempting? "You know, Liah wants a sentry system to patrol the town day and night. She also wants the Council to sit in judgment of the town's disputes, thus safeguarding against any reasons for war. There will also be funds to provide help for the sick and needy and to have a school and temple for our children. Is that so bad?"

"Yeah," scoffed Sang, "it takes lots of money to do all that. Where's it coming from?"

Professor's face was smug. "Liah said she'd finance things in the beginning until the treasury can do it." He took in a deep breath, then added, "You know, it is not Liah's responsibility to give us all that we need. The businessmen will have to contribute monies for the services, taxes in ratio to their incomes. The details are not yet set, but when the time comes, everyone will be notified."

Several businessmen moved in closer to listen, their faces solemn. One man asked outright if it wasn't illegal to force businesses to pay taxes. Professor shrugged. "Well, if you men like to repair the damage done by the Fahn Gwai each Saturday night, then go speak with Liah. Tell her you'll not pay your taxes. Besides, did you know that Liah in the short time she's been here has already started helping several families? With a little money and food? But, of course, Sang, you never took the time to find out what kind of a person she is. Well, I haven't all day to waste."

Wong Sang cried, "One more thing, what about the temple of which you were speaking? Why do we need a temple? Most people have an altar in their homes. Besides, there's a temple on Lion's Den Alley."

Chon Woo guffawed. "You don't have an altar, Sang."

Wong Sang snarled, "I don't worship and neither do you. I don't think you're very funny. And why shouldn't you pay taxes? You make enough money and those damn drunks whom you ply with liquor tear up our town."

Chon Woo got off his stool, confronting Sang with his fists. "Just because you're a ne'er-do-well and don't work, taxes based on income are all right with you. Well, it's not all right with me."

Some businessmen sided with Chon. One man asked suspiciously how they could be certain the money collected would end up in town services. The butcher and the barber demanded to know who gave Liah the right to set herself up as the authority.

"I'm positive that if you gave it much thought, sirs, you'd know that it takes somebody to step out of the rut to do something about our lives. Liah took it upon herself because of her children who she fears might come under attack by the Fahn Gwai. She isn't out to take what is not hers. She has her own money and does not need to steal. Besides, everything will be recorded, receipts given and every *Nien-Mei* (year-end), there will be a financial sheet posted listing all the expenditures and all the revenues, with each donor's name. How then can there be cheating?"

Professor's mention of Liah's own monies gave Chon an idea. He had wanted to remodel and enlarge his bar, but did not have the monies. Perhaps if he were to cooperate with Liah, she might advance him the necessary funds or even become a silent partner. The fact that Liah had money did not escape Sang either. He had long wanted to open a gambling house but lacked the necessary financial backing. Perhaps if he joined the Council, Liah might agree to back him. The first step would be to find out the truth about her monies.

Professor swung his stool around, grinning at Chon. "Does your offer of lunch still stand?"

Chon sheepishly nodded.

After lunch, Chon and Sang remained on their stools, smoking and drinking coffee. Chon looked hard at Sang and chuckled. "All right, I know you heard the part about Liah's money. I know you have it in mind to ask Liah for her patronage; so do I."

Sang squinted at Chon, his expression smug. "Yeah, but I've been invited to join the Council. That gives me an advantage over you." Sang's smile quickly turned to a scowl. "And if you're thinking of telling Liah, watch out. I can tell her of your intentions as well, Chon."

Chon was silent for a length of time, then laughed. "Okay, if you won't tell on me, I won't tell on you. Say, did I hear right? Did you get the idea that Professor means for Liah to be chairman?"

Sang scowled. "He came right out and said it to me."

Chon shook his head in disbelief. The idea of a female in the seat of authority. "Why?" he muttered. "If Liah wants to control the panel, why not Sen? We'd be the laughing stock of all the other Chinatowns. A female at the seat of government!"

Sang did not answer, for he couldn't care one way or another. The only thing that mattered to him was whether Liah was as wealthy as it was rumored and if in truth she had an illegal Apinyin trade. Apinyin was a lucrative business.

It took but a few seconds for Sang to realize his companion had other thoughts. His brow furrowed as he suddenly blurted, "I know you, Chon. You've already got ideas of how to wrest the monies from Liah. I tell you what. If you'll work with me in finding out the truth about Liah's wealth, I'll keep my mouth shut. Anything I find out, I will share with you. Together we'll be able to come up with the truth quicker than either of us alone. How about it?"

Chon glanced at the wily Sang and felt no reassurance the man would be honorable. More likely, Sang would take the first opportunity to grab the chance to align himself with Liah, obtain his own loan and open up his gambling house. Still, if the bastard squealed to Liah, he'd never get any money. "Okay," Chon scowled. "I agree, but if I catch you lying to me, I'll kill you. Understand?"

Sang nodded and left. Chon watched Sang go out the door, turning to the left. He knew he was heading toward Pig Alley. He muttered, "The bastard couldn't be honorable even with his own mother. Guess I'd better get started." He picked up the three checks and ambled up to the counter at the front of the dining room, shoving his money through the opening in the cage where Wong sat behind his cash register.

Chon, having lunch three days later, saw the deliveryman from Chew Chong Lung Groceries enter. "Hey, Lew Wing, over here," said Chon. As Lew Wing came over, Chon muttered, "The oxtail stew is good today, why not try it? And I hear the cook has a pot of special spiced soup. Come on, keep me company, I'll treat you to lunch."

Lew Wing, a stolid, hard-toiling man, shrugged and took a seat beside Chon. In addition to the oxtail stew and spiced soup, Lew ordered beef and chard. During the course of the meal, Chon artfully plied Lew with questions about his work, finally coming to the casual mention of Liah's large orders of food and liquor for her secret cache. "Don't you get backaches from lugging the hundred pound sacks of rice? I suppose it isn't easy to lug the cumbersome sacks to the secret place."

Lew Wing shook his head. "I don't know about any secret place. All I do is to leave the groceries stacked up in the kitchen."

Chon's next remark brought a dark expression on Lew Wing's face. "You'd think a woman whose Apinyin trade brings in so much money would share with the needy."

Lew stopped eating and turned and glared at Chon. "Just because Liah doesn't brag about it doesn't mean she doesn't help others. I happen to know of two people she helped a few months ago—one needed money to ship the remains of his brother home. Did you know she also gives lots of food to the outdoor people who live outside her home?"

Without another word, Lew Wing finished his meal. When at last he wiped his mouth and turned to leave, Chon reached out and took the check.

Lew Wing creased his brow and he looked hard at Chon, half-expecting to be asked for a favor. For a split second Lew waited, then nodded, muttered thanks and walked off.

Long afterwards, Chon pondered the identities of the two people Liah had aided, then suddenly leaped from his stool. Hurriedly, he paid his bill and made his way to the undertakers. Who would know better?

—

Wong Sang was luckier than Chon, for it cost him nothing for his information. However, when he casually mentioned Liah's selfishness over lunch with a friend, On Sang Faw, he was treated to the old man's fury. The man whirled on Sang and threatened to cane him if he ever uttered such an accusation again. "My son is here in Gem Sahn because of her!"

Sang wanted to ask for details, but the belligerent expression on the old man's face deterred him.

As he ate, On Sang Faw muttered, "Not only that, but she also paid for a man to ship the body of his brother back to his village for burial... selfish, indeed!"

Wong Sang blurted, "You mean Soo Sing? He's the only one in town who's leaving for home."

The old man's bushy eyebrows shot up. "I didn't say that, Sang and don't you either. No one likes others to know he can't even afford burial monies. That's the trouble with you young people. You hold nothing sacred, nor do you respect your elders. Someday, when you've aged, you will know."

Then On Sang Faw scanned Sang's face, wishing his outburst had not happened, but his pride had been wounded by Sang's forcing him to disclose Liah had given him money for his son's passage. He had no right to shame another man. On Sang Faw scrambled off his stool and continued shaking his head as he headed toward the cashier's cage.

Wong Sang cogitated for several minutes, finished his cigarette, then decided to look for Chon. Perhaps Chon had information and if he divulged what he'd discovered, Sang would tell him of On Sang Faw.

Chon wasn't at the bar, but the barmaid said he was in his office. Sang climbed the stairs, thinking 'office' indeed! More like a cubbyhole of a sleeping room. Sang rapped on the door. A voice muttered, "Go away." Sang called out that he had to speak with him.

Sang waited for the lock to be turned and then pushed his way inside the dark, stuffy room. A single light bulb hanging from a wire in the center of the room weakly shed its light. Chon sat slouched in a chair holding his head in his hands and muttering that he'd had one hell of a night. Sang started to speak nevertheless. After a moment of Sang's bubbling conversation, Chon pleaded for silence, but Sang protested. "Chon, I think Professor told us true. Liah *is* rich!"

Chon moaned, "Later, Sang, tell me later. I'm dying from a hangover."

Sang right then decided to seize the opportunity to speak with Liah herself. After all, he'd kept his part of the bargain and tried to tell Chon what he knew. It wasn't his fault the man was too hung over to care. "OK," Sang muttered, "I'll see you later."

—

Liah sat slouched in her upholstered chair in the kitchen, worried and angry at her husband. She had sat up waiting for Sen until two thirty in the morning, but he had not returned home. Finally, she went to bed thinking only to rest her eyes. At six o'clock in the morning she awakened to find he still had not returned. Her first reaction was to awaken Fifth Son and Third Son to look for their father but changed her mind. It wouldn't do to ruin their learning day. Besides, in a town as small as China Street, it was difficult to go undiscovered. Suddenly, she leaped from her chair, reached out for the calendar on the wall and tore off the date page: October eighteenth. "Oh, may the Gods make this day bright."

She plodded out to the front room, sat down and lit another cigarette, puffing nervously. Her eyelids were heavy and twitched from weariness and her stomach felt queasy. For the hundredth time in the last twelve hours, she glanced up at the clock... seven o'clock. Surely, if Sen were hurt, someone would have found him by now. Abruptly she rose, walked over to the altar and lit a taper to Kwan Koong.

The circle of light from the lamp shone on her like an arc light on an actress on stage. Liah's mind raced with emotional imagery: Sen, lying under a wagon, unconscious, perhaps bleeding or even dead. Her heart pounded; it was almost unbearable.

At seven-thirty, Eldest Daughter emerged from her room and was surprised to find her mother awake. "Mah? Are you all right?"

Liah's first reaction was to tell Eldest Daughter she feared for her father, but she bit her lips and only shook her head. "I'll prepare your morning meal. Awaken the others." Later, she thought, I will try to sleep.

After the children were fed, time dragged once again. Liah was almost in tears. Her impulse was to send for Professor. Then she heard a key in the front door and raced to the front room. Sen entered, seemingly unharmed, as Liah cried "Oh, Sen, how could you? I was half-frightened to death thinking of what might have happed to you. What's come over you?"

Her tirade done, Liah noticed happiness on Sen's face and felt its warmth. He raised his hand for silence as he grinned. "I've been hired by the train yard, Liah." In a torrent of words, he babbled on, "I couldn't come home to tell you lest they hire someone else. I am sorry you were frightened."

Liah's voice echoed Sen's joy as she grinned. "Oh, Sen, I am so happy for you. I know it hasn't been easy for you to be idle. Let me fix you some breakfast; you must be hungry having missed supper last night."

Sen followed his wife into the hallway, muttering that he was too tired and sleepy to eat, but if she didn't mind he'd have a bowl of brandy soup. It might help him sleep, for he was also excited.

Liah sat beside her husband as he slurped his soup. "Now, you can fix me a lunch too. Like you do for our sons. Oh, Liah, I feel as if a hundred-pound weight has been lifted off my shoulders. Now, I, too, have a job."

Liah, making no comment, thought how much like a child Sen was. Immediately upon finishing his brandy broth, Sen went into the bedroom. Liah tidied up and then wearily climbed into bed to sleep an exhausted sleep beside her husband.

—

Wong Sang passed by Liah's doorway several times, each time losing the courage to enter. He was angry at his cowardice, for who was Liah that he had to be afraid? Still, no matter how he talked to himself, he couldn't open the door and walk in. After the third time, Sang decided tomorrow would be a better day and he scurried out of Peacock Alley.

Chon Woo met Sang at Wong's Café that night. "What's the matter? You look as if you lost a hundred dollars at the gambling tables."

Sang scowled. He'd been cross with himself all day for being a coward. Much as he wanted to open up a gambling house, he couldn't bring himself to face up to Liah. Chon asked, "Didn't you come by this morning? I was so damned drunk I can't remember. What did you want?"

Sang nodded. "Nothing much. I wanted to know if you'd found out anything about Liah. But I don't suppose you did, or else you'd have come to me."

Chon shook his head, but his expression gave Sang to know Chon was lying. Consequently, Sang withheld his own information. Serves Chon right, thought Sang. His promises are worthless.

A week later, the morning Sen brought home his first paycheck, he felt as if his heart would burst. Liah touched the slip of paper and inquired if the numbers were the amount of his pay.

Sen nodded, feeling even more pride as he explained how Shah would accompany him to the bank to cash it. "I simply sign my name on the back of the paper and they will give me the money. Twelve dollars and thirty-five cents."

"Sen, this is foolishness. You can't write Fahn Gwai."

"I can so write. Look Liah, I'll show you. I've been practicing all week. I copied my name from my entry papers. Cousin Shah showed me how."

While Sen laboriously wrote his name, Liah looked on in awe, then began to giggle. Thomas and Shelley walked through the door, taken aback at their parent's laughter. Thomas muttered, "Now what brought this on?"

Shelley retorted softly, "Hell, I don't know, but it sure sounds better than an argument."

Though the atmosphere of the house improved because of Sen's job, Liah still had not found the right time to tell Sen of the upcoming meeting of the Council. True, the Council was not yet formed, but to Liah it was only a matter of time. She continued her campaign each time she went shopping, broaching the subject of a unified, safe China Street. Due to her zealousness, people in town began to avoid her. Worse yet, many men made light of her plans, finding sport in dubbing her 'the female dragon.'

One Sunday evening, two weeks after getting the train yard job, Sen burst into the kitchen in a rage. "Liah, how dare you insult my name? Do you realize the men are poking fun at you behind your back? I demand you cease these foolish crusades. Unification of China Street, what foolishness! Do you know how impractical and impossible it is? You're making a fool of yourself. Worse yet, you're making me look like a fool. I want you to stop it!"

Liah met her husband's wrath impassively, neither arguing nor consenting to obey. She must follow through with her plans. It crossed her mind momentarily that perhaps it might be a bad idea to ask Cousin Shah to join. She wanted no part in Sen breaking off with his cousin; however, at this juncture in Liah's life, the Council was too important to allow Sen's personal relationships to interfere. Liah consigned her fears to the Gods. If their Meng-Sui meant for them to be kinsmen and friends, nothing would change it. For her, she must not compromise, not for Sen, not for anything!

Sen recognized his wife's expression and knew she would continue. He strode into their bedroom and slammed the door. Liah breathed a sigh of relief and went about her preparations for supper.

—

The last week of October, the children brought home their report cards. There was a flurry of explanations about their grades. The highest grade was a one and failing was a five. Liah scanned everyone's card, frowning when she reviewed Third Son's card. "Why a four in Fahn Gwai?"

Theo shrugged. "I don't speak Fahn Gwai so good. I don't speak so good because every time we speak Fahn Gwai at home you hit us on the hands."

Flo was flabbergasted with Theo's lie and would have snitched on him had William not kicked her under the table, warning her to stay out of it.

Liah scanned her third son's face, scowled, and then smiled. "A more blatant lie, I have not heard, Third Son. Next time I expect to see a better grade, or else I'll really hit you."

Liah made a motion for Eldest Daughter to help with supper. Flo took the basket of Chinese peas to the table and, while she removed the strings, proudly announced to her mother she was going to a new school. "Why?" demanded Liah.

"Because, Mah-Mah," explained William, "our school only goes up to the ninth grade. Eldest Sister is going into the tenth, so she now goes to another school three blocks away from ours."

Third Son pestered his mother to sign his report card, but she refused. "Your eldest brother will sign all report cards. He will know who is doing well and who isn't. And woe to any sluggard, my Third Son."

Flo smirked at Theo. "Mah-Mah," she cooed, "I'll always bring home good grades. You don't have to worry about me. The teacher said I was a very good student."

Thomas walked into the kitchen with Shelley and glared at his sister. "Bragging again, I see."

Liah informed Eldest Son he was to sign all the report cards and to let her know whoever brought home bad grades. "You must all study hard and then perhaps the Fahn Gwai will not persecute you. More importantly, you will be able to work by the sweat of your brains instead of your backs."

FIRST THANKSGIVING

The week before Thanksgiving, Flo nagged her mother for a turkey and all the trimmings. She explained that the Pilgrims escaped to the New

World so that they might worship without persecution. Liah was shocked to learn the Fahn Gwai even harmed their own kind. "We'll see," murmured Liah. "If your father wishes turkey, then we'll eat turkey. If not, you will have to content yourself with chicken or else go hungry. Personally, I do not see why turkey. The meat is so much coarser and is not as succulent as chicken."

Thanksgiving eve, Thomas and Shelley each brought home a turkey, bonuses for the holiday from their employers. Liah gasped, "Two turkeys? Couldn't they have given you a turkey and a chicken?"

Thomas bridled. "Mah-Mah, why can't you ever be satisfied? Roast one turkey for tomorrow and ask Quon Mon if he wouldn't allow you to store the other one in his locker."

Thanksgiving morning, Liah was distressed to find her children underfoot. "All the other times I have to threaten you to finish your chores before you leave for the playground and then today you won't leave the house. If you do not leave me alone, we will not have supper tonight."

Suddenly, the kitchen was deserted. The silence stunned Liah. Such a racket her children made! As she readied the rice and vegetables, Liah wondered if the children would ever outgrow their enthusiasm. Half-aloud, she murmured, "Life has not cowed them, but that is good."

By late afternoon, her chores completed, Liah sat down to enjoy a cup of tea. Her mind ran to Professor and Cousin Shah who were invited for supper and to Madam Quock, her daughter, Yook Lan, and lastly to Liah's friend, Sen Fei.

For as many times as she thought about Sen Fei, Liah still could not keep her anger from erupting against the actress's business manager who had absconded with all her money and jewelry. Gossip had it that Sen Fei was now destitute, and Liah believed it from the sad tales she'd heard of Sen Fei's meager existence. Liah had vowed, from the moment they'd met, that the aged actress would not want for food or clothing, nor for a place to live; Liah would provide whatever she needed.

That evening, Number Three was a bedlam, the children greedily clamoring for supper. At a quarter of six, Professor arrived with Sen Fei, presenting Liah with two bottles of Ng Ga Pei. "My, but the aroma of turkey makes me hungry."

Liah grinned. "So are the children. They've been pestering me since five o'clock. As soon as Madam Quock and her daughter arrive with Cousin Shah we will sit down to supper."

Madam Quock was Liah's friend from Dai Faw. When her husband deserted her for a showgirl, Madam Quock left Dai Faw, saying the shame was too great to face.

Madam Quock's daughter, smitten by the stage, hoped for a singing career. Yook Lan, upon learning that Sen Fei would be at the dinner, could not wait to meet her. "She is the most famous singer of the Chinese Opera. I want to learn all I can from her."

"I forbid you to hound the poor woman," ordered Madam Quock. "Do it another time when it is not in Liah's house. She may take offense."

However, the moment Yook Lan saw Sen Fei she forgot her mother's admonitions and began to ply the actress with questions about voice control and the treatment of several difficult arias. Madam Quock's eyes blazed, but Sen Fei, flattered by the young girl's attention, waved aside her mother's objections.

Liah glanced furtively at Cousin Shah's placid countenance, wondering if Professor had extended to him the invitation to join the Council. She breathed a silent prayer to Kwan Yin that Cousin Shah accept and, most of all, hold no disapproval.

At the supper table, Cousin Shah chuckled as Sen attempted to quiet his children. "I remember the first time I laid eyes on them. What an overwhelming experience."

Professor agreed. His first encounter with them had been unforgettable as well. "It's little wonder the Gods gave children to young people, for certainly they'd hasten the aging of an older man."

Sen smiled. "You're right, sir. I feel as if I've aged a hundred years, not to speak of all my white hair."

Liah shot a warning glance at the children, especially toward Third Son. During supper Liah glanced several times at Cousin Shah, but he seemed not to notice. As the supper progressed, she came to the conclusion that Professor had not yet spoken to him, but she wished she knew for sure.

Liah, prodded by the uncomfortable fear of what Cousin Shah might feel about the Council, became displeased with Madam Quock. Why won't she cease acting like a simpering maiden and be the mature woman she was? Ah, perhaps her husband had reason to leave her. Liah's face reddened at the thought, but did he have to run away with an actress almost the age of his daughter? Perhaps Madam Quock acted the way she did because of her need for a man.

Sen excused himself directly after supper. "Cousin Shah and I have to work early tomorrow morning and I'm not as young as I used to be. I need my sleep. I bid you all good night."

Liah was disappointed when a half-hour later, Cousin Shah also took his leave. At nine-thirty, Professor rose and bowed slightly as he thanked Liah for a wonderful meal. "I have an early appointment to-morrow. If you'd like, I'll be happy to escort the ladies home."

It was hard for Liah not to feel a deep affection for the scholar. Not many of her countrymen would go out of their way for females. She smiled as she handed Sen Fei a paper sack containing a generous portion of turkey, rice and gravy.

Liah watched from her doorway until they had crossed the cobble-stones onto Marchesson Street and made the turn toward Mah Loo. Tired as she was, Liah then stripped the remaining meat from the turkey carcass. They would eat the meat tomorrow. The carcass she'd simmer for *jook*, a thick, rich, rice gruel. She started the jook by washing the rice and then threw a big piece of ginger root and orange peel into the rice pot. While waiting for the rice to boil, she washed the remaining dishes and cleaned the stove.

An hour later, Liah decided to abandon the cooking of the gruel; she'd finish the simmering tomorrow. Garnished with chopped green onions, egg, Chinese parsley, red ginger and sweet ginger, the turkey rice gruel was a complete meal.

Midnight. How the clock melts away the time. If only she could find a woman to help with the household chores. It seemed each day slipped away so secretively, she never knew until too late that the day was done; whatever else needed her attention took until midnight to accomplish. Of course, Liah would never complain to Sen. He'd only use it as an excuse to forbid her to dabble in town politics.

Liah readied herself for bed thinking of how the year was about to come to an end and the Council hadn't yet become a reality. Why was it so difficult to form when only good would come of it? She looked up at her private altar and whispered a prayer for Kwan Yin's assistance. Snuggled in the warm bed, Liah gave herself up to sleep. Not even her plans to unify China Street could resist the pull of slumber. Besides, there was tomorrow.

NEIN-MEI (YEAR'S END)

The secret cellar and tunnel were completed on the third day of December. Cousin Shah took Liah down the steps located under the stair well. "Be careful," he cautioned as they made their slow descent on the somewhat steep but wide stairs. "We put up a door with a lock as a barrier just in case someone discovers the opening onto the train yard. If you ever revive the shrubbery, the opening to the tunnel will be completely hidden. Although we're too tired to do so now, someday we'll dig a hook-up tunnel that will lead to Dragon's Den Road. Then in times of peril we can travel safely underground."

Liah's face shone as they returned to the house. Cousin Shah and Sen placed a huge steamer trunk over the trap door. Sen grinned. "Who'd guess there's an opening there?"

When he handed the two keys to Liah, she inquired where he had gotten such a sturdy, round cover for the door. Cousin Shah grinned an impish grin. "I found it in the Fahn Gwai's road. Just wait until tomorrow when they see the sewer gaping up at them. They'll go crazy wondering who would ever steal a sewer cover."

Contentment flooded Liah's being. Not only were they guaranteed escape in the face of peril, but also she could now set in a store of staples. There was only one issue that plagued her and that was if Cousin Shah would approve her Council and become a member. She'd have to approach Professor once again to inquire if he'd spoken to him.

It turned out that Professor, filled with misgivings, had not asked Cousin Shah to join the Council. It wasn't because the idea was not valid but because the aspect of the chairmanship with its limitless powers caused him to be fearful. Liah, who was the most likely candidate for the seat, would not violate the position, but Liah certainly could not live forever. What about the leaders who came after? Would they ever abuse the chairmanship? No, he'd wait a while before speaking with Shah. In the meantime, he'd avoid seeing Liah as well until he worked out the issue.

He glanced at the wall clock and decided to go out for a breath of air. Perhaps after he'd picked up the Dai Faw newspaper, he'd be more apt to find a solution.

Professor was leaving the newspaper office on Lion's Den Alley when he frowned. An aged priest, his arms filled with a large box of groceries, was having difficulty keeping his saffron colored robe from flying up in the breeze.

"The December chill must be freezing to the old man's limbs," thought Professor. Quickly, he ran up and reached out for the box. "Revered One, allow me to help."

The tiny man smiled as the scholar exclaimed, "Surely your attire is not suitable for this chilly time, especially in this brisk wind."

The old priest's voice sounding almost as frail as his body, trembled as he replied, "There is no use complaining about the elements since the Gods have ordained it and also since my Meng-Sui sees fit to burden me so. Besides, it is most generous of Chew Cheung Lung Grocers to give me this food donation. One must nourish the body as well as the spirit, don't you think?"

Professor noticed the old man's sly smile. He couldn't help thinking it strange that a man of God should have even a small degree of practicality and humor. All the other priests he'd met had always made him uncomfortable with their austere piety. Professor chuckled. "There is no need to place this condition upon the God's shoulders, sir. I will instruct the grocer to bring you a delivery each week. And one more thing, sir, may I remind you it is dangerous for you to expose yourself to the Fahn Gwai ruffians that roam Lion Den's Alley? Especially in your saffron robe, with your shaven head. They might make fun of you or even harm you, sir."

"The Gods will protect me from peril and if my Meng-Sui demands, I shall accept whatever fate comes to me."

"Such faith is commendable, sir, but there is no use tempting the fates."

Later, Professor and the aged priest discussed the reality of life and life after death, as well as Meng-Sui, while they shared a cup of tea in what passed for the priest's temple. The old man sighed. "Ah, when one is my age, it is easy to follow the way of Tao, for the body and mind can do nothing else. I remember the temptations in my earlier days and how great the effort required to follow passivity and purity. Now, however, the Gods and I have everything in common. Old age has made it so."

"Sir, I do not mean to be disrespectful, but I have no such faith. I am well-versed in philosophy and the logical aspects of Taoism, but I find that reality is reality. My life on earth has been a penance of sorrow and pain. The struggle to stay alive, keep a roof over my head and food in my belly is the only faith I've known. My entire family was wiped out by the Fahn Gwai infidels when they wreaked destruction on China Gai. Perhaps this is a barrier to my belief in our Gods."

One remark led to another and one question dovetailed with another until Professor spoke of Liah, the Council, the issue of the chairmanship with its limitless powers and whether the townspeople would accept the Council. The old man leaned back in his seat, his eyes closed, his hands so limp in his lap Professor feared he'd fallen asleep. A silence engulfed the room so profound Professor half-imagined he could almost hear it.

There was a lapse of fifteen minutes before the old man stirred, opened his eyes and smiled gently. "You know the principles of Feng-Sui and Meng-Sui; therefore, you know all these things are beyond our control. Madam Liah, of whom you speak, came here to worship each day and afternoon when they first moved in. I heard her soft prayers of thanks to Kwan Yin, then her pleas to be allowed to remain here in peace and safety. I heard her soft plea for wisdom, then took more notice when she prayed for all the people of China Gai. Since that time it has come to my ears the several persons she's aided, not hearsay, but from people who came here to thank Kwan Koong. So many of the outdoor residents come here to make their humble prayers of thanks. I suppose I have come to know Madam Liah better than I realized."

The old priest paused for breath, then continued. "I am struck by her countenance; she has an aura, as if the Gods have favored her with the ability to glimpse the future. Perhaps this gift balances the privations and perils of her earlier life. Whatever her destiny, time will clarify. Does that remove some of your doubts, my son?"

Professor nodded mutely, but a sense of relief pervaded his mind, even with the questions concerning the chairmanship unanswered. He reached into his pants pocket, brought out a coin and quietly deposited it in the collection bowl. "I thank you for your wisdom, sir. Hopefully, the Gods will reveal themselves to me, but, as you said, enlightenment comes from within."

The old man smiled knowingly. "Enlightenment does not come easily, my son. And it will come, for you've already begun to question. I encourage you to remain steadfast in your search and not shy away from sometimes-painful truths. In time the resolution to most troubling issues will become clear."

At eight o'clock that evening, Professor arrived at Number Three. Liah was seated in her upholstered chair in the kitchen with a basket of stockings in her lap. She and Eldest Daughter were repairing holes in the stockings. Eldest Daughter fretfully beseeched her mother to let her be done.

Liah smiled broadly, nodding for Eldest Daughter to put the basket away, they'd work another time. Quickly, Flo snatched the basket and threads and ran from the room shouting to her brothers for a game of casino.

"Is Sen asleep already?"

Liah nodded. "The work at the train yards is strenuous and he sleeps directly after supper on nights he works. I am happy you came by, for there is a question on my mind concerning the chairmanship. It occurred to me that many people might think the seat carries with it far too much authority. It will be difficult enough to get the residents to accept the Council without fear of a dictatorship. How would it be if the chairman had no power to vote except to break ties?"

Professor gaped for several moments in stunned silence, then he grinned, leaning back in his seat and began to chuckle. Liah waited courteously, scanning the scholar's face for the reason behind his laughter.

A moment later, Professor took off his spectacles, wiping them as he thought, what a waste of time fretting. The old priest was right. Meng-Sui could not be stemmed. Suddenly, as he replaced his spectacles, Professor caught sight of Liah's quizzical expression. "I'm sorry, but I must confess something. For days I've been pondering the same question about the chairmanship and did not know how to broach the subject to you, because I assume you will be chosen to head the Council. I was not sure of how you would receive my sentiments."

"Oh, sir, you must know I am a reasonable person. I only want to know the truth from you, no matter who it concerns, especially if you believe I am in the wrong. There is only one important issue and that is the Council. So promise me next time there is something on your mind, you will speak of it immediately."

Professor grinned. "I will. I must say the solution was simple, once the emotions were removed. Your suggestion is perfect." For the next hour, they discussed the laws governing the Tongs and personal disputes between parents, spouses and business partners, and deciding that there would be three levels of crimes and for each one the Council should add more stringent punishments and fines. Afterward, Professor leaned back in his seat and smiled. "Now, I'd say the Tenet of Laws will be a document of law and humanity. I defy anyone to tear it apart. By segregating crimes into three levels, we will now be able to judge and pass sentence to fit each case."

Professor suddenly shuddered. "I know that treason is unforgivable and that anyone who plots with another, especially a Fahn Gwai, deserves death. Yet the taking of a life is abhorrent to me."

Liah nodded. "I am not a monster, sir. I feel the same revulsion, but shouldn't evil people be placed under a cloud and suffer the possibility of death? There will be plenty of warnings posted and very explicit announcements of the penalties. For the crime of treason, any lesser form of punishment would be a travesty of justice."

"You are right, Liah, but I cannot go against the grain of my beliefs. Perhaps it is the earlier violence in my life that has made me so. Now that we have a decent Tenet of Laws, I think I'll speak with Cousin Shah and see if he'll join us.

Liah smiled at him. "So that's why you didn't say a word to me on Thanksgiving. I should have known."

"Speaking of the Council, did you know both Sang and Chon have been ferreting about town to find out if you are indeed rich? Lew Wing told me they have asked him the most personal questions and made derogatory remarks about you. Beware Liah. Sang has been dying to open up his own gambling parlor and Chon wants to remodel his bar."

Liah hissed, "The fools. If they had any intelligence they'd come right out and present a business proposition to me. I'm always open to new avenues of making money. I'll need money to carry out the Council's work until the treasury is able to cover the services we hope to provide the town. It was in my mind the services for the needy and the school for the children ought to be inaugurated immediately."

There was a long, comfortable silence as they both smoked. Sensing Liah was about to suggest setting a meeting date, Professor quickly murmured it was impossible, but another year was ending. "Nein Mei, year's end, where does the time go? It is in my mind that Nein Mei is no time to begin the Council. Nein How, a new year's birth, is the time for new beginnings." The scholar paused and looked at Liah. "No matter how anxious you are to start, we ought to allow the Gods their bounty. We need all the luck we can get."

Liah's face fell, her disappointment visible. "I know you are right, sir, but I cannot help my impatience. Why is it so difficult to build and so easy to destroy? It is not only the formation of the Council I'm anxious for, but I'll not rest easy until the town is protected by a sentry system."

Professor tried hard not to show his relief, but he'd bought more time, time to canvass the town, time to expose the ideas of the Council to the people and to explain the free services Liah hoped to provide. Once more, the possibility of failure crossed his mind but he quickly brushed it away. It would be difficult enough to do the groundbreaking without emotional fears. Impulsively, Professor exclaimed, "It's not that I disbelieve in what we are trying to do, but have you given consideration to those who believe in nothing free or good? Have you given thought of what it means if China Street does not want to be unified or governed?"

"No, and I'm not wasting time thinking about it. For all the good the people will receive, it just makes no sense that they will not want the Council."

Liah's positive attitude had no effect on the scholar. He rose, saying the hour was late, and that he yet had to post the daily news in the Alley. "I will let you know about Cousin Shah. Good night, Liah."

—

While Professor dealt with drumming up support for the Council, Liah was engulfed by the Christmas holiday. Eldest Daughter, in her zeal to celebrate Christmas, told her mother Christ was born in a manger because the inns had no room. Liah sighed, saying the Fahn Gwai were the most illogical people in the world. "Imagine, no place for their king."

Sen remarked to Liah one morning that Eldest Daughter was most conniving. "She told me some story about three wise men who brought gifts to their king and that was the reason that today we give gifts at Christmas."

"I do not know about the three wise men, but have you noticed the change in behavior of our children? Do you think it has anything to do with the feast day and the hope of receiving gifts?"

Sen nodded. "I think if the feast day brings such marked good behavior, it is too bad the feast day comes only once a year."

Sen couldn't ignore his wife's pride as she informed him that Eldest Son was buying clothes for the children and that Second Son planned to give gifts of luxury: toys. "Eldest Daughter told me she is making knitted items for her brothers and sister. It's too bad that that girl has such a razor-sharp tongue, for she does have a good heart."

Sen looked hard at Liah. His tone was slightly reproachful. "I'd say she inherited candidness from her mother. Well, I have neither the time nor the energy to discuss the children. Last night we worked unusually hard, for the foreman was in a vile mood and picked on everyone."

On Christmas Eve, excitement reached a fever pitch in Number Three when Thomas and Shelley brought home a six-and-a-half-foot tree. Liah gasped, "Not since the estate have I seen such a huge tree."

Emmi danced around the tree while Flo buried her face in its pungent branches, later to whine they had no ornaments. Shelley sneered, "You're never satisfied, sis. A bare tree is better than no tree."

Thomas growled, "Quit clowning. Give her the stuff."

The boys pulled out the decorations they'd also brought home.

"Can we decorate the tree now? Mah-Mah, look at the lights!"

Liah smiled, ordering the children to have supper first. "The kitchen must be cleaned and the dishes done before anyone can touch the tree."

Supper was swift though Flo was still impatient for her mother and father to finish. Liah suppressed her smile, recalling her own childhood eagerness and anticipation of feast days. The ensuing commotion and noise was deafening. Liah escaped to her bedroom, saying she'd come out after the tree was decorated.

When she emerged, Liah stopped at the front room doorway, staring at the shimmering Christmas tree. Thomas teased, "Your face, Mah, you should see yourself. Just like a child's."

Liah retorted, "It is my first tree, so in truth I am a child. Just look at that blue bird and that poinsettia. Those globes are so life-like. I remember the tree in my mistress's house. I think ours is every bit as lovely, even lovelier."

Theo turned off the ceiling lights, plunging the room into total darkness except for the tree's myriad colored lights, which seemed brighter, almost animated. Liah smiled, "Leave the tree lights on so that your father may see them when he returns home from work."

Eldest Daughter disappeared from the room and returned moments later with an armful of presents. Emmi shouted for Thomas and Shelley to put their gifts under the tree. "Emmi, what more do you want? We gave you the tree and the decorations, didn't we?"

Later, as they prepared for bed, Shelley asked if Thomas didn't think it hard on Emmi not to believe there were more gifts. "Naw," muttered Thomas. "Let her learn patience. We'd better hit the sack, 'cause you know they're not gonna let us sleep."

At eight-thirty Christmas morning, Liah was awakened by muffled footsteps outside their bedroom and heard the children's loud whispers. Turning to Sen, she said, "Sen, wake-up!" She nudged him. "The children have been outside our door for a while. They're anxious to open their presents."

Sen moaned that he was too tired and to let them open their presents without him. Liah shook her head, chuckling. "Wake up now, Sen. I'll go out and make you a cup of the Fahn Gwai *gahfeh* (coffee). You get dressed. Hurry now, just try to remember your own eagerness during our feast days at home."

Liah sat in her upholstered chair in the front room, watching and listening happily as Thomas and Shelley distributed the boxes. In her heart, she thanked Kwan Yin for the moment's joy. Although the feast day was the Fahn Gwai's, Liah was grateful for the opportunity to experience such joy. Life was too sad, too care-burdened. The sound of the children's happy excitement as they opened their presents made Liah forget her sadness, at least momentarily.

Later, the landlord visited. The children crowded around Mr. Marchesson, giggling as they tried to read the nametags on the gifts in his arms. "Silence!" ordered Thomas. "Leave Mr. Marchesson alone."

The landlord shook his head, declaring he liked the old-fashioned Christmas spirit. He winked as he put the packages down and handed out several Santa candy boxes. "Here, these are for all of you."

Sen's face was grim as he faced the landlord, trying to smile a bit when Mr. Marchesson turned. "Sen, I apologize for intruding on your holiday, but I did so much want to say Merry Christmas to your wonderful family."

Thomas translated and the cool apprehension that automatically clutched Sen eased. He reached out his hand and smiled. Mr. Marchesson couldn't help but feel the warmth of the Christmas spirit so absent in his home. Mr. Marchesson only saw the commerciality at his house, decorated inside and out by a professional decorator. Here, in Liah's home, the essence of love and warmth abounded.

"Thomas," murmured Mr. Marchesson. "You are indeed fortunate, all of you are, for having one another. I hope none of you ever loses this sense of family and, above all, never forget you're Chinese. Your ancient, civilized culture is far superior to that of us Fahn Gwai. Your mother is a rare breed, so always care for her." Then Mr. Marchesson smiled. "But, of course, I know you already know these things and as for your mother or father, it is Chinese to consider them above all else."

Mr. Marchesson saw a visible change in Thomas's face and quickly wished he hadn't spoken when Mert retorted, "Sir, fat chance we'd ever forget we're Chinese. There's hardly a day when some Fahn Gwai doesn't call us 'Chinks'."

Thomas glared at Mert. "Today is Christmas and we're not going to speak of ugly things."

The landlord smiled sympathetically. "Mert, I deplore the ignorance and lack of manners of my people, but you must remember as you Chinese say, the Fahn Gwai is a barbarian. Give him time to grow up. Your mother doesn't allow the Fahn Gwai to bother her. She's only out to see they leave her family alone. That's how you ought to consider the Fahn Gwai. Go on with your life and let him act the ass."

As Liah presented the landlord with a box of lychee nuts and a fancy box of jasmine tea, Thomas explained that she was sorry the gifts were not as grand as his. Mr. Marchesson reached out for Liah's hand, admonishing. "Little lady, don't you ever think that way. The pleasure I get each time I come here is worth more than money can buy. Thomas, be sure your mother knows how I feel."

Liah smiled and opened her gift: a porcelain peacock lamp with a fluted silk shade. She pantomimed that would occupy a place of honor on the table beside her upholstered chair. While Mr. Marchesson did not fully understand Chinese, he understood the sparkle in her eyes, her amiable tone and, above all, her pixie smile. Only after Thomas's explanations, did he exclaim, "What a lovely thought. I am honored. Well, I must leave now. My wife has invited her family for dinner and will be very irate if I am late. A very Merry Christmas, children."

Christmas dinner at Number Three was a joyous feast: roast duck, barbecued squab, tender boiled pullet in a creamy mustard sauce, stuffed black mushrooms with a pork and shrimp filling and a vegetable compote.

Professor came laden with a bottle of Ng Ga Pei for Liah, cigarettes for Sen and, for the children, a large box of chocolates. Sen Fei brought a gift of lychee nuts and jasmine tea to Liah. Liah embraced the aged actress, chiding her gently for spending her money. Liah's heart burst with joy as Sen Fei held up her gift of a woolen robe and matching slippers. "Now, this winter I will be warm because of your generosity, Liah. May Kwan Yin smile on you always."

When Cousin Shah, Madam Quock and her daughter Yook Lan arrived, the children swarmed about them to see what gifts they'd brought and for whom. Liah good-naturedly apologized for the children's rudeness. "This Fahn Gwai feast day seems to have robbed them of their manners. Children, leave them be. Do come into the kitchen; supper will be ready in a few minutes."

Toward the end of supper, Liah sighed and complained about the irony of it all. "Our first and second feasts and we celebrate the Fahn Gwai's. I can't wait until after the first of the year when we shall celebrate our New Year." Liah reluctantly admitted, even though they were Fahn Gwai feast days, she felt a gladness of heart.

Thomas retorted sharply, "Mah, how come you always separate everything into yellow or white? You know there's good and bad in both."

Before either Sen or Liah could reply, Professor interjected. "I think what your mother meant was that she would have liked the first celebration to have been one of our own feast days. Understandably so, for your mother is Chinese and born in another era. She hasn't, nor have any of us older folks here tonight, had your education. You have had exposure to the Fahn Gwai's world and we haven't. We don't understand or speak their language, nor can we read or write it."

The scholar paused, allowing Eldest Son a comment, but seeing Sen's half-angry expression, Professor quickly continued. "Your parents have good reason to distrust, even hate, the Fahn Gwai. Isolation is the only weapon we have to protect ourselves. So you see, Eldest Son, your mother doesn't separate things yellow or white, rather safe or dangerous."

William shyly addressed Professor. "Sir, I know what you mean, but it isn't just you who are not educated in their ways that the Fahn Gwai pick on. They pick on us too and call us names. It used to hurt me and make me afraid, but I know the only way I can handle it is to put up with it until I can be as good as the Fahn Gwai."

"Good for you, William!" said Theo. "Mah-Mah and Ba-Ba have to realize they have no choice but to put up with the Fahn Gwai. After all, we live in Gem Sahn. But things will change. It can't always be bad."

Sen looked up from his plate and glared at his sons. "I want no more of this kind of talk at the table. Your mother and I have just cause to despise the Fahn Gwai. It is not your place to teach us. As for change, Third Son, do not delude yourself. The Fahn Gwai will never allow you to be as good as he is. I give you a challenge: Find yourself in his court and I'll give you one guess who will be the victor. Justice is never ours. Now, no more such talk."

The Christmas spirit was replaced by a stony silence that hung over the supper table. Professor sighed, knowing nothing he could say would resolve the differences between the sons and their father. He thought that perhaps that was the worst consequence of the Fahn Gwai's treatment of the Chinese.

Thomas rose from the table, muttering he had a party to attend. The scholar watched with bemusement as Liah attempted to stop her eldest son from leaving. "Mah," chided Thomas, "just remember Second Brother and I are old enough to take care of ourselves. I'm twenty and Shel is nineteen. We can take care of ourselves against Fahn Gwai or Chinese. So do not wait up for us." He kissed her and grinned as he walked out.

Sen yawned. "I will go to bed. I work this evening and so do you, Cousin Shah. I bid you all good night."

Cousin Shah smiled and nodded. Soon he also excused himself, corted Sen Fei, Madam Quock and Yook Lan home. Professor and Liah smoked leisurely, each caught up in private thoughts. A feeling of contentment settled over the room until Liah's two younger sons returned.

At length, the children finished washing the dishes and sweeping the floor and went to their rooms to look over their new clothes, toys and books. Professor sighed. "The peacefulness, it's a balm after the night's excitement. You know, Liah, I'm inclined to agree with your two oldest sons. You ought not to worry needlessly about other people. Why not take life and live it for yourself? The Gods have provided you with enough monies, a large family and a home. Isn't all that enough? I'm afraid if you forge ahead with your plans, your life would not be yours to live, not to speak of the multitude of problems waiting to usurp your time and strength. Especially if it is your wish to include both Sang and Chon on the Council. Keeping tabs on those two will be a full-time job."

Liah wondered if this wasn't the Professor's way of backing out. Then he murmured that her plans were admirable, but the price tag too high. "Your children will do well. Eldest Son and Second Son, even Third Son, are more than capable of getting along in the Fahn Gwai's world. Soon, you will only have to wait for their weekly wages and not have to think of money."

Liah shook her head. "Of course, my sons each give me monies for household expenditures, but I want them to save their money toward a truck, which they want. As for Third Son, he must continue his education. It is too bad he is not as studious as Fourth and Fifth Sons. Hopefully, Fourth Son, who is the smartest of all my children, will decide to be an attorney. Then our people would no longer be helpless in the hands of Fahn Gwai attorneys."

They sat in silence for a moment, then the scholar knocked the ashes from his pipe. "Ah me, time flies, it's almost eleven o'clock. I do have more work to do on the Tenet of Laws if we're to hold our first meeting."

After he left, a sense of deep happiness engulfed Liah as she meditated on the twinkling star atop the Christmas tree. Through half-closed eyes she hoped that if a star could lead the three wise men to a stable to greet the bringer of peace for an entire world, she might also be guided. It was such a far-fetched myth. Still, in the myriad dancing lights that held her fascination, it seemed like it might have been so.

1914

YEAR OF THE TIGER

The morning of the Fahn Gwai's New Year of nineteen hundred and fourteen, Liah awakened, dragging herself wearily from bed. They had not celebrated the Fahn Gwai's New Year in Number Three, only as a day off for Sen. She had not slept a wink after discovering at three-thirty in the morning that her two sons had not yet returned home. She sat on the edge of the alcove wooden bed staring up at Kwan Yin's altar, her lips beseeching the Goddess for her sons' safety.

Maybe they had returned and she hadn't heard them. She rushed to the kitchen, opened the bedroom door and peeked inside. Her sons had not returned. By ten o'clock in the morning, her heart was racing with images of her sons lying helplessly somewhere, beaten, or worse yet beyond her help. Impulsively, she ran to the front room and with trembling hands lit a coil of incense, crying out for Kwan Koong's mercy.

Liah sat at the kitchen table sipping a cup of cold tea, puffing on a cigarette. She was too tired to make a fresh brew. Slowly, as her mind awakened, she stolidly went to the stove, picked up the kettle and filled it with water. She tried to divert her mind by thinking about their upcoming New Year. Was it the Year of the Boar or the Tiger? Her foggy mind refused to function. Ah, well, she would inquire of Professor.

As she contemplated another plea to Kwan Yin, she heard the key in the front door lock. Liah raced to the front room. She stopped in the doorway leading to the front room, staring in disbelief at the disheveled condition of Eldest Son and Second Son—clothes torn, hair rumpled, their faces bloodied. Second Son pitched forward and Liah ran forward to steady him. She had known her two eldest sons were men now, but never so much as now. Second Son's biceps were hard and large as she clutched his arm. Liah screamed, "Your eye is swollen shut and there's a gash on your cheek!"

Thomas grinned at his mother. His right eye was also swollen shut and turning from red to a dark purple. Liah demanded, "What did the two of you do all night?"

Thomas lunged forward, picking Liah up and swinging her around in the air, shouting New Year's greetings. He howled with laughter as his mother struggled to get free. "Put me down this instant. Do you want to waken your father? Put me down!"

Shelley burped and slumped into a chair, staring stupidly at his brother and mother. "Mah-Mah," he muttered sleepily, "we ate, we drank, we danced and we fought."

Thomas set his mother on the floor, correcting Shelley. "Aw, we did-n't start fighting until those guys tried to push themselves into our party. Then we threw them out, that's all."

Liah smoothed her robe, commenting dryly. "From what I see, I'd say the other people did some throwing around, too. Now, get cleaned up and go to bed. Mother is fatigued."

Her two sons lumbered into their bedroom and slammed the door. Liah whirled about, having it in mind to order them to clean up but decided that they were too drunk. Let them sleep.

Throughout the noisy meal that morning, Liah's head ached, pounding like a thousand anvils. As soon as the children and Sen left for the day, she'd return to bed. Angrily, she blamed her two eldest sons for her tortuous night of fright. When her two sons awakened, she'd give them a talking to.

Immediately after Sen and the children left, Liah locked the front and back doors, climbed back into bed and prayed to Kwan Yin to let sleep come. When she got into bed, the room seemed to slowly revolve and she felt a nauseous dizziness. In the silence of the house, Liah fought for sleep.

At four-thirty, Liah was abruptly roused from a deep, dreamless sleep. Far off she heard the faint sounds of her children slamming the front door and coming down the corridor. Mert rushed into her bedroom, his expression petrified, and inquired in a frightened voice if she were ill.

Her head was spinning as Mert leaned over to kiss her. She explained that she'd been up all night and was exhausted. Mert nodded, then timidly asked, was it a bad thing for her to be involved with the Council, especially when Father was against the idea? His expression was sober. "Mah-Mah, I know Ba-Ba doesn't really mean what he says when he's angry."

Liah gazed at her fifth son, so serious, so gentle; little wonder he was her favorite child. "Mah-Mah does not expect you to understand, my son, but she must do what she must do. The time has come when you children must be given a place to lead your lives without constant harassment from the Fahn Gwai. Mah-Mah does not want you to endure the terror and suffering she and Ba-Ba have lived with throughout our lives. I'd also like my grandchildren to live, learn and worship in a place of our own. Too long have the Fahn Gwai plagued us. If you would be of help to me, just give me your obedience."

"I will, Mah-Mah, but I hope you will remember we must go to school and work in the Fahn Gwai town. Do not antagonize the Fahn Gwai so that they'll want to retaliate. It will be me and my sisters and brothers who will really suffer."

Liah frowned. "I am not antagonizing the Fahn Gwai. It is they who barge into our town, gawk at us, taunt us and, worse yet, maim or kill us. If they behave themselves while in China Gai and make no sport of our traditions or our clothing or our ignorance of their language, they will be welcome."

Mert smiled. He silently remembered his own run-in with the Fahn Gwai students who called him 'Ching Chong Chinaman'. Both mother and son exchanged silent, swift glances for each knew of the other's problems. Flo suddenly burst into the room, shouting gleefully that there was a playground softball league. "If we win our division, we get to play for the city championship in July. Wouldn't it be terrific if the Chinatown team won the championship?"

"You make me sick, Flo," Mert sneered. "Mah-Mah, we don't even have a team yet and sis is already speaking of a championship."

"All right, son," Liah admonished. "Let your sister speak, however she wishes. It wouldn't hurt if *you* were to set higher goals. Then if you miss the aspired heights, you'd at least not be in dire straits. I'd also remind you that unless you study harder, you'll end up toiling with the sweat of your back. Now, leave Mother alone to get out of bed."

"Aw, Mah-Mah, I'm doing all right. What brains do I need to drive my brothers' trucks? I think sis is always trying to climb higher than she can."

"I said leave Mother alone." Liah turned to her eldest daughter, ordering her to the kitchen to clean the chard for supper. "If your father finds supper late, he'll not let us forget it."

—

A week into the New Year, Liah was anguishing over her failure to set up the Council. Why hadn't Professor been by to see her? Was it that he had changed his mind? Why weren't men driven more to action as women?

On the ninth day of January, Professor's face was wreathed in smiles as he greeted Liah. "Not only did Cousin Shah agree to be a member of the Council, he approved of the idea of unifying the town. Oh, yes, and guess who I ran into at Wong's Café? You know, Chon Woo for all his wiliness is a stupid liar. He seemed eager to engage me in conversation and as soon as we spoke, he informed me he approved of the Council, even to having you as a chairman. Isn't that a complete turnabout from the way he first ridiculed the idea?"

Liah giggled. "Not at all, Professor. I ran into him in Peacock Alley last week. He hinted about his place being too small for the amount of business he could do and that if he could find a backer, he'd offer that person a partnership. However, he made a point of saying that it would be a silent partnership."

"Well, now," said Professor, "did you offer to back him? That would guarantee you a vote for chairman."

Liah shook her head. "No, I didn't. I don't want to seem overly anxious, for that would give things away when I really ask for his vote. No, the vote must seem to come from Chon."

Liah became suddenly uneasy. Suppose the other men did not want a woman as chairman? Suppose Sang coerced the others into voting for him? Liah leaned forward, her face solemn. "I want you to promise me, should the other men not want me as leader, that you'd accept the job. Please, sir, neither Sang nor Chon should ever be in the chairman's seat. They'd defeat the very point of having the Council. Please, sir, promise."

The scholar's face paled. He shook his head. "You're being a bit too premature in your judgment, Liah. The Gods have eyes. You will be chosen chairman. I do not know how, but it appears to me the Gods favor you. They'd never allow you to be defeated."

Liah was adamant. "Nevertheless, please promise me you'll be chairman should I be rejected. Please!"

The scholar sighed, nodding his head. Suddenly, he felt the compulsion to leave. Such a turn of events would be disastrous for him should Liah's fears be realized. He must speak with the men, especially to the townspeople. Liah must be chosen chairman. He quickly reassured Liah, then took his leave.

Throughout the following week Liah had little time to think of the

Council, for the house was being readied for the New Year. Her temper was high, for while the house cleaning was tiring, cajoling and scolding the children to do their chores took far more time and energy.

Flo, who usually balked at doing extra work, silently if reluctantly helped her mother to make the *doong*. The bushel basket of Ti leaves was draining on the sink, the mung beans sorted and washed in a huge tub. The dried shrimps, side pork and barbequed pork were diced and placed in oversized bowls; the salt fish was chunked; the salted eggs halved; even the black mushrooms were ready.

Liah and Eldest Daughter started making the *doong* without Madam Quock who was always tardy, especially if the visit entailed a chore. Liah was lost in contemplation as she plaited the Ti leaves into an envelope, then carefully filled each pocket with raw rice, a little of each ingredient, then another portion of rice, building the four sides of the pyramid-shaped *doong*. A flush flooded Liah's face as she wondered what Madam Quock did without a man. Quickly, she erased the visions of intimacy between a man and woman from her mind. Anger nagged at her, for unlike Madam Quock, Liah had a husband, but a husband who scorned her, a penance it seemed she must pay until she refrained from Council matters. Frustrated, Liah ordered Eldest Daughter to pay attention, as she was being too sloppy with the folding of the Ti leaves.

An hour later, Madam Quock swept regally into the kitchen, declaring she'd been detained by a man from Dai Faw who tried to put her daughter under contract to sing in the Dai Faw opera house. "Of course, I refused to allow her to leave. Yook Lan, while talented, is not ready. Her voice has to mature."

"Mah-Mah," lamented Eldest Daughter, "I'm tired of making the *doong*. Besides, I have to play baseball today. May I go?"

Liah muttered, "Children today are not as obedient as we were nor as helpful. In my day, I wouldn't dare voice my opinions." Liah sighed. "Another half-hour, then you may leave."

Madam Quock chuckled. "It's a new era now, Liah. My Yook Lan is the same, does nothing, absolutely nothing to be helpful. I think you and I will be the ones to complete the *doong*. Let us put our minds to the task, perhaps we'll finish earlier."

Liah's grim expression melted as Madam Quock murmured, "I'm anxious to taste one. Your *doong* are the best I've ever eaten."

"You're too generous with your compliments, my friend. As soon as we have four dozen made, then we'll steam them in the cauldron, then you and I will be the first to taste them."

It may have been her imagination, but Liah thought her rotund friend seemed to perk up and her fingers moved a bit more deftly in the plaiting of the Ti leaves. Liah gave her friend a wistful smile. Madam Quock's mention of home had given Liah a twinge of nostalgia. So many years and she was still homesick.

—

Each day approaching New Year's Eve, Liah examined the porcelain jardinières, making certain the Chinese lilies and Taro bulbs were submerged in water. Two days before the celebrations, she was overjoyed to find the first blooms. The pungent fragrance of lilies increased as the yellow-centered flowers matured and the Taro leaves flared, proudly heart-shaped.

Two huge tubs of Chinese lilies and two tubs of Taro roots lined each side of the front door, scenting the Alley with their fragrance. Liah smiled, thinking now she'd no longer smell the acrid stench of the train yards. She noted happily that the hibiscus, oleanders, wisteria and honeysuckle vines were also in thick bloom. Only the ivy was yet meager with only a few creepers weaving in and out of the chain-link fence. Liah was positive that soon even the fence would be hidden from view. She frowned at the dusty fig tree at the end of Peacock Alley. Before the celebrations, she must have old Hoh Chan prune the branches and hose down the cobblestones.

Liah went inside and wrapped the good luck money, tokens of quarters, dimes and nickels, in the traditional red paper. These Liah would give to the children in Peacock Alley. For her own family and close friends, she wrapped silver dollars. The only adults Liah gave lucky money to were Sen Fei and Old Chan. She gave them five dollars each.

Sen, despite his smoldering displeasure at his wife's involvement in town politics, watched as she feverishly prepared for the feast day. Liah was worse than he remembered. Perhaps now among her own people, Liah's New Year superstitions and traditions took on a new meaning. He knew better than to mar the celebrations. "Why," he fumed silently, "did women think it necessary to purge their domiciles to change the course of their Meng-Sui? Did his wife, who fully believed in Meng-Sui and Feng-Sui, not know her fate was already decreed?" Suddenly, Sen became aware of Liah's presence, hastily went for his hat and escaped outdoors. Anywhere, decided Sen, was better than his own home. He wanted no part of his wife's frenzy of purification.

By New Year's Eve, Number Three was a beehive of activity. There were the tantalizing aromas of rich simmering soups, spiced pork steaming on the stove, roast ducks and boiled pullets cooling on platters, their skin glistening from a coat of peanut oil. Most of all, the stuffed winter melon steaming in the oversized wok mingled with the bouquet of fresh fruits, melons and vegetables. The essence of sandalwood incense and the peculiar light aroma of the ceremonial gold-flecked papers of many textures to be offered up to Kwan Koong and Kwan Yin added to the wonderful smells of New Year.

The superstitions woven from mythology manifested themselves in Peacock Alley, especially inside Number Three. It was customary to begin the first hours of the New Year, the Year of the Tiger this time, with laughter, good food and drink and family and friends. It was tra-

dition to have paid off all one's debts, settled one's personal accounts
and spread joy amongst one's neighbors through generosity. All these
ensured a happy, prosperous and healthy New Year.

In Liah's home, these beliefs were carried out to their fullest. No one
was allowed to quarrel and no one was rebuked or punished, for tears
washed away the felicity of the New Year. Liah believed fully in all this
and expected everyone who entered Number Three to behave in the
same manner.

On the morning of January 26, Liah made one last inspection of the
house and the garden, nodding each time that she was satisfied. At ten
o'clock, she flung open the double front doors. It was the Year of the
Tiger and she was ready to receive its auspicious benevolence. Then,
too, the open doors welcomed not only family and friends but also
strangers who might seek the New Year bounties inside Number Three.
At home in their village it was tradition that no one was turned away
during this time. Liah did not like that Sen limited the New Year celebrations to only one week. Longer celebrations would be too arduous
an effort, at least where he was concerned. However, one week, Liah
thought, was better than nothing. Still, she couldn't help wishing Sen
would allow the usual month, like the celebrations at home, but he remained rigid on the subject.

Thomas and Shelley, seated at the kitchen table amid the myriad
platters and compotes, moaned into their coffee. "Shel," whispered
Thomas, "is it my imagination or is Mah worse this year?"

Shelley chuckled. "Yeah, I noticed it, too, but what the hell. If it
makes her happy, let Mah do it up good. I noticed the way you bit your
tongue when you almost cussed."

Emmi declared flatly she liked New Year's celebrations. She didn't
get scolded or spanked. "Besides, I get a lot of money packets."

Thomas growled, "Get away from me, kid. Wait until you grow up,
then you'll know what it's like." He glanced over at Shelley. "If I were

you, I'd be home plenty early for dinner tonight and each night this week. Boy, will I be glad when Sunday comes. No more suffering and having to watch myself."

The morning of the final day of feasting, Emmi couldn't wait to inform her older brothers about the night's dinner. "Mah-Mah told me there's boiled pullet with mustard sauce, roast duck with plum sauce with those steamed white buns I love. Sweet and sour pork, red snapper with pickled scallions and that winter melon with that gooky stuffing. And, oh, yes, there's that minced oyster dish and seaweed soup, both dishes Mah-Mah said bring good luck and long life. I can't wait. I'm hungry now."

Shelley tousled Emmi's hair. "Me, too, sis."

The morning after the feast to close the New Year's celebrations, Liah awakened heavy with fatigue, no longer buoyed by the effervescent anticipation of New Year's. As she fumbled for her slippers, she was thankful that brunch was already cooked, yesterday's leftovers.

Professor came to see her late in the afternoon, disappointed by her tepid reaction to his announcement that all the men had consented to join the Council. Instead of being overjoyed, Liah moaned, "Ah me, it's as if I spent all my strength on the celebrations. Surely, in this town there should be one woman willing to take over my housework and laundry. Removing those burdens would make my life so much easier. But I am happy Cousin Shaw has agreed to join us. Maybe now at least I won't have to bear Sen's disapproval as well."

The scholar recalled the day when Sen had assailed his wife's efforts to unify the town. "My wife is beating her head against a stone wall. Our people are fated to a precarious life. Not only will they not raise a hand to help, but also they are at this moment ridiculing her. Don't you agree, sir?"

Liah had sensed Professor's discomfort. "I do not believe this is the time to air our differences. It's not fair to Professor."

She saw the worried expression currently darkening Professor's face and asked its cause.

"I was remembering Sen's words a few weeks earlier when he said your fatigue was due to your foolish efforts to unify Chinatown. I urge you to think now of your health and perhaps discontinue your ideas of a Council."

Liah winced, recalling that argument with Sen and her answer to his outrage after Professor had left. "You know very well I've never neglected either you or the children. Perhaps that is the reason for my fatigue. As for the Council, you also know very well it is for the children's future that I'm doing it."

She blinked to shut out the memory of Sen's retort. "Yet, it is you, my wife, who catapulted us from the estate. I tell you now, you never hoodwinked me. I know we had the option of staying on. I allowed you to move. You see, you're not the only one who thinks of the children."

Unknown to Liah, Sen's anger had been partially due to the guilt he felt. He had seen Seragio a month earlier and he'd declared Sen a smart man to leave when he did. "New people stingy. Work harder, less pay, my friend."

Meanwhile, Liah and Professor were setting a date for the first Council meeting: the seventeenth day of March. For the rest of Professor's visit, he and Liah enjoyed their tea and teacakes, consumed by their own thoughts, Liah planning for the Council's supper, Professor wondering if he was right in taking part.

After he left, he continued to worry about how the townspeople would react to the levies; he hoped they'd not see him as a partner in Liah's efforts and blame him. Unlike her, Professor had to walk the streets and face any residents' disdain or anger. Professor decided something had to be done to shield his integrity. The preservation of his name and acceptability in Chinatown gnawed at the scholar. Why had he so foolishly agreed with Liah's plans?

Late that evening, almost one o'clock in the morning, a figure emerged from the shadows in Peacock Alley and darted over to the bulletin board under the acacia tree. The man quickly tacked a sheet of paper onto the wooden board and scurried across the street, darting back into Number Four.

Back inside his house, Professor muttered, "First, we'll tell them of the services and the taxes but without details, then later we'll tell them how much it will cost." He felt guilty about not planning to lay everything on the table from the outset, but reasoned he needed to be strategic, for it was he who'd suffer the backlash of any ire people had. He was sorry for any repercussions Liah would suffer; still, she was stronger than he. And besides, weren't the plans hers? A determined expression crossed his face. "This time we'll do things my way." For the next three days, he would hole up in his room, he decided. He chuckled. "That should be time enough for Liah to cool down." Over those three days, he'd spend his time working on the calligraphy he'd not had time to do.

Professor lit the tiny lamp on his writing table. He glanced at the three characters he'd carved for Liah: health, wealth and happiness. The wooden dowels at each end of the wooden scroll were lacquered black while the raised characters were gilded gold. He thought to give them to her when they next met but rejected the idea. Why should he offer up a consolation bribe? He'd done nothing wrong. Liah's potential anger still worried the scholar, but he felt a pleasant anticipation of the next few days of tranquility and meditation during his self-imposed absence from Liah and Council issues. Suddenly, his two small rooms became a warm, safe fortress, something he'd never felt before. As he started to prepare the ink, he contemplated the ink stick in his hand, recalling the four treasures to a scholar: his ink stick, his ink well, his brush and his paper. Well, he had them all!

Sen returned home from work the next morning, entering through the back door and wrathfully confronted Liah. "What are you trying to do? No fewer than five men accosted me on my way home, demanding to know what my wife was trying to do. What's all this nonsense about taxation and free public services? The men swore to never pay taxes and said for me to tell you so."

Liah was stunned. Her curiosity about how the men had found out tortured her, but she dared not ask. She hurriedly served up his meal and fled into the front room to think. When she heard the bedroom door slam, she hurried to the kitchen to await the return of Eldest Son. He would summon Professor. Surely, he would know how the news leaked out.

By the time Eldest Son returned home from work, Liah had almost convinced herself that it had been Wong Sang who had spread the news. Liah started thinking about appropriate punishment, but she drew back, deciding to wait until she had spoken to Professor.

When Eldest Son informed her Professor wasn't home, Liah sighed. Perhaps he'd gone to Fahn Gwai town to do business or perhaps he'd gone to Wong's Café. Never mind, she told Eldest Son; she'd just have to wait.

When Fourth Son didn't find the scholar home after supper, Liah began to worry. It was unlike Professor to be gone without leaving word. She'd try again later.

The clock struck ten and Liah shuddered, hoping Sen would've lost his anger when he awakened for work. A few moments later, Sen strode from the bedroom, going directly to the toilet without a glance and without a word. Liah knew he was still as angry as before.

As he picked up his chopsticks, Sen leaned back in his chair, staring at her malevolently. In a desperate attempt to stave off a quarrel, Liah murmured, "I can't believe it's over a year since we moved here. Have you noticed the green shrubberies and even the honeysuckle vines are putting forth new shoots and flowering? To tell you the truth, I never believed a year ago, I could revive them."

Sen made no comment and the silence hung heavy between them. At length he muttered, "To tell the truth? Ha!"

Liah bit her lower lip. "Do you know there are over a thousand of our countrymen in China Street and that there are as many more in the produce area across town? Time certainly flies, doesn't it?"

"Oh," snarled Sen, "time may fly for you, my wife, but I do not spend time scheming to snatch money from our people for whatever excuse." His eyes narrowed. "And I don't have an Apinyin trade either."

Liah recoiled. While she suspected Sen knew about her illicit business, she didn't know he objected to it. Why hadn't he berated her before now? Before she could say a word, Sen released his venom. "And don't think you can patronize me, Liah. All of your constant talk about how much money you've made. Don't believe for a moment I haven't seen the scum who darken our door. One day you will bring the House of Lee down around our feet. I say desist from the trade and meddling in town politics. Quit before you get killed."

Any thought she had of telling Sen about the proposed Council vanished. Quietly, she packed his lunch of rice, garlic ribs and chards. Sen wrenched the pail out of her hand and without a word strode out the back door.

Liah leaned back weakly in the chair, automatically taking a sip of tea. For the first time in her married life she cringed at the moment when she'd have to confront Sen with the news. How, she thought, could Sen so easily forget their destitute days? Surely, he must know why she was peddling Apinyin. Surely, he must remember the terror of Fahn Gwai violence and that she only wanted to safeguard their home and their lives. She heaved herself from the chair and began to assemble the dishes. Ah, me, she moaned silently, if only she could find a woman to help with the children and the housework.

Liah made one last attempt to find Professor. When told by Eldest Son the scholar still wasn't home, Liah began to feel panic. Could he have met with foul play? But by whom and where? It couldn't have happened in China Street, for by now word would have gotten around town. If it had occurred in Fahn Gwai town, then all was lost. Did she dare to break a rule and have Eldest Son call the police? Liah shook her head no.

Immediately, she went to her bedroom, lit a stick of incense and fell to her knees, beseeching Kwan Yin for intervention and protection for Professor. Softly, she moaned. Professor was a good man, a wise man and, more than anything, she needed him to bring her plans for the Council to fruition; Kwan Yin must know how important he was.

Liah was seated in her chair the next day, trying to shake the sleep from her sluggish body and mind; worry over Professor's disappearance was beginning to take a toll on her nerves. In a lethargic awareness, she heard the front door open and close with a bang. Angry footsteps sounded in the corridor and a voice she recognized as the butcher's shouted her name. A moment later, he burst into the kitchen, his reddened face sharpened by angry eyes.

"What," Kwong Wah demanded, "gives you the right to tax us? By what authority do you scheme to fleece us?"

Her first reaction was fury at the man's audacity in bursting into her private chambers, but she steeled her anger and pointed to a seat. "Ah, sir, I'm glad you did not stand on formality and came directly into my home. Do be seated and have a cup of tea and some cakes."

Kwong Wah's anger vanished as he realized his faux pas. "I was so upset, I forgot my manners, but since I'm here, I want you to know I object to whatever taxation you have in mind."

Liah poured him a cup of tea and motioned for him to be seated. "I am happy you feel like family, sir and don't let's dwell on protocol. Let us become more acquainted. Let me explain the taxation in full detail. With your intelligence and civic interest, I'm sure you'll agree with me when I conclude my explanation." She smiled benevolently. The butcher reluctantly sat down, lowering his eyes as he battled against his own misgivings at confronting a female.

With deliberation, Liah outlined the plans for a Council and laws to govern China Street. Lastly, she adroitly asserted Professor's hand in the conception of the plan, saying he too thought a language school for the children and aid for the needy and aged were splendid ideas. Kwong Wah's defenses wavered; if Professor was the author of the plan, then it wasn't the she-devil's greedy scheme to bleed the town. Swayed by Professor's participation, the butcher nodded his reluctant agreement with the plan. His unspoken concern was the amount of the taxes he'd have to pay. He was not known for generosity or, for that matter, honesty.

"Well," Kwong Wah said as he rose, "I must go to work. I thank you for the tea and shall consult with the other businessmen and should they have questions or objections, I will enlighten them." Down deep, Kwong Wah felt pride that he was now in Liah's inner circle.

In the late afternoon, when Liah went out to the cobblestones to water her garden, she spied a notice on the trellis wall. Looking about, she spied Elder Fong On and asked him what it said. As she listened, Liah was aghast. What had possessed Professor to perform such an outrageous act and without her permission? Her anger overcame her worry. Where was that man?

By the time supper was over, Liah's anger turned again to fear for Professor's safety, but no matter her worst fears, she would not allow Eldest Son to call the police. Once inside, it would be difficult to keep them out. She'd have to wait.

Liah drew a sigh of relief after Sen left for work. While he was taciturn, he didn't berate her. She picked up his supper dishes, took them to the sink and then sat down with a cup of brandy tea. It seemed she was more fatigued than usual, but then the day had not been easy. She relived the confrontation with the butcher, wondering if she could in truth consider him an ally.

The grandfather clock had begun chiming eleven o'clock when there came a rapping at the front door. Liah's first reaction was fear, fear it was Fahn Gwai, then fear that the knock boded disastrous news. She hastily walked into the corridor, then slowly and reluctantly she approached the heavy wooden doors. She turned on the outside light, cursing the obstruction of the shutters. She cried out for identification and was shocked to hear the scholar's voice.

"Just a moment, sir," she cried, as she labored to remove the heavy four-by-four post from its U-shaped cradles. Cautiously, she peered through the locked screens and determined that indeed, it was Professor.

"What happened to you, sir?" she cried as she unlocked the screen doors. "You've half-scared me to death. I was almost ready to notify the police."

Professor helped lock the three locks, then followed Liah to the kitchen. Involuntarily, he gulped a deep breath, for the explanation he owed her would not to be easy.

Liah listened to Professor confess that he'd posted the notice in Peacock Alley, that he was sick to death with the stupid furor of people and, most of all, sick to death trying to please everyone. "For the first time, I was true to my own desires."

"It isn't you who have to contend with people." He stared into Liah's glowering face. "Also, I kept away for I wanted none of your anger, either."

Liah's anger gone, her voice was gentle. "Sir, I know I have a fiery nature, but between you and me there can always be room for compromise. I fully understand and sympathize with your position and perhaps it hasn't been so detrimental, this notice of yours."

They shared a light repast and Professor smiled as she recounted her meeting with the butcher as well as with three other businessmen who had come by to protest the taxation.

Long after Professor's departure, Liah sat in her chair, contemplating this heretofore unknown side of the scholar. Good, she thought. He'll need all his inner strength in the days ahead. With a sigh she glanced at the clock: twelve-thirty. No use wasting good sleeping time looking too far ahead. With a nod, she rose, shut off the kitchen lights and went into her bedroom.

FIRST COUNCIL MEETING

The morning of the seventeenth dawned gray and windy. Guiltily, Liah cursed her own cowardice for not having told Sen of the Council meeting that evening, but his mood had been so surly. The morning meal was noisy. Theo was belligerent at his sister's insistence that he hurry. Liah glared at Eldest Daughter, her expression clearly conveying that she'd brook no fighting this day. Theo mumbled under his breath that if Flo didn't stop badgering him, he'd see she was thrown off the team.

Liah turned her fury on Third Son. "You and Eldest Daughter had better not argue this day or else I'll severely punish the both of you."

Flo noisily banged the pots and pans when Liah walked over to the sink. Teeth clenched, Liah hissed, "Let your father berate me because of your argument with your brother and I'll make you sorry." Liah started to walk away and then turned with another warning. "If I were you, I'd make certain tonight's supper is to your father's liking. This day's inaugural Council meeting is as much for the good of you children as it is for us adults. Make no mistake; all of you had better behave."

Sen came from the bedroom at eleven o'clock. He noted only one place setting on the table. Before he could ask, Liah told him the children were already gone; they had an important ball game. Sen was furious; he berated his children for their lack of respect and consideration. "They can't wait to share a meal with their father? We can't eat as a family?"

He glared at Liah, adding caustically, "I can't really blame them, not with the example set by their mother. Disobedience is a contagious disease. If we can't eat as a family, then we are a family apart."

Liah felt goose pimples on the back of her neck. Silently she beseeched the Goddess to avert a quarrel. Gently, patiently, she asked Sen to forgive the children. "If you must be angered, then be angered with me. I gave them permission to leave. They seemed anxious to be at the playground." She paused, "Sen, if we are to remain a family we ought to allow them some independent activities. They are good children, and weekends are the only time they can enjoy their sports."

"Oh?" sneered Sen. "So now I'm not deserving of their consideration? Well, know this: I am the one who keeps a roof over our heads. I am the one who puts food on the table and clothes on their backs. I am the one who crawls into the steaming engines to clean out the smut and slime from their bellies. Let them see how their father earns his money!"

Sen shoved aside the plate Liah set before him. He leaped to his feet, declaring he'd eat elsewhere. His appetite was ruined. Abruptly, he pushed aside the chair and stormed into the bedroom, returning a few moments later dressed and with hat in hand. Liah gingerly asked when he expected to be home for supper. "To a home where children are disobedient and a wife who is deaf to her husband's orders?" He wrenched open the back door, slamming his way out without an answer.

Liah stared at the back door and shook her head. Well, there was not time to dwell on Sen's anger; there was the dinner to prepare for the men. An hour and a half later, Liah stood back, surveying the table: cold pineapple duck, cold cracked crab, barbecued pork and spiced spareribs with the marinade Cousin Quock had taught her to make in the days when they lived in Dai Faw. There was also a huge platter of deveined shrimp to be sautéed in their shells in a special spiced salt. Finally, there was a compote of sliced bamboo shoots, black mushrooms, sea urchin, water chestnuts and baby peas to be quickly stir-fried at the last minute.

She bathed and dressed in her blue satin cheongsam. The cascade of silver embroidered lotus blossoms from the right shoulder to the hem sparkled in the lamplight. So many years earlier Cousin Wah had given it to her when they lived on the estates. Now, at long last, she'd have reason to wear it. A few minutes later, Eldest Daughter, breathless from her last-minute sprint from the playground, ran into her mother in the corridor and stopped in her tracks. "Oh, Mah-Mah, you are beautiful!"

Liah, very pleased, thought how satisfying are compliments from another female were. Flo followed her mother into the kitchen, prattling on about a wonderful boy she had met at the playground.

Liah brushed a damp strand of hair off Flo's forehead and held up her hand for silence. "Not now, daughter, speak of this later. Mother has too much on her mind now. Just be certain you do nothing to rile your father. Now, you know exactly what to do?"

"Oh, I know what to do, Mah-Mah. You told me three times. I'll keep the kids quiet and have supper exactly at six o'clock. They'll do their chores quietly."

Liah frowned. "Well, do not be too overbearing or else Third Brother will be angry. We cannot have a fight today."

Professor was first to arrive. Liah was shocked when he declared they'd made an error in the budget; the figure would be much larger than they thought. Liah waved aside his lamentations that perhaps the men might not accept the large number. Too late to worry now; the outcome was now in the hands of the Gods.

Footsteps in the corridor announced that Cousin Shah had arrived. He placed two large pastry boxes on the table, declaring he'd seen them in a Fahn Gwai shop. "There's enough for the men and the children."

A moment later, Kam Fong entered, acting ill-at-ease, as if he were an intruder as he made his way into the corridor to the private quarters of the house. He raised his eyebrows in surprise when he involuntarily quickly greeted Liah. How different she looked, he thought, recalling

Liah's everyday brown jacket and pants. Liah smiled as she reached out for the bottle of Ng Ga Pei Kam held in his outstretched hand. "I thank you, Kam, but it is not necessary to bring rice wine. We have plenty." She turned. "Shall we go upstairs while we wait for Sang and Chon? I'm certain they'll be here soon."

Moments later, footfalls on the stairs announced the arrival of those two men. Chon, usually blasé, was shocked when he saw Liah's rich brocaded cheongsam. He couldn't help thinking how much younger she looked. Wong Sang's reaction to the transformation was as marked as Chon's, but for different reasons. His desire to obtain Liah's financial backing was increased by this show of affluence. Such expensive clothing and jewelry—she had to be wealthy. A sudden thought struck him as he recalled Professor's discussion of the Council with Liah as chairman. In exchange for her backing, she could be chairman or whatever else she wanted. Quickly, Sang cast a furtive glance at Chon, trying to evaluate the bar owner's thoughts. Chon's expression gave Sang to know he'd better act quickly if he wanted to beat Chon to asking first.

Liah smiled, welcomed the men and thanked them for their promptness. Eagerly, she impressed upon them that theirs was the task of promoting a safer and better China Gai in which they'd all live permanently, with free services for the needy and ill and, more importantly, a school for their children. "Before Professor outlines the Tenet of Laws, I'd like to ask each of you to think deeply about your motives for being a Council member. Not for personal gain, not for prestige, but with a total dedication toward keeping China Gai safe and to make life better for those who are not as fortunate as we."

"Liah," protested Chon. "I think you're being overly dramatic. You're only recalling the past, when Fahn Gwai were opposed to us. Why would they attack us now?"

Liah had no chance to chide Chon, for Professor rose, his face grim. "Chon, preparedness never hurt. Besides you're wrong. There will always be a need to protect ourselves."

Cousin Shah sat rigidly silent during Professor's account, then rose and solemnly corroborated Professor's story, added several grisly examples of his own. "Not only did these events occur, but the police did nothing to stop them. So, if you think today we have the Fahn Gwai's sympathy or protection, I am afraid, Chon, you are in for a surprise."

Wong Sang glowered. Why did Chon have to mention those things? In his mind, it conjured up grim memories of the men's last cries for Kwan Koong's mercy and for the ones who escaped the noose to look after their families.

Professor's eyes were misty. "The sounds of death are ever with us, submerged until they surface once again. One never forgets. Just believe Shah and me, for we speak without exaggeration."

Cousin Shah gruffly muttered it happened and would happen again. "If the Council can prevent another such occurrence, it will be worth all of our efforts. Remember this: The Fahn Gwai are fickle and, because we are aliens, many even illegal aliens, the need to keep China Gai secure is paramount."

Chon Woo lowered his eyes in silence. He was infuriated at Liah's outward show of wealth. How then, were the furnishings so shabby? Perhaps she was the kind who hoarded money. In that case, of what use was Liah to him?

Liah's warning jolted Chon from his unspoken anger. "Anyone who uses his seat on the Council to garner personal gain shall be severely punished, publicly denounced and ousted. Think well now, for later will be too late."

There was silence as Professor explained the structure of the Council, patterned after their eight-sided figure, the Baht Gwa. "Eight sides of balance with eight members. A ninth seat is provided for a young man who shows he is worthy and interested in his community. His seat, the ninth, is for representation, but carries with it no voting power until the young man has earned the right."

There was a slight stir as Professor mentioned the chairmanship with a secretary and a treasurer. "The Chairmanship carries with it no power to vote except in ties. At that time, the chairman casts the tie-breaking vote. Now, to outline the boundaries of China Gai and those areas where our protection and services will cover."

The official boundaries included the three main streets: Marchesson Street, Dragon's Den Road and Lion's Den Alley, bound at one end by Alameda South and at the other, Mah Loo. Included was Peacock Alley.

Wong Sang objected. "Why should the people who live on the other side of Ahlamedah Gai be left out?"

Professor retorted patiently. "People who live on Fargo Gai and Dahminch Gai are not being ignored, Sang. It's just that in the beginning our money and resources will not cover so large an area. We shall include them later when our finances allow."

The regulations governing public disputes and those between private parties that could not be solved were to be arbitrated by the Council. Professor noticed Cousin Shah's smile, giving him to believe the man was pleased so far. Professor readjusted his spectacles and looked hard at Chon and Woo. "Now we come to the most stringent regulation... treason. When it is proven that one of us has cooperated with the Fahn Gwai or has abetted in his penetration of our town, the penalty shall be death. In the case of such an act, hearings will be held. These will be the only Council hearings attended by outsiders; two members from each Tong will be present at the hearings and at the sentencing. These hearings will be essential before a life is taken."

"Death?" gasped Chon. "Isn't that extreme? And what gives us the power? People will never accept this."

"They will when the facts are publicized and if their lives are put in jeopardy. We cannot prevent evil-doers from residing in our town, but we can dictate under what conditions they live."

Liah's voice was solemn as she reminded the men, "The punishment must fit the crime. Shall we continue?"

It was Chon who questioned the need for a school or a temple. "After all, if we can't take care of the people on the other side of Ahlamedah Gai, how can we afford a school or a temple? And where is all the money coming from?"

"I was hoping you would allow me to systematically outline the Tenets, but if you must know, the money will come from the levies we hope will be enough."

"Taxes?" grimaced Chon. "None of the business houses will agree to pay. It's hard enough to make money without having to shell out money at the end of the month for taxes. What happens when the men refuse to pay?"

"Are you certain it is the men you're speaking of, Chon, and not yourself? Well, never mind. For the men who refuse to pay, it will be noticeable when their names are publicly listed at the end of each month. It is our intention that at each month-end, a business statement be posted, noting the money coming in and how the money was used. The contributors will be listed, along with the amount of their taxes and, for those who refuse, the amounts they failed to pay." Professor looked abruptly at Chon.

Sang grinned. "Yeah, so then the townspeople can boycott the stores who are not cooperating."

"That's blackmail, Professor," Chon snarled at Sang. "Just because you don't work or have a business, you can afford to laugh. Just you wait. People will never believe the taxes will be used for them instead of being privately pocketed."

Professor scowled. "Chon, how can you think there's a chance of discrepancy? Not only will there be a monthly accounting, but at year-end, there will be a chance for anyone to examine our books. And for each payment of taxes, they will be given receipts."

"How much in taxes must we pay?" Chon was belligerent. "How do you know the businessmen will be able to afford it?"

"The businesses are divided into types. For the stores who sell only to our people, the taxes are less than, for example, a curio shop or a bar that caters to Fahn Gwai. Because of Fahn Gwai trade, profits are higher and so will be the taxes. Services, like laundries, undertaking and herb shops will also be taxed less than the places that deal with Fahn Gwai."

Kam Fong timidly turned to Liah. "I do not think Chon means that there will be dishonesty, but in the past we've donated monies to the town's funds and never saw anything done and never were told what became of the funds. I think this plan is well conceived and in the future should anyone have doubts he can always ask to see the books. I do not think you have to doubt, Chon."

At five o'clock, sounds of the children returning from the playground distracted Liah. For a few minutes, her mind shifted to the kitchen and she prayed to Kwan Koong that Eldest Daughter would obey her. She needed none of Sen's wrath.

Kam Fong wondered how the other three members would be chosen. Professor explained, "By vote of the charter members. One more fact: The man who nominates a new member will be physically and morally responsible for his good and bad deeds. Such a provision is made to prevent collusion among members for whatever reasons."

"That's unfair, Professor," argued Chon. "Why should we be responsible for another man's bad behavior?"

Cousin Shah spoke up and said the ruling had merit. "Besides," he chuckled, "we haven't got a Council yet, so why worry about new members?" The tension broke. Shah asked seriously, "There are so many regulations, how are we to remember them all?"

"Each man," announced Professor, "will receive his copy of the Tenets and so will future members. I think if all discussion is done, we should vote whether to accept the Tenet of Laws."

Liah smiled and said, "We should have supper first, then vote. If you'll excuse me, I'll prepare the food. It won't take long."

Dinner done, Liah passed the platter of pastries Cousin Shah had brought.

Sang praised the crab, especially its unusual marinade. This gave Chon the courage to ask Liah for the recipe. Liah smiled sweetly, thinking what a scoundrel. There was no way she'd give Chon Cousin Quock's recipe to make money in his bar. Instead, she demurred, "The recipe is not mine for the giving, but if you like, I'll make it for you any time you want."

Without rancor, the men unanimously ratified the Tenet of Laws.

As they lined up to affix their signatures to the Tenet of Laws. Liah was last to sign. She glanced out of the corner of her eye as she brushed her name along side the others and saw the shocked expressions on both Chon and Sang's faces that a mere female could write! Let them think so. Who would know that in truth that Liah could only write her name and the names of her husband and children?

Wong Sang's surprise changed to an expression that made Liah feel he believed it was natural that a woman of her ambitions and force would know how to write. She handed the brush to Professor who solemnly held the document up. He gave a sigh and thought that perhaps the many days and nights of hard thought and work had been worth it.

Professor's face shone with pride as he held the document for the men to see. "We are now a town, a town with a Council and a Tenet of Laws. The next business of the day is the election of our officers."

The air became charged when Professor opened the nominations for chairman and nominated Liah. Wong Sang asked fearfully if it weren't too soon to choose their leader. "After all, we must discuss why and whom we select."

Cousin Shah agreed. "We have so many issues to address ourselves. Why not postpone the selection of officers to another time? Give us a chance to think more of the right person for each job."

Kam Fong smiled. "Yes, Cousin Shah is right. Many of us need time to think over what's taken place today and adjust ourselves to the task of government. I, for one, have never given much thought to a unified

China Gai, let alone a governing body. I need time to let things soak into my brain. At least we've ratified the Tenets. That's a beginning. Set another date for the election of officers. The hour grows late and I am an early riser. My laundry demands it so."

Chon vowed before the week was over he'd go and discuss the Council with Liah and give her reason to believe he approved of her leadership of the Council. He'd have to beat Sang to asking her first.

Liah was crestfallen, but she displayed no evidence of her disappointment. Professor asked for a calendar. "What do you say about reconvening on the twenty-seventh of April? Same hour."

The meeting adjourned. Wong Sang leered licentiously at Chon, suggesting they investigate what was ambling around town. Liah said, "I'd suggest you give sober thought to whether you ought to join the Council, Sang. See to it that in the future you are honest, or else things might not go well with you."

Sang whipped about, having it in mind to tell Liah to go to hell, but bit his tongue as he thought about opening his gambling house. He must not forfeit her friendship. They exchanged knowing glances and Sang giggled nervously as he nodded and exited through the door.

Liah remained at the table, her disappointment that she'd not been elected chairman very apparent. Suddenly, it occurred to her: Perhaps Chon or Sang might finagle the chairman's seat. No, never! Fear closed in. She fought back her tears, fought the fatigue tugging at the back of her neck and cursed her stupidity for not insisting Professor remain to discuss the meeting.

One thought dovetailed with another as Liah remembered when she asked Professor if Sen's accusation was right: that it was unflattering to women when they indulged in men's activities. The scholar had replied, "Madam, I cannot answer for you what is right and what is wrong, certainly not what is womanly. You alone can divine that answer."

It was unfair, thought Liah to involve him in a husband-and-wife argument, but she had needed reassurance. Liah shook her head now.

No, it wasn't unwomanly to indulge in a town's government, not when there was no other to take the reins. Unwomanly to ensure her children and grandchildren had a place to live, to work and to love? Besides, she thought bitterly, it did not matter if she were womanly or not. Sen no longer sought her body.

Sen's angry voice floated upstairs, jolting Liah back to reality. She rushed to the kitchen in time to hear Sen quelling an argument between Eldest Daughter and Third Son. Liah stood silently in the doorway, scowling. The argument ended abruptly. Silence engulfed the once-noisy kitchen. Liah instructed the children to go upstairs and bring the dishes. "We will share a late supper."

Liah caught Sen eyeing the pastry box and immediately opened it. "Cousin Shah brought them for the children. Here, try this one, Sen. It's filled with whipped cream and the crust is so flakey."

Sen went directly to bed after eating while Liah and Eldest Daughter cleaned up the kitchen. Alone afterwards, Liah groaned at the time. Almost one o'clock and Sen would awaken at two-thirty. Once more, she lamented not having a helper in the house. She went directly to her altar and offered up a prayer of thanks to Kwan Yin and a plea to the Goddess for a helper.

When Liah finally crawled into bed and felt Sen's warmth, desire welled within her. She deplored her lust, closed her eyes, and tried to sleep, then cursed when sleep would not come. Her body twitched, burning with desire, but knew Sen would only turn her away. "How long," she moaned, "can I take this rejection?"

Sen was punishing her for her activities on the Council, she thought. But didn't he know at the same time he was wreaking terrible punishment on himself? Finally, her body crumpled with fatigue, Liah fell asleep.

—

Liah smoked impatiently until her children left for school. Once they had left, she bolted and locked the front doors, then crawled wearily into bed. Soon she crawled back out of bed, set up her Apinyin tray and took a few light puffs. Just enough, she thought, to induce sleep.

At four o'clock in the afternoon, Liah was rudely awakened by a rapping at the rear door and faintly she heard her children shouting. Groggily, she glanced up at the clock, shocked that she could sleep away almost an entire day. She stumbled from bed, groped for her slippers, plodded into the kitchen.

Mert was first to push through the door, anxiously asking if his mother was ill. "The front doors were locked, Mah-Mah."

Quickly, Liah shook her head and said she had been tired and had gone back to bed for a rest. She was sorry she'd slept so long. "Now if you will all put away your clothing and books, Mah-Mah will fix a snack for you."

Slowly, Liah sipped her cup of herbal tea, half-listening to Eldest Daughter as she proudly told her mother she had skipped an entire grade. She was now in the twelfth grade. "Just think, Mah-Mah, one more year then I'll be finished with high school."

Theo told Flo to quit bragging at which Flo turned and angrily retorted, "Just because you had trouble with your teacher, don't take it out on me."

Theo growled, "That old bitty just doesn't like me or maybe she just doesn't like Chinese."

Liah frowned. William quickly explained that it wasn't the teacher's fault. Theo hadn't done his homework and failed his spelling test.

Theo scowled and made a threatening move when Liah reached out, grabbed his right ear and drew him close. "I will not tolerate any laziness or fighting in this house. You, my Third Son, will study and bring home good marks, or else I'll ship you back to Hong Kong where they punish lazy students." She narrowed her eyes. "And if I find you've done harm to Fourth Son, I'll whip you until you faint. He, in truth, was doing you a favor. You must study."

Liah awakened that night to the sound of rain on the skylight and tried to arouse Sen. "What shall we do? Our eldest sons are at work without their rain clothes."

Sen mumbled sleepily. "Go to sleep. I told them to take their rain clothes."

Liah cuddled up to her husband in relief. She clasped her arms about his waist and moved her legs over his. Sen ran his hand over her legs and patted her buttocks as he moved away. "Go to sleep, I have to work at three this morning."

The hours crawled as Liah fought the painful furnace in her loins, finally crying out her agonies to the Goddess. She whispered into the minhois, "Oh, please, benevolent lady, give my husband to know I can't live without him." She lamely added a postscript: "If it is within your mercy to spare me, please, please also find me someone to help with the house." Her prayers done, Liah wearily rose from her bed and went to the kitchen.

COOK COMES TO NUMBER THREE

April fifth was heady with the promise of spring and the sun fell warm on Professor's back as he crossed the street to the cobblestone walk. Liah, he mused, was indeed a privileged person with the Gods. Her life had a way of straightening out after each blind bend in the river. Professor recalled her lament for a woman to help in the house. Well, he thought, it isn't a woman, but perhaps Liah would settle. He halted at the entrance of Peacock Alley and chided himself, "Why am I trying to decide? It's her house, her problem."

Liah listened intently as Professor described a man who he thought might solve Liah's household help problem. "Quiet-mannered, soft-spoken. I understand he has excellent talents, being adept in both Chinese cooking and the Fahn Gwai's. He learned to cook Fahn Gwai when working on the railroad, later working for a rancher up north. If you're interested, I will have him stop in to speak with you."

Liah nodded eagerly and asked if Professor had warned him that she had seven children. Professor said that he had not told the man anything other than that Liah needed help. Professor was anxious to be away. "I'll have the man stop in."

"Of course, Professor. I understand that it was not your place to speak of my needs. I'll see him tomorrow if he can come. By the way, what is the man's name?"

"Taam Loong and one word of advice, Liah, give him a try. I know you're looking for a woman, but your situation demands immediate relief. However, it's your decision. I must be getting along now."

"Thank you, Professor. I am grateful for your help, sir. I'll speak with Loong tomorrow. Thank you again, sir."

The next afternoon at three o'clock a gaunt-faced, very thin man came to Number Three. He appeared fortyish, neatly dressed in a well-worn dark blue woolen suit. At once Liah sensed a sadness about him. He was very tall, looking even taller because of his paleness and his thin, bony body.

Taam Loong understood Madam needed a housekeeper. Liah motioned for Loong to be seated. While he spoke, Liah noticed his well-sculptured hands. She agreed with Professor, Loong was indeed soft-spoken and refined. His voice tensed, as it seemed he was almost pleading. "I am in need of a place to live and a job. Although I have never worked for a woman, I am willing to try. You see, my former employer was a bachelor."

He said he not only cooked but also did housework and laundry. Liah stirred in her upholstered chair at the man's mention that he prided himself on being not only a wise shopper but also a shrewd bargainer. "I am certain I can do the work, Madam."

Liah recognized the slight tremor in the man's voice, betraying the same desperation she had felt so many years earlier when waiting for Sen in the dark damp cave. She glanced up at the wall clock and murmured that it would be fine if they'd share a late lunch. "I have not eaten and we can discuss the details of the job while we eat."

Loong's meticulous use of chopsticks did not escape Liah's scrutiny; she thanked Kwan Yin for sending not only an able, talented man but also one of refinement. Casually, so as not to embarrass Loong, she asked if he minded children, a good many, for she had seven.

He shook his head, inquiring their ages. Liah was proud as she informed Loong her two eldest sons were twenty and nineteen years old, that they worked in the produce market on the other side of town. "My two eldest will not need looking after, but the others still need guidance and care. My eldest daughter, age seventeen is the one to be careful with. She not only has a temper but stubbornness as well. It will be your task to see to it she does her share of the household chores. My Third Son is sixteen, my Fourth Son is fifteen and Fifth Son is fourteen. Our youngest daughter is ten years old. Not babies, yet needing discipline."

Liah glanced quickly at the man across the table, saying very softly, "I think ten, no fifteen dollars per month for room and board. Is that satisfactory with you, sir? I shall be indeed grateful if you will take care of the laundry and the meals. The housework can be done by all of us."

"Ten dollars will be sufficient, Madam. If you will allow me time to go and pick up my things at the hotel, I will take up my duties today."

A surge of emotion engulfed Liah for reasons she did not understand. There was no certainty Loong would be suitable or even if he was able, but something about him seemed to comfort her. Ah, the Gods were good. She smiled and once more warned Loong that for the pittance he received, she did not expect him to be a slave in the house. "I want you to ensure the children do their daily chores and if they refuse, to make it known to me. You are to let them know, especially Eldest Daughter, you are here to alleviate the pressure on me and not to afford them a life of luxury, which they certainly do not deserve. In this regard, I hope you will do exactly as I ask."

Liah paused a long moment, then giggled. "Oh, no doubt you've heard about my temper; if not, you will. I am a person of little patience and when someone blocks what I am trying to do, I usually give vent to my anger Otherwise, I am usually a woman of a peaceful nature."

While he listened, Taam Loong decided Liah was forthright, surely a loving mother. In the hour and a half they'd met, Loong couldn't fathom his strange sense of being drawn to her. He also sensed her fatigue, the fatigue of someone who had labored too long, too arduously and was about to fall. Well, Loong concluded, who wouldn't be worn out with seven children to care for? Loong wondered what kind of husband would allow his wife to work to the brink of exhaustion.

When Taam Loong left for the hotel, Liah rushed into her bedroom, lit incense and knelt in gratitude before Kwan Yin. Then she returned to the front room to await Loong. She leaned her head against the cushions, thinking only to rest but fell asleep. An hour later, Liah opened her eyes, looked about and became panic-stricken. He hadn't returned. He'd changed his mind. She was almost in tears. How could she be so wrong about someone?

She felt tears of disappointment and fought to keep from sobbing. Liah felt such weakness, her body refused to move as she heaved, trying to get to her feet. With the possibility of Loong's presence and his taking over the household chores, she'd allowed herself the extravagance of feeling her fatigue. Up till now, Liah had kept that fatigue at bay.

Kwan Yin, she thought, wouldn't allow such a thing to happen. Wasn't it so that the Goddess was also a woman and knew of a woman's need for rest? Perhaps it was the seven children that had frightened Loong off? Perhaps he'd heard of the quarrel between her and Sen over her activities on the Council? Liah sighed. Surely she could not blame Loong; there were easier ways of making a living.

With great effort, she heaved herself from the deep cushions of the upholstered chair. There was supper to prepare and it would not do to anger Sen. A clatter in the kitchen sent Liah flying into the corridor.

She burst into the kitchen and found Taam Loong, his arms folded, his legs akimbo, staring at Eldest Daughter. Liah gasped. Loong turned. "I instructed Eldest Daughter to dry the dishes, that her younger brother would wash, but she had other ideas."

A scowl crossed Liah's face and Loong quickly held up his hand to restrain her. "Do not allow yourself to be angered, please. I can resolve the problem. If I am to remain, Eldest Daughter must understand my word is law."

A surge of relief flooded Liah's body. He had not only returned but had taken up his duties without fanfare. Not only was he efficient, but also the look on his face gave her to believe he actually could control Eldest Daughter. Liah didn't know whether to laugh or cry.

When her emotional reaction dissipated, Liah was filled with fury. How dare her eldest daughter jeopardize the man's decision to remain on the job? Liah walked to her daughter and pointed a menacing finger under her nose. "You will obey Loong. You will do as you're told, without questions and with haste. I demand you give the same respect and obedience to Loong as you give to me, Daughter. Is that clear?"

Liah whirled about, facing the other children. "And the same thing goes for all of you!"

Flo started banging the pots onto the shelf when Liah walked up and dug her nails into her arm. "I wouldn't damage a pot or a dish if I were you. Not if you want to live."

Liah's youngest child cried out happily that she'd finished all of her supper and that the food was good. "I ate all of it and Cook said I was a good girl."

Liah smiled indulgently, petted her second daughter's head and gave Cook an even bigger smile of gratitude. At that moment, Taam Loong became known as Cook.

It occurred to Loong that Liah's husband was not at the supper table and he asked if he should not set aside a plate for him. "Oh, I forgot," replied Liah. "If you will fix up a plate of food and leave it on the wok, I'll reheat it for him. And the lunch pail—each day when he brings it home, please make certain it is readied for another meal. I will pack his meal for work."

Sen took a taste of his late supper and looked up at his wife. Liah casually informed him that Cook had made the food. "I hired him this afternoon. He will live in one of the rooms upstairs. Do you not think he is a wonderful cook?"

Sen was shocked for a few seconds, then berated his wife. How dare she do such a thing without consulting him first? But then, what was the use? Did she obey when he forbade her to participate in town politics? He glowered. "Why the need for hired help? If you did not spend so much time on town foolishness, you would have plenty of time and energy to care for your home."

Liah rose from her seat and assembled her husband's lunch. Without another word, Sen finished his meal, put on his hat and sweater, picked up the lunch pail and walked out the rear door. Such a child, not to have said good night. Well, at least he did not rant and rave over Loong's presence in the house. Greatly relieved, but slightly guilty over what she'd done without her husband's consent, Liah went to her bedroom. It piqued her conscience to feel so light-hearted, but she could not quell her happiness.

Cook fell into their routine without trouble. Liah now had no need to go shopping, not when Loong brought home such quality food at bargain prices. Most of all, each time he went out, he brought Liah information from town and from the Tong rooms, which were inaccessible to her.

The townspeople noticed Liah's absence on the streets. Rumors flew about the new man in Number Three. Female gossips had it Liah was inflicted with a disfiguring disease, that she was bedridden; others wondered if the Apinyin had not destroyed her coordination. For wasn't it so she had a man to do her woman's work?

One afternoon, after overhearing such gossip, Cook returned from his shopping obviously angry. Liah asked the reason. When told, she replied smiling, "Oh, is that all? I wouldn't allow the gossips to annoy you, Cook. Don't you know it's ignorance or envy that directs their evil tongues? Poor souls. If speaking of my ills gives them pleasure, let them prattle."

However, Cook was not to be placated. Their unkindness and their ingratitude for what Liah was attempting to do for them rankled him. He vowed that the next time he encountered their cruel humor, he'd put them in their place.

Taam Loong not only took over the household chores, but he and Old Chan also lifted the grueling garden work from Liah's shoulders, leaving her only the pleasurable enjoyment of puttering around.

In time, Cook discovered Liah was a creature of habit. He did not find her temperamental, as people accused, but very disciplined, losing her temper only as a last resort. He was touched by Liah's generosity toward the needy, how she assisted them quietly, allowing them to retain their dignity without hint of charity. Liah, he saw, could caress her young daughter in a moment of love, but in the next moment, mete out a terrible punishment to a miscreant.

During her angry moods, Cook observed another of Liah's habits: she tapped the table with her chopsticks just before she lost her self-control. This barometer was to be Cook's most important means of measuring her moods.

One afternoon two and a half weeks later, Cook walked in on an argument between Eldest Daughter and Liah. He watched from the doorway, listening as Liah and Eldest Daughter exchanged words. Soon Liah walked to the table and sat down. Eldest Daughter was continuing her tantrum when Liah picked up her chopsticks and began drumming the table. Seconds later, without warning, Liah hurled a bowl of broth across the room.

Cook dropped his packages, rushed to the sink and grabbed a towel, which he tossed to Eldest Daughter, then bravely braced himself between the two women. Holding them at arm's distance, Cook ordered Eldest Daughter to go to her room.

Liah huffed and puffed, then fell into her upholstered chair. "She will be the death of me. I must get her married off."

Cook picked up the shards of porcelain, threw them into the trash and mopped up the spill. Without a word, he reheated another bowl of brandy broth and set it before Liah. Liah parted her lips as if to apologize, but Cook's expression dissuaded her. She sank farther back in the cushions, head bowed as she murmured, "The girl was being insufferable."

While waiting for the broth to cool, Liah picked up her chopsticks and absentmindedly began to tap the table. She caught Cook's look of disapproval and quickly informed him that she knew it was bad manners, but she couldn't seem to stop it. "It's a bad habit, I know, but in truth I'm reining in my anger."

Cook gravely retorted, "Then I'll have to take them away from you."

Liah's eyes widened until she saw Cook's perturbed expression and relented. "Yes, you do that for me. I'll be eternally grateful."

It did not happen for a long time, but the first time he grabbed the chopsticks out of Liah's hands, his heart pounded; he half-expected her to turn her fury on him. Such ferocity he'd never seen in a person's eyes, but Liah, seeing his fright, quickly backed down. "Oh, my good friend, I was not aware. I thank you."

A tender, silent look flickered between them, then Cook turned his face to hide his unmasked emotions.

As the days passed, Cook became increasingly astounded by the countless demands placed upon Liah's waking hours. It was as if the townspeople, knowing the Council's certainty, came to her for assistance and advice. He knew now that Liah was not slothful, nor was her Apinyin habit robbing her of strength. He concluded that the family's constant drain on her energies, along with putting up with a moody and sometimes wrathful husband as well as the town's problems drained her physical reserves of strength. In the days that followed, Cook found himself policing people who stopped by, preventing most from disturbing her and allowing her to give audience only to matters of emergency.

In the day-to-day management of the house, Liah and Cook were of common thought and emotions. Neither ever spoke of their new-found intimacy, but both knew they were drifting into a dangerous vortex. Despite this knowledge, Liah could not help leaning on Cook more and more. The man's invaluable information and his keen insight into the core of matters saved Liah hours of decision-making.

Liah became aware of Cook's abilities in this arena when an altercation occurred between Chan Soo and a drifter from Dai Faw, a confrontation which two rival Tongs could've gotten swept up in. When the two rivals for a woman's affections and representatives from their respective Tongs came face to face, Liah was asked to intervene. Cook informed Liah that Chan Soo's woman, Gem Lai, was a flirt and Chan Soo, a jealous, possessive lover. Armed with his insight, Liah ordered Chan Soo to punish Gem Lai, and to order her to desist from her flirtatious ways. She also ordered Chan Soo to rein in his jealousy. The drifter was warned to stay away from Gem Lai, get a job and behave, or else move on.

After this, Liah approached Cook and offered him a partnership in her Apinyin trade. With him as legman, the buyers would no longer need to come to Number Three. Perhaps, she thought, Sen might be less irate.

CHINATOWN COUNCIL

The morning of the next Council meeting dawned gray. For this second session, she had none of the pressure of having to do household chores and prepare meals. At two o'clock, she leisurely relaxed in her bath. Her eyes caught the fresh coil of incense at the Kwan Yin's altar that she had lighted and prayed silently. Please, could the Goddess make possible her chairmanship of the Council? Suddenly, the bath lost its allure. Liah rinsed her body and silently whispered yet another prayer. "If it is predestined that my husband remains my husband, please convey to him that our marriage must continue to be consummated." Even before Kwan Yin, Liah was shy to discuss human sexuality; this prayer brought a pink tinge to her cheeks.

When Liah emerged from her bedroom at three o'clock, Cook was astounded. Clad in a blue, silk cheongsam with a cascade of bamboo embossed from the left shoulder to the right hem, Liah was transformed. With her blue matching slippers and dainty jade earrings, Liah was another woman. She giggled self-consciously. "I find my loose tunic and trousers more comfortable. However, if I am to impress Chon and Sang, I must endure the confinement of tight-fitting clothes."

Liah sighed as she sipped her brandy broth. Cook smiled. "I see the rest did you a great deal of good. To respect one's body is to take care of the mind it houses. I have no doubts you will function sharply today."

"I owe you not only the fact that I am rested but that my sanity is intact. I thank you for your concern."

Cook waved aside her gratitude, saying the main thing was to weld the town into a single unit of strength. "Just a word of caution, do not jeopardize your health in the doing. You are too important to too many people."

Liah quickly lowered her eyes. Somehow his words and tone made it impossible for her to hold his gaze. Nor did she dare to read too much into their meaning. She only knew what a difference there was between Cook's calm approval now and Sen's stormy tirade the night before, which still rang in her ears. "I thought you'd given up that hair-brained idea. Well, don't say I did not warn you, Liah. Even if all the men agree, all of you will suffer the town's wrath. Nobody wants to be told what to do, especially when it comes to paying taxes."

Even now, she recoiled from the impact of Sen's words. Her lips quivered, recalling how she had fought her impulse to fight back, especially when Sen said, "What more do you want, woman? You moved us from the estate where we were safe and secure from the dangers of the outside and now you speak of wanting safety and permanence? I don't understand you. Nor do I think you understand yourself."

A smile played on Cook's face as Liah toyed with the long gold chain around her neck from which was suspended a large jade pendant. How like a woman to be vain and proud of her jewelry. Beneath her forceful determination, Liah was just a woman.

Liah caught his eyes and murmured, "Jade, life-giving, so full of promise. To think the Fahn Gwai wear it without knowing that jade is a talisman against evil."

Cook grinned at Liah's philosophical justification for her pride in her gems. "Based on what I see in the expression on your face, the men will have to name you chairman. Good! It is important to look imposing. Just remember, the men can't see the inside, so do not give yourself away."

Liah felt her tension over being chosen chairman melt away. Somehow his advice diminished her desperation; her fear of being set aside for another no longer seemed real. The men will choose her. There was no more time for further thought, as the front door opened and slammed and a few moments later, Professor entered the kitchen.

He stood at the doorway, appraising Liah and thought of her transformation to youthfulness that occurred whenever she dressed up, yet it still surprised him. It seemed Liah became a different person, as if her persona changed with the clothes.

When Kam Fong arrived, he too stood in silent amazement at the transformed Liah. A simple man, direct and open in attitudes, Kam displayed an unabashed admiration and surprise. It was difficult for Professor not to grin when Wong Sang and Chon Woo walked in and also stopped abruptly, staring.

Liah smiled. "Shall we go upstairs and wait for Cousin Shah? I am sure he'll be along soon."

When the meeting opened, Liah felt a foreboding that things weren't going to be easy, for an argument immediately ensued between Professor and Chon Woo. The bar owner objected to the high rate of taxes levied upon businesses that did business with Fahn Gwai. "Why should I pay the highest rate of taxes?"

Professor lambasted him. "Your memory is short-lived, Chon. You and the others ratified the Tenet of Laws at our first meeting. We do not have time to rehash the arguments. Do you or do you not want to be a part of this Council? If so, be quiet and allow us to carry on with the business of the day."

Sang watched and listened, thinking to himself that behind his spectacles Professor was not as passive as he seemed. This man could be belligerent, if the situation called for it. He'd better be careful.

Professor announced that the first order of business was the election of officers.

Chon Woo leaped to his feet, nominating Professor as Chairman. Apologetically, he looked at Liah. "I would nominate you, Liah, but if we are to govern, we must have the respect of the townspeople as well as other groups. A woman leader is most assuredly out of the question."

Liah was pleasantly surprised when Cousin Shah disagreed with the bar owner. "I, for one, think Liah is not only capable but has the tenacity to pursue plans to a successful end. The chairmanship needs not only a person of ability, but also one who knows how to manipulate people and situations. I also think that, while our Council is poor, Liah with her monies can assist us until such time as we can afford all the services we want to provide for our town."

Professor nodded gratefully. "Oh, one more thing, while we are on the subject of women. I'd remind you men of another woman, the dowager empress Tzu-Hsi, who brought foresight and purpose to the throne. The fact that she usurped her husband's crown was wrong, but then he was a weakling and someone had to rule. At this time, I proudly nominate Liah as Chairman of our Council."

Liah, both pleased with Cousin Shah's support and annoyed with his mention of her ability to manipulate people, tried to fathom the reason for his support, but his face was a mask. There was a moment of silence, then the scholar announced that if there were no more nominations, they'd take a vote.

The tally puzzled Liah, for she was unanimously selected. Moreover, she caught Chon Woo and Wong Sang exchanging accusing glances and wondered at the reason.

Professor was jubilant. "Ah, I am exceedingly pleased all of us have had the foresight and wisdom to choose Liah as our leader." He turned to Chon. "You did not do me a favor with your nomination, sir. I am not a leader."

Liah was stunned. It never occurred to her that Chon would blatantly desert Professor, especially after having nominated him. She smiled when Professor turned and congratulated her, but wondered what Chon expected to extract from her in return for his belated support.

The selection of Professor as secretary-treasurer came quickly and unanimously. Liah sighed and hoped that in the future the men would be as cohesive as now.

Professor smiled and raised his brush. "I shall affix our names to the Tenet of Laws and shall send a copy to the Dai Faw and Noo Yok Chinese papers. We are now officially a town."

Somewhat maliciously, Chon cautioned Professor not to be too zealous as he was now the work-horse of the Council. The other men guffawed, but Liah scowled. "I hope you do not think the title of secretary will make Professor a slave to all of your letter writing, at least not without paying his usual fees, Chon."

She thanked the men for their confidence and then abruptly turned their attention to the subject of a Chinese school. "Professor will provide the details."

"There is a vacant store on Lion's Den Alley which is suitable for a school. I do not like the public street, but later we can look for another

place in the center of town. Then the children will not have to be exposed to the Fahn Gwai."

Sang argued there were not enough children in China Gai to warrant
the expense of a school. Professor shook his head. "I personally counted
twenty-two children of school age. It has been on my mind for some
time now to do something for the youngsters. If we want them to retain
our traditions, we must teach them. As for the expenses, I shall undertake to pay the expenses until the Council has revenue."

Liah rapped the side of the table with a cane she had begun using
now and then. "You, sir, will do no such thing. The Council will not
only undertake the expense, but will pay you a wage, pittance though
it may be. The new town needs to show appreciation for your services
and your knowledge."

Cousin Shah clapped his hands. "I thoroughly agree with Liah. If
the Council cannot pay the monies, I will be glad to do what I can. You
others ought to consider helping the school, for it is our future that
hangs in the balance. The children will be the extension of our lives."

Chon Woo and Wong Sang exchanged silent glances, neither one
daring to comment. Kam Fong smiled. "If I can offer my help, I, too,
agree with Cousin Shah. The children will carry on our way of life."

Reluctantly, Chon Woo sheepishly agreed. He would also help with
the expenses. "Good!" smiled Liah. "Professor will make it a point to
make public all of your generosity. I, too, will help with the expenses.
Now, I want to speak of our temple."

Liah stated her opinion that it was not safe for the old people to travel
to Lion's Den Alley to worship. She went on to say that there was a vacancy in Peacock Alley, Number Six, and that she'd already spoken to
Marchesson. He was willing to rent it to her for twenty dollars a month.
"I shall undertake the expenses of the temple until the treasury is able
to assume the cost. The old priest surely needs a safer place to live, too."

Sang almost sneered when Chon fully agreed with Liah, that when the treasury could afford, the initial costs ought to be repaid to her. What did that scoundrel have in mind?

"Now," smiled Liah, "I suggest we have our supper and perhaps drink to the health of the Council, the school and the temple."

Cook then entered with the first of the dishes. When Chon smelled the pickled pigs' feet, Cook was accorded the position of a celebrity. "If that tastes as good as it smells, we are in for a feast."

Liah indulgently remarked, "I want you all to meet Loong. The Gods were benevolent to send him to Number Three. For those of you who might not like pickled pigs' feet, there is roast duck, steamed pork with salt fish, spiced spareribs, not to mention my favorite compote of pea pods, black mushrooms, bamboo shoots and sea urchin. Shall we raise our chopsticks?"

Supper was a festive affair. Liah was elated with her chairmanship as was Professor. Chon and Sang each silently speculated on how to beat out the other by asking Liah's financial backing first.

An hour later, Sang fell back into his seat, moaning that he'd eaten too much. He pointed to the pile of bones in front of Chon Woo. "You're a glutton, Chon, look at all the pigs' feet you devoured."

Chon sneered, "Look who's talking. I think the pile of duck bones in front of you is even larger than my pile."

Liah chuckled. "From where I'm sitting, I'd say the both of you did justice to Cook's dinner. He'll be pleased."

"Speaking of supper," announced Professor, "I think we ought to reimburse Liah for the expenses."

"I appreciate your thoughtfulness, sir, but until the treasury has more funds, I shall be happy to provide the meals. Now, if business is concluded for tonight, I think we ought to adjourn. Let us affix our names to this record of our first Council meeting, a singular event indeed."

As she signed her name, Liah caught sight of Kam Fong's face, caught between admiration and query. As she brushed her name, she murmured cryptically, "Some idiot in immigration made the error of misspelling my name. Lin Fah is my given name. I sign my given name on legal papers, but for the Fahn Gwai I must use Liah. Someday it is my hope we can have our own attorney, a young man who will see to it nobody else ever loses his or her name."

After everyone had left, Cook found Liah sitting alone at the table and grinned, "I see on your face and from the men's remarks that you have been elected chairman of our new Council. Good! Now you can relax a bit."

His grin turned to a frown as he inquired, "Now, what is on you mind?"

Liah drew back in total surprise that he had divined her inner thoughts. She confided, "You know, the Tongs have been in existence for so long and are under the guidance and protective laws of the parent Tongs in Dai Faw. I was wondering how the parent Tongs will react to us forming an organization that supersedes their powers."

"There's time enough to think of those things. Enjoy your newly won victory."

Soon, he suggested she go to bed. "It's almost two o'clock in the morning."

"I'm too excited to sleep now. You go to bed. Yours has been the hard, long day and night. I do thank you for the lovely repast. Words are inadequate now to express my feelings."

Suddenly, she averted her eyes from the naked yearning reflected in Cook's eyes, a yearning she knew was impossible to fulfill. Quickly, she rose to her feet and fled to her bedroom.

Sleep was hard to come, for the multitude of images earlier imprisoned in the shadowy recesses of her mind, fought for her attention. Sen's snoring did not help as she fought the strange feeling she felt for Cook. Liah turned her mind to the men on the Council, Chon Woo and Wong Sang emerged foremost. Strange she should now realize how short Wong Sang was. A mere two or three inches taller than she. Perhaps it was his wily aggressiveness that had blinded her; Sang was short and tiny.

Meanwhile, she was repulsed by thoughts of Chon Woo: his pale, sallow complexion made his black, bristly moustache seem even blacker. His straight black hair, shingled to lay low on his neck, made him appear effeminate. His smooth, hairless face looked unnatural, almost obscene.

In the darkness, Liah second-guessed her decision to include both men. Kwan Yin willing, she'd find no cause to rue her decision, especially since she'd argued against Professor's reasons to exclude them. Still, there was the nagging at the back of her head, as if the Gods were trying but unable to reach her.

She pushed aside the nagging feeling and turned her mind to Kam Fong, the ever-smiling gentle man with his cherubic face. His eyes were straightforward and innocent almost bridging upon naiveté; Liah could trust him. His greatest interest was the newfangled machinery in his laundry. He'd timidly informed Liah that neither he nor his men had to break their backs doing hand washing any longer.

Abruptly, Liah thought, what if Chon and Sang were to corrupt Kam? Set him against her by slandering her character and clouding her reasons for unification of China Gai? She'd have to speak to Professor in the morning.

Liah's last thoughts exonerated her choice of Chon and Sang. Who, she smiled, ever heard of weaklings winning battles? Surely not weak-kneed generals. Those two were strong even if their strength were dedicated to selfish ends. She turned on her side, snuggling into the minhois. Cook was right. Tonight she'd enjoy her victory.

—

Professor, awakened the next day by voices in Peacock Alley, lifted his shade to see a group of residents crowded around the bulletin board.

Wong Sing, his long flowing beard jerking up and down, tried to be heard above the excited voices. "Outrageous," exclaimed several businessmen.

Taxes? Who gave the Council the right? The monies will only find their way into private purses. A woman leader in Loo Sahng? It was an insult.

The butcher's wife smugly informed the group that the Council was Liah's idea, that she'd forced the men to choose her.

Professor frowned, almost ready to go outdoors to defend Liah, but was relieved when he heard some of the people speaking in support of the Council. Still, the butcher's and barber's wives whispered. He shook his head. Let them have their words; he'd wait.

A few days later, on a sunny May afternoon, Professor was given his opportunity to speak. He was returning from Wong's Café when he saw a group of agitated people at the entrance of Peacock Alley. Curious as to the purpose of the gathering, he walked over to investigate. The butcher's and barber's wives were gesticulating and screeching angrily at Sen Fei. The butcher's wife pointed a finger accusingly in the face of the aged actress. "How dare you defend Liah? It isn't your husband she's robbing to fatten her own coffers. Isn't she satisfied making money off the Apinyin users? I hear that vulgar habit has made her a rich woman."

"Not satisfied with her illicit trade, she's coerced the men to elect her leader of our town," said the barber's wife. She looked around, then continued, "That poor husband of hers is the one who suffers humiliation. And to think you, Sen Fei, would defend Liah."

Sen Fei screamed back, "You barren females to whom the Gods have given no sons! You dare slight the name of a generous, kind and wise woman? Shame on you and your clucking, evil tongues."

The butcher's wife moved forward, shoving her finger under Sen Fei's nose. "You can afford to be generous and righteous, Sen Fei. You are the town pauper who needs Liah. We do not. We have husbands to take care of us."

At that juncture, Professor pushed his way through the crowd, confronting the two irate females. "Females, bah. The two of you do your husbands an injustice, shamefully shouting like fishwives."

The crowd shuffled about, stepping away from the two women as if to signify their innocence in the fracas. Professor addressed himself to the barber's wife. "You, why don't you inquire of your husband, if you dare, where he got the money for your passage?" Then he swung about to face the butcher's wife. "And you, Madam, if you're not afraid to, why not ask your husband where he got the money to open up his shop?"

Professor relented when he saw the women's terrified expressions and he looked up at the crowd. "I do not mean to reveal secrets, but these two ladies so sanctimoniously besmirch a fine person; it disgusts me. I suggest you two ladies leave the mudslinging to the men. Meanwhile, I'd have all of you think about where you would be today if at one time or another you had not been touched by Liah's generosity. Now, I'd suggest you all return to your business."

There was a dead silence. Some were embarrassed by the scholar's tweaking their consciences, others bewildered by the scholar's ferocity. The two women glanced about furtively, not quite certain of how to leave. Sen Fei bit her lip and walked proudly out of the Alley.

Professor crossed the Alley to his place. He stood a moment in the doorway, watching the people disperse. "Women!" he spat. "They're worse than men!"

Liah sat rigidly silent as Professor described the disturbance in Peacock Alley. Afterwards, Liah asked solemnly, "How did Sen Fei take the insults? I hope those two bitches did not destroy her dignity."

"No," answered Professor as he shook his head. "For a moment I thought she'd break down and sob, but she didn't. I suppose all those years she'd been on stage disciplined her emotions."

Professor inquired if Liah wanted him to report the incident to their husbands. "I hate to think what will happen to them, but their actions were uncalled for and vicious."

"No, that won't be necessary. If I know people, the butcher and barber will have already heard about it."

Professor grinned. "You're right, Liah. In a town as small as Chinatown, it is impossible to keep things secret."

Liah hissed, "Knowing the volatile nature of the butcher, he'll give her the drubbing of her life. I say good! Poor Sen Fei."

Professor chortled. "Well, as far as the barber goes, he, too, is not known for his gentleness. I'll wager his wife will get hers, too."

"Enough of those two worthless females," said Liah. "Do stay and enjoy an afternoon snack with us. Cook will be back soon. He went to the store for some green onions and Chinese parsley."

Soon after, Cook burst into the kitchen, dropping his packages on the sink and turning to grin at Liah and the scholar. "Quan Fook, the butcher, all but knocked me down when he tried to congratulate me on your chairmanship. He asked that I convey his honorable thoughts to you. Strange though, he mentioned the fact that you being a woman in no way detracts from your competence."

Liah and Professor burst into laughter. Liah recounted the incident in Peacock Alley. As soon as the scholar was able to stop laughing, he exclaimed, "See? I told you so, Liah. And I'll wager you didn't see his wife in the store-front, did you?"

Cook shook his head. "No, come to think of it, I didn't. So that's the reason for the gift."

"What gift?" asked Liah.

Cook reached into the sack and extracted a small Virginia ham, which he handed to Liah. "The butcher's gift to you. He said it was a special smoked pork, very salty, but delicious. I suppose in a way he's saying he'll pay his levies."

The three friends enjoyed an afternoon repast, made even more pleasant by the butcher's gift. A warm, comfortable contentment filled the kitchen as they laughed from time to time over the butcher's sudden capitulation to Liah's side. Cook thought as he watched Professor and Liah, the Gods willing, neither would regret starting the Council.

Professor was back that night to share a midnight supper with Liah and Cook. His flowery prose in praise of the mandarin chicken sent Liah into paroxysms of laughter. "I never knew you to be such a flatterer, sir."

Cook frowned playfully at Liah, saying she was jealous of the scholar's praise. "It pleases me you enjoyed it, sir. I learned to make it when I was working up north...."

The front door opened, cutting Cook's remarks short. Liah relaxed. "It's only Wong Sang; don't worry so."

"At midnight?" murmured Cook. "Is that the hour to make a social call?"

Professor solemnly replied, "What makes you think it is a social visit, Cook?"

Wong Sang stopped in the doorway when he saw Professor and lamely apologized for the late call, but he knew Liah was a night person. "I hate to call on you during the early hours, but I see you are busy now. I'll come back another time."

"Oh, no," said Professor as he rose from his seat. "I was leaving anyway. Here, please take my chair. The mandarin chicken is very good. Why not have some?"

"No, thank you, I already had supper at Wong's before coming here."

Cook dished up a bit of roast chicken, spooned a few mandarin oranges over it and dished up a spoonful of rice anyway. He set another pair of chopsticks on the table and bid Sang sample it. "It isn't often I make it. It takes too long. Go ahead, taste it, Sang."

"I'll see you to the door, Professor," murmured Cook. "And then I'll board up the doors and windows for the night." He turned to Sang and bid him good night. "I rise early and cannot afford the luxury of late hours. Enjoy the chicken."

There was an awkward silence once Liah and Sang were alone. Liah knew from the look on Sang's face that he'd come to ask a favor. Well, she wouldn't make things easier by asking. Let him break the silence.

Wong Sang tasted the chicken and waxed eloquent over Cook's talents as a chef, declaring Liah fortunate for having secured his services. "What is in the sack, Sang?" asked Liah, gesturing toward a bag Sang had carried in.

"Oh, I forgot. I have some pomegranates for you." He reddened. "I heard you like them."

Liah thanked him; saying it wasn't necessary to bring her gifts. "Surely, you didn't come at this late hour just to bring them."

"Ah, Madam, you are also perceptive. First, before I tell you what's on my mind, I must say I voted for you as chairman because of your abilities. I don't want you to think I've come to collect a debt."

Liah purred, "Of course not. Speak. What is on your mind?"

"Well," mumbled Sang falteringly, "what I want to ask is whether you're interested in making more money."

Liah raised her eyebrows. "Of course, one can always use more money. What do you have in mind?" She added, "And how much will it cost? Even I may not be able to afford too exorbitant an outlay of money."

Sang did some quick arithmetic in his mind and blurted: "I have in mind a gambling house. It'll take a thousand dollars to outfit the place and set up a bank."

Sang writhed while Liah took some time to think, hating himself for needing Liah's money. Mostly, he felt guilty the figure was so large, for in truth he only had two hundred dollars to his name.

Liah creased her brow and finally replied, "I think five hundred dollars is a more reasonable sum for the gaming equipment and the bank. I'll tell you what I'll do. You match my two hundred and fifty dollars and we're in business."

Curses! Why hadn't he had the gumption to tell Liah the truth about the state of his finances? She might have agreed to finance him. Now, he'd have to 'run the block,' go from person to person, to raise the cash necessary to match her contribution. Liah asked abruptly, "Well, is that satisfactory with you?"

Wong Sang nodded. Tomorrow he'd come up with the monies. Liah went on, "Now that we've settled the finances, where do you want to set up our gambling house?" She brightened. "What about opening up in Peacock Alley? It's brought good joss to all the tenants, why not us? I could ask Marchesson to see if he'd rent us Number Eleven. The location is just right, with a cellar for escape should the police raid it."

It irritated Sang that Liah's suggestion sounded more like an order. He shook his head. "There is a place two doors down from Professor's place. I think we'll open up there."

"Very well then, Sang, you choose the location, but I hope you will give consideration to Number Eleven in Peacock Alley. We'll need good joss to make money."

"I know, I know," replied Sang crossly, "but like you I feel my Meng-Sui too. Marchesson Gai is the place."

Sang felt power in defying Liah's wishes. If she were to be his partner, she'd have to learn now that his word and authority were final. He rose abruptly from his chair. "I must get home and get a good night's rest if I am to begin arrangements tomorrow. Do you suppose you might advance the two hundred and fifty that I may rent the store and buy the equipment?"

"Bring your share of the monies, Sang, then we'll begin the partnership." She smiled. "I believe in following proper procedure in all business transactions. Perhaps that is why I am always so successful. For the moment, let us both say good night and I will see you tomorrow."

After a fretful night, Wong Sang went to see Chon Woo the next morning, at eleven o'clock. Piqued at having missed Chon the night before, Sang swore that if the man didn't loan him the fifty dollars, he'd expose to Liah that Chon only voted for her because of his own selfish desire to remodel his bar.

Sang sneered as he climbed the stairs to Chon's living quarters. His 'offices' indeed. Grumpily, Sang muttered, "More like two shabby, messy rooms." Still, Sang envied Chon's way with the females. He almost laughed, thinking what an honor it must be to be asked to Chon's rooms.

The transaction took almost a half-hour, but Sang emerged from The Dragon's Den Bar with a triumphant smile. Sang felt no compunction about his devious hint that he'd expose Chon to Liah. Quickly Sang made his way to Number Three in Peacock Alley.

Liah, sipping her morning herbal brew before taking lunch, frowned at the sound of the front door opening but the footsteps in the corridor indicated it was Sang. Somewhat breathless, Sang eyed Liah for a fleeting second, then tossed the wad of money on the table. Without speaking, Liah reached inside her tunic and withdrew a purse. She extracted three notes: two one hundred dollar bills and one fifty-dollar bill and tossed them atop Sang's. "There," she smiled casually, "we're in business."

It angered Sang to see how easily Liah had come up with the money. It was so effortless for her to make his dream come true while he had to labor and grovel. For a measly few hundred dollars Liah had humbled him to the extreme. Someday, he promised himself, he'd pay her back!

Liah's voice broke into his thoughts. "You know, Sang, now that we're partners, I hope you will be more honest with me. I don't mean just honesty about money, but the integrity between two people. If not, our partnership is doomed from the start. If you'd told me you didn't have the money I'd have loaned it to you, then you'd not have had to appeal to Chon for it."

Sang's face froze. How dare Chon expose him? The bastard. Liah shook her head. "I haven't spoken with Chon, if that is what angers you. You forget I have a web of spies. They told me you went to Chon's early this morning."

Sang began to laugh. "I should know not to try and hoodwink you, Liah. Believe me, I'll not try that again. By the way, is there a special day you'd like the grand opening?" Somehow, his deference to Liah's choice of opening day gave Sang a feeling of exhilarating pleasure; it also assuaged his guilt.

"Any day will do," murmured Liah. "Just so it is an auspicious date when your life forces and mine are strong. Why not discuss that with Professor? Oh, yes, I have spoken with Lee Wah and he has offered us the gambling tiles and furniture at cost."

Sang was flabbergasted as he gulped, "You knew I'd get the monies?"

Liah shook her head. "I already decided to finance you in any case. Just go and talk with Wah."

Long afterwards, Liah sat at the table mulling over her partnership with Sang. If she could trust a scoundrel the likes of Sang, why was she hesitant about going into business with Cook? Certainly, Cook was a thousand fold more trustworthy. Throughout the afternoon, Liah waited for an appropriate time to speak to him. It wasn't until the household had gone to bed that night that she and Cook were alone.

Straightaway she asked him to be seated. "It has been on my mind to offer you half partnership in my Apinyin business. We are favored by the Gods, for our minds and hearts run in true course. It must be so, for how else can you divine my innermost thoughts? How can I feel so safe in your presence?"

Liah paused, but Cook made no comment. "You must know there is risk involved and the possibility of being caught by the police. Those risks will be minimized once I put into effect a sentry system headed by one person to replace the separate spy systems I have in place now. Well, what do you say, my loyal friend?"

There was a hint of pride in Cook's voice as he spoke. "I will accept the partnership on one condition. If we are caught, I will go to jail. The guilt must be all mine. You must be allowed to carry out your plans and raise your children. My life is of no importance." He paused. "Well, what do you say, Liah?"

Liah had averted her eyes when Cook began to speak, but now he softly commanded, "Look at me, Liah! Before we make any further plans, there are issues you and I must resolve. I am certain you are aware of our mutual attraction. Well, have no fears about that. I respect you, your plans for Chinatown and, mostly, you as a wife and mother. I'm proud also of my feelings for you, but you shall never fail in your duties as a wife. I won't allow it." He sat back. "So! Now I have spoken of how I feel, of what is in my heart; there is not need for you to speak. I am sure your feelings are a duplicate of mine. Tomorrow, we will speak more of the details of our partnership."

Liah nodded mutely then went into her bedroom. Alone, she allowed her tears to overflow. In gratitude, she lit a coil of incense to Kwan Yin; she felt the hopelessness of a love never to be consummated but felt no less, the ecstasy. Hearing the sound of a key in the rear lock, Liah hurried out to prepare her husband's supper.

The next day when Liah came from her bedroom she felt a shy reluctance at meeting Cook. Somehow their discussion the night before left her mind ruffled and her emotions seemed to be bubbling just under the surface. She was startled when Cook motioned for her to glance at the calendar. He'd marked off the date of their partnership in bold red pencil. Liah felt a warmth deep within.

Their business partnership would give Liah a greater peace of mind. No longer would she be harassed by Sen over purchasers coming to the house. As for Cook being her partner, she would keep that fact secret, even from Sen. Of what use was it telling him?

The first changes they discussed were the places and hours the Apinyin would be sold. Liah suggested deserted locations, but Cook said that made the transactions too noticeable. "I've marked on the map the various stores and cafés where I'd like to do business," Cook said. "Since I go shopping daily, it won't be out of the ordinary for me to enter the places I've marked."

Liah, with her Apinyin trade secured, turned her focus on Eldest Daughter, wondering about the girl's aggressive attitude and her moody silence. When she spoke to Cook about her, he was tightlipped and said nothing. He suspected Eldest Daughter was having an affair, but he wanted more proof before upsetting Liah with the news. After all, he had only a few clues: the girl's exaggerated length of time before the mirror, the fussiness over her appearance. He also knew she had started using lipstick and rouge, removing the cosmetics before she entered the house.

One morning Liah was rudely awakened by shouting and screaming in the kitchen. She found Eldest Daughter and Third Son on the floor, Eldest Daughter shrieking as Third Son pummeled her and cursed. Liah roared they cease. Third Son glared, "She has no business bossing me around so much."

Eldest Daughter tearfully related that her brother had attacked her when she ordered him to dry the dishes. "Aw, Mah-Mah," complained Third Son, "eldest sister just wants us to hurry because she wants to see this boy at the playground."

William chided Theo for speaking about things that were none of his business and a second fight erupted. Liah screamed angrily, "I will have no more fighting! No one will leave the house until this disgraceful fighting is done. Now, let us have our morning meal."

The mood at the table was tense and silent. Liah was aware the children were cloaking their anger until they got outside the house. It angered her when Third Son mumbled in Fahn Gwai under his breath and Eldest Daughter grumbled back in Fahn Gwai. "I shall not say this again," warned Liah. "Put fighting from your mind and heart, or else no one will leave today." The children bit their lips; for Liah had her chopsticks poised in her hand, ready to inflict punishment.

The moment Cook returned home from shopping, he sensed there had been a quarrel. At once he announced he had a surprise for supper, but no one asked what it was. Liah leaned back in her upholstered chair as if spent and finally Cooked dumped the groceries beside the sink and slammed around pots and pans. Cook's change of behavior struck everyone at the table, including Liah.

—

The weather warmed and the May sunshine scattered glittering splashes of color along the garden in Peacock Alley. The roses, deep red, yellow and pink budded and the daffodils, golden with their proud crowns, vied for their place in sunlight with the sedate loveliness of the hyacinths, lilies and irises along the border. The chain-link fence was all but hidden by the ivy, which provided a background for the border garden.

Liah walked up and down the cobblestone walk, breathing in its wealth of perfume and stopping now and then to pluck off a withered bloom or leaf. She felt empowered because she'd been victorious in rejuvenating the shrubs and trees. She looked up at the arbor sagging now with new growth of bougainvillea and honeysuckle. By summer, the vines would have to be thinned out. Taking one more glance up and down the cobblestone walk, Liah went indoors.

Eldest Daughter sullenly slammed her chopsticks atop the rice bowls holding the morning meal. Liah's joy, dampened by her daughter's disrespect, said nothing. Cook saw Liah's frown and braced himself for another outburst between mother and daughter

Flo suddenly glanced at the wall clock. Realizing her brothers were deliberately trying to make her late for her tryst with her boyfriend, she began shouting angrily for them to hurry. Liah reprimanded her and Flo responded angrily. Liah suddenly sprang to her feet and slapped her. Cook tried to separate the two women to no avail and he lost his patience. He untied his apron, flung it on the table and slammed out the rear door.

Liah froze mid-sentence, her eyes riveted on the rear door. She shrieked uncontrollably, "You miserable child. If Cook quits, I will kill you." Liah's eyes blazed as she turned and lunged for her daughter. Flo leapt away, fled to her bedroom and bolted the door. Liah fell into her upholstered chair, limp with exhaustion. Overwhelming her fury at Eldest Daughter was her wish for Cook to come back to her. She beseeched the Goddess.

An hour later, the rear door opened and Cook quietly stepped into the kitchen. Liah rushed up, half-crying, half-laughing, but Cook's stern, solemn face brought her to a halt. She sobbed softly, "Please do not leave me. I could not go on if you did."

She turned, half-sobbing, groping her way back to her chair and sank into the cushioned depths. She felt limp and out of breath and averted her eyes from Cook.

"I see," muttered Cook, his voice unsympathetically hard. "The tussle robbed you of your strength. Well, that is what I want to discuss with you. I've had enough bickering between the two of you."

Liah's eyes opened wide, pleading silently with Cook not to leave her.

"I am not leaving you," asserted Cook. "Of that you need never fear, but you'd better give some thought to your Eldest Daughter. Two adult females under one roof—one stubborn and tired, the other a young girl who's trying to assert her natural instincts—are too much for me. These battles must cease. It is not only unpleasant for me, but it is very bad for the other children."

Liah moaned, "I just don't know what's come over Eldest Daughter. It seems she's more vile and aggressive. She's insufferable lately."

"You mean," challenged Cook, "a woman of your astute awareness cannot recognize her daughter is in love? Well, I have no proof, but even I can see the way she rises earlier, preens before the mirror and is irritable and edgy. I think she needs reassurance and understanding, which only you can give. I hope you can be gentle with her. It's up to you."

Liah was stunned. A feeling of humiliation came over her, quickly giving way to reproach. How callous on her part. Not only had she been making it difficult for poor Cook, but also she'd been blind to her own daughter's pain. "I am again indebted to you. I will mend my ways. My daughter in love! I am a failure as a mother!"

"No need for self-recriminations. Just be more patient, perhaps a bit more lenient, certainly hold your tongue."

"I know, I know, Cook," Liah said, exasperated. "I'll go now and ask the boy's name. I must know if he is husband material; I won't have meaningless carryings on."

Cook put out a restraining hand. "No! You'll only frighten her and in her present mood I'm sure she won't speak to you. Just be patient and wait until she comes to you."

"She won't tell me anything and you know it, Cook."

"You're her mother, Liah," explained Cook impatiently. "Whom would she speak to about such a serious subject if not with you? Just be patient."

Once more, Liah sank back into her chair and closed her eyes. Her mind flashed back to the day when her own mother showed Liah Sen's photograph. What joy and mostly what sorrowful fear she felt as she contemplated the photograph, her mother waiting for her daughter's acceptance. Liah recalled how unsure she had felt when she had nodded shyly that she'd accept Sen as a husband.

Now it was Eldest Daughter's turn, but Liah reasoned why should she have qualms? Unlike herself, Eldest Daughter chose the man herself, without even her mother's knowledge. Still, matrimony must loom formidably in a young girl's mind and heart. Liah opened her eyes. Yes, Eldest Daughter would surely come to her. But when? Oh, how Liah hoped the young man was suitable for a son-in-law.

That night at supper and over the next few days, Liah found herself lodged in an internal battle for patience and self-control as she waited for Eldest Daughter to confide in her. Once or twice when she was near the breaking point, Cook gave Liah a look of warning, encouraging her patience.

Just as her endurance was waning, Eldest Daughter came to her and declared she was in love with a boy named Toh and wanted to marry him. Liah was alarmed that her daughter was so anxious to marry. She asked why.

Eldest Daughter's face flushed red and she shook her head. "No, Mah-Mah, I'm not in trouble. It's just that we want to get married in June."

Liah thought, if Eldest Daughter knew what marriage was really like, she'd not be so anxious. Still, Liah remembered her own impatience to wed, to own her own house and to do as she pleased. Her face tinged red as she recalled how she had reacted to Sen's photograph and heard her mother's warning that becoming man and woman was a serious undertaking, that a wife's life was not just one of lovemaking and courtship.

The level of freedom her daughter enjoyed in Gem Sahn suddenly irked Liah. If only she had had that same freedom, she would not have abused it or thrown it away quite so easily by marrying so early. Getting betrothed, without any say-so in the ceremonies, Liah had been forced to follow strict protocols steeped in tradition. For a young, frightened girl, it had been almost too much. Even now, Liah cringed at the memory of her mother-in-law's reaction when Liah had poured the overbearing woman her ceremonial cup of tea. Liah had feared her mother-in-law would not place on the table the red packet of money signifying her receipt of Liah's reverence and her approval. No, she would not force Eldest Daughter to endure the rigid ceremonial traditions, but Eldest Daughter would have to abide by Liah's parental rights and wishes.

Liah asked her daughter if she realized what it meant, 'marriage'.

"What about your education? Are you certain you are ready to give up your freedom and any hope of a life of your own? With marriage will come motherhood. Are you ready? It isn't easy you know."

"Oh, yes! I am ready! I know what I'm doing, Mah-Mah. I love Toh. Could we have a June wedding, Mah-Mah?"

Liah shook her head adamantly. "No, there's not enough time. There's the posting of banns, the marriage contract, not to speak of the banquet planning, the notification of family and the engraving of invitations. No, there is not enough time, daughter."

"Mah, nobody these days believes in all that formality. Toh and I want a small wedding. Why can't I get what I want even with my own wedding?"

Liah's tone was harsh. "There's also the matter of picking the correct date, a date auspicious for both your horoscopes. Perhaps Professor can find us the right go-between to act on our behalf."

Flo's repeated objections brought Liah's half-angry warning. "A wedding belongs to the family. If you are to be wed, it will be done according to traditional protocol. Before anything can happen, I will first speak with your father. Nothing is possible without his consent. Now, leave me to my thoughts. We will speak later."

It was not until two nights later that Liah found the right time to speak with Sen. Sadly, she saw how his rejection of her was wreaking terrible inroads on his face. Why did he not see that by punishing her he was also exposing his own body to severe punishment? She was loath to speak of marriage to him but could not afford to remain silent. Eldest Daughter's eagerness to be wed had to be dealt with.

When Sen pushed aside his plate, Liah quickly mentioned Eldest Daughter's desire to wed. "The young man's name is Wah Kin Toh. Our daughter desires the wedding to take place as soon as wedding preparations allow. I told her as soon as I spoke with you, we'd arrange a go-between to discuss the contract of marriage and to post the banns. Of course I told her nothing was possible should you object."

She waited for a reply, but it was as if Sen did not hear her. Then she saw an almost cruel expression cross his face, followed by a supercilious sneer that he had kept a secret and he reveled in the knowledge that Liah had been in the dark.

Sen glanced sharply at his wife. Liah almost expected an angry retort, so dark was his countenance. "I know Kin Toh. He's an eligible young man, a bit too mild-mannered for the likes of Eldest Daughter, but he'll make a good husband. What objections can you have?"

"None!" cried Liah. "But we know nothing about the young man. A go-between can best find out what we need to know. Besides, there's the marriage contract to be agreed upon."

"Foolishness!" snarled Sen. "In Gem Sahn, when two persons agree to marry, that is reason enough. Why go to the expense of a go-between? I say, let them wed!"

Liah pleaded, "If you won't consent to a go-between, at least meet with his older brother. Arrange the wedding feast, get the information so we can post the banns. And what about provisions should the marriage fail? There will be the consideration for their children."

Sen raised his finger and warned, "There will be no interference from you if I speak to him! You will abide by whatever we decide. Is that clear?"

Long after Sen went to bed, Liah remained at the table. She cringed at the memory of Sen's sarcasm when she mentioned setting a date astrologically suitable for the two persons. Sen had roared derisively. "Bah, what have the stars to do with a marriage? Marriage, good or bad, is strictly between two people. Look at ours! Our marriage was consummated according to strict observation of the heavens and the Gods!"

Crestfallen by Sen's onslaught on their marriage, Liah craved the escape of her bamboo pipe, but not with Sen in the bedroom; she would have to wait until morning.

When Sen returned home from work the next morning, his mood was no friendlier than the night before. Cook, aware of impending quarrel, quietly left the house. Sen roared, "I shall pay for our daughter's wedding feast and any other expenses. Not your dirty money. And while I am on the subject of Apinyin, don't think I'm stupidly blind. I know Cook is your leg-man, but that doesn't prevent you from being caught."

The dam of pent-up emotions broke and Liah screamed back. "Oh," she sneered, "you noticed, did you? Well, then you must have also noticed that I haven't failed in my motherly or wifely duties. It also takes a husband to make a marriage a marriage. As for my sullying your precious name, have no fears. If caught, Cook has already promised he'd bear the full brunt and go to prison."

Sen leaped to his feet and Liah recoiled in fear that he'd strike her. "Enough woman. We will speak no more of this sordid situation. The consequences of your illegal trade and your disobedience in things not within your authority will surely come."

He pushed a chair out of his way with such vehemence it fell over as he strode into the bedroom, slamming the door.

ENGAGEMENT

On the twenty-sixth day of May, on a Sunday afternoon, Wah Kin Toh accompanied by his older brother, Wah Yuen Suey, came to Number Three. Sen was waiting for them in the front room. Sen introduced Liah, then motioned her dismissal with a jerk of his hand. The men, he said, would discuss the wedding plans.

Liah, stinging from her husband's abrupt dismissal, was confronted by Eldest Daughter, who demanded to know what was going on. Liah snapped that she didn't know. To ease her anger, Liah praised Toh's height. "He also has such a sensitive face," she said. "Yours is so defiant. Do not fret, we shall know what is going on as soon as the men are done." Liah sighed. "Incidents such as this one, where a father has the absolute right to act as he sees fit, are one of the freedoms you relinquish when you wed."

Toh sat on the edge of his chair, wishing he'd not made the proposal of marriage. It seemed at first so simple when he had asked Flo to marry. Now, as he listened to the bargaining between his older brother and his future father-in-law, the whole situation sounded more like a business contract.

And then there was his future mother-in-law. He had only seen her for a moment, but her piercing eyes had seemed to bore right to the core of him. If rumors were correct, she was one to sidestep. What had he let himself in for?

When the discussions were done, Toh felt total relief. His older brother smiled. "Since as you say, sir, in Gem Sahn the rules are more flexible, why not allow me to assume half of the cost of the wedding feast? If we were to keep the wedding simple, we could give the bridal couple some of the monies. The Gods know how much money it takes to set up housekeeping and, of course, to take care of babies!"

"Of course!" smiled Sen, liking Wah for his practicality. "One thing though, you know how women from the old country are. I promised my wife she'd have a free hand in the distribution of the wedding cakes."

"Yes, by all means allow your wife that honor. I still recall my own mother's frenzy. To have forgotten one person was a calamity. While I think of it, do you have any objection to holding the wedding feast in the produce section of town?"

Wah Suey was startled at the sudden change in Sen's face. He seemed hit by a bolt of lightning. Sen explained about his early days in Dai Faw, of the Fahn Gwai raids on his farms and finally when he could no longer face the risk of another attack by the Fahn Gwai, that he had moved the family to Loo Sahng. "I'll never forget the murder of my older brother. I vowed never to set foot in Fahn Gwai town and shall not do so, not even for my daughter's wedding." Quickly, Wah Suey retracted his suggestion and said the wedding feast would be held in China Gai.

Both men relaxed then and began to chuckle about the extravagant expense just to secure a nagging female on one's neck. Sen caught Toh's aggrieved expression and grinned. "Son, it is the privilege of older men to make light of these matters. Someday you too will laugh at your own daughter's wedding. Meanwhile, I will notify my wife of our decisions. No doubt both wife and daughter are at their wits end by now."

When asked the date for the wedding, Sen shrugged. "Knowing my wife, she'll consult with the astrologer to select a date auspicious to both Toh and Eldest Daughter. I will let you know as soon as I know."

When Sen entered the kitchen, Flo cried, "Where's Toh?"

Sen remarked authoritatively, "He is abiding by our customs. A groom doesn't see his bride until the nuptial ceremonies are done. Now, if you'll leave us alone, I'd like to speak with your mother."

Liah was pleased with their decision regarding the wedding cakes, but silently disappointed with their decision about the size of the feast. Why couldn't Sen allow a larger guest list? Nevertheless, she'd use her own monies to send the announcement of Eldest Daughter's wedding and to include the necessary money for the wedding feast to be celebrated in the villages. After all, this was their first wedding, why shouldn't her family and Sen's back home share in the celebrations?

Sen gruffly teased, "You know you'll have to leave the house if we are to celebrate the feast."

"I'll leave the house, Sen."

"And there's one more thing. Eldest Daughter wants a Fahn Gwai ceremony, so I've given her permission to ask Marchesson's advice and help. I don't want you to be tardy with the guest list either for there isn't much time if she is to wed in September. I'll see to it that the banns are posted in Peacock Alley."

Liah nodded wearily, her mind boggled with the numerous details to be addressed. At once, she went to Eldest Daughter's room and announced that the house must be made immaculate. Many of the relatives from out of town would be staying at Number Three. Eldest Daughter started to protest, but she didn't have time to argue with daughter. "If you are willing to face the shame of a dirty house for your own wedding, who am I to argue?"

Liah left her daughter's bedroom with a smug smile on her face. This was one time she'd not have to nag. First thing, she'd have to make out the guest list to see how many hotel rooms they'd need in addition to the sleeping rooms available at their home to accommodate family from Dai Faw, Flenoh and Bakafeh.

Eldest Son and Second Son, when told of their sister's betrothal, became wary of their mother and stayed out of her way, coming home only to sleep. As the wedding date neared, Liah apologized to Cook for the extra work and long hours. Cook's seemed miffed as he reminded her that the children were also a part of his life and that he wanted to be involved. "I've already alerted the markets and shops about the foodstuffs I will need. They said to offer you their felicitations, that the Gods favor you. They said they'll provide the freshest of poultry, meat and produce for this auspicious event."

Liah couldn't help but compare Cook with Sen. Unlike Sen, Cook seemed more paternal, even loving, while Sen only groaned how hard he worked in order to keep a roof over their heads and food in their bodies. Liah felt a pang of guilt that perhaps this was Sen's way of getting seeking revenge for her disobedience.

NUMBER THREE MARCHESSON STREET

Wong Sang ended up renting Number Three on Marchesson Street for the gambling house. He worked day and night helping the carpenters and as soon as they were done, he did the painting himself. While he painted the front door, Sang was struck with a pang of guilt. Although he'd promised Liah he would, he had not reinforced the door as she had instructed. How could Liah be certain the Fahn Gwai police would try to force entry? Besides, he was the headman and she only a silent partner.

To assuage his guilt, Wong Sang nailed extra screening across the two windows in front and the window in the rear of the building. That night, when he'd finished work, Wong Sang tested the front door, kicking it viciously from the outside. "Nah," he muttered, "nobody can kick it in." Then he glanced at his watch and decided to get dinner.

By the time he'd reached Wong's Café, Sang had convinced himself Liah was being extravagant. A new, stout door would only cost them an unnecessary outlay of money. Sang was almost finished with his meal when Chon Woo walked in. "Hey, Chon," he shouted, "can you give me the telephone number of your bookkeeper? I will need his services."

Chon scowled and thought, what a pompous ass. Not yet opened and already he wants everybody to know he's a businessman. Chon took the stool next to Sang and listened sullenly as Sang gushed. "Professor told us the twentieth day of June is the peak astrological time for Liah and me."

"I thought you said you weren't superstitious?" Chon added, with a sneer on his lips, "Tell you what I'm going to do. On your opening day I'll come and challenge the two of you. Your Meng-Sui against mine. Or should I say, *Liah's* good joss against mine, it certainly can't be yours."

Sang chafed in the worst way to insult Chon, but knew the bar owner wouldn't hesitate to expose to the diners that Sang owed him money. Sang was impatient to open up. He'd show the bastard. Sang again felt jealous of Liah's wealth, for if he'd had the capital, Chon would not now be riding him about her good joss.

Sang was later more irritated when he dropped in to see Liah only to be told that Professor had made an error in the calculations. The twentieth-*eighth* day of June was the correct date for the opening.

"What's the difference, Liah? I've made plans to open up on the twentieth. Now I'll have to notify the musicians and all. Not to speak of going around town to change the date on the posters."

Liah was adamant. The twentieth-eighth day of June or nothing. In the end, Sang grumblingly consented. After all, if their luck was good, and it'd better be, he'd no longer be beholden to Chon. Boy, at first chance he'd repay the bastard his money.

Opening day, Wong Sang felt foolish as he set off strings of firecrackers. "Liah and her Goddamn lurking devils," he thought. Still, if it brought good joss he'd set off more; in fact, he'd even set off the Fahn Gwai's fireworks. He stood watching the flurry of red paper, his ears ringing.

He turned to make a last minute check on the food for the buffet they would be serving during the first day's celebrations. Chon's voice startled him. "Hey, are you ready to lose your money, Sang?"

"Lose? Shit, you'd better be prepared to pay up."

The men who had crowded around the doorway as the firecrackers exploded went indoors to witness the grudge bet. They pushed and shoved to get a better view of the betting. Sang grinned, "Okay, Chon, let's not keep the Gods waiting. Let's see who the Gods favor."

Two spectators placed money on the table, but Chon shook his head. "Nobody joins this game. When I beat Sang, it'll be all my luck. I want no excuses from him." Chon reached into his pocket and brought out a wad of greenbacks, peeling off a hundred dollar bill.

Sang handed Chon the dice and pointed to the black tiles set up in stacks of four. The dice rolled a five. Sang counted off the five rows, handed Chon one stack of four and himself the next row. The Pai gow tiles were arranged with the lower-value pair in front and the higher-value pair behind.

Chon's face was grim as he glared at Sang.

Sang flipped his four Pai Gow tiles face up on the table. A sympathetic moan went up for Chon. On the table were two twelve's, a six and a three. Arranged with the two twelve's in back and with the six and three in front, the hand was unbeatable. Chon gaped disbelievingly for a second, turned and stomped out the door. Sang grinned and picked up the hundred dollar bill, shoving it into his pocket as he yelled for the men to try their hand. "Surely, with such a phenomenal hand, the bank can't be as lucky now."

By noon, the place was crowded and noisy. There were a few gamblers at the table, but most of the men were there to partake in the free meal and liquor. The elderly were there in numbers, impatiently awaiting the food. Shortly after twelve, not only was there the delivery of food from the Golden Dragon restaurant, but also the Chinese orchestra had set up the bandstand and was tuning their instruments.

Sang gawked as Sen Fei entered, dressed in an elaborate stage gown, complete with a spangled, flower-studded headdress. His first reaction was to laugh, but for the tongue-lashing he'd certainly get from Liah, he wordlessly nodded and pointed to the bandstand and to the musicians. Lord, he thought, he'd be glad when the day was over.

By six o'clock that night, Sang felt the blood pounding in his head and an uncanny flow of good joss in his fingers as he dealt the dominoes and raked in the money. He felt exhilaration but nausea at the same time. Perhaps it was the pressure of gambling, or the rich odors off the food. For sure, the strident noise of the orchestra and Sen Fei's staccato high notes abused his ears.

Sang was shocked when, at eleven o'clock, Chon Woo strutted back through the door. "Okay, Sang!" he shouted. "How about another bet, this time double or nothing. Well, are you afraid Liah's luck is waning, how about it?"

Sang's eyes narrowed and his anger flared as he tossed the dice to Chon. The Pai gow were dealt and Chon swore, "Well? Turn your God-damned Pai gow over."

Sang did so, then Chon followed suit. Chon's face paled. While Sang's hand was bad, his was worse. The bar owner clenched his teeth and his eyes blazed with barely controlled wrath. He swore to himself and then raged, "You sonofabitch! Wipe that grin off your face before I wipe it off for you. Not another cent will you get from me!" Chon then slammed his way back out.

Sang just had to tell Liah of his encounter with Chon. Like a child, Sang was eager for Liah's praise. He was eager for the night to be over, but time dragged on and not many gamblers remained. At the stroke of three, Sang padlocked the front door and hurried to Number Three. As he made his way around the corner, he hoped Liah's spies had not already informed her that he was coming. For once, he wanted to see the look of surprise on her face.

But she was ready for him when he arrived, even had a plate of supper prepared and waiting for him. While he ate, Liah smiled broadly, her expression indulging Sang, telling him she thought he was a big man. "While I heard we did well, I don't have any details. You can tell me later."

Wong Sang pushed away his plate, wiped his mouth taking care to dry his moustache and reached inside his coat for the moneybag. His spirits soared and his ego swelled as he emptied the contents on the table. Liah eyed the pile of coins and bills and declared there was close to four hundred dollars. Sang cried, "Madam, your eyes are indeed sharp. Actually, there's four hundred forty-two dollars and eighty-five cents." In the back of his mind, Sang not only made note of Liah's eagle eyes, but her razor sharp mind.

When Sang's slightly exaggerated and long drug out story about Chon was done, Liah murmured, "Yes, the Gods do favor us." Her expression sobered. "To alienate the Gods would be asking for disaster, but to alienate Chon places the Council in jeopardy. Let there be no more animosity."

Sang's retort was fiery. "He didn't have to be so arrogant and insulting. He was so certain he'd beat me. I can't help it if I'm luckier. Still, you're right, Liah."

The two partners agreed to keep the first night's money intact for good luck. When Sang was about to leave, he giggled nervously as he asked Liah for a loan of ten dollars. "The initial layout of money has left me almost broke."

Liah grinned. "Sang, you are now a businessman. You cannot be without funds. Take this fifty dollars. It should carry you until the end of the month when we will divide the profits. We'll deduct it then."

Afterwards, Cook mused, "Somehow Sang doesn't seem so belligerent. I suppose now that he has his own gambling house, he is content."

"No, Cook, men like Sang are never satisfied. Sang will never change, and never will he be trustworthy. However, until the next bidder happens along, we can rest a bit easier."

She cautioned Cook to be on the alert. "I have a feeling Chon will be coming around for his portion of financial help now."

"Well, do you not want to be his partner? The Dragon's Den Bar is a moneymaker."

"Yes," murmured Liah, "the profits from the bar would help me pay for the new temple I hope to move into Peacock Alley. I do so want to buy Kwan Yin a jeweled incense urn. So many years ago I promised."

Cook listened and thought, "No wonder the Gods favor her."

—

Throughout the month of July, despite the warm weather, Liah harangued the children over housecleaning. Their home must not be a disgrace when friends and relatives came for Eldest Daughter's wedding. Each time she stepped outside into Peacock Alley and saw the banns rifled by the gentle breeze, Liah's spirit rose. Discord arose when Eldest Daughter cried when her mother forbid her a white wedding gown. "White is for mourning, I shall not invite bad joss. Why not wear blue, your favorite color?"

In the end, Eldest Daughter sullenly chose a blue silk brocaded cheongsam. Not even her mother's permission to purchase matching shoes and purse relieved the girl's disappointment. Once more, she lamented that it was her wedding, so why couldn't she choose the time and the clothing? "Yes, yes, I know! The wedding is a family event, but I have always dreamt of a white gown and a June wedding."

Yook Lan watched as her mother, Madam Quock, pinned the hem of Flo's blue silk afternoon dress. Yook Lan was also caught up in the flurry of preparations, but vowed never to marry, at least not until she'd made her mark in the Fahn Gwai movies or was acclaimed as a Chinese opera singer. If only she could persuade her mother to pay for more singing lessons.

Flo saw Yook Lan's face and wondered if it was true that Yook Lan was running around with a Fahn Gwai boy. Rumor had it that she planned to run away and get married. Yook Lan must be brainless. Even Flo wouldn't dare. Flo looked down at Madam Quock, only to have the plump woman scold her to stand straight. How could Yook Lan dare to come up against her mother, in fact, come up against the entire town? In the end, Flo pushed aside the thought. That was Yook Lan's problem.

On Friday, the sixteenth day of September, Liah's third cousin, his wife and their two sons and a daughter arrived. She hadn't seen them since they moved to Fresno. The oldest son, now sixteen, was a tall, thin shy boy; the second son, fourteen, was a lively rambunctious one. Third cousin's thirteen-year-old daughter was the image of her mother and just as aloof.

Later the same day, Sen's fourth uncle and wife arrived, creating a stir when the taxi pulled up to the entrance of Peacock Alley. Sen felt pride when he saw his three nephews, such strapping, big boys, aged nineteen, seventeen and fifteen, towering above their parents.

By five o'clock there was a group of residents milling about the Alley waiting for the wedding festivities to begin. The youngsters were especially eager as they hung around the doorway in hopes that the lady of the peacocks would give them lucky money or candy.

Throughout the day, Sen had watched for the arrival of Cousin Quock. By six o'clock, he was despairing. There was a trace of tears in his voice when he lamented to Liah. "With my older brother no longer alive and Elders Lee and Wong unable to attend, I had hoped Cousin Quock would be here to represent that earlier part of my life in Dai Faw."

"He'll be here if he promised," soothed Liah. "Cousin Quock is a man of his word. Be patient, Sen."

Sen flared, "Look who's speaking of patience!"

"The wedding is not until tomorrow, Sen. Be assured Cousin Quock will be here. Now, please help me with the gifts. There are so many, we are running out of space."

Liah glanced over at Cook, busily deboning chicken for supper. It appeared he was feeling as happy as she was. Liah cast a furtive glance at Sen moodily sipping his cup of tea. Her comparison of Cook to Sen made her feel guilty and Liah quickly went into her bedroom. She had to give thanks once more to Kwan Yin.

The family was gathered in the front room for the social hour before supper when Mr. Marchesson pushed open the door. The guests were silent as Liah proudly introduced the landlord. He'd come to inquire if there might be something else he could do. He saw Flo's somber face and asked if she were afraid. "A little, sir," answered Flo, almost in tears. "It's just that there are so many people and rituals. I'm scared."

Mr. Marchesson reached out and patted Flo's shoulder. "There, there, try not to think of it. Tomorrow, after the wedding, you and Toh will be able to take up your lives. Just put up with the commotion until then."

As he was going out the door, Mr. Marchesson stopped. "Flo, does your father understand he has to give you away?"

Flo giggled, "Yes, sir, but he doesn't know why."

Dinner was halfway through when a loud knocking at the door brought a halt to the laughter. Liah was alarmed at first, but Sen shouted in joy. "It's Cousin Quock! I recognize his voice."

Cousin Quock roared as he burst into the room, bear-hugging Sen as he congratulated him. It seemed to Liah her husband was transformed into a different person. The first moments of reunion done, the fisherman roared for one of the children to help him. "I have two huge gunny sacks outside. Bring them in."

Liah made room for Cousin Quock at the table, insisting he sit beside Sen. "All day he's watched for you, sir. Sen was so afraid you wouldn't come."

Liah had forgotten Cousin Quock's size. The roar of his voice had not diminished. In fact, he'd not aged and his strength hadn't weakened. If anything, Cousin Quock seemed younger and stronger. Quickly, Liah went to the cupboard for another wine cup. She felt full of pride as she held out the cup and urged Cousin Quock to eat and drink. "I will make the marinade and Cook will prepare the crabs. It'll be like the first time in Dai Faw!"

Dinner took on a boisterous mood, Cousin Quock reminding Sen of earlier days when they had fished together on his junk. For the first time since he left Dai Faw, Sen thought of Dak, Elder Wong's younger brother. Sen wondered if Dak was a happier man than Elder Wong.

Thomas and Shelley told him of their trucking line and Cousin Quock nodded his approval. "Do you remember," roared Cousin Quock, "when I said I'd take you fishing with me? Now, look at the both of you. Sen, you are a fortunate man. Not one but five grown sons!"

When Sen inquired where he was fishing these days, Cousin Quock's face darkened. "Not in Dai Faw! The Fahn Gwai bastards chased us out. I fish now in *Montelay* (Monterey)."

The men visited and drank in the front room after dinner.

Saturday morning, the wedding day, the townspeople came to pay their respects, to offer thanks for the moon cakes, to wish the bride well and to leave their small packets of money wrapped in red paper. At eleven o'clock, Liah and the family, accompanied by the groom's family, went to the temple. An entourage of well-wishers shouted joy as Liah walked down the cobblestones onto Marchesson Gai. For a fleeting moment, Liah wished the temple were already moved to Peacock Alley. In the future, she prayed, when her sons would wed, she'd only have to walk a few doors down on Peacock Alley.

A murmur rippled through the crowd as they spied Marchesson walking alongside Liah's Eldest Son and envied Liah her friendship with such an important Fahn Gwai. Sen, caught up in the wedding emotions, seemed to walk taller beside his wife. Flo was the only one who dreaded the temple ritual, wishing the tea ceremony done. Out of the corner of her eye, Flo sought Toh's eye, but he was looking down at the ground, his face grim, resolute.

Once the ceremony was done, Liah stepped into the street and felt triumphant as she headed back toward Peacock Alley. Kwan Koong and Kwan Yin willing, she would make the wedding trip many times.

She stepped into the front room of Number Three, frowning at the tall, huge baskets of roses and lilies decorated in their white ribbons intermingled with pink and shuddered at the lack of red. Fahn Gwai! She'd never understand them. Why did they use the dismal color of mourning white for weddings? The bride and her bridesmaids went to change into their Fahn Gwai clothes. Such a hilarious racket arose that

Liah went to investigate. Flo's cheeks flamed red and Yook Lan turned away. It was clear the girls were enjoying a ribald joke. Liah chided them that the guests were arriving.

Suey Wah, uncomfortable with prattling females, wished the second part of the wedding ceremony were done. Why, he thought, did females demand such a splashy affair, when in truth a man was only acquiring a nag? Sen, standing beside Cousin Quock, nodded with a grim expression. "Come now, Sen. Weddings are primarily for women, so let your wife have her day. You and I know it's a lot of fuss for getting an eternal nagger."

When Liah reappeared in the front room, she was wearing a brown brocaded cheongsam, embroidered with gold chrysanthemums. Cousin Quock gaped. Sen retorted wryly, "Cousin Wah gave it to her."

The bridal march sounded as Mert placed the phonograph needle on the record. Flo gently took her father's arm as he awkwardly led her to the simple altar. A silence hung over the room, the minister smiled and Thomas was heard to clear his throat.

The ceremony was simple, taking exactly ten minutes. Then Flo found herself crushed by her brothers and tearful sister. Guests and family pressed red packets of money into her hands. William was the only unsmiling one as he gently wished Flo well and shook Toh's hand. Liah watched her daughter, thinking to herself that she was the epitome of the docile bride. Thank Kwan Yin for that!

The minister remained long enough to drink a toast to the bridal couple, then departed, leaving Mr. Marchesson the only Fahn Gwai sharing in the noisy camaraderie. At the conclusion of the buffet, after the cake was cut, Mr. Marchesson whispered to Flo to throw her bouquet. Flo aimed the flowers at Emmi who stood silently by the doorway. She caught the ribboned bouquet, but then ran into her bedroom, sobbing that she'd lost a sister.

After the evening banquet, Liah turned to Flo. "May you and Toh find a lifetime of wedded joy."

Toh and Flo both blushed furiously and fled outside to their waiting taxi. They drove off to the apartment Toh had just rented for them in the produce area of town.

The next day, Sunday, a huge noon feast closed the three days of celebrations. Flo and Toh, flustered by talk of grandparenthood, blushed. Liah saw Sen earnestly speaking with Cousin Quock, but could not overhear their conversation. Each time she passed them in the kitchen, their talking ceased. Once she heard Cousin Quock reprimand Sen and wondered why. Later, as Cousin Quock said good-bye, Liah noticed his grim expression was devoid of his usual joviality.

By late Sunday night, Number Three was deserted. Liah was left with the task of picking up Eldest Daughter's room. She hoped Eldest Daughter would be a better housekeeper for Toh. A stray pair of stockings, a blouse, a petticoat. Sen growled, "No matter now. She's Toh's responsibility." Sen's voice was harsh and somehow he seemed to have shed the joyful mien and resumed his surly ways.

Sen dropped back into his remote, moody ways, refusing all Liah's attempts to inveigle him into conversation. There was a new aura about Sen as if he harbored a secret and was waiting for the right moment to spring it on her. The days passed and on the twenty-fifth day of September her suspicions were confirmed. Alone at the supper table, she placed her arm on his, but Sen drew away almost angrily. "We must talk Sen. About us."

"Not now." he growled. "I am tired, perhaps tomorrow."

Fury gripped Liah after the first moments of hurt disappointment. Not even as she readied for bed would Sen come near her. Several hours later, through a fog of sleep, Liah heard the sounds of drawers opening and closing. She raised her head and saw Sen with an armful of clothing. "Clean out your closet tomorrow, Sen."

Sen turned and dumped the clothes into a huge valise and snapped the lock. "It won't wait till tomorrow. I'd planned on telling you later, but you might as well know now. I'm moving into Eldest Daughter's room until...."

Liah cut Sen short. "You can't do that!"

"It's only for a short time. I've booked passage home. Gem Sahn is no longer bearable, at least not under this roof."

Suddenly it hit Liah that Sen was not including her in his plans. Liah's fury ignited. "I suppose you have in mind a young concubine. A man of your age and with seven children." Liah paused, then demanded, "I suppose you have the money for your passage?"

Sen slammed his way out of the bedroom, returning a moment later to snatch his overcoat, raincoat and hat from the hook behind the door. He lurched to the alcove bed, leaning over. "My passage is already paid for and not with tainted money." He snarled, "And one more thing, when you speak to me from here on out, use a civil tongue or else do not speak." With that parting shot, Sen whirled about, slamming the door as he left.

Liah gaped at the shut door. How dare he? Just like that, cut off a marriage and with no thought to his children. Liah grabbed a teacup on the night table and hurled it against the wall separating her bedroom from that of Eldest Daughter's. "Oh, my outraged master. If that is your wish, go! Beget your bastards! You're certainly of no use to me, you eunuch!"

The commotion awakened Emmi and Liah commanded her daughter to go back to sleep. "Mother is saying good night to your father."

Once again in her alcove bed, Liah felt pent-up emotions leave her body and felt a new freedom, a new strength, something she'd not felt for a long time. She murmured sleepily, "I'll tell him tomorrow I didn't mean all the ugly things I said."

Liah awakened at noon and, remembering her promise of the night before, rushed from her room. She rapped on her daughter's door, then pushed her way in. Sen was gone! The valise was gone! She felt anger against herself. She should have told him yesterday! Ah, well, the Gods did not mean for them to part on friendly terms.

Later in the day, Liah learned through Professor that Sen was staying with Cousin Shah. The scholar was somewhat embarrassed as he related the heated argument between Cousin Shah and Sen. "Do not hold these words against me, Liah. I am only relating what Cousin Shah told me. Cousin berated Sen for his leniency with you and said Sen should have whipped you. Sen said he couldn't blame you, for he had not been able to provide the family with the necessities as well as you could. He said he had not been the man he should have."

Liah listened sorrowfully and felt the pain Sen must have felt admitting this to his cousin. Ah, moaned Liah silently, that humans had to suffer so. Whose fault was it that their marriage had fallen apart? Certainly it was not her fault and perhaps not even Sen's. That fate could create such victims!

Professor felt acute discomfort as he blurted out the promise Sen forced his cousin to make: that Liah would need protection following the path she was on and that Cousin Shah must promise to give Liah his strength and stand beside her in times of trouble. "If you want me to return home in peace, you'll grant me this," Sen declared.

A lengthy silence engulfed the scholar and Liah before she asked when Sen was leaving. Professor replied, "I don't know for certain, but probably around the end of month, seeing as the steamer from Hong Kong will dock in Dai Faw just before that time and it usually takes a week for the steamer to reach Loo Sahng after that. I will make inquiries at the travel agency if you'd like."

"Not necessary, sir. The only reason I ask is for the children. They will want to say good-bye to their father. I sincerely hope they will understand their father's leaving." Liah sighed, thanking Professor, who gratefully bid her a hasty good-bye.

Sen's leaving home left Thomas, Shelley and Theo sullen and silent. The younger children were shattered and for the first time did not have their mother's comfort to turn to. Liah retreated deep into a shell and mentally seemed miles away. Cook tried to assuage their sorrows but knew he could not. When Eldest Son asked if they'd had a quarrel, Liah snapped, "Certainly not. You're old enough to ask your father. You know the ways of men. He didn't tell me why he was leaving."

Thomas quickly apologized. "I meant no disrespect, but Ba-Ba's going is so sudden. I guess I'd better take the kids to say good-bye to him. I hear he's at Cousin Shah's place."

The sight of his seven children wrenched at Sen's heart. Emmi ran forward and clutched at Sen's arm, begging him not to leave. Thomas reached out, jerked Emmi to his side and gave her a warning look. Cousin Shah glared fiercely as he listened to Sen explain why he was leaving. At one point, Cousin Shah started to speak, but Sen gently motioned for silence.

Sen leveled his finger at his children. "I want you to promise me all of you will care for your mother. Everything she is doing is because of you children. It's just that Ba-Ba has never been happy in Gem Sahn. I seek peace for the remainder of my life in the land of my birth. Now, if you really love me, you will allow me to leave in peace."

He turned to his youngest son. "Someday, you and Second Daughter will come to know why I had to leave. Meanwhile, study hard and make something of yourselves. Perhaps you might even come and visit me. You ought to see the land of your origin."

Sen gravely turned to Eldest Son and Second Son. "You two understand the situation, but promise me you will look after your mother as well as your sisters and brothers. Father thanks you both for assuming the task he is now unable to finish. May Kwan Koong protect you and make your lives easier than mine. Now, take the children home."

Thomas shook hands solemnly with his father, then embraced him, as did Shelley. William and Mert, almost in tears, grabbed their father's hand, then shamelessly hugged and kissed him. Emmi suddenly broke loose from Thomas, ran up to her father, sobbed and begged him again not to leave. With anguish on his face, Thomas went up and again pulled Emmi away. With one last silent look, Sen waved and went inside.

The walk home was miserably silent. As they approached Peacock Alley, Thomas stopped and commanded them to listen to what he had to say. "All you guys know Mah's birthday is coming up. Be sure you don't ruin her day by crying. Like Ba-Ba said, everything Mah does is for our good."

William wiped away a tear and said softly, "The twenty-ninth of September is Mah-Mah's birthday. The same day Ba-Ba is leaving"

Shelley muttered, "Not in a million years will we ever forget that date. Neither will Mah."

Theo glowered as Thomas further commanded them to smile when they saw their mother. Shelley muttered, "Yeah, and all of you will have to quit being selfish and stupid babies."

Thomas nudged Shelley roughly. Shelley exclaimed, "Aw, lay off, guy. It's hard on all of us!" He looked down at Emmi's tearstained face and tousled her hair. "Okay, sis? Are you okay?"

Supper was dismal, silent and tense. Everyone struggled to remain cheerful. At the meal's end, infuriated with the sorrowful faces around the table, Liah silently accused her husband of cruelty. Her voice was gentle. "Your father was never happy in Gem Sahn. Should we demand he stay and be wretched? He's toiled long and hard for us. Now he ought to be given the right to return to his land of birth. Won't you children allow your father the desire of his heart? Please, let him go in peace. You're grown up enough now to understand it takes sacrifice to make another person happy."

Cook listened and, glimpsing Second Daughter's eyes brimming with tears, fumed silently at Liah and Sen. Why couldn't the two of them resolve their differences without hurting the children? Still, he had to agree that Liah was right in trying to unify the town. Because of her efforts, her children wouldn't face the perils their elders had. Ah, well, children heal easily. Cook sneaked a glance at Liah, wondering if she, too, would soon shed the pain of her husband's departure.

Immediately afterwards, the children kissed their mother good night and went to their rooms. Only Eldest Son remained, exchanging sympathetic glances and reaching out for Liah's hand. Silently, he kissed her good night, then went to his room.

The night before Sen sailed, Cousin Shah held a farewell dinner. Liah's children, led by Thomas, went, to share the last meal they would have with their father and to say farewell. The dinner was solemn. Emmi's tears as she clung to Sen almost made him change his mind, but his recollection of Liah accusing him of being a eunuch steeled his resolve. Gently, Sen pushed his youngest daughter away from him and motioned for Thomas to take the children home.

As they left, Sen waved from the doorway and shouted, "All of you remember your father loves you dearly. Farewell! To be sure, I will know of you and your behavior. Farewell."

Sen remained at the doorway waving until his children turned the corner onto Alameda South, then shut the door, figuratively closing the door on his life in Gem Sahn. Tears coursed down his cheeks as he half-murmured, "Cursed land which robbed me of all I value."

Liah awakened at eleven o'clock, depressed that it was her birthday and also the day her husband deserted her. She was forty-four years old and alone, with so many unfulfilled dreams. Had Sen planned this as punishment? If so, he had succeeded, for on each succeeding birthday she would be reminded of her disobedience, which had ultimately caused him to return home. It was very difficult not to hate Sen.

When she entered the kitchen, Liah smelled the aroma of chicken frying. Cook, without turning, said good morning and continued frying. "I thought it might raise the spirits of the children. They love fried chicken."

In one blinding moment, Liah realized that with Sen's departure she was free. A shyness accompanied her as she took her seat, waiting silently. When Cook set her cup of herbal tea on the table she could read nothing in his opaque eyes. It was not until late afternoon that the tears, which Liah had repressed, fell down her cheeks. Very gently, Cook touched her arm. Liah reached out blindly, clung to his arm, her head on the table, sobbing convulsively.

The crest of her emotions passed and Liah became aware of her clinging to Cook's arm and abruptly pulled away. Her cheeks flushed crimson and she turned her face away. Sensing her guilt, Cook sighed and spoke softly. "The Gods destined our love, Liah, or else circumstances would not be ours to consummate it. Liah, it is yet too soon, but since we are confronted with the issue, let me speak.

"A thousand daily whiplashes have I endured in my love for you. I shall not press you, rather, when you are ready, I shall be waiting. You will come to me freely and without contrition."

He began to chuckle. "I have something else to confess. While I am frying chicken for supper in an attempt to raise the children's spirits, that is not entirely the only reason. The children want to surprise you for your birthday. I tell you this now, because I want you to pretend you are surprised, that you are happy. So, fortify yourself as there will be guests, too."

"Oh, Cook, I hope they've not invited too many. My heart is too tear-sodden and I am filled with shame. Professor might understand, but I'm certain none of the others will. They'll probably gloat and condemn me."

"Foolishness, Liah! You can no more control Meng-Sui than swerve the course of a flood. You will live out your life as decreed by the Gods as shall Sen. Neither of you have anything of which to be ashamed. Enjoy this feast day of yours, your first day on earth."

She lowered her eyes, pursed her lips and was silent. A faint smile played around the corners of her mouth as she stole a glance at Cook. Liah felt a quiver of joy, thought how paradoxical to feel both sorrow and joy at one time. Perhaps in time she would put aside her sad memories of Sen. She shook her head in disbelief that Sen could actually leave her.

A STRANGER IN TOWN

Life in Number Three returned to normal several weeks after Sen's departure for his village in the Kwangtung Province of China. The children, caught up in their schoolwork and play, seemed to have forgotten their grief. Liah was calmer than she'd ever been since coming to Gem Sahn. Certainly her heart was more at peace.

She turned to Professor with whom she was sharing lunch. "See how easily the children have forgotten their father? It's as if Sen never was. I am prone to believe I'm wasting my life trying to ensure their safety. I should forsake them before their ingratitude destroys me."

Professor smiled knowingly. "That is what you say now, Liah, but let any one of them be in need and you'll be by their side in an instant."

He leaned back in his chair and asked gruffly, "What did you expect? Your children have seemingly forgotten their father, but in their hearts Sen will always be there. They are wiser than you. They sense that life goes on despite grief. Be grateful they are resilient, otherwise how could they ever weather the vicissitudes of life?"

Cook smiled smugly at Professor and gave Liah an I-told-you-so glance. Liah pulled on her cigarette and did not answer. Presently Professor gave Cook a nervous glance, took in a breath and asked if Cook had seen the stranger who was rumored to have come from Dai Faw.

Liah's eyes flew to Cook. "What stranger? And what is he doing here?"

Cook shook his head. He'd only heard rumors. Professor cleared his throat again and said, "I meant to tell you, Liah, but thought I'd try to find out more beforehand. I hear he's surrounded by a bevy of females. Does that give an inkling as to what he does?"

"Professor, you know I dislike strangers in town. Why didn't you at least mention it? You must check out the rooming houses and the hotel. We must know more."

Professor shook his head. "You know how touchy Sam Chew is about giving out information on his guests. I'd hoped to catch the hotel janitor alone and to ask him, but we must not make people suspicious of our motives. We don't want to look like we're policing."

Cook chuckled. "I too, was hoping to glean more information. I saw Kam in Lion's Den Alley last week and he said he'd seen the man. According to Kam, he surmised the stranger was a northerner, perhaps from Peking. He is said to wear the long robe and high-soled brocaded slippers of the Manchu. Kam said he didn't like the man, as he seemed arrogant, glib of tongue and has cold, shifty eyes. That's all I know."

Changing the subject, Cook cautiously informed Liah that Eldest Daughter was very upset over her father's departure. "She suspects you had a fight with him. The next time you see her, please explain the facts, or perhaps have Eldest Son do it."

Liah pushed her plate away, frowning. The news of the stranger and Eldest Daughter's displeasure took Liah's appetite away. Professor continued, "You know, Liah, we cannot prevent anyone who wishes to live here from doing so. If our authority is to prevail, we must not be seen as overbearing or tyrannical. Let me do some more looking around." He smiled. "I promise not to withhold anything again."

Liah grinned. Cook sighed. Why couldn't he manage to placate Liah in the manner Professor did?

Professor took his leave and Cook followed him out the door as he had groceries to purchase.

Four days later, Professor came early in the day to inform Liah the stranger was to be her neighbor. "He's taken up residence at Number Ten. He told one of the waiters at Wong's Café. Although he didn't mention his profession, the waiter also noticed all the ladies he parades about town."

Somewhere in the recesses of her mind, Liah felt an uneasiness. Experience had taught her these feelings bespoke of misfortune and she wondered about the stranger.

"If, in fact he is a pimp, to have him open up a public brothel in Peacock Alley wouldn't be good for the neighborhood," said Cook. "What are you going to do about it?"

"Nothing," replied Professor. "As long as he doesn't parade his females up and down the cobblestone walk."

Professor turned. "Liah, I think you ought to ask Chon Woo about the man's plans. I hear they drink together every night in Chon's room."

Liah shook her head. "In that case, I'm certain Chon has told him of the levies and the initial fees. We'll just have to wait."

When Wong Sang came that Saturday night with the receipts, he raved about the stranger's beautiful girls. "God, I've forgotten how delicate and lovely our women are. One gets used to the brash Fahn Gwai females."

"Oh, so you're familiar with this stranger?" inquired Liah.

Wong Sang shook his head. "No, I have just seen him with the women when they walk around town. Chon knows him and said his name is Lee Tzu Tzo. He claims to be from Peking, wears northern-style clothes and is arrogantly proud of his northern birthright, as if he is a member of Manchu royalty. Stupid, isn't it?"

"Yes, yes. Go on. What else did Chon tell you?"

"Only that the man was born in Peking, but when his father died his mother took him back to her village in Kwangtung. That's all I know."

Liah pondered this, then asked, "Isn't it strange that he should have returned to Kwangtung? Usually, a son remains in the father's village. It's also strange that his mother was allowed to leave with him."

Wong Sang shrugged as if such a fact was unimportant. He grinned. "I can't wait until the guy opens up. Well, here's the night's take. I have plans to go to Chon's bar. I'd like to see this guy."

Liah scowled, warning Sang to keep his distance until the man's mo-

tives were ascertained. "Work hard, be thrifty, then you will be able to
have a woman of your own."

"Yeah," quipped Sang, "meanwhile I'll use his."

—

On the last day of October, Lee Tzu Tzo paid Professor a visit. The
scholar was surprised by the man's height, dramatically emphasized
by his thin, pale, angular face and long blue mandarin robe. The man's
high forehead contrasted sharply with his straight black, slicked-down
hair. Professor turned his gaze to the man's long, pale, sculptured
hands, his gestures almost effeminate. "My name is Lee Tzu Tzo, but if
you'd feel more comfortable, you may call me Lee Chu Cho."

Professor felt an instant dislike for the man's condescending manner,
but guardedly he nodded and said he'd use whatever pronunciation
Lee Tzu Tzo wanted. The man simply said, "Call me Lee Cho." His
voice irritably bullish, Lee Cho inquired about the levies. "I understand
I cannot open up for business unless they're paid."

"That is so, sir," replied Professor, deriving a slight pleasure from
the man's frown. "Oh, by the way, my name is On Wei, but most folks
here call me Professor. I welcome you to our town. Perhaps you'll share
tea with me?"

While they sipped tea, the scholar plied Lee Cho with as many questions as he could without arousing suspicion. He learned that indeed
Lee Cho had been born in Peking and that his father had been an officer
in the Manchu army. Upon his father's death and his mother's re-mar-
riage, the family moved to Kwangtung where his stepfather owned a
mercantile store. His tone silkily superior, Lee Cho murmured, "That
accounts for my speaking both Mandarin and Cantonese."

As the hour wore on, Professor felt increasingly irritated by Lee Cho.
Not only did he not like the man's glib tongue, but somehow the scholar
also sensed evil lurking in the man's aura. In his mind, Professor re-

called the recent disappearance of a concubine in Dai Faw and wondered if Lee Cho were involved, had come to Loo Sahng to hide out or
perhaps his parent Tong had even sent him. His train of thought was
broken when Cho started inquiring about Liah.

"She is wife of Lee Fook Sen, who recently returned to Kwangtung.
Who knows, you might even be related."

Lee Tzo's expression clearly indicated that he deplored the idea of
his being related to a commoner. Wasn't it so that the blood of the
Manchu flowed through his veins? At least on his father's side. Tzo, recalling where he was, shook his head and politely said he doubted there
was any relationship. "While we are speaking about Madam Liah, may
I inquire about the unusual fact that a woman heads the Council? Is it
not also audacious that you all chose to separate yourselves from the
parent Tongs in Dai Faw?"

"It isn't strange at all, Tzo. Liah is a capable woman, tenacious in
her actions and stubborn of nature. Not only that, she has the foresight
and dedication to make this town a safe place for us. I'll offer one word
of advice, Tzo. If you plan to reside on China Gai, you'd better know
Liah is not a person to toy with. Anyone who jeopardizes the town's
well-being automatically becomes her enemy."

The pimp said nothing as he leisurely drew on his cigarette. Ugh,
thought Professor as he watched the smoke disappear for a long moment only to reappear suddenly out Tzo's nostrils. The man almost
looked like a fire-breathing dragon. Professor was also offended each
time Tzo waved his long, ivory cigarette holder to make a point or
flicked a long ash, the gesture made almost as if he were conferring a
royal favor.

"I do intend to remain here; and do not worry, I shall do nothing to
enrage the lady. I intend to call upon her to find out how much the initiation fees are and the amount of my monthly levies." Lee Tzo paused,
then abruptly asked, "Can anyone be a member of the Council?"

"No, sir," replied Professor, suddenly suspicious. "A man must be nominated by one of the existing members and approved by the other members. Of course, to ensure against mischief, the nominator stands equally guilty should the new member prove a liability. Punishment for any crime committed by the new member will also be meted out to his sponsor. Does that answer your question, sir?" Lee Tzo daintily folded his napkin and pushed aside his teacup. He sensed the scholar's irritation and quickly rose. "I fear I have overstayed my first visit and for that I apologize. I am not usually so rude and insensitive. I thank you for your hospitality, sir. Perhaps you'll allow me the opportunity to reciprocate. For now, I'll say good-bye."

Professor watched from his doorway as the pimp made his way across the street to Peacock Alley. He shuddered as Lee Tzo raised his robe as he walked much like a woman raises her skirt to avoid soiling its hem. Professor felt a foreboding about the man. If only he could put his finger on why, he'd feel better. Kam Fong was right. Lee Tzo was an unpleasant person with an unspoken purpose.

As soon as Lee Tzo disappeared into Number Ten, Professor put on his coat and made his way to Number Three. Perhaps Liah would be able to penetrate his dubious feelings.

—

It was not until the second day in November at ten-thirty in the morning that Lee Tzo paid a visit to Number Three. A stranger, he didn't know the hour was too early, that Liah never received callers until after twelve noon. Lee Tzo rapped on the screen, then rapped a second time when no one appeared. The heavy glass-panel doors were open, indicating someone was home. Once more he rapped, then opened the screens and stepped inside.

He came face to face with the peacock and the peahen. Startled by the pimp's entrance, they sent up an earsplitting shriek followed by angry screams.

In the kitchen, Liah's mouth flew open as she dropped her teacup and raced into the corridor followed by Cook shouting for caution. There she came face to face with Lee Tzo, an astounded expression pasted on his face. "What," demanded Liah angrily, "do you mean by frightening my pets? What do you want and who are you?"

Standing behind her, Cook poked Liah in the back. All at once, she noticed the mandarin robe and realized the man must be Lee Tzo.

Dumbfounded by the peacock and peahen and now astounded by the tiny woman before him, Lee Tzo stuttered, "Er, ah, I am very sorry, Madam, my name is Lee Tzo. I'm sorry to have frightened your koong jeks, but in truth they frightened me as much as I them. I have come to pay my respects."

Liah nodded, smiled slightly and invited him into the kitchen for tea. As they walked down the corridor, she thought that Kam Fong and Professor were right; she didn't like the man either.

Tea was no more successful than his entrance. Lee Tzo sat on the edge of his chair, still unnerved by his abrupt entrance. Liah leaned back in her seat, explaining that she never received callers until after the noon hour. "I am sorry you were made so unwelcome by my pets. They are good as watch dogs."

However apologetic Liah's mien appeared, her tone gave Tzo to know she'd brook no deviation in visiting hours nor would she tolerate any other infractions. He shuddered at her eagle eyes and wondered if she were as hard as reputation in Dai Faw had her. Such power to be held in the hands of a mere female. Outrageous, thought Tzo, fighting to keep his displeasure from showing. However, if he were to live in this wretched town, he'd better kowtow for the time being.

Liah became annoyed when Tzo mentioned that they might be distantly related, both having come from Kwangtung. "Oh," smiled Liah. "Are you Hakka?"

Tzo held himself slightly rigid and shook his head. He—a lowly villager?

Liah saw him fidget with his gold chain and knew the man was about to ask a question.

Tzo leaned forward. "Madam, I understand before I can open up my doors I must pay not only levies but an initiation fee?"

"Quite correct, sir." Liah's tone now shifted from a friendly, sociable pitch to brisk and businesslike. To be so easily set aside and made to feel inferior angered Tzo. If he lived long enough to repay her insults, his sojourn in Loo Sahng would indeed be worthwhile. His eyelids drooped and his tone became silky again. "How much will my levy be, Madam? I hope it is not beyond my reach to pay."

"Sir, the rates of levies were agreed upon by the Council. I am sure yours will not only be fair but well within your reach. Such is your business, I doubt you will be unduly burdened."

Lee Tzo informed Liah he already had his own two sentries who kept order in the brothel, but also acted as watchdogs in case of police raids. "Will I still pay as much in levies?"

"I also have my own sentries, many more than you, but I pay my levies. Sir, we are not robbers. It takes considerable money to provide welfare for the town's aged, sick and needy, for the temple we hope to move into Peacock Alley as well as for the school for the youngsters."

A moment of silence ensued, then Liah, exasperated by Tzo's effeminate gestures, allowed herself the luxury of dropping any guise "Sir, if conditions here are not to your liking, I suggest you return to Dai Faw. We are doing what we must."

An uncomfortable silence hung in the kitchen. Cook untied his apron and quietly left by the rear door, a signal to Liah that she was not acting in her own best interest. Before Liah had a chance to soften her remarks, Tzo began to giggle. "Madam, I did not mean to quarrel. As a newcomer, I find it unusual, these fees, these levies and laws, which do not exist in Dai Faw. You are indeed farsighted. Your town is indeed fortunate."

Liah began to squirm in her seat, wishing the man would conclude his visit. Her head, which had ached only slightly when he arrived, was now throbbing unbearably. The scoundrel—to have come so early in the day!

Lee Tzo, delighted with Liah's apparent discomfort, waxed eloquent again, murmuring, "It seems your town will never have to do without. Not with all the monies flowing into its coffers."

Liah poured Tzo another cup of tea and wished Cook would return. Her eyes were steely as she reiterated how peaceful China Gai was and that she hoped nothing would change that.

"The heavens strike me dead if I mean any mischief, Madam. You have my word, I shall be a credit to your town."

Liah's lost her self-control. She pointed a finger at Tzo. "What do you mean, sir? My town? You've said that three times now and I resent the implications. Nobody owns this town, unless it is the residents. Not today, nor tomorrow not ever, will anyone use our town for selfish purposes. Now, if you do not mind, this visit is done. I am weary and I bid you good day."

Lee Tzo's face was a cold, hard mask as he gaped. It angered him that he'd overextended his good judgment. Foolish of him not to know that she'd catch his innuendoes. He rose, bowed and went into the corridor.

Lee Tzo left Number Three fuming to himself at Liah's curt dismissal. Nobody, let alone a woman, could treat him as if he was a commoner. A thought crossed his mind that he might fail in his mission. Damn! Why did he allow himself to become ensnared in such an audacious scheme to begin with? Perhaps he could still back out, he thought. But deep in his heart he knew once committed to the gang, there was no escape. He shuddered. The only way to leave was death. Secret society or no, there had to be a way.

The pimp was so engrossed in his dilemma that he did not notice Professor until the scholar was abreast of him. The man's voice startled Tzo and he lurched and would've stumbled had the scholar not put out an arm to steady him. "I'm sorry, I didn't mean to frighten you, sir. I thought perhaps we might have lunch at Wong's. However, perhaps this is an inopportune time."

Lee Tzo giggled nervously, admitting he was a bit shaken. "I made the error of calling on Madam before the hour of noon. You are absolutely correct. She is forthright and determined. I don't know which shocked me more, Madam Liah or her koong jeks."

"Oh, my," murmured Professor sympathetically. "You indeed had an encounter. Well, after all that, you need a chance to recover."

They walked off the cobblestones, turned left onto Marchesson Street, took the Pig Alley shortcut and entered Dragon's Den Road. It did not escape Lee Tzo's notice that several people stopped them to wish Professor good health and to say good day. Some of Tzo's self-esteem was restored when Mr. Wong welcomed them, even if his greeting was mostly for Professor.

Once they had ordered, Lee Tzo postulated that perhaps all the attention Professor received was due to his seat on the Council. "A seat on the Council surely brings honor and recognition, sir."

Professor shook his head. "No, it's because I do their letter writing and, in so doing, know their lives intimately. Because I am literate, they bring me all their problems; we've shared their woes as well as their joys. Perhaps too, our countrymen here revere a scholar as they do in the old country."

"Be that as it may, sir," argued the pimp, "you are a man of distinction, while others such as myself, given the business I'm in, are not. If I were to be a member of the Council, perhaps the stigma of my owning a brothel would diminish."

Professor gaped and reined in his impulse to reject such a notion out of hand. It would not do to have a pimp on the Council. The very thought ruined his appetite. He must see Liah immediately and tell her of this conversation.

Throughout the rest of their lunch, Professor felt uncomfortable and wished he'd never invited the man to join him. He became weary of dodging all of his queries about the Council and Liah. Finally, he looked at his watch and shook his head. "Time has escaped me. I must get to the newsstand to pick up my paper. If I am to post the news on the bulletin board, I must hurry."

On his way to the newsstand, Professor mulled over what had taken place at Wong's and prayed to Kwan Koong that the pimp would not press his wish to join the Council. Harrumph, he thought, as if anything could erase the stigma of his brothel!

The news posted, Professor crossed the cobblestones to Number Three. Liah listened without a word. Professor chuckled. "At first it appalled me, but now that I think of it, isn't it ridiculous? A pimp on the Council?"

Liah's brows were knitted and at length she murmured, "I had a strange feeling Tzo had ulterior motives when he called on me. It struck me as impractical that he'd move to Loo Sahng when there are so many more of our people in Dai Faw. We must pull aside the veil to discover Tzo's real motives for coming here and wanting to join our Council. Just be alert and keep your guard up as you watch him. Cook is already doing so."

The next night at midnight, when the two were together again having a snack, the conversation returned to Tzo. "I've been thinking, Professor. It might not be as impossible to allow Tzo a seat on the Council as we first thought. Of course, we'd have to check out his background and his motives. But if the report on him is good, we could make him pay an exorbitant fee for his seat. We need a new school for the children and the temple needs to be relocated to Peacock Alley. Why shouldn't we consider it?"

"A school funded by a pimp? Liah, surely you are joking!"

Liah gently replied, "A school funded by a pimp is better than no school. The children of Chinatown would be the losers if we allowed our emotions to overrule good sense. Besides, it's only a passing thought."

When Professor left for home, he thought, passing thought indeed! Nothing ever crossed that woman's mind without the possibility of it becoming reality. Professor fumed to himself that a pimp on the Council would be outrageous.

When Cook returned from shopping the next day, Liah saw his grim expression and asked why. It turned out Cook had been in Wong's Café where he'd seen a woman begging for a job just for room and meals. Cook shook his head, "It's bad enough to see a man in those straits but a woman? I felt degraded by my inability to offer help. I fled from the café and ran into Professor but didn't stop to talk. Liah, I felt so sorry for her and ashamed of my own shortcomings."

Liah tapped the table with her chopsticks as she listened, her face stony. "I know how you must have felt, but the Gods have been good to me. I can help her. I want you to return to Wong's and bring her to me. Surely, she can do little chores around the house and help me with my bamboo pipe. The Gods know how hard and long you work."

Cook's initial reaction was to veto the idea, but he couldn't help recalling his own desperation when he too had at one time begged for work and for the exact same wages. Just then, the front door opened and Professor hurried into the kitchen. He stared at Cook as if to ask if he'd seen the woman. Cook nodded. Liah smiled. "Do sit down, sir. I was asking Cook to bring the poor woman to me. Perhaps you might do it for me instead?"

Professor cautioned, "Liah, I know the goodness of your heart, but have you thought of what it means to have a distraught female around you all day and into the night? She appeared very unstable."

"How can she be anything else, sir? It's bad enough for a man to claw for subsistence, but a woman? I think it's disgraceful of our people to allow her such a piteous life, but as Cook pointed out, our people all have their own money problems. Do bring her here, sir."

While waiting for Professor's return, Liah ranted, "I know it is not callousness on the part of our people to close their eyes to another's pain, but it still angers me. The Fahn Gwai shut us out of their world, hound and attack us. Fahn Gwai legislation keeps us apart from our loved ones in China, strips us of any justice we might hope to have and now we do not come to the aid of this unfortunate woman? Sometimes I think the Gods have no eyes."

The front door opened and Cook motioned for silence. Professor entered, lugging two battered suitcases, a tiny woman trailing behind him. Liah noticed she wore the long, dark brown tunic and trousers associated with Hakka women. "Do sit down," cried Liah as she rose to welcome the woman. "You must share lunch with us. And how about you, sir?"

The scholar held up a hand and informed Liah that he'd already eaten at Wong's Café. The woman softly informed Liah her name was Quan Yik Bo and that she'd been living in Dai Faw. The bubonic plague epidemic after the earthquake had taken the life of her husband. Since then she'd seen precarious times. Yik Bo broke down sobbing. Liah gently touched her arm and handed her a handkerchief.

"Cry all of your tears today, for tomorrow will be filled with nothing but joy. How would you like to live here? I need a woman to help me; certainly my two youngest children need constant looking after. When I smoke Apinyin, I need someone to attend me. Cook is already burdened with the duties of the house, laundry and cooking. Will you do this for me, Yik Bo?"

Yik Bo looked up disbelievingly, her mouth agape. In a quick motion, she fell to her knees before Liah. Liah sprang from her chair, yanking her to her feet. "No one in my house ever kneels to another, unless it is before Kwan Yin or Kwan Koong. You will not be a charity case, Yik Bo, but a necessary extra hand in the house."

Rivulets of tears streamed down Yik Bo's face as she mutely nodded. Liah touched her arm, indicating she should follow Cook upstairs to choose her room. "After you've settled in, come downstairs and I will give you two minhois and linen. It gets chilly in the late night and pre-dawn hours."

Once upstairs and in a bedroom, Yik Bo sighed and looked around the spacious room, still not believing she'd found a home. Presently, she noticed Cook's speculative glance and lowered her eyes. Cook told her, "I want you to know Liah is a loving and generous woman, but she is also capable of violent temper tantrums. Please be on your guard and try to read her moods."

Cook paused and then went on, "Because you live in Liah's home, there will be those who will use cunning to try to glean information from you. Whatever you see or hear in this house is not to be spoken of outside of it. Do not be the one to weaken Liah's strength, making her prey to her enemies. Understand?"

Yik Bo nodded her lowered head. Her female curiosity was aroused. Was Cook Liah's lover? Was that the reason her husband had deserted her? And what of her children? How did they relate to him, the usurper of their father's affections? Yik Bo shook her head. No matter, nothing Liah could ever do would be wrong in her eyes.

Liah's children addressed Yik Bo as Amah, as did everyone else as time passed. Amah spent much of her time mothering Liah's youngest daughter. She also took over the mending and picking up after the children, relieving Liah from having to nag them.

In the beginning, Cook felt slightly jealous but slowly realized how much more time he had, now freed from trivial chores. Yik Bo's fierce protection of Liah pleased him and together they formed a barrier against the endless stream of residents who came to Number Three for help or with complaints.

On the nineteenth day of November, Amah was puzzled when Cook circled the date on the calendar. Liah chuckled. "Cook is the historian of our home. Every auspicious date is entered on his calendar. This day is yours, Amah. The day you became one of our family."

Cook's face was grim as he put away the pencil. Luckily, Liah hadn't remembered it was also the day Lee Tzo had paid his initial fees and had become an official resident of town. Although Cook knew that Yik Bo had struck up an acquaintance with Mei-Mei, Lee Tzo's concubine, he didn't think it advisable to speak of it to Liah, though he thought she might be able to furnish vital information about what went on inside Number Ten. Neither had Cook informed Liah that the pimp planned to open his brothel on the twenty-first day of November. There was no need to upset her new-found calm. Liah found out one day as Yik Bo was mending clothes. She mentioned in passing that Mei-Mei's amah had told her the girl was not a prostitute but rather Lee Tzo's concubine. "She told me how he caters to Mei-Mei's every whim and that a wife could not be treated better."

Liah was surprised that Yik Bo had struck up a friendship with Mei-Mei's amah. She nodded and listened as the woman went on, broaching the subject of Wong Sang being a nightly guest there.

"I thought Tzo was friendly with Chon? Rumor had it that they drink together every night in Chon's private room. I wonder why he'd changed and started befriending Sang. Perhaps Wong Sang is more pliant than Chon."

Yik Bo's face revealed her discomfort as she wrestled with a promise she'd made to Mei-Mei's amah not to tell Liah, but she sighed and blurted, "Please do not repeat this, but I was told that Tzo is pressuring Sang for a favor. Amah told me she overheard Tzo wheedling Sang about town politics and asking how you ever got such a hold over the town." Yik Bo's face puckered. "I am worried about you, Liah. Do you suppose that man has evil plans against you?"

"Do not worry about me, Yik, but do be careful about yourself. Never let it appear that you are eavesdropping. You know I have my spies whose job it is to garner information; however, I am grateful to you."

"Oh, Liah," murmured Yik Bo, her head lowered. "I am glad to be of service. It has sat heavy on my heart that I have been such a burden and an object of charity."

Cook, preparing food at the sink, turned to Yik Bo, his face soft. "What a foolish idea. You will never know how much happier Liah is now that you've lifted the heavy work from her shoulders. The children have an extra mother in you. That alone counts for a lot, not to mention all the information you bring. Now, think no more of charity."

Liah felt a deep compassion for Cook in his remarks. It was more meaningful being echoed this time by him. Yik Bo was put at ease.

Amah was not the only person who noticed that the pimp had shifted his attention to Wong Sang and was spending a great deal of time with him. At first Chon had been miffed, but later felt he was better off without Tzo. The man had more on his mind than friendship. Should he warn Wong Sang? No, thought Chon, Wong Sang is old enough to take care of himself and if he's greedy, he'll deserve whatever consequences he gets.

One afternoon, Chon ran into Professor at Wong's Café and mentioned the fact that he feared Lee Tzo had ulterior motives in coming to Loo Sahng. Professor creased his forehead. "Well, if anyone should know, it's you. You're with the man all the time."

"Not anymore, sir. It bothered me the way the man asked so many pointed questions about the Council, about you and mostly about Liah. Well, I haven't all day to chat. My bartender Charlie is away and I have a lot of work to do."

Professor's tone was matter of fact as he advised, "If that's how important Charlie is, you'd better give him a raise. Rumor has it Louie Him is thinking of enlarging his place and putting in a bar. I heard he asked Charlie about finding a bartender."

Taken aback, Chon frowned. Damn, was Professor hinting that perhaps Louie had offered Charlie a job at higher pay? Even though Sang had beat him to the punch, it'd been on Chon's mind to still approach Liah for financial backing, to enlarge his place and maybe modernize it, making it more attractive to the Fahn Gwai. Of course, Lee Tzo had hinted that he would finance him, but Chon had decided that Tzo's price would come too high.

Now when Wong Sang dropped in at Number Three with the night's receipts, he hardly had time to chat and left immediately. Liah murmured half-angrily, "No time these days for conversation? I don't like it. And suddenly Sang is pushing to enlarge his gambling house. Sounds like Tzo has sowed that seed. I wonder what Lee Tzo has in mind."

After one such brief visit, Liah was surprised to see Professor at so late an hour. Liah motioned for him to join her at the table. "Sang was just here and in a hurry to leave. I don't like the way he's been lobbying for us to open a larger place or perhaps even another place."

Cook frowned as he informed Professor they were afraid perhaps Lee Tzo had propositioned Sang to open another place. "Of course for a favor in return."

"It's the favor that bothers me," said Liah half-angrily. "It can't be anything good. I've got the feeling that Wong Sang already has his mind made up to accept Tzo's patronage if I happen to refuse him."

Professor sighed. "That's crossed my mind as well. Chon has told me he refused Tzo's help for fear of what might be asked of him. If Chon of all people can sense that Lee Tzo has ulterior motives, we must be right."

HOLIDAYS WITHOUT SEN

Thanksgiving and Christmas were celebrated at Number Three, but there was an overtone of sadness, for it was the first time without Sen. Although no one mentioned him, everyone missed him and they all knew he was on Liah's mind. Several times Thomas caught his mother's eye and held her gaze as if to say he understood and for her not to worry. However, he knew neither he nor anyone else could bring her comfort or happiness. This was a battle she had to fight alone.

It was not often Thomas brooded over unalterable circumstances, for his was a practical mind. Now, however, he found himself wishing he were a magician so that he could magically bring a smile to his mother's face. He glanced covertly at Cook. A thought that came unbidden to his mind: Was he now his mother's lover?

It was none of his business, Thomas told himself, but he felt a warm flush on his cheek as he banished the vision of his mother in Cook's embrace. Suddenly he was struck with a pang of guilt. Who was he to judge his mother or his father? In the next instant, however, Thomas grinned. Surely, both his parents were no strangers to passion, not with seven offspring!

Thomas glanced at Shelley, then at the rest of his brothers and sister, stopping to stare at Mert. Of all the children, he alone with his soberness and sensitivities missed their father most. Thomas wished he could speak with Mert, but conversation had always been difficult between them. It wasn't just the difference in ages, but also that Mert almost always seemed to be in a world apart. Damn it, thought Thomas, surely William, who was closer to Mert's age, could offer him solace.

Mert noticed his older brother looking at him and Thomas quickly smiled and turned his thoughts to Christmas dinner. When it was over, he and Shel could go out and do up the town. That was one way to forget.

On New Year's Eve Liah was chagrined at having to host Eldest and Second Sons' New Year's Eve party. She complained about the barbaric music they planned to play. "Mah," teased Thomas, "you know you're glad we're not going to go out and get drunk. Besides, by the time our shindig begins, you'll be in bed. We'll not disturb your dinner."

Professor, Sen Fei, Madam Quock, her daughter Yook Lan, Kam Fong, Toh and Eldest Daughter shared the night's supper. Flo was pleased when her mother suggested they stay the night. "Too many drunks out tonight. You can sleep upstairs in the guest room."

Flo was eager to dance. Since her wedding she'd not been to a single party. Thomas frowned. "Sis, you're a married woman now. If I catch you acting up, I'll throw you out. Understand?"

Supper concluded at a quarter to eleven and Professor walked Sen Fei, Madam Quock and her daughter home. "I don't mind, Liah. I have an errand to do, besides having to stop in at Wong's to discuss business with On Lei."

Professor was returning from Wong's Café at one-thirty in the morning when he met Wong Sang in Peacock Alley, the man reeling from one side of the cobblestones to the other. "Sang, in your condition you'll never make it home. How come you're leaving Tzo's so early?"

"Tzo made me leave. He said he didn't want me puking all over the place. The bastard."

"Well, you're welcome to stay at my place, Sang."

"No thanks. I'll make my way home."

Professor watched Sang weave his way down Marchesson Gai and chuckled to himself, "By the time Sang gets home, he'll have walked three times the distance."

—

Wong Sang closed his gambling house a bit after midnight on New Year's Day and came by with the receipts. Liah noticed his unusually quiet demeanor. She knew he was still suffering his debauched drinking on New Year's Eve, but held her impulse to berate him for the early closing. All she said was, "Closing so early? Weren't there men anxious to test their luck in 1915?"

Sang tossed the heavy money sack on the table, muttering that they had already had a great night, so closing early wouldn't hurt their profits. Without another word he walked out and headed to Tzo's. Soon he wished he had stayed at Number Three. At least Liah's verbal drubbing would have been better than listening to Tzo droning on about how the two of them would share in future monies. Sang began feeling fearful, not only of Tzo, but also that Liah might discover what he was doing with the scoundrel.

The pimp pressed Sang for his decision regarding his offer of a partnership in another gambling house. Sang begged for more time to think. Tzo frowned. "I'd hate to think there is cowardice in you. Are you afraid of what Liah might say?"

Sang scowled and Tzo quickly changed his tactics. It would not do to humiliate the man. "Ah, well, I know it's hard not to fear Liah. I myself was in awe of the she-devil. When you've sobered up, we'll discuss this issue more. Let me call one of my girls Mei Wah for you."

After that, Lee Tzo adopted a different strategy, allowing Wong Sang the use of his house for several days without mentioning Liah or his offer of a gambling-room partnership. Then, on the fifth of January, Wong Sang, lethargically drunk and in bed with Mei Wah, was jolted out of his stupor by Lee Tzo appearing in the room and making an abrupt demand.

Sang gaped stupidly, his mouth open and saliva dripping. He pushed Mei Wah away in her attempt to wipe his lips. "You want to be a member of the Council? You're joking, Tzo."

The pimp's face darkened and his fists clenched as he fought the desire to smash Sang's face. Then his voice became silky. "Surely you have but to nominate me, Sang. I'll do the rest. If the men reject me, you'll still get your finances to open a second gambling house. Think of it, Sang. You'll have two gambling houses and you won't have to share the profits of the second one with Liah. You'll be able afford a woman of your own. Who knows? I might even give you Mei Wah."

Wong Sang, still fuzzyheaded, blinked. He could not think. Even in his drunken state, Sang knew fear—fear of Liah. Tzo continued his wheedling: "Let us not talk anymore, I'll call for more wine, then you and Mei Wah can indulge again."

It wasn't long before Professor came to Liah about the persistent rumors that there was to be another gambling house in China Street. No one knew who the owners were, but from what he could gather, everyone believed them to be Sang and Tzo. "And why not?" asked Professor. "He and Tzo are thicker than flies. It is also whispered that the pimp has made some sort of proposition and for accepting, Sang's reward is Tzo's financial backing."

Professor paused to fill his pipe, then asked, "Has Sang asked for a meeting of the Council yet? If he has, perhaps it is to petition a seat for Tzo."

Liah's face creased thoughtfully. "If that is the case, we must have our own candidate also seated to counter Tzo."

"You mean you'll allow that scum to sit on the Council?"

"You forget, sir, I am powerless to prevent it. I do not have voting rights. I have been considering Lim Tao as a candidate, even before knowing about Tzo."

"Do you think you can dissuade Sang from naming Tzo? I mean, you are his partner," cried Professor.

"No, sir, but I will make it expensive for Tzo if indeed he has a mind to join the Council. Our school needs expansion and we do need funds to move the temple into Peacock Alley and to refurbish the shrine."

Professor shook his head.

"Professor," placated Liah, her voice gentle, "I'm not asking for you to put aside your principles. We have the Tenet of Laws to control Tzo's behavior and you and Cook can both keep a sharp eye on Sang and Tzo."

"Enough talking on this sordid subject for now," said Cook. "The two of you have been through too much to allow the likes of Tzo to come between you. Let us share a hot meal on this dismal day."

He placed a covered porcelain tureen on the table and lifted the cover. Up surged the aroma of the hot pot, filled with shrimp, scallops, squid and lobster simmered in a rich broth with sliced bamboo shoots, black mushrooms, water chestnuts, snow peas and young tender shoots of chard.

Professor smiled broadly, nodding agreement. Silently, he gave himself up to the reality of Meng-Sui and Feng-Sui. What will be, will be! At the meal's end, he sighed and thanked Cook for brightening his day. To Liah he said, "I've decided to allow Meng-Sui to prevail. It doesn't, however, ease my prickly conscience, but as you said, it is the children's loss if I hold firm."

Hours after Professor's departure, Liah was thoughtful. "I'm distressed that Professor is having such a furious battle with himself. If only the man wasn't such a strict Confucian, then his morality would not now be assailed."

Liah knew Cook's silence indicated he felt the same way about Tzo's membership in the Council as Professor did and she was disturbed. In all their previous decisions, Cook had always been one to give her courage. She hoped now it was no evil omen.

In the days that followed, Liah's mood was dark. The two men with whom she'd shared so much and held in high esteem were now on opposite sides of the river from her. It was during this black moodiness that Cook received unpleasant news, but was loath to speak of it to Liah. As the days passed, Liah began to notice his reticence each time they spoke alone.

The following week it rained heavily. Professor had not called at Number Three for four days, but before Liah could ask Cook to investigate the matter, the scholar walked into the house one afternoon. After exchanging greetings, Liah inquired if Professor had spoken to Lim Tao.

"No, I have not had the chance. It has been too wet to venture outdoors for the past few days, but I plan to speak with him sometime in the upcoming week. I want to speak to him privately."

Professor lit his pipe, then turned to Liah. "It has been on my mind all these days of rain to make the suggestion that during the wet season we do not hold Council meetings, not unless there is an emergency."

"A splendid idea, sir. It'll also give us time to ask Lim Tao and to inform him of Sang's upcoming nomination of Tzo. Lim ought to know what is in store for him, should he decide to join."

1915

YEAR OF THE RABBIT

L iah's celebration of the New Year of the Rabbit in the Fahn Gwai's year of nineteen hundred and fifteen was unusually elaborate. It seemed to Cook that she was celebrating something more than the New Year, her freedom perhaps, or her anticipation of becoming a grandmother? Whatever the reason, both he and Amah made certain the festivities did not drain her strength.

The afternoon following the feast that closed the ten days of celebrations, Liah knelt before the Goddess in thanksgiving. Her concentration was shattered when the front doors opened and slammed shut, followed by the boisterous voices of Eldest Son and Second Son. Their coming home at all hours for meals was causing Cook to work harder; she'd have to have a talk with them. Quickly, she ended her prayers, lit her coil of incense and met her errant sons in the kitchen.

Liah's voice barked, "You know lunch is served at noon. If you want to eat, you'll have to be home at that hour, or else spend your money and eat at the café."

Eldest Son stopped in his tracks, lifted his mother and plopped her into the upholstered chair. "Now, you must take care of yourself, Mah, and not get so angry. I hear you are to become a grandmother. Is that so?"

Liah gaped, unable to bring herself to scold him. Liah asked how he was so certain of his sister's pregnancy. He shrugged. "I don't know, Mah, guess Toh has let it out around the café. Why not ask him?"

Cook sneaked a glance and saw that Liah was deep in speculation. A grandchild? Oh, if only the Gods were so generous. Liah, impatient to confirm her son's news, chafed as she realized it was only Thursday and Eldest Daughter and Toh would not be visiting until Sunday. For the first time Liah knew how isolated she was on China Street. Without the Fahn Gwai's instrument of conversation, she now had to wait three days for Eldest Daughter and Toh's confirmation.

—

In April Liah knew Sang was ready to ask for a Council session. It was no surprise then, when on a late afternoon he came to see her. He was laden with a huge sack of mangoes, pomegranates and a huge sprig of lychee nuts. His posture was rigid with self-conscious guilt. Mostly, however, it was his nervous giggle that gave her to know he was about to make his move.

Liah sat in her upholstered chair, leisurely smoking a cigarette. She did not ask him the purpose of his surprise visit. Why should she make it easy for Sang? Upon seeing Sang, Cook untied his apron and headed to his room for his wallet, saying that he had to go out to pick up the day's groceries.

"Liah," muttered Sang timidly, "can one person really know another person after only a brief friendship? What I mean is, can one know someone well enough to name that someone for a seat on the Council? A man whose wealth might benefit our people?"

Liah shrugged her shoulders. "Before you think of naming a man to the Council, remember that his behavior, good or evil, will also reflect on you. So, who is this man of whom you think so highly?"

A feeling of doom came over Sang and he quickly shook his head. "No one in particular, Liah. I was merely thinking aloud."

Liah's eyes narrowed, becoming opaque and flinty, and Sang shriveled. Damn! He never should have come. Instead of trying to enlist Liah's help in seating Tzo, he should have surprised the others by making an outright nomination. Quickly, he leaped to his feet, excused himself and giggled that he hoped Liah would enjoy his gift of fruits.

Cook came downstairs, surprised at the rapid conclusion of Sang's visit. Liah chuckled. "You won't have to leave now. Sang got scared and left."

Liah paused and motioned for Cook to be seated. "I've given considerable thought to our Apinyin trade since Tzo's arrival. We should be more cautious and change the locations of deliveries more often."

"I have been thinking the same thing. I think I have a solution to better guard the hiding place of our supplies. As for the delivery sites, I've not used the same place any more than a week."

The next day, Liah awakened to the sound of hammering and went into the kitchen to investigate. It was so unlike Cook to allow noise before eleven o'clock. Despite her sleepiness, Liah gaped disbelievingly at the two unhappy, mewling kittens on the kitchen floor. The hammering was coming from inside the bathroom. "What," she demanded, "are you doing, Cook? And what of the two kittens on my kitchen floor?"

Cook emerged from the bathroom, grinning. "They are a part of my plan. Now, no more questions. Go sit down, I'll fix your morning brew."

Liah tried to shut out the din of the hammering as she sipped her herbal tea, half-playing with the kittens. It seemed to her that the larger one, the orange tabby was the smarter of the two. His brother, a black and white ball of fur, did not try to grab the string, but lapped at the saucer of milk. Liah thought, littermates yet so unlike. Wonder where Cook procured them?

An hour later, Cook called for Liah. "A cat box in the toilet room?" asked Liah.

Cook carefully pried off the top portion of the box, revealing a deeper box below the cat box. Liah smiled. "How clever of you, Cook. No one would ever suspect what is under the cat box."

Cook's face was solemn as he warned Liah never to lift the false top. "If it isn't flush with the floor, it will be noticed. Once we put the sawdust in it and the kittens use it, our cache of Apinyin will be safe."

"How will the cats know that is where they must go?" asked Liah, as she again glanced at the two kittens.

"Cats are smart. You don't have to teach them anything. When they are ready, they will seek out the box. Now, if you are satisfied, I'll fill the box with sawdust."

Cook poured a bit more milk for the kittens. The orange tabby having had his fill, walked away, sniffing about the kitchen. When he wandered through the door to the corridor, Cook picked him up and put him in the bathroom. He grinned and pointed as the tabby kitten stepped into the cat box. His brother, finished with the milk, played with the string near Liah's chair. "Do you think he needs to go, too?"

"Leave him alone, Liah. He has to learn like the other one. Once they know their place, you'll never have to worry."

A half-hour later, Cook called for Liah. He grinned, pointing to the cat box. "Not only did he urinate, but did the other too."

"Now, who is going to clean the mess? I'm certain the children won't."

Cook frowned. "I'll clean it from time to time, but the idea is to leave it messy. The Fahn Gwai won't think of dirtying his hands. They won't look more than they have to, let alone fiddle with the top."

The front door opened and slammed, cutting their conversation short. Liah frowned. "It's Wong Sang."

Cook scooped the two kittens back into their carton. Sang heard the mewling and Liah pointed to the box. "We have mice in the house. When they grow up, they can keep the rodents out."

Sang nodded, taking a chair at the table. Straightaway he blurted, "Liah, please call the Council for a meeting, I want to nominate Tzo for a seat."

Sang read Liah's silence as disapproval. He immediately launched into a defense of Tzo. "If you knew Tzo like I do, you'd know he is generous and with his money we could do a lot for the town. He told me he was in error the last time he called on you so early in the morning and without notice. If you'd like, Tzo said he'd come and speak with you. You can ask him whatever questions at that time."

"Why?" retorted Liah. "We've already met. I see no need for a second meeting."

Sang felt despair. "He's afraid that because he's a pimp the others may reject him. He said his being a pimp has always resulted in shabby treatment. Now he'd like to try to be a lot more than he's been. Will you speak with him?"

"Very well, Sang, I'll speak with him. If he is earnest and has nothing evil in mind, there is no need for him to be afraid."

Wong Sang drew a breath of relief, thanked Liah and scurried out. Liah sat silently for a long time, thinking of questions and conditions she'd have to lay down if she allowed Tzo to be nominated.

—

The first week in May, Lee Tzo again called on Liah, this time at three in the afternoon. She accepted his gift of guavas and alligator pears, bade him to be seated and indicated that they would share a cup of tea. He waxed a smile, lifted his brocaded skirt to sit down and draped the skirt around him. Ugh, she winced, so much like a woman.

After his first sip, Lee Tzo breathed pleasurably, "Ah, my favorite brew, lychee tea."

Liah nodded wordlessly, hoping he would come to the point and mention his bid for the Council. He made trivial talk, looking about him as if holding court. Liah inwardly fumed with the waste of her time, but forced herself to endure his company.

A half-hour later, Tzo's eyes narrowed and his body tightened imperceptibly. Liah braced herself and vowed to listen without rancor. "I am certain you know the purpose for this visit, Liah. Sang intends to nominate me for a seat on the Council. We thought if you were favorable to the idea, the men would accept me, too. Perhaps it would help if I made a donation to one of your charities?"

It rankled him that Liah forced him to wait for her answer. How dare she? No woman ever dared to keep him waiting. Without a preamble, Liah asked, "How big a donation, sir?"

"Whatever amount you designate, Madam."

"Three hundred dollars then."

Three hundred dollars! Lee Tzo added that amount to what he had already paid in initiation fees and levies and fumed. How dare Liah! This was outright thievery. With a controlled voice, he murmured, "That is quite a large sum of money for the badge of respectability, but if that is your demand, then most assuredly I will pay it."

He fluttered his hands in a show of helplessness and was reaching inside his robe for his wallet when Liah held up a restraining hand. "No, pay the monies to Professor. He'll give you a receipt for the amount and, should the men reject your bid for membership, you will be refunded the same amount." Liah felt a surge of pleasure at Tzo's concerned expression when she raised the possibility of his rejection, that despite his women and his money he still might be found unsuitable.

Lee Tzo felt his anger rising but held his tongue. He rose ceremoniously from his chair saying, "I know you are a busy woman so I shall take my leave. I hope the next time we meet, we'll be partners in Chinatown government."

"Not partners, Tzo, fellow Council members," Liah said, almost displaying exasperation. "Furthermore, please do not forget we are in the service of the townspeople. Next time do not feel the need to come with gifts. If your business concerns the Council, feel free to come any time, sir."

Lee Tzo coughed daintily. "It is rumored you have purchased a ruby eye for the teakwood dragon, which will grace the altar in the temple. Allow me to assume part of the cost. Although your coffers do not want for monies, everyone has their limits."

"Certainly not, sir!" Liah snapped. "It is generous of you, but I owe the Gods much for what I have today. No one shall share in my gesture of gratitude, but I thank you." Liah then leaned back, scrutinizing Lee Tzo through half-closed lids and went on, "Are you perhaps dangling ripe fruit before my eyes? If so, please don't."

Lee Tzo's face froze, unable to hide his fury. The outright accusation of bribery was an affront to his dignity and silently he vowed to avenge his honor. Liah, seeing his clenched fists, said quickly, "Let us not act as children. If I seemed forward, it is just that I want it understood between us that bribery is unnecessary. Please accept my apologies. I am a forthright woman and sometimes not too diplomatic, sir. Now, as you said earlier, I am a busy person."

Seething, Lee Tzo, bowed and marched out.

Throughout the remainder of the day, Liah was preoccupied with whether she'd done the right thing in asking for the three hundred dollars. The man definitely had ulterior motives and by Kwan Yin's mercy, she'd find the reasons. By nightfall, Liah was troubled and by bedtime, Cook gave in to her pleas for her bamboo pipe, knowing how desperately Liah wanted deliverance from the stress.

DISSENSION

Two days before the Council meeting on the eighteenth day of May, Cousin Shah paid his first personal visit to Liah since Sen's departure. While he had sent the children packets of money for Christmas, Cousin Shah had not been present for either Thanksgiving or Christmas. Liah surmised that Cousin Shah had surely come to complain about the possibility of Lee Tzo becoming a member of the Council and his disapproval was not long in coming.

"What do you have in mind, allowing a man of Tzo's evil nature to join? Lee Tzo is rumored to be a member of a newly formed dissident faction of the House of Lee, composed of cutthroats, smugglers, thieves and blackmailers. Have you not heard about the many countrymen now being bled of their monies to safeguard exposure of their immigration irregularities from Fahn Gwai authorities? Elder Lee Ting as much as said that to the elders."

When asked for documented proof, Shah leaped to his feet, narrowed his eyes and pointed an accusing finger. "Proof? The faction is so secret, not even the members know exactly who their leader is. Extortions are not reported in fear of reprisals. Surely Professor told you this."

"Cousin Shah, why not speak to the other men? If they believe Lee Tzo is unsavory and dangerous to us, they will not accept him. You know I can do nothing. I do not have the power of vote."

"Do not parry with me, Liah!" Cousin Shah's eyes were slits of burning anger, his face flushed. "A word from you and the men will reject Tzo. Of one thing you can be sure: If that scoundrel is admitted, I will resign from the Council and if Tzo proves evil, I shall not lift one finger to help you. Heed my words!"

Liah had it on her tongue to thank Cousin Shah for his information, but he turned on his heel and stomped out. Liah, head bowed, sat stoically staring at the floor.

Liah sought the pleasure of her Peacock Alley, but the aromatic loveliness could not penetrate her sorrow and anger. Shah's threat to desert her brought to mind her husband's return to Kwangtung. She searched her heart and mind, trying to justify Sen's and Shah's opposition to her actions and beliefs. Was she wrong? Each time Liah probed her motives, a stronger conviction rose from the depths of her doubt and she shook her head. With or without their support, she must continue.

Caught up in her web of conflict and pushing aside the fearful possibility of Cousin Shah's desertion, Liah sought her bamboo pipe. In the arms of the opiate, Liah felt herself emptied, as a bamboo stalk with the pith removed, free of pressures, free from any emotion. If the Gods had deserted her, life was no longer meaningful and oblivion was the only way out.

Cook watched helplessly each day as Liah seemed determined to

shatter her sanity. Amah, too, saw the inroads on Liah's face and beseeched Cook to stop her. "No food and constantly drugged. How long
can her body and mind withstand the punishment?"

"We can do nothing, Amah," murmured Cook softly, "not until she
can withstand the reality of things. We can only stand by while she
seeks escape. Cousin Shah's threat to quit the Council should Tzo be
admitted is soul-shaking for her. He is all that is left of her life that is
tied to Sen. Surely, you understand the alienation Liah feels."

Amah berated Cousin Shah for his cruelty, but Cook shook his head.
"Cousin Shah is right and what's worse, Liah knows it. It is only for the
money she even allows the thought of Tzo being on the Council. She's
trapped by what the monies can do for the townspeople. Mostly, she
feels guilt for stripping Cousin Shah of his face, especially when he's
done so much for the family."

There was a clatter inside Liah's bedroom and Cook glanced up at
the wall clock. It was almost three in the afternoon. He shook his head.
"At least she's slept the night and half the day. Perhaps after the meeting
she will ease up on the Apinyin. Now, no looking sad or worried. We
must help her break this mood."

Amah sobbed. "To think I thought my life was travail. Liah's pain,
which I cannot alleviate, torments me. She who made my life possible."

Cook was quick to console Amah. "Don't torment yourself needlessly, Amah. Your caring has repaid Liah a hundredfold. As for you
feeling in Liah's debt, which one of us has not had her help?"

Tears coursed down Amah's face as she fled upstairs to her room.

—

The day of the meeting, the twentieth day of May in the Fahn Gwai's
year of nineteen hundred and fifteen, the Year of the Rabbit, Liah sat
before her mirror. Her eyes were slightly swollen, clouded and seemed
sunken deeper into their sockets. Curse the Apinyin, she thought, and

curse, too, her weakness. Angrily, she reached for the jar of rouge and lightly applied the tint to her high cheekbones. There, now her eyes didn't look as ghastly.

An hour later, clad in a silver chrysanthemum-brocaded cheongsam of light gold, Liah walked into the kitchen. Liah's transformation never ceased to amaze Cook. Amah embraced her. "Oh, Liah, you are so beautiful."

Liah smiled and Cook sadly winced, for her eyes still betrayed her sorrow. Quietly, he placed a bowl of brandy broth on the table. It was on her mind to refuse, but his stricken expression forced her to nod. "I'll drink it, but please do not hurry me. It is too early for me to rush."

Amah smiled, placing a plate of meat filled pastries before her. "While you are waiting for the broth to cool, just taste one. Cook baked them especially for you, Liah."

Liah giggled. "Between the two of you, you'd have me fat as a pig. All right, Amah, I'll taste one, but you too must not rush me. I have a good deal of last-minute thinking to do before the men arrive."

Cook's voice was gruff. "Well, if you like the flaky crust, you'd better not wait too long."

Without comment, her expression guilty, Liah reached out for the meat pie. There was a shocked surprise of pleasure as she bit into the flaky depths. "Ah, I'd forgotten how exquisitely flaky and tasty your pies are."

Liah leaned back in her chair, spreading her hands in a gesture of gratitude. "Ah, the Gods have not rejected me, or else why you two loyal, loving friends? If only my courage today is as strong as your love, I'll be victorious."

Cook turned from the sink, waving a ladle at Liah. "You not only have the courage to do what is right, but I must say that you look like a fire-breathing dragon, a dragon who'd slay anyone who dares get in your way. Well, get the ugly task done. Accept the men's decision, if you think them responsible. Whether Cousin Shah remains, or leaves, is already decreed by the Gods. Waste no emotion on that over which you have no control."

The front door opened and Liah placed a finger to her lips for silence. The men were arriving. Professor entered first, a sober tautness on his face. "It's the barber's wife again. She's saying you are in alliance with the devil and have a pimp for a partner."

"Barren bitch!" snorted Liah. "We'll have to speak to her husband again. This time, a beating will not be enough!"

The front door opened and slammed and Chon burst into the kitchen. "Liah, is it true Sang is going to name Tzo to our Council? Tzo's no good and dangerous. You'd better stop things."

"Chon," retorted Liah impatiently, "you seem to forget I have no power of vote."

Chon snapped, "I don't know what's gotten into Sang. Throw a girl at him without charge and he's ready to sell us out. He does exactly as he's commanded."

"What do you mean, Chon? Commanded?"

Chon flushed pink and bit his lips, trying to evade the question. With a visible sigh of relief, he was rescued when Kam Fong and Cousin Shah entered the kitchen. Cousin Shah demanded, "Where's Sang?"

Liah pointed to the wall clock. "He has five more minutes. Let us go upstairs now."

—

Liah dispensed with the reading of the minutes and announced that this meeting had been called at the request of Wong Sang. The gambler was nervous as he stood up and walked to the head of the table to stand beside Liah. He cleared his throat, looking straight ahead, for the set, rigid faces of his fellow Council members were too much for his eyes to confront.

The men waited silently. Wong Sang shifted his feet, glancing furtively at Liah whose impassive face infuriated him. He blurted his nomination of Lee Tzo to the Council, then walked defiantly to his seat.

Sang had hardly sat down when Cousin Shah shouted, "No! I say no. A pimp on the Council will destroy any respect the people might have for us. Since Sang has already publicly spoken of the nomination, people have already started to complain to me, asking me to convey their disapproval to all of you."

Cousin Shah narrowed his eyes and pointed an accusing finger at Sang. "Tell me and tell the men here why you agreed to name Lee Tzo." He paused. "As I see you don't want to answer, then I'll explain. It is rumored Lee Tzo has offered to set you up in a second gambling house in return for his nomination."

Cousin Shah turned to the group, his eyes blazing. "Lee Tzo is a member of a newly formed dissident group who is out to unseat the elders of the House of Lee. Their excuse is that the elders are too old to meet the needs of the younger generation or to control them. There is another rumor that Tzo was sent here by the group to carry out a secret mission. We must demand that Sang inform us of that mission. Well, speak up, Sang!"

Wong Sang's face paled. Cousin Shah's accusation evoked panic in him. Was he Tzo's pawn? Was he being used by Tzo to get a foothold in Chinatown? It chilled his blood to realize the implications; if true, he'd become ensnared in a huge political nightmare. He shook his head.

Professor fervently wished he could be as forthright as Cousin Shah, but a promise was a promise. He held his hand up for silence. "Men, I quite agree with Cousin Shah about not allowing Tzo to join our group. We know nothing about the man or why he is here. In the face of Cousin Shah's accusations, we should exercise the greatest caution."

With discomfort, the scholar continued. "Nevertheless, at this time I'd like to bring up a point of expediency. We are in dire need of money

for the school, and, for reasons of safety, it is imperative that the temple
be moved to the center of town. All these things take money and our
treasury is depleted. Lee Tzo has made an offer in good faith to make a
sizeable donation, enough to take care of these important items."

Professor held up his hand for the men to hear him out. "I, too, objected to Lee Tzo's candidacy as I thought a school funded by a pimp
would be an outrage. However, I could not dismiss the fact that a school
funded by a pimp is better than no school at all. So, for the youngsters
to have a school and the aged to have a safe place to worship without
Fahn Gwai taunts or harm, I will be a traitor to my principles and en-
dorse the nomination."

"Professor!" cried Shah. "We will get the school for the children and
certainly we'll labor to move the temple to a safer place *without* Lee
Tzo's money. No! No pimp shall sit on the Council."

Chon Woo sat stoically silent throughout the discussion. He was disgusted with himself for allowing Tzo to slip through his fingers and
doubly so now that Tzo was setting Sang up with another gambling
house. It was insufferable that Sang would soon have two places. Liah
was not the only avenue of help for Chon. He was stunned when suddenly Cousin Shah turned to him and exclaimed, "So! You didn't know
either, Chon? Well, that makes two of us. Are we going to allow Tzo to
come in?"

Liah's face betrayed no emotion, but she was seething. Sang had disobeyed her. In return for financial backing, he'd sell out his fellow members. Sang quavered under her blazing stare, bit his lips and looked
down at the floor.

Kam Fong timidly urged everyone to remain calm. "Unity in the
Council is vital if we are to gain the authority and respect of the people.
That Lee Tzo is a pimp, that he is alleged to be a member of a dissident
faction in Dai Faw and plans mischief in our town are rumors unless
we can prove his intentions. If the man is willing to put up monies to

aid our civic projects, I say let him join. We have the Tenet of Laws to punish him if he proves evil, as well as Wong Sang who named him."

Wong Sang cringed as he heard Kam linking him to Tzo. His palms were sweaty and his heart was pounding in his ears. It was all he could do to remain seated.

There was a dead silence when Kam sat down. Liah glanced around the table, then faced Cousin Shah. Her voice tremulous, her face stoic, she said, "There is no one here who has not known the aid of Cousin Shah, who has found housing, work, even financial help for people whenever needed. It is now distressing to disagree with you about Lee Tzo. It is oftentimes difficult for us to separate good from bad, for sometimes good and bad overlap. Life does not give us just good people like Cousin Shah, but also unscrupulous, distasteful men like Tzo. If we must blame someone for the likes of Tzo, then blame the Fahn Gwai government. If they would allow you to bring your wives from our homeland, pimps would not play such a dominant role in our lives. As Kam pointed out, Lee Tzo's monies will bring a good deal of comfort and pleasure to our townspeople. I ask all of you to think with a wider perspective before you make up your minds on Lee Tzo."

At this point Professor rose, cleared his throat and timidly asked if he, too, could make a nomination. Wong Sang eyed him suspiciously, mirroring Chon Woo's stare, indicating they both were wondering if the scholar's nomination was really Liah's idea.

Cousin Shah, upon hearing Lim Tao's name, leaped to his feet. "Now, there is a worthy man—a man who is not only hard-working and law-abiding, but has not forgotten his wife and four sons in our homeland. He sends money home regularly for their support. Is that not so, Professor? You do his letter-writing, don't you?" Cousin Shah's voice rang with pride as he gave Wong Sang a withering glare, then sat down.

For a long moment, not a word was said, as if the men were mute statues. No one wanted to break the unanimity of the moment yet all of them knew the outcome of the confrontation with Wong Sang would soon be determined with their ballots. Chon sat furiously cursing Sang for having put him in jeopardy with Liah. His vote, he knew, must admit Tzo, that is, if he wanted Liah's support.

It was Professor who finally broke the awkward silence. "I would also add to Cousin Shah's commendation of Lim Tao. Not only is he a good husband and father, but also he is an assayer whom many of us who do not trust the Fahn Gwai's bank have entrusted our savings. His honesty is impeccable."

Liah glanced up at the wall clock. "Let us have supper before we vote. Perhaps the extra time will give us the perspective we need before the votes are cast."

Chon Woo sniffed the air pleasurably as Cook placed a huge tureen on the table. "Is that pickled pigs' feet I smell, Cook?" Cook lifted the lid and the steaming, pungent aroma of sweet and sour escaped. Chon leaned forward and grinned.

"Not only do we have pigs' feet tonight," murmured Cook, "but there is cold cracked crab with Liah's secret marinade, pan-fried spiced shrimps in the shell and spiced spareribs."

Cook eyed Liah sternly as he added, "And for those of you who favor black mushrooms sautéed with unborn peas, water chestnuts and sea urchin, I might add this compote is done to perfection."

Cook looked at Liah, making a silent plea for her to eat; her eyes were bright with gratitude. "Ah, are we not fortunate to have all of our favorite entrees. Let us raise our chopsticks."

Liah did not miss Chon's move to sit beside Professor rather than Sang. If Sang noticed, he gave no sign but ate silently. At one point, Chon caught Sang's glance, but Sang turned away.

It was impossible at the table not to overhear the conversation between Wong Sang and Kam Fong. It amused her, Kam's noncommittal retort. To Kam, Lee Tzo's Meng-Sui had already been decreed. If he were to be accepted or not was of no great concern. He, for one, was not going to allow Cook's supper to go to waste.

The ensuing balloting was brief but very tense. Cousin Shah and Professor tallied the votes and Lim Tao was unanimously accepted while Lee Tzo was accepted by a three-to-two margin. Cousin Shah gaped. He couldn't believe the men would allow the pimp to be seated. He reached out, grabbed the pieces of paper and flung them at Liah. "Be it so! Lee Tzo will surely bring disaster to this town. Madam Chairman, you may consider this my resignation from the Council."

Liah met Cousin Shah's fury silently although her inner self was shattered. "I beg of you sir, to please reconsider. Resigning is exactly what Tzo would want."

She never got to finish her plea, for Cousin Shah strode from the room, slamming the door behind him. Professor's face paled as he quietly stooped and picked up the papers strewn about the floor. He silently cursed his weakness; if only he'd had the courage of his beliefs, Lee Tzo would not now be a member. Blood pulsed in his ears and Professor felt deep grief for the first time in a long time. He could not help wondering who had cast the two negative votes. One for certain was Cousin Shah's, but which of the other men had rejected Tzo?

A heavy, brooding silence hung over the room, like an unspoken grievance against Wong Sang. Sang dropped his eyes, squirming in his chair. Liah murmured, "We have lost a good and big-hearted friend. Which of us in this room has not had his life eased because of Cousin Shah's caring? He was always helping someone find a job or a place to live and he always lent a helping hand even with money to tide one over until their first paycheck."

She narrowed her eyes. "Woe to Sang and Tzo should Cousin Shah's predictions come true!"

Chon sneered. "Well, Sang, now that you've succeeded in bringing about Shah's resignation, perhaps your pimp might have a nomination of his own."

Liah's cane came crashing down on the table. "Chon Woo, your humor is ill-timed. I recall it was Cousin Shah who also found you your first employment. Even in jest, we shall not speak of Cousin Shah. Until this day next year, we will cool our anger."

The men waited to be dismissed, but Liah seemed to have forgotten their presence. Professor motioned for the men to sign the record, and afterwards each man solemnly left the room. The scholar remained, waiting for Liah to speak.

A harsh silence ensued until Liah spoke, saying they ought to think of a replacement for Shah's seat. Professor was shocked; he silently rebuked Liah that her first concern was not with Cousin Shah and his resignation.

Liah, catching the fleeting expression on the scholar's face, sighed. "Sir, I do not have the luxury of giving in to my grief. Cousin Shah's leaving leaves me bereft of Sen's family. I thought you already knew the depths of my despair. Yet I have the welfare of Chinatown to consider and the Council's future."

Professor nodded mutely, feeling shame. If he could feel the gravity of Cousin Shah's resignation, what must it be like for Liah? Nevertheless, she did not allow her emotions to control her, but rather stood stoically by her duties. For that, she was the more courageous and he the weaker.

When he gained control of his voice again, Professor softly reminded Liah of Meng-Sui. "As Kam Fong said earlier tonight, this night's events were already decreed by the Gods. We were only carried on its forceful flow. Now, you're right, we must think of a replacement. Do you have someone in mind?"

"Lee Wah seems the right choice, but you must search your mind for another person; perhaps someone else might be better a choice."

Cook quietly entered the Council room, glancing anxiously at Liah. Professor was calmly and thoughtfully puffing on his pipe, which shocked Cook who'd expected an explosion. Professor asked who might nominate Lee Wah. Liah shook her head. It was too soon for her to consider the details. At the moment, she was too sorrowful over Cousin Shah's rejection and his ominous predictions concerning Lee Tzo.

Cook calmly suggested Chon Woo nominate Lee Wah. "He's jealous of Sang's relationship with Tzo and will feel revenge in nominating a man of his own. There is a rivalry between those two and, in this instance, you can make use of it."

"Splendid idea!" cried Professor. "But how are you to approach him, Liah?"

"My heart is heavy with sorrow now, but when I put aside the grief I feel, I shall invite Chon Woo to lunch and at that time hint for his help." She smiled. "Of course, I'll have to bait him first with the idea that I might finance him in his plans to enlarge and modernize his bar."

After another lapse of silence, Liah asked if Professor wouldn't write a letter to Elder Lee Ti of the House of Lee in Dai Faw. "Inquire into the nature of Lee Tzo and the reason he left Dai Faw for residence in Loo Sahng. Tell him it's imperative we have a quick reply to our questions. Come downstairs, I will give you Elder Lee Ti's address."

—

Immediately after the Council meeting ended, Wong Sang hurried to Number Ten, stopping several times to catch his breath. The traumatic session had left him slightly fearful and very weary. Tzo, seated on the divan in his private chambers, sipped warmed rice wine spoonful by spoonful, fed lovingly by Mei-Mei, his concubine. When Sang entered, Tzo roughly pushed Mei-Mei aside. "Ah, by the expression on your face, I see we won."

Lee Tzo clapped his hands. Mei Wah appeared from behind the curtained door to kneel at Sang's feet. "Enjoy yourself," murmured Lee Tzo imperiously. "I know the session must have been stormy. I'll wager Liah was livid."

"No. It was Cousin Shah who was most outraged and he resigned because of you." Wong Sang's voice lost some of its bravado when he informed Lee Tzo that both of them would have to be careful. "I was warned that should you commit evil, my fate and punishment would be the same as yours." The pimp's eyes narrowed and Sang saw for the first time Tzo's unmasked flinty hatred. Lee Tzo quickly recovered his control, motioning for Mei Wah to lead Sang from the room.

Several hours later, Sang awakened from his drunken lovemaking, his head reeling from the potent, warm rice wine. He felt Mei Wah's body heat and reached out for her again. Much later, as he awakened, his eyes swept the pale red glow of the pink-shaded lamps. In his sleep-sodden drunkenness, Sang saw a painting of a nude on the wall, not quite life-sized like the one in Tzo's chambers, but nonetheless suggestive, with a reddish glow of lamps on her sensuous curves.

All the while Sang was indulging in his drunken orgy, Lee Tzo remained in his private quarters, fuming at the monies he was losing because Sang was occupying the best room in the house, and gratis at that. Once he put his plans into operation, he would shed Sang like a snake shedding its skin. Lee Tzo, in anticipation of relegating Sang to his house's public cubicles, smiled derisively.

—

When Professor appeared at Number Three the next day, Liah asked him if a good night's sleep had not diminished some of his painful guilt.

"You are fortunate, Liah, for your Apinyin draught afforded you a few hours respite. I must admit I spent the entire night in nightmarish self-recrimination." His voice faltered. "I especially suffered because if I'd had the courage of my convictions, I, too, would have voted against Tzo's acceptance and today would have been different." He held up a hand. "Oh, yes, I know we have the Tenet of Laws, but nonetheless I lost my own fight."

Liah sighed sympathetically. "Cook and I were discussing the enlargement of our sentry system. We are afraid if it were known we were doing this, the townspeople would think we might be taking over. You know how Tzo and Sang would spread the rumor."

Liah allowed the scholar to finish several cups of tea, enjoy the meat pies and, when he appeared more relaxed, asked if he would not pretend to own the sentries. "Just say that since you opposed Tzo's entry onto the Council, you've had two attempts at your life. People would believe you opposed Tzo and believe the story of the attempts on your life."

Cook smiled. "Professor, it's only for a short period of time. When the furor dies down, we can gradually allow it to be known that the sentries proved too expensive for you and that Liah took over the men rather than let them go. By then, it won't matter what Tzo and Sang say."

Liah continued, "It will be fine for the town to know you have body guards, but it won't be necessary to tell them how many."

"How many men," asked Professor, "do I have, Liah?"

"Only three men, sir, and they will arrive from Dai Faw in a few days. Cook has procured jobs for them and when they arrive you will take them to meet their employers. Oh, also here are the keys to the rooms we've rented for them in a rooming house on Mah Loo. Since the men will have different hours of employment, there is no fear of them becoming too well-acquainted."

Cook handed Professor an envelope. "Inside is enough money to pay the men for meals and their first month wages. The men get ten dollars a month, a room and two meals daily at Wong's Café. You can make arrangements with Wong."

Professor looked at the three keys in his hand and the envelope of money. "Never would I think of owning a sentry system. I hope it will not usurp too much of my time."

Liah smiled. "I hope not either, sir. Hopefully, we can take the men over sooner rather than later."

When Professor departed for Wong's Café, Liah sighed in relief. "I almost believed Professor would refuse to help. I feel so much better."

"Never fear, Liah. Professor would never refuse you a thing. Of this, I am positive. It's just that Cousin Shah's resignation has jolted him. As for that matter, it has jolted all of us."

Liah dropped her gaze, fighting hard to stem the tears that sprang to her eyes when Cook mentioned Cousin Shah. Quickly, Cook remonstrated, "Let us not look backwards, Liah. Shall we have our late tea?"

That night at midnight, Sang's gambling house was almost deserted except for a few stragglers chatting at the buffet table, enjoying the last of the night's free supper. Sang, looking up from the gaming table, became aware of a stranger who'd loitered inside the house during the night without once placing a wager. As the stranger approached, Sang instinctively drew back, readying himself for an attack. The stranger smiled as he saw Sang's apprehension and shook his head. "I notice you handle a good deal of money. Are you not fearful of robbery or bodily harm?"

"That's why I braced myself now. Yeah, I'm fearful. What's it to you?"

"I cannot expect you to trust me, a total stranger, but if I told you my name is Wei Tan Wong, a Kung Fu master from Hong Kong, would it allay your fears? I've just arrived from Dai Faw and am looking for employment."

Sang relaxed, a grin slowly creasing his forehead. The man's mention of being a Kung Fu master from Hong Kong recently arrived from Dai Faw awakened a fuzzy memory of a bit of news Sang had read in the papers.

"Are you not the Kung Fu master the *Dai Faw See Bo* featured in an article some weeks back?"

Wei Tan Wong nodded. Sang grinned now. "You're the one who exposed imposters who were offering their services and then absconded after receiving advance payment."

Suddenly suspicious, Wong Sang asked, "Why then are you looking for employment? I thought you dedicated yourself to helping people without money?"

Wei Tan Wong frowned. "Yes, but unfortunately in Gem Sahn one has to pay for one's food and one's rent, not to speak of sundries which also cost money."

"Okay, Wei Tan Wong," declared Sang. "I'll hire you as my body-guard beginning tonight. I'll give you five dollars a week and meals at Wong's Café. How does that suit you?"

Wordlessly, Wei Tan Wong nodded his approval. Wong Sang smiled and informed his bodyguard that he was a favorite patron at the brothel. "I will not need you after I've deposited the night's proceeds with Liah. When I go to the brothel, it is usually an all-night affair. Understand?"

Sang's voice sounded proud as he confided that Liah was his silent partner in the gambling house. Wei Tan Wong frowned, warning, "It was foolish of you to have divulged this secret to me, Sang. Some things are better left unsaid; however, I'll keep your secret."

"Yes, yes, you're right. Well, let's close the place, then I'm off to the brothel."

That night, Sang entered Lee Tzo's place feeling braver and less threatened. It was then he realized how much he feared Tzo and wondered why. Somewhere in his mind, an answer tried to surface, but Sang quashed it as he entered Tzo's private quarters. Tomorrow, he'd give it his attention.

—

An unusual spate of bad weather turned the streets of Chinatown into soggy mires, making travel impossible. To walk on the streets was to be ankle deep in gooey mud. The only advantage of the inclement weather was that neither the Fahn Gwai nor the noisy wagons could make their appearances. During the three or four days of rain, China-town was like a ghost town; doors and windows remained barred against the wet and cold, and not a person ventured onto the boards laid across the muddy streets.

Professor opened his door, peered out at the leaden sky and shook his head. Another murky day and this the middle of May. The streets surely could not absorb any more water. If the rains did not cease, he'd have to barricade his doorway with burlap sacks. He glared at the water not a foot and a half away and cursed. Why couldn't the Fahn Gwai pave their streets or put in drains to catch the excess water? Even as he cursed, Professor knew the Fahn Gwai wouldn't spend the money, at least not in Chinatown. The welfare of the Chinese and Mexicans were beneath consideration. His temper flared as he glared outside one more time, then slammed the door.

At noon Professor thought of the aromatic warmth of Liah's kitchen and decided to brave the slushy street and the rain. He scooted across the planks onto the damp cobblestones and rapped on her door.

Cook exclaimed, "My, but you are a brave man to go outdoors. Come in, sir. I hope the rains let up. Liah is tired of leftovers and tinned goods. The shrimp and curry pies are almost done, so please come in."

Professor closed his eyes in sheer delight as he bit into the flaky pies. "Ah, you've revived my spirits, Cook. The rains were making inroads into my morale."

Cook confessed that he'd been preoccupied that morning. "Those stupid birds are huddled under the shrubbery outside, but won't come out for me."

For the next half-hour, Professor relived for Cook how he and Liah first met and how she trained the peacock and peahen not to leave the cobblestones. Cook glared, "Not half as trained as I'd like them."

Liah emerged from the bedroom at twelve-thirty. Cook jerked his head in the direction of the front of the house and muttered that the stupid birds were outside in the rain. Without comment, Liah went out, returning shortly with the peacock and his mate following close behind.

She threw a lettuce leaf on the kitchen floor, which the birds devoured ravenously. "Stupid koong jeks. You could have eaten sooner and been warmer if you had obeyed me!" scolded Cook.

"Never mind, Cook," Liah murmured, placating. "Their feathers keep them dry and now they are eating. Let us enjoy the pies, shrimp and curry, aren't they?"

At the end of their meal, Professor leaned back in his chair. It wasn't often Cook lost his temper and he hoped what he had to say now wouldn't cause more emotional spillovers. "Have you heard that Sang has hired Wei Tan Wong as a body guard? Wei Tan Wong whispered to me that Sang didn't want it known though, the better to provide protection. He doesn't want people going through Wei in order to get at him."

Cook snorted, "Well, anyone who has a friend of Tzo's caliber needs protection. It's Sang's own fault."

It didn't escape Professor's notice that Liah was silent, just inhaling her cigarette and watching the smoke trail upward to the ceiling. Cook refilled the teapot and filled Liah's cup again, handing her a plate of meat buns he had just removed from the oven. His tone was tense. "Perhaps Sang knows something we don't. Perhaps Tzo has taken him into his confidence. I wouldn't be surprised if Sang isn't against Tzo's plans and perhaps wants to pull out but can't. Perhaps Sang fears for his life."

Professor sneered, "I can't say I feel sorry for the man. He didn't have to nominate Tzo for the Council, just as he didn't have to be taken in by Tzo's flattery or favors." Abruptly, he turned. "Let's not ruin our meal speaking of snakes. Liah, did you know that Cousin Shah is leaving for Dai Faw?"

Liah exhaled, watching the smoke drift toward the ceiling, and said nothing. She was fighting hard to overcome her feelings of loneliness, half-angry at her own weakness, half-sad because an era of her life was coming to a close. Without glancing at her companions, she murmured,

"You know, I still can't get over the deep pain of Shah's rejection, mostly of his accusations regarding my approval of Tzo. And his threat that he will not raise a hand to help. I hope time will prove that wrong. Meanwhile, I will light a taper to Kwan Koong each night for his well-being. Who knows? Someday our paths may cross again."

Professor raised his arms to stretch, suddenly drawing them back in pain. Liah rose, went into her bedroom and returned moments later with a bottle in her hand. "This is the Het A Dew (herb alcohol) I brought from my home when I first came to Gem Sahn. Use it each day and night, sir, and it will relieve the rheumatic pain."

Professor held the bottle up to the light, gently shaking the murky amber liquid. He uncorked the top, sniffed it and in an instant the pungent herbal alcohol smell permeated the room. "This indeed is the real brew, not at all like the watered-down potions in the drugstore."

Liah smiled. "When I left home for Gem Sahn, my mother insisted I take a jug with me. At the time I felt her overbearing, but time has proven her wise. The children are forever spraining an ankle or a wrist and it provided relief for Sen's aching muscles. When we farmed, I used it every night on him."

At the mention of Sen, Liah fell silent again. Professor knew if this was the original gallon she'd brought, there couldn't be much left. He handed back the bottle, but Liah shook her head. "Please take it, sir. I have two gallons aging which soon will be ready for use. In another half-year, I'll have more than I can use."

Liah lapsed into reverie. "It's been over twenty years since I left home. Time flies on the wings of an eagle."

Cook glared despairingly. "How is it each time you're hurt, or things do not go your way, you always blame the passage of time? I, for one, will be relieved when Cousin Shah leaves. Perhaps then you'll be less moody and morbid."

Liah recoiled at Cook's gruff retort until she saw his face. The pain she felt was mirrored in his eyes, but he had cloaked his own sadness with anger. A sad smile played on Liah's face. For as long as she had Cook beside her, she could never be alone. Just the same, she yearned for the heartache to be borne away by the wings of the eagle.

CHON WOO'S PACT WITH LIAH

Liah, not yet reconciled with her guilty feelings over Tzo's acceptance into the Council, chafed against the day when the pimp would be officially seated. Only afterwards would she feel any calm. It was during this restless time she and Chon Woo had a private meeting.

It was late afternoon on the twenty-sixth day of May in the Fahn Gwai's year of nineteen hundred and fifteen, a crystal clear, mild day, warm and vibrant, not at all like the previous rainy days. She breathed in the pungent, sweet and sour aroma of pigs' feet simmering on the stove. She knew it was Chon's favorite dish and the atmosphere must be perfect if she were to exact a favor from him. She also must be careful that this meeting not seem like a bribe. Chon was an unpredictable one.

In the midst of her contemplations, a fight erupted between Third and Fourth Sons. Liah swiftly rose, reached for their ears and pulled them apart. Fourth Son shouted it was Third Brother's fault and Third Son hotly denied it. "Enough! Get along or else your skin will peel off from the flogging you will receive!"

During the fracas, Chon entered the front room. What a ruckus, he thought. Liah's children were at it again. While they squabbled in the kitchen, he paced back and forth in the front room, wondering what to do. Should he go back to her private quarters or wait until Liah should come out?

He glanced about for an answer, then he spied a brass planter sitting atop a brass tray and several bats leaning against a wall. He lifted the planter off the tray, grabbed one of the bats and struck the tray as if it were a gong.

When the low, moaning sound flooded the corridor, all squabbling ceased. Cook, followed by Liah and the children rushed into the front room. Chon grinned foolishly. "I called out several times, but no one heard me. Guess you folks were too busy fighting."

Liah's face relaxed and she smiled benevolently. "Oh, Chon, you needn't have waited in the front room like an outsider. Next time, just walk straight back to the kitchen."

Liah's reassurance that he was not an outsider pleased Chon and his ruffled dignity vanished. He muttered, "Still, it's an inconvenience. Why not install a bell or something?"

"There's no need, Chon. Anyone who has the right to come here knows to go back to the kitchen. We'd have heard the doors opening if it hadn't been for the boys battling." She glared at Third and Fourth Sons who quickly disappeared.

Back in the kitchen, Liah took her seat, motioning for Chon to sit down. Chon's pride rose by several notches at being considered family, and he smiled. He sniffed the air. "Am I wrong or is that pigs' feet I smell?"

Cook brought the covered tureen to the table, lifted the lid and smiled. Chon's eyes glowed with eager anticipation. Liah ladled a generous portion onto Chon's plate. Cook chuckled. "Be sure to leave room for the rest of the meal, Chon."

Chon grinned, "I'll need nothing else, Cook. Pigs' feet is my favorite food and it's so difficult to find it cooked properly."

Neither Liah nor Chon uttered a single word as they occupied themselves with the sticky, gooey, syrupy pigs' feet. Once Liah caught a glob of syrup running down her cheek. Such an unusual and undignified sight struck Chon as funny and he roared with laughter. Chon, a few moments later, was caught in the same predicament and grinned as he wiped away the syrupy drip. "No need to worry, Chon," said Liah. "Afterwards, we'll have a hot towel to clean up. Enjoy yourself."

Why, thought Liah, did food somehow bring people closer together?

Right now, she almost liked Chon. An hour later, Chon leaned back in his chair, groaning he couldn't eat another bite. Cook held up a custard pie, but Chon shook his head. "Not for me, Cook. I'm so stuffed with pigs' feet, roast duck and the northern noodles, I'd burst if I took one more bite."

Liah refilled his wine cup as a strained silence engulfed the room. Now that the meal was done, Chon wondered again why he'd been summoned. He impatiently pulled on his cigarette, inwardly cursing for Liah to make the next move. Once she'd spoken her piece, he'd then bring up the partnership he hoped she'd enter into with him.

Liah leaned forward and smiled. "I know you were the other person who cast a vote against Lee Tzo. I think it was a very commendable thing. It has occurred to me that once Tzo is seated, he will want to name a man of his own to the Council. This must not happen."

All at once Chon was on his guard. His answer must be exactly what Liah wanted to hear. "Er, ah, how can we stop him?"

"I thought because you rejected Tzo's assistance, you might like to be the one to name a man to the Council. You know of course, if Tzo were to seat a man of his own, we'd be plagued with tie votes all the time." She paused. "To hear Sang speak, you'd think Lee Tzo threw you over for him."

Chon's eyes smoldered. How dare the bastard say such a thing! "Well, I wasn't thrown over. I rejected Tzo because I smelled a rat. Also I was afraid of what the man had in mind. Liah, he's up to nothing good. If only I had known what." Chon paused. "If there is someone to name, I'll do it, if only to show Sang up. He's getting too big in his head."

Liah proffered a decanter of rice wine, but Chon said no. His head was already awhirl and he had yet to broach his proposition to Liah. How to ask her? Damn it, if he'd stayed with Tzo, he'd not now be currying Liah's help.

To his shock, Liah casually mentioned she'd heard he wanted to modernize and enlarge his bar. "Lee Wah is in the import business. Why not ask him to help you? I'm certain he can save you a lot of money. Just tell him I told you so."

Chon swiftly caught Liah's meaning. So, Lee Wah was the man Liah wanted on the Council. Well, why not? What she said was true. And her mention of him created the perfect opportunity for him to make the proposition. She leaned forward and smiled again.

"I have always admired your business acumen and your ability to appeal to the Fahn Gwai. Is it not so that your business is growing at a rate that necessitates your enlarging? I have monies that I'd like to put to work. Would you be interested in a partnership, Chon?"

Chon's mouth fell open. So easily done when he'd fretted all day! He grinned, but then a frown crossed his brow. His voice cautious, with just the right amount of friendliness, he said, "You know, Liah, I have been sole owner of The Dragon's Den Bar too long to have to worry about a partner, even you. I do not like to be accountable to anyone, nor to have my honesty questioned when it comes to the profits."

"Have no fear, Chon. If we become partners, I shall not bother you. It matters not how much profit I receive as long as I get an amount enough to make my investment worthwhile. The only reason I am anxious to earn more monies is for the charities I want inaugurated for the town's children, the aged and the needy. Well, what do you think?"

Chon grinned. "Of course we will have a partnership, Liah. As for nominating Lee Wah, he is a splendid choice and, as you said, he can save me a lot of money." He glanced at the wall clock and then rose from his chair. "Time flies when one is enjoying one's self. I have to relieve Charlie at the bar now, but could we speak further of the arrangement another time?"

Liah nodded and Chon left Number Three in high spirits. Now that Liah was his partner, he would have all the money he needed to renovate his bar. He could hardly wait for opening day. He'd show Tzo and Sang!

—

Lee Tzo chafed and cursed waiting for the Council's next meeting, positive that Liah was deliberately delaying seating him. As the days passed, Tzo's temper rose and his need for revenge against Liah grew. His anger turned to fear, however, whenever he received one of the telephone calls from Dai Faw inquiring whether he'd yet gained a foothold in Chinatown. It was after one such telephone call that Lee Tzo took Wong Sang to task.

Wong Sang glared even in his drunken state as Tzo unleashed his fury over the delay in his being seated. "Why the hurry, Tzo?" he asked, his slurred speech further infuriating Tzo. "You've been accepted; Liah will call a meeting soon. Nobody rushes Liah."

Lee Tzo narrowed his eyes but not enough to hide his hatred and Sang cringed. "We shall see, Sang. Nobody stays on top forever and even Liah can topple into the gutter." Lee Tzo noticed Sang's startled expression and quickly backed off. "What I mean is that with time Liah might change, maybe mellow and weaken with age."

"Not that woman. She will be as strong and stubborn as an ox until the day she dies."

Lee Tzo smiled. "You are so right, Sang. Right up until the day she dies."

—

June sixth, the first Sunday of the month, the Council met at exactly three o'clock.

The men arrived with grim expressions on their faces. It angered Liah that Lee Tzo arrived punctually. He seemed anxious to be recognized formally and was peeved when Liah just casually nodded. She had vowed she would not welcome him and had asked Professor to do the honors. "The memory of Cousin Shah is yet too fresh," she said. While waiting, the men conversed in whispers and Sang was taut with discomfort speculating that the men were speaking of Cousin Shah. When Liah and Tzo eyes met, she held his eyes until he dropped his gaze. Sang watched the battle of wills, wishing he'd not nominated the bastard. What was in Tzo's mind?

Sang was further disturbed when it was the scholar who welcomed Tzo and not Liah. The scholar handed Lee Tzo and Lim Tao their copies of the Tenet of Laws, instructing them to sign the official copy and then turned the meeting over to Liah.

Liah briefly acknowledged Lee Tzo, then she warmly welcomed Lim Tao. Tzo was furious Liah pointed to the Tenet of Laws, and reiterated that the document governed members' behavior and spelled out that punishment would be meted out to both the perpetrator and the nominator should a member break a law.

A slightly proud smile played on Liah's face as she turned to announce that on the second day of the Fahn Gwai's month of July, their school would re-open. "The school will now have one room for the younger children and one for the older students. A dedication ceremony will be officiated by our priest at one o'clock in the afternoon. Professor, you will escort the priest to and from the ceremonies. It is not safe for the old man to traverse Lion's Den Alley by himself. When the temple in Peacock Alley is ready for him to move in sometime in the next year, he'll be freer to come and go. It is expected that all members of the Council will be present for the rites."

Liah's face shone. "The good residents of China Gai have been donating monies to buy a teakwood altar for our new temple. Lee Wah has generously procured for us a teakwood altar carved in the likeness of a dragon at cost. As soon as Number Six is ready, the altar will be delivered. Hopefully the ruby I purchased for the dragon's eye will arrive in time."

Lee Tzo leaped to his feet and asked if he could not help defray the costs for the trappings for the temple. Liah's face darkened with irritation that he would bring this up again and in front of the Council. "No thank you, Tzo, it will not be necessary."

"Why should you donate all of the trappings for the temple? It belongs to all of us."

"Long ago, when I struggled to keep alive, I promised the Goddess the best urn money could buy. It was my promise and mine alone to keep. The subject is closed."

There was an uncomfortable silence afterwards. Sang cursed Tzo's stupidity and his show of arrogance. As usual, it was Professor who spoke first. His steady stare reminded Liah to control herself. "Gentlemen," he glanced around the table, "for the past year we've enjoyed many meals here and I think it is time that the Council repay Liah and assume the future costs of meetings. I know Liah will not accept payment, so I propose we make a monthly donation for the children or to any charity Liah desires." He reached into his wallet and withdrew a fifty-dollar bill.

Chon Woo exclaimed as he saw the money, declaring that it was a pittance. "And what about Cook's work? He ought to be paid for his efforts on behalf of the Council meetings."

Professor frowned. "You didn't give me time, Chon. I would have given Cook recognition." He handed Liah another fifty-dollar bill. "You have no choice but to accept it. The fees each month have fattened our treasury and we can now afford to pay for our meals." He readjusted his spectacles. "I will now read the financial status of our treasury."

When he was done, Lee Tzo asked why he had not heard the log of his donation. Professor held up his hand for silence. "Your donation was not made until the end of the month, therefore, it won't appear until the next report. If you'd waited, you would have known."

Tzo fumed. Not because his generous donation received so little fanfare, but because he felt rebuked by Professor. For the remainder of the meeting Tzo was icily aloof.

Chon waited impatiently for business to conclude, then got to his feet. He had a nomination to make. Liah hid her smile as he waxed dramatically about Lee Wah's qualifications, glancing fleetingly at Tzo when he said Lee Wah was a man worthy to be Council member. "As I see it, our Council needs not only progressive ideas but conservatism too. Lee Wah is of the old school and will give us the balance needed. I therefore propose Lee Wah to the Council."

Lee Tzo's fury was almost too great to conceal. His mouth contorted and his eyes blazed. Chon Woo had upstaged his chance to fill the eighth seat by nominating a man of his own.

Liah, he glared, must have been the instigator. Wong Sang also knew by Chon's arrogant manner that Chon was doing Liah's bidding. Jealousy flared as he realized that Liah must now be Chon's partner. How he wanted to wipe that smug expression off Chon's face. Another realization hit Sang. If he'd had the wisdom, he'd have rejected Tzo and gone to Liah for more financing and now not be cowed by Tzo. If he'd known the peril of being beholden to Tzo, Sang would have spurned Tzo's favors in his brothel too. Sang lamented what he'd done, but it was too late now.

The balloting was quick and Lee Wah was unanimously elected. It was on Tzo's mind to cast a 'no' vote, but that would have declared himself on the opposite side. It was too early to be obvious. His time would come.

In his frustration, Lee Tzo congratulated Liah on seating another of her choice. There followed a stunned silence, then Sang cried out, "Liah, pay no heed to Tzo! He didn't mean what he said. Censure him for lack of good judgment, for stupidity, even arrogance, but nothing more."

Professor coughed gently, a reminder to Liah that she must remain in control. Liah's stony anger dissipated and her tone was silky as she smiled. "Lee Tzo must know by now I am not mild-mannered, but if he promises to hold his impetuous tongue, I'll keep a leash on my temper. As a new member, I would advise Tzo do less talking and more listening. Now, if all the business is done, let us sign the records."

Wong Sang giggled as he stood up and held a thimble-sized cup of rice wine in the air. "A toast to our Council. We have eight members and are complete now. I drink to our success."

Lee Tzo, yet smarting from Liah's reprimand, murmured just loud enough to be heard. "Wrong, Sang, there is yet the ninth seat for a deserving young man. I say, why not give it to one of Liah's sons? I hear Fifth Son is a fine young man meriting recognition."

It was not his words that outraged Liah but his snide tone. Her cane crashed down on the table, barely missing Lee Tzo's fingers. "You, sir," she hissed, "insult me with your insinuation. Now, hear this. None of my sons will ever serve on the Council. I don't want them to suffer your warped sense of values. As for anyone who believes I am furthering my own gains, let me say now and forever, I have all the money I need. Kwan Yin and the Gods have been generous with me."

She eyed Lee Tzo, indicating to the others that her tirade was directed against him alone. Unable to counter, Lee Tzo offered an abject apology. Liah impatiently waved aside his apologies by looking up and asking if there was any more business. If not, they'd sign the records.

Lim Tao wondered at Liah's signature of Lin Fah and Liah explained once again that some Fahn Gwai idiot at immigration had misspelled her name.

It did not escape Lee Tzo's eyes that Liah could write. He wondered, was there anything that witch could not do? Quickly, he signed his name and took his leave, not even waiting to speak with the men nor to invite Wong Sang to his brothel.

—

When the Council chamber was deserted of all but Liah who remained in her chair, deep in thought, Cook entered and quietly removed the oilcloth, revealing the gleaming, ebony-black surface of the table below. Liah, without actually thinking, ran her fingers over the intricate carvings there, a smile of pleasure on her face. "Sit down, my friend. There is something that we must discuss. I gather you already know of the stormy session?"

"Yes, I heard the crash of your cane. Was it something Tzo did or said?"

"Yes, the snake had the nerve to insinuate the election of Lee Wah was my doing and that the final seat, the junior seat, was meant for one of my sons!" Liah leaned back in her chair. "But I dispelled any doubts on that score. I said never would one of my sons sit on the Council. Also I told them I needed no Council to fatten my purse as the Gods have already showered me with enough bounty."

There was a prolonged silence, then Liah began to giggle. "You should have seen Tzo. He was so comical, sitting there in shock. I thought Lim Tao and Kam Fong would burst into laughter. I barely missed his fingers."

Cook's countenance was grave as he warned Liah not to go too far in her dislike of the man. "Do not take Tzo too lightly. He is here for no good and we must prepare ourselves for anything."

"I know. That's why I've been sitting here thinking about our private sentry system. We must put more men on if we are to protect our Apinyin trade."

"We will discuss things tomorrow. At the moment, you are worn out and should take your rest."

Wordlessly, Liah nodded. Words would not come for the overwhelming warmth that rushed into her tired spirit, wondering at her age how love could be unexplainable. An abiding peace replaced the earlier feeling of desperate panic of exile, with a tinge of sadness clinging to the fringe of her mind. Their eyes met, kindling, then Cook reached out a hand to help Liah to her feet. Gently, he led her down the stairs, both smiling at the realization that despite the many times they'd spoken about the railing, it hadn't yet been put in.

The next day there was no discussion about their sentry system, nor was anything said about safeguarding their Apinyin trade. Liah's mood was dark. She seemed not to care about a thing, refusing food but begrudgingly drinking her brandy broth. Cook recognized this as the withdrawal symptoms from Apinyin and, not wishing her to suffer the usual fasting, tried to divert Liah's attention from her plight. "The Chinese lilies in the Alley need thinning. They're pushing themselves out of the border and onto the cobblestones."

Without a word, Liah went to her bedroom and donned her pointed straw hat and returned to the kitchen for the shears. Cook handed her a trowel, remarking how much a peasant woman she looked. Liah glowered back and stomped into the corridor.

The abundant rains and sunshine had transformed the garden into an explosion of color and pleasant aromas. Liah walked up and down, stopping now and then to pluck a dead leaf or to examine a rose bud, but mostly she scanned the Chinese lilies and agreed with Cook. Liah knelt and began the tedious job of thinning out the lily bulbs, carefully separating them and placing them in a basket.

The peacock and peahen began a raucous shrieking and Liah looked up to see Chon Woo approaching, his arms filled with catalogues. She felt peeved that the man had come to collect his reward so soon. Nevertheless, she smiled. There was at least one good aspect of Chon's visit: he'd rescued her from this tedious task.

Two hours later, after Chon departed, Cook scowled. "He didn't waste any time, did he?"

Liah replied without rancor, "You must understand Chon. He has waited a long time for this financial opportunity. Besides, he is driven by a desire to go one better than Sang. Anyway, the sooner he improves his place, the sooner I'll be getting dividends." She paused. "Oh, I know what you're thinking and you're right. Chon's loyalty is good only until a better financial backer comes along, but for the time, he will be important to me."

Later that afternoon as they shared tea, Liah confided to Cook that her mood was dark because Fifth Son had outright refused to go to college. "He also said he wouldn't go into law, even if he decided to go. He said for me to pin my hopes on Fourth Son, that he was the studious one."

"Well, if it's your children's happiness you have in mind, you will not force them into a life they do not want. Besides, according to Meng-Sui, they'll end up being exactly what their fate decrees."

Liah frowned. "Are you telling me I should allow them to go their own way, even if it is not good for them? For me not to urge them to take the right path?"

Cook smiled indulgently. "No, not if all you do is urge."

For a moment Liah scowled, then began to chuckle.

—

The summer, which only a few months earlier Liah feared would not come, had arrived full force by August. On the twentieth day, Liah celebrated her second son's twenty-first birthday. It was shameful the way her two eldest sons ignored her heart's desire and, more importantly, set such shabby examples for their younger brothers and sister. If only they would agree to betrothals, she'd feel more assured of a continuance of their family name. It required a good deal of self-control for Liah not to tongue lash her two errant sons. Only her promise to Cook that she'd only urge her sons to take the right path kept her from forcing a confrontation. Liah's eyes accused Cook of taking unfair advantage of her.

She was saddened to think that her youngest child also might soon no longer need her. Most distressing was her recollection that on the tenth day of next June, Eldest Son would turn twenty-three years of age and was yet unmarried. Nevertheless, there was one bright spot. Eldest Daughter, who had turned twenty in July, was heavy with child—not a grandchild carrying the name of Lee but a grandchild nonetheless.

After the festivities, when they were alone together, Liah burst out in anger. "See what you have forced me to do? Now, having promised you I would leave the children alone, I can't even speak to them of marriage."

Cook replied, "I didn't make you promise to be mute. I only asked you to be civil. Quarreling and fighting are different than a civilized discussion."

Liah moaned, "It seems so long ago that I was burdened with seven helpless children, fleeing for our lives. Now they're grown and they turn a deaf ear to me. Even Eldest Daughter fails to let me know how she is. Ah, time is my greatest enemy."

Cook impatiently retorted, "Every time things do not go your way you dwell on the past, bemoaning the passage of time and that you are being pushed aside by time and that you are not needed. Cease this childish complaining. A woman who is to become a grandmother does not whine so."

—

Five days after her second son's birthday, Lim Tao made his first social call to Number Three. Liah was overjoyed to see him, for it had been on her mind to become better acquainted with him. At the outset of the visit, Lim Tao, ill-at-ease, fidgeted in his chair, worrying he had acted too rashly in coming. "Please," urged Liah, as she handed him a plate of freshly baked pastries, "make yourself at home. My home is yours and until you are reunited with your wife and sons, please consider us your family."

Lim Tao thanked her. He shook his head, deploring the complexity of the immigration process. "I've almost given up hope, Liah. It's been almost eight years since I first made application for their entry. And all I've gotten are heartache, anger and expenses."

Afraid that Liah might think him niggardly, Lim explained the number of times the agent in Hong Kong has pressed him for more money. "I sometimes think he is not only stalling but raising a family on my toil."

Liah sympathized and cursed the Fahn Gwai's inhumane treatment of her people. She confided that one of the reasons she was adamant her sons go to college was to have one become an attorney. "Perhaps then we might be given fairer treatment."

Lim Tao shook his head. "Perhaps for later generations, but for the time, it does not help my situation, Liah."

At the conclusion of their visit, Liah leaned forward and lowered her voice, a habit she'd acquired in the early days when secrecy was a means of self-preservation. "I know a man in Dai Faw who is honest and works hard to help our people. I will have Professor write on your behalf. Keep remembering Meng-Sui and the favors of the Gods make all things possible. Do not despair, sir."

Lim Tao smiled. "I am not a believer like you, Liah, but if you can facilitate my family's entry to Gem Sahn, we shall all be forever in your debt."

"No need for that, sir. We all do whatever we can to better the life of another. Isn't that the way we survived the perilous years in Gem Sahn? I shall let you know the moment I hear from Dai Faw."

Liah gave word to Professor and he wrote. Over the ensuing weeks, however, they did not hear back. Liah became increasingly distressed when she heard rumors of trouble brewing in the House of Lee. She feared for the life of Elder Lee Ti and wondered if Lee Tzo had anything to do with the dissension.

As the heat of summer became unbearable, Liah put aside her anxieties, succumbing to the vapors of her bamboo pipe. The air of tranquility vanished when the month ended and school vacation arrived and with it the children home all day, constantly underfoot, arguing and fighting. The commotion strained Liah's patience and caused her to lash out.

Usually self-controlled, even Cook exploded one morning, when an argument between Third and Fourth Sons broke out. Cook grabbed his broomstick and began swatting Theo and William, shouting, "I'm sick and tired of you two! You are brothers but act like enemies. I will not have it! Understand?"

Theo and William gaped at Cook's irate attack. They shouted that they were sorry and begged for the thrashing to end.

Cook's anger quickly cooled. "You two made me lose my temper. I not only have to deal with you kids, but also with the Council's problems, the town's problems and most of all your mother's health. Her bad appetite, lack of rest and Apinyin are going to kill her. Is that what you want?"

Theo's belligerence dissolved and his eyes opened wide in fear. "Oh, Cook, I'm sorry, but Fourth Brother makes me so mad! He's always being so goody-goody." He turned to William and grunted sheepishly, "If you promise not to act like a know-it-all, I'll try to remember we're brothers."

William's eyes filled with tears and he bit his lip, whispering, "Sir, I'm sorry, too. I'm also worried about Mah-Mah. She looks so tired and pale. I thank you for being so good to her and for being like a father to me."

MYSTERY TENANT IN NUMBER ONE

September ninth, nineteen hundred and fifteen was a record hot summer day with the temperature soaring above one hundred degrees. Liah's mood teetered dangerously on the brink of exploding into violence, and the presence of the outdoor people in her front room did not help. Cook threatened to ask the people to leave, but Liah shook her head. "The poor souls are freezing in the winter and now are roasting in summer. The Gods are good to me; therefore I must share my bounty with them. I'm truly sorry for my disposition, but this unrelenting heat is a constant torment. Please bear with them a little longer, and bear with my vile mood as well."

"I do not begrudge the extra work, nor do I mind the vile mood you're in. It is your not eating that bothers me and bothers the family. If you'll agree to take a bowl of brandy broth at least twice a day, I'll be satisfied. Then I'll not even mind your uneasiness about your daughter's first birthing."

"I'll eat more, I promise, Cook."

"Harrumph!" he muttered. "I will believe it when I see it. All I ask is that when I put food in front of you, you do not bite off my head."

The heat and humidity turned Chinatown into an oven. The Fahn Gwai schools even closed. In Chinatown, the fierce humidity sent residents indoors, barring and boarding up their windows and doors against summer's onslaught. In the hours between high noon and evening, the streets were deserted, the town barricaded against the heat. Only the youngsters were outside, playing listlessly in Peacock Alley and in the muddy swimming hole at the playground.

Professor avoided Number Three. He had not yet decided whether to assume the responsibility of the extra five men Liah wanted to add to her sentry system, but knew this would not be a good time to deny her. Professor chuckled to himself as he thought that there was no good time to deny Liah's wishes.

One day toward the end of September, Cook returned from the meat market excited, bearing important news. Liah almost screamed. "Now what? I can not endure any more problems, what with the outdoor people and the children."

"There you go again, thinking the worst,"

His hands on his hips and his eyes glaring, Cook announced he was not going to divulge a thing until after supper. "Whether I tell you or not will depend upon the way you eat. Besides, having to wonder about the news will be good for you. Instead of fretting about the heat, you can fret about what the news might be." As he went about his work, Cook wondered how Liah had withstood the heat as a farmer's wife. Had she suffered as much then as she did now?

After dinner, the house was quiet, the outdoor people having returned to their makeshift dwellings and the children having gone to bed. The slight breeze flowing through the house began to revive Liah. "Well?" she eagerly demanded. "Tell me the news."

"Someone has rented Number One. It is rumored that the tenants are Mexicans. Several people saw swarthy foreigners coming and going and it seemed there was a lot of remodeling going on inside."

Liah cried, "A foreigner in our town? That's unfortunate. We must do something about that. I was hoping one of our people would rent the store."

Cook shook his head. "Well, no use getting upset. The place is rented and nothing can be done about it."

Liah fumed. "Marchesson is to blame. He had no business renting to outsiders. He knows how we feel about keeping the town to ourselves."

Cook chided, "No use fussing." He changed the subject. "Has Eldest Daughter sent any word yet?"

Liah shook her head. "I've a mind to put in the Fahn Gwai telephone."

Cook snorted. "I was not supposed to tell you, but Eldest Son has already made arrangements to have a telephone installed. After the lines are connected to the house, the workmen will put in our instrument."

The next time Liah saw Eldest Son, she accosted him. "When did you say the telephone was to be installed?"

Thomas glanced at Cook then shrugged. "I told Cook not to tell you. I knew your impatience would drive us crazy. They'll be here soon. I'm not certain. There are wires to be connected and we aren't the only customers the company has. You must be patient."

"Be patient? Do you realize I am waiting on the arrival of my first grandchild?"

"Aw, Mah-Mah, to hear you talk, you'd think this is to be your first birth."

Liah snapped, "It might as well be my first. After all, it is my first *grandchild* and I'm all the more nervous not knowing what is happening."

—

The first day of October arrived, bringing with it cooler weather. The outdoor people finally returned outdoors for good. On the first night after they'd gone, Liah asked if Cook had provided supper for two of her favorites, Wing On and Sam Lew. "Did you see how those two always came to life when you offered them food this summer? At eighty-one and seventy-two, meals are all they have to look forward to. We must never forget them."

"It's no wonder the Gods favor you, Liah. Your thoughtfulness when it comes to others makes up for all of your temper tantrums."

Liah grinned, then her voice became soft, "There was a time in my life when I was completely dependent on the love and charity of others. This is my repayment to the Gods and to those generous souls who made my current life possible. That is partly why I am worried sick about Elder Lee Ti and Elder Wong in Dai Faw. Without their help back then, neither Sen nor I would be alive today. I'll be glad when we receive word from Dai Faw."

Late in the afternoon, on the fourth day of October, Liah was slouched in her upholstered chair, when the front door opened and closed gently and she heard the sound of footsteps, high-heeled Fahn Gwai ladies' shoes. Cook grabbed a cleaver, but Liah shook her head. "It is a woman, Cook."

A moment later, a red-haired Fahn Gwai young lady appeared in the kitchen doorway. Liah just stared. The woman had happy, flashing green eyes and the most infectious smile Liah had ever seen. She was obviously wealthy, given her expensive softly tailored green wool suit and matching green shoes. Speechless, Liah was further shocked when the young woman addressed her in Cantonese. Her Chinese, though spoken by a foreigner, was both fluent and grammatically flawless. Although the young lady had taken the liberty of walking straight into her private quarters, Liah could not find it in herself to be angered.

Liah regained her composure and motioned for her guest to be seated. The young woman accepted, saying her name was Selah Wang and she'd come to make Liah's acquaintance. She was also there to seek permission to do business in Chinatown and to inquire about the associated fees.

"What kind of business are you in?" inquired Liah. Selah giggled and then asked if Liah could believe that she was a madam and that she wanted to open a brothel. For yet a third time, Liah was flabbergasted. If she lived another hundred years, she would've never believed such a beautiful, educated lady could be the owner of a brothel. Liah became giddy as she listened to Selah's story of her five-year stay in Hong Kong where she had studied and absorbed the culture of China.

As they talked, Selah was somehow drawn to the stern-faced, tiny woman. Could she really be the head of the Council? Liah's insight into people gave Selah to know that Liah was not the average, run-of-the mill female, that the little woman had brains and was not to be trifled with.

Liah smiled. "I like you, Selah. I hope we can be good friends." She invited Selah to join her for a meal.

As they shared tarts fresh from the oven, Selah spoke of her parents. "My father was a coolie and my mother a worker in the railroad camp. Father died ten years ago and now Mother lives in Sonora."

Sensing Selah's pain, Liah quickly consoled her. "Your mother must be comforted to know your father's Meng-Sui is good. It had to be so, to have had a loving wife and daughter. Your father is now resting in eternal peace, his Feng-Sui blessing you and your mother." Liah paused and then asked if Selah had any sisters or brothers.

"I have three younger brothers. Presently they are here to help me furnish and clean out Number One. My older brother is married and the father of five children. My mother lives with him, and while my father is undoubtedly resting in peace, my mother will never be the same again without him."

Selah's voice dropped to a whisper. "Such devotion between two people I've never seen. I owe my parents a great deal, especially my mother who insisted none of us ignore my father's culture. It was her doing that I went to Hong Kong and it was through her efforts that all of us speak the tongue of our father."

Cook, touched by Selah's filial love and respect, awed by her beauty and elated because Liah liked her, smiled broadly as he thought, the Gods are good. Now Liah will have someone to talk to, a woman who can match her brains and strength.

Cook was pleased when Selah waxed eloquent over the flakiness of the tarts' crust. "You must give me the recipe, sir." Her eyes twinkled as she added, "But I suppose like all good chefs, you do not give out recipes. I'd sure like my chef to be able to make them."

To Liah's surprise, Cook not only volunteered the ingredients but offered to show Selah's chef how to make the tarts. "The secret is in the handling of the dough, Selah. I'd be happy to teach him, if you like." There was a hint of pride in Cook's voice.

For the first time since coming to Peacock Alley, Liah realized how isolated she felt. She had no other female with whom to talk, let alone share a secret. While Amah was big-hearted, loving and loyal, she didn't have the scope to understand Liah's feelings; besides, she was too caught up with the children and spent her leisure hours with Mei-Mei's amah. As for Madam Quock, Liah couldn't tolerate her for too long a spell; the woman was without a brain in her head.

Cook listened to Selah's laughter, also thinking to himself: this beauteous one is just what Liah needs. Liah was indeed favored by the Gods. He had a feeling Selah was bright and no weakling. She wouldn't falter in the face of trouble. As he thought of trouble, Lee Tzo came to mind. Cook realized he should warn Selah.

"Lee Tzo, recently from Dai Faw, is someone we believe to be dangerous. Be wary of him. He might resent your opening another brothel and might try to do you harm."

Liah gasped. "I forgot. Cook is right, Selah. Be very wary of Lee Tzo!"

Selah took Liah's hands in hers. "Don't worry about me. I can take care of myself. Besides I have two half-breeds and a dwarf who would do battle for me. I'm used to fending for myself, so please, Liah, do not fret."

Liah suggested Selah pay the same fees as Lee Tzo. "I'd ask less, but we must not give the scoundrel anything with which to make an issue. Also, please be sure there is no gambling or Apinyin."

Selah nodded. "I did not mention it, but my brothel will not be open to the public. That is why I chose Number One. With the exorbitant prices and the well-known personages that will come, we need an entrance and parking place in a protected area. What is more deserted than the train yard? If Tzo complains, just tell him that my prices are too far above the reach of Chinatown residents."

Selah glanced up at the wall clock and then leaped to her feet. "I have overstayed. Amah will be furious to know I came to see you alone. If I might, after I've opened, I'd like to come and visit you again. I like you too, Liah. Goodbye, and please do not worry on my account."

As quickly as she came, Selah was gone. The room held her sparkling aura long afterwards, especially her sandalwood essence. Liah blushed when Cook remarked that Selah certainly didn't appear to be the ordinary madam.

"That one will bring excitement into your life." Cook reddened slightly as he wondered if the lady had a husband or patron.

Liah giggled. "Not that one. When you went out to the garden, she told me she had no time for men. I suspect she had a tragic love affair early in her life and now rejects men. Seems hard to believe that one so young and lovely doesn't need a man or marriage." Liah averted her eyes while speaking, for even in Cook's presence it was hard to speak of things male and female.

Liah paused, then proclaimed that she and Cook must keep Selah's identity secret for now. "She doesn't want any vandalism at her place nor does she need Tzo to know what kind of place she's opening."

"What about telling Professor?"

Liah shrugged. "I know he's dependable and loyal, but in this instance the secret is not mine to divulge. It is up to Selah to tell him. Meanwhile, see to it no one defaces her property."

Cook was thoughtful. He'd not seen Liah so vibrantly alive or happy. She exuded a lightheartedness that was almost foreign to her. She hadn't even been this happy with the formation of the Council. Whatever Selah was, Cook vowed to protect her. He could do no less for a woman who made Liah feel such elation.

Meanwhile, Selah had returned to Number One. Her amah demanded to know where she'd gone. "You scared me half to death. I searched everywhere for you."

"Oh, Amah, I went to see Liah. I had to tell her of my intent and to find out about the fees. She's wonderful. You'll love her too."

Amah's face dropped and she threw her hands up in despair. "Aiyah! You went to call on her and did not take me? You know it isn't safe or proper to be on the streets unescorted. Well, what did she say to you?"

Selah reached out, drawing Amah into her arms and kissed her. "We got along beautifully. She's not at all like the rumors have her. She's a shrewd, fairly good-looking woman with a pair of eyes that miss not a thing. Amah, how old did you say Liah was?"

Amah clucked. "I do not know if it is her true age, but they say she's forty-two. People say her husband deserted her because she's too strong willed, especially with her activities in the town Council. Personally, I think she's wrong to be disobedient to her husband."

Selah chuckled. "You're still living in the Middle Ages, Amah. I think Liah's right in trying to improve conditions in Chinatown. I don't know if she'll succeed, but she'll have my assistance. Now, my old-fashioned friend, go unpack my trunks, and do be careful with my gowns."

The old woman grimaced as Selah impudently tweaked her nose. "Now run along. I've got to speak with the carpenters."

The following day, Liah fought a sense of apprehension she could not fully fathom. What was the Goddess trying to tell her? Toward noon, Liah turned to Cook for the tenth time and moaned that her daughter must have miscalculated. "Here it is the tenth day of October and she said she would deliver at the end of September or surely by the first week of October."

Cook chuckled. "Well, miscalculation or not, this is one event you will not hasten. Sit down and have lunch. The baby will be born when it will. Why not take a nap after lunch? It'll pass the time."

Liah awakened with a start at four-thirty when the front door opened and slammed. Through a fog, she heard footsteps and then muffled conversation in the kitchen. Groggily, she sat up in bed and listened but heard nothing intelligible. Finally, she groped for her robe. Entering the kitchen, Liah stared at Toh and asked fearfully, "Is my daughter all right?"

"She had a baby girl, born three hours ago. Both your daughter and baby are fine."

Toh's face flushed with pride as he apologized for the delay in coming. "The street cars are slow and the connections are problematic, otherwise I'd have been here sooner."

Liah grinned. "Tomorrow we shall have a telephone, Toh. Now, tell me about the baby."

"I stared at her for several minutes before I realized that I was actually a father." Toh's voice was jubilant. "She will be an independent child. She cried so lustily, and your daughter could not offer her breast fast enough. She so tiny, so, fragile."

Normally reserved in manner, Toh now appeared youthful in his joy. As she watched her son-in-law's animated face, Liah thought that it was the first time she'd seen him so excited.

"Have you named her yet, Toh?"

"Not yet, Mother. We thought perhaps you or Professor could give her an appropriate Chinese name and my wife and I could give her a Fahn Gwai name."

Liah motioned for Toh to sit down, but he refused. He had to go home. Liah cried that Toh must wait while Cook prepared the traditional chicken brandy broth and pickled pigs' feet.

"It is not necessary, Mother. The midwife has already cooked the chicken broth, which my wife will probably be drinking now and the pigs' feet will be ready this evening. The midwife said these two dishes are necessary for my wife's recovery and for her milk for the baby."

Footsteps in the corridor interrupted their conversation as Thomas and Shelley burst into the kitchen. Thomas extended a hand in congratulations. He'd heard the news at the produce market. "Your older brother has been handing out cigars, Toh. Congratulations again!"

Liah wrapped up a dozen meat tarts, several portions of barbecued pork and a spiced chicken. "Take these home with you, Toh. I'm certain the midwife will not have time to cook meals for several days. Eldest Son will drive you home."

By the time Liah returned from the front room, Cook was carefully encircling the tenth day of October on the calendar with his red pencil. "Well, now you have your first grandchild." He paused, then softly inquired if she was disappointed it was a granddaughter.

"Certainly not. A grandchild is a grandchild. Now, if you'll step across the Alley and ask Professor if he would come and see me, I'd like a horoscope made for the child. I hope today is an auspicious date."

A crooked smiled played on Cook's face and his eyes shone mischievously. "I do not think even the Gods would dare to thwart your auspicious grand-motherhood."

Liah made no comment for she was deep in thought calculating the date, year and symbols. Strange, she thought, how time fades the data in one's mind. Important as birth signs are, she had forgotten them. Cook seemed to divine her thoughts, saying quickly that it was currently the Year of the Rabbit.

Professor was not at home and did not arrive at Number Three until nightfall. "I was in Fahn Gwai town with Wong Kan and what a time we had! The immigration red tape is bad enough without having to pantomime. I was never so frustrated trying to make ourselves understood. I returned home just a few minutes ago and Cook told me of your granddaughter's birth. I congratulate you, Liah. The Year of the Rabbit is an auspicious time to be born. I know you want a horoscope drawn up for the infant, and if you'll give me a few days to do the calculations, I'll have it for you."

"Oh, sir, please have supper with us. We can discuss my granddaughter's birthday while we sup. Are you positive today is a good day to be born?"

"Liah!" admonished Cook. "You heard Professor. Today is a very good day." He gestured a warning with his chopsticks as he pointed at her. "Besides, she is born, therefore today must be a good day. Now, if you'll pour the rice wine, we'll drink a toast to the baby. Then, we'll have supper."

Filled with excitement, Liah was unable to eat and plied Professor with questions. "Was the child to be favored by the Gods?" she asked. Without waiting for an answer, she went on that she was certain the baby would be an unusual and gifted child as the family genes ensured that. She then inquired if Professor would please think of an appropriate name for the baby. Cook scowled and Professor chuckled. "Liah," he said indulgently, "there is a piece of advice I'll give at this time. Enjoy your newfound role of grandmother. Take your life and live it more fully instead of spending so much of it on the Council. Only the Gods know how much life you or I have remaining."

"I suppose you think me foolish, but in truth this is my most important moment on earth to me. Do you realize this is the propagation that ensures that the House of Lee will not perish?" Suddenly, Liah's eyes sharpened. "In my joy I'd completely forgotten Sen. He must be told of his granddaughter. Sir, will you write the letter?"

Professor nodded. He wondered if Liah yet considered Sen her husband. If so, where did Cook stand? Surely, they must be more than friends. His face flushed and he pushed the question from his mind.

"Liah spent this afternoon making plans for the distribution of the red eggs, chicken, roast side of pork and all the trimmings to mark the baby's month-old birthday," said Cook.

Professor laughed. "Only a few hours old and you would have her a month old already, Liah?"

"Be that as it may, sir, it does take a good deal of time to draw up the list of people we must remember. Forget one person and you will have an enemy for life." Liah added, "I shall not make that costly mistake."

Speaking of enemies, Professor asked about the sentries Liah had hired. "I have rented the rooms, but to date, no one has contacted me."

Cook reassured Professor that the men would arrive soon. Professor listened without comment. Although he'd had time to think about it, it was still an audacious move for him. Still, Professor could not help feeling important when the town discovered he had bodyguards. Again, he reiterated, "I hope people believe my need for sentries."

Liah scowled. "Just tell them that since Tzo's arrival in town you've received threats on your life and that there are strange happenings. That ought to keep Tzo and Sang on their guard. Once the men arrive, I'll definitely feel better."

Cook sighed. Was Liah never to learn patience? She caught his eye and smiled. "I know, I know, I am being impatient, but I can't help it.

Too much is at stake for action at a snail's pace."

As Professor took his leave, Liah reminding him of his promise to generate the baby's horoscope. "I want to read it at the month-old celebrations, sir."

Professor smiled and nodded. "It shall be done Liah. Have no worry. It's not often I'm called upon to do a baby's horoscope. Mostly, I do horoscopes for prattling women who want to know if gambling fortunes are at hand, or if their sons will sire grandsons."

CHANGES AND CHARGES

Liah awakened the day after her granddaughter's birth and remembered that this was the day her telephone was to be installed. She donned her robe, fumbled for her slippers and rushed into the kitchen. Cook motioned for her to be seated and said that he'd have her brandy broth ready shortly. Where were the telephone men? It was eleven o'clock!

"I do not know and don't want you to bother me today," said Cook. "I have too much to do, including laundry. So sit down and don't make me have to coax you to eat."

Shortly before two o'clock in the afternoon, she watched curiously as the uniformed men strung and tacked wire all around the baseboard of the kitchen, boring a hole into the wall where the telephone was to be installed. She marveled at the Fahn Gwai's miracle. How could a few feet of wire make it possible for her to speak to Eldest Daughter across town?

Just before the installation was done, Eldest Son and Second Son came home. Thomas scribbled down the numbers and handed them to Cook. "This series of numbers is our telephone number. Here is another set. That's my sister's telephone number. When I have time, I'll look up any other numbers that Mah wants or she can have one of the kids do it."

As soon as the men left, Liah telephoned Eldest Daughter. Thomas stood beside her as she made the call. Liah grinned as she heard Eldest

Daughter's voice and shouted back she now had a telephone. Thomas nudged his mother, saying she did not have to yell. For ten minutes, Liah half-shouted her conversation while Thomas stood by, a look of consternation on his face.

Cook muttered, "Be patient, your mother isn't used to a telephone. She'll eventually learn not to shout; for the time being, let her be."

Shelley whispered that now that they had a telephone, neither Flo nor Toh would get any peace since his mother would be calling them two or three times a day.

Thomas grinned. "If it were only two or three times daily, Flo would be lucky. Well, let's get to bed. Every time she talks to Flo, Mah usually gives us hell for being single."

Shelley agreed and both sons disappeared into their bedrooms.

Over the ensuing weeks, Liah's impatience to see her new granddaughter grew. Cook complained to Eldest Son that he, for one, would be relieved when Liah finally got to hold her. "It's incredible the way she's so fixated on touching her. Perhaps it's a good thing your sister is confined at home for the standard month-long recuperation. She'll need her strength to deal with your mother's over-zealousness. Can you imagine how much more uncontrolled she'd be if the baby were one of yours?"

"You too, Cook?" moaned Thomas. "I thought you were on our side."

"I am neither on your side nor on your mother's," Cook said soberly. "While I can see your point of view, I can also see your mother's. She is from an older generation, one that feels entitled to expect daughters-in-laws and grandsons." Cook sighed, "Life is difficult enough when it only involves reconciling duty to one's parents and being true to yourself, but when these issues are complicated by two different cultures, the problems multiply sharply. Anyway, if you don't want her to harass you about marriage, I'd eat and go to bed. She is still sleeping."

On November ninth, the tokens announcing the birth were ready for distribution. The perfectly simmered pullets, shiny with a coating of peanut oil, were wrapped in wax paper. The red-hued eggs were neatly assembled in boxes and the slabs of barbecued pig were also neatly packaged. Only the sliced ginger remained to be wrapped.

Eleven-year-old Emmi whined that the wrapping of the red ginger was boring. Thomas growled and told her to shake a leg. He didn't want to wait all day.

Liah smiled at her youngest child with affection, urging her to finish. "Mother will give you a reward if you'll hurry."

Cook sighed with relief when Thomas left with the many boxes for distribution in the produce sector of town. Cook and Amah would distribute the boxes to the various business houses and families in China Street. Professor entered, offering to help. "You'll get them delivered faster if I were to help. Suppose I were to deliver the boxes to all the places on Lion's Den Alley? Then Cook and Amah can do the rest of the streets."

On November tenth, Number Three was a beehive of activity; for today the family and close friends would feast in honor of the infant's month-old birthday. It was the first time Cook felt the pressure of the event, having three females constantly under foot. Amah, although helpful, was not efficient or meticulous enough to keep up with him. Madam Quock talked too much and was too bossy. Liah, too excited, could not or would not eat and barely managed to drink a bowl of brandy broth and only after he threatened not to cook if she didn't.

Throughout the morning and early afternoon Cook smiled to himself as Liah beamed at the many residents who came to give her granddaughter lucky packets of money and gifts. Her spirits soared and Cook had to admit that perhaps a granddaughter would transform Liah's life into a happier one despite Council matters. Everyone bubbled with happiness except Professor, who appeared tense and very speculative.

Professor knew the infant's horoscope had to be full of glowing predictions, but he also knew the facts did not bear it out. At one point Professor almost decided to gloss over the infant's faults, but decided in the end to tell the truth. Liah must know Meng-Sui was not to be denied. Frustrated, he realized Liah for all her worldliness still believed in the old superstitions involving the moon, the stars and the Gods.

Liah awakened from a nap at four o'clock and wandered into the kitchen. The aroma of roasting ducks, simmering pullets, spiced ribs and especially of the rich, savory shark's fin soup brought a smile to her face. "All these wonderful aromas make me hungry."

Cook carefully hid a smile and motioned for her to be seated. He ladled out a bowl of shark's fin soup, laced it with a bit of vinegar and placed it before her. He dipped a fork into the pot of simmering spicy soy sauce and brought up a side of spareribs. Carefully, he sliced off two ribs. "Eat these and then you can go out to check the garden. Afterwards you should bathe and dress."

Liah was standing at the entrance to Peacock Alley when Toh and Flo arrived by taxi. Liah ran forward excitedly and yanked open the door. Before her daughter could alight, she reached out for her granddaughter. Gently, softly, Liah raised the pink blanket and cooed. "My heart sings. She's light as a feather." She stroked the baby's face, murmuring to herself. "My heart sings."

Moments later, as she became aware of someone staring, Liah stole a glance out of the corner of her eye to see Toh's beaming face, surely happier than she'd ever seen him. Liah lifted the infant's finger. "Ah, such a long tapered hand. Can it be she'll be an artist?"

The taxi sped off leaving a cloud of dust in its wake. Liah scowled. Even in winter, the dust could not be avoided. "Come, let's go indoors. I don't want the baby breathing in the impurities in the air."

Just as they turned to go inside, Liah saw Professor cross the cobblestones. Cook saw his worried expression. The Professor had confided in him his dilemma. Cook surmised that Professor had decided on telling Liah the truth. Cook waved for Liah to enter, then waited to speak with the scholar.

Cook and Professor remained outside a while watching the dwindling curls of dust left by the taxi. Cook quickly offered his support. "I know you're going to tell Liah the facts instead of dressing them up. That is both commendable and very courageous. I wanted you to know how I feel. The child will undoubtedly have a good life with Liah at her side. However, as you well know, Liah, though normally a very logical person, is nevertheless very superstitious."

Their gazes met and held for a fleeting moment of sympathetic understanding. Why, wondered Cook, couldn't the man stretch the truth just a bit? By the time the infant grew up, his predictions wouldn't even be remembered. Professor's response answered Cook's question. "You and I both know that if I were to paint a rosy future, Liah would hold me to account for each thing that goes awry. Liah has the memory of an elephant." With that, they entered the house.

On the way to the kitchen, Cook stopped to gaze at the baby. He murmured, "I don't believe such a beautiful creature would ever grow up to be stubborn and willful."

"Neither do I, Cook," said Liah as her eyes scanned Professor's face for confirmation.

Professor was saved from answering as the front doors flew open and effusive Madam Quock rushed forward, her arms outstretched. "Let me hold her!" With an accusatory glance at her trailing daughter, Madam Quock lifted the baby's blanket and cooed. "Liah, it's natural for you to think your granddaughter is perfect, but the Gods know otherwise. If she inherits your stubbornness, it might turn out to be a god-given gift. One needs perseverance if one is to obtain what one wants in life."

Professor, who believed Madam Quock flighty and stupid, was nevertheless grateful for the interruption. Liah scoffed, "That's how much you know about Meng-Sui! Anyone can see the infant has an aura of good fortune about her." She glared defensively at her friend. "No matter, Madam Quock, as long as she has me, she'll never want for anything."

Liah reached out for her granddaughter. "Quock Lan, give her to me. Your time will come. Let me enjoy my granddaughter before the guests arrive."

Flo and Toh glanced at each other and Flo whispered, "Mah-Mah is being over-zealous. This is the first time she's spoken so to Madam Quock. Also, did you see Yook Lan squirm?"

The family and guests were seated at the supper tables in the front room when Selah entered. Liah grinned and rushed up to embrace Selah. Conversation stopped and people stared at the red-haired beauty who evoked such a show of welcome from Liah. Yook Lan covetously ogled the heavy gold chain around Selah's neck from which hung a flawless jade heart and thought that such a necklace must be worth a good deal of money.

Liah seated Selah beside her and casually murmured Selah's name, indicating that they were friends. Flo, on the verge of speaking, was thwarted by Liah's warning glance. Professor gazed at the red-haired Fahn Gwai, shocked at her height. Seated beside Liah, who was a mere four feet six inches tall, Selah appeared to be a giantess. There was also something strange about the woman. She was obviously Fahn Gwai, yet somehow she wasn't. He was stunned when Selah addressed him in flawless Chinese, not in the idiomatic language of townspeople, but in the precise, grammatically correct style of the educated.

Once or twice during the ensuing meal, Liah scowled at her sons who insisted upon discussing world conditions and the possibility of American participation in the war in Europe. Thomas, whose tutelage under Ted Crosset on the Dobney Estates had gotten him interested in the affairs of the world, now spent his leisure reading up on world politics. Thomas was amazed that Selah was so informed about the impending war and world politics.

"German soldiers," murmured Thomas, "are not only superior soldiers and trained impeccably, but Germany has the best railroads in the world too. They can move their troops and supplies to the front without effort. I'm afraid it won't be long before Gem Sahn will be pulled into the war."

Professor cast Thomas a furtive warning glance. It wouldn't do to ruin Liah's celebration. Thomas bit his lip and remained silent for the rest of supper. Selah patted his hand, whispering for him not to worry.

"It's all right for you, Selah, but my trucking business will be forced to shut down if Shelly and I have to go to war."

"Dear one, don't worry. What will be will be. Trust in the future. I see a long, successful life ahead for you."

"Yeah," muttered Thomas. "I suppose Third and Fourth Brothers can hold down the fort if Shell and I have to go. In fact, Third Brother, Theo, has been chafing to drive for us, but Mah-Mah would kill both of us *and* Theo, if he quits school."

"Your darling mother is absolutely right, Thomas. Theo must get his education, or else he'll be stuck doing manual work for the rest of his life."

All conversation ceased with Liah's announcement that Professor would read the infant's horoscope. As Professor rose, Tom nudged Shelley. "Look at Professor's face. I'll bet he's sweating blood trying to divine a future that will suit Mah."

The scholar adjusted his spectacles and looked around the room, his gaze coming to rest on Liah. "You know, of course, that a horoscope is not a perfect prediction of a life to come. To a greater or lesser degree, the day of birth, the hour and the relationship of the stars and planets reveal facets of the character of an individual and hints about his or her future. For the most part, a person's happiness and success in life are the direct result of a person's own abilities and perseverance."

With one last glance at Liah, Professor began to read. "The Year of the Rabbit is an auspicious time to be born. You can expect that the child will have artistic talents and a keen mind, but will also fall victim to hardship and heartache because of her ability to discern the truth in all matters. She will see through superficiality and deceit. Her greatest source of unhappiness will come from her stubborn nature, which will make it almost impossible for her to compromise her values and positions. While it is very commendable that she will be highly virtuous, she will have to learn to moderate speaking her mind. That is your granddaughter's horoscope, my newly blessed grandmother."

Liah moaned, "I believe you, sir, but another stubborn one?"

Selah giggled, leaned forward and cooed, "Liah, if you don't want her, I'll take the darling."

"Who said anything about not wanting her? I just don't want her to be stubborn."

"Well, now," teased Selah. "The baby comes by it honestly. From what I've heard, her grandmother is stubborn, outspoken and ferocious when crossed."

There was a stunned silence at the table and Professor flinched, waiting for the tongue-lashing that was certain to come, but Liah just grinned. Selah concluded, "Seriously, Liah, you and I both know that in this life it is necessary to be tough, to stand up for one's rights and not be downtrodden. I am happy that both you and your granddaughter have been given a stubborn streak."

An explosion averted, Professor leaned back in his chair, contemplating the red-haired stranger and wondering who she was and where she was from.

At ten o'clock, Toh announced they had to leave for home, as he had to work the next morning. Liah reached out for her granddaughter's hand and caressed the sleeping infant's face. "Toh," she declared, "you and your family must visit me every Sunday. I want to get to know my granddaughter." She looked at Thomas and said, "You must drive them home. The night air is not good for the baby."

Before they left, Liah pointed to a bowl filled with small red envelopes. "Those are for baby Aileen. See to it she has an account opened at the bank. By the time she's grown, she must have enough money for her education." Liah then glanced at Eldest Daughter. "And by the way, I will want the baby's bankbook. I want to put money into her account from time to time so it'll be more convenient if I have the passbook."

Flo frowned and then giggled, "Auntie Selah, Mah-Mah just says that because she's afraid I'll spend the money."

Liah glared. "No matter, I want the bankbook."

As soon as Toh and Florence took their leave, the party broke up rapidly. The Council members congratulated Liah one last time, then went out the door. Fifth Son walked Sen Fei, Madam Quock and Yook Lan home. The front room became deserted except for Liah, Selah and Professor. "Let us go back to the kitchen. We'll share another cup of wine and chat."

As they drank their wine, Professor finally blurted, "You're the resident of Number One? Liah has said nothing of it."

"She was not at liberty to say anything," Selah informed Professor. "I made her promise me. Now I can tell you myself and ask that you also keep my confidence until I have moved in. I don't want any vandalism done. Besides, the decorations and alterations are not complete."

"Miss Wang, I do not mean to pry, but where did you learn to speak such fluent Cantonese?"

Selah giggled. "I think what you really mean to ask, sir, is how did a mixed-breed Fahn Gwai learn Chinese? Well, my father was a coolie with the railroad when he met my mother and they were married. After my father's death, it was my mother's idea that I learn the language and culture of my father. As a consequence, I lived and studied for five years in Hong Kong as well as for several years in Paris."

Professor, duly impressed, wondered if the young lady were a writer, a teacher, or even a government worker. "Miss Wang," he murmured, "it appears you're spending a good deal of money in the remodeling of Number One. I take it you intend to live here permanently? If I am not being too inquisitive, could you tell me what line of business you are in?"

Professor thought Selah's sudden peal of laughter most charming. "Oh, Professor, I hope you and I will become good friends, so please call me Selah. As for your inquiry, would you believe I am opening up a fancy and expensive brothel?"

Professor was once again stunned. Selah giggled. "Oh, sir, please do not hold my profession against me. While I am educated enough to be a teacher and equally trained as a dancer, I find that kind of work too exhausting and a drain on my creativity. I like to be free and that includes my spirit. Dancing and teaching are too restrictive."

Liah quickly allayed the fear she saw appear on the scholar's face. "Selah will in no way cut into Tzo's business. Her place will not be open to the public and the prices will be too exorbitant for our people. She will entertain a clientele of rich and powerful men. So please, if you would, see to it our people do nothing to harm her or her place."

Professor sat forward with a jolt. "I've got to get word to the residents that Number One is to be occupied by one of us. Some people had it in mind to do mischief to drive the foreigner out."

Selah smiled. "Oh, then, some people must have seen my brothers. Well, don't worry about me. I have my two brothers who are staying in the place and by this weekend my chef will arrive as well. I also have a dwarf who lives there." She paused. "I hope, sir, you will not hold it against Liah for not having told you about me. I wanted to meet you and introduce myself."

Professor's face flushed with pleasure. Selah received a shock in return when Professor inquired if the college she had attended in Paris was the École de Françoise. Selah nodded, amazed that the scholar had guessed. She suddenly realized that if Professor had had the same opportunities as she, he would be so much more successful today. Damn it, she thought.

Misty eyed, Liah listened once again to Selah telling Professor the tale of her mother and father's relationship. Oh, to be so passionately in love! Liah wished she and Sen could have been so blessed. For the first time, Liah's belief in arranged marriages wavered slightly. Perhaps she was wrong. However, as the concept of free-choice marriages came to mind, she brushed the thought aside. Grandsons should be the product of more than chance meetings and emotional reactions.

Selah's voice had dropped, filling with sadness. "I do not think Mother will ever get over Father's death. Theirs was a marriage made in heaven. Of course, my brothers and sister and I try to keep her morale up and encourage her to remain engaged in life, but I suspect in private she yet grieves."

Liah's hand reached out and gently touched Selah's wrist. "Kwan Yin is merciful. Your mother will ultimately find peace, although it may be a long, hard and painful process. Memories tend to be dreadfully stubborn."

Selah smiled wanly, glanced at her wristwatch and leaped to her feet. "It's almost one o'clock! Amah will skin me alive!" She reached out, embraced Liah and planted a kiss on her forehead. To Professor, she held out a hand. "Now, good sir, I must hurry home. When I'm open for business, I expect you to drop in and allow me to buy you supper and drinks. If Liah would ever leave the house, I'd do the same for her. Now, my newly found friends, adieu."

"I will walk you home, Selah."

"Thank you sir. However, it's just a short distance. I'll be fine."

In the afterglow of Selah's departure, Cook, Professor and Liah sat quietly. It seemed the kitchen was suddenly drab in Selah's absence. At length, Professor murmured as if he were thinking out loud, "I wonder how Selah hopes to handle Tzo. He won't like it, Liah."

Liah tersely replied, "We shan't tell him a thing. Let him discover things for himself." She leaned forward. "Sir, I hope you like Selah enough to look out for her safety. While she professes having the ability to take care of herself, Tzo is not ethical. She means a good deal to me and I don't want anything to happen to her."

Professor nodded. "You didn't need to ask, Liah. I've already planned to keep surveillance on Number One. When does Selah intend to open for business?"

"Not for another two or three months. She's already paid the same fees as Tzo, so there'll be no trouble on that score." Liah smiled, her expression mischievous, as she said, "I would love to see Tzo's face when he finds out there's to be another brothel in Chinatown!" Laughing, Cook realized that even he had caught Selah's lighthearted attitude. Bless Selah!

Professor pointed to the wall clock, indicating that all three of them ought to think of rest. "I will let it be known that Selah is one of us and that she is not to be harmed." Professor raised his hand to head off Liah's cautions. "Fear not. I'll be discreet. I won't give out her name, or that the tenant is even a woman. Good night, Liah, and you, too, Cook."

—

Professor brought word to Liah that Tzo was miffed because he hadn't been invited to her granddaughter's month-old celebration. "Well," hissed Liah, "too bad, sir. I wanted nothing to blight that day, and his sarcasm and evil aura would have displeased the Gods. Let him be miffed."

As Christmas drew near, Cook urged Liah to include Tzo in the celebrations. "It does no good to offend the man. Either invite him or do not invite any of the other Council members." Liah vented but in the end decided to allow Tzo to attend the Christmas dinner. "He'd better behave, or else I'll tear into him."

On Christmas Eve, Thomas grinned and whispered to Shelley that their mother seemed like a small child experiencing her first Christmas. She was holding a Teddy bear and a doll whose eyes opened and closed and said 'Mama'. "I don't care, Thomas," smiled Shelley. "Mah can act any way she wants, just so she leaves me alone. I say thank God for Aileen. Mah seems like a new woman around the baby." Cook eyed

Eldest Son and Second Son. "If I were you two, I'd be home on time for supper on feast day. Your mother's mood can change as rapidly as the winds."

Christmas morning found Liah waiting impatiently for her eldest daughter to arrive with baby Aileen. Liah smiled as she mouthed the name, 'Aileen,' and thought that the infant's Fahn Gwai name was almost like a Chinese name. She was proud she could speak the Fahn Gwai name of her granddaughter. Liah's anticipation of the three-day stay of Eldest Daughter's family grew by the minute as she waited at the entrance of the Alley for the taxi to arrive.

As soon as Eldest Daughter arrived, Liah took her granddaughter into her arms. Later, she made the Teddy Bear squeak as she tried to teach Aileen to clasp it. Flo laughed. "Mah-Mah, she's too young to do that. You're wasting your time."

Liah scowled, "That's how much you know about babies. They are never too young to learn. You'll see!"

Theo quipped, "Aw, Flo, leave Mah alone. Aileen is just an excuse for her to play with the toys."

"Look who's talking. Who set up the electric trains and who got baseballs and bats for Christmas?"

Later, Liah sat back and watched her family as they crowded around the table for brunch. She was thinking how kind the Gods had been to her when, without warning, her mind flashed back to that first Christmas morning here when Sen surprised the children with fried chicken. My, she recalled with pain, they were poor. Wistfully, Liah pushed aside the memory, turning her attention to her granddaughter.

Only once that day did Cook see a frown cross Liah's face. As the hour for the Christmas dinner party neared, he knew for certain the frown was due to Lee Tzo. Just before six-thirty, Cook drew Liah aside and whispered that she must try to maintain her self-control. "Lee Tzo is not worth having a feast day ruined. You enjoy yourself. I will keep vigil on the man."

The supper was almost over when Selah entered, her arms filled with packages. Lee Tzo was shocked at the entrance of the red-haired lady and looked to Liah for an explanation, but Liah ignored his glance.

Selah laughed gaily, instructing Thomas and Shelley to bring in the rest of the packages. "I couldn't carry them all."

It did not escape Selah's notice that Liah didn't make any comment to Tzo nor did she introduce her to him. Good for Liah, thought Selah, let him stew.

Selah handed Flo a huge box. "It's a Raggedy-Ann doll just like the one I had when I was a girl. I hope Aileen will love it as much as I did. Mother had to wrestle it away from me in order to launder it."

Cook shyly handed Selah a gift box as she handed him a gift. "I must truthfully tell you I do not know what's in the box. Eldest Son purchased it for me."

Madam Quock and Yook Lan watched enviously as the gifts were distributed. When Selah turned to them with gifts, they giggled with delight. Liah watched Madam Quock's effusive delight and thought, wait until she discovers Selah is the owner of a brothel.

Selah exclaimed, "Little Lady, aren't you going to open my gift?"

Liah replied, "I'm waiting for you to open my gift first. I hope you like it."

Selah squealed with delight as she held up diamond earrings. She took off her jade ones and carefully put on the diamond ones.

Liah in turn closely examined the earrings Selah had given her. "Well, you and I certainly do think alike. I have never seen jade earrings in the shape of the Buddha, but I like them."

Selah grimaced, then confessed, "I could not find a suitable set for you, so I reached into my own jewelry box for those. Do you mind? Jewelers today are not as artistic or as proficient as when I was a girl. I bought those in Hong Kong during the time I lived there."

Liah smiled approvingly, saying she'd treasure them all the more.

By then, Lee Tzo had pushed his way forward and Liah begrudgingly introduced him to Selah. However, there was no opportunity for any conversation between them, for Selah had just opened Cook's gift. Cook's face reddened as she held up a frothy negligee. "Oh, sir, I'll enjoy wearing this. How did you know I love lounging wear?"

Cook gasped, "You'll have to thank Eldest Son!"

Liah mused out loud, "I wonder where Eldest Son learned about female clothing since he is not married."

It did not escape the Council members that Selah did not forget them. Each man received an earthenware jug of rice wine, wrapped in green cellophane paper and tied with the shiniest of red bows. As the evening wore on, Tzo, fascinated with Selah, tried to probe for information. Was she going to locate permanently in Loo Sahng? Where did she learn to speak such flawless Cantonese and also the northern language of Peking? Selah glibly evaded all the personal queries and only confirmed that she was going to be a permanent resident.

The last guest departed at eleven o'clock. At Liah's whispered request, Selah and Professor remained. "Did you see Tzo's amazed look when you spoke to him in Mandarin?" asked Liah. "I wonder if he has any inkling as to your brothel. You can be certain Sang will be his ferret. Nevertheless, beware of both Chon and Sang. Both men are weak enough and greedy enough to be bought by Lee Tzo."

Liah gently waved aside Selah's attempt to minimize the danger. "No, Selah, you do not know how cruel these men can be. Never underestimate them. For that reason, I am planning to enlarge my sentry system even more. The three men I've hired and placed under Professor's name are not enough. I wonder if you'd mind if I were to hire five men and assign them to you. No one must know they work for me, not even the men. Until we can establish a centralized sentry network, I do not want people to say I am making a play for power. I will pay their wages and their room and board, but it will look like it's all coming from you."

Selah thought for a few moments, then leaned over and smiled. "Of course, Liah, if you think that it's necessary; but do not do this on my account." Liah shook her head. "No, this is for all of us."

Selah rose from her chair. "Now, I must get home before Amah turns into an angry ogre." Turning to Cook she said, "A man of your culinary talents could easily turn me into a fat, contented female. One reason I don't come more often is that I fear Amah's tyrannical efforts to keep me in shape. That little woman has the toughest, strongest hands and her massages are murder. Good night, all of you, and Merry Christmas!"

There was a short silence after Selah's departure finally broken by Liah giggling and eyeing Professor and Cook. "That young lady certainly leaves one speechless, as I'm sure you noticed." Turning serious, she went on, "I should tell you that I have not told her about my Apinyin trade and that part of the reason for the extra guards is to safeguard my business. It's too early to burden Selah with my activities. I'll tell her later."

Professor refilled his pipe and took a meditative puff. "It seems that Selah is not afraid. That means she will not be as vigilant as she should be, so it remains for us to be on the alert for her."

Liah's heart filled with warmth knowing Professor could divine her thoughts. She nodded. "Well," sighed Cook, "it's been a long, hard day and night. I will say good night." He smiled ruefully. "It was strange having an infant under our roof. I awakened each time she cried."

Liah's eyes twinkled. "I can see you've never been a father, or else you would have known that a baby just cries sometimes, not because it is hungry or wet but just out of a need to talk."

Cook's face tinged pink, as he shook his head. "Even if I were a father, I'd not have known. Baby rearing is the province of mothers."

"You're right, sir." Professor chuckled. "I, too, will take my leave. I thank you for a wonderful dinner, as usual, and for sharing your family with me, Liah. Good night."

—

Two days after Christmas, on the twenty-seventh day of December in the Fahn Gwai's year of nineteen hundred and fifteen, Liah had a visitor from Dai Faw. The big man's name was Wong Cheung and he carried a letter from Elder Wong of the House of Wong. Liah thanked him, tucking the letter inside her long, brown tunic, saying she'd read it later, then bade him to take a seat. "I would appreciate it greatly if you would indulge me for a bit. I'd very much like to hear the news from Dai Faw. It's been ten years since I lived there."

Liah's mind raced as she listened to him and surreptitiously observed that Cheung's face was sun burnt like that of a farmer or a fisherman, definitely not a storekeeper. She speculated about the real reason for the man's visit, waiting for him to speak of it. She asked, "Do you know Fatt On? He and my husband exchanged places. Fatt took over our store off an alley next to Du Pon Gai." Her voice wavered, "He was very good to us, but we haven't heard a word from or about him since the quake. We pray to Kwan Koong that he is yet alive."

"No, Madam, I don't know him, and Du Pon Gai has now been renamed Grant Gai; however, our people still refer to it as Du Pon Gai. After the quake, the Fahn Gwai tried to relocate our people to another site, but they refused and so Chinatown is yet situated on Du Pon Gai. Nevertheless, Fish Alley was destroyed and since the quake Dead Man's Corner is no more."

Liah sighed, shaking her head. "So much time, so many changes. Who can predict tomorrow?" Cheung divined Liah's sense of loss, and said nothing further, waiting for her to recover. "It is sad that time is so swift an adversary. Blink your eyelids and an entire lifetime can be lost. Well, no more dwelling on the past, let us speak of you."

Cheung's face softened slightly as he informed Liah of a farm he planned to lease near the ocean: forty acres he hoped to plant in celery and onions. "At the moment, I am awaiting word from the land owner. If he agrees to my offer, I will move to Loo Sahng."

"Then the Gods must direct your course to that end." Liah saw his disbelief, then reiterated, "The Gods have always shown me the way and most assuredly will guide your course as well. Meng-Sui and our ancestors' Feng-Sui have always seen to my well-being and safety. You must hold the same faith. Are your relatives in Dai Faw or in the old country?" He had not mentioned his wife or family, and not knowing his marital status, Liah didn't want to commit a faux pas. Liah saw tenderness flash fleetingly across Cheung's hard face as he suddenly spoke of his wife and four sons. Why, she wondered, did the man have such a fierce countenance? Nor did it escape her notice that his fists slowly clenched and unclenched. Slowly, a foreboding flickered to life in Liah's mind.

"My wife and sons are with me now. My sons are aged nineteen, seventeen, sixteen and the youngest, is ten. At this moment they are lodged at the Lotus Garden Hotel."

"Then, please bring them for supper tonight. There is not a better meal than one prepared by Cook."

The big man hesitated a moment, then smiled and asked the hour. "Is seven o'clock suitable for you, sir?" asked Liah. "I'd like to introduce you to my two eldest sons, who work in the produce area of Loo Sahng. They truck the produce for the farmers. They might be able to give you information that might help you sell to the wholesalers."

Wong Cheung nodded his acceptance of her invitation. Liah still sensed his tension and saw a curtain drop over his eyes. Her curiosity was heightened. Why was he so?

Wong Cheung paused then leaned forward in his chair and softly confided that his surname was not really Wong. "Although my sister is married to Elder Wong Hing's brother, I am of the Hua Family. My entry papers are false. I apologize for not having told you in the beginning; but you can blame my caution on my past experiences in Gem

Sahn when keeping one's family status a secret was a matter of self-preservation."

Liah made no comment, feeling the big man had more to say. He went on. "There are those," he muttered angrily, "among us who would report such a situation to the Fahn Gwai. I tell you this because Elder Wong thinks highly of your husband and he has heard of your efforts to unify the Loo Sahng settlement. He has also heard of the charity work you have done. He fears your efforts to unify and aid our people will be difficult and perhaps dangerous, therefore, he asked me to offer my assistance."

"Have no fear, Cheung, your secret is safe with me. I, too, abhor those among us who'd curry the favor of the Fahn Gwai even to the point of destroying the very lives of their own people. In our Tenet of Laws, there is a provision that such acts are punishable offenses."

The big man's visit ended as abruptly as it had begun. He said he would return at seven o'clock with his family. As soon as Cheung left, Liah raced back to the kitchen and announced that there would be guests for supper that night. "I must contact Professor. Wong Cheung brought a letter from Elder Wong. Perhaps it will enlighten me as to what sort of a man Cheung is."

As Professor scanned the letter, his facial expression changed from mild interest to utter surprise and finally to disbelief. "Aiyah! It seems we have a hatchet man in our midst! Here, let me read the last paragraph exactly as Elder Wong has written it. It is important you hear it word for word."

Liah's brow knitted and her lips pursed as she listened to Elder Wong's fears that a headstrong, youthful rebel gang was trying to unseat the elders of the House of Lee in Dai Faw. Wong Cheung, he suggested, might be a valuable man to have at her side should the hooligans spread to Loo Sahng.

Liah stiffened, as Elder Wong confided, "Although Cheung was, in his youth, a paid executioner, his behavior in his adult years have proven him sound of judgment, stable and loyal. As a brother-in-law, I can ask for no better. For the past eight years, he has served on the panel of Wong elders with an excellent record. Perhaps he learned valuable lessons from his earlier years of violence."

Cook's face was solemn and his glance troubled as he looked at Liah. Liah made Professor swear to secrecy. "Cheung confided to me that he is not really a Wong, but rather a Hua. He and Elder Wong are only related by marriage to his sister."

Professor suddenly became animated. "Here! Here is your replacement for Cousin Shah's seat. You did say you wanted to include on the Council a man from the Four Families Association. True, the man's beginnings were violent, but as Elder Wong pointed out, Cheung has been a very reliable man as an adult. Perhaps his presence on the Council might deter any mischief Tzo has in mind."

Liah's eyes widened in surprise. "A hatchet man on the Council? The others wouldn't allow it. Besides, I didn't tell you earlier, but I feel a foreboding about Cheung that I can't explain."

Professor nodded. "I understand. I just thought that seating Cheung might deter any plan Lee Tzo might have to seat a candidate of his own.

Cook frowned. "Why not have a New Year's Eve party, Liah? Professor can meet the man and judge his character for himself. We'll have an early supper before your sons destroy our sanity with their Fahn Gwai music."

"Splendid idea, Cook. I'll invite Selah, too. She has a canny sense about people."

It was agreed that Professor would answer Elder Wong's letter and introduce himself. It wouldn't do for Liah to be receiving mail from Dai Faw, lest Tzo begin to suspect something. Professor frowned. "I never thought the time would arrive when we wouldn't feel safe in our own town!" As the scholar rose to leave, he stopped and grinned. "I almost forgot. Tomorrow I, too, will have a telephone. When I get the numbers, I'll give them to you.

Cook sighed. "It'll not be the same, telephoning you, sir, instead of crossing the Alley to call you."

Liah tersely retorted, "Don't be silly, Cook. We'll yet summon Professor the same way we always have. Only when the reason is social or inconsequential will we telephone. You can never tell who might be listening in on the telephone."

Dinner with Wong Cheung and his family was uneventful. Liah noticed that his wife was almost mute, uttering only a few words. The sons were also restrained, not at all talkative like Liah's children. There was little time for conversation anyway as the meal was over quickly. Shortly after eating, Cheung excused his family, saying his wife was tired. Liah was frustrated because she'd learned nothing from their dinner.

—

On the twenty-eighth day of the Fahn Gwai's last month of the year of nineteen hundred and fifteen, the Council met at a *Nien-Mei* (year-end) session to resolve all business and to close the year's financial ledgers. It was sad, for Liah missed Cousin Shah, and in her grief turned her glance to Lee Tzo. Wong Sang watched out of the corner of his eye, breathing an involuntary sigh when Liah turned to address the members. "If there are no other issues, I'll have Cook bring our supper."

Lee Tzo quickly got to his feet. "Madam, do you not think we ought to discuss who might be a replacement for Lee Shah's seat?"

Liah's eyes blazed and her tone was brittle with displeasure. "The year of waiting is not yet done. You might show a bit of respect, if not restraint, for a man who has done so much for us. And while I'm on the subject of discretion, the innuendoes you've made about me recently have not escaped my notice. I hear you've been insinuating that I am using the Council to further my hold over the residents of China Gai and that I'm filling my coffers from the fees they pay. Up until now,

I've said nothing, hoping that you would use your good judgment and desist on your own, but now with the other members as my witnesses, I warn you. Cease such talk immediately!" In the face of such a forceful tirade Lee Tzo was unable to respond and remained silent.

Without a further word, Liah turned to the others and commended them for their cooperation and diligence in performing their civic duties during the past year. "Now, let us share supper after we sign the records."

Liah was first to affix her signature to the records and was aware of Tzo stonily watching from behind her.

At the supper table, Liah flicked the long ash from her cigarette, silently cursing Sang and Tzo for their whispered conversation. At one point, Tzo became aware of Liah's displeasure, smiled and desisted. Harnessing all of her self-control, Liah smiled back, then offered him the compote of black mushrooms and sea urchins, sautéed with chestnuts, unborn peas and pork. "I do believe this is your favorite dish." It sickened her when Tzo, his pride seemingly restored, simpered as he daintily spooned a portion onto his plate.

If Liah could have read his mind, she'd have been enraged to know Tzo's ultimate plan: to get revenge and oust her from the chairmanship. Tzo's sweet dreams about revenge were dampened when it hit him, sitting at the table that evening, how little he'd accomplished since his arrival. A distinct discomfort overwhelmed him. Should he fail in his mission, his cohorts in Dai Faw would have his life. Tzo's appetite was suddenly ruined.

Lee Tzo rose the moment supper was done, nodded curtly to Liah, then went out the door. Wong Sang and Chon Woo soon took their leave and shortly thereafter the chamber was deserted save for Liah and Professor.

Cook entered the chamber in time to see Liah with her hand raised in self-defense. "I know, I know, don't tell me. I should not have reprimanded Tzo, but the man is insufferable. It will not happen again. I promise, sir." Liah gritted her teeth and continued, "I tell you what, sir. What if I were to invite the man for tea? Of course, you'll also have to be here as I can't stand to be alone with Tzo."

Cook cautiously informed Liah that he'd overheard Tzo invite Chon to his brothel for a drink, but Chon had refused.

"Tzo invited Chon to his bar? I'm glad he refused, but I'm not afraid of Chon. He is a crafty one, but he isn't a fool like Wong Sang. He'll not become ensnared by Tzo, not for a few drinks."

Professor assembled his papers and books to prepare to leave and uttered a warning. "Chon is not altogether without a price tag, Liah. Keep that in mind. Well, I must say good night. Tonight's meeting was arduous."

When Amah returned at one o'clock from a Chinese show, Liah was yet sitting at the kitchen table. She was discussing with Cook the enlargement of the sentry system. Amah exclaimed, "Aiyah! Just look at your face! I'll bet you had another ugly session with Tzo, eh?"

Liah smiled weakly. "I'm fine, Amah. Once I get a good night's sleep, I'll be fit again. It's you and Cook who should get to bed. You are the ones who work the hardest around here."

—

At three o'clock on New Year's Eve afternoon, Liah's children were busily but noisily decorating the front room for the night's festivities. Streamers were strung from the gaslight chandelier to the four corners of the room. The phonograph had been dusted off, the needle cleaned and the records sorted. The floor had been swept and the jar of dance wax was standing by to be used just before the dancing began.

Theo was in the kitchen tasting the punch and grinning. He boasted to his younger sister that once they'd spiked it, the concoction would be perfect. Emmi pouted as she wiped the punch glasses, waiting for her invitation to the party. Cook watched Theo mixing the punch, thinking to himself that the Fahn Gwai had such outlandish tastes.

Mert bounced into the room in time to hear Emmi complaining to Theo, "You're being mean, Theo. Why can't I come to your party? There'll be other girls here and they're almost my age."

"But they're different. You're our sis. I tell you what, when you're seventeen, you can come."

"But that's six years away!"

"That's the idea!" Theo roared with laughter.

Mert scowled, "Lay off, Theo. Remember when Thomas and Shell did the same thing to you?"

William, standing in the doorway, chimed in, "Yes, I also overheard you ask Thomas if you could go with them tonight and they laughed you off." Theo made a lunge for William, threatening to take on his two brothers, when Liah's bedroom door opened bringing the scuffle to an abrupt halt. Cook glared, warning the boys that they'd better not ruin New Year's for their mother. Liah scowled as she took her seat and waited for her herbal brew and the party preparations continued in huffy silence.

Selah and Professor arrived sharply, at seven o'clock, then sat down to enjoy a cup of rice wine. At ten minutes after seven, Cook stole a glance at the wall clock, thinking to himself that it was rude of Wong Cheung to be late.

Just then a red-faced Wong Cheung entered the room followed by his two older sons. "I am most sorry to be tardy, but the cafés are so busy tonight. They kept me waiting for over half an hour for the food I had ordered for my wife and two younger sons."

Liah smiled sympathetically. "Never mind, you are here now, sir. Allow me to call my sons. They can entertain your two sons while we chat. And don't worry about their supper. There's a lot of fried chicken and all the trimmings on the buffet table in the front room." She turned to his boys and inquired if they would prefer to eat with their father, but they solemnly shook their heads. What serious youths, thought Liah.

Liah introduced Cheung to Selah and Professor. During supper, Selah inquired if this was Cheung's first visit to Loo Sahng. He replied that this was actually his second trip, that he had visited Loo Sahng nine years earlier. Hearing this fact, Cook was struck by a bolt of intuition, and it was all he could do not to cry out. The same thought must have occurred to Professor, too, as his face mirrored Cook's amazed look. Fortunately, Cheung did not notice.

At ten o'clock, the sound of music from the phonograph in the front room grew louder. Liah smiled at her guests and said, "My sons are reminding me that their turn to celebrate is at hand. I know it is not yet midnight, but later it will be too noisy for us to do so. Shall we drink a toast to the New Year?"

"Good idea, Liah!" cried Selah as she raised her glass. "I would like to make the first toast." Liah's eyes sparkled as Selah winked. "To all of us in this room: I drink to our health, wealth and, most of all, to our happiness. May nineteen hundred and sixteen find all of us blessed by the Gods." Selah paused after drinking and raised her glass a second time. "And if I'm not being too brash, I'd like to drink a special toast to the most amazing and big-hearted woman I've ever had the privilege to meet. To Liah, may she obtain everything her heart desires in the coming year."

Liah then raised her glass. "I, too, have a toast. I know our Year of the Dragon does not start until late February, but I want to salute the Gods and wish all of us a most satisfying New Year."

They could hear the front room filling up with boisterous girls and boys and at ten-thirty, Wong Cheung rose to say good night. "I thank you for this night's celebration. I, too, wish all of you felicitations of the New Year. It is time my sons and I rejoin the rest of my family. I shall say good night." Selah also took her leave, hugging and kissing Liah, saying, "I gotta go too. Good night all and Happy New Year!"

Cheung gave his two sons the choice of staying at the party or leaving; they chose to follow their father. Liah murmured half-aloud that the two youths were far too serious for their ages. One's carefree period of life only lasted for the short duration of childhood.

It was difficult to speak over the blaring music, but once Selah and Cheung had departed, Cook blurted out his speculation about Wong Cheung. About nine years earlier, there had been a scandal in Dai Faw concerning a concubine who belonged to a rich merchant who had fled with her lover. The merchant had paid for the services of a highbinder (Chinese assassin) to find the couple and bring them back for punishment. It was reputed that they had eloped to Loo Sahng.

Liah was fascinated. "Don't keep us in suspense. Tell us what happened. Were they caught? What happened to them?"

"I don't really know. The couple was never seen again. Some say they were caught, executed and their bodies disposed of in the celery bogs outside Loo Sahng. Others say they were brought back to Dai Faw, tortured and slain. Some believe the executioner allowed them to escape. No one really knows."

"And you suspect it was Cheung? How do you know? Couldn't the timing be a coincidence?"

Professor heaved a big sigh. "I, too, recall the event of which Cook speaks. The executioner was described as a big man, with flinty eyes and a taciturn manner. Of course, it's not certain proof, but Wong Cheung did say he was here nine years ago and he was a hatchet man.'

Nothing more was said as the three friends sat at the table, each lost in his or her own contemplative silence. At length Professor murmured, "You're right Liah, it might not have been Cheung. And even if it were, he was only acting in the line of duty. The girl was wrong to break her contract."

Liah's mouth opened and then snapped shut. Her eyes were blazing as she snapped, "How is it that all men, no matter how learned or passive, seem to think nothing of owning and disposing of women as they choose? However wrong in her actions, that girl was a human being who possessed hopes and dreams and the right to give and receive love.

Whatever contract she broke, it was likely not of her making, nor her choice. Torn from her familiar surroundings, sold and forced into a sordid existence, I don't blame her if she chose love and ran away. My sympathies are with the girl."

Realizing he'd touched upon a nerve, Professor swiftly tried to soften his position, but Liah motioned for silence. "I am not reprimanding you, sir, rather I assail the cruelty of our ancestors who instilled such an inhumane philosophy."

The scholar's face became tinged pink with embarrassment. "I apologize, Liah. You are absolutely correct. I was thinking out loud and thinking none too clearly at that. Perhaps I was making excuses for that highbinder since it might have been Cheung and I do so want him to fill Cousin Shah's seat."

Liah acknowledged Professor's apology as Cook placed three thimble-sized cups on the table. "We are going to drink a private toast to the three of us. Then we'll escape from this ungodly din. Midnight is approaching and the hour of the Fahn Gwai's New Year is nigh. May this coming year of nineteen hundred and sixteen bring us most, if not all, of what we dream of and hope for."

They watched as the hands of the clock touched twelve and heard the striking of the hour. The three friends raised their cups and drank. Simultaneously, there was a loud commotion in the front room followed by the sound of clattering footsteps in the hall as Liah's children burst into the kitchen shouting "Happy New Year!"

Liah clapped her hands over her ears, nodded and waved the merrymakers back to the front room. She pantomimed that she was going to bed. Professor motioned good night, then took his leave.

—

Late the next afternoon, Liah awakened to the first day of the New Year, groggy but relaxed. The Apinyin she'd partaken of the night before had

made sleep possible despite the children's noisy celebration. She heard
the sound of running water in the kitchen and the muted sounds of pots
and pans being carefully put away. She knew by the time she went into
the kitchen, every vestige of the children's party the night before would
be gone. She wondered how Cook managed on so little sleep. She must
make certain the children did something special to show their appreciation for Cook's efforts.

An hour later, Liah was seated in her upholstered chair in the
kitchen sipping her herbal brew while Cook prepared their brunch.
During their meal, she felt Cook had a question to ask but did not know
quite how to ask it. Finally, he blurted, "Do you know the nature of
Cheung's wife's illness?"

Liah's cheeks turned pink and she was silent for a moment. Quietly,
she murmured, "She has a problem that afflicts the females of our
species." This brought the discussion to an abrupt end.

Cook realized that despite their intimacy, Liah would never confide
the secrets of the feminine world to any male. He nevertheless felt a
warmth and tenderness toward Liah, but she did not see his glance as
her eyes were yet lowered.

1916

YEAR OF THE DRAGON

THE LAST SEAT

The Fahn Gwai year of nineteen hundred and sixteen was already well into its first week, and Liah had still not decided whether to allow Wong Cheung a seat on the Council. It was partially because she was still suffering over the alienation between herself and Cousin Shah. Life was bitter enough without breaches within the family. Sen, too, was on her mind.

However, it was mostly the fate of the young girl that haunted Liah. The idea that Wong Cheung might have her blood on his hands was disturbing if not outright revolting. Yet something about the man led her to believe that, if he had been involved, he had allowed the couple to escape rather than executing them

Meanwhile, she bedeviled Professor to come up with an alternate candidate, something she had already done several times. Finally at his wit's end, Professor cried, "I told you Wong Cheung must be our man despite the cloud over his name. He, if anyone, can contain Lee Tzo. You allowed expediency to seat Tzo, then why not Cheung?"

Liah sighed and finally relented. "All right, sir. I reluctantly agree. Go notify him of his candidacy and tell him I'll not hold it against him should he refuse."

Once the decision was made, Liah relaxed. Once again she turned her mind as to Lee Tzo's presence in Loo Sahng. Later that day, she implored Cook to help. "With Dai Faw having so many more people, why did he come here? You must do more to find out the truth."

Cook sternly gazed at her. "Waste no more time or thought on that man!"

Their discussion was cut short with the opening and closing of the front door. It was Professor, returning.

Liah was relaxed as she pleasurably inhaled and exhaled the cigarette smoke, watching as the smoke wafted slowly in lazy curls to the ceiling. As Professor watched, it seemed to him that Liah was another person. He knew no one else who could wring the last ounce of enjoyment from a single cigarette.

The afternoon quiet was eerie, broken only by the occasional raucous call of the peacock and the distant sound of someone shouting. Even when the trains rolled into the yard, the noise sounded somewhat muted behind the closed doors. Suddenly, Liah's voice broke into Professor's thoughts.

"It always heartens me when the Fahn Gwai New Year is done. This year, our New Year of the Dragon, is appropriately named for the times. For in truth, Wong Cheung is truly a fire-breathing dragon. By the way, has either of you noticed his finely sculptured hands?"

Professor murmured. "More like hands of death! It makes me shudder thinking about it. I hear he was a proficient killer." Slightly flustered, he went on, "The man is unpredictable. He's friendly and open one moment, then without warning withdrawn and cold as ice. It's as if the man tries to keep himself shut off from the external world."

Liah poured Professor a cup of tea and offered him a plate of freshly baked tarts. "I suppose Cheung's earlier years as an executioner forced him to be so. Cheung could not allow himself any weaknesses."

"Enough of this kind of talk!" Cook said sternly. "Let's put his past aside." Cook sat down, took a tart and placed it on Liah's plate, beseeching her to eat. "Did Cheung accept the invitation to join the Council, Professor?"

"Yes, he did. He said it would be an honor and that he'd do whatever he could to be a credit to the group. Now we need to think of someone we can ask to nominate Cheung, someone who will keep our information secret until the right time."

Liah replied, "You're right, Professor, but it won't be easy. It must be someone the men respect, someone who is neither afraid of Lee Tzo nor needs the man's favors."

Professor suddenly blurted, "I think Lim Tao fits those qualifications exactly. Would you like me to ask Lim?"

Liah replied, "No, sir. I'll ask him. There are facts we must tell Lim, as he should know what kind of man he is nominating. Also, he must be willing to keep secret all that I tell him. And none of the other members must find out we have a candidate in mind, not until Lim names Cheung You can be certain Tzo will have the name of his man ready too."

A week later Liah invited Lim Tao for tea. He came reluctantly, suspecting the visit had something to do with filling Shah's vacant seat. He wanted to avoid any involvement with Liah's political maneuvering if at all possible.

After the meal, Lim relaxed, warmed by the heady chrysanthemum tea, Cook's flaky curry tarts and custard pie. Liah asked about his progress in getting his family's immigration papers approved and his face darkened.

"I am at the end of my patience. I rue the day I decided to bring the family to Gem Sahn. Never have I been so confused by government forms and questions. Then there are the demands for more and more monies by my representative in Hong Kong and by my cousin here in Dai Faw with whose relatives my family is staying in Hong Kong. I swear sometimes I suspect my money is not only supporting my family but my cousin's as well. I don't know where it'll stop." His face then hardened. "Perhaps when I am broke."

Liah was understanding and her tone sympathetic. "I've always contended that if we had an attorney in Chinatown, one from the ranks of our people, the expense and headache of immigration would be greatly minimized. Kwan Yin willing, someday we will."

Lim Tao shook his head, saying for him it would be too late. Either he continued with the money payments, or else he'd lose all the monies he'd already paid. "Besides, my family would then be barred from coming to Gem Sahn."

Liah murmured, "If you believe that your man is not being effective, perhaps I can help. I have a cousin in Dai Faw who might assist you. I cannot give you his name, as he does not want to be deluged with requests from desperate people. He does not work in immigration but is an agent for one of the Fahn Gwai companies and knows the Fahn Gwai's process of law."

"Oh," smiled Lim, "if that were only true. My family and I would be forever in your debt, Liah. Can you speak to him on my behalf?"

Liah consented and Lim leaned back in his chair and let out a deep sigh of relief. He reached out for another of Cook's tarts. In his newly found peace of mind, Lim vaguely heard Liah mention a name and something about wanting Lim to nominate him at the next meeting. Suddenly, his attention focused on what Liah was saying, that the candidate had been a hatchet man. What could Liah possibly have in mind nominating such a man? Lim sighed as he realized that if she would facilitate his family's entry into Gem Sahn, he would be obligated to do whatever she asked of him.

He readily agreed, but Liah shook her head. "Do not agree so quickly, Lim. I want you to think the matter over thoroughly, but be assured that I will have Professor draw up a document absolving you of any guilt if Cheung proves to be a detriment to the Council. In the meantime, I'd appreciate it if you didn't speak of the nomination or anything I have told you about Cheung. I want it to be a surprise to the other Council members. Then Tzo cannot destroy Cheung's chances in advance."

Lim was loath to ask, but his impatience made him inquire, "Do you know how long it will take for you to find out if your cousin can help me, Liah? It's not that I'm impatient, but you must understand my anxiety." Liah smiled. "This very night I will have Professor dispatch a letter. It will likely be about ten days to two weeks before I hear back. It's too bad we cannot use the telephone, but security concerns force me to be discreet. No one must know that I am helping you with your family's immigration and there are too many stool pigeons around."

Lim Tao nodded. Feeling that he was being invited into Liah's inner circle to some extent emboldened Lim enough to inquire why she had allowed one as evil as Tzo to join the Council. Liah replied, "Since Tzo was allowed to join the Council, the children now have their school and we now have sufficient monies to care for our elderly. Mostly, however, it was decided that if Tzo were within our ranks, it would be easier to monitor his actions."

Lim Tao nodded solemnly. "I pray to Kwan Koong the man will not necessitate the use of the treason clause in the Council's Tenet of Laws. However, I believe you are wise to use his money to satisfy the needs of our children for a school and the needs of our aged and needy.

When Lim Tao left for work, Liah admitted to herself that she was more worried about the nomination than she had let on. There remained two more issues to deal with: the document exonerating Lim in case Cheung proved unworthy and the letter to her cousin Wah Sui Lum in Dai Faw.

—

When the Council met in late January, however, everything was not yet settled regarding Lim nominating Cheung. It was evident to Liah that

Lee Tzo was ready to make his nomination though, for he chafed for the business of the day to be done so that the nominations could begin. Liah was urging the Council to underwrite the costs of the upcoming Chinese New Year celebration including not only the dragon imported from Dai Faw but also the dancers, the fireworks and the daily free buffet meals at noon.

Lee Tzo leaped to his feet as soon as it was agreed. "Madam Chairman, I think we ought to discuss the prospects of a replacement for Shah's seat on the Council. While it is true that his term will not expire until the fifth month of this year, in order to select the best man, should we not discuss potential candidates?"

Liah had no chance to reply, for Professor immediately vetoed the suggestion. "We will not discuss the replacement at this time. I know you are anxious to see our Council complete, but it is not the way we do things. Be patient, Tzo."

Supper was swiftly served and consumed, the men swearing the food was the best they'd ever tasted. As soon as the records were signed, Lee Tzo bowed to Liah and without a backward glance walked out. Sang breathed a sigh of relief, averting his glance as he passed Liah on his way out. Liah hardly noticed. Her mind was on Tzo. It was obvious that he had a candidate in mind, but whom? She began to fret again. The thought that Wong Cheung might not be selected if Tzo was successful with his candidate nagged at her. Liah pushed frowned. "I was just thinking that we must find out who Lee Tzo has in mind to name."

"I agree, Liah," said Professor as he held out a sheaf of papers. "However, before I forget, here is the document you asked me to draw up." Without speaking, she knew it was the statement absolving Lim Tao in case Wong Cheung did not prove worthy—one more issue to weigh heavy on her mind. He went on. "Also, Pong On's family is due to arrive in Dai Faw around the first week of May. He has instructed me to write another letter to his wife to ensure she is prepared for the questions the immigration agents will ask. One incorrect answer and she will be deported and incarcerated in the detention shed until the departure date."

Cook frowned. "The Fahn Gwai certainly go to great lengths to prevent our people from coming into Gem Sahn. They asked me stupid questions like: Where is my village located? How many feet is the compound wall from the well? Is the compound wall made of concrete or mud? How high is the wall? It takes luck and patience to answer the multitude of inane questions correctly. I've often wondered what would have happened to me if, during my transit to Gem Sahn, a flood had washed out our well, and another was dug elsewhere."

Professor laughed. Turning serious, he said, "By the way, Liah, if you would give me Cousin Shah's address in Dai Faw, I'd like to write to him and ask that he check into Lee Tzo's background. I'll tell him we have grounds to suspect he is part of the dissident group infiltrated into Loo Sahng." Wordlessly, Liah nodded.

—

The beginning of the celebrations ushering in the New Year of the Dragon fell on the fifth day of February. Chinatown was transformed into a colorful fairyland. Each store was newly painted or brightly decorated with exotically shaped lanterns; windows were decorated with gold banners emblazoned with the Chinese characters signifying long life, wealth and happiness. On tall bamboo poles fishes, birds and dragons swayed in the breeze. Every doorway was lined with pots of Chinese lilies, Taro roots and flowers; and the sound of laughter was heard all over the town.

Inside every store and home were the traditional Baht Gwa, an eight-sided lacquered dish filled with red melon seeds, black melon seeds, candied ginger, coconut candy, melon preserves and sesame seed can-

died squares. Pyramid-shaped compotes of oranges, mangoes, tangerines, apples, sweet meats and moon cakes were displayed for guests
and family.

During the day and into the early evening, the acrid odor of firecrackers filled the air and exploded bits of red paper covered the sidewalks and streets, a carpet of good luck not to be swept away. Wagon
wheels and tires would help the breeze scatter the lucky color throughout Chinatown. The laughter of children filled the air along with the
explosions of their incense-lit firecrackers. Children shrieked as the
older boys set off giant firecrackers, many of which were placed underneath cans and upon exploding sent the cans flying high into the air.
Occasionally, an adult shouted warnings to be careful. By afternoon
each day, the elders of Chinatown had escaped into their windowless
rooms for a respite from the earsplitting, lightning-bright flashes of the
firecrackers. Despite the noise, everywhere one could feel a carefree,
happy spirit and the colorful landscape was filled with the sounds of
jubilant laughter. Everyone got into the act of welcoming the Year of
the Dragon.

At Number Three Liah, was awakened by the muted sounds of fireworks and reached groggily for her slippers. Her first concern was to
check the sky for the weather must be clear for their opening day festivities. Cook met her at the door. "The sky is gray, but I don't think it
will rain. Sit down and have your morning brew, then you can turn
your mind to the day's celebrations."

She yawned, then went to the kitchen and settled into her upholstered chair. She caressed the soft nap on the arm of the chair, as usual.
It was now a long time ago that her mistress had given them the furniture in the bungalow, including this chair.

A half-hour later, at one o'clock in the afternoon, Professor came to
report that he'd escorted the old priest to the new temple in Peacock
Alley. "The old man's eyes started misting and I almost expected him

to cry. He said that this was a day the Gods would never forget and that their blessings will fall upon us forever. There was a fair-sized crowd in the Alley when we arrived and he proclaimed this day to be truly auspicious."

Cook smiled indulgently at Liah's haste with her brunch, much like a petulant child eager to join the festivities. An hour later she emerged from her bedroom, beautifully gowned in a pink and silver cheongsam, a pair of sculptured tapers in hand. She gazed lovingly at the red, gold, yellow and green raised carving on the tapers. "This pair," she murmured wistfully, "is the last of the tapers I brought from China. It has been such a long time before I could fulfill my wish and burn these in a permanent place of our own. Fulfilling my promise to Kwan Yin is like being born anew. Oh, I wish you could know how I feel at this moment!"

Cook opened the trap door under the stairwell. "Take care that you pay attention, or else you might stumble. And take the turn to the right or you'll end up exiting in the train yards." After navigating the tunnels, Liah lifted the trap door at the other end, which opened into the temple's kitchen pantry. She listened for a moment before entering, then cautiously made her way to the temple.

She remained on her knees, bowing in the temple, for a long time, her head touching the floor. Her obeisance and prayers done, she reverently reached out and touched the tapers to the already lit tapers in the brazier. She stared, mesmerized by their bluish-green flames until they turned yellow, and then softly she whispered, "Ah, gentle lady, I've kept my promise. These incense urns are the finest money can buy, and with Kwan Koong's will, they will always contain a lit taper in your honor." Suddenly, Liah sensed she was not alone and turning she saw the aged priest coming toward her. "Ah, Madam," his voice quavered. "I never believed I would finish my earthly days in such a beautiful abode. I know it is mainly through your efforts and I am grateful."

Liah felt annoyance at her embarrassment. Why was it she always felt guilty receiving a compliment? She bowed low. "While you are generally safe in Peacock Alley, sir, you must still exercise caution at night. Do not venture outdoors and do not open the doors to anyone. No one has the right to worship at night. While the Fahn Gwai usually respect religious places, when they are drunk, they become barbarians. Nevertheless, my heart is light knowing how pleased you are with your abode."

Each day at noon and again at six-thirty in the evening during the ten-day celebration of the New Year, the townspeople crowded the streets, the balconies and rooftops to watch the dance of the lion. There was a long string of paper money, gaily tied to red bows in front of Number Three. Each time, Liah stood behind the door screen waiting for the arrival of the lion.

The men who maneuvered the colorful lion danced to the cadence of drums and cymbals, the lion's head moving up and down and side-to-side, cavorting in the pleasure of the New Year. After concluding the dance, the lion's mouth finally reached out for the long string of contributions. Liah felt a sense of pride, for the length of time a lion danced before a doorway was in direct ratio to the amount of money the dancers saw. In front of Number Three, the lion had danced for twenty-five minutes. It amused Liah each day to see the coquettish antics of the lion after he'd snatched the string of monies, especially when he roguishly scratched his ear and his rump. Peacock Alley became carpeted in red paper and, as the days passed, the depth of the carpet reached several inches in depth.

Near the end of the festivities, the altar in the temple was overflowing with incense sticks and burnt tapers. As she prepared to light another offering, Liah saw two nubs, the remains of her special tapers, which she had offered on the first day of the festivities. A sadness entered her mind as she wished she had more. Perhaps she could ask Lee Wah to order some from Hong Kong. She quickly lit her coil of incense, knelt and touched her head to the floor three times. The old priest entered, then upon seeing Liah in prayer, backed his way out. Her prayers done, Liah glanced proudly at the teakwood dragon and its fiery ruby eye and nodded. Yes, she'd kept her promise. Swiftly, she began making her way through the tunnel back to Number Three.

Professor did not altogether share Liah's child-like enjoyment of the New Year of the Dragon. "It's easy for you to speak of it as enjoyment. You don't have to dodge the firecrackers the children toss about so thoughtlessly."

"Oh, Professor, in another few days the celebrations will be over. It's such a short time to relive the traditions of our people and, in doing so, remember our homeland. I truly hope that I may see my home once more before I leave this earth. Although I've found peace, security and even wealth here in Gem Sahn, my heart still belongs to China."

It struck Professor, as he listened to Liah speak, that his own memories of home had become like a dream. Indeed, he felt as if he had become a displaced person with nowhere to call home. A sadness stole over him, but as suddenly as it came, it was dispersed by the concussive sounds of more lightning firecrackers. Liah was right. In another few days, Chinatown would return to its everyday drab existence. He lit his pipe and smiled. "You're right, Liah. A few days of inconvenience is an inconsequential price to pay for heart-warming nostalgia. At least the acrid odor of gunpowder smells better than garbage."

On the fifteenth of February the celebrations drew to a close. That day the lion danced three times: at noon, at four-thirty and at seven-thirty. As Liah awaited the arrival of the lion, she felt a reluctance to close out the celebrations and promised herself that when the next New Year came, they'd not only have the lion dance, but the dragon dance, too. In her mind's eye, Liah recalled the 500-pound satin and papier-mâché dragon of her childhood, glittering with spangles, beads and fluttering shiny ribbons. She remembered the gymnasts cavorting around the dragon, the jugglers tossing brilliantly decorated ribboned balls in the air and a comic who taunted the dragon into a frenzy of dance. It had happened so many years ago, yet the memory of it remained as clear as if it had been yesterday. She held her hands out in front of her and sadly nodded. Time was passing swiftly and, with it, her youth.

Soon the cymbals and drums announced the lion's arrival and Liah walked to the door. She did not feel the same joy she had on the first days of celebrations. In her heart there was a heaviness as she said a silent farewell to the lion, fervently wishing that the next year would quickly find them together again. Farewells, however short, always saddened her. Quickly, she turned her gaze to the throng of people inside Peacock Alley. It seemed to Liah that the many Fahn Gwai with their children enjoyed the lion dance as much as the residents. She smiled as she spied a Chinese youngster hand a Fahn Gwai child his punk stick and instructed him on how to light a firecracker and toss it into the air. She murmured, "Well, it's a beginning. It will be children who will make a difference in our lives. Fahn Gwai and Chinese alike. Pray to Kwan Yin for that miracle."

At eight o'clock, the Year of the Dragon was properly ushered in. At Number Three, family and friends sat down to an elaborate feast. Beyond their boarded up doors and windows, they could still hear firecrackers yet sounding their greetings to the New Year.

It worried Cook and Amah when late that night Liah's mood darkened and it was necessary to administer a draught of Apinyin. Amah cried, "She's so elated one moment, then in despair the next. Oh, how that women suffers. What can we do, Cook?"

Cook softly replied, "Nothing, Amah. We must allow Liah to pull herself up again. Liah does not like to end anything and the end of the New Year celebrations is no different."

At four o'clock in the morning, Liah was startled from a deep sleep by raucous shrieks in Peacock Alley. Initially groggy from Apinyin, she suddenly became wide-awake. Her pets! Slipping hastily into her slippers, Liah fled into the corridor and out the front door. Cook, already in the Alley, was returning from his inspection.

Liah pushed past him, screaming for her peacock and his mate. Cook cried for her to return. She found the peacock roosting in the acacia tree, but there was no sign of his mate. Liah ran up and down the cobblestones rustling the shrubbery as she tried coaxing out the peahen. The door to Number Ten opened and Lee Tzo, dressed in a blue satin robe, stepped onto the cobblestones, asking what was the matter.

Liah turned to face him, screeching vengefully, "As if you did not know. My peahen is gone!" The pimp stared and then asked if Liah in her flimsy, nightdress wasn't cold. Liah halted in her tracks, suddenly feeling naked. Cook narrowed his eyes at Tzo, then escorted Liah indoors where she collapsed in her chair, in a paroxysm of sobs.

Thomas, Shelley, Mert and Theo, hearing the commotion all arose and hurried to the kitchen. Awakened by the earlier noise out in the Alley, Professor soon came through the door. They stared hard at the sobbing Liah. The scholar had never seen Liah in tears and could not reconcile the image he saw before him with the forceful Chairman of the Council. Thomas coaxed, "Mah-Mah, we'll find her for you, just do not cry. If we don't find her, we'll buy you another."

"No!" shrieked Liah. "We shall not buy another. My mistress gave her to me for joss. Another will not do."

Liah's sons and Cook went out to Peacock Alley to continue the search. Liah could hear their voices calling but knew in her heart she'd never see her pet again. She had no proof, but every fiber in her body told her it was the evil work of Lee Tzo.

Outside, Mert confided to Theo that it was scary to see Mah-Mah cry. Theo muttered, "Yeah, and if I find out that bastard Tzo killed the peahen, I'll kill him!" Cook warned them about taking precipitous action, but his eyes belied his emotions, for he, too, wanted revenge. "Do not act in anger, boys. It's a heinous act, but we must think of the repercussions. Life is too short, as far as your mother's life is concerned, to waste it in fighting. If you want to help, just keep your eyes and ears alert. Go about your business yet be watchful; that is the best way to help your mother." His eyes clouded. "And in the coming months, be kind and obedient."

In an intuitive flash, Thomas saw Cook's outpouring of love for Liah and felt a sharp pang of guilt. Cook loved his mother more than he; at least in a way that made his mother's life so much warmer and more meaningful. "Yeah, Cook's right, Shel. Let's hit the hay and think on it when we're more rested." With one last scan of the area, they all headed back inside.

The following weeks found Liah morose, constantly looking out of the window in the hope she'd see the peahen. Once, seeing a movement in the oleander bushes, she rushed outdoors crying for her pet, but it was only a scraggly cur, and it frightened her when it darted away, racing out of Peacock Alley.

Liah sorrowfully spent time with the peacock, feeding him tidbits of lettuce hearts, ripe strawberries and seasoned rice. "Ah, my long-time companion, we both are alone now. Does your heart pain for the absence of your mate?" Even as Liah whispered, she felt slightly traitorous, for unlike her peacock, she had Cook.

The loss of her peahen awakened memories she had not thought about for a long time, memories of the Dobney estates, her mistress and her generous master who had nevertheless also deserted his wife. She suppressed a sigh, for now there was no more estate, no mistress and no master. Even her children were now grown up and leading lives of their own. It was as if time had brushed her aside. Soon even her life would be a thing of the past.

She suddenly took hold of the peacock, fiercely admonishing him, "Well, not for us. Neither circumstance nor Meng-Sui will toss us around like dolls. I've too much to do before I join my ancestors." With that, Liah marched into the house, walked up to Cook and gently smiled. "I've put aside my grief, knowing that anger and thoughts of revenge will only rob me of precious time. We must think of tomorrow."

An overwhelming sense of relief came over Cook and he let out a long deep sigh. "If that is so, you've lifted a burden from my heart and given me back ten years of my life. These past weeks have been an agony for me." Liah sighed. "If only I could protect the peacock, I'd not be so anxious." Cook was silent for a while, then asked if she would like to have a medallion made for the peacock. It would declare him to be her property and warn anyone seeking to harm him that bad joss would surely follow.

Liah's face suddenly lit up. "Yes, a gold medallion and a chain! I'll ask Wong Dak, the jeweler, to make them." The very next afternoon the peacock wore a gold chain from which dangled a medallion inscribed with a dire warning of bad joss for anyone who dared to harm him. "He is now truly my peacock." Her tone suddenly saddened as she mourned, "If only I had had the foresight to have made medallions sooner. Perhaps the peahen would yet be with us." Cook replied, "Waste no time on things that are unalterable, Liah. The peahen's Meng-Sui decreed her end. Light a taper for her eternal peace and accept the Gods decree."

—

On the twenty-first day of March, Lee Tzo was on his way to Wong's Café and he saw the red-haired Fahn Gwai woman giving instructions to workmen laying a flagstone walk in front of Number One. Although he'd met Selah briefly at dinner at Liah's, he was shocked to find out that she lived in China Street.

Tzo forgot his hunger and instead rushed to Chon Woo's place. If anyone knew the town's gossip, it was he. When Tzo was finally able to rouse Chon, the bar owner glowered and angrily shouted, "You woke me up to answer that stupid question? If you're so curious, why not ask Liah? Selah is her friend. Now, go away and let me sleep. I didn't get to bed until dawn."

Chon pulled the blankets over his head as the pimp pursed his lips. Someday he'd make Chon sorry he'd been so abrupt and cocky with him. Tzo marched from the room, slamming the door behind him, then smiled broadly as he heard Chon's agonizing moan and made for the stairway.

Lee Tzo, his curiosity piqued, broke his habit of sleeping until noon and was out on Marchesson Gai at ten the next morning. Tzo saw two men removing the front door to Number One and replacing it with a massive, six-inch thick, black lacquered and exquisitely carved door adorned with huge brass knobs. He gaped at the foyer, which he could see through the open door. Beyond the mosaic floor of the vestibule with its oversized unglazed ceramic ollas overflowing with massive philodendrons and gardenias, he spied an ebony bar, its huge mirror reflecting shelves of shiny bottles, decanters and glassware. What luxury, he thought. The chandeliers alone must have cost a fortune. He wondered what kind of place this was going to be. He concluded it must be an exclusive Fahn Gwai restaurant.

Lee Tzo's curiosity mounted as the week progressed and he almost swallowed his pride and did go to ask Liah for information, but in the end he decided he did not want to give that bitch the satisfaction. At the end of the week, Lee Tzo stood outside Number One, inspecting the newly finished flagstone walk and deciding once more that the place was going to be a restaurant. Otherwise, why would there be a red canopy covering the distance from the curb to the entrance? Surely, it had to be restaurant and bar.

Soon after, two huge vans pulled up to the entrance and began unloading furniture. By noon, it seemed all of Chinatown was lined up along the street, gawking at the bright, shiny, cushioned lounges, satin-covered settees and tables of various shapes and heights. It was when the workmen started to unload fancy bed frames, mattresses, vanities, chifferobes, and lamps with pink shades that Lee Tzo realized that this was gong to be a brothel. He was incensed. How dare Liah allow such a thing? For all the monies he had poured into her coffers, he deserved the exclusive right to the town's business.

His rage mounted as he saw the women's envy and heard the men's ribald interest. "The mattresses are so thick and so large!" Another bandied, "Hell, who cares? A willing body is all you need and then even the floor would be fine." Lee Tzo's expression turned vicious when Wong Sang nudged him and said, "Look at what she's done to the front of the place and all that expensive furniture. Looks elegant, doesn't it?"

Selah watched the crowd from her second-story bedroom window, frowning as she spied Sang and Tzo. A sudden danger signal flashed in her mind when she saw them huddle together. The pimp sneered and moments later stalked away. She stared at them a moment longer, then dismissed her misgivings. There was too much to be done before she could open her doors to bother about them now. Nevertheless, even after she turned away from the window the nagging sensation remained.

What with the daunting amount of work facing her before she could open and Tzo and Sang's interchange nagging at the back of her mind topped with her extreme exhaustion, it was no wonder that missing workers caused her temper to boil over. Where were Chelo and Lalo? She thought that for two cents she'd fire them, but then immediately knew that wasn't true. Where would she ever find two more loyal, efficient and honest workers? She smiled as she nodded to herself: Or at least they were when they weren't loafing or drunk.

Selah pushed aside her aggravation and decided to have a bite of lunch. She passed the tiny cubicle under the stairwell, smiling as she saw the crippled, deaf mute dwarf asleep on his cot and pushed open the swinging kitchen door, smiling. "Chateaubriand. Ah, Renee, it smells heavenly."

Selah indulged in a leisurely lunch and was relaxing with a second cup of coffee when she heard the back door open followed by the sound of laughter. She marched into the pantry in time to see Chelo reaching out for a loaf of freshly baked bread. "Get your filthy hands off of Renee's baking! If you want food, go sit down in the kitchen and eat what he sets before you. I'll not have Renee given extra work because of you two laggards."

Chelo grinned, his teeth uneven and very white. "Boss lady, me 'n Lalo pow'ful hongry."

Selah's green eyes blazed fury. "You were supposed to be here yesterday to stock the bar."

"Me 'n Lalo heah now, boss lady. We work velly hard today."

She studied the two half-breeds, marveling at their differences. Lalo was lithe and almost six feet tall, with red hair that was both curly and unruly. He was smooth-skinned with a tanned complexion. Chelo, whose skin was dark almost to the point of being swarthy, was half-a head shorter than Lalo and his body squarely built and knotted with hard muscles. His hair was black and straight but cut raggedly. How could anyone take them for brothers, she thought. Perhaps it was because of their Polynesian heritage, their demeanor and perhaps their pidgin English that most people mistakenly assumed they were brothers.

Lalo grinned at Selah. "Hones', boss lady, me no dlink on job. Me too dlunk fo' two months. Aiyah, me no wanta dlink no moh."

Selah's anger melted. How could anyone stay mad at these two clowns? In short order, she had briefed them on Lee Tzo and warned them to be alert in case the pimp might take umbrage at her opening up a competing brothel in Chinatown.

Chelo's face darkened and assumed a fierce expression. "We fix him!"

Selah immediately replied, "No, please, Chelo, no rough stuff. Promise me you and Lalo will not harm Tzo. Just be alert and keep an eye open for anything suspicious. That's the best way you can protect me."

Chelo's anger did not subside but he nevertheless nodded. Lalo, the happy-go-lucky of the two nodded. "Yessum, boss lady, me do lak yo wants. Me sees Chelo do too."

Following his discovery of Selah's brothel, Tzo took his anger and frustrations out on his girls, exhorting them to go beyond their normal efforts to please their clients. In addition, he told them that he expected them to bring in more income each week. His slitted eyes blazed cruelly. "Unless you want to find yourself out on the street with no protector, or worse yet, dead!"

Several days later, no longer able to contain his wrath, Tzo stormed into Number Three. He waved his arms, narrowing his eyes. "That red-haired Fahn Gwai female means to show me up. How could you, Liah? Why allow another brothel in town when there are not that many people."

Liah felt sheer pleasure at Tzo's burst of anger. She allowed him time to fume, then in a calm tone urged him to sit down. "Selah will, in no way, diminish your profits. Her place will be too high-toned and expensive for our people. She already has a clientele made up of well-to-do and powerful Fahn Gwai men. Many of them are government officials and financiers. Her business will be done by appointment and her girls are not everyday streetwalkers. Now, let us enjoy a brunch. Cook has baked the curried shrimp tarts of which you're so fond."

Between mouthfuls of tart, Lee Tzo, much like a pouting child, asked, "Has she paid her initiation fees yet?"

"She has not only paid all the fees, but insisted that they be the same as yours."

Lee Tzo accepted another cup of jasmine tea and then leaned back in his chair. "I suppose she's opening up soon?"

Liah raised her eyebrow. "She didn't say, Tzo. Why do you ask?"

Lee Tzo reached out for another curried shrimp tart and complimented Cook on the subtle seasoning and especially for the flakiness of the crust before replying to Liah. "No reason. I was curious, that's all."

For the next hour, Liah suffered the pimp's company, wishing he'd take his insipid smile and go home. Once Cook gave her a warning glance, and Liah smiled weakly at Tzo's most recent lame joke. Silently, she cringed at his feminine mannerisms.

—

In April, Selah's Place was formally opened. Although there was no fanfare, free food or a Chinese orchestra, she did set off several strings of firecrackers for good joss. Several residents milled about the door, hoping to catch a glimpse of the interior.

Late that night, Chon Woo was holding court at Wong' s Café and bragging that he'd not only seen the inside of the luxurious brothel but had even paid fifty-dollars for his pleasure. Wong Sang, not to be outdone by Chon, scornfully replied, "So what? I paid the fifty dollars, too. My girl was named Sophia and she was magnificent!" Sang gestured lasciviously and the men laughed. Annoyed that Sang had become the center of attention, Chon snapped, "You're a fool Sang. They're all the same. It's just that for fifty dollars they tease you more. Sex is sex!" "Maybe," smirked Sang, again drawing a large curvaceous figure in the air, "but I've never seen such big tits before."

One man called out, "Hey, are you guys going to switch brothels now?" Chon growled, "I only went there out of curiosity and like I said sex is the same no matter where you go." Wong grinned. "Yeah, Chon's right. Everything is pretty much the same, only it's cheaper at Tzo's, much, much cheaper."

—

The Council met on the last day of May to select a replacement for Cousin Shah's vacant seat. Lee Tzo sat rigidly in his seat as Liah told them of the news from Dai Faw and denounced the dissident group of youthful rebels for their efforts to unseat the elders of the House of Lee and the other family associations. She scowled and reported that these same dissidents would try to extort money from the Chinese illegals in Dai Faw by threatening to report them to the immigration authorities if they refused to pay. "It is even rumored," she declared, "that an agent from this rebel group has been sent here to set up this system of extortion and to try to take over our Council and run things for their own selfish ends. I vow that whoever cooperates with these despicable men or aligns themselves with the Fahn Gwai authorities, will be punished by death."

Lee Tzo met Liah's glance combatively, but not so Wong Sang, who squirmed as he wondered if in truth Tzo were the secret agent.

Liah turned the meeting over to Professor. The scholar sighed, adjusted his spectacles and quietly announced that nominations for Shah's seat were open. "We shall go clockwise around the table. If you have a candidate in mind, please give us his name when it is your turn. However, before you name a man to take Cousin Shah's place, remember that you will be held responsible for that man's future actions. We shall begin on Liah's left."

Kam Fong shook his head, as did Lee Wah. Lee Tzo then leaped to his feet, nodded to Liah and immediately launched into his speech. "I consider it an honor to nominate a man whom I believe will be a great asset to our town. I am certain all of us know how expensive, confusing and aggravating the immigration process is. If we were to have among us an agent from the immigration department, the process of bringing our families to Gem Sahn would be eliminated. I, therefore, nominate Yang Tsue to take Shah's seat."

Lee Wah gasped. He recovered his self-control and, leaping to his feet, challenged Lee Tzo. "Is this Yang Tsue from Dai Faw? Does he have an office on Washington Gai and Kearney Gai?" When Lee Tzo nodded, Lee Wah shouted, "He is no immigration agent. He's a crook! I know for a fact he's bled many of our people dry and bankrupted them. Yang Tsue is a crook, I tell you!"

"You're a malicious liar!" screeched Lee Tzo. "What proof do you have? You're only trying to prevent my nominee from joining the Council. I demand a retraction of these accusations."

"I have proof enough, Tzo. My cousin was bilked by Yang. To begin the immigration process, my cousin gave him two hundred dollars. A month later, Yang asked for an additional fifty dollars, saying that my cousin's wife's papers contained irregularities and that he needed the extra money to pay for an agent in Hong Kong to straighten them out. The same thing happened multiple times, costing my cousin another fifty dollars on each occasion. When my cousin ran out of money, Yang just shrugged and told him that he could not complete the process unless he was paid more money. It cost my cousin over a thousand dollars with nothing in the end to show for it." Lee Wah, usually a mild-natured man, shook a fist at Tzo. "I know of many more cases like this, should you care to listen. Yang is nothing but a crook. We should not allow him a seat."

Lee Tzo suddenly rose and threw a punch at Lee Wah but missed. Chon Woo shouted, "Hey, you guys! Stop it! We can settle this by having Professor write to the Four Families Association in Dai Faw and to the *Dai Faw See Bo* to check Yang out for us. If he's seated and if he is indeed a crook, we'll throw him out. However, I am sure Lee Tzo knows about the death penalty for traitors and would not name such a man."

When order was restored, the nomination process continued and neither Chon nor Sang had a candidate. Lim Tao then rose from his seat. "I have a man to name. He is also from Dai Faw, but is now residing in Loo Sahng. His name is Wong Cheung, an elder from the House of Wong."

It was Wong Sang's turn to gasp. "Is he the same man who people are saying was a hatchet man many years ago?" Lim Tao nodded. "What has a man's past got to do with his present life? For the past eight years, Wong Cheung has been a highly respected elder of the House of Wong. He carries exemplary testimonials as to his character, not only from the panel of elders but also from many of Dai Faw's civic leaders. I, for one, am not going to refute the word of so many outstanding leaders."

"But a hatchet man?" cried Wong Sang. "Once a killer, always a killer."

Chon sneered, murmuring under his breath but loud enough to be heard, "What's the difference? Why not a hatchet man? We have among us all sorts of people, even a pimp." Upon hearing this, Lee Tzo roared and lunged for Chon. "You, Chon, hold yourself above me? How much better are you? You cloud the heads of Fahn Gwai, sending them out into the streets to destroy our houses and maim our people. Damn you! You're scum!"

Liah rapped her cane forcefully on the table leg, her voice commanding. "Gentlemen, no more quarreling! The nominations are before us. Shall we proceed?"

After this second outburst concluded, Professor murmured that there were no other nominations. Liah nodded, suggesting supper be served before the balloting. "Our emotions will have simmered down and our minds will be clearer."

At the supper table, the lines were clearly drawn. Liah secretly exulted, for based on the way the men were grouped, Wong Cheung was as good as elected. Only Lee Tzo and Wong Sang sat together as they talked in subdued voices. Once dinner was done and the dishes removed from the table, the meeting continued.

Downstairs, Cook could hear the buzz of angry voices as the sounds drifted down the stairwell. To relieve the tension he felt over the election, Cook worked himself into a frenzy cleaning the stove, wiping down the walls, even cleaning out the litter box in the toilet room.

At midnight, the long wait ended with the sound of footsteps on the stairs. Cook dropped his dishcloth and sprinted to the corridor in time to see Lee Tzo marching stiffly out the front door. Wong Sang was next to push through the corridor without so much as a word to Cook, who stood by the kitchen door. A little bit later, Lee Wah and Lim Tao came down the stairs and Lim Tao grinned at Cook. "I suppose you must have guessed by now, that Wong Cheung is our replacement for Cousin Shah. We could hear the front door slamming."

Lee Wah apologetically told Cook that it had been his exposing Yang Tsue that had infuriated Tzo. "Well," he commented, "I'm not going to lose a night's sleep over the likes of Tzo or Yang. Like it or not, Wong Cheung is our new Council member. Good night, Cook. I must tell you the supper was superb as usual." Together, Lim Tao and Lee Wah took their leave.

Upstairs, Liah warned Chon. "I wouldn't needle Tzo about this. He is dangerous. Moreover, the five to two vote means that Sang and Tzo are in league together. You better be careful."

"What do I have to fear from a pimp? If he tries anything funny, my Kung Fu men will kill the bastard. I'm not beholden to him; I owe him nothing."

At Cook's appearance in the Council chamber, Chon grinned. "I overate, Cook. The Peking roast duck and rolls were delicious! Good night, Liah, and good night to you too, Cook. Professor, are you coming?"

The scholar shook his head. "There are several points I wish to discuss with Liah. As a friend, Chon, I, too, caution you not to infuriate Tzo any more than he already is. That man is insane when it comes to saving face."

There was a frown on Cook's face when the three were finally alone. "I saw the dishes and I know neither of you ate well. What do you say we carry on our discussions in the kitchen and perhaps have a late snack?"

Later, Professor pushed his plate away and his eyes sparkled and his tone reflected his pleasure. "You know, it's very strange. At the meeting, I couldn't seem to swallow and I could not taste the food. Now, however, look at all the food I just consumed. I should be ashamed of my gluttony."

Cook poured Professor another thimble-sized cup of Ng Ga Pei. "Nothing strange about it, sir. When one is tense or unhappy, one cannot focus on anything else, even good food."

Liah grinned. "I don't know that I've ever felt happier than when Chon quipped about having a pimp on the Council, so why not a hatchet man? For a moment, I thought Lee Tzo would tear Chon's eyes from his head."

"How about the way he tore into Lee Wah?" asked Professor. "If Lee Wah had not ducked, it would have caught him full in the face."

"Good thing that Lee Wah kept his composure," said Liah. "He's well-trained in the martial arts. Do not allow the man's placid personality to deceive you. Lee Wah is very tough underneath it all."

The meal done, Professor lit his pipe and prepared to leave. "I will notify Wong Cheung about his being selected tomorrow. Good night, Liah, and thank you, Cook, for allowing me a second chance to eat my dinner."

The next afternoon at four o'clock, Professor returned to Number Three. "Well?" asked Liah. "Was Cheung happy about the seat? What did he say?"

Professor shook his head. "I really do not know how he feels. It's hard to fathom that one. One moment he is friendly and open and the next he is remote and silent."

"I suppose his past has made Cheung that way. It would have been difficult to do the killing if one could not wall off one's emotions." Liah's voice softened. "It's too bad he has to wear such a hard exterior. Underneath, Cheung is a loving and kind man. I've seen this in the treatment of his children and, especially, his wife."

Their conversation ended abruptly when Cook burst into the kitchen. "The news is out. No fewer than eight men stopped me, asking

'Why a hatchet man is on the Council?' Two of the men were outright insulting and said it could only mean you were out to control Chinatown. I wanted to punch them in the mouth, but instead merely asked why they didn't come and speak directly with you. They instantly shut up and stalked off."

Professor was greatly relieved Cook had broken the news to Liah, as he had been loath to do so. He chimed in and told her of an incident in Wong's Café earlier in the day. "When I entered, I saw Wong Sang flailing his arms about and shouting. You know how he gets when he's excited. However, upon seeing me, he clammed up and said not another word. I'll give you one guess what he was telling them. The men dispersed immediately and didn't say a word to me on the way out."

"When I went into the meat market this afternoon, the butcher greeted me effusively and seemed eager to make conversation," said Cook, "but he said nothing about Wong Cheung. However, I know for a fact that he's done his share of mud-slinging. I got the feeling he was trying to cover up."

Professor sighed. "I hate to think what Lee Tzo will say when he finally shows himself. I noticed his door is yet closed. I, myself, was politely queried about Wong Cheung by some of the people I met on the street, but I suppose people will not get too huffy with me because they might need my letter-writing skills in the future. Liah, what do you plan to do?"

"Nothing! The sooner the people tire of the novelty and sensationalism of the situation, the sooner we can get back to normal activities. Meanwhile, I do not need either of you to defend me. No one will believe you're not under my sway anyway. Just let time take care of things."

THE NEW SESSION

The air was alive with tension given the way the last meeting had gone and the Council members were eager to be done with this session lest there be a repeat performance. Kam Fong and Lim Tao had arrived first and sat waiting for the others and making small talk, Lim complaining about his family's difficulties in gaining entrance into Gem Sahng, Kam lamenting that the huge boiler in his laundry needed repair. Everyone else soon arrived.

Liah waited a long moment before she opened the session with a welcome for Wong Cheung. It didn't escape her notice that Lee Tzo sat scowling in his chair. Seated opposite him, Wong Cheung gazed directly back at Tzo with an implacable look on his face, then turned away and ignored him. The big man's response to Liah's welcome was brief but hinted that he would not be tolerant of violence of any kind and that he would defend the welfare of Chinatown with his life. Lee Tzo, with his eyes lowered, snickered something to Wong Sang. With little business to conduct, the meeting was quickly adjourned much to the relief of everyone.

A week after the meeting, Professor found himself annoyed by the apparent apathy of the populace. The people's initial furor over Cheung's appointment, verging almost on violence, had all but disappeared. "Resignation to one's Meng-Sui has its drawbacks, especially when people allow their lives to be totally governed by the will of others. Do they not know they must make some effort to help themselves?"

Cook sighed. "If our people did not follow the way of passivity, they'd have perished at the cruel hands of the Fahn Gwai. You can't ask them to change their attitudes now."

Liah chimed in, "You're both right, but I have more pressing issues to think about. Professor, I'd like you to write a letter to Elder Wong of the House of Wong in Dai Faw to notify him that Wong Cheung has been seated on our Council and to ask on my behalf for his support in case anyone in Dai Faw thinks badly of this action. Be sure to inquire as to his health and tell him that we have entreated Kwan Koong's benevolence upon him."

Professor nodded. "That's a good move, Liah. I've also been thinking lately of Cousin Shah. We haven't heard from him in a long while. Surely he'd not turn his back on you if you were in need of help."

Liah shrugged her shoulders. "I feel in my heart that Shah would never do such a thing, especially not after promising Sen; however, perhaps he hasn't received your letter yet or it may be that he is elsewhere at the moment."

In the weeks following Professor's mention of Cousin Shah, Liah fretted, making only feeble attempts to eat. Cook watched Liah, her face immobile, her eyes staring without seeing. As many times as he'd seen her so, it always left him with a sense of inadequacy. If he could not divine her innermost thoughts, how could he be of any service? It was as if he was dancing with shadows and he liked it not at all. In desperation, he turned to Eldest Son and Second Son for help, but neither of them wanted to approach their mother either. By late June, Cook squared his shoulders and threatened to leave unless she snapped out of her lethargy.

So deeply entrenched in her Apinyin habit, Liah was unable to appreciate the impact that such an event would have on her. Cook shook his head sadly, seeing that his threat was falling on deaf ears. He put a cup of brandy broth in front of her, silently untied his apron and went to do the day's shopping. There was no use trying to converse with her; Liah was unreachable.

Late that afternoon Selah telephoned and asked Cook if she could come by for a visit. Cook's response was one of sheer relief. "Most assuredly, Selah. Since when do you need an invitation? The Gods are surely smiling on Liah today. Your visit might be just the thing to break her out of her lethargy. Please hurry."

Selah, who'd never seen Liah in an Apinyin stupor, was shocked. She bent over Liah, kissing her on the cheek and was shocked at the coolness of her skin. "My dear friend. What have you been doing to yourself lately? You've lost weight."

Cook feared Liah would lash out, but to his surprise, she just smiled. "Oh, Selah, I've been deep in the doldrums." She glanced up at Cook. "I've been indulging myself and neglecting my meals, but the pressures of life have been too great to bear lately. I needed the Apinyin. You do understand, don't you?"

"Of course, darling," smiled Selah. "But you mustn't forget that the body needs comforting too. If you'd remember to eat, you could then indulge in your Apinyin without doing yourself so much harm. If Apinyin gives you comfort, then take it. I am not one to judge you."

Cook sensed that Selah had finally coaxed Liah from her cocoon and he set a platter of pastries on the table and poured tea for the two of them. Selah smiled gently as she placed a tart on Liah's plate. "If I'm going to gain weight eating Cook's delicious treats, then you will have to join me."

After they had both eaten their fill of Cook's pastries, Selah exclaimed, "I almost forgot the real reason I came to see you. I have a letter addressed to you from a Lee Shah. Do you know anyone of that name with a return address in Second Town (*Sacramento*)?"

Liah leaned forward, suddenly alert. So that's why Cousin Shah didn't write sooner! She leaned back in her upholstered chair and murmured, "I thought he had abandoned me." Her guilty, almost childlike, expression tugged at Cook's heartstrings. He thought, "You endured all that self-punishment for nothing, Liah. Next time have more faith and patience."

It was two o'clock and Professor had gone to Fahn Gwai town on an errand. Liah smiled impishly. "I know I'm being impatient, Selah, but could you read Shah's letter to me?" Selah scanned the letter quickly and told Liah, "The letter indicates that Cousin Shah has moved to Second Town and now owns a café in partnership with his second cousin. It also says that he's making plans to bring his wife and sons to Gem Sahn."

Liah's brows furrowed as she further learned that the Six Companies Association had recently participated in a joint investigation with the House of Lee relating to a murder in Dai Faw where one of the accused was a youth from the House of Lee. Selah continued, "During intensive questioning, the dead man's younger brother broke down and admitted that his older brother had been involved with a secret group bent upon changing the power structure of Chinatown. Upon finding out the group's real intent, the older brother had tried unsuccessfully to quit the gang. Ultimately, death had been his way out. The younger brother then provided the judges with a list naming the members of the group except for the leader. It seems that the leader of the group was unknown even to the senior members of the group as he had always taken pains to hide his identity."

Selah paused, took a deep breath and went on, summarizing, "Cousin Shah warns you to be cautious and on the alert, as he suspects that Lee Tzo might just be that escaped leader from Dai Faw. He says he has no proof, however, as all his inquiries have turned up nothing. He also says he has spoken with Elder Wong of the House of Wong and urges you to accept Wong Cheung's friendship. Apparently, Cheung is extremely reliable and knows how to deal with violence and even warfare."

Liah sighed when Selah mentioned Shah sending his regards to the children and his promise to send additional information as soon as he was able to obtain it. She also felt a slight twinge of fear when Shah said that he held no great hope of finding out the truth, as the secret group was extremely well organized and the leader astute in cloaking his identity as well as that of his henchmen.

Liah turned to face Selah. "I worry about you. You are not used to men like Tzo. He will not stop at anything, even at taking a life, to get what he wants, and I know he's already afraid you will steal a lot of his business. I must warn you, we have had our own suspicions that he might be that secret agent from Dai Faw. You must keep this information to yourself and not tell anyone lest it get back to Tzo."

"No chance of him harming me, Liah, but you must be careful yourself. We can't get along without you. However, if it will put your mind at ease, I'll be extra careful. Now, I'll run along, but, darling, will you promise to take better care of yourself?" Selah lowered her voice and added softly, "You mean a lot to me."

Cook smiled as Selah leaned over and kissed Liah on the cheek. Then she was gone. Cook inhaled deeply and said, "Each time Selah visits, the house smells of lilac and jasmine, the scent lingering long after she's gone. You are fortunate to have her affection. That one does not give the same to all."

Liah nodded absentmindedly and mused, "Do you think we might be able to add more men to Professor's bodyguard?"

Cook shook his head adamantly. "People will know for certain that the men are yours. If you want more men, just go ahead and add them on to our force." Liah's mention of adding more guards bothered him, as it indicated that Liah was now even more concerned about Tzo.

Suddenly, the peacock shrieked from outside on the cobblestones. Liah sprinted into the corridor and out the front door screaming for her koong jek. Trailing her, Cook shouted for her to be careful. Up and down the cobblestones Liah shouted for her peacock, until Cook grabbed her by the arm and pointed up at the acacia tree. In the topmost branches, the peacock was noisily giving vent to his fright.

So engrossed in their search were they that they hadn't seen Professor rush out from Number Four. Coming up to them he said, "When I heard his shrieks, I wondered what terrible thing had happened to him." Liah paid no heed to him, but went up and down the cobblestones pulling at the shrubs and bushes. Cook then got a broom and began beating on the oleanders. Suddenly, a mongrel dog scampered out of hiding and darted away.

Professor pointed and shouted at Liah. "There's the culprit that frightened your koong jek!" Liah gaped at the scholar, seeing him for the first time. "Sir, I thought you were in Fahn Gwai town today?"

"I was. I got back half an hour ago. When I heard the peacock, I came out to investigate."

Recovering her composure, Liah whispered for Professor to come inside saying that she had received a letter from Cousin Shah. Once inside, she told him of Selah's visit and the contents of the letter. Professor agreed that they needed to be extra vigilant while waiting for further word from Cousin Shah.

—

Liah, though relieved to have heard from Cousin Shah was now plagued by the mystery of the unknown agent from Dai Faw and found it difficult to resist the escape of her bamboo pipe. However, each time she was ready to succumb to the Apinyin vapors, she thought of Selah's pleas for her to take care of herself and stopped short. By the end of June, when Wong Cheung came to say good-bye, she was distraught. Cheung was leaving Chinatown to take up residence on his leased land near the sea. "Although I will be absent for a while, do not think I will forget the promise I made to Elder Wong. I will make arrangements to telephone you each Monday and Thursday afternoon. Should there be a need for me, I will be in Chinatown in two hours. Have no fear."

Toward the end of their visit, Liah saw the big man's face suddenly tighten as he leaned forward and said in a low and husky voice, "Before I go, I want to address the rumors that I slew a young girl and her lover here when I was a hatchet man. It is important to me that you know the facts, as I very much wish to have you as a friend."

While Cheung was presenting his story, Liah became fascinated by Cheung's beautifully sculptured hands. She found it impossible to believe them to be the hands of an assassin. When, finally Cheung concluded, Liah saw the pain etched on his face as he muttered, "It is that unsuccessful attempt on my life that caused my wife's unstable condition today. I shall live with that burden for the rest of my days."

Liah sighed, "I thank you for telling me. I am grieved to have evoked such ugly memories for you. Know this, our Meng-Sui, yours and your wife's, dictate the circumstances of our lives, so do not burden yourself with unnecessary feelings of guilt. You did what your Meng-Sui ordained. Embrace your new life and make it as fruitful and peaceful as you can. As for the Council, it will not be necessary for you to attend the meetings, unless there is an emergency. May Kwan Koong guide your footsteps." With that, Cheung took his leave.

The very next day, Liah confided Cheung's story to Professor. "I will tell you because it will set your mind to rest about Cheung, but it must remain a secret. It seems Cheung's wife was not aware of her husband's line of work, at least not until the highbinders came to their house looking for him."

"What did the highbinders want with him? I thought he had been hired by the merchant to bring the girl and her lover back to Dai Faw for capital punishment."

"The young girl's parents learned of the death decree and hired their own men to kill Cheung."

When Professor asked if Cheung had indeed killed the couple, Liah shook her head. "He never said and I did not ask, but I got the feeling he allowed them to escape."

Liah told Professor not to mention that Cheung was out of town. "He will still maintain his two rooms at the Lotus Garden Hotel. However, he will not attend all the Council meetings. If the men ask why he's not present, I'll tell them he's in Dai Faw on business. That ought to keep Lee Tzo guessing."

However, Professor was skeptical. "In a town as small as ours, it is common to know who is doing what. It'll leak out sooner or later. What will you do then?"

"By then," declared Liah defiantly, "I hope it will make little difference."

"I hope you're right, but then you're always right." Professor smiled shyly and Liah thanked Kwan Yin for the scholar's friendship. It would be more than she could bear if she didn't have that man's support.

SUMMER IS HARD

Temperatures during the summer of nineteen hundred and sixteen reached record-breaking highs in Los Angeles, with the thermometer hovering at one hundred degrees. It was not only the heat but also the oppressive humidity that plagued the residents of Chinatown, the majority of the outdoor people living in flimsy wooden structures and the aged in outdoor areas. Cook stood by helplessly as Liah gave in to one Apinyin escape after another, abstaining from even nourishing soups. The four or five hours a day when the outdoor residents escaped the worst heat of the day within Number Three robbed the family of privacy and while Cook did not mind cooking extra meals, he yearned for the return of peace and quiet.

Each night as he handed Sen Fei, Wong Fah and Wong Sing their cartons of leftovers, he felt satisfaction knowing that the three oldest residents of Chinatown would now be able to eat a morning meal, a fact that also gave Liah comfort. Cook found it ironic that Liah worried about the oldsters having food to eat when she so flagrantly ignored her own meals.

Cook observed Liah's sons as they came home from work, hot, tired and in ill humor, especially Fifth Son who wanted only to fall into bed. One night, Cook asked Fifth Son with some concern if he shouldn't consider quitting the job at the garage. Surely by now he knew all that was necessary to repair automobiles. His mother waited only for his word to set him up in a business of his own. Mert shook his head, saying there wouldn't be enough business among their people. Besides, the wages were building his nest egg. He didn't want his mother's backing, not if he could help it.

It both irritated and worried Mert that his mother was constantly in-quiring about William's future plans for college. She kept asking if Fourth Son was certain that he didn't want to be a lawyer, knowing how badly their own people needed legal representation. One evening, more tired than usual, Mert snapped at her. "Mah-Mah, I have told you Fourth Brother has plans to become a teacher. Please don't make things hard for him by trying to push him into doing something he doesn't want to do. He has wanted to be a teacher ever since we lived on the Dobney es-tates. He says his teacher has told him that he might be able to win a scholarship to study in Hong Kong if his grades are high enough."

Liah was silent, Fifth Son's mention of Hong Kong bringing thoughts of Sen to mind. For a moment she wondered how he was far-ing, but pushed the thought quickly from her mind. Whatever his cir-cumstances, it had been his choice to return to China. Liah's voice became somewhat harsher, as her enduring anger with Sen caused her to be harder than she intended on her fifth son. "All right! If being a teacher is what Fourth Son wants, let him become a teacher!" Then her voice became sarcastic. "However, if you don't mind, Mother will speak to him anyway, if only to point out how badly we need legal represen-tation in Chinatown."

Mert tensed up as he replied. "No, of course not, Mah-Mah. You know, don't you, that all of us really want to please you. It's just that we need to manage our own lives"

Half-angrily, Liah muttered, "Yes, please me in all things except marriage and grandsons."

Mert, physically and mentally exhausted, did something he rarely did: he lashed out at his mother. "Mah-Mah, every time we talk, we always end up fighting about marriage. I'm too dead tired to argue tonight. I'm going to bed."

"Son," cried Liah in alarm, "aren't you going to eat? I'll reheat the beef and greens for you. Cook also cooked your favorite dish, steamed pork with hot preserved herbs."

Mert shook his head and, much to his mother's displeasure, went into his room and shut the door rather forcefully.

—

The grueling summer slowly passed. By October, the outdoor people had returned to their shelters. Cook and Liah, on that first day alone, relaxed leisurely with their morning tea. A cool breeze blew through the front doors, drawn by the opened rear door. Cook smiled ruefully. "Soon, the summer heat will be forgotten and we will be complaining about the cold. The Gods vary the weather from one extreme to the other. Why can't they let us enjoy a period of moderate weather?"

Liah smiled. "The Gods are not our friends, Cook. We must fight to survive. Just the same, I agree that it would make our lives easier to bear if, once in a while, the Gods would soften the elements. By the way, I want to thank you and Amah for bearing with me during this summer. Not only were you pressured by having to cook for the outdoor people as well as our family, but also by having to put up with my unreasonable outbursts brought on by my discomfort."

Cook smiled gently and said in response, "I have thought of a method whereby next summer we can keep the front and back doors open the entire night to admit the cooler night-time air without fear of someone forcing entry. I am going to install iron grilled doors."

The telephone suddenly rang and Liah froze in fright, as she was still not used to the Fahn Gwai technology. Cook's eyes cautioned her to keep calm as she rose to answer it. Liah murmured, "Good news never comes at this hour."

Cook hovered beside Liah as she spoke cautiously into the mouthpiece. After listening for a few seconds, Liah suddenly shouted, "Praise Kwan Yin, daughter! Now, you must be certain to take good care of your body, for it houses the new life Kwan Yin has blessed you with. Be sure you come this Sunday for a visit and come early."

When she had replaced the earpiece onto its hook, Liah smiled broadly and said with a self-deprecating shrug, "Well, I guess I cannot always be right. Eldest Daughter is again with child. Kwan Yin is truly generous."

—

Life returned to normal with the colder weather and, by Christmas, Liah was eager to show her granddaughter the new-fangled toys she had purchased. She could hardly wait until Eldest Daughter and Toh arrived for lunch.

At eleven o'clock on Christmas morning, much to the delight of Second Daughter, Liah ordered the entire family to be awakened. "I want to have lunch and then immediately open presents." Cook tried to hide his mirth, but Liah saw his expression and scowled, "This is my granddaughter's second feast day on earth and I want her to fully enjoy it."

When Flo and Toh arrived at noon, her brothers were sitting grumpily at the table. Thomas growled, "It's about time, sis. Hurry and eat so we can open up the gifts, then I'm going to hit the sack again."

Liah sat with her fourteen-month-old granddaughter on her lap, opening up the gifts she'd bought for her. Liah wound up the red, white and black rooster, put it on the floor and watched as it strutted about flapping its wings. All the while she was explaining what it was and how it worked to Aileen. Flo shook her head and told her mother that she was just wasting her time because Aileen was too young to understand. Liah chose to ignore her.

There was also a red, white and blue soldier which, when wound up, walked up and down, moving its rifle forward and back. Aileen reached out, as babies do when they're interested in something, and Liah joyfully placed it between her hands. Once Liah let go of the toy, it fell to the floor. Eldest Daughter leaped up, picked up the soldier and murmured that she'd put it away until Aileen was old enough to play with it.

Liah scowled. "Give it back!"

"But Mah-Mah, she'll break it!"

"Then Eldest Daughter, we'll buy her another. Give it back!"

William's, Theo's and Mert's gift to their niece was an electric train. Theo moved everything off the table and set up the tracks while William and Mert assembled the train cars, hooking the cars to each other. Cook grinned, "Are you boys sure you bought the train for Aileen?"

Theo took the infant from Liah, held her near the table and explained that the engine would pull the train around the track, going over the mountain and through the tunnel. Liah giggled, "I think my three sons did buy the train for themselves. Aileen doesn't understand yet."

Flo hotly challenged her mother. "I thought you said she understood everything!"

"Only because it is a boy's plaything," snapped Liah, "does she not understand. Do not underestimate the intelligence of your first born!"

Later, after supper, other guests including Selah made an appearance. Again, Flo and Yook Lan were taken in by the mysterious aura of the red-haired woman and envious of her expensive clothes and jewelry. It wasn't fair that one woman had so much, they thought to themselves. Yook Lan felt a stab of jealousy and, when she felt Selah's gaze, she quickly turned away.

Selah began to hand out presents and her gift to Liah immediately ignited envy in both Flo and Yook Lan. How, wondered Yook Lan, could anyone afford such an expensive pair of earrings? Yook Lan watched as Liah took off her jade and pearl earrings and replaced them with her new diamond ones.

Flo squealed happily as she unwrapped Selah's gift to Aileen, a delicately wrought gold bracelet. Flo giggled, "Oh, Auntie Selah, such generosity. Aileen is such a lucky baby. I wish I were so fortunate."

Liah scowled at that, recalling that Eldest Daughter had recently asked her for a pair of Liah's jade earrings and that Flo had frowned when Liah informed her that the earrings were to be part of the dowry for her brother's bride. Eldest Daughter is too greedy, thought Liah.

Liah felt gratified when Selah placed her arms about Sen Fei and kissed her before handing her a large, long red-ribboned box. The aged actress grinned. "For me, Selah? That wasn't necessary."

Selah smiled. "I know that, Sen Fei, but my heart urged me to share with you the bountiful happiness of this feast day. Open it, dear, see if you like it."

Madam Quock was parading about, showing off her silk brocaded jacket but stopped and looked covetously at the beautiful satin cheongsam Sen Fei had received. Madam Quock had to fight even harder to keep the envy from her face as Sen Fei reached for something underneath the cheongsam and grinned. "Oh, Selah, how did you know I needed a warm winter coat? It even has a fur collar! May Kwan Yin bless you."

Selah's eyes twinkled, slightly misty as she hugged the aged actress. "Wear them in good health, Sen Fei. May Kwan Yin walk beside you, too."

1917

YEAR OF THE SNAKE

L iah's sons did not celebrate the New Year of nineteen hundred and seventeen. Although Thomas and Shelley wanted to enlist in the army, they couldn't just give up their trucking business. Theo, however, was the one most affected by the world's events. He sulked and cursed his mother's over-protective nature, her forbidding him to even think of going to war.

The New Year of nineteen hundred and seventeen was a hard one for Thomas, who was positive the United States would sooner or later enter the war. Although Thomas had told his mother about the World War going on, Liah just could not conceive of a struggle of such magnitude that it would involve the entire world. Surely, her eldest son was exaggerating. Liah, having decided as much, turned her mind to the celebration of the New Year of the Snake. Her first move was to make a promise to Kwan Yin that she would use her bamboo pipe less in the coming year if the Goddess would see to it that one of her sons would wed.

Liah begrudgingly acknowledged her third son's twentieth birthday on the eleventh day of January; and on the twentieth day of the same month, Fifth Son's seventeenth birthday. It made her heart ache and infused her entire being with sadness to know all her sons were now of marriageable age but as yet unwed.

In her desperation to see at least one of her sons wed in the coming year, Liah considered writing to Sen to suggest that he, as their father, consult a matchmaker. However, she knew that Sen would never do anything she wanted. It was one way he could get even with her. What galled Liah most, however, was the absurd promise she'd made to Cook not to pressure the boys. Liah thought about breaking her promise, but her fear of alienating Cook outweighed her desire for married sons. She knew he was not one to take lightly a broken promise.

When the celebrations of the New Year of the Snake concluded, Liah held a dinner in honor of her youngest child's thirteenth birthday. Her heart was heavy, for soon even Second Daughter would reach marriageable age. At the same time she became incensed at the thought that perhaps Second Daughter might wed before any of her older brothers.

Immediately after Emmi's birthday celebration, Liah's mood turned dark and heavy. It was on Cook's mind to cheer her up by reminding her of her second grandchild's impending birth, but something held him back. There was a worried expression on Liah's face as if she sensed there might be potential problems with the birth of this grandchild. One afternoon when she lamented about the tardy birth, Cook without thinking, chastised her for being impatient.

Liah retorted, "What do you know of childbirth? I am deeply worried, for Eldest Daughter has violated every regimen of good prenatal care. The Gods will surely show their displeasure with her. I'm worried, not impatient, sir!"

Amah giggled. "Cook meant no ill-will. Besides, children born in Gem Sahn seem to be stronger than people of our generation were. This infant will be born when the time is right and even you cannot hasten it."

Liah's eyes reproached Amah, but she merely said, "I suppose you and Cook could be right, but I'm too old to change my way of thinking."

"Hah!" Cook challenged. "Did you hear that, Amah? Have you noticed every time Liah is at fault she uses age as an excuse? In this case, age should provide wisdom, not an excuse for impatience or stubbornness." Liah glowered but could not utter a comeback when in her heart she knew Cook was right.

The ensuing days dragged by and with each new dawn, Liah became more concerned about the birth of her second grandchild, but she was careful to hold her emotions in check. Neither Cook nor Amah shared her fears.

Finally, at four-thirty in the morning on April the sixth, the telephone began ringing, its shrill jangling seeming louder than usual in the sleeping house. Liah awakened with a start and sat bolt upright, consumed with fear. She sprang from her bed and ran barefoot into the kitchen. Cook shouted at her from the top of the stairs, cautioning her to slow down lest she trip in the dark kitchen.

Liah grilled Toh, demanding three times to know if the infant were normal and whether Eldest Daughter was all right. Upon hearing that both were fine, Liah admonished Toh to ensure Eldest Daughter ate the pickled pigs' feet and drank the brandied chicken broth. She added, "Be certain the midwife puts enough liquor in the soup. Eldest Daughter will need to build up her strength besides making enough milk for the infant." Before hanging up, Cook heard her tell Toh that perhaps next time he would be blessed with a son.

When Liah hung up the receiver, she turned to see Cook circling April sixth on the calendar and commented, "I still say you will have done all that record-keeping for naught if you were to lose the calendar." Cook smiled smugly and said, "I keep a copy upstairs."

A short time later, Liah pushed aside her cup of tea. "I don't want any more. I'm too overjoyed to sleep, Cook. Will you come to my bedroom?" Cook pointed upstairs. "She'll hear us." Liah replied, "Amah sleeps the sleep of the blessed. Will you?" Wordlessly, but smiling ever so slightly, Cook helped Liah from her chair.

—

The next day at eleven o'clock, Thomas and Shelley arrived home and bolted into the kitchen crowing that they were uncles again. "Wow!" Shelley shouted. "A brand new niece and a war, all in one day!"

Cook frowned and Thomas tugged sharply at Shelley's sleeve. "Come on, stupid, let's hit the hay. We'll tell them about the war later."

At the supper table, Thomas informed his mother that America had entered the war. "They will be conscripting men and, if our names come up, Mah-Mah, we will be forced to go." It angered him when Liah shook her head in denial, saying that Kwan Yin wouldn't allow her sons to fight.

Theo knew then that if Mah-Mah wouldn't let Thomas join the Army, he wouldn't be allowed to either. Theo thought of his buddy, Harry Myers, who had enlisted immediately after the President's declaration. He felt again the shame he had experienced when he had refused to go sign up with Harry and their friends. Theo winced as he recalled the incredulous look on Harry's face when he told him that for a Chinese, parental obedience outweighed even a war.

Theo could hardly contain his frustration until Liah went into her bedroom. "How can Mah-Mah be so deaf to our wishes? How can she so callously turn her back on America's problems, yet be so sensitive to the way we Chinese are treated? It isn't right!"

Cautiously, Mert tried to console his brother, but it wasn't easy. Theo was extremely touchy and could turn violent when his pride and manhood were challenged. Mert offered, "Theo, you must try to understand that Mah's just afraid one of us might be killed if we go to war. Moreover, you can't expect Mah to understand world events. For one thing, she was born and raised in China where women were not typically given an education. For another, her experiences with Fahn Gwai have been so negative that she wouldn't really mind if they killed each other as long as they didn't kill us."

"That's bullshit!" exploded Thomas. "I can still remember her outrage when we told her about the Twenty-one Demands Japan made on China in 1915. Remember? It was back on the estates when Mr. Dobney told us about it. She blew her cork!" William, who had been silently listening to his brothers, timidly suggested that the situation was different then because the Japanese were the aggressors on China and China was Mah's homeland.

Silence engulfed Liah's sons, each contemplating his own thoughts. William recalled reading about the Japanese's Twenty-one Demands as well as Ted Crosset's outrage. However, he also recalled that Ted Crosset had said that China was in part to blame. He believed China's corrupt government had weakened her internal power and made her vulnerable to exploitation. Japan, William faintly remembered, had also declared war on Germany as a way to obtain the port of Tsingtao. William's face was grave as he timidly asked if he would be forced to go if called up. He would hate to halt his studies.

Theo glared and, for want of another way of dissipating his frustration, tore into his younger brother. "You make me sick, William! Is it even possible for you to forget your schoolwork? There's a war going on and we're sitting on our asses! Doesn't that mean anything to you?"

Mert instantly came to William's defense. "Aw, Theo, shut up! Don't get on William's case because you're sore at Mah-Mah." Then Shelley growled, "You shut up, too, Mert! Theo's right, but William is right about Mah. It's just that Theo, Thomas and I feel like we'll be shirking our duty if we stay home." Theo nodded in violent agreement, causing Shelley to add, "Just because you feel that way, don't go getting stupid ideas about sneaking off. Family still comes first, then the war."

Cook's voice was stern as he warned the boys that they ought to desist talking about the war. "I hear your mother moving about the bedroom. One thing I know for sure is that if any of you are called up, it will kill your mother. Please think again before you do anything that you might be sorry for later. Now, no more talk. I think she's coming out."

Thomas, his face mottled with pent up emotion, muttered that he had to get out of the house to think. "Come on, Shell, let's go to Selah's. Let's have a long drink where we can talk things out."

Theo wistfully asked if he might go along. Shelley was on the verge of denying him but saw his brother's pain-etched face. "Sure, Theo," he said and put his arm around Theo's shoulders. "Why not? It's not like we're going to make any decisions."

Mert and William were quiet after their brothers left, each lost in his own unspoken thoughts. William feared his education would be curtailed and Mert was fearful that Theo might do something foolish, like enlisting. Cook, sensing the boys' inner conflicts, said softly, "I have one thought for you. Meng-Sui is real. If it is meant for you to get something you want in life, you will get it. Please advise Third Brother that if his Meng-Sui decrees he will go to war, he will. If not, then nothing will cause it to be so."

It was when Cook murmured that they all owed their mother much that Mert jumped up and exclaimed, "I think I'll go over to Jui Jinn's Café. Do you want to go, William?"

—

Number Three Son put aside his thoughts of war and his frustration when Liah celebrated her second grandchild's month-old feast day. Flo proudly said, "What a difference between the two children, Mah-Mah. Mary Marie is such a gentle baby. She's not at all like Aileen."

Aileen in her lap, Liah flashed a warning to Flo that she'd better not make any more derogatory remarks against her first-born grandchild, especially in Liah's presence. Flo quickly changed the subject, lamenting her inability to produce a man-child for Toh. Liah counseled that there would be other children. "Just offer up a prayer to Kwan Yin. She will bestow upon you a son."

At the supper table, Thomas joshed with Toh about his partiality to girls. Toh smiled. "Son or daughter, I do not care. After all, we're not in China. Besides, isn't it so that when a daughter marries, she brings home a son?"

Everyone guffawed except Flo, who averted her eyes. When Toh touched her gently on the arm she pulled away violently. Liah frowned at the exchange, wondering what was the matter. Just then, the front door opened and Selah came into the kitchen exclaiming, "Now, where is the little darling?"

Selah handed Flo a tiny jewelry box containing a beautiful necklace. "I hope she will wear it in health and peace. Meanwhile, allow me to carry Mary Marie." Selah then turned to Professor, asking if the horoscope had been read yet.

Liah shook her head. "Not yet, Selah. Why not sit down, as we are about to hear it. It must be a good reading, otherwise Professor would be as tense as the last time."

After the auspicious reading, Flo exclaimed, "Well, thank God Marie won't be as stubborn as someone else I know. Two stubborn ones would drive me mad." Liah clasped Aileen a bit closer and defiantly retorted, "Eldest Daughter, you are in no position to speak of stubbornness. If Aileen is stubborn, she comes by it honestly." Liah's eyes blazed. "Now, leave my first-born granddaughter alone."

Professor helplessly shook his head. "Eldest Daughter has taken my horoscope reading too literally. An inclination is completely different than a certainty." Liah waved aside the scholar's explanation, saying that it didn't matter. "As long as I have life, no matter what life holds for them, I shall provide. Now, no more such talk. We shall drink a toast to my newly born granddaughter."

Selah smiled broadly. "Good for you, Liah. Now, if I might, I'd like to propose the toast. To Aileen and Mary Marie, two beautiful girls who are fortunate to have the world's loveliest and most generous grandmother. You will need no other boon in life, and may Kwan Yin always walk beside you." Selah then produced a second gift from her bag. "Aileen, this is for you, darling. Shall I help you with the ribbons, dear?"

"Auntie Selah!" squealed Flo as she held up the red pinafore dress. "Gosh, this makes me wish I were a little girl again. They are making such cute clothes now." Cook warned Liah with a glance not to make a retort, but it was too late. Liah scowled, "Being born twice would be too much for your mother. Not even Kwan Yin would punish me thus."

Liah unbuttoned Aileen's dress to put on her new one. "Red is a lucky color, my child." Aileen did an awkward pirouette in her new dress and ran over to her father. After hugging her, he gently pushed her toward her mother, but Flo just glared and pretended not to see her.

When the festivities ended, Liah ordered Thomas to drive the family home. Flo took the opportunity to complain. "I told Toh we need a car. Now that we have two children, it is too difficult to ride the street cars and taxies are too expensive." It surprised Flo when her mother agreed. "I am sure that when the time is right, Toh will purchase a car. Now, be sure to cover the baby so she will not catch the night air and be sure that Aileen is warm." Liah leaned over once more to hug Aileen, then pushed her toward her father.

Alone with Cook, Liah confided that she was worried about Eldest Daughter. "Did you see the way she pulled away from Toh almost hatefully? Moreover, it pleases me not the way she derides Aileen."

Cook sighed. "You are not trying to control the state of you daughter's marriage, are you?"

"No, but it worries me. Eldest Daughter is a tigress and with her spiteful nature life would not be bearable if she held something against Toh or Aileen."

BIGGER SCHOOL

On the twenty-fourth day of May, in the Fahn Gwai's year of nineteen hundred and seventeen, the Council met to discuss the enlargement of the school. Professor informed the men he'd found a suitable place situated on Marchesson Street, right in the center of town. Not only was it an ideal, protected spot where the children would not have to traverse the Fahn Gwai's cross streets, but also it was a large store. "If perhaps

Marchesson owns this property, Liah, you might ask to rent it. For you he'll charge a lower rent."

Lee Tzo muttered that it was too bad he could not join the Council twice, for then he'd supply the monies needed to outfit and move the school. He looked up to see Wong Cheung's fiery eyes glaring at him. Liah quickly placed Professor's request open for discussion before the silent confrontation erupted into a not-so-silent one.

The ensuing discussion was short and the appropriations were agreed upon, then supper was served. At the supper table, Wong Sang engaged Cheung in direct conversation. "Where is your farm, Cheung?"

"Near the ocean," replied Cheung.

"Why then do you still retain your rooms at the Lotus Garden Hotel?"

Wong Cheung's eyes hardened as he stared at Wong Sang, sending chills down Sang's spine and making him wish he'd not asked the questions. "I am as yet living here, as I'm still negotiating the lease on the farm. In fact, it will be a few more months before I leave. Besides, there is no reason to leave now; it's too late to put in the crops I want."

The big man turned to Liah, notifying her that while they were waiting to move, it was a good time to send his family back to the village to visit his wife's parents. "Once we move in, she will not be able to leave."

Liah murmured that it was generous of Cheung. Many men would think twice about the expense of such a trip. Wong Sang and Lee Tzo eyed each other but said nothing. Wong Sang, especially, did not want to chance again provoking the formidable Cheung.

After the meeting was over, Cheung thanked Liah for her silence when he had announced his family's departure. "I needed a plausible reason to explain their absence, as they are already ensconced in our new home. I have vowed to never let any enemy wreak havoc on my wife again."

Professor and Liah nodded and Professor made note of Sang's inquisitiveness. "I wonder why? It isn't like him to care what happens to anybody. Do you suppose he's asking for Tzo?"

The big man shrugged, answering Professor, "Whatever the reason, I warn you again to stay alert. I do not like the way I feel about Tzo. I am almost sure he's the secret agent in Loo Sahng, but I have no proof. We shall have to wait for time to point him out. Well, I must leave now. Once again, don't be hesitant to ask for my help, Liah." Cheung bowed slightly to Professor and took his leave.

For some time Liah was lost in thought. The scholar puffed meditatively on his pipe and at length asked Liah what she thought of the big man's parting words. "It's as if he was warning you, but I wish he'd come right out and say it plainly and with more specifics. It'd save you and me a good deal of mental work."

"Perhaps he can't give us facts, sir. All we can do is be on our guard and stay alert. As Cheung said, time will unmask the culprit."

"I suppose you're right, Liah. I was being wishful. Well, I must be leaving now. If we are to have our school opened soon, I'll have to make inquiries into furniture and supplies for the students. As soon as you hear from Marchesson, I'll begin to pack the books and furniture. On behalf of the students, I thank you again for providing them with the proper space to learn."

"Sir, no need to thank me. The men approved your new school. Now I, too, will be going downstairs. I would be grateful if you will walk ahead of me in case I trip. Cook left for a meeting after serving the meal. He wants to be certain that if there's any news about Tzo or the mystery agent, he'll get it first-hand."

—

The gentle warmth of spring gave way to the harsh heat of summer. For Liah, it always heralded a time of personal volatility and ill temper.

This summer her mind focused on Third Son, who Liah feared might run off to the war.

It was a warning from Eldest Son that forced Liah to allow Third Son to quit his education and start driving a truck for his brothers. Liah couldn't believe Third Son would sneak off in the dark of night to go to war, but she couldn't be certain. She cursed the Fahn Gwai and lit an extra taper to Kwan Yin, asking for the Goddess to intervene.

An unexpected argument between the brothers erupted when Thomas asked William to join them in the business after he graduated from high school. William thanked Thomas, but declined, saying that he had made an application for a scholarship in Hong Kong. Thomas narrowed his eyes suspiciously and demanded to know if William had intentions of visiting their father.

William shook his head adamantly and retorted, "No. However, if I were to visit Father, it would be my business and not yours. After all, Mah-Mah never intended that we ostracize Father."

"It is our business, William. We do not want Mah-Mah to be hurt by your going. After all, Father is the one who deserted us."

After Thomas left, William sat alone at the kitchen table, deep in thought. It was thus that Liah found her fourth son and anxiously asked him if something was wrong.

"Mah-Mah, it's just that I'm confused. My elder brothers want me to join them in the trucking business, but I want to continue my education and someday get my teaching credential."

Liah smiled wanly at Fourth Son. "I am certain your brothers will understand. If it will ease your mind, Mother will speak to them. It is a fine thing that one of my sons will go for the Fahn Gwai's higher level of leaning. And a professor in China holds the highest honor among all the professions. I am proud of you son."

Mother and son sat for a while in a comfortable silence, then William asked cautiously, "Mah-Mah, are you happy? What I mean is, do you miss Father? I have always felt guilty loving Father and knowing that you were sad about his departure. However, you did tell us that Father toiled hard and long for us. My brothers make me feel like a traitor because I think of Father once in a while."

"Oh, son!" cried Liah as she leaned forward to draw him closer. "Mah-Mah did not know of your pain. Of course, I am content, and why should I not be? My children are obedient and loving; and all is well with the Council, the temple, and the school. Moreover, we have monies set aside for the aged and needy. As for loving your father, you should continue to do so. I shall inform your brothers that I do not want any of you to feel alienated from your father. It's just that he neither felt comfortable nor safe in Gem Sahn; and he felt that my position on the Council demeaned him. Now, think no more sad thoughts. Mother shall speak to the rest of the children. All of you should revere and love your father."

That night Liah was upset by Fourth Son's intention of going to Hong Kong for college and could not sleep. Although Eldest Daughter was married and out of the house, that was different; she was yet in town. Cook found her seated in her upholstered chair in a pensive mood. "Now," he asked, "what is the trouble?"

Liah sighed, her voice tremulous, saying he'd not understand. Seeing Cook frown, Liah blurted out that she was thinking about how much she would miss Fourth Son if he left home for Hong Kong to study.

Cook said not a word, but touched her lightly on the shoulder. "Come. I'll prepare your bamboo pipe. While I do not like you smoking the Apinyin, it is better for you than brooding."

—

The twelfth day of June, nineteen hundred and seventeen would be a date Theo would never be able to erase from his mind. It was on that

day that he found out that Harry Myers, his best friend in school, had
been killed in battle. It had never occurred to Theo that Harry might
die. So crazy a youth, Harry was too strong and too young to die. Consequently, Harry's death disoriented Theo, dampening his devil-may-
care attitude and leaving him shocked and confused.

In the days that followed, Theo tried to cope with his sorrow, crying
into his pillow long after his brother William had fallen asleep. Half of
him still wanted to go to war, but the other half clung to his mother's
belief in Meng-Sui. Exhausted from the mental conflict, Theo decided
to obey his mother, but with that capitulation something deep inside
Theo snapped and forever after he felt estranged from the family.

—

Liah was delighted when Eldest Daughter announced to the family that
Toh had purchased a new car and as soon as he learned how to operate
the machine, they would drive to the house for a visit. Cook grinned,
for now the family could visit Liah more than once a week. Perhaps if
Liah had more time with her granddaughters she wouldn't need the
bamboo pipe as much.

Sharing a knowing glance with Cook, Liah thought again of Sen.
How vastly dissimilar they were. There was so much more sharing between herself and Cook, while there had always been a barrier between
Sen and herself for almost as long as she could recall. Her cheeks tinged
pink as she recalled her first two years of marriage. The both of them
had been so naïve and then came the birth of their first son. Sadly, the
rapid deterioration of the marriage soon followed.

Cook was reflecting rather on the nature of women from the villages
and how fiercely proud they were of their possessions. He saw the same
pride now on Liah's face. Ownership of anything new or valuable was
to be flaunted amongst their people. And why should it not be? The

warrior God gave them so little with which to be identified as individuals. Only through their boasting about their men-folk's ability to provide for them did they feel any importance. Yes, underneath all the wisdom, strength and vision, Liah was still a woman, a vulnerable woman.

On the twenty-eighth day of June, Liah waited impatiently in the Alley for the arrival of Toh and his family, not only to welcome her two granddaughters but also to see Toh driving his brand new Hupmobile. Finally, at two o'clock in the afternoon, she saw a blue, shiny automobile draw up to the entrance and was aghast to see Eldest Daughter at the wheel.

For a moment she stood transfixed, staring. Flo tripped gaily from the car, giggling at her mother's amazement. "Mah-Mah, isn't the car beautiful? Is Mert home? I want him to check it out."

Liah recovered her composure enough to inquire if it wasn't dangerous for her daughter to drive, to have control of the vehicle.

"Oh, Mah-Mah, don't worry. I am a good driver. The salesman told me so. Toh was having trouble manipulating the gears, but I did it easily. Toh said one driver in the family is enough."

"Well," muttered Liah, not quite believing Eldest Daughter, "come inside. Lunch is ready. There are now no excuses that you can't visit more than once a week." Liah reached out for Aileen's hand, murmuring that she had a surprise for her. Flo crossly accused her mother of spoiling Aileen. Liah glowered, "She's my granddaughter and my first grandchild. I can do anything I want. I'll hear no more of this kind of talk from you, or else I'll lose my temper and you will suffer."

It did not escape Liah's notice that a small crowd of people had gathered around the car. Mert had the hood up and, after checking the motor and all the wires, announced that it was a well-built car. Cook touched the shiny, smooth fenders and thought the vehicle elegant.

Once inside, Liah pointed proudly to the new heater in the front room. "It was installed two days ago. Your brothers generously had a gas line installed in the front portion of the house. Now we won't freeze this winter." Deep down, Liah's heart overflowed with joy. Kwan Yin was indeed being generous with her bounty: a new granddaughter, a new car and a new heater! Such are the things that enrich one's life.

On the tenth of October, the family shared a sumptuous supper honoring Aileen's second birthday. Liah seemed as excited as her granddaughter with the new toys and gifts. Throughout supper, Liah noted again Eldest Daughter's distress and her angry rejection of Toh. Just before they left for home, Liah pulled Eldest Daughter aside and demanded to know what was going on. Flo burst into tears, confiding to her mother that she was with child again. Half blushing and half-angry, she spoke of Toh's incessant passion. "He always seems to need me."

A flash from her own past leaped to Liah's mind. Pressing Eldest Daughter into a chair, she cooed soothingly, "Is that all? When your two older brothers were mere babies, I, too, found myself again with child. I felt the same fright, the same humiliation and dreaded to tell your father. It was already so hard for him to take care of us."

Once again Liah's gratitude toward the family friend Fatt On overwhelmed her. "If Fatt On had not consoled me, telling me that Sen was blessed by the Gods, and promising to help us in any way he could, I do not think I could have faced the pregnancy. Daughter, you too, are blessed by the Gods, so wipe your tears away and thank Kwan Yin for this blessing. Mother will always help you."

As Liah was speaking, Flo realized that her mother was unaware of the real reason for her distress. Moreover, she couldn't tell her mother that she did not experience passionate fulfillment in sex with Toh lest her mother think her lustful. Amidst her turbulent thoughts, Flo heard her mother calculating the birth date of her next grandchild. "If your calculations are right, daughter, the child ought to be born sometime next July."

—

The cooling breezes of November relieved Liah's weariness. No longer suffering from the humidity, the oppressive heat or the torment of abdominal pains she'd been having, Liah happily turned her mind to the forthcoming winter. Even if the Gods were relentless in their endowments of extreme weather, she'd not suffer cold this winter. The open-hearth heater in the front room would provide comfort. She wanted to light it now, but since the winds were not blowing or rain falling, she couldn't bring herself to be so wasteful.

—

One morning while waiting for her brandy broth to cool, Liah was talking to Cook, her mind focused on Eldest Daughter, who continued to be tense, angry and unhappy about the pregnancy. If only she could pinpoint the real problem then maybe she could help. It was good for neither her unborn child nor her two young children to have a distraught mother.

Cook impatiently retorted that it could not be easy for Eldest Daughter to be carrying an unborn baby while two more clung to her skirts, demanding attention. Liah's eyes suddenly opened wide and she berated herself for not having thought of this idea sooner. "What if, for the duration of her pregnancy, I take care of Aileen?"

"Why not take the two?" asked Cook sarcastically. "Surely, you can't be serious? Aileen will drain your energies." Amah, who had been silent up until then, cried, "That little bit of a child couldn't be a chore! In any event, I'll help with her." As she spoke, a beautiful, joyful smile settled upon Amah's usually drawn face.

Thus, it was that on the twenty-eighth day of December, Liah paced the front room waiting for Fifth Son to arrive with Aileen. Presently, she heard the sound of an engine and ran outside. Aileen, bewildered and somewhat reluctant to visit her grandma alone, clung to her uncle's hand as Liah ran up. Her arms outstretched, Liah gathered up her granddaughter and would have carried her indoors if Cook hadn't leaned forward and picked Aileen up, growling, "You know she's too heavy for you."

Amah laughed, "How could such a child weigh more than a feather? Let me hold her, sir."

Cook ignored both women and walked into the house with Aileen.

1918

YEAR OF THE HORSE

PEACOCK ALLEY AND AILEEN

Aileen's coming to Number Three filled Liah with almost forgotten memories of motherhood. Caught up in the daily care of her granddaughter, Liah was eager to celebrate the New Year of the Horse. There was so much traditional lore to pass on to the new generation, for Aileen was indeed the span that connected Liah's generation to the future and gave her earlier privations and toil deep meaning, The brighter future her granddaughter's generation held made up for all the Fahn Gwai's cruelties Liah had suffered. When Aileen took her rightful place in the world, it would be a more just world.

Cook was not as farsighted, his only concern being that the child not drain too much of Liah's strength. As he watched her cajoling Aileen to drink her brandy broth, Cook shook his head. Why could not the Gods be more generous with their boons? On the one hand, Liah was eating and sleeping more regularly since the coming of the child, but on the other hand all her time and energies were spent on the child.

Their eyes met and Liah smiled. Cook's eyes left unsaid how happy he was for her newly found joy and the diminished use of her bamboo pipe. He cloaked her from the sadness he felt; Amah's and Liah's constant attention to Aileen's needs left little for him.

—

The first time Liah bathed her granddaughter, she was shocked to find so many bruises on Aileen's body. Lovingly, she cautioned Aileen to be more careful. Did she want to get hurt? Liah was aghast at the child's terrified reaction. As Aileen cowered and trembled, Liah gathered her into her arms, cooing comfortingly. She told Aileen over and over that Grandma would never allow anything to hurt her.

On Eldest Daughter's next visit, Liah inquired about Aileen's bruises, her fitful sleeping habits and her sudden crying out for her father. "She also exhibits such terror when I mention the word 'hurt'. Why is this?"

Fear flashed across Flo's face and Toh dropped his eyes, but not before Liah caught a glimpse of his own fearful expression. Liah said nothing more, but she was disturbed by Toh's nervous manner. She made up her mind to query Toh without Flo around.

Two weeks later, Cook approached Amah about Aileen's presence in the house. He smiled sheepishly. "It seems to me that Aileen drains too much of Liah's time and strength. Perhaps you might take over more of her care."

Amah thought for a long moment, then impulsively blurted, "Oh, Cook, you are not jealous of a small child, are you?" Immediately realizing her faux pas, she added, "Of course, I'll do as you say, sir." Cook stared open-mouthed, then untied his apron and fled upstairs. Amah sighed, hoping that she had not overstepped her limits with Cook and angered him.

Alone in his room, his heart beating hard and his mind jumbled with flashing images, Cook tried to get a grip on himself. A half-hour later he was struck by the realization that Amah was right. He was jealous. How ridiculous that a man of his years should be afraid of a child stealing away Liah's affections. His cheeks reddened and he grinned. At least he was not so old that he could not yet feel the pangs of jealously.

With that, his tension dissolved away and Cook knew that to love Liah was to also love Aileen.

When Cook returned to the kitchen, Amah dropped her eyes as he entered. He very much wanted to assure Amah that he was ready to take Aileen into his heart but had no opportunity to speak. Amah avoided his glance and finally gathered Aileen to herself, saying they were going to the playground. As Amah stood at the doorway leading to the corridor, Cook smiled. "You were right, Amah. Have no fear. I will love Aileen as I love Liah. I am beholden to your enlightenment."

Tears sprang to Amah's eyes. In her whole life, there were no two people she loved as much as Cook and Liah. If her thoughtlessness had marred her friendship with Cook, she could not have borne living one more day.

After that, Cook experienced an emotional jolt as he found himself caring for Aileen as if she were his own child. Though it was an amazingly good feeling most of the time, every now and then he felt guilty when he so wanted to put her on his knee and spank her for being naughty. Something held him back, for he, too, sensed something was amiss. He wondered at Aileen's erratic sleep, her sudden screaming as if awakening from a nightmare, only to sob inconsolably in her grandmother's arms.

Finally, the celebrations for the Year of the Horse arrived. Liah, with her granddaughter in tow, tended the garden each morning, checking the pots of taro roots and Chinese lilies, explaining all the while to the three-year-old that taro blossoms and Chinese lilies were the traditional flowers of New Year. Aileen mimicked her grandmother, taking in long breaths of the plants' fragrance and peering under each leaf looking for the telltale bulge of buds.

Passersby stopped to chat with Liah, paying special attention to her three-year-old granddaughter. Theirs was the knowledge of Liah's deep pride in Aileen. Besides, words uttered half in interest couldn't fail to further their esteem in Liah's eyes and it was a known fact that those in

Liah's esteem always came out the richer for it.

The day Liah and the ladies began the making of the *doong*, Aileen provided everyone with a chuckle. All thumbs, Aileen was trying to shape the Ti leaves into a cone to fill it with the small plate of ingredients Liah had given her. "She'll learn," smiled Liah. "Just wait and see. She's a smart child." This brought a round of smiles from Sen Fei, Madam Quock, Yook Lan and Amah.

Later, Liah cast a quick glance at her granddaughter, still stubbornly manipulating the Ti leaves, trying to get them to retain the rice and sausage and then trying to pleat them together. Aileen's lower lip protruded in a silent promise that she was going to make at least one *doong*. Professor's prediction of Aileen's stubbornness flitted across Liah's mind. An inaudible sigh escaped her lips, then she turned her mind to the completion of the tokens of the New Year.

Mid-April brought the sunshine, and with it warmth that dried out many of the puddles and the rain-soaked streets and alleys. Aileen clamored to go outdoors. Liah relented, grinning as she kissed Aileen, saying "Just for a little while." She allowed Amah to take Aileen on walks around Chinatown more often. On one such outing, while Aileen was playing on the slides at the playground, the butcher's wife assailed Amah with catty remarks about Liah having only granddaughters. She asked Amah if she thought the Gods would ever favor Liah with a grandson.

Amah raised her head in a proud manner and replied in a haughty voice that the Gods had smiled on Liah so far and would bless her with a grandson at the proper time. With that spiteful repartee, Amah led Aileen home, seething with anger and anxious to tell Liah of the incident. Amah returned home and, in an irate outburst, told Liah about the butcher's wife. "She was so sarcastic as she mewled about whether the Gods would favor you with a grandson, since your daughter has only given birth to girls. I told her in no uncertain terms that it was only a matter of time."

Liah smiled at Amah's vehemence and replied, "Pay no heed to that childless female, Amah. She's only striking out in frustration. Come, let us have tea."

—

Liah was complaining to Cook of being in the doldrums when she suddenly caught the hint of a conspiracy in the house. Once her suspicions were aroused, she spared no mercy in questioning Cook. Usually her persistence yielded information, but this time Cook adamantly denied there was any such conspiracy in progress.

As the weeks passed, Liah's ill temper mounted. How dare they shut her out! After a stormy session with Eldest Son, the family held a secret discussion and decided to inform Liah that their sister's upcoming birth would take place in the Fahn Gwai hospital. Once the decision was made to tell Liah, Thomas groaned, "God, life for us will be hell until the baby's born. I wish Mah wouldn't carry on so. Let's just hope it's a boy, then she'll calm down."

Hearing the news, Liah was aghast. "What nonsense! What do Fahn Gwai doctors know? In China, women even have babies out in the rice fields."

At ten-thirty in the morning on the twenty-eighth of May, the telephone rang shrilly and Cook raced to stop the caterwauling. He listened a moment, then heaved a sigh of relief. "A baby girl, seven pounds. Fine," he responded. "I'll inform Liah."

At noon, Liah glared balefully at Cook from her chair. "Such a powerful draught I had last night. Because of that, I missed speaking with Toh. Now I'll never know the details of the baby's birth."

Cook frowned as he placed a steaming cup of herb tea on the table. Tempted to take out her frustration on him, Liah quickly changed her mind, for his expression seemed to dare her. Inwardly, she smiled.

Surely Cook was, when necessary, a forceful person. Instead, she fretted over the whereabouts of Professor, as she wanted him to chart the infant's horoscope. Just then the front door opened and boisterous voices floated back to the kitchen as Eldest Son and Second Son shouted out the news of their newly born niece.

Behind her back, Cook warned them not to tarry seeing as their mother was not in a good mood. Thomas and Shelley consequently ate a quick meal, then retreated to their bedroom. Listening to their half-audible laughter, Liah frowned and glared. One day, she vowed, she would take them to task for disrespecting their mother. Cook smiled to himself as he caught a fleeting glimpse of Liah's face. Before she could rail at him for cooperating with her sons, Cook untied his apron and told her that he had shopping to do. As Cook went out the door, he heard Liah call out to him, "Coward!"

At four in the afternoon, Professor stopped in to see Liah, and was joyfully informed of the birth of her third granddaughter. It was during their tea that Liah noticed an anxious expression on the scholar's face and asked him what was the matter. Professor shook his head. "We'll speak of matters later. Right now, allow yourself the ecstasy of being a grandmother again."

"Never fear, sir. I have had my moments of relief and joy. Eldest Daughter and infant are both doing well. Now, tell me what is weighing on your mind."

Professor mumbled, "Well, Old Chan told me last night that whatever evil Tzo has in mind, it is now about to occur. He couldn't hear all of Tzo's conversation with the stranger he spoke to, but he did overhear something about a delegation from Dai Faw and something about a meeting to be held tonight at eight. Tzo seemed angry when Sang shook his head, declining an invitation to attend and he ordered him to be present."

Cook muttered disgustedly, "Delegation indeed! More like a gang."

Liah looked steadily at Cook, warning him to alert Old Chan. "Tell him not to expose himself to danger, but ask him to keep his eyes and ears open. Perhaps he might glean some more information."

Liah then turned to Professor. "I think it's time you wrote another letter to Cousin Shah to ask if he has any information about this delegation from Dai Faw. Please ask him to notify me as soon as he has any news." The scholar nodded silently.

—

On June twenty-ninth, the day after the celebration of her third granddaughter's month-old feast day, Liah lapsed into silent moodiness. The time was quickly arriving when Aileen's visit would come to an end. Liah creased her forehead in thought, wondering why Toh had been so reluctant when he had arranged for his daughter's return in the middle of August. Something was amiss and Liah was angry that what it was still eluded her. She berated herself for not probing into the matter further.

On the eighteenth day of August, Aileen returned home. The first night without her, Liah and Amah were bereft. At eleven o'clock, Liah retired, begging for the use of her bamboo pipe. Afterwards, Cook gazed down at her calm face, begging Kwan Koong to erase the pain in Liah's heart. Very softly, he turned out the lamp and gently closed the bedroom door.

Soon the hot and humid September weather brought the outdoor people to Number Three. But it was mostly the painful absence of Aileen that led Liah into one of her darkest moods. The increasing amount and frequency of her Apinyin use began to frighten the family. It was during this time that Cook heard about the dueling youths of the House of Quan and those of the Four Families Association. As the public fights escalated in violence, Cook forced himself to face Liah with the news.

As Cook expected, Liah's reaction was violent. "I should sanction

Wong Cheung to use his hatchet on the entire lot of those ungrateful hoodlums! Even more so, we should punish their parents who are probably behind these fights."

"You can't mean that, Liah!" Cook exclaimed angrily. "You can't thrust Wong Cheung back into his violent past. Until you can control your emotion, I'd suggest you put Professor in charge. You're only talking like this because of your sorrow at Aileen's departure."

Stunned, Liah replied tearfully, "You're absolutely right, but I can't seem to help myself. I miss her so much." Cook, however, did not relent. "Your black mood has jeopardized the well-being of this entire family as well as your own well-being. Stop now and do some serious thinking before you allow this day to pass."

Liah recoiled from Cook's tongue-lashing. For once, though, she wasn't even inclined to fight back. She nodded and her voice was hard as she struck out, "You'd think our people would learn from the long years of Fahn Gwai persecution not to hurt each other. We must stand united or else the Fahn Gwai will wipe us from this earth."

—

The week following Liah's receipt of the news regarding the eruption of gang violence in Chinatown, a Council meeting was called. Two members from each of the Tongs involved were invited to air their grievances. The two elders from the House of Quan and the two from the Four Families Association were openly hostile glaring at one another. The atmosphere became heated as two of the elders lashed out at each other and Liah was hard pressed to quiet them. Finally, she demanded silence. "You shall each have your turn to express your grievances."

Allowed to speak first, Elder Hua Fong from the Four Families Association accused the youths of the House of Quan of aggressive behavior, of actively seeking out the youths of the Four Families

Association to taunt them into fights. Elder Hua's voice quavered with anger. "Moreover, the Quan youths have been insulting and molesting our elders, both women and men alike. They push in when there is a line waiting for services, and they shove the women and old men off the sidewalks. It is making life miserable for our families."

Once given the floor, Elder Quan, a scant two years younger than his seventy-year-old counterpart, pleaded with the Council to make the Four Families youths desist from disrupting business in the meat markets. "They shout from the doorways to the customers, saying that the meats are tainted and not fit for dogs. In cafés, they gather in groups to harass our people by standing beside their booths or tables, putting pressure on them to leave. I do not want this fighting to persist or to become personal, as I hold nothing against Elder Hua. However, the years weigh heavily on my shoulders and because of my years, my opinion is no longer heeded in the House of Quan. The Council will have to enforce whatever action is taken with these youths. I am too old to fight anymore."

After listening to both sides, Wong Cheung rose from his seat. First, he apologized to Elder Hua on behalf of the House of Quan and then apologized to Elder Quan on behalf of the Four Families Association. Both sides, he said, had legitimate complaints.

Chon Woo applauded and suggested that perhaps Wong Cheung could publicly drub the youths from both Houses. At that, Wong Cheung raked Chon with a flinty glance, causing Chon to immediately drop his eyes. Lee Tzo seconded Chon's suggestion, saying that he, too, had suffered at the hands of the youths. "They spit on the ground as I walk by and make disparaging remarks about me. Worse yet, they harass my girls. It's gotten so bad my girls find it safer to walk on Peacock Alley and to stay away from areas that are not close to home."

Wong Cheung's eyes then bored into Lee Tzo who giggled nervously. "No need to take this personally, sir. I only speak the truth. It won't be necessary for you to personally mete out the punishment. The Council can appoint a panel to issue the decree and afterwards select an enforcer."

Liah rapped the table for silence. Looking at Lee Tzo, she said, "I find your remarks out of line, as are Chon's. It is not for one person to take the mantle of peacekeeper onto himself or even for two. The Council will act as a group. You keep your girls in line and we will keep the peace."

The Council unanimously approved the publication of warnings throughout China Street, stating that anyone found to be aggressively looking for a fight whether by pushing, shoving, teasing, taunting or making insulting remarks would publicly be given ten lashes.

The two elders were friendlier during the ensuing supper. Elder Hua sighed that a tremendous weight had been lifted from his shoulders. He smiled sadly. "Life does not endow us with the strength of our youth. Madam Liah. We are both grateful for the Council's intervention."

At the end of supper, Liah surprised the men with a warning to Lee Tzo. "It has come to my attention that your harlots are themselves half to blame for the demeaning treatment from the youths. From this day forward they will walk on the streets but must keep their hands to themselves. Did you not know they were aggressively marketing themselves and making themselves conspicuous? Did you also not know your girls are being overly friendly with the Fahn Gwai? See to it they refrain from consorting with the Fahn Gwai in Chon's bars or on the streets. That is an order."

Liah held up her hand, forestalling any comment from the pimp. "Nothing you say will change the facts, sir. Now, let us sign the records. As soon as the elders have signed, my Fifth Son will drive you all home. I thank you for coming."

—

A secret surveillance on Lee Tzo was initiated following the Council meeting. Cook, Professor, Liah's two Eldest Sons and Old Chan kept watch on Number Ten for strangers who might enter or leave the brothel. One afternoon, Liah noticed Professor was being a little testy and asked why. Professor wiped his spectacles, saying that the heat was almost too much for him. "These daylight vigils drain my energies. Indeed, I feel somewhat feeble and senile."

"You are none of those things, sir. You're right though. We will abandon the vigil at least during the heat of the day. Nobody is going to be about at that hour anyway."

"The heat during the day is bad enough," moaned Professor, "but even at night the house is so warm and close, I can't sleep. Of course, I really wouldn't mind the watches if only we could come up with a shred of evidence against the man."

Cook nodded his agreement. "I tell you what, sir. I'll have Fifth Son measure your door and transom for screens. We have noticed that by leaving the doors and windows open at night, the house is cooler by fifteen or twenty degrees during the day, and it diminishes the stale air at night."

Liah nodded. "I can imagine your situation, sir. I find after the outdoor people have been here and the doors and windows are closed and shuttered, I always get a headache. Only after the night air has blown inside the house do I find relief. Allow me to help with the installation of the screens. I'll speak to Fifth Son this very night."

—

On Monday morning Liah complained that as much as she wanted to see Aileen, she found Sundays tiring. "It might be my constitution, but I'm certain Eldest Daughter's abrasive attitude affects me the most. I sometimes wonder how Toh can endure that girl."

Professor, whose mood had noticeably lifted since the installation of the screens, chuckled. "In another two weeks the heat will abate and then we'll be complaining of the cold and wet. However, the outdoor people will no longer be spending so much time here. So have patience, Liah. I must thank you again for the newly installed screens. They have made my life so much more endurable. You were absolutely right; the late night breezes do relieve my tension."

Late that afternoon, Chon Woo dropped in for tea with Liah. It was Professor's habit to read aloud the day's news to the outdoor people as well as to Liah and any visitors in order to keep everyone up to date regarding the war. After his reading, he commented that he thought the war would soon end. Chon Woo took the opposite view, believing that the munitions manufacturers would keep the hostilities going, so as to keep making their profits. Professor argued back and tempers rose. Finally, Professor, irritated by Chon's arrogance, blurted, "If you're so sure of your position, Chon, why not make a bet? Each of us will put up fifty dollars, and the loser will donate his share to the Chinatown Adversity Fund. How about it?"

Chon threw a suspicious look at Professor and demanded to know if Professor had inside information or if he were a fortuneteller. Professor shook his head. "I only know what I read in the newspapers and journals. You say the war will drag on and I say the hostilities will cease at the end of this year or within the first three months of the next Fahn Gwai year.

Listening to the argument, the outdoor people began to chatter amongst themselves. Some agreed with Chon Woo while others lined up with the scholar. There was an electric excitement among the oldsters, and Liah was pleased, for it wasn't often that the outdoor residents had a diversion in their drab lives. "Done!" Liah cried, "Each of you put up your money and we'll consider this wager official."

Cook then entered the front room carrying a huge tray. "Chon, please stay and share our meal. I've made Fahn Gwai potato salad and fried chicken. For those of you who need rice, there is also fried rice." The ensuing meal was almost festive, with the old men excitedly asking Chon or Professor questions about the war. For a time, their lethargy and discomfort with the heat vanished, and it seemed to Liah that the oldsters appeared youthful and filled with vitality once again. She thought that win or lose Professor and Chon had brought some excitement into the oldsters' lives.

As Professor had forecast, the cool, autumn breezes soon slipped into Chinatown and the outdoor people returned to their shelters. Peace reigned once more in Number Three and Liah made her yearly apologies to Cook and Amah for the extra work and inconveniences brought about by the presence of so many outsiders.

On a blustery November eleventh, the people of Chinatown were amazed to see Professor racing down Marchesson Street, waving a newspaper and shouting to the people he passed that the war was over. At the entrance to Peacock Alley, a small group of people gathered around the usually decorous scholar, now animated with a huge smile on his face. "The war is over! I told Chon it would be so!" The oldsters who had sided with Professor wore smug expressions, as if to tell the others how smart they were. Professor thanked them for believing in him, then hurried to inform Liah of the news.

Liah, sipping her herbal tea, smiled at the scholar as he opened up the newspaper and laid it on the table. He traced his finger along a line on the map from the English Channel to Switzerland, explaining to Liah that that line was called the Western Front and that the Eastern Front had extended from the Baltic to the Balkans. He then explained about the Battle of Turkey. "I can't read Fahn Gwai, but our papers used the same map. The foreman who told me about the battles said the oceans were of the greatest importance in the war. The country that held dominion over the seas ensured its use for the movement of armaments and men. These blue areas indicate the oceans."

Liah was still skeptical that the war was really over so she asked Professor timidly, "Are you certain of your facts, sir? I must know, for I fear my Third Son still might do something foolish." Professor, reining in his impatience, explained that the Armistice had been requested by the Germans who agreed on a treaty based on fourteen points proposed by the Fahn Gwai president. "I do not understand what the fourteen points are, but when our papers come out tonight, I'll try to find out the details. Believe me, Liah, the war is truly over."

Liah flashed him a wide smile, declaring Professor to be a genius. Professor shook his head and demurred, "I merely read whatever journals and papers I could and tried to think things through. It was a journal from Hong Kong that first hinted at the war's cessation when the Russians pulled out of it." He grinned mischievously at Liah as he admitted that when he had made the bet with Chon, he was speculating based on that information.

Cook then inquired if Professor was going to see Chon to officially request the money for the Adversity Fund, but the scholar retorted, "No! Chon lost, so let him come to me."

"I don't think," murmured Cook, "that Chon will be a very happy man. It's not the loss of the money so much as the loss of face he will suffer."

Liah snapped, "Then Chon had no business making the wager, especially in public!"

Over tea, Liah confided to Professor and Cook that she felt as if a hundred-pound weight had been taken from her shoulders. "You will never know the feeling I had every time I'd look into Third Son's room, checking to see if his suitcase was gone. Now the war is done, thank Kwan Koong!" Both men shared in Liah's newfound peace of mind.

1919

YEAR OF THE RAM

It seemed to Cook, as he watched Liah preparing for the celebration of the Chinese New Year, the Year of the Sheep, that her spirits were never so blithe. Perhaps the armistice had something to do with her elation, for no longer did she have to fear Third Son would sneak out to join the Fahn Gwai army. Cook, too, felt a release from the worries of nineteen hundred and eighteen and took in a deep breath as he hoped nineteen hundred and nineteen would be less burdensome.

After the weeklong celebration, Liah turned her mind to the problem of filling the vacant junior member's seat on the Council. There were two leading candidates: Tom Soo, whose Chinese name was On Ping and Jui Jinn. She was discussing with Professor some way that they might help Tom with his law school expenses without seeming to be giving him charity. "The young man is not only admirably ambitious and hard-working, but I detect a great deal of pride in him. We must be discreet."

Professor smiled self-consciously as he confided to Liah he referred to On Ping by his Fahn Gwai name 'Tom'. "Your youngest daughter told me he preferred it so." Liah grinned, saying Younger Daughter had also spoken to her about it.

"Did you know Jui Jinn opened his new café today?" asked Professor. "He ought to do well, situated on Ahlamedah Gai. He plans to serve not only our people but also the Fahn Gwai who work in the train yards, the stockyards and the stores around Chinatown. The place will be open twenty-four hours a day to catch all the different shifts of workers."

Liah nodded, saying she'd sent him the traditional evergreen plant with a ribbon expressing good fortune. Professor leaned back in his chair, taking a long draw from his pipe and slowly exhaling the gray smoke. "You know, I sense a profound change in Jui since he served in the war. I saw him on that first morning he returned home from the army. During our conversation, he spoke of how glad he was to be Chinese and how proud. He said he no longer feared the Fahn Gwai, for they were no better, no stronger and no braver than we are. In fact, he said he felt he was superior. He expressed anger at the discriminatory attitude of the Fahn Gwai even during the war. For example, he and the colored men were not welcome in the Fahn Gwai barracks and always drew the menial dirty work."

The scholar paused, then chuckled softly. When Liah asked what was so humorous, Professor told her how Jui Jinn had once been ordered to go to the river and draw water for the storage tanks. "It was an arduous task, but this day as he knelt at the river's edge filling the water buckets, he heard a deafening explosion behind him. When he turned his head to look, he was aghast. An enemy bomb had just leveled the entire camp."

For a long while, Liah waited for additional details, but Professor remained silent. It was as if he wanted to spare her the grisly information. When it was evident the subject was closed, Liah nodded and murmured, "Jui Jinn's Meng-Sui so decreed it."

Liah broke into Professor's silence and asked if he thought Jui Jinn should be their candidate for the vacant junior seat on the Council. Professor thought for a second, then shook his head. "No, despite Jui Jinn's maturity, I think Tom should be our junior member. With his training in the law, he can not only help our people with legal work, but he can also represent us and act as our liaison between Chinatown and the Fahn Gwai. However, there's still time for us to make up our minds."

A week after Jui Jinn's Café opened, Professor stopped in to wish him luck. True to his promise, Jinn insisted that the scholar be his guest for breakfast. When his plate arrived, Professor exclaimed, "My, what a huge slice of ham, and those eggs look so fresh with their deep yellow yolks."

Jinn's face reflected unspoken pride as he informed the scholar that the ham was imported from Chicago and that the eggs came fresh daily from a nearby ranch. "They are brown eggs, which are larger and better tasting. Would you like another serving of our freshly baked rolls? My brother is an accomplished baker. How about a taste of his egg custard pie? Nobody in Chinatown has as fine a custard pie." Professor assured Jinn that he believed him, but said that once he ate what he already had in front of him he would surely be too full. "I'll try them at another time. Thank you."

Professor glanced around the dining room and inquired if Jinn needed any employees. "Perhaps you could use a dishwasher or a waiter for the late shift? I happen to know a worthy young man who is trying to work his way through college. His name is Tom Soo." Jinn replied that indeed he'd heard about Tom and that if the young man needed it, Jinn would be more than happy to help.

—

Shortly after the opening of Jui Jinn's Café, two new Tongs opened their doors in Chinatown: the Hop Sing Tong located on Dragon's Den Road just off Blind Man's Alley, and the Bing Goong Tong headquartered in Lion's Den Alley. Attending the lavish free buffet luncheon celebrating the establishment of both Tongs, Professor smiled as he spoke to the attendees and admitted to perhaps having drunk too much of the fine liquor present. As the representative of the Council, he welcomed each Tong and stated that he hoped peace would continue to prevail, as there was ample room for two more Tongs in Loo Sahng. Though he did not say it directly, he strongly hinted that the Council would not tolerate any violence between feuding groups.

A short time later, Liah was shocked to learn that her son-in-law, Toh, had joined the more aggressive Tong, the Bing Goongs. When confronted, Toh said, "That is not entirely true, honorable Mother. My older brother put me up for membership without my knowledge. I do not attend any of their meetings or functions because it is all I can do to work and support my family."

—

Chinatown during the year of nineteen hundred and nineteen grew more rapidly than at any other time. The new people, unable to find lodging in the heart of Chinatown, overflowed onto Fargo Alley and even to the far lengths of Alameda South.

Liah, with the influx of new people, was faced with problems of employment. It was, therefore, a great relief when the two competing butcher shops both enlarged and modernized their equipment and when two more grocery stores opened their doors. The competition between the two butchers was kept friendly until a third shop opened its doors on Marchesson Street. Then the owners of the two established butcher shops banded together to lower their prices in direct competition with the new shop. Professor just grinned at hearing the news and remarked, "Well, at least our elder residents will get to eat more meat."

One day, Cook came home from his shopping and announced that another café was going to open up the following month. "It seems because Jui Jinn is doing so well, a group of investors rented that empty store next door to the Fahn Gwai saloon on Ahlamedah Gai. Wong Sing is fronting the group, although I think the money is coming from the Soohng family."

"Nonetheless," murmured Liah, "the opening of so many new establishments will mean work for all the new people. I was becoming worried about the jobless newcomers."

"Well," sighed Professor, "I hear many of our people are now being hired by the meat packing companies along Mah Loo. That's where Tom's father is working."

During the ensuing lull in their conversation, Liah reached inside her tunic and brought out a letter. "I think this letter is from Cousin Shah, sir. Will you read it for me? Just skip the formalities and get straight to the news. What's going on in Dai Faw?"

Professor scanned the two pages, sighing as he shrugged. "Cousin Shah has confirmed the existence of a secret society, but as to the membership and the identity of the leader, he has reached a dead end. No one is talking or else they don't know anything."

Disappointed, in a resigned tone Liah said, "I was hoping he could shed some light on the situation, but if Cousin Shah can't find out anything, then nobody can. I suppose we must just do as he has counseled us, keep a sharp watch and take precautions."

"I was just thinking, Liah," murmured Professor, "in his earlier letter, Cousin Shah spoke of the investigation in which the Four Families Tong was involved. I can't help but think the punishment decreed for the perpetrator was death. Remember the newspaper article I read to you recently, about the two youths found slain in Ross Alley? Well, one of the youths was from the Four Families Tong and the other from the House of Lee. Can it be a coincidence?"

Cook was solemn; for it bothered him that nobody had stepped forward to give the two youths a proper burial. He shook his head. "Never to know eternal peace. I don't care what crimes they may have committed, at least one of our people should have done something for them."

Liah's rebuttal was fierce as she denounced the two murdered youths. "If they were cooperating with the Fahn Gwai authorities against their own people, they deserve what they got! What frightens me is that perhaps this secret society has gone underground. I wonder how Elder Hua Fong of the Four Families Tong can be so certain that the dissident group has been disbanded."

Professor prepared to leave. "Liah," he advised, "worry does not help and also saps your energies. Let time reveal the answers to these mysteries. Always, no matter how clever or how careful they are, some-one will slip up and the truth will come out. Meanwhile, Cook, do not grieve over the two dead youths. Their Meng-Sui will decree their fates in the hereafter. Well, I'll see you two tomorrow."

The next day, when Professor came for tea, Liah straightaway an-nounced that the time had come to read Cousin Shah's two letters at the next Council meeting. "I did a lot of thinking during the night and the conclusion I came to is that we should allow Tzo and his cohorts to know that we are aware of this secret dissident group and that their ac-tivities are not as secret as they think." Holding up a hand to forestall Professor's objection, Liah went on. "They don't know how little we re-ally know, so when you read the two letters it might frighten them into giving something away. You might even say we've received other in-formation, but that we can't divulge it lest we give away the name of our informant. I'm almost positive it will work, sir."

Professor thought for a moment and then reluctantly nodded his as-sent. "I suppose it can't hurt our cause. I don't think Tzo is shrewd enough to see through our bluff. He is overly confident and focused on what he sees as certain success."

Cook, noticing Professor's obvious tension, gave Liah a look and then changed the subject. "Let's discuss the nomination of Tom for the junior seat on the Council,"

Liah's face brightened. "Yes, let's think of Tom Soo instead of that scoundrel Tzo. We need to think of a good reason to justify the token pay-ment we're going to attach to the seat; otherwise Tom will think we're taking pity on him. That young man's pride makes this so difficult."

"What about Tzo and Wong Sang? Won't they object to Tom?" Cook asked.

Liah's face darkened. "Neither man would dare to object, not at the risk of a public tongue-lashing." A silence descended as each of them tried to work out a solution to the problem of how to help Tom without Tzo or Sang making it sound like charity. Finally, a smile crossed Liah's face. "I know! At our next meeting I want you, sir, to recommend amending the Tenet of Laws. Explain to the members that the young man who serves as the junior member on the Council will be serving an apprenticeship and apprenticeships typically come with a token wage. If the men want to know why we should pay a token wage, just tell them that young men of that age commonly do not have much money and to serve on the Council would diminish their wage-earning time. The token wage will be compensation for their service to the Council."

Professor smiled. "Excellent idea! I also had it in mind to find out if Tom reads or writes Chinese. Since my classes are larger now, I'd like to hire him as my assistant teacher. For that, I will pay him twenty dollars a month."

Liah quickly objected. "No, sir! If you need an assistant, the Council will pay for one. It is not necessary that you take money from your own pocket." Surprisingly, Professor shook his head and responded, "Liah, I don't want to appear unappreciative, but I'd like to help Tom personally. In that way, when Tom becomes an attorney, I would feel in some small measure that my life would not have been in vain."

Suddenly, Liah became keenly aware of Professor's feelings of futility with respect to his accomplishments in life and her compassion surged. In China, Professor's position in the village would have been one of prestige and honor. That his life in Gem Sahn was so humble and anonymous both saddened and angered Liah. Why couldn't the Gods have been kinder to such a man? She smiled at once and agreed.

Professor voiced his thanks and then said, "Would the tenth day of December be suitable for a lunch with Tom? We can then seat the young man at our *Nien-Mei* (year-end) meeting."

"Yes, that will do nicely. Please forward the luncheon invitation to

Tom for me. And if you do not mind, sir, I'd like you to be present as well."

LIAH, PROFESSOR AND TOM

The day was cold, windy and dark with low clouds threatening rain as Tom made his way down Marchesson Street to Number Three in Peacock Alley. He had not wanted to go, but his uncle had insisted. "She is not one to ignore, Tom. Who knows? With her patronage, your goal of becoming a lawyer might become a step closer."

Tom was thoroughly chilled by the time he reached Peacock Alley. His vest and sweater provided but little insulation against the biting winds. As soon as he set foot inside Number Three, he saw Liah sitting in her upholstered chair. Noting his red hands, Liah smiled and urged him to come into the kitchen to warm up. Tom followed without a word, finding Liah's piercing eyes somewhat disconcerting.

As he stood in front of the stove warming his hands, Tom fought the impulse to bolt and run. He could think of no reason why Liah should want to entertain him socially. If this was so, then why was he here? When the front door opened and shut, Tom was surprised to see Professor enter. Well, he thought, at least he would not be alone with Liah.

During their luncheon, Professor was impressed by Tom's knowledge of the Chinese classics and by the young man's manners. Liah also approved of Tom's polite use of chopsticks, taking food only from the section of the serving dishes immediately in front of him. Her observations revealed Tom's preference for steamed pork with squid and she repeatedly plied him with generous portions until he politely declined any more.

As they ate, Professor spoke briefly of Chinatown's history, starting with the ugly massacre by the Fahn Gwai to the present day. It surprised Tom to learn that Liah was a comparative newcomer, having only been a resident for the last six years. When he learned that the Council was Liah's conception, including the Tenet of Laws, Tom's admiration for the tiny woman began to grow. Professor concluded his historical summary, saying, "Peacock Alley was a drab, dusty little alley when Liah, against all odds and in the face of ridicule, revived both the greenery and the neighborhood."

Tom's ears perked up as he heard Professor lament that he had been born too soon. "I would give anything to have been born in your generation, Tom. It must be wonderful to be able to speak, read and write the Fahn Gwai's language, and to be able to go to college and take up the law. I envy you."

Tom frowned, having it on the tip of his tongue to contradict the scholar, but he remembered where he was. Life for him was not so different from previous generations; he was still a yellow man. His voice was respectful as he replied, "Sir, I have not lived through the perils of your generation, but in my short life I, too, have felt the Fahn Gwai's prejudice and suffered their scorn and injustice. I understand what it means to be Chinese."

This discussion suddenly brought to mind his mother's untimely death and melted his usual reticence. "I vividly recall my mother's illness and her sudden death after the Fahn Gwai took her to the Fahn Gwai hospital over my father's objections. As a young boy, I saw the fear in the eyes of our people who stood by passively as they carried my mother out on a stretcher and put her into the ambulance. It was as if our lives and desires meant nothing to the Fahn Gwai. Once I am a lawyer, I will devote my time to prevent just such injustice. I swear it!"

As he spoke, Tom's voice had become laden with emotion and charged with anger. When the force of his emotions crested, Tom blushed. Heretofore, he had never allowed anyone to catch a glimpse of his unbridled anger. Liah gently touched his wrist. "Let us speak no more of sorrow or anger for now. Please eat some more. How about another serving of steamed pork? The lobster is also very good."

Tom relaxed and his shame over having lost his self-control subsided. Somehow Liah's touch, her voice, but mostly her eyes seemingly filled with understanding, put him at ease. Tom felt a sudden release of the tension he had felt since he had arrived. At the end of the meal, Cook announced that there was custard pie for dessert. Tom responded, "Oh, sir, I've overeaten and have no room left, not even for custard pie, which is my favorite dessert." At Cook's look of disappointment, Tom grinned and capitulated. "However, I'm sure I could handle just a small piece."

Touched by Tom's sensitivity to Cook's disappointment, Liah smiled. She searched her mind for a way to bring up the junior seat on the Council without arousing Tom's suspicions that she was trying to help him. The opportunity came when Professor asked Tom how he planned to support himself. Tom's smile vanished as he confided that he was waiting for word from a Fahn Gwai department store regarding his application for a job as a night janitor. "If I do not get that job, I'll probably work nights in a café or restaurant in Chinatown, that is, if I can find such a job."

Liah exclaimed, "Oh, Tom, you're so thin now. What will those long hours do to your health?" Tom chuckled and replied, "Madam Liah, I've always been thin. I'll be fine, I'm used to long hours and hard work."

"Tom," continued Liah, "you said you wanted to help our people after you got your law degree. Perhaps you wouldn't mind working with your own people even now."

Tom tugged his left ear, a habit Liah was later to recognize as signifying serious thought on Tom's part. "I know perhaps my hopes are too high," Tom said, his voice dropping to almost a whisper. "But I would like to try. If I fail, I will at least have picked up enough knowledge to be of help when I am a lawyer. Besides, by helping someone now, I'll be making up for not being able to help my mother before."

Professor caught Liah's glance. Now was the time to speak of the junior seat on the Council. Professor carefully chose his words. "Tom, it just so happens that we have a seat on the Council for a deserving young man who will represent the youth of Chinatown. By accepting the post, you would be in a position to make known the problems faced by our youth. You could also identify the needs of the young and help determine how best to satisfy them. Would you like to join us?"

Tom tugged at his left ear again and thought a moment. He then blurted, "Are you forgetting I am only nineteen years old, sir? Don't you think I'm too immature and inexperienced to take on such an important assignment?"

Liah smiled and Professor shook his head. "I think you're more intelligent than you give yourself credit for, Tom. You will do fine. I should also mention that there is a token wage that comes with the job. It's not much, just twenty dollars a month."

Seeing the uncertainty on Tom's face, Liah quickly explained. "Tom, the seat is really just a method to train young men in the workings of government and to make them aware of their duties toward our people. That is something I think you have already learned. The seat carries with it no voting power. It is really just an apprenticeship. Why not give it a try?"

Tom then smiled. "Fair enough, Madam Liah. I'll accept, with the understanding that if the duties of the seat interfere with my studies or if I cannot do the job, I can quit without ill feelings."

Professor chuckled. "Fair enough, Tom. There is, however, one more thing I'd like to speak to you about. How is your knowledge of the Chinese language?"

Tom paused, tugging at his left ear again. "My Chinese, sir? Well, my uncle forced me to go to Chinese school as well as Fahn Gwai school, and I attended for almost five and a half years. While I can read and write and I know a little of the classics, I am not what you would call an expert."

"Well," explained Professor, "with the influx of new residents into Chinatown, my classes are now too large for one teacher. We also have a new, larger school, currently being refurbished, that will open soon.

I badly need an assistant. Would you be willing to give the post a try? There is not much money involved, again only twenty dollars a month. While I'm certain you'd earn more with the Fahn Gwai, I hope you realize the great impact you could have on our youth. By teaching in the Chinese school, you would be in a position to teach the kids not only Chinese but English as well. You know of course that too many of our children struggle in Fahn Gwai school because of the language barrier. Will you at least think on it, Tom?"

Liah intuitively knew the youth was calculating in his mind how far the twenty dollars from the Council seat and the twenty dollars from the school would go toward meeting his monthly needs. Tom asked, "Are you positive there would be no adverse feelings if I find that I cannot continue in either position? I do not want to make enemies, sir."

A sudden loud clap of thunder drowned out Professor's answer, but Tom saw the scholar nod. A bright flash of lightning was followed by another clap of thunder, and suddenly a torrent of water hit the room's skylight. "My, such a cloudburst. I hope our streets won't be washed out again. It gets so messy," continued Professor.

Just then the front door opened and slammed. A few moments later, Fifth Son burst into the kitchen, water sluicing down his slicker. Rain that had collected on the brim of his rain hat also poured onto the linoleum floor. Liah shrieked, "Son, go take off your rain clothes, and mop up the floor!"

Mert handed his wet clothes to Cook and then turned and gazed at Tom. Although he'd met Tom when his family had visited Liah on an earlier courtesy call, it surprised him to see Tom having lunch with his mother. Mert grinned, "I hope you wore rain clothes, Tom. It's pouring cats and dogs now."

Tom shook his head and said that he'd be all right; he was used to wet weather. Mert told Tom he had an old raincoat and boots that did not fit him any more. "You're welcome to have them if you want. I'll get them and you can try them on."

Tom grinned as he tried on the raincoat and boots. "Hey, they fit, Mert. The boots are a little big, but I can stuff a bit of newspaper in the toe."

"Great, Tom. Look inside the pocket. I think there may be gloves, a scarf and a hat, too. I'm always too lazy to go looking for them, so I just kept them in my pockets."

Tom found the items and glanced up at the skylight. Smiling to everyone he said, "Thanks again. Now that I'm all prepared for the weather, I'd better get home. I've got a lot of studying to do. I thank you, Madam Liah, for lunch and I hope to do justice to the trust you and Professor have placed in me."

Cook stood by the kitchen door leading to the corridor. He held out a box to Tom and said, "This is a custard pie. I thought your aunt and uncle might enjoy it. Perhaps you should consider waiting until the rain subsides a bit. The pie might get soaked."

However, just then Professor handed Tom his umbrella. "I have no intention of venturing out in this downpour, so please use my umbrella, son. I have another at home."

Once Tom had left, Liah embarrassed Mert by commending him on giving his rain clothes to Tom. He demurred, saying, "What's so great about giving away clothes that don't fit me any more? I'm just happy Tom can make use of them. He'll need something during the rainy months." At that, Cook motioned for Fifth Son to be seated. "I'll just re-heat some food for you."

Liah and Professor then turned their attention to coming up with a strategy for seating Tom on the Council. Listening, Mert glanced up, looking pleased. "Tom on the Council, Mah-Mah? That's great. He'll make a fine addition."

Liah smiled and warned her son to keep the news to himself, at least until the Council members had accepted Tom. Liah chuckled. "I think we should get Wong Cheung to nominate Tom. I'd like to see Tzo's face when Wong Cheung makes the nomination. What do you think, sir?"

Professor, having considered Wong Cheung himself, beamed. "An excellent choice, Liah. Will you ask Wong Cheung or shall I?" Liah replied, "I will do it as he is due to telephone me this week. When he does, I'll ask him to be present at our Nien-Mei meeting to perform this task."

Professor glanced up at the wall clock, moaning that he still had so much to do. "I must get home to finish the bulletin for today, but I fear it is still raining heavily."

Cook cracked open the rear door and peered out. A sudden blast of cold air brought in a sheet of rain, which soaked both Cook and the floor. Fifth Son guffawed and said to Professor, "Sir, this weather is only fit for ducks. Who will go outdoors to read the bulletin anyway? You might as well stay here and enjoy our hospitality."

Professor settled back in his chair, agreeing that this was not exactly the right moment to leave.

LIAH'S TRIUMPH

The Council met on the twenty-eighth day of December in the Fahn Gwai year of nineteen hundred and nineteen in a Nien-Mei meeting to close the books on the year. When notified of the session, Chon informed Professor that he and Lee Tzo had conceived a plan that would lessen Liah's Council burdens. In a hurry at the time, Professor merely nodded and advised Chon that there would be time to speak of it when the Council met.

Liah frowned when Chon and Lee Tzo arrived at the meeting early. So, she thought, their strategy was to present the plan to her before the others got there. That way she would have no one to come to her aid. Thus, when Tzo silkily purred that he had a plan that would lighten her duties as chairman, Liah waved him off. "We shall hear of your plan after the others arrive. Save your breath for them, Tzo."

Tzo, however, was not to be deterred and rushed on. "We just wanted you to hear the idea first. We thought that, if the town were to be dissected into four parts with two Council members overseeing each sector, your job as chairman would be lightened. Only for emergencies or grave policy matters would the Council need to act as a whole. Once a month, each pair of Council members would report to the Council as a whole on the status of their sector. What do you think, Liah?"

Liah, seeing clearly what the outcome of such a move would be, merely shrugged her shoulders. "It doesn't matter what I think, Tzo. The Council members will decide on the issue."

Lee Tzo's eyes narrowed and his tone hardened. "You know very well that if the men know you approve of this plan, they'll vote for it."

Liah stiffened, her eyes glittering. "Are you insinuating that I can sway the voting?"

Chon Woo glared at Tzo and attempted to placate Liah. "We mean no such thing, Liah. Lee Tzo is clumsy and doesn't express himself very well. Frankly, I don't know how he inveigled me into sponsoring such an idea, but he did. You're right, we will let the membership decide."

The pimp glowered and the expression in his eyes left no doubt that Lee Tzo thought Chon was a cowardly traitor. However, the opportunity for further discussion disappeared as the other members of the Council had started to arrive and were coming up the stairs.

Professor had already started going over the ending ledger balances when Wong Cheung entered the chamber. Liah motioned for him to be seated and a motion of her hand indicated that it was unnecessary for him to explain his tardiness. At the end of the accounting, the men signed their names to the record. Then Professor casually picked up a page from the *Dai Faw See Bo* and began to speak. Lee Tzo's face paled slightly when he heard the scholar's account of how a secret dissident group of hoodlums had tried to unseat the elders of the House of Lee, threatening violence and threatening to expose those who would not cooperate as illegal immigrants to the Fahn Gwai authorities.

The room quieted as Professor next read the two letters from Cousin Shah, which fleshed out the details of the news item. As he read the letter detailing the hearing conducted in the Six Companies headquarters in conjunction with the House of Lee, there was a sudden outbreak of oaths. Professor continued reading. "The joint hearing was necessary because one of the youths involved was a member of the Six Companies as well as a member of the House of Lee. After the investigation was completed, it is rumored that grave decisions were rendered, but no one except the judges know exactly what punishments were handed down. A writ has now been issued that the dissidents disband, or else they will be subject to dire consequences."

Finally, Professor picked up another newspaper and read a clipping dealing with the two bodies that had been discovered in Ross Alley. "I do not know if these deaths were a result of the joint hearing, but the dates coincide too closely to be mere coincidence. Liah believes that the hearing and the presumed punishment ought to serve as an example for anyone who involves themselves in subversive activities."

When Professor suggested that the Council consider protecting Liah from harm, Lee Tzo eagerly leaped to his feet. "You're right, sir! I think a guard should be posted in front of Number Three. That would surely set my mind at ease."

Liah almost laughed at Lee Tzo's transparent effort to exonerate himself. "I thank you, sir, but a guard will not be necessary. Besides, I do not want the stupid ruffians to think I might be afraid. No, no guard! My sons and Cook are all the protection I need. Now, Professor, let us proceed with business."

Taking his cue, Professor began, "It has been on my mind that the Tenet of Laws should be amended with respect to the junior seat. The amendment would better reflect the value we place on that member of the Council, There is a clause in our bylaws that stipulates that the junior

Council member shall receive a token payment of ten dollars a month, which I feel is not sufficient. I propose that we ratify a change of that sum to twenty dollars a month. Because it is such a small issue, I think a vote by show of hands might be in order. Are there any comments?"

Chon, who had not missed Lee Tzo's previous effort to put himself in a better light by suggesting a guard for Liah, now leaped to his feet. "Why bother with a discussion, sir? I think the idea is a good one. Even twenty dollars a month might not be enough. We need to encourage our youth to serve their community."

With that, the men quickly and unanimously ratified the amendment, and a twenty-dollar token wage was established for the junior member. Liah then glanced at the clock and suggested that they have supper before continuing with the rest of the Council business. Lee Tzo, however, declared that he had an issue that should be discussed first. Without waiting for agreement, he began spelling out his idea.

"Chon and I have come up with a plan to alleviate the stress placed on Liah by her duties relating to the Council." Lim Tao and Lee Wah gaped at the pimp as he proceeded to outline his plan to dissect Chinatown into four equal parts, with two Council members to administer to the needs of each sector. Lee Tzo finished up by saying, "In this way Liah and the Council wouldn't be constantly burdened with petty problems."

Wong Sang gasped, leaped to his feet and pointed an accusing finger at Tzo. "Relieve Liah? It's obvious that you and Chon just want to divide up the town and grab more power for yourselves. The Council was formed to prevent exactly this kind of divisive action. I say no!"

Professor then whirled on Chon Woo. "You ungrateful man! How could you side with another to strip Liah and the Council of its stated purpose? I know Lee Tzo probably conceived this plan, but did you have to stoop so low as to be a part of it? I, too, say no. Throw this plan out! It does not even merit continued discussion."

Lee Tzo, already shocked by the scholar's vehement outburst, was astounded when Professor actually lunged for Chon Woo. Kam Fong and Lee Wah restrained Professor as he turned his anger on Lee Tzo, asking, "I would like to know why you came to Loo Sahng, Lee. Surely there are more of our people in Dai Faw, and you could make so much more money there. Why come here?"

Wong Sang shouted, "Yeah, answer Professor's question. Why did you come here, Tzo?"

In the midst of this conflict, Wong Cheung quietly stood and admonished the group to remain calm. In the ensuing silence he said, "I believe that every motion, good or bad, should be voted on. That way, it becomes an official part of our records. I recommend that at this time we take a vote on the proposition."

Once the votes were counted, the final tally was seven to one and the plan was defeated. Lee Tzo glared fiercely at Chon and silently vowed revenge on the bar owner. Chon returned Lee's combative stare.

After the vote, Liah glanced around the table and asked for a moment of the Council's time. "For those of you who do not know me well, I'd like to tell you a bit of my history. In my earlier days in Dai Faw, I suffered Fahn Gwai persecution and even attempts to kill my family and me. On the fifth such attempt, after the Fahn Gwai had burned our house and ruined our crops, we came to Loo Sahng, only to find the same circumstances prevailed here. That is why I conceived the idea of the Council and a sentry system to protect ourselves from the barbarians and to ensure a permanent peaceful place for our children to live and bring up their children."

She stopped, took in a deep breath and continued. "With Kwan Koong's help, we shall reach our objectives. I am more determined than ever that our security needs be met. We should let no one undermine us, for if we do not stand together, we shall perish apart. I am, and shall remain, dedicated for the rest of my life to a unified Chinatown."

Once Liah finished, Kam Fong, usually silent, stood up and faced the men. "I would like to tell you what I know of Liah as well. I am not as well-versed as some of you in politics nor do I possess much power or prestige. I am but a simple man who wants only a safe place to live, without fear of Fahn Gwai violence. I remember how things were before Liah came. Each person was out for himself, acting without regard for any other. Now we sleep undisturbed; now we have a temple and the Adversity Fund for the sick, aged or needy; now our children have a decent school. Moreover, I think of all the jobs and lodging she's secured for our new residents. That is all I have to say."

Lim Tao was mindful as Kam spoke of how Liah had also helped him establish his store in Peacock Alley. She had told the landlord that Lim was her friend so that he could receive lower rent.

In the reflective silence that followed Kam's speech, Wong Cheung stood and solemnly asked if he could make an additional motion before breaking for their meal. Lee Tzo frowned and waited, ready to attack whatever plan was put forth. He knew Cheung was only doing Liah's bidding. "As we discussed previously, there is a provision in the Tenet of Laws that provides that a deserving young man can hold a seat on the Council. It happens that I know of just such a young man. His name is On Ping, the nephew of Soo Dack On. On Ping is going to law school; he aspires to become a lawyer so that he might help his people in the Fahn Gwai courts. The fact that he is working to put himself through school without accepting financial aid from his uncle is exemplary. He is a good role model for our youngsters. Therefore, I offer up his name for consideration for the junior Council member seat."

Professor informed the men that On Ping's Fahn Gwai name was Tom and that he preferred to be called Tom. "Shall we take a vote on Tom?"

During the vote, Liah took note of the sneer on the pimp's face that implied that he knew that Tom was really her handpicked choice. No matter, thought Liah happily, Lee Tzo could no longer do any harm.

There was a murmur as the men congratulated Cheung on seating Tom. Professor noted how fitting it was that their year-end session should seat a youth who would someday represent the next generation. Chon Woo was first to quip, "Now that we will have an attorney in our midst, we can get our legal work done without cost. Cheung, that was a smart nomination."

Liah raked the bar owner with fiery eyes. "There shall be no such arrangement, Chon! We shall pay for all our legal counseling as usual. The only difference will be that Tom will charge our people less than the Fahn Gwai charge us, and he will have our best interests at heart. Is that clear to everyone? Now, let us have supper."

At the supper table, Wong Sang maliciously needled Tzo and Chon. "Come on, the two of you. Be good losers. Just because your plan to partition Chinatown failed, that's no reason for such a hostile attitude. Enjoy your supper, it's delicious."

Chon fawned over Liah and with a certain unease she observed the vengeful look Tzo gave him. Chon's quick shift in loyalty was a dangerous move and Liah made a note to herself to warn the bar owner.

Supper done, the records were signed by each member. Lee Tzo hurriedly brushed his name, nodded curtly to Liah and without a word strode from the chamber. Only when he was outside on the cobblestone walk did Lee Tzo allow his fury to emerge. Cook saw him repeatedly smack his fists into his palms as he marched toward his brothel. However, if Cook could have glimpsed Tzo's thoughts, he'd also have seen Tzo's fright as he recalled Professor's mention of the two dead men in Ross Alley.

When they were alone, Professor apologized to Liah for his outburst. "The man is infuriating! I know it was stupid to show Tzo how I really feel, but I am not a saint."

Liah smiled gently. "No harm done, sir. I think the others all felt the same way. I feel sorry for Mei-Mei, for certainly Tzo will take out his fury on her."

Professor made no comment. He yet recalled how Liah had railed at him for making a derogatory remark about another concubine. He was of the belief that, since Mei-Mei received so many jewels and gowns from Tzo, she had no call to complain of mistreatment once in a while. However, he wasn't going to allow Liah to know his feelings. Experiencing her disfavor once was enough.

Fortunately, Liah did not divine his thoughts as she said, "Professor, why don't you stay and share supper with Cook and me? I know you did not eat much due to the stressful nature of tonight's meeting."

The scholar nodded, thinking that Liah had correctly sensed his need for more conversation to alleviate the tension of this night. Besides, he really hadn't eaten much at supper.

1920

YEAR OF THE MONKEY

A YOUTHFUL BEGINNING

Tom Soo was officially seated at the first meeting of the Council in the Fahn Gwai year of nineteen hundred and twenty, the Chinese Year of the Monkey. Lim Tao and Kam Fong flanked Tom at the table, a precaution Professor felt necessary should Lee Tzo be unfriendly or, worse, whisper falsehoods against Liah or try to enlist Tom in his schemes.

Liah, her face wreathed in a smile, officially welcomed Tom and in turn introduced all the Council members around the table. "Although On Ping is his Chinese name, Tom is usually known by his Fahn Gwai name. So, if we call him Tom, all of us will speak at least one Fahn Gwai word."

Wong Cheung, sitting opposite Tom, smiled his welcome. "If only one of my sons were half as studious, half as hard-working and half as knowledgeable of our traditions, my heart would be overflowing with pride, and I would thank Kwan Koong eternally. I'd deem it an honor if, in the future, you'd come to me with any of your needs, Tom."

Liah did not miss Lee Tzo's frown as the big man voiced his support of Tom. She also suspected that the big man knew well that his open patronage of Tom provided some protection against anyone who might object to Tom's presence on the Council.

Following the introductions and welcome, Professor asked for each member's copy of the Tenet of Laws in order to add Tom's signature. Lim Tao watched as Tom brushed his name onto the copies and remarked, "Young man, I must commend you. You not only know how to write Chinese, but you do it very well." Tom smiled as he handed the assayer back his copy of the Laws. "Sir, I have my uncle to thank for that. He was the one who insisted that I attend Chinese school for over five years."

Wong Cheung, last to sign the records, turned to Tom and said, "I want you to know that I meant what I said earlier about helping you. I truly would consider it an honor to help such a fine young man as yourself."

Tom smiled, thanking the big man. Liah asked Tom to stay a moment; she had something for him. After Cheung had left, he turned to Liah and Professor. "I know that man's name is Wong Cheung, but who is he?" A twinkle in his eyes, Professor replied, "He is a former hatchet man, but is now an upright, loyal member of our Council, as well as having been an elder in the House of Wong before coming here. He is the man who nominated you to your seat, Tom."

Seeing concern appear on Tom's face, Liah quickly added, "Do not worry, Tom. Wong Cheung was a hatchet man in his youth but has not been in that profession for years. Nevertheless, with him on your side, you need never worry about yourself. He meant it when he said he would provide you with whatever assistance you need."

Alone with Professor and Liah, Tom suddenly felt uncomfortable once more. What did Madam Liah want of him now? He thought briefly of excusing himself, saying he had more homework to finish before he called it a day, but just then Liah leaned back in her chair, reached inside her pocket and withdrew a pouch. She then proceeded to take out two crisp ten-dollar bills and laid them in front of Tom. "This is your consideration for the month as the junior Councilman. You will receive the same amount on the first of each month."

Professor chuckled. "I think tonight might have been your lucky night. You got paid and you received the patronage of Wong Cheung."

Tom stared at the twin ten-dollar bills and suddenly felt reassured that he'd done the right thing by joining the Council and assisting with the Chinese school. Then Liah's voice penetrated his thoughts. "Tom, please consider this house as a second home. It would be our pleasure if you would take supper with the family whenever you like. We usually eat about six-thirty or seven o'clock at night. If work or college keeps you from coming at that time, there is always food in the house and Cook would be delighted to reheat some supper for you. Promise me you will make it a point to come."

When Tom nodded his agreement, Liah smiled and exclaimed, "Good! You need to put some meat on your bones. You're too skinny to have the strength to withstand long days of work and study. A young man also needs a family, a place he can call home and someone to lean on in times of crisis. I should be proud if you'll allow me to do for you what your mother is no longer here to do. Now, I'll bid you good night as I'm sure you have studies to complete."

Professor and Tom went down the stairs and made their way to the cobblestones. Shrouded in darkness, Peacock Alley looked like myriad shadows piled on top of more shadows. They proceeded to the entrance of the alley where Professor suddenly asked Tom if he had time for a walk. "What about you and me take a walk around Chinatown? That way you'll have an opportunity to meet some people you should get to know as a member of the Council. Let's surprise Chon at The Dragon's Den Bar."

Tom was not in the mood to drink but did not want to hurt the scholar's feelings, so he agreed. When they entered the crowded bar, Tom immediately clapped his hands to his ears as the sound threatened to overwhelm his senses. The scholar steered him through the noisy crowd and pointed to the stairs. Once on the landing, Professor explained, "Chon calls this his office, but in truth it's his bedroom. I should also caution you that Chon likes to brag a lot, so pay little heed to what he might say."

Tom shouted back, "Sir, how does Chon manage to stand this noise?" Professor smiled and responded, "It's all about the money." Chon opened his bedroom door and saw Professor and Tom. He motioned for them to follow him down to a somewhat secluded area of the bar below. "The crowd will thin out soon. What an honor to have you two in my establishment. The drinks are on me."

Around one o'clock, Wong Sang came through the door, stopping in his tracks when he spied Professor and Tom. "You, sir, out on the town? Professor, are you changing your habits in your old age?"

Tom's head was spinning and he'd lost count of the number of drinks he'd consumed, but he did know that he hadn't paid for a single one. Tom giggled and replied, "Elder Brother Sang, I am afraid I'm to blame for Professor's late hours. He suggested that I should acquaint myself with the town, but I must confess that we've not been anywhere else but here."

The gambler roared. "Well, Tom, this is the only worthwhile place in town to have a drink. Say, how would you like to go to Tzo's brothel? I'll introduce you to some of the girls." Tom's face flushed as he shook his head. "No thank you, sir. I don't want to get used to luxuries I cannot afford. I'll be better off embracing my books rather than a woman."

Professor had stiffened, fearing Tom might insult Sang, but he relaxed as he listened to Tom's polite refusal. Tom, he thought, was going to be just fine. "How's that, Sang, for knowing his priorities?"

The gambler laughed self-consciously and leaned forward to nudge Tom. "So what do you think of our chairwoman?" Without waiting for an answer, Sang went on in mock seriousness. "I'd advise you to walk a straight line when she's around or else our empress will take you to task." Slapping Tom on the back, Sang roared at his own joke. "An empress of Chinatown! What a laugh, eh?"

Professor pursed his lips, his expression warning Sang to watch his tongue in front of Tom. However, Sang just sneered back, indicating to the scholar that he would say anything he pleased. Despite his tipsy condition, Tom became aware of the sudden tension in the air. If there was one thing he didn't want, it was to get embroiled in Madam Liah's conflicts. Tom simply shrugged and muttered a simple, "Yeah." Professor suggested that they take their leave and visit some of the other establishments in Chinatown.

Later, at Wong's Café, Professor beamed at the junior Council member. "Tom, you've survived your first encounter with one of the senior Council members and I must say you acquitted yourself admirably. Sang was obviously baiting you, but you neither insulted him nor backed down. I am most impressed!"

Tom ate wordlessly, thinking hard about what he'd just gotten himself into. Professor continued, "As for Liah, I would not expect you to fully understand her or her motivations. However, in time I'm sure you'll come to know Liah for what she is and what she stands for. You should know that I believe that she is an exceptional woman with a large heart despite having a fiery temper. If I were to have to balance Liah's character on the scales, I'd say her good traits outweigh her bad ones."

After leaving Wong's Café, the cool night air helped to further clear Tom's head and he inquired about the expensive-looking establishment at the junction of Marchesson Street and Peacock Alley.

"Oh, that's Selah's place," said Professor. "You'll like her, Tom. Between Selah and Liah, it's hard to say who has the bigger heart or sharper mind."

"Selah? That's an unusual name. What kind of place does she run?"

"A brothel, Tom. Not an ordinary brothel, like Tzo's, but an expensive and very exclusive brothel. Selah caters to the Fahn Gwai, with many famous and powerful Fahn Gwai among her clients. Say, let's go inside and I'll introduce you."

Tom was reluctant, but once again he did not want to insult the scholar. "All right, sir, but just for a short while. I yet have studies to finish."

Standing on the landing of the stairs, Selah squealed with delight when she saw Professor come in. Tom stood frozen in the entryway, awestruck. Selah, her flaming red hair accentuated by a jade green silk cheongsam, took him utterly by surprise. She appeared to be nothing less than a fiery goddess in the flesh. Selah rushed up to embrace Professor and then turned a radiant smile on Tom. "Ah, let me guess. You must be Tom. Liah has spoken highly of you and told me that tonight you were to be officially seated on the Council. Congratulations, Tom. Let's have a drink to celebrate."

She linked her arms with Professor and Tom and led them into the dimly lit bar. Tom was grateful for the semi-darkness, as he was sure his face must be beet red. He toyed with his drink, thinking about how gorgeous Selah was.

Selah, seated between the scholar and Tom, sensed a reticence in Tom along with a strange sadness and wondered at the reason. The ensuing conversation was mostly one-sided, with Selah asking questions and Tom answering with one or two words. It wasn't until Selah asked about his curriculum that Tom's reserve broke momentarily. He told her excitedly that he was pursuing a career in law and that he wanted to help the people of Chinatown upon graduation. For a moment, Selah thought she'd breached his wall, but Tom's shell closed again.

After a bit, Professor tapped Tom on the shoulder, pointing to the time. "Is it really already two o'clock, sir?" gasped Tom. "We really must be going." Selah leaned over, kissed Tom on the cheek, and whispered, "Darling, I like you. If ever you need a shoulder to lean on, I'd be honored if you would call me." Seeing reluctance in his eyes, Selah giggled and said, "Don't worry, darling, I don't bite."

Tom relaxed and murmured, "I thank you for the offer, Miss Selah, however, you might regret making it in the future."

"Call me Selah, please, dear. I meant what I said. Call me."

Once more on Marchesson Street, Professor noticed Tom's relaxed mood and said, "Didn't I tell you she was a force of nature?" Tom nodded and replied, "Selah is everything you said she was and more. Somehow she made me feel less nervous and less afraid; she seemed to understand my inner self better than I do. Do you know what I mean, sir?"

Professor chuckled and nodded sagely. Seeing Professor's sly smile, Tom stopped suddenly and whirled. "You were intending to take me to meet Selah all along, weren't you?" The scholar burst into laughter. "It was only a matter of time before you asked about Number One, so I thought I'd accelerate the process." Then turning serious, Professor continued, "I hope you will make a friend of Selah, Tom. Please do not allow her profession to deter you. You will find that she can be a valuable ally."

"Professor, do you think I'm a snob? Like Selah? Why, I think I love her!" Embarrassed, Tom lowered his voice and asked if Professor thought it would be proper for him to see Selah from time to time. "Tom," murmured Professor softly, "I believe Selah needs someone like you as much as you need her. Selah was educated not only in Gem Sahn but also in Hong Kong and Paris as well. Therefore, it is difficult for her to find people to converse with on her level. No, I think this friendship will serve you both. Go see her as often as you like, Tom." With that, Tom shook Professor's hand and bade him good night.

—

Jui Jinn's Café had quickly become a favorite hangout for the young men of Chinatown soon after it opened. Open all day, it was the kind of place where for twenty-five cents a person could eat a hearty meal anytime and afterwards sit and chat for hours. Jui Jinn's influence on the youths was only natural since he was a veteran of the Great War, he had traveled beyond California and China and he had served a tour of duty in France. As a consequence, Jinn was frequently sought out for his advice on many problems. In addition, as much as the youths loved hearing his adventure stories, they also resonated with his inner struggle between his allegiance to his Chinese heritage and his allegiance to Gem Sahn. The fact that Jinn was proud to be Chinese boosted their morale and gave them a sense of worth they had been lacking.

Tom felt a kinship with Jinn. Each morning before classes, Tom had breakfast at the café, bonding with the others his age. Most of the youths, if not all of them, were, like Tom, struggling to establish their identities. During their discussions, some of the young men plied Tom with questions about the difficulties associated with going to college and about the opportunities one had upon graduation. Some of the pessimists among them challenged Tom's goals, saying that he was a dreamer heading for a big fall. After all, why would a Fahn Gwai hire a Chinese lawyer over a Fahn Gwai lawyer? Such pessimism only hardened Tom's resolve and he redoubled his efforts, for not only did he have to succeed for his own sake but also for the sake of the youths who were watching him from the sidelines.

Mert, too, had discovered a kinship with the café owner. A month after his election to the Council, Tom entered Jinn's Café to find Mert and Jinn chatting at the counter. Tom joined them and listened as Mert spoke of his secret love affair with a girl named Cora. Mert despaired of the idea of letting his mother know of the affair inasmuch as the girl was too modern for his mother's taste. He just knew that his mother would never allow him to marry such a girl. Like Mert, Tom never confided in his uncle or aunt either. The older generation of Chinese could not and, in some cases, would not even try to understand how Tom and his generation felt. Tom felt sympathy for Mert. It was difficult straddling two such different cultures.

Mert asked Jinn if his older brother had ever tried to force him into marriage. Jinn laughed and said, "Yeah, many times, and we got into several fights about it. However, ever since I got back from the war, he's left me alone. He hasn't brought the subject up, even when our mother sends letters deploring my bachelorhood. I suppose your mother, Mert, is no different than mine. They expect us to be obedient children and to do whatever they think is best for us."

Jinn refilled their coffee cups, then poured a cup for himself before continuing. "You know, when I was in the trenches, I spent a lot of time thinking about death. If I had been killed, my family's bloodline would have stopped right there since my brother has no children. At first that made me sad and sorry that I had not married, but then I considered Meng-Sui. If my fate were to die without an heir, then it would be so. At that point, I made up my mind that I'd never marry unless I was in love."

Mert turned to Tom and remarked, "You're lucky, Tom. Your uncle and aunt aren't pushing you to get married. I suppose it's because you're still in school. You don't know what it's like to have your mother constantly on your back about marrying the right girl and having children to carry on the family name."

Tom took a sip of his coffee and considered his words before speaking. "In that way I guess I am lucky. However, I wish my mother were alive today and could see me graduate from law school. I'd put up with a lot to have that wish come true." There was a long silence, and then Tom glanced at his watch and said, "I've got to get to work, guys. Thanks for the coffee, Jinn. I'll see you later."

After Tom left, Jinn reached out to fill Mert's cup again, but Mert shook his head. "I have to get home. I promised Mah I'd put away the supplies, and you know how mothers are."

Jinn's last words of advice occupied Mert's thoughts as he made his way along Alameda South and onto Marchesson Street. "I'd advise you to stand by your convictions, Mert. The next time the subject comes up, tell your mother you'll marry only when the right girl comes along. If she persists, tell her you don't want to fight about it any more and you'll just have to move out. Your mother is a smart woman. She'll know you mean it. Either face up to her or shut up and do what she tells you. You have no other choice, Mert. I know that this situation is not easily resolved, but no one can help you except yourself. Good luck!"

As soon as Mert pushed open the doors to Number Three, his resolve to face up to his mother crumbled. Damn! He just couldn't bring himself to cause his mother pain after all the love and devotion she had shown him, even if it meant that he would continue suffering her incessant nagging and that he might not get to marry the girl he loved. By the time he entered the kitchen, it was as if he had never even entertained the idea of facing up to his mother.

Tom Soo's election to the Council erased Liah's fear that Lee Tzo might seat a man of his own, even a junior member. However, she was still worried that Lee Tzo might try to ensnare Tom in his schemes with a promise of personal rewards or by maligning her whenever he was alone with him. Cook instantly came to Tom's defense. "Have confidence in the young man's intelligence. Tom is too smart to be inveigled into Tzo's schemes. And as for Tzo maligning you, Professor will ensure that Tom gets the whole picture. You should put aside your worries."

Cook silently thanked Kwan Koong for bringing Tom into Liah's life. She now had another young man to mother which somewhat eased the burden on her other sons. Liah took to making certain Tom ate several meals a week with the family and was constantly checking on his health, as she was concerned that the weight of Tom's schoolwork, his teaching duties and his night janitorial job might sap his strength.

It occurred to Cook, however, that should Tom fail in his attempt to become an attorney, Liah would become inconsolable. When Cook brought up this concern with Professor and suggested that they explain to Tom just how much it meant to Liah that he succeed in becoming a lawyer, the scholar shook his head. "We cannot lay an extra burden on the poor boy. Liah is a strong woman and has survived heartbreak before and can again. Besides, it is my opinion that Tom will succeed in his endeavor. The young man is smart and has fully dedicated himself to his goal."

RAID ON WONG SANG'S PLACE

Hans Weigen arrived on the nineteenth of April to take responsibility for the Chinese settlement in Los Angeles. He had reluctantly left his home in San Francisco where, for the past twenty years, he had patrolled the Chinatown there. He reflected that he had been comfortable there. He knew every Chink by sight and he knew the area like the back of his hand, all the hideouts, all the escape routes and all the best restaurants. He had managed to keep his finger on the town's pulse and for the most part kept the Chinks in line. There was only one reason he had come to Los Angeles and that was to please his superior, Police Chief Walter Fields.

Chief Fields had informed Hans two weeks ago that Los Angeles Police Chief Henry Dobbs wanted to borrow his services for six months. Chief Fields had urged Hans to take the assignment, admitting that he owed Chief Dobbs a favor. "Who knows, Hans? You might even wind up liking the place. Didn't you say just last week that Frisco has gotten too tame for you? I guarantee that if you take the job and you don't like it, I'll get Chief Dobbs to return you no questions asked." Hans' first thought was that if he took this job, Chief Fields would wind up owing him a big favor, which was a handy thing to have in the bank. Then there was the fifteen percent raise in salary he would be getting along with blanket authority to handle things in Chinatown as he saw fit. The promise of getting his old job back if things didn't work out had sealed the deal and Hans accepted.

It was six in the evening when Hans walked into Chinatown and he had covered no more than two blocks on Marchesson Street when he spied a group of men converging on a dilapidated-looking doorway.

Hans recognized them as cops despite the fact that they were wearing plainclothes. He guessed correctly that they were about to raid a gambling joint. The man in charge pointed and four of the officers swiftly charged the door and kicked it in.

Inside, Wong Sang raised his hands over his head, staring blankly at the officer frisking him. How could this have happened? Where were his sentries? Why was there no warning? He watched helplessly as other officers efficiently cleaned off the tables by merely bundling everything up in the tablecloths. Sang's first impulse was to rush forward and claim everything as his personal property, but to do so, Sang realized, meant admitting ownership of the gambling house, which would surely land him in jail.

Finally, the officer in charge shouted, "Chop, chop. Everybody outside!" All the men in the gambling house were led out and loaded into the waiting paddy wagon. Wong Sang sat dejectedly in the heavily screened wagon, glaring at his two sentries, his eyes accusing them of having failed in their duty. The two men lowered their eyes as Sang sought to understand how this raid could have taken place without at least some forewarning. The only thing that made sense was that someone had tipped off the police and perhaps paid off his sentries to look the other way. Having come to that conclusion, a wave of anger swept over him along with an overwhelming desire for revenge.

Old Yin, Sang's cook, had been preparing supper when the raid had erupted. He had peered from behind a greasy curtain to see what was going on and startled an officer who had been standing with his back to the curtain. Without thinking, the officer swung his billy club and Old Yin fell to the floor, moaning. Seeing Yin fall, the officer in charge bellowed at the officer, "Why the hell did you have to hit him so hard? Well, put him in the wagon and we'll drop him off at the hospital on the way to the jail."

Professor watched the scene unfold from his doorway and cursed when he saw them carry Old Yin out on a stretcher. When the police and the paddy wagon had left, he hurried over to Number Three.

Liah was consumed with fury as she listened to Professor tell her of the raid. As soon as he had finished, she promptly ordered Fifth Son and Eldest Son to get down to the jail to bail the men out. She looked directly at Thomas and told him under no uncertain terms to let Mert do the talking. "Your temper will only get us deeper into trouble." She then asked Professor to find Tom, lamenting, "Of all the times for Cook to be absent, this is by far the most inconvenient. Otherwise, he, too, could look for Tom."

Ten minutes later, Cook rushed in lugging a rice sack, which he promptly opened, dumping the contents onto the kitchen table. "This bag of petty cash and the three sets of Pai gow tiles were hidden in the rice bin. The police confiscated everything else." Cook shook his head and remarked how strange it was that the Fahn Gwai knew exactly which door to kick in. "Some of the bystanders told me that there was no hesitation on the part of the police whatsoever. Do you not think that suspicious, Liah?"

Liah's face was florid and her voice shrill with fury as she shrieked, "If someone stool-pigeoned on Sang, I'll have his hide." Seeing how agitated Liah was, Cook tried to calm her down. "Well, there's no use fuming until we know the facts. Beside, it doesn't do any good anyway. I'll make a pot of tea. It will help calm you down."

"Forget the tea!" commanded Liah. "Make me a pot of the Fahn Gwai *gafeh* (coffee). Professor ought to be here soon with Tom, and Eldest and Fifth Sons should be back from the jail shortly as well, so you'd probably better prepare some food, too."

Liah was sipping coffee when Professor returned and informed her that Tom had gone directly to the jail. Together, they waited almost two hours for the boys.

As soon as they were through the door, Liah leaped from her upholstered chair and demanded to know if Old Yin was all right. Thomas growled, "Aw, Mah-Mah, we're starving. Can't we eat and talk at the same time?" While the boys ate, Tom informed Liah that the arrested men were now back in Chinatown, but that Old Yin had been admitted to City Hospital. With regard to Old Yin's condition, Tom told Liah, "I met a Chinese doctor there, a Dr. Sung, who said he wanted to keep Old Yin overnight to make sure that there was no concussion. He told me to tell you not to worry, that he'd personally watch over Old Yin."

"A Chinese doctor? In a Fahn Gwai hospital?" queried Liah. She then turned to Professor and asked, "Didn't Dr. Sung and Sung Tang Hai have a son who was studying medicine? I wonder if it could be him." The scholar closed his eyes and did some mental arithmetic before he nodded and responded, "I'm not sure, but I believe it has been eight years since we heard that, so the doctor could very well be Sung Tang's Second Son."

Tom smiled gently. "I had not met him before, but I have a favorable impression of him. When we spoke, I happened to mention the circumstances of my mother's death, and he said that the hospital was a good one and that there may not have been anything more the doctors could have done for her. We agreed, however, that perhaps if he or another Chinese doctor had been present, we might not have been so frightened and we would certainly have understood what was happening better. He confided to me that one of the main reasons he chose to become a doctor was in fact to help our people. Dr. Sung's words helped to ease my guilt over my inability to help my mother in her time of need. I also do not feel as bitter toward the Fahn Gwai."

Tom lapsed into a thoughtful silence and quietly finished his supper. Once everyone was done, however, he suddenly blurted, "Madam Liah, someday when I'm an attorney, I am going to do something about the way the Fahn Gwai officials treat us. The officer at the desk at the police station was extremely rude to us tonight and made no effort to help us at all. You know the officer actually made me feel guilty, as if I'd committed a crime when I tried to find out about the men who were arrested and about Old Yin. Only when I lied and said I was Old Yin's relative did he finally tell me where the old man was. Yet that officer readily gave out the same information to the Fahn Gwai reporters. I swear I will do whatever I can to help end this discrimination."

Wong Sang suddenly entered the room, cutting short Tom's tirade, and the focus shifted to the somewhat subdued yet visibly angry Sang. "The police got everything. The raid happened so quickly there wasn't time to save a single thing. I have a feeling that someone stool-pigeoned on me and if I catch the sonofabitch, I will kill him!"

Liah replied, "Don't be too surprised, Sang, if the stoolie turns out to be someone close to you. If I were you, I wouldn't continue to be so intimate with Tzo, at least not until we clear this matter up." Sang's eyes widened in shock and then narrowed as he demanded, "Are you trying to tell me it was Tzo who stooled on me?"

Liah shrugged her shoulders. "I did not say that. As for our losses, didn't I recommend that you should put in a sturdier door? You didn't even put up screens or make provisions for stashing the tiles and money in case of a raid. I believe you and the Fahn Gwai police are equally to blame for our losses."

Wong Sang became incensed at her rebuke, but just then Cook began to chuckle. "Professor, I thought you said nineteen hundred and twenty was supposed to be a year of peace and serenity. If this is an indication of how things are going to be, I think you may need to adjust your forecast." Professor started to defend his prediction but thought better of it and just nodded. Liah effectively ended the conversation when she scowled and said, "Well, Sang, what is done is done. However, when we catch the stool pigeon, he shall be dealt with severely."

After the raid, many in Chinatown began whispering that Liah had failed in her promise to secure Chinatown against outside intrusion. In an attempt to avoid another such incident, Sang's bodyguard Wei Tan visited each sentry post and issued a stern warning. Any sentry failing to be alert and ready to sound the alarm when needed would be subject to instant dismissal and appropriate punishment. Meanwhile, Liah pondered over whether this was part of Tzo's campaign to discredit her.

When Hans saw the old man who had been clubbed during the raid being carried out on a stretcher he had cursed quietly to himself He had it in mind to reprimand the officer in charge, but remembered that this was not his jurisdiction, at least not yet. The thought occurred to him, however, that if these idiots continued to alienate the Chinks, it would make his job all but impossible. Hans knew from his experiences in San Francisco Chinatown that the Chinks would cooperate, within limits of course, but only if they were treated with some respect and honesty. Damn it! While still at the scene, he had become aware of several bystanders glaring at him. Some of them spat on the sidewalk in his direction and Hans decided it was time to leave.

Back in his hotel room, Hans couldn't sleep. Too many images were flashing through his mind. He lay on his back, hands behind his neck, staring upward as if the darkened ceiling were a movie screen. Images of Los Angeles Chinatown flashed before him. It was a dirty, dreary little settlement by the train yards, composed mainly of rundown soot-covered buildings and dark, narrow alleyways. The spaces between the buildings were filled with rubbish and reminded him very much of San Francisco Chinatown. As a matter fact, if you didn't know where you were, you might come to the conclusion you were in San Francisco Chinatown. It certainly stank the same!

Hans recalled the police report he'd read earlier on Los Angeles Chinatown and murmured to himself, "Gambling, prostitution and opium—Apinyin." He chuckled at the Chink pronunciation of opium. Heaving a sigh, Hans reflected that at forty-six maybe he was getting too old to start something like this all over again, but then considered that the alternative might entail riding a desk until he could retire. Well, speculated Hans, perhaps his boss was right. Perhaps he ought to give L.A. a chance. Toward dawn, he finally fell asleep.

The next morning, Hans made his way to the office of a Lt. Swanson.

According to the information he had been given, he would first meet
with the lieutenant, who would be his new commanding officer should
he take the assignment. Subsequently, he'd meet Chief Dobbs. Hans
stood in front the office, stopping a moment to straighten his tie and
button his coat before rapping on the door. Out of habit, Hans glanced
nervously at his watch and determined that he was indeed on time.

A curt drawl gave him permission to enter, and once inside Hans
found himself looking at a thin-faced officer with a high, receding hair-
line seated behind a desk. To one side sat a tallish, heavy-set, slightly
gray-haired man in a business suit. The air of authority surrounding
this man left little doubt that this must be Chief Dobbs. The young officer scrutinized Hans in a less than friendly manner without speaking.
Hans, in turn, stared back and took stock of the officer. What he saw
was a man in his early thirties with steely blue eyes; thin, pursed lips;
and a pale, sallow complexion. Hans classified him immediately as part
of the police bureaucracy and instantly disliked him. Chief Dobbs rose
and stretched out his hand in welcome. "Glad to see you, Hans. I'm
Chief Dobbs and this is Lt. Swanson," indicating the man behind the
desk. "Chief Fields thinks very highly of you. Why don't you have a
seat and we can talk?"

Taking a seat, Hans became wary, a habit he had developed when
speaking with the brass. He reminded himself to watch his language,
since his normal speech was geared for the street and usually filled with
idiom and four-letter words. For a fleeting moment, Hans considered just
being himself so they could see what he was really like but quickly decided that he owed it to Chief Fields to try and make a good impression.

Chief Dobbs proceeded to outline the problems they had in Chinatown, while Hans, having already read the file, paid scant attention. Instead, his eyes took note of the lieutenant's extremely orderly desk. A
brass nameplate was centered exactly at the head of the blotter, and
there was a shiny brass letter opener lying perfectly parallel to a ruler,
itself positioned parallel to one side of the blotter. Already turned off

by the man's unnatural neatness, the moment Hans saw the unscuffed soles of Swanson's shoes protruding from under the desk, Hans knew for sure that they'd never get along. His attention snapped back to focus on Lt. Swanson as that officer mentioned something about a Chinatown Police Squad and that perhaps Hans could learn the ropes from them before the group disbanded.

Hans' retort was succinct. "If the squad you're talking about is the same bunch of idiots who raided that gambling joint in Chinatown yesterday evening, then they can't teach me a damn thing. Those guys don't know anything about Chinks." Lt. Swanson's eyes became angry narrow slits in his pale face. He snarled, "Just what do you mean by that? Those officers are damn good. Do you think you can do better?" Hans replied calmly, "Yeah, I know I could and with one hand tied behind my back."

Chief Dobbs tried hard to suppress an amused grin at the heated exchange, but took the opportunity to intercede after Hans made his claim with such certainty. The chief asked Hans, "Would you like a chance to prove that, Hans?"

Realizing he had maneuvered himself into having to accept the challenge, Hans tried to make the best of it by dictating the terms. "Sure, sir, if my conditions are met."

Lt. Swanson asked disdainfully, "What conditions?"

Hans shot back, "Your chief knows what they are. First, I work alone. When my life is on the line, I don't want to have to worry about a bunch of idiots doing something stupid. Second, I handle trouble the way I see fit. I don't want someone second-guessing my actions."

At that, Lt. Swanson almost came out of his seat and shouted, "You've got to be joking! That would be tantamount to giving you blanket authority to do whatever you pleased. Not even our best men have that much power. That is absolutely out of the question."

"Well, then," Hans replied, "I won't take up any more of your time. I guess I'll be heading back home." As Hans rose to leave, he paused and casually asked, "You mentioned you had a lot of crime in Chinatown. Out of curiosity, what crimes are being committed? Chinks, by and large, usually abide by the law because they don't want the police coming into their section of town."

"There's a lot of gambling, prostitution and opium use," snapped Swanson. "In addition, probably half the Chinks there are illegal immigrants." Hearing that, Hans grinned. "Oh, is that all? Those activities are a normal part of life in every Chinatown I've every heard of. If I were you, I'd leave them alone and you won't have any trouble with them."

Chief Dobbs thought that Hans was exactly the man he wanted. He appeared to be street-smart, practical and extremely knowledgeable about the Chinese. Before he had a chance to speak, however, Lt. Swanson curtly retorted, "It's a damn good thing you're not going to work here. As long as I'm in charge, we will do things according to the book. The law states that gambling, prostitution and drug use are crimes, so in my territory, they will be treated as crimes."

Chief Dobbs suppressed another grin, as Hans was clearly unimpressed by Lt. Swanson's speech. Hans turned to shake hands with Chief Dobbs, who said, "Hold on Hans. What if I were to meet your conditions, would you consider coming to work for me? The Chinatown Squad is disbanding at the end of this year and you could start the New Year with a clean slate."

Out of the corner of his eye, Hans caught the look of utter amazement on Lt. Swanson's face and smiled to himself. Hans considered the offer for a moment, then replied, "Sir, I'll have to think about it. I'll let you know my decision before I leave town." Shaking hands with the chief, Hans took his leave.

Alone with Chief Dobbs, Lt. Swanson commented, "Surely you can't be serious about hiring him, sir. He's an insolent, insubordinate sonofabitch. He's a lone wolf and won't fit into the department at all."

Chief Dobbs tossed a manila folder onto Lt. Swanson's desk and said, "Read this. Hans has built up a very impressive record. As for his insolence, his insubordination and his ego, he's entitled to some slack in light of his accomplishments. Don't let your dislike of the man blind you to his strengths, Swanson. A man of his caliber is rare these days. He took the time to understand the Chinks and that's why he's been so successful. It wouldn't hurt if some of our younger officers emulated him. Oh, and one more thing: If I were you, Swanson, I wouldn't lean on Hans too hard. He might take it into his head to flatten you. If that happens, don't come running to me. I won't raise a finger to help you. Do you understand me?"

Lt. Swanson nodded meekly and watched his superior officer stride out of the office. Alone, Swanson glared angrily at the closed door, frustration and fury enveloping him. Finally, he cursed, picked up the manila folder, flopped in his swivel chair and began to read.

Hans, meanwhile, made his way back to Chinatown. He wanted to survey the place in daylight and maybe get a bite to eat in one of the cafés. Myriad familiar sights, sounds and smells stimulated Hans' senses as he entered Dragon's Den Road. He saw that Wong's Café was busy and decided that boded well for the quality of its food.

He took a seat at the counter and noted that the menu was, as usual, only written in Chinese. Glancing around he saw he was the only Caucasian in the place, although there was a black deliveryman at the end of the counter chatting with one of the waiters. As had happened when he first set foot in San Francisco Chinatown, the waiters here also pretended they didn't see him and he had to wave his arm until they couldn't ignore him any longer. He pointed to the plate of the customer to his right, indicating he also wanted a plate of oxtail stew and rice. The waiter raised his eyebrows but said nothing.

Following his solitary lunch, which Hans had to admit was pretty good, he signaled the waiter again and asked, "How muchee, lunchee?" "Flee," grinned the waiter. Hans was surprised, not that the meal was free but that they had already pegged him as a cop. He nodded, left a dollar tip under his plate and walked out.

When he neared the end of Dragon's Den Road, Hans knew he was nearing the slaughterhouses; the putrid, acrid odors were unbelievable. He hurried down a dirt side road and entered Marchesson Street, seeing a fancy-looking place ahead that he decided to check out.

As he made his way, Hans peered into the narrow little alleys and shuddered when he peered down Pig Alley. At the time, he didn't know it was called Pig Alley, but Hans knew it'd be a long time before he'd have the nerve to enter that one. Dark and clammy, he surmised, like Dai Faw, people lived within those dark alleys.

When he finally reached the building he was heading for, Hans peered down the adjacent alley. The well-kept garden and walk was decidedly out of the ordinary, but he decided to save investigating that for another day. For now, he focused his attention on the fancy building before him.

He stood in front of the ornately carved and highly lacquered ebony door for a moment, wondering if he should just enter or knock. As usual in Chinatown, there was no address or nameplate to give the uninitiated any indication of whether this was a public or private establishment. His gut told him it was probably a public place so Hans turned the oversized knob and walked in.

As his feet sank into the thick, plush carpet and he observed the opulent decor, his first thought was of a high-class brothel. However, in San Francisco Chinatown, brothels were little more than dark, dirty hovels. So then what was this establishment? As his eyes adjusted to the dim interior lighting, his gaze took in the ebony bar to his right, the huge mirror running the full length of the bar and the expensive crystal chandeliers. Impressed, he walked over to the bar.

Selah, sitting there having her morning tonic, caught Chelo's subtle nod. She swung her barstool around to face Hans and inquired, "May I help you, sir?" Hans stopped in his tracks, feeling somewhat like a little boy caught with his hand in the cookie jar. He shook his head. "Not really, I'm new in town and was just walking around when your building caught my eye. I just had to see if the inside was as impressive as the outside. Do you mind?"

Selah shrugged her shoulders. "Well, now that you've seen it, what do you think?"

"I like it. It's real classy," replied Hans. Selah motioned for him to have a seat and told Chelo, "Give the gentleman whatever he wants and I'll have another of my usual." To Hans she said, "It's on the house."

As Hans sipped his beer, he snuck another look at the red-haired beauty beside him. She obviously wasn't a Chink so he couldn't help wondering what she was doing in Chinatown and how had she gotten here. Trying to strike up a conversation, Hans asked Selah, "Do you mind if I ask what kind of establishment this is?"

Selah turned to him, smiled and caught him completely off guard by replying, "Why, it's just what you think it is, a whorehouse. Of course, it's not your usual run-of-the-mill whorehouse. My clientele consists of the most wealthy and influential men in the city. However, I'm sure, as an officer of the law, you had already figured that out."

Hans could only nod and admit who he was. "You got me. I'm Officer Hans Weigen from San Francisco." Selah replied with a grin, "Well, I hope you're not a kick-in-the-door-first-and-ask-questions-later kind of cop."

Hans roared and slapped the bar with his hand. "I think I'm going to like you!" Turning serious, he said, "You're beautiful, evidently well-educated and smart, so what the hell are you doing in Chinktown?"

Selah's demeanor turned somewhat frosty as she replied, "Sir, I am proud to say that I am part Chink and only too happy to be living among my father's people. Would you care for another beer?"

Hans, embarrassed by his faux pas, shook his head. He placed a five-dollar bill on the bar, nodded to Selah and walked out. Hans stepped into the bright afternoon sun and looked down the cobblestone walk. He decided that, since his visit to the brothel had been cut short, he might as well have a look.

As soon as Hans stepped onto the cobblestone path, he felt as if he had been transported to a different place entirely. Something about the alley captured his full attention. Whether it was the front doors of the buildings, each painted a different color, or the relative neatness of the area, or the presence of well-tended greenery, Hans could not say. He took note of the wooden sign posted at the entrance to the alley and be-rated himself for never having learned to read Chink.

As he slowly ambled down the cobblestone path, Hans encountered not a single person. He began to wonder if this were a private walk. Glancing at his wristwatch, he saw it was only three-thirty and was thinking about what to do next when the hair on the back of his neck bristled. Hans knew he was being observed. Although he didn't see anyone, he was certain there were eyes peering at him from behind the blinds and shutters. Suddenly, he realized that, even in the short time he had been here, this Chinatown was stirring up feelings he thought were long dead. By the time he reached his hotel, The Alexandria, Hans had decided to accept the assignment.

—

Two days after the raid on Wong Sang's gambling house, Tom dropped in to chat with Selah. He was still chafing from his rude treatment at the police department and needed to vent to someone. Chelo greeted Tom and shouted for Selah to come down. She shrieked with delight as soon as she saw Tom and ran up to give him a big hug. As she embraced him, she whispered in his ear that there was a reporter at the end of the bar trolling for a story so he had better be careful of what he said.

Tom tried to keep his voice down as he told Selah about his experi-ence at the police station. However, as he retold the incident, the anger surged within him again and he cursed the cops in a voice that could be heard all over the bar. The reporter, who introduced himself as Joe

Banyon, took the opportunity to slide down the row of bar stools to sit beside Tom. "So, what do you have against the cops, kid?"

Selah squeezed Tom's arm firmly, warning him to keep quiet, but Tom's wrath against the desk sergeant would not be stemmed. Tom told the reporter in a heated voice about what had happened during the raid on Wong Sang's gambling house, including the clubbing of Old Yin. Then he related how he was given little to no information while the reporters were told everything. Tom's voice became strident. "Why did the cops have to raid a two-bit gambling joint in Chinatown in the first place? Why not one of the big Fahn Gwai gambling houses? I'll tell you why! It's because we're Chinks, that's why!"

Tom's anger crested and he looked apologetically at Chelo and Selah, then fell silent. The reporter tried to elicit more details from Tom but to no avail. Realizing the interview was over, Banyon asked Tom for his name. Tom replied in a disgusted voice, "Just call me Joe Chinaman. Better yet, let's just forget the whole damn thing. I was just letting off some steam."

"Okay, kid," muttered Banyon. "Just read tomorrow's issue of the *Press*. Maybe I can do something for you, Joe Chinaman or whatever your name is. So long."

The moment the door closed behind the reporter, Chelo leaned over to Tom and said, "Mebbe, man, you talk too muchee. Say too many tings no oughta say. Joe Banyon, him one big mouf paper man."

Selah smiled sadly. "Come on, future lawyer-man, drink up. You're tired and I think you ought to get home and get to bed early tonight." Tom heaved a big sigh and looked guiltily at Selah. "You also think I said too much, don't you? I'm sorry, but I just couldn't help it, Selah. I lost control of myself."

Selah patted his arm sympathetically and said, "Tom, it's okay to have strong feelings about things. However, if you're going to be a good lawyer, you have to learn to speak about those things when it's appropriate and when the right people are listening. Joe Banyon is definitely not one of the right people. For your sake, I hope nobody ever finds out who Joe Chinaman is."

After Tom left, Selah continued to sit at the bar, thinking. She wished she could do something to relieve the obvious tension building up in the boy and even thought of letting him have one of her girls for a night. Knowing Tom, however, she discarded the idea. Tom's pride wouldn't let him accept what he perceived as charity even if it was just a gift. Nevertheless, as wound up as he was getting, something was going to snap unless he found some kind of release.

Tom returned to Selah's the next day when he got word that Selah wanted to see him. She was sitting at the bar and waved him over, motioning to the seat next to hers. "Sit down, darling, and relax. Chelo, please fix Tom a drink."

After ten minutes of small talk, Selah pulled a newspaper from behind the bar and gave it to Tom. "Here, my talkative friend, read this." As he read Banyon's article, Tom's facial expression changed from incredulous to righteous indignation. "Goddamn! I didn't say this! The guy's a liar!" He turned to Selah. "You were here. You heard me. I was mad, sure, but I didn't say all these things."

Selah replied, "I warned you, Tom. Banyon is a loose cannon. His need for drama outweighs his need for accuracy. Maybe the next time, you'll be more circumspect in his presence. Well, done is done. Let's hope nobody finds out who Joe Chinaman is."

Chelo leaned over the bar and grinned at Tom. "Man oh man, when you talks, you surely do talk." When he saw Tom's angry face, he quickly added, "Doan worry. I not say nuthin'. Go on, finish you drink."

Tom was still seething and slapped the newspaper onto the bar. "Selah, listen to this self-serving garbage."

"Despite the hard-line tactics used by the police, this reporter has found no crime, to speak of, in Chinatown. There have been no burglaries, no rapes, no murders or riots, not even a case of wife-beating. The police allege there is

opium trafficking and use, but this reporter has neither seen nor smelled any evidence of this. The police also say that prostitution is prevalent in Chinatown, but once again this reporter has found no proof of such. In fact, this reporter has only seen little children playing in the streets, much like children every-where, and housewives shopping, bargaining or gossiping much like house-wives everywhere. This reporter is inclined to believe the irate young man who confided to me that he'd been rudely shoved about by the police and ignored when he attempted to locate an old man who had been brutally clubbed over the head by the police during a raid. The young man's name? When asked, he angrily retorted, "Joe Chinaman!" This self-derision underscores the depth to which the police of this city have belittled the Chinese residents of this fair city. This reporter, who has up until now turned a deaf ear and a blind eye to the reports of outrageous police conduct in Chinatown, now has cause to wonder what is really going on."

"Wow! Dat man one good story-teller, eh?" Chelo grinned, but see-ing Tom's scowl quickly returned to his chores.

Selah plucked the newspaper from Tom's hand and told him, "That's enough about Banyon, Tom. The other reason I asked you to come over is that I need your help. I would appreciate it if you could quietly inquire if the police have a Hans Weigen on their payroll. He's a big hulk of a guy from San Francisco. I'd like Liah to know about him if it turns out he is on the force."

Tom's first impulse was to tell Selah that he had absolutely no desire for another encounter with the desk sergeant, but realized deep down that he wanted to find out if he now had the patience to tackle situations like this. Once he graduated with his law degree, he'd have to go in and out of the police department on a regular basis, so he might as well start learning how to handle the prejudice. Tom smiled at Selah and agreed to make the inquiry. "But," he told her with a grin, "if that desk sergeant gives me the same treatment this time, I'll deck him!"

A LETTER FROM CHINA

One afternoon, Selah had occasion to chat with the mail carrier when he dropped off a package that required her signature. He complained about how difficult his route in Chinatown was, owing to the absence of street names and numbers and the fact that almost no one spoke English. He told her, "It takes me three times longer to deliver the mail here and even then I have to take two or three letters back as undeliverable because I can't find the right place or the right person."

Selah listened sympathetically, but when she heard about the undelivered letters, she said, "How horrible for those people who don't receive their mail. I'll tell you what, if you'll trust me, I'll deliver the mail for you. I know most of the residents here and, if I don't, Professor surely will."

"Lady," said the mailman enthusiastically, "you've got a deal."

That very day, he left her with all of the mail for Chinatown. After he left, Selah sat at the bar and sorted through it all. She set aside a few items for Professor to distribute on Dragon's Den Road, Lion's Den Alley and on the far end of Marchesson Street. Her curiosity was piqued, however, when she discovered a letter addressed to Liah. She decided to deliver it right away. She called out to Lalo, "I'm going to Number Three. Keep an eye on things for me."

On the short walk down Peacock Alley, Selah reflected on how solitary her life was. Although she was far too busy to be lonely, Selah wished she had at least a few other women to talk to. Besides Amah, Liah was her only female friend. Selah wondered if Liah felt the same way.

Liah's joy at seeing Selah was cut short when she saw the red, white and blue letter in Selah's hand. "Is that for me, Selah?" For some unknown reason, Liah had a strange feeling that the letter was from Sen. However, she couldn't fathom why he would be writing a letter after such a long time. After six years, she had difficulty even remembering what he looked like. Liah took the letter and tucked it inside her tunic as she invited Selah to sit and have tea with her.

Although she was still waiting for Tom to confirm the facts, Selah decided to tell Liah about the rumors she had heard concerning the police. "Liah," murmured Selah, "I have heard a rumor that the Chinatown Police Squad is going to be disbanded by the end of the year. It is also rumored that a new cop from Dai Faw will be brought in to patrol the town. I don't know if the stranger from Dai Faw I met a few days ago is the replacement cop, but we should be on the alert. He is reputed to be no dummy."

Liah knitted her brows as Selah went on to describe the cop she'd met, Hans Weigen. Hearing that this cop was bulky, had large hands and affected an unlit cigar dangling from meaty lips, Liah dredged up an image from her time in Dai Faw. It was too much of a coincidence for this cop not to be The Cat!

"Selah, if this is the cop we called The Cat in Dai Faw, you must be cautious. If you have any interaction with him at all, don't push him. When he get's angry, he acts like a wild animal."

Selah shook her head. "It's not me who needs to be cautious. You must secure your operation. There's not much he can do to me, but I do fear that he could hurt you." Although Selah never spoke explicitly of Liah's opium business, Liah understood what she meant. Selah paused, then continued, "I wonder how the man got the nickname 'Cat?"

Liah giggled. "I gave him the name when I lived in Dai Faw. Despite his great size, that man walks as swiftly and as silently as a cat." Selah replied, "A tiger is more like it, Liah. Hans is no pussycat, I assure you."

After that, their conversation drifted from topic to topic, coming to rest at last on Tom. Without telling Liah about Tom's outburst in the bar and the resulting article in the paper, Selah shared the opinion that Tom was too intense and too serious for his own good, as well as having too much foolish pride. "I agree," Liah said. "However, it is most likely

Tom's Meng-Sui to have to suffer in order to grow wiser and stronger. I do have the feeling that Tom will achieve his goals and be successful in his life, if Kwan Yin and Kwan Koong are willing."

Selah sighed and replied, "I hope you're right, Liah. If nothing else, he has us on his side. I know that you've offered him your shoulder and your home as have I, and that's probably as much as we can do for the time being. Well, I should be getting back. If Amah learns that I've sneaked off without her again, she'll tan me."

As Selah was leaving, Liah said, "Selah, don't be alarmed if you see a strange man lurking around your place in the near future. I've ordered one of my sentries to watch over your place. I hope you don't mind."

Selah's face softened as she stooped to kiss Liah. "Honestly, Liah, I really can take care of myself, but thank you anyway."

Professor arrived at Number Three shortly after four that afternoon. Liah apologized for the summons, but told him that she had a bad feeling about the letter. Professor replied, "No need for apologies, Liah. I'm glad to be of service." He quickly scanned the letter, saying that it was indeed from Sen, then suggested that he read it verbatim.

My Revered Wife,

I pray to Kwan Koong this letter finds all of you in good health. I send you my regards, and hope your life is all you would wish it to be. I am writing this letter with mixed emotions. My life with you and the children is still fresh in my memory; however, these things must be said. I have married a woman from my village who is twenty-four years old. I know you will say it is outrageous, since I am over twice her age. However, you know our customs are different here in China. By our standards, she is beyond her prime, but she is all I need and want in a woman. I am very happy, for in a few months, I shall become a father again. That, too, you might think foolish, but my heart is full. Tell my

*children that their father looks forward to the day when they will visit.
I request that you help our children to accept my marriage. It is, after
all, my moral privilege to wed again. You are very good at getting people
to adopt your point of view, so you should have no difficulty convincing
them that this is for the best.
Your husband,
  Sen*

Liah fumed at the last sentence. It was clear that even after all this
time, he had still not forgiven her for her Council activities. Then a tinge
of jealously colored her thoughts. How dare he marry another woman!
Liah recalled her many nights of unfulfilled passion and desire, and she
had a sudden urge to strangle Sen. Regaining control of her emotions,
Liah thanked Professor and declared, "The children must be told."

When Liah glanced up at Cook and Professor, she saw concern
etched on their faces. She quickly assured them that she was fine, saying, "I'm glad Sen's started a new life. He was never happy in Gem
Sahn. However, I would be most grateful if the two of you could think
of a good way for me to inform the children. As a matter of fact, Professor, I would appreciate it if you would have supper with us tonight. I
am afraid Eldest Son may lose his temper, and you know he has a
strong influence on the other children. I need someone outside the family present tonight so he will temper his response."

Liah watched her children closely at the supper table that night,
waiting for the right moment to mention their father's letter. In particular, Liah kept an eye on her eldest son and her youngest son, for they
possessed the fiercest and the meekest of temperaments. Liah longed
to shield them from the hurt, which they would surely feel, but knew
that she had to tell them of their father's remarriage.

"Children," Liah began when she sensed an appropriate lull in the
conversation, "I have asked Professor to read you a letter that I received

from your father today." Bedlam erupted as each child immediately bombarded Liah and Professor with questions. Liah raised her hand and demanded silence. Professor appeared uncomfortable but bravely stood up and began. "Before I read his letter, I would ask that you withhold any snap judgments until your Mother has a chance to discuss the contents of the letter with you." Hearing that, the children looked at one another with worried expressions and waited apprehensively.

As Professor read the letter, Liah had to put a restraining hand on Thomas and shoot a threatening look at her second son, both of whom displayed mounting agitation. When Professor finished reading, there was a moment of silence, which was broken when Thomas swore vehemently, "Goddamn, he's no father of mine!"

Emmi mused, "You mean we're going to have a stepbrother?"

"Not necessarily, sis. It might be a girl," growled Shelley.

"Good grief, another sister?" shouted Theo angrily. "If she's going to be anything like Em, I'm glad I'll be far, far away." Emmi kicked viciously at Theo under the table and the room erupted into a shouting match.

Liah rapped her chopsticks on the table, bringing the fracas to an abrupt end. "Now, I want all of you to listen to me. None of you should pass judgment on your father. While it is normal for us to feel jealously or sadness or even anger, you should not hate your father. He truly loves you. It's just that in China your father has the right to take on as many wives as he can afford. I do not object to your father's actions and I hope you will not object either. I will tolerate no more anger on your part."

Liah scowled at her three oldest sons, who were obviously not accepting the situation. Thomas shouted, "Mah, what kind of father is he to desert us, then have the nerve to tell us he's remarried and going to be a father again? How can you expect us to feel anything but anger? I don't want to have anything to do with them." Thomas eyed his sister and brothers. "Isn't that so?"

Emmi and Mert merely hung their heads in silence, while Shelley, Theo and William nodded agreement. Emmi pouted and then asked why Bah-Bah could not have stayed with them, and had a baby with Mah-Mah? Liah blushed and gently told her that it had not been possible. Theo, meanwhile, continued to make snide remarks, causing Mert to shout at him to shut up. "Didn't you hear Mah? She said we were not to get mad at Father!" Thomas then glowered at Mert and reiterated, "I told you. He's no father of mine!" Liah glared at him again, and Thomas motioned to Shelley. "Come on, let's get out of here." So that Liah could not understand, he added in English, "It's a good thing he's out of reach, otherwise I'd belt him good!" Mert lowered his head and Emmi sympathetically reached out to pat his arm, but Mert suddenly pushed his chair back from the table and ran to his room.

Professor broke the ensuing silence by saying that he ought to be getting home. Suddenly embarrassed, Liah immediately apologized for having involved him in the awkward family situation. "I thank you for your time and patience, sir. The children's outbursts are due to their youthful emotions and their loyalty to me. They meant you no disrespect." She hesitated and then said, "If you do not mind, I would like the news of Sen's marriage to remain a secret, at least for the time being."

The scholar nodded understandingly and said good night. After Professor had left, Liah began to worry about the rift that had opened up between Fifth Son and the rest of his brothers. The worry eventually led to her feeling renewed anger against Sen for having written. Why couldn't he have gone on with his life without notifying the family? Did he do it out of spite, expecting that Liah would feel remorse and jealousy? Didn't he realize how much his actions would hurt the children?

Cook's stern voice suddenly broke into her thoughts, "Done is done, Liah. Before you try to reason with them or try to mend the split between Fifth Son and the others, let them cool down first." Liah glared and choked off the impulse to tell Cook to shut up and mind his own business. In truth, Cook was more a father to her children than Sen ever had been. At least he was trying to understand their behavior and act in their best interest. Liah lowered her eyes lest Cook see the rejection and anger that she was feeling. Her face burned as she recalled the many nights she had tried to arouse Sen to satisfy her sexual needs. Now he dared to tell her that he had taken another wife!

Over the ensuing weeks, the rift between Fifth Son and his siblings did not heal itself and it began to frighten Liah. In the past when the children fought, there might have been a few days they gave each other the silent treatment, but never so long a period as now. She wanted to put her arms around Fifth Son and comfort him, but knew that the boy would be angered and reject her. Instead, Liah lit tapers to both Kwan Koong and Kwan Yin, beseeching them that her children would unite as a family again.

On the twenty-third day of June in the Fahn Gwai year of nineteen hundred and twenty, Fourth Son William graduated from college. Liah's heart sang and her joy overflowed, as the family held a celebration feast to honor William's accomplishment. Professor, Selah and Toh's family all arrived at six-thirty and, as they all greeted one another, Liah was glad to see that the children were once more at peace. However, it saddened Liah that she would be saying goodbye to Fourth Son, for he had won a scholarship to attend graduate school in China. Selah noticed Liah's moist eyes, leaned over and whispered, "Don't mar your son's party, Liah. You can think unhappy thoughts later. Smile, darling."

During supper, Flo barely touched her food and seemed thoroughly worn out. Selah inquired if she was not feeling well but Flo shook her head and replied, "It's the three girls, Aunt Selah. All day long, I'm either chasing after them, feeding them or bathing them. I'm exhausted."

Hearing this, Liah frowned. "I've told you, daughter, that I would help take care of the girls, but you've always rejected my assistance. At the very least, you should allow Aileen to come and stay. After all, you are always saying that she is the worst of your three children."

Flo lifted her chin defiantly. "It's not me, Mah-Mah! Toh doesn't want them to leave. I've told him repeatedly that if Aileen were with you, at least I wouldn't have to deal with her tantrums." Toh cast a furtive eye in her direction, but Flo gave him a look that warned him to mind his own business. Liah felt again that something was amiss between her daughter and Toh, but was at a loss to put her finger on it. She decided she would confront her daughter later and turned her attention back to the celebration honoring Fourth Son.

At supper's end, Liah rose, lifted her glass and told everyone, "Now, we shall all drink a toast to Fourth Son. He has brought great honor upon our family, not only with the completion of his studies, but also with his scholarship to study in Hong Kong. Mother is very proud of you."

After the toast, William fixed his eyes on his mother and murmured, "I truly wish you would attend my graduation exercises, Mah-Mah. It would be an honor to introduce you to my professors." Taking great pleasure in her son's display of filial piety, Liah reassured Fourth Son that her heart was full and that her pride in him would not be diminished if she did not attend. "Selah and your older brothers will be there to applaud you, son, and I shall be there in spirit. Now, you should open up your presents."

Emmi clamored for William to open up her gift first. "It's from Theo, Mert and me." William dutifully undid the ribbons and paper to find a toiletry kit. Emmi then urged her older brother to open it, saying excitedly, "There's soap, toothpaste and everything!" Emmi grinned with pride when William promised her that he would think of her every time he used the kit.

Professor gave him a bilingual dictionary, saying with a smile, "Fourth Son, you are a splendid model for our young people in Chinatown to emulate. Your graduating with such high grades and winning a scholarship to graduate school will give others a sense of confidence that they, too, can do what you have done." He then looked at the rest of Liah's children and continued in a more serious tone. "I'd like to make one further point if I might and then I'll be silent. One of the reasons Fourth Son was able to graduate from college is because he was able to remain in one location for the entire period. You should honor

your mother, for it was she who insisted upon and oversaw the unification of Chinatown." Everyone applauded, filling Liah with happiness
yet again.

Selah then embraced William and, as she handed him a traditional
red money envelope, whispered in his ear, "Spend this foolishly, darling. You are much too serious and you should relax a little and have
some fun. I, too, am very proud of you."

When Selah walked away, Toh timidly handed William another red
envelope. "I am not a learned man, but through you I see better times
coming for us. Good luck, brother-in-law, and may your stay in Hong
Kong be a pleasant one."

Then it was Liah's turn and she solemnly faced her fourth son, reaching into her tunic and withdrawing a tiny jewelry box. "Mother wishes
to give you a gift, too." William's pulse sped up as he untied a red ribbon securing the jewelry box and lifted the lid. His eyes became misty
as he recognized the jade ring his mother had acquired some time back
and that he had always admired. He remembered the time he had asked
her if he might have it, but Liah had shaken her head and replied, "You
may have it when you become a man." Their eyes met for an instant
and they exchanged an unspoken mutual understanding. William then
gathered his mother into his arms and whispered a teary thank you.
Liah wordlessly squeezed his arm and pulled away quickly lest she give
in to the emotions threatening to overwhelm her. Emmi chose that moment to ask if she, too, might go to college.

William laughed, tousled her hair and answered, "Why not, sis? Just
study hard and get good grades."

Thomas interjected, "Come on, sis, you don't need to go to college.
Once you graduate from high school, you'll probably get married just
like Flo."

"I'm not like Flo, and I do not want to get married!" Emmi protested
angrily. Liah frowned at the vehemence with which her youngest child
spoke. However, she mostly wondered why her youngest had drawn

such a sharp contrast between herself and her older sister.

Selah giggled, "Emmi, darling, pay Thomas no heed. He's just teasing you. You go right ahead and plan on going to college. Women have the same right to an education as men do."

Flo jealously retorted, "It's easy for Em to plan on going to college. She's lucky. Being the youngest, she gets spoiled. When I was her age, we had nothing and I had no choices." At that, Liah rapped the table with her chopsticks and declared, "Enough of this talk, Eldest Daughter! Being poor had nothing to do with your getting married. As I recall, marriage was entirely your choice, so don't make excuses. Second Daughter will get her chance to choose between college and marriage, just as you did. Now, let us have dessert."

"Wait, Mah-Mah," said Shelley. "Thomas and I haven't given William our gift yet." Thomas handed William a long, thin package, which William opened, revealing a pigskin wallet tooled with his initials. Inside was a section for identification cards, another for pictures and a secret compartment for money.

"Thanks, guys," said William smiling, broadly. Then, looking at each of his siblings, William went on, "I really want to thank you for all the wonderful gifts, but I think more than anything else tonight, I am thankful that we've put aside our differences and become a family again. Now that I'm about to leave home, I want you to know how important it is for me to know that we are one and that nothing can break us apart."

Liah's eyes misted as she listened to her son speak and everyone became a little introspective after he finished. Finally, Thomas broke the silence by saying, "You're right, William. We might get mad and yell at each other, but it is never for long. We're all family. By the way, did you look in the secret compartment?" William investigated and found a crisp hundred-dollar bill tucked neatly inside the tiny compartment. The money brought a tear to William's eye, knowing that it was his brothers' way of helping him with expenses without William being able to refuse.

Once the celebration was over, Liah took Eldest Daughter into her bedroom and demanded to know why she was exhibiting such a negative attitude. Flo burst into tears and shook her head, saying she didn't know why. After trying unsuccessfully to get to the bottom of the situation, Liah gave up and called Toh in, then talked both Toh and Eldest Daughter into agreeing to allow Aileen to come and stay with Liah.

Within a week of Aileen returning to Number Three, Liah laughed to Cook, Amah and her children. "We have only one small child to take care of and not one of us has a moment to ourselves. It makes me think of when I had seven young ones to care for and had to do all the cooking and cleaning myself. I wonder how I managed."

Thomas grinned and replied, "You had us to help and you didn't spoil us as you do Aileen." Cook chuckled in agreement while Amah cried, "Oh, the poor baby, she needs as much love as we can give her, doesn't she, Liah?" Liah smiled and reassured Amah that they were indeed doing the right thing. "Pay no mind to the men. What do they know about childcare? Eldest Son, don't the Fahn Gwai have portable swimming pools? We could set one up in the back yard and when it's not in use, we could store it upstairs."

—

The July heat aggravated Liah, but, for her granddaughter's sake, she kept her temper in check. Much to Cook's delight, her need for her bamboo pipe did not increase as it usually did. Although she did smoke once or twice a week, she did it for the enjoyment it brought her, not to escape reality. What distressed her more than the heat was her granddaughter's frequent nightmares and the unexplained terror she exhibited whenever she was scolded. Liah could not fathom why Aileen got so terrified.

It was during this time that Professor and Cook heard rumors that Lee Tzo had started to sell Apinyin in competition with Liah. Neither

Professor nor Cook wanted to destroy the serenity Liah had acquired, but they realized it would be wrong to withhold the knowledge from her. In the end, it was Cook who bravely informed Liah of their suspicions.

Upon hearing the news, Liah immediately asked them, "Do we have proof? Before we can punish a person, we must have incontrovertible proof." When Cook shook his head, Liah became furious and barked, "Well, get some! I suggest you inquire amongst our customers or have one of our sentries shadow Tzo. I don't care how you do it; get me proof!"

When Professor found three of her customers who promised to testify that Tzo had sold them Apinyin, Liah called an emergency meeting of the Council. The day of the meeting was extremely hot and humid, making everyone in attendance short-tempered. Upon being confronted with Liah's accusation, Tzo hotly denied he was dealing in Apinyin. Liah just smiled and then had the three informants brought into the chamber. As soon as Lee Tzo saw them, the color left his face to be replaced moments later with a flush of anger. In turn, each of the three men pointed Lee Tzo out to the Council as the man they had done business with. Having provided their testimony, the witnesses were then dismissed and Lee Tzo was left to face the other members of the Council.

At first, Lee Tzo tried to discredit the witnesses. He said, "How dare you accept the word of those three nobodies over mine? They have distorted the truth, which is that I merely suggested a possible source of Apinyin to them when they asked." Judging from the disbelieving expressions around the table, he saw that this approach wasn't likely to get him very far. Thinking quickly, Lee Tzo decided to go on the offensive and complained, "Anyway, why should Liah be given the right to monopolize the Apinyin trade?"

Kam Fong normally liked to listen to everyone else's opinion before making any comments. However, this time he responded immediately to Lee Tzo's question: "I do not care if you feel that Liah is monopolizing the sale of Apinyin. What concerns me is that if the Fahn Gwai catch you, we will all suffer the consequences. You know that the Fahn Gwai authorities allow Liah to deal small portions of Apinyin as part of everyday Chinatown life. However, if you were to be caught, there would be an investigation by the Fahn Gwai, which would mean all of us would come under their scrutiny. This would obviously not be to our benefit. I, for one, strongly suggest you desist from any involvement with Apinyin."

Lee Tzo became even more belligerent and snapped back, looking directly at Liah, "This is one time you will not impose your will on me or anyone else! Just as there are several cafés, butcher shops, bakeries and every other kind of business in Chinatown, there should be more than one source of Apinyin. You have no right to prevent someone from doing business!"

"We have the right and the means!" shouted Chon Woo. "None of us wants to have the Fahn Gwai running around Chinatown, poking their noses into our affairs just because you want to make money selling Apinyin!"

At that point, Tom Soo rose and politely requested permission to speak. The other members saw an opportunity for calm and signaled for Tom to continue. "Elder brothers," he began, "before we speak further on the subject of the Apinyin trade, let me tell you what happened to me when the Fahn Gwai police raided Wong Sang's gambling house. When instructed by Madam Liah to inquire about what had happened to Old Yin and to the men who had been arrested, I approached the Fahn Gwai authorities and was treated like a worthless piece of trash even though I speak their language. They think they can do anything they want to us and there is nothing we can do to prevent it. We should think very seriously before condoning any illicit activities that might catch their attention. The Fahn Gwai are not stupid, merely prejudiced. Some of them understand very well how Chinatown works and can take away our livelihoods as well as our freedom in the blink of an eye. That is all I have to say. Thank you for allowing me to speak."

A thoughtful silence followed Tom's speech and Liah allowed Tom's words to sink in while she gazed steadily at Lee Tzo, who sat stolidly with his eyes focused somewhere in the distance. Wong Sang, who had nominated Lee Tzo to the Council, squirmed in his chair and cursed Tzo's stupidity and greed. It was Chon Woo who broke the silence by offering his opinion that Tzo's business associates were rank amateurs and were therefore very likely to attract the notice of the Fahn Gwai authorities. Chon Woo was looking straight at Sang as he spoke, causing Sang to snap back, "I wouldn't be so self-righteous, Chon! You, too, endanger us with your illegal liquor sales to minors and by keeping your bar open after hours."

Chon lunged toward Sang but was held back by Wong Cheung. Shrugging off Wong Cheung's restraining arm, Chon warned, "Don't forget, Sang. It was you who nominated Lee Tzo. If he does something to earn the censure of the Council, his punishment will also be meted out to you!"

Professor stepped in and suggested that both Chon and Sang take their seats so that the Council could get back to deliberating the issue of increased Apinyin trade. In the end, the Council voted overwhelmingly to ban Apinyin sales by anyone other than Liah. As Lee Tzo was signing the meeting records, Liah murmured, "I hope this closes the Apinyin issue as far as you're concerned. I truly hope that everyone obeys the Council's edict." Lee Tzo merely glared at Liah and departed.

Once she was alone, Liah sat in her chair going over the Council session in her mind. Although she had won, she decided to have Cook change their Apinyin delivery schedule. If she was any judge of character, Lee Tzo certainly wasn't to be trusted.

—

The next morning, as Liah was sipping herbal tea and attempting to sweep out the cobwebs in her mind, the telephone began ringing shrilly.

Liah cursed at the instrument but resigned herself to the noise since the machine did allow her to communicate quickly with whomever she wanted. She heard Cook answer the phone and exclaim, "Congratulations, Toh! The God's have answered your prayers and delivered you a son. Let me get Liah."

As soon as she reached the phone, Liah happily shouted into the mouthpiece, "The Gods have been most generous, Toh! How is Eldest Daughter?" After listening to Toh's reply, Liah's voice took on a note of concern. "What? She's not breast-feeding? Why not? Is something wrong?" After they hung up, Liah became concerned. Although her son-in-law had assured her that nothing was amiss, Liah was not convinced. She mulled over her knowledge of traditional Chinese medicine and was stymied. In China, mothers always breastfed their babies unless there was something wrong. "The Fahn Gwai doctors," Liah told Cook, "do not want Eldest Daughter to breastfeed the newborn because the time between babies has been too short." Liah lapsed into silence, shook her head and muttered, "I just know something is wrong."

Suddenly, Aileen began to cry and Liah rushed into the bedroom. Cook sighed. Liah was totally committed to caring for that child. He prayed to Kwan Koong that Liah never suffer pain as a consequence of loving Aileen so much. Cook reflected that love made one so vulnerable. Sighing again, he searched the drawer for a pencil and carefully circled the twentieth day of July. As he did so, Cook thought how favored by the Gods Liah was to have four grandchildren already.

Liah came into the kitchen, carrying Aileen in her arms, one hand clutching the child's shoes and stockings. Cook frowned and rebuked her. "You know she's too heavy for you to carry." He reached out, took Aileen from Liah and sat the child on a high stool. While Cook steamed a meat-filled bun for Aileen to eat, Liah struggled to put on Aileen's stockings and shoes. "Stop wriggling, child! You must get dressed before you can eat. Cook, will give you the bun as soon as it is warm? Now let Grandma put on your stockings and shoes." As Aileen greedily reached out for the bun, Cook smiled and told her, "It's still too hot for you, child. Let it cool, and then your grandmother will break it in two for you. It's too big for you to hold." When Aileen pouted and shook her head, Liah smiled and told Cook, "Let me have a plate. I'll cut it in two for her now. I'm afraid patience will not be one of her virtues."

Cook watched the affectionate exchange between Liah and Aileen and thought how wonderful it was not to have the burden of Liah's health on his mind. Aileen's presence had given Liah new life. It could have been his imagination, but he thought Liah may even have put some flesh on her bony face. When he had mentioned this to Amah earlier, she had agreed with him and her eyes misted as she confided, "Up until recently, I've been so worried about her, Cook. I don't know what I'd do if something were to happen to her. Liah is my life." Surprisingly, Cook had replied in a stern voice, "Don't ever say such a thing again! Liah will outlive both of us." He turned away but not before Amah saw the pain in his eyes and knew that without Liah Cook's life would also end.

—

The extreme August heat that year affected not just Liah. Throughout Chinatown, tempers flared, businessmen and their customers argued and the smaller Tongs quarreled with the larger ones over accusations of unfair treatment. A frown was the expression seen on most of the residents' faces, and their voices were curt to the point of rudeness. Inside the Council chamber on the eleventh day of August things were no different. The session had been called at Lee Tzo's request. He'd come to see Liah earlier, complaining about the rude and disrespectful treatment he had been receiving from the youth of the Four Families Association.

Hearing his complaint, Liah had lashed out at him, "Are you certain it is not you who is in the wrong here? Word has come to me that you have approached several youths of that Tong in an attempt to get them to work at your illicit activities. I haven't yet mentioned this to the

Council lest Wong Cheung decide to put you in your place. His methods as you know aren't gentle." Lee Tzo responded meekly that it seemed like Liah always took the other parties' side against him, regardless of the circumstances. Liah curtly dismissed his accusation, saying, "I cannot help it if you're almost always in the wrong. Furthermore, if you had not vetoed the consolidated sentry system, we would now have men patrolling our streets and you would have witnesses to corroborate your story. Perhaps the next time this issue arises, you will support it. However, I will ask Professor to schedule a Council meeting so that you may air your grievance."

Once the Council had been called to order, Lee Tzo took the floor and lodged his complaint, which he admitted was a minor matter but one that should be addressed before it got worse. He then pleaded for a lenient punishment for the youths, looking at Wong Cheung as he did so, saying, "They are young and do not fully understand that their elders are owed respect. I believe the Council should have the youths gently reprimanded so that they learn this lesson."

Throughout Lee Tzo's speech, Liah's face remained expressionless, giving Tzo no hint as to whether she would expose Lee Tzo's supposed offer to the youth of the Four Families Association. When he finished, the pimp reached into his pocket, withdrew a creamy white silk handkerchief and daintily mopped his brow and cheeks. Watching, Liah again noted the femininity of his mannerisms. She stole a glance at the other men and thought that they, too, agreed with her assessment. Only Wong Cheung sat impassively, seemingly affected by neither Lee Tzo nor the hot humid weather.

Wong Sang rose the instant Tzo finished and said he, too, wished to air a grievance. "The more I think about the raid on my business, the more I think I was the victim of a stool pigeon. The police knew exactly when and where to conduct the raid despite the lack of street numbers on the doors. They wrecked the place so thoroughly that I couldn't salvage a thing. I am ruined! I tell the Council this not because I want help, but to let you know that should I find out who did this to me, I shall kill him!"

Lee Tzo could barely hide the satisfaction he felt at his erstwhile ally's loss and Liah spoke up, "Whoever takes pleasure in another's loss shall be dealt with, not only by the Gods but by the Council as well. Our purpose is to aid one another's successes not to revel in one another's failures." Having delivered her rebuke without naming names, Liah went on, "I, too, thought that the raid was extremely well-orchestrated and swiftly executed, so much so that it could only have been prompted by a stool-pigeon. That being the case, it should be the Council's business to discover the perpetrator and mete out the appropriate punishment. I hope you will defer to the Council in this, Wong Sang."

The smirk on Lee Tzo's face had vanished as he decided he had better join the majority on the issue and he declared, "Death is too lenient a punishment for a stoolpigeon. I hope we catch him soon." Liah smiled and said mysteriously, "I wouldn't worry. We already have a good idea who the stoolpigeon is. It's only a matter of time before we expose him." The Council members all looked at one another with the same question in their eyes, but Liah said no more.

Wong Cheung then rose and faced Lee Tzo, saying, "You can be certain I shall obtain the facts surrounding your grievance and if the youths of the Four Families Association are guilty as charged, they will indeed be taught a lesson. Of course, I hope I find that you did nothing to justify their displeasure."

Lee Tzo's face paled slightly and he lowered his eyes. Once the meeting was over, Tzo quickly signed the records and departed. Wong Cheung remained behind to ask Liah if she had any details to add to Tzo's account. Liah smiled at the big man and said, "There is nothing for you to act on now. I suggest you merely keep an eye and an ear out and let me know if you see or hear anything. I'll tell you more once I have more information. For the time being, I would say nothing to the youths in question. I, for one, do not think they are guilty of Tzo's charges. Before you go, I must also express my appreciation for your volunteering to deal with this matter. Please understand that I do not want you to feel you are obligated to do this. We can find another if you wish to abstain." Wong Cheung merely shook his head and took his leave.

A delicate peace settled over Chinatown as the overt sale of Apinyin from the other source ceased. However, Liah was still concerned, since Lee Tzo wasn't the kind of man who gave up so easily. Liah thought that perhaps he had taken his Apinyin business underground and she decided to have discreet inquiries made.

—

One afternoon while Liah was taking a nap, Cook sought out Fifth Son in the front room and engaged him in a quiet conversation. He spoke in a low, guarded tone. "I've been wanting to speak with you alone for the past few days, but each time your mother has been around." Selecting his words carefully, Cook went on. "You know, of course, that I treat you children as if you were my own. For isn't it so, that I've shared in all of your successes and provided support when you encountered problems?" Mert nodded warily, concerned that a lecture was in the offing.

Cook continued, "I need to speak to you about the young lady you are seeing. I am not asking you to quit seeing her. I am merely asking you to tell her to stay away from here. She has come looking for you three times already, and it has been fortunate that each time I was able to intercept her before your mother found out. You must realize that your mother is very old-fashioned and would not approve of your gallivanting around."

"You mean to tell me that Cora actually showed up here?" gasped Mert. "Do not worry, sir. I'll make sure that it doesn't happen again. She must be an idiot not to know she shouldn't be coming around here. However, you do understand what I'm going through, don't you, Cook? Mah-Mah is constantly pressuring me to get married and have children, but I'm just not ready for that. I want to learn what women are all about and have some fun first. If she doesn't let up soon, I'll be forced to consider moving out."

Cook replied sympathetically, "I understand. However, you cannot expect your mother to understand. She grew up in a time when children were expected to obey their parents without question. A son would be betrothed to the girl chosen by his parents, married on the date set by his parents and would, if the Gods were willing, produce heirs soon thereafter. Since I know you and your mother love each other very much, for both her sake and yours, I ask that you exercise patience in this matter. I promise you that when the time is right, I will try to reason with her."

Mert heaved a big sigh, nodded and promised that he would do his best. Mert looked at Cook somewhat guiltily, realizing what a delicate position he had just put Cook in and feeling a sudden surge of admiration for the man, having to keep the peace in this house.

—

The heat and humidity became unbearable as the end of August drew near. Each morning, Cook sloshed pails of water onto the cobblestones to keep the dust down and cool the stones. This particular morning, as he was sloshing the water around, he cursed softly as he realized that if it was already this hot this early, it would be like an oven by noon.

Suddenly, a booming voice greeting Cook shattered the stillness of the early morning. Cook looked around and noticed a gnarled wisp of a man with a flowing white beard perched atop a ladder, evidently trimming the overgrown wisteria and honeysuckle vines lodged amidst the interstices of the wooden arbor. "A good day to you too, Hoh Chan. What a miserable summer day it's going to be. Eight o'clock and already the cobblestones are hot."

The old man chuckled and replied, "You youngsters shock me with your frailty. If it is not hot in summer, then when should it be hot? You eat the bountiful fruits and vegetables ripened by the sun and enjoy the beauty of the flowers and shrubs nurtured by the sun and yet you still complain about the sun. Why not allow the sun to do its work and keep quiet?"

Cook smiled at the friendly rebuke and then, addressing him using the formal word for "Sir," asked Hoh Chan how he managed to keep so agile and energetic. "You must be in your seventieth summer season at the very least, yet it appears that you have more strength than I."

"Work, rice wine and women and in that precise order!" roared Hoh. That's how I do it. Enjoy those three pleasures freely and it will keep the blood flowing strongly. By the way, why are you wasting all that water? The cobblestones will dry up in minutes."

"That's true, sir," explained Cook, "but it will keep the dust and soot from getting indoors. Besides, I've got to keep the cobblestones clean for the outdoor people who choose to sleep on them." Hoh nodded his understanding. "The Gods do not spread their generosity evenly among us, do they? I hardly ever give much thought to the outdoor people. They bake in summer and freeze in winter. Nevertheless, I still maintain that if we want to enjoy the bounty of summer, we must endure the heat."

"Well, Ancient One," Cook said, "when your work is done, come inside and have some lunch." Taking mock offense, Hoh Chan tossed down a hefty branch, which landed at Cook's feet, and scoffed, "Ancient One? Speak for yourself Cook. I'm not old. I am a wise seventy years of age. As long as I can work and play, who dares to say that I am old?" When he finished speaking, he sent another branch crashing to the cobblestones to emphasize his point. Cook smiled and went back in the house.

Liah came out of her bedroom with a sullen expression and silently sank into her upholstered chair in the kitchen. Cook hastily placed a bowl of brandy broth on the table, said good morning and went back to the sink. Moments later, Liah suddenly giggled. Startled, Cook turned to see what Liah found so amusing. Liah just grinned and said, "Even with your back turned, I can read your thoughts. You're thinking what a vile mood I'm in this morning, and you're praying to the Gods that today will not be too terribly hot. Am I right?"

Cook laughed and nodded. He then told her, "Hoh Chan is in the Alley today, and I took the liberty of inviting him for lunch. You know how he favors meat-filled rolls and tarts." Liah replied, "That's fine. You know, that old man amazes me. At his age he's still scampering up and down that ladder like a young man. He has to be over seventy."

Cook smiled and responded, "It's all right to admire him for his longevity, Liah, but I wouldn't let him hear you say that he's old. I made that error earlier and he threw a branch at me that just barely missed. In fact, he hurled a second one just to make his point. That ancient one is indeed vigorous for his age."

Suddenly recalling something she had once heard concerning Hoh Chan, Liah asked Cook, "Did you know that in his youth Hoh Chan predicted the weather for the old miners? It has been said that a Fahn Gwai weatherman once kept track of Hoh's predictions and confirmed that Hoh's rate of accuracy was far higher than the weatherman achieved despite the scientific instruments the weatherman used. When the Fahn Gwai asked him how he did it, Hoh just pointed to his head and said 'brains'." Liah chuckled. "If Hoh Chan were to predict rain for today, I, for one, would carry an umbrella in spite of the clear sky." Just then they heard the sound of the front door opening and banging shut, followed by the sound of brisk footsteps in the corridor. Liah smiled and remarked, "Here comes our energetic miracle man now."

Hoh Chan burst into the kitchen, nodded to Liah as he plopped himself onto a chair and said, "I have transplanted some of the shrubbery to the end of town along the wooden fence separating us from the barns and corrals. Perhaps in time the area won't reek so badly of horse and cow shit."

Liah replied, "Thank you, Hoh. Perhaps when you have the time, you could also transplant some of the oleanders and maybe some hibiscus to the rear of the Alley. That will serve to hide the trashcans from view. For now, however, have some of the rolls Cook has baked. How about one with black mushrooms, pork, shrimp and sausage?"

Liah watched approvingly as Hoh drank his tea and gobbled down four meat buns and three sweet tarts seemingly before stopping for a breath. He refused when offered a plate of spiced ribs and chard but asked if he could take them home for supper. Liah smiled broadly, saying, "Of course, Hoh. Cook will wrap up not only the ribs and chard, but also some rice and more of the pastries."

"That would be most kind, Liah. I thank you." Hoh Chan wiped his lips carefully and made sure nothing had gotten lodged in his beard as well. Rising, he declared that it was time to leave, saying, "I still have much to do. Right now I've got to go shovel some horse manure into the vegetable patch and mix it in. Thanks again for this meal and the one I'll enjoy tonight with a cup or two of Ng Ga Pei."

They heard the front door slam behind him and Liah nodded, "You're right, Cook. That one will live a very long time. Did you hear the timbre of his voice? That is one of the signs of longevity."

A week later, Hoh Chan brought a pot of geraniums to Number Three. In the course of his third helping of stuffed bean cake and barbecued pork, he informed Liah that he had observed Apinyin peddlers using the temple to meet with their clients. Liah's sudden rage took the old man by surprise. He had never before seen Liah so angry. She spat, "Sacrilegious barbarians!" Liah's tone was menacing as she uttered, "Death! Death to the dogs! Death, do you hear?"

After his initial shock, Hoh Chan sat impassively and let Liah vent. When she finally wound down, she apologized to her guest for her loss of self-control, but Hoh merely shrugged. Liah's voice took on a note of concern as she cautioned him, "You know that I revere our place of worship, so I thank you for your constant vigilance. However, you must be careful. Those men are evil and will not hesitate to kill you if they think you are a danger to them. You should also be prudent when visiting me."

The old man scoffed saying that no one dared touch him, as he was a long-time student of the martial arts. Liah smiled back and replied, "No one doubts your ability to take care of yourself in a fair fight, Hoh Chan. However, these dogs will not fight honorably. They will ambush you or come at you from behind with several men. Outnumbered, you will be unable to defend yourself. Please take care, old man."

It was on the tip of Hoh Chan's tongue to reprimand Liah for calling him old, but the concern evident on her face dissuaded him. He knew that Liah only had his welfare in mind. Instead he said, "I thank you for you concern. I will be on the alert." He, in turn, warned Liah to be certain that she had adequately protected her own Apinyin business. Then he said, "Now I must return to pruning the arbor. Never would I have believed that the honeysuckle and wisteria could be restored to such vigor that it threatens to overwhelm the fence."

Aileen chose that moment to enter the kitchen, rubbing her eyes as she clambered onto Liah's lap. With deep pride in her voice, Liah informed Hoh Chan that her granddaughter was staying with her while her mother recuperated from childbirth. The old man grinned and replied, "She is a fine-looking granddaughter, Liah. I hear this latest birth has finally brought forth a grandson for you. The Gods have truly sent you their blessings." With that, Hoh Chan returned to his work.

That night at the supper table, Liah angrily told Professor that Hoh Chan had observed Apinyin sales being transacted inside their temple. Seeing her stony expression, Professor braced himself and asked if she wanted him to call an emergency meeting of the Council. Liah shook her head and replied, "We do not have sufficient proof yet. We only have Hoh Chan's word, and we can't use his testimony anyway without compromising him and putting him in danger. Lee Tzo and his men would kill him in an instant. We must set a trap to catch Tzo in the act. Then we'll convene the Council and demand a stiff penalty."

Cautiously, Professor disagreed. "Catching Tzo alone will solve nothing. We must also identify his cohorts or else another will take his place and the Apinyin trade will continue." Liah thought for a moment and agreed. After discussing how best to conduct the surveillance, Liah said, "I am reluctant to place the burden on you and Cook, but it is not wise to share this plan with anyone else at this time. Will you do it?"

Professor nodded and replied, "We have no other choice, Liah. We will do what we must do. I only hope that the surveillance will not be a lengthy one. While it will be bad enough in this heat, I don't relish watching in the cold, wet and windy weather." Liah nodded in silent sympathy and prayed that the Gods would be merciful and bring this dangerous task to a speedy conclusion.

So it was that Cook took to patrolling during the morning hours, since no one would question his being on the streets at that time; they would think that he was simply doing the daily shopping. Nevertheless, Liah warned him to make certain he did indeed do some shopping, lest someone become suspicious. For his part, Professor took to patrolling during the evenings. Despite their efforts, Liah was concerned that they might be missing anything that happened late at night. It was Professor who came up with the solution to have Chon's two Kung Fu masters patrol the streets after work. Liah cried in delight, "That's perfect! They could even start lodging with the old priest inside the temple under the pretext of providing for his welfare and safety. With the addition of the two Kung Fu masters, I'd say we will be well-served with regard to both the surveillance and our added protection."

Toward the end of August, Aileen returned home and a great sadness overwhelmed Liah. After pushing aside her own grief to console the bereft Amah, Liah's first impulse was to reach out for the comfort of her bamboo pipe. However, Cook cautioned her that she needed to remain clear-headed in the event something occurred concerning the Apinyin peddling. Liah retorted, "No one has uncovered a shred of evidence so far. Why do you think something will turn up now? Besides, one or two puffs will not rob me of my lucidity." Cook had shrugged in resignation and had started to walk toward her bedroom when Liah cried out, "No, no Apinyin, not yet, Cook. You're right, I must keep my faculties sharp."

On the morning of the twenty-fourth of August, quite by accident, Professor caught sight of a known opium user entering the temple by the rear door only to emerge a few moments later. Professor ducked back into the cover of shrubs and watched as the man furtively glanced up and down the cobblestones before slipping through an opening in the chain-link fence into the train yards.

The scholar immediately sought out Cook to tell him what he had seen and to discuss what to do. Inasmuch as they really didn't know much, they decided not to involve Liah just yet. Instead, they asked Selah to let them observe the temple from her roof terrace. Over the following week, they saw no fewer than six suspected opium users or sellers come and go from the temple in the same fashion, as the one Professor had seen. The second week they noticed the same men frequenting the temple again along with several more they'd not seen the first week. Having determined that the first sighting was not an isolated event, they now decided it was time to tell Liah.

It shocked both men when Liah did not erupt immediately in a fit of anger, but rather sat silently, deep in thought. They waited patiently until finally she nodded to herself and informed them that she had concocted a plan. Liah told them that they would raid the temple one morning and bring witnesses to observe the proceedings.

Hearing this, Professor countered, "A raid will not nab all the men involved, since they do not all arrive at the same time." Liah replied, "It's not necessary that we get them all, Professor. From what you and Cook have observed, the hour between eight-thirty and nine-thirty seems to be the preferred meeting time for most of them. We'll get the few men we miss later on. Now, I think we should use Wong Sang, Chon Woo, Lim Tao and Tom Soo as our witnesses." Cook immediately expressed concern and said, "Aren't you afraid Chon or Sang will alert Tzo?"

Liah shook her head and replied, "Here is what we will do. Professor will awaken Chon and Sang at eight o'clock on the morning of the raid and escort them here. Lim Tao and Tom will be notified in advance to be here at eight-thirty but without us divulging what we are planning to do. Once they are all here, then we will inform them of the raid. If we do it this way, no one will be able to give Tzo advance warning."

On the first of September, the sleepy-eyed and somewhat grouchy witnesses assembled in Liah's front room and were told of the Apinyin raid. Wong Sang paled and stared at Liah. "You can't be meaning to make stoolpigeons out of us, are you? Why us? Why not some of the others?"

Liah hissed, "Quit whining, Sang! You are a sworn member of the Council, so do your duty!" Then Liah asked if everyone understood their roles and finished by saying, "It is important that we catch not only the peddler but the customer as well. We will need both to testify against Lee Tzo." Chon Woo glowered at Liah and retorted, "This is a lousy job you've got us doing, but let's get on with it. I've got to get some sleep afterwards. I sure hope you know what you're doing, Liah."

Liah was waiting impatiently in the front room for the men's return when the sound of gunshots echoed down Peacock Alley. Before she could prod herself to go outside to investigate, she heard the men's agitated voices and moments later they burst into the front room. Seeing their faces contorted with shock and fear. Liah cried out, "What has happened?"

Wong Sang's voice trembled as he said over and over, "He's dead! He's dead!" Tom Soo fell into a chair and provided, "He's dead, Madam Liah, shot." Cook, also visibly shaken, took several deep breaths and gasped, "Liah, somebody shot the man." Not one of them was seemingly up to giving her a complete account of what had happened.

It was Lim Tao who finally recovered enough to give Liah some of the details. "We were closing in on two men when suddenly a volley of gunfire rang out. The young man we took to be the opium seller fell to the floor while the customer fled out the back door. The old priest is hysterical. What shall we do, Liah?"

Liah took a deep breath and then turned to Professor. "You must lock the doors of the temple and calm the old priest as best you can. Stay with him until he has recovered. Quickly, go!" Liah then instructed Cook to call the mortician, Lung Sam, and send him to the temple immediately, making him swear to remain silent until the facts of the event were made clear.

At that point, Wong Sang recovered his composure enough to scream at Liah, "Now look what you've done! You've involved us in a murder!" Liah bristled and cursed at Sang, telling him, "Lee Tzo is the one who bears the blame for this death. If he had abided by the edict of the Council, none of this would have occurred. If I were you, I would start figuring out how to defend myself in front of the Council, or have you forgotten that you were the one who vouched for Tzo in the first place." Sang's expression suddenly changed from angry to concerned and he shut up.

Liah then turned back to Cook. "Are you certain Lung Sam will act at once?" Cook nodded but said, "I'll go outside and watch for him."

Tom was still hunched over in a chair with his hands covering his face. He shook his head and spoke to no one in particular, "The guy who got shot couldn't have been more than a year or two older than me. We could even have been the same age. Oh, God!" Lim Tao shook his head in sympathy and went to make coffee. When the brew was ready, Lim Tao quietly handed each man a steaming cup.

Tom, hollow-eyed and pale, grasped his cup with both hands but did not immediately take a drink. Wong Sang nodded his thanks as he accepted his cup from Lim Tao, gulped it down with one or two swallows and then suddenly slammed the cup down on the table. Facing Liah, he said sarcastically, "Now that you've managed to get a man killed, can I leave now?" Liah scowled at him but nodded, saying, "Yes, just remember to keep your mouth shut. If you leak any of what happened, you will earn whatever punishment we mete out to you." After Sang departed, Chon Woo also rose and left but without asking permission. As he was walking out, he gave Liah a harsh scowl and shook his head.

Twenty-five minutes later, both Professor and Cook returned. Cook nodded at Liah's questioning look and indicated that they had taken care of everything. After having a cup of coffee, Professor quietly asked Liah, who had lapsed into silence, if there was anything else she wanted him to do. Receiving no answer, Professor took Tom by the arm, nodded to Cook and silently left.

When Thomas and Shelley awakened shortly afterwards, Cook told them of the raid and the ensuing murder of the young man. Shelley cursed and immediately asked about his mother. Cook replied, "She understandably holds herself responsible for the man's death and was quite distraught, so I gave her a strong draught of Apinyin. She will sleep until early evening." Thomas's eyes were blazing with anger and Cook, concerned that he might do something foolish, said, "Eldest Son, if you want to help your mother, you will do nothing foolish. For the time being, there is nothing that can be done. I suggest you be here for supper tonight to keep your mother company." Both boys nodded their understanding and decided to go to Jui Jinn's for breakfast. As they were leaving, Cook cautioned them to keep quiet and not get into any arguments.

Professor arrived at Number Three at eight o'clock that evening. There were dark circles under his eyes and he uncharacteristically declined the offer of supper. He reported, "I've been all over town and nothing seems to be amiss. I saw Wong Sang hanging out at Chon's bar as usual, but neither man said a word to me. The only person I didn't see at all today was Lee Tzo."

Liah did not at first acknowledge Professor's presence and remained huddled up in her upholstered chair. However, when Professor mentioned Lee Tzo's name, she stirred in her chair and murmured, "Professor, I have suffered the worst twelve hours of my life today." Her eyes were pained as she whispered, "I have condemned myself a thousand times over for this unfortunate young man's death. I had not foreseen such a tragedy."

Cook gently chided her, "Do not place too much of the blame on yourself, Liah. The young man's Meng-Sui decreed his death." Professor then chimed in, saying, "The young man was dealing with dangerous people, and it is that which got him killed. Cook is right, Liah, you should not blame yourself."

Liah then shifted her thoughts to Tom Soo, to how badly the event had affected him and to how helpless she had been to comfort him. Professor again shook his head and told her, "He's young and he will recover, Liah. After we left this morning, Tom told me he was thinking of resigning from the Council, but I pointed out to him that doing one's duty is not always pleasant and that he owed it to us and to himself to see this thing through. I think I convinced him to stay. It may be that the emotional impact of this young man's death was exacerbated by memories of his mother's death. Time will tell."

The scholar then relit his pipe and told them that he was going to take one last walk around Chinatown before retiring. Before he could leave, however, Liah apologized and asked him to remain a moment more. She told the scholar, "I want you to call an emergency meeting

of the Council for tomorrow morning at nine o'clock. I believe we
should confront Tzo now. If Chon or Sang refuse, remind them of the
punishment for dereliction of duty. Also warn them not to alert Lee
Tzo." Professor reluctantly agreed and took his leave.

Lee Tzo appeared at Number Three, sleepy-eyed and irritable,
shortly before nine the next morning. Although he was extremely curious about the reason for the meeting, he refrained from asking. By nine
o'clock the Council members were all present except for Wong Cheung
and Professor called the meeting to order. He began by explaining that
they would start without Wong Cheung because "there was no way to
notify him since he was nowhere to be found. Now, I will turn the meeting over to our chairwoman."

Liah's voice was hard as nails as she succinctly informed the members of the surprise raid on the temple in an attempt to capture the
Apinyin peddlers and their customers. Lee Tzo exchanged harsh
glances with the Council members who had been witnesses to the event
but he remained silent. Liah concluded by disclosing the murder of the
young man by unknown assailants. This drew a number of gasps from
around the table. Professor then shared his theory that the murder had
been prearranged by the gang leader for just such an event to prevent
the young man from talking. As Professor spoke, Liah observed Lee
Tzo and saw him clench his fists in his lap and harden his stare even
more. Despite Tzo's obvious anger, however, she thought she detected
a momentary flicker of fear in his eyes, giving her to believe that he was
indeed involved. Liah's eyes met Tzo's for a moment until he finally
glanced away.

When Professor finished speaking, Liah went on, "This outrageous
crime has brought shame on our community and I vow that the murder
shall not go unsolved or unpunished." Looking at Tom gently, Liah
continued, "The unfortunate young man's body is currently at the mortuary and, when his identity is known, he shall be buried with the ap-

propriate rites to ensure his eternal rest. I want it known that none of you men who were present at the raid are guilty of anything. I commend your sense of civic duty and am truly sorry we have been confronted with this dark deed."

Suddenly, Wong Sang lunged forward to attack Lee Tzo. Lim Tao deftly deflected the blow and held Sang back as he screamed at Tzo, "I told you months ago not to dabble in Apinyin, but no, you had to do it anyway!"

Lee Tzo had leapt to his feet when Sang first attacked but now sat back down in his seat. With a glint of moisture on his forehead, Tzo glared at Liah, pointed his finger at her and shouted, "So! You dare to accuse me of trafficking in Apinyin without any proof. Well, you're not going to make me the scapegoat for your mistakes. If you had not meddled in this affair, this murder would never have happened. You, Madam, are trying to divert attention away from yourself by sullying my name and you shall not succeed. This raid was unsanctioned by the Council and is your sole responsibility. I shall not sit here and listen to lies." With that, Tzo rose to leave.

"You shall remain in your seat, sir," hissed Liah and Kam Fong roughly pulled on Lee Tzo's arm forcing the pimp to sit down. Glaring back at Tzo, Liah replied, "Although Sang has prematurely accused you of complicity in this affair, you will pay with your life should our investigation determine that you were indeed involved."

Kam Fong then asked, "Liah, are there any clues as to the identity of the victim? Perhaps there is something on the young man's body that might reveal his family association." Professor shook his head. "No, nothing. We believe that the lack of identification was also part of the gang leader's plan should the young man be caught. I'm afraid we'll just have to wait for the culprits to trip themselves up."

Liah saw, or, imagined she saw, a look of smug relief on Tzo's face. Infuriated, she snapped, "That notwithstanding, we do have proof that one of our own is at the bottom of this business. And perhaps not at this moment, but soon, he shall be apprehended and tried by the Council." This statement brought on instantaneous silence in the room.

Professor was shocked at this. He wondered if Liah had gotten information that she had not shared with him. For his part, Lee Tzo seemed unaffected, but Liah saw a momentary flash of fear cross his face and she smiled to herself. Despite it being a bluff, Liah felt in her heart that the Gods would provide the needed answers.

After letting the silence stretch out for a bit, Liah abruptly changed the subject and said, "Let us put this subject aside for now and speak of happier things. The population of our town has now grown to over three thousand people. It is time that we have our own lion to celebrate the feast days instead of renting the lion from Dai Faw."

Tom gasped and Wong Sang cried out, "Liah, how dare you speak of death in one breath and feast days in the next? Don't you care that a young man lies dead in the mortuary? Are you that insensitive?" Although Professor's initial reaction was much the same as Wong Sang's, he saw the sorrow and remorse deep in Liah's eyes and realized that she was trying to break its grip on each of them. Immediately, he countered Sang's outburst. "While we all mourn the young man's death, Sang, I think Liah is right in speaking of our feast day and the lion. Life is bittersweet. If we do not temper sadness with happiness, life would become unbearable. By my estimates, the money we save from not having to rent Dai Faw's lion and their lion dancers will pay for our own lion in a short few years."

Tom heaved a big sigh. Although he knew Professor was right, the horror of the young man's death haunted him. Perhaps someday he'd learn to accept the sad with the happy, but right now his heart felt only sadness. The ensuing discussion was brief and the Council members sanctioned the purchase of a lion. Lee Wah, as he was an importer, offered to make inquiries in Hong Kong. He said that as soon as he received the quotes, he'd notify the Council. The session ended with a quiet, sober supper, the signing of the records and the adjournment.

—

The Sunday following the Council meeting, Wong Cheung returned to Chinatown and immediately came to see Liah. Professor saw by the foreboding in his expression that the visit was not merely a social call. Straightaway, the big man addressed Liah. "I have reason to believe the slain youth was one of ours. Our Tong just received a request for help in locating a Hua Lam Li. The description we got fits the youth in question. I also received a report from the elders in Dai Faw. It's too bad I was not here for the raid or to confront Tzo with the accusations contained in that report." Professor immediately apologized for not waiting for his return and explained that they had hoped to shock Tzo into making a false move but to no avail.

As the big man continued, his voice terrified Liah. She'd never heard such menace in a voice in her entire life. "My elders in Dai Faw tell me that certain of their youths have been approached with an offer to peddle Apinyin in Loo Sahng in return for large sums of money. They do not know if any of them have accepted the offer, but when Hua Lam Li disappeared, his younger brother went to the elders and told them of his fears. I wish to confront Lee Tzo as my elders have asked. Can you call another meeting?"

Before answering, Liah rapidly explained what had led up to her decision to conduct the raid, the role of the witnesses and the how the event unfolded. Cheung's expression was grim as he heard about the confrontation in the temple and the volley of shots that had rung out. After concluding with an account of the Council meeting, Liah pleaded, "Wong Cheung, can you please allow us a few more weeks to watch Lee Tzo? We hope he will slip up, but failing that, we hope to trap him.

If Tzo has included Wong Sang in his plot, we can perhaps maneuver Sang into incriminating Tzo. It won't hurt to wait a little longer and when we have definite proof that Tzo is guilty, the Council will undoubtedly demand the death penalty. I am sure the members will not issue a death sentence on the basis of what we have so far."

The big man's face remained impassive and Liah was afraid she'd failed to convince him, but moments later he heaved a big sigh and said, "You are perhaps right, Liah. I will bide my time for now. However, I must inform the elders in Dai Faw about your plan and get their approval." Wong Cheung then reiterated his earlier offer of support. "I again make available my services should you have need. You have but to ask."

A few days after Wong Cheung's visit, Liah received a telephone call from the big man positively identifying the slain youth as Hua Lam Li. Sorrowfully, Liah passed on the information concerning the youth's family and village to Professor and requested that he make the necessary arrangements to ship the body back to China for burial in his ancestral plot. Liah enlisted Tom Soo to do the associated paper work and asked Wong Cheung to have the elders contact the youth's family. Liah herself paid all the expenses, including a sum for the parents of the slain youth.

Although consumed with remorse, Liah prodded Professor to contact the Four Families Association for any shred of information concerning the Apinyin trade in Dai Faw and any hint of a connection with Loo Sahng. When nothing turned up, the scholar was irate. He harbored a strong suspicion that the Four Families Association and the other Tongs were withholding information, perhaps out of fear of retaliation or Fahn Gwai intervention. Finally, he threw up his hands in frustration and muttered, "I give up, Liah! Never in a thousand years will we succeed. There is a conspiracy of silence. I know it."

During this time, Liah redoubled her efforts to unify Chinatown. She reasoned that if there was no help to be had from Dai Faw, they must survive on their own and this could only be done if Chinatown were united. However, Lee Tzo was not passively waiting for her to act. Word soon came that Tzo had started a smear campaign against her. Professor told Liah and Cook, "It's not a direct condemnation of you, but rather of your power over Chinatown. His snide insinuations are beginning to make people wonder and I don't like it, Liah. He is making people believe that your money has enslaved the town and that you believe you can do anything you want."

Liah listened attentively but remained silent until after he had finished. Professor cried, "If only Lee Tzo had said these things in front of me, I'd have put him down." At this point, Liah shook her head. "No, Professor. Neither you nor Cook should try to defend me. It will only add a measure of credibility to Tzo's remarks." She lapsed into silence again and both men waited for her next words.

"I'm thinking," Liah murmured to Cook, "that we are under attack and that we'd better secure our Apinyin deliveries. Perhaps we should allow our customers to purchase a month's supply instead of a week's supply. That would significantly cut down on the risk of being caught. For those who cannot afford it, we will allow them a month's credit. Until we catch Tzo, we must be extra cautious."

Although Liah seemed to be speaking and acting in a rational manner, Cook understood the pain she was feeling over having initiated the events that led to the death of the youth. He nodded his understanding and hoped for her sake that the matter resolved itself sooner rather than later. Her spirit would suffer grievously until then.

A CHANGE OF DICE

It was during this time that Liah and Cook decided to provide financing for Wong Sang to open another gambling house. Professor agreed with the decision, saying, "I know that Sang is capable of being bought, but this will lessen the chances that Tzo will be able to bribe him. Moreover, since his place was raided, Sang's gone back to being surly and argu-mentative. Have you spoken to him yet?"

"No, he's coming by tomorrow afternoon," replied Liah. "I entirely agree with your assessment of him, by the way. His attitude was most disagreeable when I asked him to meet with me, especially since I didn't tell him why I wanted to speak with him."

On the fifteenth day of September, Wong Sang arrived at Number Three and almost immediately began to lament about his bad fortune. Liah, already in a bad mood, railed at him. "I don't recall hearing you praise the Gods when business was good so don't blame your setback on them now. Besides, you brought the disaster upon yourself. Didn't I recommend that you install a stouter door and put up iron grills on the windows? I also recall suggesting that you should locate the busi-ness in Peacock Alley. If you must blame someone, blame yourself. Now, are you or aren't you going to open another place?"

Somewhat chastised, Sang moaned, "How can I? Everything I own is gone. I've only got seventy-five dollars to my name." Exasperated by Sang's sniveling, Liah snapped, "Cook managed to retrieve a bag of cash and several sets of gaming tiles that the Fahn Gwai police missed. I'll finance the rest and you can pay me back as business develops. So, what do you say, Sang? It's hot and I don't want to listen to you com-plain anymore."

Hearing Liah's offer, Sang grinned widely and said, "I'm in. I'll go talk to Marchesson about a new location immediately." Liah nodded, but added, "If I were you, I'd keep the knowledge of our partnership to your-self for a while. Tzo may not like the thought of you getting back on your feet again and might put obstacles in your way. I know he wouldn't hes-itate to sacrifice you or anyone else if it helped his own cause."

Sang snarled angrily, "If I find out that he was the sonofabitch who snitched on me, I'll kill him." Liah responded evenly, "There's no need, Sang. Why dirty your hands when the Council will do the work for you? Oh, by the way, do you still employ Wei Tan?"

Wong Sang shook his head and answered, "Not anymore."

"Well, rehire him," snapped Liah. Noting Sang's displeasure over her order, Liah admonished, "I'm tired of your childish resentment each time I offer you good advice. Do you or don't you want to reopen?" She allowed Sang to think things over for a bit, then added more diplomatically, "I think you should not only consider rehiring Wei Tan, but you should also consider leasing half of the new building to Wei's three cousins to open a café. The café will help to mask the coming and going of so many men to the gambling room. However, you should decide for yourself."

Wong Sang muttered something inaudible and took his leave.

—

Wong Sang's surly attitude vanished as soon as he rented Number Eleven and, in accordance with Liah's "recommendations," rehired Wei Tan and rented out half the store to Wei Tan's three cousins. It hurt his pride to admit Liah was right, but the café would help to camouflage the gambling room.

A week into the renovations, Sang frowned as Cook walked into the store and said that he had a good idea that would prevent the police from confiscating all the money and gambling tiles if there should be another raid. Seeing the keg in Cook's arms, Sang growled, "That barrel is your good idea?"

Cook said nothing. He looked around the back of the room and pointed to a place in the corner. "I think you should put your wok stove there along with a barrel each of soy sauce and peanut oil. This rice keg will then look perfectly natural." Sang started to object but thought better of it and said, "Please show me how it will work."

Cook explained, "This keg has a false top, which will be filled with rice. In an emergency, you would lift off the false top, shove the tiles and money into the keg and it will all fall through a chute to the ground below. In fact, I would just bunch up the tablecloths with the tiles and money, and shove each one into the keg."

Sang grinned. "This is really an ingenious idea, Cook. Now, even if the Fahn Gwai police grab the keg if they raid us and break the place up, they won't get all the money and gambling tiles." Cook accepted the praise but warned Sang, "If I were you, I'd keep the knowledge of the secret chute to myself. That way a stool pigeon won't be able to tip off the police."

Sang scowled and lowered his voice. "Cook, can you tell me if it was Lee Tzo who snitched on me? I promise I won't do anything without Liah's permission." Cook shrugged and replied, "I'm not at liberty to divulge secrets. Let's plan out how to design the chute. We want to be certain it works properly."

—

Lee Tzo was shocked when he saw Wong Sang working on Number Eleven. It was immediately evident that Liah must have refinanced Sang and he cursed. It had been his plan to refinance Sang but only after seeing the man beg. The pimp walked up to Sang and sneered, "Well, I see you've partnered with Liah again."

Sang fought his strong desire to have a confrontation with Tzo and managed to hold his tongue. Fear of Liah's wrath won out over his desire for revenge. He merely grunted, "Yeah."

Tzo went on, "Three locks this time? Isn't that a sure sign that this is a gambling house?" Sang's face darkened and he muttered, "Only we would know it's a gambling house, Tzo. The Fahn Gwai police wouldn't know unless someone told them."

Lee Tzo giggled nervously, nodding his head. He looked at his watch and invited Sang for lunch. Sang ignored Tzo, turned and opened his door to go inside. Lee Tzo followed him and angrily demanded to know why Sang had ignored his invitation for lunch. Seething at Tzo for entering without an invitation, Sang curbed his temper and muttered, "Didn't hear you. Thanks, but I got no time. Not if I want to open on time."

Tzo silkily responded, "When is that?"

Sang narrowed his eyes, faced Tzo and shrugged, "I don't know the exact date yet. Professor will tell me which day is likely to be most auspicious."

Tzo followed Sang around the room as Sang installed paneling on the walls. The pimp kept up a one-sided conversation all the while. "I had been thinking lately," murmured Tzo, "that I should be your partner. We are surely alike in nature and I wouldn't boss you around like Liah. Just think, Sang, no kowtowing to that bitch and we'd split the profits fifty-fifty."

Tzo correctly read Sang's silence as a refusal and quickly told Sang that this, of course, was not the right time to be speaking of opening a second gambling house. Perhaps after he'd opened up, then Sang could think of another place. "Am I right, Sang?"

Sang reached for the box of nails and muttered dismissively, "Sure, sure, Tzo. After I've opened up this business, we can talk. Right now, however, I'd like to concentrate on my work without any distractions."

Lee Tzo recoiled as if he'd been slapped in the face and vowed to himself that he would repay Sang's slight with interest. With great effort Tzo casually inquired if Sang was going to visit the brothel that night, saying, "Mei Wah misses you, Sang." Wong Sang shook his head and his tone was impatient as he replied, "No, not tonight. It's not a good idea for me to be seen too often at your place. People might draw the wrong conclusions. Besides, I don't want to get Liah mad."

"What?" taunted Lee Tzo angrily, "You'd allow a woman to dictate

your actions? Surely, Liah can't fault you for going to a brothel." Lee
Tzo's voice was filled with disdain as he concluded, "I'll talk to you
again when you're not cowering in fear of a woman. You can be sure
that if you and I were partners, you'd not have to worry about what
you could do and who you could see."

As Lee Tzo went out the door, Sang drove a nail into the panel with
such force that he put a hole in the panel. He cursed both Tzo and Liah
as he ripped the panel down and started over.

—

When Professor declared that the twenty-sixth day of September in the
Fahn Gwai year of nineteen hundred and twenty was the astrologically
propitious date for Wong Sang to open his new gambling parlor. Sang
merely shrugged and said, "As far as I'm concerned, any day will do.
My luck will be determined by my ability to play the tiles." Nevertheless, he agreed to open on the twenty-sixth.

Wei Tan's cousins opened up their café four days before Sang and curious patrons jammed the café to try out the food. On the morning Sang
opened his gambling parlor behind the café, the cobblestones were already red with firecracker confetti left over from the café opening. Sang
grinned and said to one of Wei Tan's cousins, "If these bits of red paper
summon the luck of the Gods, all of us ought to do great!" Turning serious, he continued, "Are you certain the buzzers are in good working condition? I don't want to be surprised if there's another raid. You should
also keep your eyes open for any strangers or people acting funny."

The firecrackers, the passing trains, Sen Fei's shrill falsetto voice accompanied by moon fiddles, reeds, cymbals, lutes and drums all contributed to the cacophony filling the air as throughout the late afternoon
and evening, Peacock Alley celebrated the opening in traditional Chinese style. Everyone was having a good time except for Lee Tzo, who
was cursing the commotion behind his closed bedroom doors. At one

point, he vowed vengeance on Sang and Liah for forcing him to endure the unending noise.

At eleven o'clock on opening night, Lee Tzo made his appearance in the gambling house. Mei-Mei obediently and respectfully walked in a few steps behind him, her body swaying with a sensual grace. She seemed to glide over the floor and the men ogled her as she passed by, her tiny-toed slippers peeking out from under her skintight cheongsam with the slits on the sides almost reaching her waist.

Wong Sang spotted Tzo and shouted out a challenge. "Are you brave enough to wager against the house on this most propitious day?" Lee Tzo's pride in his grand entrance disappeared and he frowned as he responded, "Are you so certain of your good joss, Sang? I don't know if you should risk squandering Liah's monies by betting against me."

Wong Sang was momentarily taken aback by Lee Tzo's brazen mention of Liah's involvement in his business, but retorted, "Name your wager, Tzo. I'll meet it, or should I say Liah and I will meet it." Furious that he had failed to embarrass Sang, Tzo sneered, "Very well. Let us find out whose luck is stronger this day."

Three times Lee Tzo flung money on the table and three times he lost. Although livid with fury inside, Tzo managed an outward calm. "It is said," Tzo commented as he declined to make another bet, "a wise man knows not to continue gambling when three times in a row he loses. I will return another day, for even Liah's luck cannot always be this good."

Flush with victory, Sang couldn't resist needling Tzo when he again brought up Liah's involvement in the business. Loudly enough for everyone to hear, he said, "The word is you want to open up a gambling house to compete with ours. Beware, Tzo, the Gods do favor Liah. However, I suppose if I were you I would also take my chances with a gambling house instead of peddling Apinyin. If you do open a gambling parlor, be sure no stoolpigeon does to you what one did to me."

Lee Tzo froze in his tracks, then turned abruptly and started to make a move toward Sang. Remembering where he was, however, he managed to get a hold of himself and turned his move into a graceful bow. Just then Old Yin, now back on his feet and healthy again, announced that supper was ready and the background noise of the gambling parlor resumed.

Sang called out to the throng, "You all know Old Yin. He was clubbed on the head when one of our people sold us out to the Fahn Gwai police. Well, he's back with us and has prepared a fabulous meal to celebrate our opening. Come, everybody, food and liquor is on the house."

Speaking to Tzo in a voice only loud enough for him to hear, Sang added, "You of all the people here should definitely have supper. The Gods know you lost enough tonight to pay for the entire feast." Sang felt exhilarated as he saw Tzo clench his fists, his lips turning pale with fury. The pimp drew in a sharp breath, glared at Sang and stalked out.

Sang retired to his office, slumped in a chair and reached for an open bottle of whisky. He savored his triumph over Tzo for several minutes before the continuing din outside intruded once again. Sang moaned, "For a whole week I have to listen to this? Sen Fei's voice could shatter glass."

—

The heat of the last days of September drove the residents of Peacock Alley into the streets at night to escape the stifling air indoors. Three days after the grand opening of Sang's gambling house, Tom and Professor were cooling off outside Number Four. Although it was two in the morning, it was still too hot indoors to sleep.

Slouched in his rattan chair, Professor puffed quietly on his pipe as Tom lay sprawled atop the wooden bench. Suddenly, the scholar leaned over, tapped Tom on the arm and pointed up the street. "I thought Sang and Tzo were at odds again."

"Yeah, I thought they were too," muttered Tom, as he sat up and saw the gambler and the pimp walking toward them. Tom whispered, "Maybe it's just a coincidence. Maybe they're as hot as we are and are both just out for a walk. I know that Sang has been telling everyone in Chinatown that Tzo was the stool pigeon who turned him in to the Fahn Gwai police. However, they certainly look friendly enough now."

Sang was first to spot Professor and Tom and cursed, "Damn! Wouldn't you know those two would see us together? Now Liah will have my head." Lee Tzo whispered to Sang as they approached the pair, "Just keep your mouth shut, I'll handle this."

Tzo stepped off the cobblestones, hailing Professor and Tom. "Sang and I are on our way to Wong's Café. Why don't the both of you join us? It's too hot to sleep." Tom remained silent and looked to Professor for a cue. "Why not?" chuckled Professor. "Come on, Tom. Tomorrow is Sunday and you can sleep in."

Lee Tzo smiled at Tom. "We'll stop off at Chon's first. My treat."

As they entered the bar, they noticed Chon's arm fall from a young girl's shoulders as he stared disbelievingly at Professor, Tom, Wong Sang and Lee Tzo. He recovered quickly, however, and shouted out a greeting. "Now, this is a great honor. A great honor. Not one but four Council members. My establishment is honored. The drinks are on me tonight." Chon signaled the barmaid and guided his guests to an empty booth.

After the barmaid had brought them their drinks, Professor inhaled the aroma emanating from his brandy snifter and offered a toast, "To the Council!" Chon then raised his glass, toasting the health, wealth and happiness of Chinatown. Toast after toast followed in rapid succession. An hour later, Tom rose unsteadily to his feet, raised his glass and started to propose yet another toast but was abruptly interrupted by Tzo, who had also lurched to his feet. In a somewhat slurred voice, Tzo said, "This night would not be complete if we did not drink to the health of our Council leader, a dictator and self-promoter. May Kwan Koong reflect on her deeds and heap disfavor upon her head."

Professor lowered his snifter and Tom stared at Tzo dumbfounded. Wong Sang's mouth dropped open in shock while Chon quickly walked away to speak to other customers. Tom looked around the booth, noted Professor's rigid face and Sang's open mouth, and sought to defuse the situation. He raised his glass and muttered, "Yeah, I drink to Madam Liah."

Lee Tzo swayed on his feet and shouted for the barmaid to refill their glasses. Wong Sang scowled and nudged Tzo saying, "That's enough. You're already drunk." The pimp viciously shoved Sang's arm away, leaned forward to tug at Professor's sleeve and asked, "Am I drunk, Professor?" The scholar gently disengaged Tzo's hand and murmured, "You'll be fine once we get some food into you, Tzo. Let's all go over to Wong's Café."

Lee Tzo's face immediately took on an injured look and he declared loudly, "So, you think I'm drunk too!" He then turned unsteadily to face Tom, who was seated across the table from him. "What about you, lawyer man? Do you think I'm drunk?" Just then Chon walked up somewhat nervously and suggested that it was time for them to leave. Professor, Tom and Wong Sang nodded their agreement, rose and attempted to steer Lee Tzo toward the door, but he angrily pushed away Tom's arm and screeched at them, "You weak, obedient slaves of the all-powerful Liah! You make me sick. All of you toady up to her and do her bidding without a thought of your own."

A small crowd began to gather around the booth and Chon angrily snapped at them, "Haven't you guys ever seen a drunk before? Go on, everybody, drinks are on the house." At that, the crowd quickly dispersed toward the bar and Chon whispered to Sang, "Get that miserable bastard out of here!"

Lee Tzo began to laugh uncontrollably but managed to blurt, "Say, Professor, would you like to hear something funny? Do you think Liah knows about everything that happens in this town? Well, she doesn't. Ask Wong Sang. Go on Sang, tell them, or I will."

Wong Sang's eyes shot daggers at Tzo and he hissed, "Shut up, you drunken fool!" The pimp laughed in delight at Sang's discomfiture and he shrieked, "Tell them, Sang! Okay. If you won't, I will." However, before Tzo could say another word, Sang smashed his fist into Tzo's face. The pimp's head recoiled at the impact and he stared in glassy-eyed astonishment for a second before falling forward onto the table.

Wong Sang hastily apologized "I'm sorry about this, Chon." Chon merely nodded and whispered to them, "Take him out the back door. It will be less noticeable." Professor, Tom and Sang lifted the unconscious Tzo and carried him out. Once outside, they decided to take him back to his brothel.

After they managed to half-carry, half-drag the still-unconscious Tzo home and had dumped him on his bed, Wong Sang beat a hasty retreat as Mei-Mei's curses filled the air.

At three o'clock the next afternoon, Sang stopped in at Number Three to drop off the previous night's receipts, fully expecting Liah to lash out at him for his role in last night's debacle. However, Liah gave no hint that she knew what had occurred. The thought flashed through his mind that Liah was just toying with him as a cat would with a mouse. However, Liah continued to act as if nothing were amiss. Sang realized that Professor had not yet told her about it and quickly took his leave.

After Sang left, Liah became thoughtful. It was obvious from Sang's demeanor that he had done something that he expected to be chastised for, but she had no idea what. Just then Cook returned home from shopping, an amused look on his face. Grinning, he said to Liah, "I was in the meat market just now and ran into Professor who told me a most interesting story. It seems that last night Lee Tzo invited Tom, Sang and Professor to have dinner with him at Wong's Café but made the mistake of stopping off at Chon's first."

Before Cook could continue, they heard the front door open and a moment later Professor walked into the kitchen. Cook smiled and said to him, "Sir, you are just in time to tell Liah yourself what happened at Chon's. I've only told her that Tzo invited you, Tom and Sang to supper at Wong's." Liah smiled and replied, "I was wondering why Sang seemed so guarded this afternoon. He must have thought that you had already told me what happened last night."

Professor related what had occurred. He finished by saying, "I'm sure that Tzo, drunk as he was, would have said something incriminating, but Sang knocked him out before he could utter a word. In any event, Tzo seemed to think that whatever it was would reflect badly on you, Liah."

Cook commented thoughtfully, "I wonder what Tzo is planning. Wei Tan has been watching Tzo for us and has informed me that he suspects Tzo is about to make some move. He said he saw Tzo pacing in front of Number Ten the other day, as if he were expecting some important visitors. Unfortunately, Wei Tan couldn't stay and see who showed up without someone noticing. He said that Sang has also been on edge of late."

Despite their premonitions, nothing of significance transpired the rest of the year nor all of the following one. Overall peace seemed to have settled over Chinatown.

1922

YEAR OF THE DOG

TROUBLE AND STUCKEY

On Saturday nights Chinatown was a busy and boisterous place. Consequently, it was an exciting place to go slumming with a girlfriend and the white population of Los Angeles did just that. For the timid, there was the exotic Tea Garden Café at the entrance to Lion's Den Alley or The Noodle House, a popular eatery that, as the name implies, served all kinds of noodles. For the more daring, there was The Dragon's Den Bar, or the Eastern Café, both situated in the center of Chinatown. Two other cafés in front of Blind Man's Alley were also favorites of Saturday night revelers.

"White people who venture into the alleyways of Chinatown have to be daring, drunk or just plain crazy," Hans said to his partner. "I can understand them visiting places on the fringes of Chinatown, but to go where it's dark and there are no other white people around, they're just plain asking for it. Don't they know that the Chinks consider their presence an intrusion upon their privacy? Worse yet, some of the whites actually make fun of the Chinks, thinking they don't understand. Mark my words, someday a Chink is not going to take kindly to the insults. Then watch out."

Hans and his partner, Little John, were the only policemen assigned to the Chinatown area. Chief Dobbs had suggested that Hans train a few men to support them, but Hans had vetoed the idea. "No, Chief. If we send too many men in, the Chinks will see it as the police meddling in their business. As it is, they're only barely tolerating Little John and me. I'd hate to see what would happen if they decided that they had had enough of us. We're better off leaving things as they are."

Chief Dobbs decided not to pursue the idea, at least for the time being. He remembered how a previous Chinatown raid had resulted in a major upheaval within the Chinese settlement and a hue and cry in the press. He didn't need the newspapers on his back again. Once had been enough. However, he cautioned Hans, "You must get them to understand that we're there primarily for their benefit and that they're better off working with us than against us. The bigger the town gets, the more police we'll have to assign there."

Hans laughed, "Boss, can you picture me trying to explain to a suspicious Chinaman who can't speak English that we're there to help him? Don't you realize that they not only distrust us but despise us 'White Devils'? I can't say I blame them much, in light of all the violence that's been done to them. However, one reason so many of them are coming into town from up north is that we treat them better here than they do up there. Don't worry. Little John and I can handle things no matter how big the town gets. Outside of gambling, prostitution and some probable opium use there really isn't any serious crime in Chinatown."

The Chief retorted, "Okay, I can't say I understand them like you do, so for the time being, I'll go along with your approach. However, I'm telling you straight out that the first time things get out of hand, we're going in there whether they like it or not."

—

One Saturday night in early August, The Dragon's Den Bar was bulging with lusty, laughing, shouting men, all hell bent on relieving pent-up emotions that had accumulated all week. They were lined up at the bar five deep and it was a wonder that the bartender and barmaids could keep all the orders straight. Adding to the din was the musical offerings of a jazz combo in the corner.

Seated at a small table against the wall were two burly white men, huddled over their drinks. The larger of the two had a scowl on his face and was becoming increasingly belligerent at the occasional jostling that occurred in the tight quarters. Once he even took a swipe at a barmaid. His companion, concentrating on keeping his drink from being knocked over, pleaded with his friend, "Aw, Trouble, sit down, will ya'? It don't pay to get so riled up over a few Chinks."

Trouble eyed his friend malevolently, then flopped back in his chair. "Okay, Stuckey. But I promise you someday I'm gonna kill me one of these bastards!"

Stuckey shrugged and replied, "Yeah, yeah. Come on, drink up."

Trouble was a hulk, a railroad foreman with the fiery temperament of his Irish and German heritage. He had been sixteen years old when he first came to work on the railroad. Years later, when the rails pushed westward, Trouble became a foreman for the Union Pacific Railroad. When the Transcontinental Railway was completed, Trouble was kept on to maintain the tracks, but he soon missed the blood, brutality and excitement of laying the rails.

It was the competition with the Central Pacific Railway that first caused Trouble to develop a hatred of the Chinese. He resented the chiding and ridicule he endured from his boss about how much more track the Chinese coolies laid compared to his own crew. Back then, he routinely got drunk as a way of dealing with things and when drunk would brutally attack any coolies he came across. That pattern had continued right up to the present. His ugly disposition soon lost him the companionship of most men, for they didn't like to be embroiled with the police every time they went on a binge. Stuckey, who had been with Trouble in the early days of the railroad, remained the only man who would go out with him.

Stuckey was not overly bright and didn't make friends easily. He found that following Trouble's lead saved him from making decisions, so he stayed with him. However, once in a while, Trouble became too brutal, even for Stuckey. At those times, he would warn Trouble: "Don't push things, Trouble. I'll paste you one if I have to." Usually, Stuckey was able to keep his friend in check, but he was afraid that sooner or later Trouble's temper was going to get the better of him.

Trouble blamed all of his present woes on the "damned Chink coolies" again. In his mind, they were now stealing work from him by undercutting the wage scale. Trouble stared into his glass and brooded. Emptying it, he raised his arm to attract the barmaid's attention, but she was too far across the room to see him. He then waved his hand at the bartender, "Hey, Chink! Bring me another bottle! Chop! Chop!"

It made Trouble feel superior when he ordered the Chinks around. He liked to see them cringe or scurry out of his way. The bartender soon brought over a bottle, set it on the table and stood with an open hand waiting for the two-dollar payment. Trouble emptied the bottle into his glass and ignored the little man. Sensing Trouble was not going to pay at that moment, the bartender made a move to leave, but Trouble's arm shot out, grabbing and holding the man by his collar. Trouble then stood up and threw him against the wall as he roared, "Stay there! Don't you move, you yellow rat!"

The little man landed on the floor and tried to signal to the bouncer, but Trouble grabbed him again and yelled in his face, "I don't like you Chinks! You're always taking our jobs away. We ought to ship you yellow bastards back to where you came from!" Trouble grabbed the man again and made a feeble swipe at the little man but missed. Someone yelled from the end of the bar, "Oh, shut up, Trouble! Leave that Chinaman alone. We want our drinks, too."

Trouble dropped the bartender and weaved his way over to see who it was that had dared to yell at him. When he saw that it was his former friend Murphy, he shouted, "Murphy, you shut your own mouth! Why the hell are you sticking up for a Chinaman?"

Murphy lowered his voice in an attempt to defuse the situation and replied, "Okay, okay, Trouble. I know you're mad and you're drunk, but do you have to take it out on poor Charlie? He works for a buck just like you and me. Besides, we all want to get drunk, too."

Trouble glared at Murphy and shouted, "You got to be a pretty big man because of them Chinks, didn't you? Well, you might love them, but I hate them!" Murphy again tried to calm Trouble, saying, "Come on, Trouble. Let's just forget it. I'll buy you a drink. How about it?"

Trouble shook his head. "Keep your lousy money. I'll tell you what I'm going to do. First, I'm going to get real drunk. Second, I'm going to find a Chink and kick the shit out of him. Finally, I'm going to carve him up." To emphasize his point, Trouble used his right index finger and drew it across his neck.

By now, the bar had become eerily quiet and the jazz combo had stopped playing. Stuckey went over to his friend and tried to pull him back to his seat, but Trouble knocked him across the room. At this point, most of the customers moved away, leaving an open space around him and Murphy. No one made any attempt to leave the bar because Trouble stood between them and the door, looking like an angry bull.

Murphy glared at Trouble. "You do that and they'll hang you for it. There are witnesses here who heard you make the threat. For your sake, I hope you'll just go home and sleep it off."

Charlie had crept along the wall and, as he cleared Trouble's reach, he got up and ran back to the bar. Trouble took a swipe at him, but missed as Charlie ducked behind the bar. Murphy took a menacingly step toward Trouble and warned him, "I told you to lay off, friend." Trouble's right arm shot out at Murphy, but in his tipsy condition, he missed yet again. He raged, "Friend? You ain't no friend of mine, Murphy. You're no better than the Chinks. You can't tell me what to do!"

Trouble turned to look for Stuckey and seemed surprised to find him lying on the floor, leaning against the wall. With a concerned look on his face, Trouble reeled over to help him up. Stuckey shook free of Trouble's arm and waved a fist at him, saying, "One of these days I'm going to plaster you so hard, they'll have to use a broom to sweep you up. Oh, hell, let's just get out of here!" The two men lumbered out of The Dragon's Den Bar, but not before Trouble swiped one hand across the bar, sending glasses flying in all directions.

Everyone in the bar continued to hear Trouble's ranting as the pair walked unsteadily down the street. Murphy turned to Charlie and said, "Better warn Chinatown! Looks like Trouble might just do something this time!" Charlie nodded and caught the attention of his two bouncers. He spoke a few words and the two quickly departed. Each man took a different route to notify all the sentries, then returned to their posts at The Dragon's Den. Within fifteen minutes, all of Chinatown had been alerted and the citizenry went inside and barricaded their doors.

BODY IN PIG ALLEY

August third would be a day no one in Chinatown would ever forget. Sunday dawned pink behind the night's dark clouds, casting an eerie glow over the sleeping town. Aileen was sound asleep beside her grandma, but soon began to toss and turn. Try as she would, Aileen could not get back to sleep. She opened her eyes and spied her red, white and blue soldier standing on the shelf nearby. She got out of bed slowly and carefully so that she wouldn't wake her grandma. She tiptoed over to the shelves, climbed on a chair and took the toy off the shelf. Suddenly, however, Aileen realized it was Sunday! She hurriedly replaced the soldier on the shelf, threw on her clothes and tiptoed quickly down the corridor. She had to be at the playground early to claim her favorite set of rings. As she stole down the corridor, she half-expected Cook to call out for her to come back and eat first.

This morning she was lucky. Cook had risen early to do errands and unbarred the doors. When he had left, he had locked only one door lock. Aileen quietly slipped outside, making sure not to slam the screen door, and walked slowly until she was two doors away, then she broke into a run.

Willie saw Aileen from across the street and waved to her to cross over. Willie was only a few years older than Aileen, but he was more mature. His mother had died when he was young and he was being raised by his father, who still grieved for his wife and consequently paid little attention to him. Therefore, Willie was usually on his own when he wasn't working in his father's market.

When Aileen reached him, Willie said, "Aileen, why are you going to the playground so early? It's only eight o'clock." Aileen eagerly explained, "I know, but I wanted to get there early to get my favorite set of rings. Are you coming to the playground today, Willie?"

"Yeah," replied Willie, "if I finish my work in time. I'm on my way to the store now. Maybe I'll see you there." The two of them then began walking. As they approached the alley where they would go their separate ways, he said, "Hey, walk with me to the store and I'll give you some lychee nuts. It's only three blocks out of your way." Aileen thought for a few minutes. She loved lychee nuts but going to the playground by way of Pig Alley would take more time. In the end, her love of lychee nuts won out and she replied, "Okay, Willie. Let's go."

They traversed Pig Alley coming out on Dragon's Den Road, then entered another alley, a short cut to Lion's Den Alley where Willie's father's store was. They were leaving the alley when they saw a man lying half in the street and half on the boards of the sidewalk. Willie and Aileen ran up to investigate. Before Willie realized what they were seeing and could shield Aileen from the sight, she saw the blood seeping from beneath the body. Aileen started screaming uncontrollably and Willie grabbed her arm and dragged her away. They fled back the way they had come until they reached Professor's house. Willie banged insistently on the door and called loudly to Professor, then he turned to Aileen and shouted, "Quit your screaming, will you? I can't hear anything else!"

Aileen stared at Willie for a second and bit her lip to keep from crying. She trembled as the discovery of the body replayed itself in her mind. Willie's grip on her arm was beginning to hurt and she cried, "Willie, let go of my arm! You're hurting me." Willie didn't seem to hear her, however, and continued pounding on the door.

Finally, they heard movement inside the house and the door opened. Willie and Aileen rushed inside and hurriedly spilled out their story to Professor. Professor immediately went to phone Liah's Fifth Son, Mert and instructed him to call for Dr. Sung and an ambulance, saying, "Tell them to hurry. The man could be very badly hurt from what the children have told me. I'll meet them in the alley."

Professor then turned to Aileen and demanded, "What are you doing out so early, young lady? Your uncle Mert says you should return home right now." Aileen was speechless. She bit her lip again, trying hard not to start crying again, but she couldn't get the bloody picture out of her mind. Professor saw her distress and his voice softened as he said, "Now child, you be a good girl and go on home. Your grandma is waiting."

Professor instructed Willie to wait until he got back, then opened the door and he and Aileen stepped out into the pink daylight. He motioned for Aileen to go home, then headed toward Pig Alley. When she reached Number Three, Aileen found her fifth uncle waiting for her at the front door. He gave her a stern look and in an angry voice said, "Your grandma is waiting for you. She wants to see you right now." Aileen flew through the door to number Three, ran down the corridor and collapsed sobbing into her grandma's arms. Mert raced over to Pig Alley. He caught up with Professor and the two men hurried to where Willie said they had found the body.

When they got there, Dr. Sung was already administering first aid. As they stared at the body, Professor heard Fifth Son gasp, "My God, it's Sam Yin! He's been beaten to a pulp." Professor looked down at the battered, bloody body and winced. His face paled as he hoarsely cried, "Who could have done such a heinous thing to Sam, of all people?"

Mert regained his senses and he asked, "Dr. Sung, will Sam be all right? We have to tell his wife Sui something, but what shall we tell her?" Dr. Sung sucked in a deep breath and replied, "Sam's life is in the hands of the Gods." Feeling Sam's pulse again he added, "However, I think you better get Sui here as soon as possible. I frankly don't hold out much hope."

Professor nodded and turned to Mert. "Fifth Son, you stay here with the doctor, I'll get Sui." Mert shook his head and replied, "No, I better go get Selah. She'll be able to handle Sui better than we can." Professor agreed and ran as quickly as he could to Sam's store. He shuddered as he saw the shambles of what used to be a door. The hinges hung from the jamb, half-torn off and bent. The door itself lay on the ground, splintered, with razor sharp pieces of wood strewn everywhere. Professor stepped carefully over the debris, calling out for Sui as he went but received no answer. He made his way to the living quarters at the back of the store where he encountered more destruction. The bedstead lay almost dismantled among the bedclothes. Chairs and tables were strewn about amid myriad broken bottles and dishes. One of the window curtains sagged, nearly torn from its rod.

Professor's panic grew as he continued to yell out Sui's name. He dreaded the thought that Sui, too, might have suffered the same fate as Sam. He ran out behind the store and started pushing aside the many crates and boxes piled against the side of the building. Suddenly, Professor thought he heard a soft sob and he yelled for Sui again. He noticed a small shed. He ran over and opened the door, finding Sui huddled next to a wooden crate, her head cradled in her arms, rocking slowly back and forth.

As Professor tried to rouse the traumatized woman, Fifth Son and Selah arrived. Selah immediately nudged Professor aside, knelt beside Sui, touched her arm and said in a soft voice, "Sam's still alive, Sui. Please come with us. We will take you to see Sam before the ambulance leaves." However, Sui did not respond and continued to rock back and forth. Selah then motioned for the two men to pick her up.

As Professor and Mert attempted to lift her to her feet, Sui suddenly became agitated and struggled to fight them off. Selah shouted, "Just pick her up, Professor. You take her legs and Mert take her arms. She's in shock and can't help herself. We have to hurry to get her there before the ambulance leaves!" As they started to carry her away, Sui blurted, "They've killed him! My Sam! They've killed him!" Then she fainted and went limp. Fifth Son carried her the rest of the way himself.

The orderlies were about to carry Sam's stretcher to the ambulance when the trio arrived with Sui. Dr. Sung gave her a quick slap on the cheek and Sui opened her eyes and looked around. When she saw Sam lying on the stretcher, she broke away from them and rushed over to him, falling to her knees and imploring, "Sam, it's me, Sui! Oh, please, answer me, Sam!" She pressed her cheek to his and continued to talk to him softly through her tears. When Dr. Sung motioned for the orderlies to load Sam into the ambulance, Sui tried to fight them off. Professor and Mert had to physically restrain her as Selah tried to calm her down, saying, "Let them get Sam to the hospital, Sui. Let Dr. Sung help Sam."

The orderlies placed Sam in the ambulance and Dr. Sung got in and tapped on the window telling the driver to go. The ambulance lunged forward down the dirt road, its shrill siren shattering the otherwise quiet morning. Mert and Professor watched the ambulance drive away holding Sui upright, as she had gone limp again. "Every time I hear a siren," Mert said softly, "it gives me the creeps. A siren sounds so desperate and forlorn. Knowing that it's for Sam, it's even worse."

Professor agreed with a nod of his head, then asked Selah, "What shall we do with Sui?" Selah replied, "We should take her to Liah's. She can decide what's to be done about Sui and the baby." As soon as Selah mentioned the baby, she gasped, "Oh, my! The baby!" The two men were equally stunned. In the rush of getting Sam to the hospital and finding and bringing Sui in time to see him, they had completely forgotten the baby. Professor immediately said, "Fifth Son, you and Selah take Sui back to your mother's house. I'll go find the baby. God, what a mess!"

Professor returned to Sam's store and began searching through the ransacked place, consumed with dread that he would find the child dead amidst the debris. However, his search turned up nothing. Then Professor remembered where he had found Sui and reasoned belatedly that she would probably have taken the baby with her when she fled. He dashed outside to the shed, his eyes quickly scanning its dim interior. Seeing nothing, he hastily started moving stacks of crates and cardboard boxes when he thought he heard a faint sound. He stopped and listened closely, determining that the soft intermittent sound seemed to be coming from outside the shed.

He rummaged through the rubbish there, pushing aside broken crates, empty cartons, dented barrels and all manner of trash but to no avail. Professor was almost ready to give up when he noticed a narrow space behind the shed separating it from the next building. On a hunch, he removed a few crates stacked in front of the narrow passage and found the baby. Sui had hidden him inside a wooden crate and covered him with paper.

Professor looked down at the peacefully mewling infant and shook his head, thinking how tragic it would be to be so young and already fatherless. However, he quickly banished the thought, as it was bad joss to even think of death. Superstitiously, Professor turned and spit for good luck. He then picked up the baby and carried him to Liah's as fast as he could. On the way, Professor began to feel the toll the day's events had taken on him and ruefully acknowledged once again his advancing age.

He entered Number Three and went directly to Liah's bedroom where Liah and Selah were attending Sui. Sui was lying on Liah's alcove bed and Selah was wiping Sui's tear-stained face with a damp cloth. When her eyes focused the baby, Sui sat up suddenly and cried out, holding her arms out for her child. Selah took the baby from Professor and handed him to his mother. Sui gently lifted away the blanket covering the infant and pressed his face to her cheek. She then began rocking back and forth, her tears spilling onto the baby's face.

The three friends looked on helplessly for a bit, then Liah motioned for them to step outside. They gathered in the kitchen and Liah said, "I think we must ensure Sui has people to watch over her and the baby at all times. In her traumatized condition, we can't trust her to take care of herself let alone the infant. Moreover, the men who attacked them might come looking for her. She is, after all, a witness to their crime. Selah, can you keep them at your place? I'll pay the expenses for both of them."

Selah nodded and replied. "I'll be more than happy to take them in and it isn't necessary to pay me. I'll take care of everything. You folks concentrate on preserving Sam's life and apprehending the fiends who did this horrible thing."

Liah murmured, "Thank you, Selah. I would keep them with us as we have the room and Amah would be only too happy to have a baby to care for, but my granddaughter is in such a state that I already have my hands full. You know, of course, that she and Willie were the ones who found Sam in the alley. Right now, she's sleeping off the bowl of brandy broth I poured into her. I think Sui and the baby would only make it harder for her to deal with what has happened."

Selah nodded in agreement and Liah said, "You make the arrangements for her living quarters, Selah, and when my eldest son returns tonight, we'll bring Sui and the baby over. Thank you again."

—

Word quickly spread through Chinatown that Sam Yin had been viciously attacked. Everyone wondered who could have done it, how they could've done it with the sentries on high alert and most especially why. It couldn't be a Tong matter, for Sam was a quiet, devoted family man who worked hard to make a living from his little produce store. He was well respected and didn't have any enemies. Nor did he gamble. Since his wife's arrival from Hong Kong several years before, he didn't even attend his family association meetings. Rumor spread that the attacker or attackers had to be outsiders, perhaps drunken white revelers or thieves.

When Charlie heard about Sam, he immediately went to tell Liah about the ugly incident in the bar the previous night. Charlie pantomimed how Trouble had grabbed him by his collar and thrown him against the wall. He then gestured with his index finger mimicking how Trouble had said that he would "carve him a Chink!" Charlie declared, "I'm sure Trouble was the one who did this. He also has a friend by the name of Stuckey. Even though Stuckey was also mad at Trouble last night, I'm sure he would help Trouble. He always does what Trouble asks."

Liah listened impassively, but her eyes had turned steely hard and somewhat opaque. She unconsciously tapped her chopsticks on the table in a steady staccato beat all the while Charlie spoke. Cook watched silently and didn't make any move to remove the chopsticks, for he thought it was better for her to release her pent up fury. When Charlie finished his story, Liah sat as still as a statue in her chair for several minutes without uttering a word. Finally, she leaned forward to pour a glass of brandy for her guest saying, "Please have a drink and a bite to eat before you leave, Charlie." Charlie took the brandy but replied, "Thank you, Madam Liah, but I must get to work." Downing his drink, Charlie rose and asked, "Madam Liah, is there anything you wish for me to do? I would be honored to be of some assistance."

Liah shook her head and graciously replied, "No, Charlie. We must do some thinking on this before any action is taken. In any event, this matter must be brought before the Council and it will be up to the

Council members to decide the course of action, not me. Nevertheless, I thank you for the offer."

After Charlie left, Liah remained at the table, deep in thought. Cook hovered within earshot in the event she might need him. He couldn't remember a time when she had remained so uncommunicative and fretted that she might be contemplating some violent response. He tip-toed to Eldest Son's room to see if Aileen were awake and, as he opened the door, Liah stirred from her trancelike state and asked anxiously, "Is she still asleep?" Cook took a quick peek into the room, quietly closed the door and replied, "She's still sleeping. I think she'll be so for a long time. The brandy broth was very potent."

Liah spoke with concern in her voice, "I hope this shock doesn't give her more nightmares. She has enough of them as it is. Why did the Gods ordain that she would be the one to find Sam? Well, we'll just have to deal with it. I'll have the priest make up a good health amulet for her and while I'm at it, I'll have him make up a protective amulet as well." Such amulets were parchment papers inscribed with magical text by a priest. These papers were sewn into triangular red cloth bags then pinned to the recipient's clothing. There were magical amulets for a multitude of purposes, including health, wealth, happiness, love, sexual potency, fertility and protection from harm, to name but a few. As long as the recipient kept the amulet pinned to their clothes, the amulet would retain its potency. Liah would ask for an amulet to preserve Aileen's mental and physical well-being and another to keep her from physical harm.

Dr. Sung telephoned late the next night and informed Fifth Son that Sam had just died as a result of the beating. He said that, despite his best efforts and those of the hospital staff, Sam had been too badly injured and that the internal bleeding could not be stemmed. Fifth Son thanked the doctor and told him that everyone understood he had done his best. After relaying the message to his mother and Cook, Fifth Son went silently to his room. Liah remained at the table, taking deep breaths as she clearly fought to keep calm. Cook waited for the inevitable order to convene the Council.

A DAY OF MOURNING

Word of Sam's death covered Chinatown like a pall. Silence hung over the group of people clustered in Peacock Alley reading the news on the bulletin board. Women wiped their eyes, held on more tightly to their babies and moaned in sympathy for Sui Yin. Even the children playing in the Alley seemed less boisterous.

Sam's funeral was solemn. A band led the procession, playing a mournful dirge. After the musicians came the hearse with a life-size photograph of Sam mounted on top. Next came the car carrying his widow, her brother and her brother-in-law and Selah who was there to comfort Sui. A long line of mourners followed behind. The police motorcycle escort rode up and down the line of cars, making sure no outside traffic broke the continuity of the cortège.

The procession wound its way through the length and breath of Chinatown, taking Sam on a final tour of his beloved town. The cortège entered town from Lion's Den Alley and made its way slowly down the street until they reached the dirt road in front of the stockyards. It then turned left and entered Dragon's Den Road from which it proceeded back out onto the city street, Alameda South and re-entered Marchesson Street where the cortège came to a halt at the entrance to Peacock Alley. People lined the streets in silent farewell to Sam; many women openly crying as the widow passed.

The rest of the way had to be made on foot. The band marked time as the coffin was taken out of the hearse and the waiting pallbearers carried it through Peacock Alley. Selah helped Sui out of the car. When Sui saw the coffin, she tried to break away but was held back by her brother and her brother-in-law. Selah whispered to them, "Let her walk beside him. In that way she can remain with Sam a little longer."

The band entered the Alley with the procession following. Unseen, Hans and Little John watched from a vehicle parked a little way down on Marchesson Street. They were hoping that no white people, however well meaning, would be stupid enough to interrupt the funeral. That would undoubtedly lead to a full-scale riot.

Aileen stood in front of her grandma's house, watching the sad procession approach. She didn't understand it all, but she felt the sadness and was crying uncontrollably. She moved away when she noticed her grandma's face at the window. Liah, however, didn't see her. She was too intent on the cortège about to stop in front of Number Three. It wasn't until they stopped directly in front of her door that Liah stepped out and went over to Sui. Sui clung to the casket as Liah took Sui by the shoulders and leaned over to whisper words of comfort. She patted Sui gently on the back then immediately re-entered Number Three.

The procession moved on down the Alley, left the cobblestone walk and continued on to the dirt road that would lead them to the alley where Sam's store was located. Here they halted again and the pallbearers carried Sam's coffin into the house for his last visit. Fueled by memories of that horror-filled night as she gazed at the shambles around her, Sui finally broke down. She fell to the ground shrieking and began banging her head on the floor over and over. Gentle but firm hands picked her up lest she do herself harm. Sui's continued shrieks echoed in the store as the procession picked its way through the ruins, left by the rear door and solemnly made its way back to Peacock Alley where the pallbearers lifted the coffin back into the hearse and the driver began the last leg of the journey, to the cemetery. The line of cars slowly drove down Marchesson Street behind the hearse, entered Alameda South and wound its way to the cemetery located on the west side of town. Once the procession left, the musicians climbed into a van and proceeded directly to the cemetery so that they would be there when the cortège arrived.

The Chinese cemetery was a stark utilitarian place. There were no marble tombstones, no grass, not even a tree to soften the finality of death. It was as arid and as dusty a place for the dead as Chinatown was for the living. But the cemetery was merely a temporary way station until the remains could be shipped back to China for proper burial in the family plot. For some mourners, the trip to the cemetery piqued their consciences, as some of their relatives were still there, awaiting the trip home.

A high wooden fence walled in the burial grounds, hiding the gravesites from public view and also preventing looting of the graves. Row upon row of wooden markers, with only the name of the deceased and the date of death, dotted the dreary cemetery. In the center of the grounds was an area enclosed by a fence constructed of wide wooden slats. At one end of this enclosure sat an incinerator. The worldly goods belonging to the dead, or their favorite things, were offered up in flames to follow the departed to their new life. To one side was a wooden stand for the casket and an altar on which offerings of food and drink for the deceased could be placed, along with urns for the burning of incense and the sacred parchments and trays for candles. At the end opposite the incinerator benches were set up for the mourners.

When Sam's casket was placed on the wooden stand, Sui rushed up and threw herself atop the coffin. They left her there as the rituals began. Professor gave the eulogy, concluding with a reminder to the mourners. "Sam was a good man, but he has now gone on to a better life. If he were here now, he would surely urge you to forgo a lengthy bereavement or thoughts of revenge and instead to focus on taking care of his wife and son and doing what he is now unable to do."

While Professor was speaking, the custodians were feeding into the incinerator Sam's favorite belongings and all the things he would need in the next life: his pipe, tobacco, fan tan cards and money followed by his clothing, bedding, eye glasses, books and a few reminders of his wife and son. His favorite easy chair had been broken down earlier and now the pieces were also burned.

Large molded and decorated candles and incense were lit in the urns and sacred papers and parchments were burned at the altar to light the way for Sam's soul. All his favorite foods and drink were set out on the table to sustain him until he reached the new world. For days, fresh offerings of food and drink would be set out for him until his soul no longer returned to visit his body.

Sui's brother and brother-in-law walked over to her and tried to raise Sui to her feet. When their attempts failed, Selah rose and whispered in Sui's ear. "Light the incense, Sui," she urged. "Start Sam on his journey!" Selah then took the incense sticks from Professor and placed them in Sui's hand. However, Sui kept shaking her head, refusing to place the incense into the urn. Finally, Selah guided her through the ritual while the men supported her inert body. They then let her return to the coffin for one last farewell. Then Selah gently pried Sui away, saying softly, "Let him go, Sui. Let Sam go. He cannot remain here any longer."

A line of mourners passed in front of the casket, each person pausing to bow and offer a final farewell while the band softly played a final dirge. When the last person had left, Selah whispered to Professor, "Let's leave her for a few more minutes."

As the mourners left the cemetery, a family friend posted at the gate thanked them for attending and handed each person both a coin wrapped in white paper to symbolically enrich the person's life for having shared the family's sorrow and loss and another white packet containing brown sugar to sweeten the hour's sorrow.

Later that day, Sam's embalmed body would be returned to the mortuary where it would remain until it could be shipped back to his village for proper burial in the family plot.

—

Back in Chinatown, Hans and Little John sat in their vehicle parked on Marchesson, waiting for people to return from the funeral. Hans thought a police car would infuriate the grieving residents, so he had borrowed a truck for the day's patrol. He made it a point to remain outside the town boundaries out of respect for their grief. More importantly, he didn't want anyone to focus their fury on them. If it were not for the fact that Hans feared repercussions from the murder, he would not even have patrolled the outer perimeters of Chinatown.

When the hearse finally returned, Hans straightened up and told Little John, "Okay, keep your eyes peeled." Little John replied, "I hope you don't plan for us to sit here all day and night. I won't last that long."

Hans remained silent and observed each car as it entered Chinatown. Finally, he replied, "Naw, I just want to stick around a few more minutes. It's really too soon to expect something to happen. I'm guessing it'll take them a week or two for them to figure out how they're going to respond. Liah's the key, but she isn't showing her cards yet."

WAITING IS DIFFICULT

An uneasy quiet hung over Peacock Alley. People walked softly by Number Three, glancing quickly at the closed doors, then looking fearfully away, lest the doors suddenly open. A few old men and women sat around the Alley, but most of the town's inhabitants stayed away. The days of silence chilled Chinatown like a frozen glacier. Three days of silence and still no word. The inhabitants knew that the longer it took, the more violent the revenge was apt to be. In their sorrow and fright, some hoped that Liah would let things go. They reasoned that retaliation would only bring them more pain. However, some of the bolder citizens began to talk among themselves that violence was the only way to take their revenge. However, they all knew that however they felt, it was Liah and the Council that would decide what to do. They could only hope that it would be the right decision for everyone.

Across town, Lt. Swanson barged into Hans' office and asked, "Any action in Chinatown yet?"

"Not a peep," replied Hans. "I was just on my way out to check on it again."

"What a Goddamn mess. No telling how much blood will be spilt, but sure as hell there will be some. Of course, I don't give a damn about their blood; it's our blood I'm worried about." The lieutenant had gotten word that Trouble and Stuckey were likely responsible for the murder, and thus they were likely to be the target of any retribution. He knew the men from previous run-ins with the law and didn't have any use for either of them. He considered Trouble a vicious, ignorant drunkard and he liked Stuckey even less. Stuckey was an idiot for associating with Trouble. Both of them were worthless, as far as he was concerned. The only reason he was wasting his time looking out for them was the fact that they were white. No white man deserved to be killed by Chinamen!

However, the thought of his men putting their lives in jeopardy just to save those two bums enraged the lieutenant. He barked at Hans, "What have you done about protecting Trouble and Stuckey? We should bring them in for their own protection."

Hans slammed the sheaf of papers he was reading onto the desk and said sarcastically, "I don't see in these orders where it says to bring in Trouble and Stuckey. It says here we're to 'apprehend the killer or killers of Sam Yin as soon as possible'. Are you telling me that Trouble and Stuckey are the killers?" Hans had deduced as much himself, but he wanted to know if Lt. Swanson had definitive proof.

The lieutenant quickly tried to backpedal. "No, I didn't say that. What the hell's the matter with you?"

Hans exploded, "What's the matter with me? A man has been brutally killed without provocation! Even a Chinaman doesn't deserve that. A woman and her baby have been left without a husband and father! Even as we speak, an old lady in Chinatown is maybe planning a bloodbath, which could get me and a lot of others killed. And you ask me what's the matter?"

The lieutenant stared open-mouthed at Hans as he vented. However, he had to admit his officer had pretty well summed up where things stood. The situation stank. In a rare moment of humility and candor, he apologized. "I'm sorry, Hans, but the brass upstairs have been on my case to take care of this before things get out of hand. I've seen those Chinamen explode before and I never want to go through that again. I just don't know what to do."

Hans was surprised by the unexpected apology and gruffly replied, "Yeah, I know what you mean. Those Chinamen are an unpredictable bunch. Every time I go down there, I'm looking over my shoulder. You never know when or where or what will set them off, so you're always on edge."

The lieutenant left and Hans continued turning the case over in his mind. He knew almost to a certainty that Sam's murder had not been committed by a Chinaman or even a group of Chinamen from one of the Tongs. He knew the Tongs did not commit murder without good reason. Nor did they brutalize their victims. A Tong death was usually clean and quick. Hans had also heard about the incident at The Dragon's Den Bar Saturday night. It didn't take a genius to figure out that Trouble had probably been responsible.

He picked up the orders he had slammed on the desk and re-read the typed instructions. When he read "apprehend as quickly as possible," he got angry again. He thought, "Why did everything dangerous require immediate action?" He thought fleetingly thought of quitting, but admitted to himself that he always thought of quitting whenever things got out of control. He also had to admit that he was beginning to like these Chinks. There was something admirable about the way they were able to persevere in spite of all the adversity they were forced to endure. He didn't understand how they managed to survive and even maintain a certain human decency. For this reason, Hans both admired and feared them at the same time.

Dropping the orders into one of his desk drawers, his thoughts turned to Liah, the reputed Opium Queen and Boss of Chinatown. He realized that gaining an understanding of who she was and what she was would go a long way to understanding Chinatown itself. Briefly Hans wondered why the Chinamen also called her 'The Old One'. She couldn't be more than about forty-five or so. He shook his head and wondered if he would ever understand the Chinks. Shrugging, Hans grabbed his coat and left to make a sweep of Chinatown.

As he walked down Peacock Alley, he felt a strange foreboding. The place was still deserted, and the usual laughter and noisy chatter were still absent. He wondered where all the residents were. He figured that after three days they would surely have to come out at least to buy food and necessities, but he noticed that all the stores were still closed with their doors and windows shuttered or boarded up. "Shit," murmured Hans. "It's like a ghost town."

When he approached Number Three, Hans was surprised to see that the front door was open. That put him in a quandary; should he or shouldn't he go in? He wanted to express his condolences to Liah, but he didn't know how she'd take it. He might just stir up a hornet's nest. Glancing at Selah's place, Hans decided to have a drink and get Selah's take on things.

As soon as he had stepped inside the cool and plush foyer, a woman's voice from the bar invited him in. He passed through the velvet drapes flanking the doorway and walked up to the bar. Selah raised her glass in greeting and asked, "What'll you have, Cat?"

"Scotch, plain," replied Hans. "What's new, Selah? I haven't seen a soul around here since the funeral. I hope things have calmed down. What do you think?"

Selah shrugged her shoulders and motioned for Lalo to pour a Scotch for Hans. "On the surface, everything is calm, but the atmosphere is still tense. Sui is still taking Sam's death very hard." Selah then resumed nursing her own drink in silence.

As Hans sat quietly at the bar, he realized how much he missed Little

John's company. He hadn't said more than a couple of words to anyone except the lieutenant since his partner had left on his vacation right after the funeral. Doing some mental arithmetic, Hans figured Little John would be gone for another ten days or so. Abruptly, Selah asked, "How about something to eat? I'm about to have a bite, will you join me?"

Hans grinned. "Sure. I get lonesome sitting by myself, especially in hostile territory. I sure will be glad when Little John returns from his vacation."

Selah couldn't help feeling a little sorry for the big hulk of a man. Although she understood that he was just doing his job, her Chinese heritage reminded her of the terrible stories she had heard about police mistreatment of the Chinese. Lalo, the bartender, grinned at his boss and announced, "Me tink yo dinnah is ready, Missus."

It was late afternoon when Hans returned to the station. He had no sooner shed his coat when the lieutenant walked in unceremoniously and asked, "Well, how did it go? What did you find out?" Hans bristled but kept his anger in check. From his demeanor, it was obvious that his boss must have gotten called on the carpet by the brass and was now looking to take his frustration out on someone. Well, he would try his best to avoid being the one. Hans answered curtly but without anger, "No one is stirring down there. Everyone is waiting for the other shoe to drop."

NIGHT OF THE GODDESS

On August fourteenth, the night before the Moon Festival, Liah watched as Cook finished scrubbing the white skin of the winter melon to remove the grime. He then carefully cut off the top and put it aside. Next, he scooped out the seeds and filled the hollow center of the melon with a mixture of diced ham, chicken, pork, lotus seeds, ginkgo nuts and water chestnuts. After replacing the top, Cook positioned the melon on a rack in the middle of a deep pot partially filled with water. Finally, he covered the pot and placed it on the stove to steam.

Cook then turned his attention to the stuffed chicken. First, he mixed various seasonings with the salt that would be rubbed on the chicken, then he placed the bowl on the table and said, "Please give this a taste and see if the proportions are right." With Liah's approval, Cook then went on to describe the stuffing, "I want to make a mixture of shrimp, pork and black mushrooms. If I stuff the chickens today, I'll have more time tomorrow to get everything else done." Liah's eyes sparkled at Cook's mention of black mushrooms, which were among her favorite foods.

Liah suddenly looked around and frowned, "I do not see the fresh fruits. Did you forget them?"

"No," replied Cook, slightly exasperated with Liah's lack of patience. "Willie's father said he'd have them for us tomorrow morning. He knows how you like the lychee nuts on a branch and the tangerines with stems and leaves. He didn't have any today."

A slight excitement ran through Liah as she envisioned the feast table. Her family was right that she should celebrate the Moon Festival in spite of the tragedy; life was indeed for the living. Still, in the back of her mind she couldn't help being a little sad thinking about Sui Yin's plight. The sadness must have shown on her face, for Cook counseled that she should not allow sadness to interfere with her preparations for the Moon Festival. "Kwan Yin would not feel too kindly if you do not honor her as is her due. It is, after all, her special day. You can feel sad after tomorrow."

Liah looked guilty and nodded in agreement. "If you wouldn't mind, I think I'd like to use the porcelain compotes and platters from the cupboard for the feast. I promise I'll try not to think sad thoughts, but it's hard." Cook gently replied, "Meng-Sui governs our lives, Liah. Allow the Gods to direct the course of our lives as they see fit."

The next morning, Cook's preparations for the feast continued in earnest. Liah blew the smoke from her cigarette and reached out for the cup of herbal tea that Cook proffered. Just then, Aileen ran into the kitchen and leaped onto her grandma, clasping her sticky hands about Liah's neck and planting an equally sticky kiss on her cheek. "Child," cried Liah, "please wash your hands and face! Your kisses taste like loquats."

Cook smiled ruefully and mumbled about how every day he had to threaten not to let her go to the playground until she finished her food. "Of course, today when I have so much to do, she won't budge from the house."

"Leave her to my care, sir," smiled Liah. "I'll keep her busy with chores."

Liah beckoned to her granddaughter. "Right after Grandma finishes her tea, you and I will assemble the prayer papers. It's time you learned how."

Later, Aileen stood at the table in the front room, fascinated with the array of parchment papers, some rough-textured brown, beige and white, but mostly captivated by the orange- and gold-speckled papers, and the red, brilliantly gold-speckled ones. She begged for a sheet of each. Liah looked at her and picked up a sheet of each kind of paper, but refused to give them to her, saying, "If you behave and not be a bother, Grandma will give them to you later."

Liah then summoned her second daughter, Emmi, now all of eighteen years old. "I need your help to lay out the prayer papers. Afterwards, we'll gather the different kinds of incense." Emmi reluctantly emerged from her bedroom, grumbling that she was busy sewing her new dress. Liah sternly replied, "The sooner you help, the sooner you'll be able to get back to it."

Aileen watched as her grandma and aunt meticulously counted out each kind of paper, piling them into a prescribed order. As Emmi assembled the prayer papers, Liah used her fist to gently knead each pile into a bowl-like fan. Aileen soon grew tired of the monotonous procedure and ran into the kitchen to help Cook, who scowled and ordered her back to help her grandma. Aileen pouted, angry at being shunted from Cook to Grandma and climbed into the upholstered chair in the front room behind her grandma to sulk.

Cook entered the front room with a fresh pot of tea and placed it onto the caddy. Noticing Aileen's discomfort as she squirmed in the upholstered chair, he told her, "Come with me, Aileen. I have a chore for you. There are Chinese peas that need stringing."

When Liah returned to the kitchen a little later, she noticed her granddaughter's sullen expression and she winked at Cook. "I don't suppose the spiced ribs are ready for sampling?"

Aileen's eyes suddenly lit up. "I'll taste them for you, Cook!"

As soon as she had finished two spareribs, Aileen reached out for the bag of loquats again. Liah chided her, saying that Kwan Yin might become angry if she saw her eating all the loquats.

"But Grandma," argued Aileen, "I thought you said Kwan Yin didn't come out until the moon appears? How will she know I ate the loquats?" Liah burst into laughter. "Child, I didn't think of that."

At a quarter to seven, Aileen bounded from the bedroom, crying that she'd overslept and wondering if she had missed the festivities. Liah shook her head. "No, we haven't started yet. Go put on your shoes and stockings. The party will start soon."

While Aileen was admiring the compotes of shiny fruit, beautifully arranged in pyramids, she was overcome with hunger as she spied the artistically arranged platters of duck, chicken and spareribs. As she reached out for a tangerine, Emmi grabbed her hand. Startled, Aileen screamed and Liah came running to see what was the matter. Glaring at the pair she said sternly, "One more fight and the two of you will spend the night in your rooms and go hungry.

Lee Tzo arrived first. Liah noticed that Mei-Mei had not accompanied him as she usually did to feasts. At seven o'clock, Madam Quock entered Number Three, accompanied by Sen Fei, with Yook Lan in tow.

It amused Liah to see the younger woman fawn over Sen Fei. It was clear that she was trying to ingratiate herself to the opera singer in the hope that she would get free music lessons.

The entire Council was present shortly after seven. Liah acknowledged Lee Tzo's generous gift of six bottles of Ng Ga Pei, saying, "While we are waiting for Eldest Daughter, why don't you men open up the rice wine and taste the appetizers Cook has provided?"

Selah arrived and infused the room with an air of festivity. Yook Lan scarcely concealed a covetous expression. Liah noticed and wasn't pleased. True, Selah's shimmering green satin cheongsam was obviously expensive, but Yook Lan's eyes were on her diamond and jade pendant and matching earrings, Liah was certain. Lee Tzo took note of Liah's challenging stare and decided not to cause a scene.

Liah glanced up at the clock. Eldest Daughter still had not arrived and her tardiness irritated Liah. "Well, we shall begin without my eldest daughter," she announced. Liah took Aileen's hand and led her and the guests outside to the arbor. Aileen gaped at the red brocade tablecloth and the array of porcelain platters and compotes heaped with food and fruits. She was particularly captivated by the new brass incense urn; it was embossed with a golden dragon that matched the golden, fire-spitting dragon on the red tablecloth.

Liah lit several incense sticks, then took her granddaughter's hand and whispered to Aileen to kowtow (bow) three times toward the image of the Goddess. Next, Liah placed the incense into the shiny urn. "Now we shall offer a prayer to the Goddess," Liah said. "Come, child, let Grandma show you how."

Aileen gingerly held the bowl of burning prayer papers and stared in fascination at its gentle flames. Her grandma stood behind her and gently guided Aileen's hands in the offering to Kwan Yin. In her heart, Liah fervently prayed for her granddaughter's health and happiness. Then Liah deposited the burning prayer papers into yet another fancy dragon brazier.

The sound of a car engine signaled Eldest Daughter had arrived. Liah ignored her and urged her guests to offer up their own prayers. Aileen raced to her father, saying excitedly, "Daddy, I made my prayers to Kwan Yin."

Flo muttered that she hoped the prayer was for an improvement in Aileen's behavior. Mert glanced furtively at his mother and Thomas scowled at Flo. "If I were you, I wouldn't let Ma hear you," he said. "It's bad enough that you're late."

Madam Quock pushed her way to the front with Yook Lan in tow and placed prayer papers in her daughter's hand. She whispered that she ought to ask Kwan Yin for a nice young man. Liah watched Yook Lan as she offered up her prayer. It seemed to her that the young girl instead beseeched the Goddess for a successful career as opera singer.

Each of her guests took a turn to offer up their prayers. Several un-invited ladies then darted in to use Liah's altar. Eldest Son made a move to restrain them, but Liah gently held him back. She was inclined to let the poor souls be, for the comfort they would feel would be worth far more than the cost of incense and prayer papers.

At nine o'clock, Liah, her family and friends went indoors for the family dinner. Liah presided at one table. Selah at the table where the Council members were seated. Halfway through supper, Liah noticed that Aileen was being unusually quiet. Selah had seen Flo snub Aileen earlier. She watched as Liah walked over to the child and whispered something in her ear. Suddenly, a smile broke out on Aileen's face. It warmed Selah's heart. How, she thought, could Flo harbor such hatred for her first born?

After dinner, the men began a game of dominoes while the ladies played mah-jongg.

On the other side of the room, Liah was asking Yook Lan with amusement if she had pleaded with Kwan Yin to become a famous singer. Yook Lan scanned the room to ensure her mother was out of earshot, then nodded. "Well," smiled Liah, "it doesn't matter if you asked for a career instead of a husband. It is not imperative that girls marry in order to find happiness." Liah's face hardened, "In fact, many girls ought never to marry, they bring such unhappiness and suffering not only to themselves but their spouses as well."

Flo was sitting nearby and overheard what Liah said. She froze and panicked. Was her mother on to her secret? She quickly rose from her chair and told Liah that they had to leave as Toh had to work early the next day. Liah hugged and kissed her grandchildren and told them she'd see them Saturday. Toh embraced Aileen. He whispered to her that he'd see her again as soon as he could. The child's sad face pained him and he quickly led the others out to the car.

Sen Fei's face was also sad as she dwelled on memories of her tragic love affair, how her lover had betrayed her and stolen her money and jewelry. Liah noticed her sadness and invited her to sing for them. Much to her distress, Liah heard Yook Lan request the famous aria from a play of unrequited love. Liah's eyes beseeched Sen Fei to not to focus on her past, but her silent pleas were futile. After the performance, Yook Lan lamented that she could never dream of singing with such con-trolled emotion. Liah's voice was cryptic as she murmured, "You will, child, as soon as your heart is broken."

By eleven-thirty Aileen was curled up, asleep in her grandma's up-holstered chair, covered with a shawl someone had draped over her. The sound of dominoes slapping down on the table, the clack of the mah-jongg tiles as they were "washed," and an occasional quick curse or ripple of ladies' laughter filled the front room.

Lee Tzo tried to initiate a discussion on the issue of retaliation for Sam Yin's death, but none of the other Council members would hear of it. Kam Fong gave the pimp a harsh glance and changed the subject. Seeing the interchange, Mert whispered to Theo that Lee Tzo must be really dense. Why else would he persist in bringing up things not apro-pos to the celebration of Kwan Yin?

The long evening finally came to an end and Liah thanked everyone for coming. She offered special thanks to Professor for his gift of kumquats, to Selah for the Fahn Gwai liquor and coolly thanked Lee Tzo again for his Ng Ga Pei. Professor escorted Madam Quock and Yook Lan home and Cook began to clean the tables.

Soon afterwards, a drowsy Aileen heard footsteps, a murmur of voices and the sound of locks turning and boards being fitted into the windows. A moment later, someone lifted her up and carried her to her grandma's alcove bed. Something warm and cuddly snuggled up to her; Wowo, the puppy she'd just been given, gave her a wet kiss then it was blissful oblivion.

Liah knelt long at the altar of Kwan Yin, offering up a prayer of thanksgiving. She then pleaded with the Goddess for Sam Yin's eternal peace, and for Sui Yin's merciful guidance in the years she must live without her husband. She prayed that Sui Yin's life-waters, her Meng-Sui, would carry her to a happier place, perhaps even to a new marriage.

Her prayers done, Liah prepared for bed. She smiled down at her granddaughter and Wowo, leaned over and gently placed the puppy on the floor, then climbed wearily into bed and closed her eyes.

At ten o'clock the morning after the festival to Kwan Yin, the telephone jangled like a thousand demons. Or so it seemed to Cook as he cursed, racing down the stairs to quiet the ringing. He was chagrined when he recognized Lee Tzo's voice on the phone, but it quickly turned to shock as he listened. He gasped, "Mei-Mei is gone? Are you certain?" Once he got the whole story, he refused Tzo's pleas to alert Liah immediately. "Of course Liah's abed. I'll tell her when she awakens. No! I will not disturb her rest. If you need someone to talk to, go see Professor."

SPECIAL PATROL

In Number Ten Peacock Alley, Lee Tzo was in a towering rage. He screamed at representatives of the tongs in Dai Faw, Chicago and Noo Yok, accusing them of doing nothing to locate his concubine. "It's been a week and there has been no word. She is just a worthless and ungrateful female. She can't have vanished from the face of the earth. I demand that you find her immediately along with whoever took her!"

At police headquarters across town, Hans was also furious but for a different reason. He exploded at his superior. "The Chinks are not finished with Sam Yin's murder. The longer it takes them to retaliate, the greater the violence will be. I know these Chinks. They're patient and it's only a matter of time."

Lt. Swanson's face exhibited an all-knowing smirk as he shook his head. "I disagree. The Chinks, I've been told, seem to have settled back into their normal routine. I think you're being overly dramatic. I know all about their patience and their desire for revenge when it comes to that bunk about ensuring eternal rest and saving face. However, I'm certain that they won't jeopardize their necks to commit murder on a white man. Now, let's hear no more about this."

Hans forced himself to remain civil, but his emotions seethed below his surface calm. He curtly responded, "Okay, but don't say I didn't warn you, sir." He left his superior's office and marched down the corridor to his own. He plopped into his swivel chair and threw his hat across the room, expertly landing the disreputable-looking chapeau on the top branch of his hat tree. A few moments later, he glanced at his watch and growled to himself. Tom was late. He flung his soggy cigar into the wastebasket, and lit another. Tom was the only one in Chinatown with whom he'd managed to establish any sort of relationship, not that it had amounted to much. At least Tom would talk to him.

At four o'clock, Tom finally rapped on Hans' door. Entering, he apologized profusely, explaining that an immigration interrogation had taken longer than usual. "It pisses me off when an immigration officer makes an appointment, then fails to keep it. We waited almost two hours for him to return from lunch."

Hans relit his cigar, ignored Tom's apology and pointed to an empty chair. Tom, irritated by the man's rudeness, sat but said nothing, waiting for the cop to speak first. However, Hans merely sat and stared at Tom. After a lengthy silence, Tom became uncomfortable as Hans had intended. He fidgeted in his chair, then blurted, "You might be interested to hear I transacted some business for Madam Liah recently. Sui Yin is going back to her family in Canton. Her brother is accompanying her along with the baby. Isn't that great?"

The cigar almost fell from his lips as Hans considered the implications. He could not believe that he might be wrong, that the Chinks really weren't going to exact retribution. His gut instincts were almost never wrong. "Yeah, that's great, but do you actually think this business with Sam Yin is done, Tom?"

"I don't know, Cat, but I'm hoping it is. However, I must admit that Chinatown seems almost too quiet. Moreover, lately the Council has been behaving more secretively than usual. They clam up whenever I come around. On the other hand, there is no talk of revenge and everyone has gone back to their daily routine."

Hans scrutinized Tom's face as he spoke but couldn't read anything there. He wondered again whether he could trust Tom to tell him the truth. "So you're saying it's over with?"

Tom shrugged and replied, "Madam Liah is the only one who can say for sure."

At the mention of Liah's name, Hans lost his self-control and he abruptly rose from his chair. He began pacing up and down, coming to a stop in front of Tom. He shook his finger in Tom's face and said, "Who the Goddamn hell does she think she is? A female *taipan* (wealthy businessman)? Liah's nothing but an opium-smoking manipulator and you can tell her for me that if she's planning anything, I'll throw her in jail faster than she can blink!"

A long silence followed, then Hans went on, "I'm warning you too, Tom. If I find out that you haven't been square with me, I'll fix it so that you will never practice law in this town. You know I can do it."

Tom's face paled, but his temper flared. "Yeah, I know the law. The law is for the Fahn Gwai and I'm nothing but an alien. Well, I'll be square with you. I'm glad there's somebody like Liah around who sticks up for us Chinks. What do you think of that?"

As quickly as his temper had flared up, Hans' temper vanished and was replaced by frustration, knowing that perhaps he'd just alienated the only semi-friend he had in Chinatown. Somewhat mollified, he said, "I'm sorry for the outburst, Tom. I've been under a lot of stress lately. If anything happens in Chinatown, the brass will blame it on me because I didn't know about it and didn't do anything about it. I just need to know the truth."

Still angry, Tom replied, "I've told you the truth!" He pointed his finger at Hans. "Here's another thing to think about. The next time you want to see me, don't go around town broadcasting it. Just leave word with Selah. I don't mind being helpful, but I don't want to get killed in the process." Hans stared incredulously and retorted, "Don't try to fool me. They would never kill one of their own."

In a matter-of-fact tone, Tom replied, "Believe it. If they thought I was a threat to the security of Chinatown, they wouldn't hesitate. If you don't understand that, you don't know a damn thing about us." With that, Tom rose and headed for the door.

Hans sat there for a while, mulling over their meeting. Finally, he swept aside the mess of papers on top of his desk and spread out his map of Chinatown. He and Little John would start patrolling the streets using the patrol cars as a visible reminder of Fahn Gwai authority. Hans smiled ruefully, admitting to himself that it wouldn't matter much if the Chinks decided they were going to seek revenge.

The first day of patrols, on the twenty-third of August, the fifteen men handpicked by Hans, were in the briefing room. "Twenty-four-hour surveillance. For your own safety, remain inside your patrol cars.

Look over the map, acquaint yourselves with the marked-off areas, then check your schedules. Are there any questions?" Hans waited a minute, then warned, "If you don't want a hatchet in your back, do not take chances and use your most polite manners; the Chinks do not like rudeness. First and foremost, never say 'Chink' to their faces."

That first day of patrols, Liah was besieged with residents' reports of Fahn Gwai police. She finally issued a bulletin informing the town to ignore them and not give the police cause to run anyone into jail. The Apinyin users and gambling houses, in particular, should beware.

Toward the end of the week, Sim was returning home from work, tired and deep in thought, when he ran into Tom. "Sim, so late and you aren't in bed? Are you okay?"

"I just got off work at Dragon's Den. Tomorrow is Saturday, no school, so I worked later."

Tom smiled. "Say, how about you and me having a snack at Wong's? My treat."

They made their way toward Wong's. Hans, seated in his patrol car, muttered to John, "Betcha those two are headed for the café."

John stared, recognizing Sim as the young boy who had helped him get his vehicle out of the mud while other residents had stood around, smirking at his situation. He felt inclined to tell Hans he knew the kid but wasn't sure his partner wouldn't approve of fraternization.

Tom and Sim walked in silence. Both were tired; both agreed to supper because each thought the other needed companionship. Tom's thoughts revolved around Sam Yin's senseless murder, the Council's demand for retaliation, Liah's stoicism, but mostly his feeling sick to death about Hans' suspicions and rudeness. If Sim hadn't nudged Tom he would have passed the café.

They took seats at the counter and exchanged no conversation while they ate their pork noodles. Afterwards, Tom asked Sim again if something was the matter.

"Oh, Elder Brother," murmured Sim, addressing Tom with the polite title reserved for times when speaking to someone older, "it's just that Officer John and I had lunch and he has now asked me to supper at his house and I said yes. Now, I don't want to go."

"Why not, Sim? Officer John is a very nice man."

"I'm not like you, Elder Brother. I'm not used to the Fahn Gwai's ways and I can't speak his language. I don't want his family to think I'm stupid. I can't even use the Fahn Gwai's knife and fork correctly."

Tom felt a wave of sympathy, recalling his own discomfiture during his early contacts with the Fahn Gwai, but he wasn't going to make things easier for Sim. Sim would have to learn the same painful way Tom did. That was the only way Sim would truly learn. "Sim," he said, "when you and Officer John had lunch, did you order? And did he eat what you suggested? And did he enjoy what you thought he ought to enjoy? I'm sure he had never eaten salt fish steamed with pork and garlic sautéed snails before, but I bet he never said a word. He ate them to please you. You mean to tell me you can't be as good a friend and accept his world for just a night?"

Sim's eyes pleaded for Tom to understand, even say it was all right to cancel the supper, but Tom was adamant. "Why not go and try it once? You know when you've finished your education, you will inevitably turn to the Fahn Gwai for your livelihood. Might as well start learning about them now."

For the next twenty minutes, Tom instructed Sim on how to use a knife and fork, warning him that to pick up or cut small pieces of meat was one thing, but the technique was a bit more intricate when cutting steaks and chops. "Use the fork to hold the meat in place and then with a jerky, push-pull action, slice the meat off into a bite-size piece and eat only one piece at a time. It's not that hard. It's easier than using chopsticks, in fact."

At the end of the session, Tom smiled gently at Sim. "I know you were tired when we met and I thank you for sharing my supper. I miss my meals many times because I don't like eating alone, but I promise you, Sim, we won't always be alone, nor lonely. Just be patient and study hard and don't be so stand-offish with the Fahn Gwai. They aren't all bad, nor are they all ignorant." As an afterthought, Tom chuckled and added, "It just seems that way."

On his way home, Tom spied Hans' armored car parked down the street from the café, behind a delivery truck. As he walked by, he raised his hand in a deliberate salute. Hans scowled back, muttering something about their cover being blown and started the engine. Tom reached Blind Man's Alley and suddenly remembered he'd promised Madam Liah he'd stop in to see her. He sighed and turned toward Peacock Alley.

—

The heat had become nearly intolerable by the end of August and on a muggy hot day, Mert returned home from work, peeved his mother was sleeping off an Apinyin smoke. Not even Cook's explanation that she needed the escape seemed to placate Mert. "The stuff is no good for her, sir."

Cook nodded, "I know, but it's better than driving herself into a frenzy over Sam Yin's murder. Sit down. I will fix you something to eat."

The front door opened and slammed. Minutes later, Sim burst into the kitchen, stopping abruptly when he didn't see Liah. "Hi, Sim," smiled Mert. "Why the hurry? Are you in trouble?"

Sim shook his head. Cook smiled, "Well, in that case, sit down and you can share a meal with Fifth Son. I'm just heating up some ribs, spiced the way you like them."

It seemed that Sim did have something on his mind and he finally he blurted, "I came to see Madam Liah. I have something to tell her, but now I'm not sure I ought to tell. Officer John is my friend and I don't want to betray him."

Mert looked at Sim. "Did Officer John tell you a secret?"

Sim shook his head. "I overheard Officer John and Hans talking, something about that they didn't think Trouble and Stuckey would ever be brought to trial. They said only a miracle would bring in a guilty verdict. The police are looking for them now. Lots more things, but I did not understand and I forgot. Do you think it is wrong for me to tell of these things, Elder Brother?"

Cook shook his head, thinking how unfortunate one so young had to be so mature and without a mother. Mert smiled gently. "Sim, you are Chinese and you must never forget that. What the men did to Sam Yin was cruel. And what about Sui Yin and Sam's young son, who will have no father to care for him? Have you thought of that?"

Sim's face was miserable with doubt. "I know all that, but Officer John is very good to me."

"Yes, Sim," Mert sighed. "However, Officer John is only one of millions who like the Chinese. As you are a boy now, you do not run into much discrimination, but as soon as you finish college you will experience many ugly situations with the Fahn Gwai. Maybe you will not suffer the bodily pain and harm our ancestors did when they came to build the railroad or dig for gold, but there will be even uglier discriminations, which you cannot see and therefore cannot fight against. I will tell my mother what you told me and, Sim, don't worry. My mother is not a mean person."

Both Cook and Mert were silent after Sim left. Cook deplored the lad's sadness, his wisdom beyond his years. Mert nodded wordlessly. Their eyes met and Mert blurted, "You know, sir, I just can't help feeling guilty every time I see Sim or Tom that I don't have to struggle so hard because of Mah."

Cook sighed, nodding. His voice was patiently gentle. "Just remember it isn't easy to live with your mother. In your own way, you've also struggled."

"Thanks, sir, but what you really mean is for me to be lots more patient with Mah whenever she has a temper or tries to get me to do what she wants. I know all this, but gosh, it's hard sometimes to remain calm and quiet."

Cook looked Mert directly in the eye, his voice firm, purposeful. "But Fifth Son, you will be able to do the right thing, I know it. Now, would you like more spiced ribs?"

Sim returned the next day to Number Three. Liah saw his guilt and saw the lines melt from his face as he haltingly confessed that yesterday he did not tell everything to Fifth Brother. "I do not want to help the two evil men, but your son asked me to think of Aunt Sui Yin and her son and that's why I'm back."

Liah smiled compassionately at the young boy, wishing she could take him into her house, but then he had a father, even if the man did not properly care for him. "Sit down, child. Do not fret so. I cannot expect you to behave as an adult, although you've shown more courage and brains than most grown ups."

Sim lowered his eyes and informed Liah that the two men were already caught and were now in jail. "Officer Cat said Stuckey and Trouble were put in jail for their own protection. Otherwise our people would kill them."

Liah reached inside her vest, removed a purse, extracted two dollars and handed them to Sim, who shook his head. "I do not want money. That's not why I came to tell you. Fifth Brother said we are Chinese and should protect ourselves from the Fahn Gwai."

Liah nodded. "True, Sim, but this is not a reward. This is for your bank account, as I know you are saving money to go to college. You and Tom are to be commended for working such long, hard hours and being so frugal. It is on my mind that when the time comes, I should help you."

Sim made a gesture to refuse, but Liah held up her hands for silence.

"Sim, we all need help at one time or another. Do not be proud. That is the way our ancestors survived the ordeals of persecution and privation. When you are doing well, after college, you can turn around and help another worthy boy. By doing that, you will have repaid me for whatever help I provide you now. Just remember that, son."

Sim smiled weakly, cautiously asking if Madam Liah might declare war on the Fahn Gwai, for that meant he could not go to school. Liah laughed. "No, Sim, at present there are no plans. War does not solve anything. It is only a last-ditch measure and we will do nothing until after the trial. Now, please wait a few moments. My granddaughter should be home and the both of you can share a snack. Now, put away the two dollars, Sim."

Just then they heard Aileen shouting as she opened and slammed the front door. "Grandma, Grandma, I'm home and I'm hungry." While the two youngsters ate, Liah calculated Sim must be about fourteen or fifteen. His mother, who died in childbirth, had spent no time with her son, while his father, grief-stricken, had left the son almost on his own from the beginning, blaming Sim for his wife's death. Sim's care had fallen to the women around Chinatown and by the time he was nine years old, he was foraging on his own. Liah shook her head. It was a wonder the boy had any moral fiber.

Cook smiled as he handed Sim a paper sack. "It's some rice and spiced ribs which you might eat later on today and a slice of custard pie."

Aileen hugged her grandma, asking if she couldn't go to the playground. "Aileen, you're a lucky girl. Poor Sim has almost no one to look after him."

Aileen's face fell. She anxiously asked her grandma if she might not take Sim into the house and take care of him as Grandma took care of her. Liah shook her head. "Not while he has a father, my child. We can, however, be kind to him and, each time we see him, make certain he's well, happy and full of food. Now, no more talk. Go and enjoy yourself at the playground."

WRATH OF A MAN SCORNED

Ten days after the disappearance of Mei-Mei, Lee Tzo remained secluded in his private chambers, drunk and demonic. His girls tiptoed quickly past his door, fearful they might meet their master. The obscenities heard through the closed door communicated his insane fury, but even more so the whirring of his whip as he flailed it in the air. Not even Wong Sang made a visit.

Frustrated by his inability to find Mei-Mei and mete out her just punishment, Lee Tzo instead focused his hatred on Liah. Vengeance would be his when he evened the score with Liah. Soon even his patrons were staying away and Lee Tzo's hatred turned to Selah, convinced that it was her fault his business had fallen off. The two she-devils, they'd pay for his pain.

Mei-Mei's amah secretly went to see Liah, warning her of Tzo's threats. Liah thanked the old woman, asking if perhaps she'd not like to find new employment, but the old lady shook her head. "Perhaps if the Gods allow, the new young girl will need my protection. Ah, the Gods are cruel. Besides, the other girls need me, especially the new one from Macao. I must hurry back in case my master should emerge from his chambers. I tell you, he is insane!"

The girls dreaded the nights most of all, when their master writhed and moaned about his lost honor. Mei-Mei and her lover must be found and brought to their tortured deaths. The runaway couple had to be in Dai Faw or else in Noo Yok and the Tongs were doing nothing to find them. May the Gods send thunderbolts and kill every one of the bastards!

About two o'clock one morning, Lee Tzo awakened from a drunken stupor, sitting bolt upright in bed. So great was his need for revenge, he fumbled in his jacket pocket for a ring of keys. Stumbling out of bed, he strode across the hall, cursing, and fumbled with the lock. When he wrested the lock from the door, he charged inside.

Asleep on the silken covered bed was Tzo's latest import from Macao. He'd planned to tutor the young girl in the art of erotic love-making, then auction off her virginity to the highest bidder. In his drunken madness, none of these plans mattered, only his desire for re-vengeful satiation.

He yanked off the coverlet and swept the bedclothes off the bed. Curled in the sleep of innocence, the young girl brought back memories of Mei-Mei's virginity. With a savage motion, he clutched her long black hair, dragging her from the bed. Mei-Tai screamed, her eyes wide, filled with terror. With one motion, Tzo ripped away her gown, pinning her arms behind her and pressing her nakedness against his body. Half-un-balanced by the girl's body in his drunken state, Lee Tzo went through the door, stumbling his way toward a huge gong mounted on a stout carved teakwood frame. With his free hand, he seized the brass mallet and slammed it against the brass gong. Mei-Tai's screams rose above the low sonorous roll of the gong and, in an instant, doors opened and pa-trons and girls alike came out into the hall. As they watched, several men leered; the girls were terrified, recalling their own brutal initiations.

"Look!" screeched Lee Tzo, his voice as high-pitched as a woman's. "Look, a virgin who, after I'm finished with her, will do anything for your pleasure." Without another word, Lee Tzo dragged Mei-Tai back into his chambers and kicked the door shut.

Mei-Tai's screams and pleas for mercy rent the air, but mostly it was the whirring, cracking of the whip that filled the hallway and the win-dowless, stuffy rooms where men, whetted by the sounds of pain, wreaked their own punishment on the girls. Inside his private cham-bers, the sight of the girl's swollen lips and blackening face, impelled Lee Tzo to even more violence. He picked Mei-Tai up, tossing her onto the silken coverlet, then took her without tenderness, without pleasure, without conquest, with only raging vengeance.

When at last he lay exhausted, Lee Tzo was aware of a burning pain in his back and discovered Mei-Tai's fingernails embedded in his flesh. He yanked her hands free and rang for Amah who appeared instantly. He demanded she tie Mei-Tai's legs and arms to each bedpost. Lee Tzo howled with demonic laughter, feeling a resurging passion as he viewed Mei-Tai's body spread-eagle. He shoved Amah out of the way, shouting, "Now, we'll see if you can run away!" Staggering across the hall, he fell onto Mei-Tai's bed in a senseless, drunken sleep.

He snored fitfully through the day and in early evening awoke in a daze, wondering where he was. In a flash, he recalled Mei-Tai's punishing treatment. An enormous sum would have come from a movie mogul who craved the services of a young virgin. Well, reasoned Tzo, it would take longer to earn that sum now, but then the girl had many good years to perform. Shouting from his half-reclining position, Tzo roared for his bath. Amah laboriously strained to keep Tzo on his feet as she helped him to his room. "After I've refreshed myself, I shall instruct the worthless whore in the art of serving wine."

Tzo scowled as he picked up his cash box, half-expecting the receipts to be bad. Instead, he smiled broadly as he found his business had returned to normal. With a moan from his bed, Tzo locked up the box and walked over to inspect Mei-Tai. He reached out, pinching her thighs. Getting no response, he slapped her face and mounted her. His fingers roughly tweaked her nipples; Mei-Tai's eyes opened as she shrieked.

When he could no longer perform, Lee Tzo rang for Amah, ordering the bath. Quickly, silently, efficiently, the men servants carried in a hot steaming tub of water. Amah added oils and attar of jasmine, tested the water then looked to Lee Tzo. He motioned the cords to be cut, and the men carried Mei-Tai, gently immersing her body into the fragrant water.

Mei-Tai let out an agonizing scream as the water touched her bruised body, then collapsed and gave herself over to the bath. Amah appeared instantly, tending to Mei-Tai's face, arms and neck, applying a soft herb gel; with her eyes Amah warned no more crying out.

Lee Tzo lolled on his silken settee sipping brandy, daintily nibbling dim sum, grinning at Amah's repairs. Mei-Tai's head wobbled, her eyes swollen shut. She lay almost senseless in the healing water. For an hour, she endured Amah's ministrations, wincing each time more warm water was added, wanting only to sleep.

Finally, Lee Tzo leaped impatiently from his settee, pushed Amah aside and reached in and yanked Mei-Tai from the tub. Amah left the room as Mei-Tai beseeched mercy, hearing the pimp's cruel laughter as he roared, "Later, worthless whore. Pay heed, for I shall only show you once how wine is to be served to your patrons."

He reached for the carafe and held it over the flames, cautioning but for a moment. Then he took Mei-Tai's hands, placed them around the neck of the carafe and lifted it to her lips. "Sip it, hold it, then transfer the warm wine to my lips. Quickly, girl!"

All the time Mei-Tai fed Lee Tzo wine from her lips, his hands explored her body, pausing each time on the welts and swollen bruises, feeling excited as Mei-Tai winced. "Good!" he muttered. "Your pain brings me excitement, arouses my senses. I must say I did a good job. Pain is pleasurable, peaks my performance. You shall know more of it later, after we've finished with the lessons of wine. Now, heat some more and gently, ever so lovingly, feed it to me."

Amah knocked lightly on the door and entered with fresh linens. Quickly, she made up the bed, perfuming the sheets and pillows. The men servants entered noiselessly, removing the bathtub with Amah following hurriedly behind them.

Revived by the warm rice wine, Lee Tzo fondled Mei-Tai's nudity and felt a resurgence of desire. In one sweeping motion, he lifted Mei-Tai and carried her to the bed, laying her face down. Throughout the late afternoon and night, as Mei-Tai's screams and pleas for mercy rang throughout the brothel, the other girls shuddered.

Business was brisk, as word circulated through Chinatown of the pimp's madness. In the fevered atmosphere, a scream issued from one of the rooms. Instantly, the guard went to investigate. While Lee Tzo was abusive, he allowed no other man to harm his girls.

Tai-Tai, the oldest girl in Tzo's harem, huddled beneath her quilt as the naked man was forcibly lifted from the bed and dragged from the room. Another shriek rang out from the private chambers. Tai-Tai scrambled from the bed, knelt before her altar and beseeched Kwan Yin that Mei-Tai's torment cease. In her tearful prayer, Tai-Tai prayed for her master's sexual release, for only then would he relent in Mei-Tai's tortures.

An insistent jangling bell summoned the two men servants. At Tzo's command, they tied Mei-Tai's arms and legs to each of the bed posts. Impulsively, cruelty blazing from the depths of his eyes, Lee Tzo leaned forward and pinched her nipples, but Mei-Tai, unable to scream any longer, only moaned, a long, futile moan like that of an animal whose spirit is broken. Lee Tzo mounted her again, cursing and screaming for satiation. Finally, Lee Tzo achieved his vengeance fueled torrent of release. The young girl from Macao had suffered a long, bloody penance for Lee Tzo's Mei-Mei.

SUMMER IS HARD

Summer vacation was drawing to a close and for the first time since coming to live with her grandma in Peacock Alley, Aileen was beset with panic. Grandma had told her she had to decide where to go to school. If she returned home, she dreaded the squabbling between her mother and father, and more than anything her beatings, which usually followed. If she remained with Grandma and went to the new school, would the teachers be nice? She didn't know anyone at the new school except Willie. In fact, she didn't even know where the new school was. Throughout the day and into her dreams at night, Aileen pondered the situation but couldn't make up her mind. She feared making the wrong decision.

Liah peeked out of the front room window and saw her grand-daughter seated on the bench under the acacia tree, listlessly fiddling with a string, half-heartedly playing cat's cradle. Liah agonized over her granddaughter's dilemma, but remained determined that Aileen must face the ordeal alone. Stern warnings were issued to the family: Aileen must make the decision by herself. Liah told Cook that it was for her growth. At the window, recalling her words, Liah moaned, "But she is only six."

Lingering at the window took Liah back to her own youth, when as a bride she also had to make an excruciating decision alone: whether to join her husband in Gem Sahn. True, her decision was of greater mag-nitude and she was much older, eighteen, at the time. Her terror of un-known Gem Sahn, leaving forever the family and people she loved, helped Liah to understand the sense of aloneness her granddaughter must be feeling now. Half-aloud, Liah moaned, "Aileen must learn to face life for I cannot be there forever to protect her. Ah, Kwan Yin, but it's hard."

Suddenly, Aileen became animated; she had spied Viola walking past the entrance of Peacock Alley. Aileen rushed to her, calling out questions. What was the school like? Were the teachers kind? Not only did Viola refuse to answer, but also her nose went up in the air, a smirk playing on her lips as she kept walking. Aileen's inquisitiveness disap-peared in an instant and was replaced by anger She thought to herself, "Just because her father owns an ice cone machine, she thinks she's above everyone else."

From the window, Liah was also infuriated, more so because Viola's parents had borrowed so much money from her to set up shop. Well, she'd just have to tell Viola's parents to punish her for such bad manners.

Viola indeed did feel superior. Having been born in China, she felt she was more Chinese than those who were American-born. She was also jealous of Aileen's athletic abilities and that her grandma was a powerful woman. Out of the arrogance of China-born kids over the American-born, a rivalry had grown. To bring them down a peg, Aileen's friends called Viola and her friends F.O.B., Fresh Off the Boat.

Every weekend, the Chinese youngsters from the produce section of Loo Sahng challenged those who lived in Chinatown to a baseball or basketball game, played with the fervor of warring nations. In the heated arguments that followed whenever the Chinatown group lost, Viola was particularly callous, especially with the insults she hurled at Aileen.

One afternoon after Aileen's team had won a baseball game by only one run, tempers erupted and a fight ensued. In the scuffle, Viola screamed over and over that Aileen's grandma was a peddler of "Apinyin."

The taboo word chilled the air and the children stopped mid-fight to gape at Viola. Their anger forgotten, most of the other children slunk away, then ran home. Aileen, stunned at first, suddenly erupted with a doubled-up fist which shot out and caught Viola in the eye. Willie jumped in, pulling Aileen away while threatening Viola he'd finish the job if she didn't quit hollering. "If I were you I wouldn't tell my mother how I got that black eye. She might give you the whipping of your life. Now scram!"

Willie walked Aileen home. He grunted his disapproval of Viola, trying to soften the blow to Aileen's hurt pride. Aileen was silent. Willie snorted, "Why let Viola get to you? She's stupid and jealous. Besides, she's a girl."

Aileen stopped and, in a pout, retorted, "But Willie, I'm a girl, too."

Willie stopped in his tracks, grinned, then reached out to tousle her hair, "Yeah, I forgot, but you're different."

Aileen almost grinned. Her heart sang and somehow Viola's snobbery and derogatory accusations of her Grandma didn't seem as important. Besides, Aileen smiled, "I gave her a black eye, didn't I?"

Just as quickly as the enmity between the rival groups had exploded, it dissipated when they no longer had enough players for two teams. Snub-lines were forgotten and the downtown bunch and Chinatown bunch started trading players. Viola alone had stubbornly clung to her animosities.

Aileen watched Viola trudge down Marchesson Street, finally disappearing into her father's confectionary shop, then returned listlessly to the bench to resume playing cat's cradle.

Why, wondered Aileen, was Viola so mean? Why couldn't she answer her questions? Perhaps if she knew what kind of teachers and where the school was, Aileen might be able to make her decision. Viola's unfriendliness only reminded Aileen that at this unknown school she might be faced with antagonistic students. Just then she heard voices shouting her name. The Lee brothers appeared and asked if she'd like to play ball. Aileen sprang from the bench, "Okay, if I can pitch."

Liah smiled from her window. Her granddaughter would have a respite from her inner struggle if only for a while. Liah went to the kitchen and asked that Cook dial the confectionary shop; she had a complaint.

To Aileen's disappointment, there were not enough players for a ballgame, so she returned home. Wowo ran ahead of her, scampering up to the door of Number Three. Aileen half-heartedly followed. Yanking the screen doors opened, Aileen made straight for her grandma's bedroom. There, she stopped, uncomprehendingly, then let out a scream. There was a man in Grandma's bed! Nobody ever slept with her except Aileen. She turned, raced down the corridor and back out onto the cobblestones, and ran blindly down Marchesson Street.

Wowo was hard on her heels. Aileen ran without knowing why she was running or where she was going. She only knew she had to get away. When she reached the playground she ran past the wading pool, the gymnastics rings and bars, and out to the baseball field. Tears flowed like rivers down her cheeks. Aileen was devastated; she had no place to go.

In her torment, Aileen heard the boys and girls riding high on their swings, laughing and shouting to each other. Their laughter deepened Aileen's despair and she shouted for them to shut up. No one heard her and the merriment went on. Aileen felt even more alone. She dropped to her knees and hugged her dog tightly. "You are my only friend in the world. I wish I was dead."

This didn't satisfy her need for comfort. Aileen leaped to her feet. She had to see Willie. He'd understand and explain things to her. Willie knew everything!

She retraced her steps, racing toward Willie's store on Blind Man's Alley. By the time Aileen arrived, she was sobbing uncontrollably. Willie looked up, staring. "What's the matter? Did Raymond hit you again?"

Raymond was the town bully and Aileen his favorite victim. "No!" Aileen cried and shook her head, sobbing harder. Willie dropped a crowbar he was holding, dug into his pants pocket and handed her a handkerchief. "Hey, turn off the water works, will you? How can I help you if I don't know what's the matter?"

He turned over an empty celery crate, motioning for Aileen to sit. She tried to stop sobbing, but the harder she tried, the more she cried. Willie's father walked in, saw her grief and backed out again. Willie chuckled. "You see? Now you've got the hiccups."

Aileen told Willie what had upset her. "Oh, Willie, Grandma doesn't love me. I don't know what to do. That's why she gave me Wowo, not because I was good. She doesn't need me like I need her."

Aileen's sobs started anew. Willie stared, his face flushed, and he sighed hard. It was the first time he felt inadequate. What could he tell her? His face became redder and redder as he grappled with what he could say. Finally, he gruffly muttered for her to stop crying so he could think.

He reached into a lug box, picked out an apple and thrust it into her hand. Aileen took it automatically, but made no attempt to eat it, just twirled it around by its stem. Willie, finally blurted, "Okay, so you saw someone in your grandma's bed. So what? That's grown-up stuff. When you grow up you will understand, only now you have to know she loves you very much."

"Willie, what do you mean grown-up stuff? Please tell me."

Willie's face tinged pink. Again, he reached over, this time plucking a branch of lychee nuts from a box. "Here, if you don't want to eat your apple, eat these. I'm not saying one thing more; it's none of my business. And if you know what's good for you, you won't ask any more questions, especially of your grandma."

Willie's face was crimson now. Aileen pondered this as she pulled the lychee nuts from their branch, peeling them and sucking the succulent fruit from the pod. Why, she thought, did adults always tell her it was grown-up stuff whenever they didn't want to answer her questions? Aileen attempted to ask Willie one more time, but he scowled.

While Willie was speaking with Aileen, his father telephoned Number Three, informing Liah that her granddaughter was in his store and that she was crying. Perhaps Madam Liah would know what to do.

Feeling better, Aileen began helping Willie cull produce, tossing all but the unblemished and firm, and neatly stacking crates. She tried a last time to ask Willie about adults, but Willie whirled about angrily. "I told you no more questions, not to me, not to your grandma, not to anybody, if you know what's good for you."

"Willie," asked Aileen half-tearfully, "I'm scared. Do you ever get scared?"

Willie, almost sixteen years old, suddenly felt penitent. He gently replied, "Yeah, I used to, especially when my mother first died. I was so lonely and scared all the time. Okay, no more stupid talk. Help me with the green onions."

An hour later, Mert walked into the store, saw Willie and Aileen busily stacking fruit. "Say, Willie, sell me a branch of those fresh lychees. They look great."

Mert, lychee branch in hand, motioned for his niece to follow him. As they walked home, he offered some lychee to Aileen who refused. "I ate too many while I was helping Willie. Thank you."

"Well, then," Mert relied gruffly replied, handing Aileen a handkerchief, "wipe off your face, it's filthy."

When they emerged from Blind Man's Alley, Mert asked if Aileen would like to stop at the confectionary for a Popsicle or an all-day sucker.

"No thank you, Fifth Uncle, I will never go to Viola's store again."

Mert glanced down at his niece, and Aileen quickly explained, "She said Grandma was a crook, that she sold Apinyin. I gave her a black eye for that."

"Good for you, Aileen. I don't believe in fighting, but she deserved it and I'm proud you did it. One more thing, kid, no matter what people say, Grandma is a good woman and has a very big heart. Remember that."

"Oh, I know that," muttered Aileen and for the rest of their way home she pondered the truth of her words. When they approached the entrance of Peacock Alley, Aileen broke away, ran to the bench under the acacia and pretended to pet Mr. Fantail, the name Aileen had given the peacock because he looked like a fan to her when he spread his tail feathers.

Mert scowled, motioning for her. "Your grandma wants to see you, She said she was worried about you. Go see her before you play with Mr. Fantail."

Aileen looked up, miserably shaking her head. "Honest, Fifth Uncle, I can't go in yet. I just can't!"

Mert snapped, "Aileen, if something is the matter, tell me and I will see if I can help. Otherwise go inside."

Aileen began to cry as Mert grabbed her and dragged her toward

Number Three. "God, kid," he shouted, "don't you ever run out of tears?"

Suddenly, Aileen stopped in her tracks. "Wowo. I left him at Willie's."

She was halfway down Marchesson Street when Willie appeared coming from the other direction with Wowo at his heels. "Thank you, Willie. Thank you, too, for telling me about grown-up stuff even if I don't understand." Willie's face turned pink again and he scowled, turned and fled.

Aileen finally returned to Number Three, but she did not run directly to the kitchen as she usually did but instead flopped in her grandma's upholstered chair in the front room. Soon Aileen heard the thump, thump of Liah's cane as she approached down the corridor. Aileen did not look over. Liah stood quietly a moment in front of the chair, then gently tapped Aileen on the head with her cane. Aileen felt a rush of mixed emotions: anger, sadness, mostly bewilderment. She just couldn't understand why Grandma would want somebody else in her bed.

She scooted over and Liah sat down. She reached for Aileen's hand, drew her close and began gently stroking her hair. At the touch of her grandma's hand, Aileen collapsed, sobbing wildly. Liah allowed time for her granddaughter's tears to crest, holding her close, saying not a word.

Mert, hearing the sobs, rushed from his room. Liah motioned for him to carry Aileen to the bedroom. Aileen felt her grandma tucking the blanket around her and turned her face to the wall. Liah leaned over, whispering, "Silly child, to think anyone could ever take your place. Grandma loves you and will forever. You must believe that."

Aileen, her face still averted, nodded. Liah sighed; this too, was a lesson her granddaughter had to learn. Aileen sobbed herself to sleep. When she awakened some hours later, Wowo was beside her. Impulsively, not knowing why, Aileen began to scream for her grandma.

Footsteps outside the bedroom door announced Cook was coming. Aileen threw the minhois over her head. For some reason, Aileen did not want to see him. Cook lifted the minhois, asking with bemusement, "I thought you called for your grandma. Now that you're awake, you might as well get up. I'm fixing wonton for supper."

Aileen gaped. Was he the man who had been in Grandma's bed? She wanted to ask him so badly, but Willie's warning rang in her ear. Instead, she asked if she couldn't have pork, too.

"Come on, put on your shoes and take Wowo outside."

She scrambled off the bed and, on her knees, searched for her shoes. Cook scolded, "If you hadn't kicked them off, you'd not now be on your knees. Here's one shoe. You find the other."

Aileen glanced up at Cook, wondering again if he was the man, but he met her gaze unflinchingly. "And hurry. Wowo can't wait forever."

Aileen scampered into the kitchen. Wowo followed but stopped in the middle of the kitchen floor and piddled. Cook glared. Aileen pursed her lips, muttering defensively that it wasn't her fault, Wowo couldn't help it.

Liah's eyes signaled for Cook to relent, motioning Aileen to the door.

Once she was gone, Liah glanced speculatively at Cook, speaking low. "Do you think she recognized you?"

"I don't think so, but from here on out, we'll have to be very careful."

In the days that followed, Liah was exceedingly loving toward her granddaughter, oftentimes scrutinizing the child's face to convince herself Aileen did not comprehend what she had seen. Or that she knew it was Cook. For weeks afterwards, Aileen wanted to question her grandma, but Willie's warning stopped her. Willie was so much older, so much smarter; she decided to obey him.

On Monday of Labor Day weekend, Aileen in her lap, Liah asked Aileen if she had made up her mind about school. Aileen made a pained, sad face, declaring she was too tired to think any more. Could her grandma make the decision for her?

Liah removed her arm from around Aileen, shaking her head.

"Grandma is not helping you, nor is anyone else. All I can say is that you're fortunate you have a choice. Most of the time, life commands us to do what it wants us to do. Each time you make a hard decision, you will lose something. You want to live here, but you also want to go to your old school. You cannot have both, so when you choose one, you lose the other. I know it is hard. Grandma is sorry, child, but you must make the choice."

Aileen's eyes were full of pleading. "Grandma, can't I live here with you and go to my old school? Uncle can drive me to school when he goes to work."

Liah sighed, shaking her head. "You have to make your decision by this evening, child."

Aileen hung her head but then raised it and in a firm voice said, "I'm not going to suffer anymore. I will tell you now what I will do. I'll stay here with you and go to the new school."

Liah drew Aileen to her, crushing in a close hug. "Grandma is so very proud of you child. It was a difficult choice to make. You did a very grown-up thing."

Aileen recoiled. "No! I don't ever want to grow up!"

Liah tousled her hair. "Now that's a foolish thing to say, child. Just think, when you are grown up you can stay up as late as you wish. Nobody will force you to go to bed or take naps. Now, why don't you go to the playground?"

"Can I have a nickel to buy a sucker, too?"

Cook dug into his pants pocket and drew out a nickel, handing it to Aileen. "Now go and don't pester your grandma anymore."

Aileen darted into the corridor. They heard her shouts as she slammed the door. Liah sighed. "One more day of misery and I'd have gone back on my word and made the decision for her."

Cook murmured, "I know. Several times in the last two weeks, I saw you waver. You should indeed be proud, knowing how you suffered with her."

Liah's eyebrows shot up, her eyes quickly filling, for it was true. "I pray to Kwan Yin that in the future I can be as strong, for I cannot bear to see that child suffer."

Not wishing Liah to be lulled into a false security, Cook retorted, "There'll be many more such decisions, some of even greater gravity, but I know you'll use your head. You can't shield the child for the rest of her life. Now what shall we have for supper?"

Aileen ran out of Peacock Alley, feeling the impact of the hot afternoon September sun on her face. The Chinatown streets were sun baked, cracked, the wagon ruts crumbly and dusty. Each time a horse-drawn wagon lumbered down Marchesson Street, dust whorls rose from beneath its wheels like rising smoke. Aileen stood in the stifling heat, debating whether to go to the playground or to see Willie. Wowo pranced about the street, running up and down, impatient for Aileen to follow. Heat did not diminish her puppy's energy.

Willie probably wouldn't be at the store and the wading pool would be cool, so Aileen turned and ran down toward the playground. Kids jammed the pool. Aileen removed her socks and shoes, held them high, and pushed her way in. She grimaced at the feel of the tepid, muddy water, and pushed her way out again. She'd go see Willie.

At the store, Aileen was flabbergasted when Willie's father said that he'd gone to register for school. "Register, sir?" asked Aileen, "Do I need to register?"

Willie's father shrugged, suggesting she wait until Willie returned. "He should be here about five o'clock. Here." He handed Aileen a sprig of lychee nuts.

Returning home, sprig in hand, Aileen peered into the darkness of Pig Alley and shuddered. She'd not been inside the alley since she and Willie found Sam Yin's body, no matter how long she had to walk to get home, but today the heat was oppressive. For almost five minutes she stood at the entrance, hoping someone would come along and enter the darkness, but there was nobody on the streets. In a sudden burst of courage, Aileen closed her eyes and plunged into the dark alleyway.

When she emerged on Marchesson Street, Aileen half-expected to see Sam Yin's ghost; some residents said they'd seen his form. She proudly ran home to tell Grandma of her bravery.

She burst into Number Three. Cook and Liah, hearing her shouting, looked with alarm at each other. Both remembered the last time she came home unexpectedly. Forgetting her news of Pig Alley, she shouted, "Grandma! There were too many kids in the pool, so I went to see Willie, but he's in school registering. I've got to go back at five to tell him I'm going to his school and he can take me to get registered."

Aileen extended the sprig of lychee nuts, but Liah refused them, suggesting Aileen eat them.

Liah noticed Aileen's stocking less feet and exclaimed, "What happened to your stockings, child?"

Aileen dug into her dress pocket and brought out the gritty wad of stockings. "Ugh," grimaced Cook. "Did you wash them in mud?"

Liah screwed up her face, ordering Aileen to remain exactly where she was while Cook brought her a basin of water to wash her dirty feet.

"But I've got to go back to Willie's!"

Liah growled, "You can go back at five. Meanwhile, you'll have a meat bun and a glass of milk and take a nap. Then you can go back."

At five o'clock, Aileen ran out of Peacock Alley with Wowo close behind and darted into Marchesson Street. Again, she felt an eerie reluctance as she approached Pig Alley, but as before she closed her eyes and dashed into the dark alley. When she reached the store, Willie was working. Again forgetting her news of Pig Alley, she asked Willie if he wouldn't take her to register at his school.

"I thought you were going back to your old school."

Aileen shook her head, launching into a fusillade of questions. "Willie, I don't know anything about the new school: where the toilets are, where to eat lunch, where the classrooms are, not even where the school is. Will you show me? I'm kind of scared. I don't know anybody at the new school."

"You know kids. What about Viola, May, the Lee boys? And me?"

Aileen screwed up her face, "Having you there will be great, but I don't like Viola and she doesn't like me and neither do her girlfriends."

"Don't worry, Aileen, you're smart, you'll get along. You might feel a little alone at first, but you will make friends. Here, if you're going to stay, you might as well help me cull these green onions."

There was a lapse of silence as they worked, then Willie cleared his throat. "You know the other day when you came in here crying? I don't think you were as mad or hurt as you were surprised. Isn't that true?"

Aileen sobered and stuck out her bottom lip. "Yes."

"Well, Aileen, I've been thinking and it's hard trying to explain woman stuff, I mean man and woman stuff. It's something grown-ups have to do, it's not a bad thing, just that you're too young to understand that your grandma needs a man every now and then and not because she doesn't love you." He paused. "Okay, we will not talk about this again."

Aileen nodded, relieved. She was tired of hearing about grown-ups; it just made her feel more mixed up. She muttered, "But she's got me, Willie."

A moment later Aileen sighed. "Willie, I'm scared. Will you promise to show me everything?"

"Aileen, I told you I would. For the first week I'll show you not only where everything is in school, but I'll teach you the way to school and back. Promise me one thing though, promise you won't shout my name each time you see me, okay?"

Aileen nodded and glanced at the clock then leaped up from the crate box where she was sitting. "I've got to go home. It's supper time."

"Okay, remember tomorrow you be ready at eight o'clock and I will take you for registration. Be sure to tell your grandma."

Aileen nodded and darted out of the store. Willie heard his father shouting a warning to her that there was a wagon coming. Willie listened, shaking his head. Crazy kid, always in a hurry.

AUTUMN WROUGHT

September brought the excitement of the first day of school: seeing old friends again and swapping vacation stories, but for Aileen this year it meant trepidation; she was not excited. This year, September meant going to an unknown place with strangers and, even more so, her dependence on Willie. Suppose they got separated? Though he had shown her the way, what if she couldn't find her way home?

The night before the first day of school, Aileen went to bed at eight o'clock without coercion from her grandma. She lay in the alcove bed, listening to the murmur of voices in the kitchen, wishing she did not have to go to school. She stared at the new blue dress laid out on a chair for her, with its fancy embroidered bodice, her brown shoes and blue stockings beneath the chair and her fears only increased.

Presently, Liah entered the bedroom and was surprised her granddaughter was yet awake. She quickly went to the bedside. "Do you want Grandma to rub your back?" Aileen nodded gratefully. With Liah's hands warm on her back, she suddenly felt safe, and quickly fell asleep, not even waking when her grandma climbed into bed.

Mert tiptoed into the bedroom at seven-thirty the next morning. He tapped Aileen several times on her cheek, gesturing silence.

Aileen dressed carefully, feeling lost without the assistance of either her grandma or Amah, especially when she went into the kitchen to wash up. Mert steamed two meat buns, poured glasses of milk and admonished her to eat.

"I don't like this kind of breakfast, Uncle."

Mert glowered, "Well, tomorrow we'll have Cook fix a plate of food, but for today, eat."

He picked up a quarter from the table and handed it to Aileen, saying it was for her hot lunch. "Willie will show you where the cafeteria is and Grandma said to be sure and eat all of your food."

Impulsively, Aileen reached up and grabbed her uncle's neck. "I don't want to go to school. I'm scared."

Mert, taken aback by his niece's embrace, quickly unclasped her arms. "Come on, you're a big girl now. Besides, Willie will be there to take care of you. Come on, let's go out and see if he's here."

As they walked to the entrance of Peacock Alley, Aileen wailed that Willie would probably forget to come. They waited and Aileen lamented, "How will I go to school now?"

"You worry too much, kid. See? There's Willie now." Mert pointed. Willie was emerging from Pig Alley, heading for Peacock Alley. Aileen dashed out to meet him then stopped and turned to wave good-bye to her uncle and shouted for him not to forget to take care of Wowo. As Aileen and Willie approached Alameda South, her fears of school were overwhelmed by the dread of entering the Fahn Gwai's world.

Willie, noticing her sudden silence, asked what was the matter. "Come on, Aileen, there's nothing to be scared about. Now pay attention as we go, for inside a week you'll be coming and going all on your own. You won't need me. You're smart."

Aileen smiled gratefully. Although school was only nine blocks from Chinatown, today it might as well be nine miles. Though preoccupied with thoughts of what could go wrong, Aileen heard Willie pointing out landmarks. He soon became impatient. "Come on now, pay attention. How are you going to recognize the streets you need to take if you don't memorize the stores and buildings?"

When they arrived at the school, Aileen's curiosity overtook her apprehension. She spied Viola, Sue and May on the swings and shyly said hello. Viola stopped swinging, looking dumfounded at Aileen. "I thought you were going to go to your downtown school? Why do you have to come to our school?"

Willie glowered. "Viola, you're not only nosey, but you're stupid. Aileen's going to show you how smart a downtown student can be."

Sue sneered unkindly. "Pretty dress, Aileen. Your grandmother must have gotten it with the money from you-know-what."

As Aileen lunged for Sue, Willie caught her. "Pay no attention to them. They're jealous."

He turned to the three girls. "I hate to say this, but your attitudes and words are dangerous. I should snitch to your fathers about your mentioning Apinyin, but I won't. Still, Sue, why don't you ask your father who paid for your mother's passage to Gem Sahn? He might get upset and punish you but don't say I didn't warn you. And you, Viola, why not ask your father who put up the money for his confectionary shop? Both of you ought to know this—Madam Liah did. What do you think of that?"

Viola gaped. Sue accused Willie of lying, but May was silent. She didn't want Willie talking about her family.

Willie saw Aileen's wounded expression and whispered, "You cry and I'll brain you."

The school bell rang, effectively ending the confrontation. Willie tugged on Aileen's arm. "Come on, I'll show you where to go. See that building? That's the cafeteria. Meet me there at noon." Then he led her to the office.

A clerk there took Aileen's name, address, her parents' names and her birth date. "We will send for your records at your old school. Now, come along with me. I'll show you to the nurse for your physical examination. After that you will be tested to determine your learning level."

A tall, thin spinster of a woman, the clerk smiled. Aileen smiled back and followed her down the hall. In the nurse's office, Aileen's eyes, ears and throat were examined, and the nurse put a stethoscope on her chest to listen to her heart. Upon finishing she was returned to the clerk's office.

After giving Aileen three aptitude tests, the clerk checked them while Aileen looked around the room. Oversized pictures of old Mexico hung on the wall: boys wearing serapes and sombreros, a donkey cart and donkey, oversized cacti. Aileen decided the office was no different than the one in her old school, only more cheerful.

Having reviewed the test results, the clerk told Aileen, "Now we'll take you to your classroom. Your tests indicate you are capable of doing third-grade work, but perhaps we'll try you in A-2 for a while. If the work is too easy, we'll move you up. In any case, the A-2 and B-3 students are in the same room. Mrs. Raphael will show you where to go."

Mrs. Raphael glanced at the clock and saw it was almost lunchtime. "Dear, why don't you have lunch first? Afterwards you come back here and I will show you to your classroom. Do you know where the cafeteria is?"

Aileen nodded and just then the bell rang. Doors banged opened and with a cacophony of boisterous chatter students raced down the halls toward the cafeteria. Aileen's heart pounded as she joined the exodus, feeling like an outcast. When Aileen arrived at the long line outside the cafeteria, she cast a frantic eye around for Willie.

A stubby, spectacled teacher noticing Aileen's anxiety, walked over to inquire if this was her first day in the school. "Yes, Madam," she replied in a tremulous voice. "I am new here. I'm waiting for Willie. He said we'd eat lunch together on my first day, but I don't see him."

"Willie Lew? He's a nice boy. I am Miss Early. You wait in line and I'll see if I can find him."

A few moments later, Miss Early returned with Willie beside her. Aileen was ecstatic. She was no longer alone. Miss Early made room for him in the line, explaining to those behind Aileen that he was with her on her first day in school.

Aileen chose a plate of beef and chard over rice and would have passed up the bottle of milk if Willie hadn't plunked it on her tray. She started to protest, but Willie growled that her grandma had demanded that he see to it that Aileen drank her milk.

When the bell rang ending lunch. Willie pointed to the gate through which they had entered the school grounds. "Wait for me there after school. I'll walk you home."

From the office Mrs. Raphael led Aileen to the second floor. "You're in Room 5." She opened the door and Aileen was surprised and happy to see Miss Early at the front of the room. Miss Early was delighted too. She welcomed Aileen and took her by the hand to an empty desk. "You'll find all of your books, pencils, pens and paper inside the desk. Right now, we're practicing penmanship. Please take out your book and turn to page eleven."

Viola, Sue and May stared blankly at her. Miffed, Viola leaned over to whisper, "How come she got to be in our room? She's younger than we are."

Miss Early walked up and down the aisles, stopping now and then to correct a student's hand or pen positioning. When she came along-side Aileen's desk, Miss Early watched a moment, then complimented her beautiful letters. "Who taught you to write so well, my dear?"

Aileen heard Viola's snicker, but didn't care as she informed Miss Early that it had been her teacher in her old school and her uncle.

Next Aileen was enthralled with Miss Early's geography lesson. She listened as the teacher traced the Tigris River, flowing over 1,000 miles through Mesopotamia to join the Euphrates River near Basra, then flowing on to the Persian Gulf. The Arabian Nights stories came to life for Aileen as she listened to Miss Early describe the two rivers constantly overflowing onto the plains, making Baghdad accessible to commerce and world trade. The traditions of the old world especially fascinated Aileen: the women, mysteriously veiled, dressed in gossamer gowns, living their cloistered lives.

Toward the end of the day, Aileen became worried. What if she couldn't find Willie? How would she find her way home? At the thought of being left alone in Fahn Gwai town after dark, Aileen almost panicked, almost to the point she would've been willing to force herself on Viola and her friends.

When the bell rang at three o'clock, Aileen sprinted to the school gate and breathlessly waited for Willie. A half-hour passed, the playground became deserted but still no Willie. Suddenly, Aileen spied him across the yard. She screamed for him in relief. Willie scowled as he ran up. "I thought I told you not to shout out my name!"

Almost tearfully, she explained she was scared. "I thought you forgot about me. I'm sorry."

On the way home Aileen complained that she'd never learn the way, that there too many things to memorize. Willie chided that she needed to pay more attention. Aileen then wailed that she was too nervous to remember anything.

It wasn't until Aileen set foot on Marchesson Street that her fears ebbed. They took the long way home, dropping in at Willie's store where his father gave Aileen some apricots and lychee nuts.

Aileen's courage was fully restored as she ambled down Marchesson Street munching on the fruit. She spied Uncle Mert waiting at the entrance of Peacock Alley and rushed up to him, gushing about her day at school, about Miss Early and how Viola and her friends were mad because she had been assigned to their room. "And Uncle Mert, I was scared walking on the Fahn Gwai's street, but I didn't get hurt."

Aileen felt as if her heart would burst with good feelings. She had Willie to watch over her, Fifth Uncle waiting, and Grandma and Cook and Wowo. She bounded into the house, ran into the corridor and shouted to Grandma that she was home.

Aileen couldn't talk fast enough to her grandma, recounting her first day at the new school. In her heart, Liah gave thanks to Kwan Yin.

"And Cook," Aileen said, "I had beef and greens and rice for lunch, but it didn't taste as good as yours. Willie made me eat it all anyway. The Fahn Gwai do not know how to cook our kind of food."

Aileen was too excited to notice, but Liah saw the pleased expression on Cook's face.

Liah frowned when Aileen mentioned how the girls sneered at her new dress, asking if her Grandma had bought it with her Apinyin monies. "But Grandma, please don't tell their fathers, then they'll never be my friends. Willie said Viola only acts like that because she's a stupid girl and because she's jealous. I want to do as Willie said, ignore them."

A smile played on Liah's face as she agreed. It warmed her heart, for her little girl was going to be fine and again she breathed a silent thanks to Kwan Yin.

Throughout her first week of school, Aileen was grateful for Miss Early's protection. When Aileen found herself shut out of a baseball or a kickball game, the teacher pushed her in. Because of the teacher's efforts, Viola branded Aileen the teacher's pet. Aileen didn't care. She had someone; she was not alone. It did cross Aileen's young mind to wonder why Viola so disliked her.

By the end of the second week of school, Aileen was the most popular player on the playground and it seemed to her she'd always been friends with these kids. Her relationship with Miss Early only grew to be more special. The teacher seemed to understand the child's need for affection. Whenever Aileen felt at odds, Miss Early was there to reassure and affectionately encourage her and the teacher reveled in her student's tremendous curiosity and response to instruction.

It was Miss Early who detected Aileen's artistic talents, encouraging her with books about famous painters and their impact upon history and civilization. The message: Above all, hard work and believe in your abilities. Each time Aileen achieved something remarkable, the teacher felt a sense of reward that heretofore she'd not experienced in her long years at Macy Street School.

Miss Atwater, the principal, suggested Aileen be placed in a school for gifted children, but Miss Early shook her head. "There is something deeply rooted in the child, something she's found here and if denied, could irreparably damage her creativity. I think we ought to leave her here and nurture her."

Miss Atwater asked, "Do you suppose Aileen's advanced knowledge comes from having lived in a Caucasian community? After all, the children who are confined to Chinatown speak only Chinese and have no outside contact with the outside world."

Miss Early shook her head. "To a certain extent you may be right, but I think Aileen has a lot of innate intelligence. Although the local Chinese children start out slow owing to their lack of English language skills, they quickly catch up; so Aileen has competition."

"Do you think it's true that the Chinese are inherently smarter than us? It's a fact that their civilization is much older than ours. Perhaps their culture has ingrained certain academic skills into their subconscious."

Miss Early shook her head again. "I don't think they're smarter because they're Chinese. However, in most of their homes where I have been a guest for supper, there was a high level of parental guidance and discipline. I think their respect for their elders makes the children more apt to listen to and obey their teachers. Moreover, I'm told that teachers themselves are highly respected in China."

It was decided that Aileen would not be pushed one grade ahead but would instead receive extra instruction from the art teacher, Miss Wadsworth. Viola and her girlfriends were shocked when they discovered Aileen taking art classes in the sixth-grade room, but they didn't make any snide remarks. Mary's and Sue's parents had already punished them, warning them of more dire punishment the next time they dared insult Liah's granddaughter. Both girls wondered why Viola didn't get punished. They didn't know that Viola kept her punishment to herself. Her parents had not only warned her, but her backside was bruised from the tanning her father gave her with a strap. What feeble remarks Viola did make after that were only amongst the three of them.

—

Throughout the hot, humid days of fall, life in Chinatown was strained. Businesses grumpily offered their services; wives railed at their children and husbands at their wives. In Number Three, everyone walked on tiptoes, evading Liah in her foul mood. Aileen was no exception, going uncomplainingly to bed and eating her meals quickly lest her grandma lose her temper.

One exceptionally hot morning, Cook whispered a warning to Fifth Son: "This is the worst I've ever seen her. Her Apinyin intake is alarming. If only she'd eat, she wouldn't feel so bad."

Mert nodded. "There's nothing we can do and I'm certainly not getting my head cut off for saying anything. If she weren't my mother, I'd walk out on her."

Both men looked at each other, both knowing the other was just letting off steam. Neither could ever walk away from Liah. Mert continued, "The outdoor people jamming in here every day doesn't help matters. Even Professor and Tom have stayed away."

Cook continued shelling peas and asked Fifth Son if he'd heard anything about Mei-Mei. "I hear Lee Tzo has given up the search. Five long weeks and still no trace of her. Strange, isn't it?"

"Yeah," muttered Mert. "I'm glad she got away. Her life with Tzo was no bed of roses. Still, I'm as curious as you are. I wonder where she went."

Cook took the strainer of peas to the sink. "I hope for her sake she's never caught. If Lee Tzo ever catches her, she would beg for death. Of course even if she is not caught, she'll spend the rest of her life looking over her shoulder. She won't even be able to live among her own people again. It will be a living death."

Mert disagreed. Being a slave to Tzo was no life. Cook frowned, "Slave or not, Mei-Mei had a roof over her head and Tzo did pamper her. He was generous. I only hope the young man she spoke to the night before she disappeared can take care of her. Professor said the young man looked intellectual, like a scholar or teacher."

Mert gasped, "Does Mah-Mah know this?"

"No, and I am not telling her. Professor will do so when he feels the time is right. Besides, what good will it do now?" Cook heaved a sigh. "I know, Fifth Son, it's not easy for you living with your mother. I know you want a life of your own and, in trying to be an obedient son, you are restricted and…."

Mert sensed a lecture coming on and gruffly interrupted, "What are you trying to say, sir?"

Cook hitched up his apron and sat down to face Mert. "Well, I don't want to make trouble between you and your mother, but that girl who has been coming to the house. I'm afraid one of these days she'll run into your mother. I don't know what will happen."

Mert scowled and asked if the girl he was talking about wore a colored scarf over her hair and very high heels. Cook nodded, remarking she had come by only two days earlier.

"That stupid girl! I warned her not to come here. All right, Cook, I'll tell her again and this time I won't be so soft-spoken. Thank you for the warning."

Cook sighed. "That's one reason your mother wants you to go back to China. She's afraid you'll marry such a girl. She has said such girls are uncouth and are barbarians."

Mert clenched his fists, "Yeah, if Mah had her way, I'd be married to a dumpy, stupid girl from the village. No thanks! When I am ready for marriage, I'll choose my own bride and one from Gem Sahn not China. Tell her that for me!"

"You're right in wanting to choose your own wife, but your mother is from the old country and only wants what's best for you. I've been warned to leave you children to her, that I have no right to interfere."

Mert listened thoughtfully. "I thank you again, sir, and in case my brothers and sisters have never thanked you, let me tell you they are grateful to you too. You are more of a father to us than our real one."

The tall, lean man sat up stiffly in the chair for a moment and his eyes misted, for Fifth Son's gratitude had caught him by surprise. Up until now he'd worried about how the children felt about his taking their father's place. He looked at Fifth Son and wondered if he knew about his intimacy with his mother and, if he did, whether he resented him.

His voice husky, Cook sighed. "I thank you for your kind words. I have long tried to make it clear to all of you that I never meant to usurp your father's place. You are grown up now so I will say this: until your father was gone, never was there anything between your mother and me. I hope you believe me."

Mert's face flushed. "Yes, sir, I believe you, sir. I think all of us know that, even my flighty older sister Flo."

They heard movement inside Liah's bedroom and both men tensed. Mert picked up his keys, motioning that he was leaving. Cook was left alone to face Liah.

The following afternoon, Mert was not as lucky, for when he returned from work, he came face-to-face with his mother. Liah, still groggy from Apinyin sleep, glared angrily at him as she puffed on a cigarette. Mert quickly said hello and went to his room, saying he was tired from a hard day at the garage.

Cook placed a bowl of brandy broth before Liah and went back to the sink to finish up the chard for supper. The two remained in deadlocked silence, both waiting for the other to speak. At last Liah retorted, "I know you think I'm an ogre. Don't think I didn't hear you warning Fifth Son about that hussy. I've known for a while about her visits to the house. You two thought you'd fooled me."

Cook didn't answer. Liah crushed out her cigarette and lit another, only to angrily grind it, too, into the ashtray. "The disgraceful hussy. I will let my son know I won't tolerate her or his bachelorhood. In fact, I'll go tell him now."

Before Cook could stop her, Liah left the kitchen and thumped her way to the front room, her cane beating short, staccato taps on the floor, a sure barometer of her pent-up anger.

Mert, his body flung on top of his bed, was sound asleep and snoring and didn't hear his mother's approach. By the time she pushed open the door, it was too late. "Well!" she said. "Now, we'll have things out."

Mert turned his head and growled, "Aw, Mah, I'm tired. Couldn't you see I was sleeping?"

"I want to speak to you about that cheap slut who darkens my door in search of you. She may be Chinese but she is from a low caste, and is ill-bred and headstrong. What kind of a wife and mother would she make? Is that the kind of female you want to grace your home and raise your kids?"

Fifth Son sat up, boiling mad. Mother or not, she had no right to barge in and awaken him. He shouted back. "She's not going to be my wife. Nobody is. I'm not ready to get married, so leave me be. How come you never pick on my brothers? Why me all the time? Or is it because you think me a weakling? Please, Mah, leave me be!"

Liah's face blanched, furious at the memory of her two older sons who had threatened to move out unless she ceased her nagging. This only fueled her temper and she tapped her cane. Cook, listening from the kitchen, shuddered. A moment later, he heard the cane crash along with the splintering of glass then angry shouting.

His first reaction was to stop the fight, then he sighed. Perhaps it was good that the two of them were venting their pent-up feelings. He decided that he would intervene only if injury to Liah seemed imminent. He heard Liah scream: "Don't you dare, Fifth Son."

Aileen, returning from the playground, came into the house just in time to hear something smash against the wall. It came from Uncle

Mert's room. Aileen's heart raced, then she heard another crash, followed by Fifth Uncle warning his mother that if she didn't leave his room, he'd be forced to hurt her. "Mah," he shouted angrily, "please don't push me. I will hurt you if you don't leave!"

Aileen's initial impulse was to run; then she heard her grandma shriek, "Put me down this instant! Cook!"

Footsteps sounded in the corridor as Cook rushed into the front room. There he saw Aileen looking stricken. He ordered her to go outside and play, then rushed past her to the bedroom door, flung it open and grabbed Mert by the arm, shouting, "Leave your mother alone. Whatever occurred, it's not cause enough for you to harm her." Aileen gaped in dismay. Mert had his mother's arms pinned behind her, suspending Liah halfway in the air, kicking and screaming to be set free. A lamp was on its side on the floor; the ukulele, broken, lay atop scattered sheet music. Liah's cane had been flung into one corner of the room.

Cook continued to persuade Mert to free his mother, promising that Liah would inflict no further harm if he just let her go. Just then, Liah managed to free one hand and raked her youngest son's face. The bloody streaks made Aileen scream and she turned and fled out the front door.

She stood just outside the door and jammed her fist to her mouth to keep from screaming again. Torn between her love for Grandma and Fifth Uncle, she felt almost as terrified as when her father and mother fought. Her world crumbling, her desire was for flight, but to where? Wowo leaped about her feet and Aileen stooped and clasped him tightly to her chest. He was her only true friend. Mr. Fantail, pecking nearby, issued his customary greeting, but Aileen angrily shouted for him to shut up.

She plopped herself onto the bench under the acacia tree, hugging Wowo as tears streamed down her face. Selah came out of Number One and smiled when she saw Aileen. "Darling," she cried, "why aren't you at the playground? Well, never mind. I have a letter for Fifth Uncle. Will you give it to him?"

It wasn't until Selah came nearer that she saw Aileen's tears and the panic on her face and asked what was the matter. Aileen collapsed against Selah, sobbing wildly. Selah cooed, allowing time for Aileen to unleash her tears. "Darling, tears are for grown-ups, not children. You ought to be carefree and happy. Want to tell me about it?"

Selah raised Aileen's head, reached for a handkerchief and wiped away the tears. "Tell you what. We'll go buy a Popsicle, then talk things over."

Aileen shook her head, explaining why she didn't go to Viola's store anymore. "Good for you, darling," approved Selah. "Then we'll go to Jui Jinn's Café and buy ourselves an ice cream cup."

Seated once again on the bench under the acacia, Aileen carefully spooned up the ice cream while Wowo climbed into Selah's lap to lick the condensation from her cup. As Wowo tasted the coldness of the ice cream container, he sat on his haunches and growled. That made Aileen smile.

"Now, that's the way I want to see my little girl. Just remember, you're a child. Don't worry about grown-up troubles. Even when they fight, your grandma and uncle still love each other. It's because they love each other so much that they fight, darling. In fact, when you go home, I bet they won't even be angry any more."

Aileen shook her head. "No, they will still be angry. Besides, I'm not going back. I'm going home to live with my father and mother!"

Selah was stunned. Angrily she bit her lip and decided she would have a serious talk with Liah and Mert. She couldn't just standby and allow the frightened child to return home to abuse. Just then, Professor came out of his house and saw Aileen's tear-stained face. Selah nodded a greeting and whispered to him: "Well, it's happened. Nearly scared the poor child to death, they did. I'm going to confront the two of them and tell them to think of Aileen."

Aileen couldn't hear Selah, but clung tighter. Professor shrugged. "You're braver than I am."

"Well," Selah whispered fiercely, "somebody has to pound some sense into those two. I blame that Cora. If that hussy really wants to marry Mert, why doesn't she try to win Liah over instead of sneaking around? Why can't she behave with decorum, at least until after she's married?"

Professor retorted dryly, "I can't say I blame Liah much. I wouldn't want a daughter-in-law like that girl. Well, I wish you well. I am on my way to Lim Tao's with more forms to complete. Immigration is such a long, tedious not to mention aggravating process."

Just then Mert shouted for Aileen to come to supper. Selah felt her stiffen. As Mert came closer, Selah saw bandages on his face and pain in his eyes, but her concern for Aileen was greater. She ordered him to be quiet. Couldn't he see how distraught the child was? Didn't he know she was torn between her grandma and him? "Tell Liah I will bring Aileen in when she's ready."

Selah paused, then in a gentler tone, apologized for her anger. "It's just that I can't stand to see a child suffer. It unhinges me."

When Mert turned to go home, Selah ran her fingers through Aileen's hair, cooing, "Now, I know you're a brave girl. Auntie Selah wants you to go home and eat your supper."

Mert heaved a big sigh. Selah beckoned him and the two of them watched as Aileen slowly made her way to Number Three. Selah reached out and pulled Mert to sit on the bench. "Don't worry so, Mert. Just stick to your guns. I know your mother; she's stubborn and strong-minded, but I know positively she is only doing what she thinks best for your well-being and happiness. When she finally realizes her threats will not work, she'll leave you be. That's how your older brothers did it. You were too young to know what was happening, but you aren't the only one to suffer Liah's tongue-lashings and temper."

Mert tried to speak, but Selah raised a finger for silence. "Oh, I know all you younger children think Thomas and Shelley had an easy time, but you are wrong there. Many were the times the two boys moaned and cursed and drank themselves senseless. So just continue to stand up to that loveable ogress and time will be on your side."

Mert turned to go. "One more thing, Mert," Selah said and narrowed her eyes for emphasis. "Your mother is from the old country. It's her birthright and privilege to expect daughter-in-laws and grandchildren. However, I shudder to think you might choose Cora. That girl has no class or brains. If I were you, I'd break up with Cora. She will badger you until she gets her way. Since your mother is adamant that Cora won't get you, if you continue to see her, you'll be choosing her over your mother."

"That's not fair, Selah! Mah shouldn't be able to tell me who I can see and who I can't. However, I understand what you're saying. Just let me think for a while."

Selah nodded and said, "That's a start. Now before you go home again, let me fix you a bracer. I'd hate to see the two of you go at it again, for you'll surely come out second best no matter what happens."

Lalo said nothing when he saw Mert's bandaged face as Selah's eyes silently demanded his silence. She went behind the bar, mixed a strong shot of scotch with some soda, then handed it to Mert. "Drink up, Mert, and promise me you'll see to it that that hussy Cora doesn't visit Number Three anymore." Mert nodded wordlessly and Selah hugged him tight then pushed him out the door.

Dinner was a dismal, silent affair. Neither Thomas nor the others said one word. The tension at the table made it impossible for Aileen to sit still, let alone swallow. Suddenly, she picked up her plate and took it to the sink, complaining she was not hungry. Before Liah could question her or admonish her to eat, Aileen had fled to the bedroom. She burrowed into the minhois, clinging to Wowo, new tears wetting the pillows.

Two hours later, Aileen woke up to find her grandmother sitting beside her. She placed a hand on Aileen's forehead. "No fever, that's good. Was it something you ate that made you ill?"

Aileen shook her head, ducking back under the covers and turning her face to the wall. Liah leaned over and gently rubbed her back. Soon Aileen sat up and cried, "Grandma, I want to go home."

"Why, child?" exclaimed Liah fearfully, "I thought you liked being here with me. Tell me what's the matter."

Aileen burrowed her head into the minhois again, sobbing wildly. Liah, gently rubbing her granddaughter's back again, allowed Aileen to unleash her tears, then pulled the child to her. "I want you to quit crying now and tell me. Is it because Grandma and Fifth Son were fighting? It does not concern you, my child. We both love you."

Aileen only sobbed harder and shook her head. Aileen repeated her wish to go home.

"Go home, child? I thought you were happy here and doing so well in school?"

"I don't really want to go, Grandma, but when you and Fifth Uncle fight, I feel awful. I love both of you and nobody loves me. I wish I were dead!"

Liah tightened her arms around Aileen, rocking her gently back and forth like a baby. "So that's it, child. Well, don't worry. Things are not as bad as they appeared. Grown-ups, like children, fight when they can't agree. Fifth Uncle and Grandma don't agree and so we fight, but that doesn't mean we don't love each other. I must admit the hot weather has made Grandma cross. In fact I was thinking of going to apologize to Fifth Uncle about my bad mood."

Aileen clung to her grandmother for a long time. Then Liah disengaged her arms, reached under her pillow and pulled out a flat, rectangular box wrapped in blue paper with a blue ribbon. "For me?" gasped Aileen as she eagerly reached for it.

Cook, eavesdropping at the doorway, was immensely relieved. The tension was broken. He frowned as Aileen impatiently tugged at the ribbons. In two long strides, Cook stepped into the bedroom, demanding, "How many times have I told you to be patient. Here now, let me help. I won't open it, I'll just untie the string and wrapping."

Aileen tore off the seals and opened the package. It was a handicraft set. "Oh, look, Grandma, needles, yarn, crayons, patterns and even a small pair of scissors. And look at the instructions. I can't read all of it, but Fifth Uncle can help me or maybe Auntie Em."

Upon further investigation Aileen exclaimed to her grandma that she didn't need her uncle or aunt. "I've done this before. First you color in the picture, then you use the matching color of yarn to embroider all around the picture, then you cut the picture out and put it in a frame. Can I start a picture now?"

"Yes, it's Saturday tomorrow and you can sleep later, but do it in the kitchen. The light is better there."

In the kitchen with Aileen, Liah leaned back in her upholstered chair, tired from the scuffle with her fifth son but more relaxed now. She watched her granddaughter utterly immersed in her coloring and thought how cruel to have inflicted such fright in the child. Suddenly Liah realized her fifth son must be even more miserable. She must speak with him. Liah touched Aileen on the arm. "Child, Grandma is going to go and speak to Fifth Uncle, but do not fear. I am no longer angry. We won't fight. You color your picture, then when I come back we will all have a late supper. I know none of us ate too well tonight."

As Aileen fidgeted nervously, Liah urged her to continue with her coloring. Reassuringly, Liah reiterated, "Grandma isn't mad anymore."

Aileen searched her grandmother's face for a long moment, then continued coloring in a clown's red hat. Cook remarked cryptically to Liah, "Just remember when you face your son, you're on a mission of peace. You promised."

Liah grimaced. "You heard what I said to the child." Then she marched out.

Mert, cleaning up from the earlier battle, heard the taps approaching along the corridor and opened his bedroom door, standing defensively to barricade his mother's entry. Liah said gently, "I didn't mean for things to get so out of hand, but with the hot, humid weather and the extra people in our home, I couldn't help myself."

Mert turned from her and continued picking up pieces of broken ceramics and glass and tossing them angrily into the wastebasket. A pile of sheet music lay on the bed waiting to be sorted. Liah tugged at her son's sleeve. "Let's talk. I want to make a pact. Will you please stop and listen?"

Mert sighed, sat down on his bed and silently waited. Liah pursed her lips, then straightaway declared she would tolerate her son's girlfriend if he would promise to go to China the following year. "While you're there, you might even find a girl you like who would be more suitable than that hussy."

There was a prolonged silence as Mert weighed the deal. While he knew his mother was still trying to out maneuver him, he decided that a visit to China wouldn't commit him to anything. Nodding his agreement, "OK, Mah, but don't get your hopes up too high. And you promise not to fight with me anymore about this, right?"

Liah's eyes sparked with anger, but she clung to her self-control and nodded. "Oh, by the way," she murmured, "when you see the child, please reassure her that we still love each other despite our fight. She was heartbroken, torn between loyalty and love for each of us."

"Yeah, I know. She was with Selah earlier, crying her eyes out. Mah, while we're on the subject of Aileen, don't you think you're spoiling her? She can't go through life crying over every little thing."

"Son, give the child a little more time. The sorrow and pain inflicted upon her by your older sister must be healed before we can begin to discipline her."

As she walked out of Mert's bedroom, she smiled guiltily and placed several twenty-dollar bills on his pillow. Mert acknowledged her peace offering and nodded his thanks.

Cook noticed Aileen's worried face while Liah was in Fifth Son's bedroom. "I see," he said, "you're almost done with your coloring. How would you like some spiced chicken and wonton soup for a snack. I noticed you didn't eat much at supper. Why don't you ask your fifth uncle and grandma if they would enjoy some, too?"

In a flash, Aileen leaped off the stool, shouting as she ran toward the front room. Cook fervently hoped that tranquility would once more be restored to the family.

—

Life in Number Three Peacock Alley was at least peaceful, even if Mert felt nothing had changed. While his promise to make a trip to China had caused his mother to cease badgering him about Cora and marriage, he worried that she might be setting him up. He was concerned enough to seek out Cook.

Cook told him, "You've bought yourself a measure of peace, assuring yourself there'll be no further arguments, so why not enjoy it? Perhaps by the time next year arrives, something might change. Remember, Meng-Sui will not be denied."

Accepting the truce, Mert's moodiness disappeared and in time he forgot to worry. So improved was his family life he no longer stayed away from home and even took his niece and sister to the Hippodrome Theatre to see Rin Tin Tin and Tom Mix in two movies showing as a double feature. The only irksome time was when Aileen started crying when Rin Tin Tin was being cruelly whipped by his master. About to scold her, Mert remembered his mother's advice and instead softly told Aileen that it was only a make believe movie and that she shouldn't cry so much over everything.

Both girls declared it was so sad that they couldn't help it. When they returned home, Liah ordered a late supper from Wong's Café. Sim delivered a roast beef dinner, complete with entrees, side dishes and hot coffee. He toted the entire meal and utensils atop his head on a huge wooden tray with three-inch raised sides. Aileen, always intrigued by this manner of portage, asked if Sim could teach her how to do it.

Liah shook her head. "Child, leave Sim be. It takes a long time and lots of practice." She smiled, "I see Mr. Wong didn't forget to send both rice and potatoes. Tell him thank you, Sim."

She reached inside her tunic, withdrawing several dollar bills and fished fifty cents from her coin purse. "This is for our supper and the fifty cents is for you, Sim." On the verge of refusing the large tip, Sim was silenced by Liah's stern stare and he instead offered his thanks.

Halfway through supper, Aileen rubbed her eyes, complaining she was too sleepy to eat. Auntie Em, eighteen years old and filled with the superiority of an elder, shook her head. "You eat what's left on your plate Aileen."

Liah sighed. "Allow the child to go to bed, Second Daughter. This is not supper but an extra meal. Now run along to bed, Aileen, and be sure to brush your teeth."

Em pursed her lips and started to argue when Mert laughed. "Forget it, sis. Besides, now, you'll have a double-portion of potatoes."

Em glared balefully at her older brother and sulkily ate in silence.

THE CAT GOES GATE CRASHING

The surprise predawn raid on Liah's place scheduled for the twenty-fourth of September almost didn't come off. Hans feared it was too soon after Sam Yin's murder to risk stirring up more adverse feeling, but Lt. Swanson wouldn't hear of it. "A day, a month or a year later wouldn't make much difference in their feelings toward us. They'll still hate our guts. Get on with the plans. Besides, the men's schedules have already been changed and I'm not going to rearrange them again."

In the afternoon of the twenty-third, Hans held a briefing in the lieutenant's office. Lt. Swanson first told the men about the importance of the raid and emphasized that any man who couldn't follow orders should back out now. "Any man who disobeys and jeopardizes this raid will answer directly to me. Now I'll turn you over to the officer in charge." Lt. Swanson didn't want to introduce Hans as Hans but neither did he want to anger him, so he merely pointed in Hans' direction. Whatever he wanted to be called, Hans would surely make it known.

Hans slowly scanned the officers, recognizing two of the men as the officers he'd seen raid Wong Sang's gambling house. He chomped down hard on his cigar then said in a loud voice, "I'm known as Hans. I'm known as a cat because of my ability to kill rats. And if I catch any of you lousing up my detail, I'd just as soon kill you as I would a rat. I've had the chance to observe several of you on a previous raid and I don't want the same stupidity to occur on this operation." His partner sucked in a quick breath, thinking to himself that Hans was being unwise to antagonize these officers.

However, not a man flinched, not even the two officers involved in the previous raid. Only a sneer from the two officers let Hans know they got the message. He turned to the blackboard. "This is a diagram of Chinatown. Memorize the streets, especially the location of the building I've marked. That is Peacock Alley and the intended target is Number Three, the one with the red door. You will notice I've marked most of the streets in red; that means stay out. We are only interested in this one place. Does everyone understand?"

For the next hour, Hans took the men through the plan. Each man was given a map, his position and warned to stay alert and not to move until signaled. "We want to take them by surprise. Until you see my car crash into the front door, stay hidden. Those of you guarding the entrance and exit of the alley, keep your eyes peeled. Grab any Chink running out."

The men were assigned in pairs: Derrick and McGavin would be backing up John and Hans; Small and Rogers would be guarding the exit of Peacock Alley while Poppers and Stander would be guarding the entrance. Several plainclothes men would be stationed along the train tracks in case some of the Chinks tried to escape over the chain-link fence.

"One last thing, there's to be no shooting and absolutely no clubbing. Lt. Swanson informs me you're good men, but based on what I saw on the last raid, you'll have to prove it to me."

The two officers responsible for the clubbing squirmed in their chairs, looking away. "Very well," ordered Hans. "Tomorrow morning, six a.m. sharp. Are there any questions?"

"Yeah," drawled Rogers, his tone tinged with sarcasm. "What's this raid for? What are we looking for?"

Hans recognized Rogers as the man who had clubbed the old man. Staring straight at Rogers, Hans said tersely, "I'll tell you when I'm good and ready. Watkins and I know what we're after and that's all you need to know for now. Any more questions?"

Hans' brusque manner drew a murmur of protest from Lt. Swanson who remarked that Hans need not be so unfriendly. Hans retorted, "This ain't no popularity contest, sir. I don't give a damn if the men don't like me. They just have to do what I tell them to do."

As Hans was leaving, Lt. Swanson gave him a stern look and said, "I don't care how you do it, just be sure you bring me results without getting any of our boys hurt. If you have to mess up a few Chinks to do it, don't hesitate."

Sunday mornings in Chinatown were always extremely quiet; nothing moved and no one was about. On the twenty-fourth day of September, it was no different. All the doors were securely bolted, locked, shuttered and barred. All the windows were boarded up from within and barred. Not until almost eleven o'clock in the morning would the town begin to stir.

At seven thirty the police were deployed to their assigned places. Hans and John slowly drove an armored car to the entrance of Peacock Alley and up onto the cobblestone walk. Hans then maneuvered the vehicle to face Number Three's double doors and revved the engine. As he released the clutch, the car shot forward and up the three cement steps.

On impact, Hans and John were thrown against the dashboard and for a moment Hans felt as if his ribs had been broken by the steering wheel. John had braced himself with his legs and had suffered no damage.

"Shit!" bellowed Hans, glaring at the broken screen doors and splintered wood scattered over the cobblestones. The screens hung crazily on their hinges, but the stout front doors had remained intact.

Inside Mert awakened with a start, leaped from his bed and raced up the stairs to the mezzanine, his bare feet not making a sound. He opened the hexagonal window overlooking the cobblestones and gaped at the scene below. Hans looked up and seeing Mert, yelled, "Open up in the name of the law!"

Angrily, Mert shouted back, "Goddamn you Cops! You won't even leave us alone on your own Sabbath? Where's your warrant?"

"What the hell do you think this is, toilet paper?" Hans waved the warrant while his men snickered.

Mert slammed the window shut, locked it and went downstairs. He threw open the doors, shaking his head at the ruined screens. Then he followed the stream of men pouring into the house, shouting that they'd have to pay for any damage they caused.

Hans ignored Mert and assigned two men to each part of the house. He indicated that he would search the bedroom at the end of the corridor himself. As the men dispersed, he shouted a warning, "Search thoroughly but I don't want any of you destroying property just for the hell of it!"

Hans and John proceeded down the corridor, made a right turn and threw open the door to Liah's bedroom. Cook, awakened and standing in the corridor, was panic-stricken. He made a lunge to enter too, but John who was standing guard, held out a restraining hand.

Liah sat boldly upright in her bed, clutching her minhois, blankly blinking her swollen eyes. For an instant, she and Hans stared at each other. Hans grinned, "Ah, Mama, Apinyin?" Liah scowled, "Quai Miaow!"

Hans grinned, "Mama, how come you Numbah One? Apinyin, yeah? Me savvy you!"

Liah understood Hans, recalling his Apinyin raids in Dai Faw, and resigned herself to yet another. Despite her irritation, she was flooded with a sense of satisfaction as she recalled the many past raids Hans had made that hadn't produced any evidence. A frown crossed her face. He had, however, caught her once and she had been forced to attend the Fahn Gwai rehabilitation program, where she had been allowed a bit of opium each day to cope with the withdrawal pain. Well, she thought, he wouldn't catch her today!

When Hans had burst into the bedroom, Aileen had ducked underneath the bedclothes and neither saw nor heard what transpired between Hans and her grandmother. By the time she came up for air, she couldn't understand why Hans and her grandmother were chuckling. It seemed one of the officers searching through the bins and cupboards had come across some dried duck gizzards and preserved ducks' feet. He grimaced and tossed them on the floor. Mert cursed, demanding the officer put them back where he found them. Hans ordered the officer to do as he was told. "Goddamn it, I told you not to mess anything up."

The officer's partner then found a jar of sulfured duck eggs. "Hey, Hans, what the hell are these? Looks like eggs with some kind of crap on 'em."

Hans swore. "Leave them be. They're pickled duck eggs. Thousand year-old eggs from Hong Kong."

Fifteen minutes later, Hans yelled for his men to assemble in the kitchen. Their search, which had turned up no Apinyin, infuriated Hans and he erupted in anger. "Keep looking! It's got to be around here somewhere!"

Hans motioned for John to follow him. "I'll introduce you to the boss lady. If she knows you're a friend of mine, it might be of some help to you in the future ."

Liah was still sitting in bed when the officers re-entered her bedroom. "Mama, this is my friend, John. Savvy?"

Liah's eyes raked over John Watkins. A moment later, she murmured, "Needo Yahn!" Hans turned to his shorter partner and laughed, "Well, now you have a nickname too, Needo Yahn. It means Little John in Chinese. Did I ever tell you that she's the one who nicknamed me Miaow, Hans when we were in San Francisco? When we barged in just now she called me "Quai Miaow." That's Bad Cat in Chinese."

When the search turned up nothing, Hans reluctantly ordered the officers to leave. Sticking his head into Liah's bedroom to say goodbye, Hans saw Aileen duck under the covers again. "What's the matter with the kid?" Liah shrugged her shoulders and pointed an accusing finger: "Miaow! Quai! Quai!"

Hans pointed back, "Mama, quai! Apinyin quai! You savvy?" With that, Hans stomped out.

Mert followed Hans through the house, demanding to know who was going to repair the door. Hans ignored him until he stepped outside and immediately made an obscene gesture with his finger, shouting, "Nobody!"

Hans climbed into the armored vehicle, started the engine and worked to maneuver it out of the alley. Mert roared with laughter as the car bounced crazily over the cobblestones, with Hans' head hitting the roof of the car once or twice.

All day people came to examine the damaged doors and to smile at Liah's successful resistance against the police. Hoh Chan grinned as he swept up debris, holding up several large splinters to show folks. "See?" he demanded, "This is why you people should fortify your homes. Now get out of here so I can clean up." There was a sense of importance about the old man as he went about his work.

Cook, peering out of the window, smiled to himself. He returned to the kitchen and informed Liah of what Hoh Chan had said. "Now, with the raid and Hoh Chan's warning, the people are more likely to take heed and fortify their homes." Cook chuckled. "That old one, the way he talks you'd think that this was his place." He added with a chuckle that Lee Tzo had barely missed being hit by debris hurled by Hoh Chan. "I think the old one intended to land that junk as close to Tzo as he could. I almost broke into laughter as Hoh pretended to be so penitent."

Liah grinned. "That ancient one will outlast all of us. I wonder if he really meant to hit Tzo?"

—

Hans and Little John rode back to the station in utter silence. Little John wasn't going to chance his partner's wrath by making any comments about the failed raid. At the station, Hans bolted out of the vehicle, yanked open the door to the building and stomped upstairs to his office. Little John slipped out of the vehicle and hurried down the ramp leading to the level where his car was parked. It wasn't until he was well away from the station that Little John took a deep breath and chortled at the memory of the men grimacing at the preserved ducks' feet and dried gizzards. If Sim hadn't introduced him to those foods previously, he wouldn't have known what they were either. As he recalled, they didn't taste half-bad.

Little John thought of Sim, wondering where the kid was and how he was doing. For several weeks Little John had not run into Sim. He smiled as he recalled how that skinny, pathetic kid came to his rescue when he was mired in mud while the residents stood about, enjoying his predicament. Little John wondered where Sim had learned to use a board to gain traction. He remembered Sim placing one beneath his mired wheel and hollering, "Hokey!"

Little John frowned, also remembering how Sim refused his financial assistance and wouldn't hear of having a nicer place to live in. "Me okay, honest, lib heah long time, b' me self, me get job, mek mo money, den me mov alla same good." Little John quickly dropped the subject, knowing the Chinaman's pride.

Back at the station Hans angrily strode down the corridor and slammed into his office. No sooner had he flung his hat on the rack than the door opened and Lt. Swanson walked in. Hans dropped into his chair, fighting back the urge to curse. Try as he might, he couldn't wipe away the images of the Chinks laughing at him and the thinly veiled sneers of the officers. To make matters worse, Lt. Swanson started in on him immediately, ""I just heard from some of the men that your raid was a failure. Is that true? Give me the details. A lot of time and money went into this raid and I want to know what went wrong. You better not be trying to make me look bad to the brass."

Hans chomped down hard on his cigar and glared at the Lieutenant saying nothing. He knew Lt. Swanson could make his life hell, but at the moment he just didn't care. Raising his voice, Lt. Swanson ordered, "Tell me what happened right now!"

Finally Hans spat out, "Nothing happened. We broke in, searched the place, and found nothing. Either they hid the opium damn good or else there was none to begin with. As for this being my fault, as I re-member, it was you who wanted to conduct the raid!"

Seeing the anger on Hans' face reminded Lt. Swanson of the warning he'd been given by Chief Dobbs: "Don't rile Hans unless you're prepared for a full scale fight." Consequently, he ended the argument by saying, "All right, I'll let it go this time. But don't you forget that I am your superior officer. If you don't start showing me some respect, I'll have your badge!" Turning on his heel, Lt. Swanson abruptly left.

Hans, caught off guard, was slow to react. When he regained his senses, he leaped from his chair, opened the door, and shouted at the officer's receding back: "If you want my badge, come and get it! Anytime!"

Hans glared at the Lieutenant's back as the man disappeared into his own office. Livid, he recalled how his martinet of a father used to bully him the same way and he reentered his office and slammed the door shut. Almost inaudibly he cursed, "Goddamn it, he's just like my old man!"

TOM'S DAY IN COURT

One afternoon in the middle of September, Liah called Professor and said, "Last night I promised Tom I would see to it that the residents would cooperate with him and testify at the hearings into Sam Yin's murder. If they don't, he's afraid the case against the two Fahn Gwai won't be as strong. Please post the notices around town."

Professor agreed to do as Liah asked; however, he felt compelled to complain about the inequities of the Fahn Gwai legal system. "There's no doubt in anyone's mind that Trouble and Stuckey murdered Sam. Yet they get a trial. If one of us were even suspected of murdering a Fahn Gwai, there would be no trial, only a hanging from the nearest tree."

Liah concurred but told Professor, "Tom feels it is of the utmost importance for us to follow the Fahn Gwai legal procedures. He said it would show the Fahn Gwai that the Chinese are law-abiding citizens. We should follow his advice in these legal matters. After all, this is why we encouraged him to become a lawyer."

September twenty-seventh, the day before the hearing, was scorching hot. The early morning dew evaporated but the clouds hung low in the sky, threatening rain, and the day became sticky. By nightfall, it was unbearable. Tom had gone to bed at nine-thirty, but sleep would not come. His body was tied up in knots stretched far beyond the elasticity of his muscles. The bedclothes clung to him, damp with his perspiration and, by eleven o'clock, the agony had driven Tom from bed. He sat up, moaning. "God, I've got to get out of here or I'll go out of my mind."

Tom decided he needed to talk. He needed to be with someone else to forget his feeling of impending failure, the dread that had been gnawing at him all week long. He decided to go see Professor knowing the scholar kept late hours. Within a few minutes, Tom was plodding wearily toward Professor's house.

Professor, propped up in a chair leaning against the side of his house, called out as soon as he saw Tom. "Too hot for you, too? Well, come sit by me and we'll cool off together."

"Yeah," moaned Tom, "my bed feels like the top of a stove and my nerves are killing me. That's why I'm here to talk. Do you mind?"

Tom lit a cigarette; Professor pulled thoughtfully on his pipe. The two friends sat silently, each waiting for the other to speak. Tom took an impatient last puff of his cigarette then dropped it on the ground, grinding the butt into the dirt. Professor felt sure Tom would speak, but Tom only sighed and squirmed in the cane chair. Eventually, Professor sighed, "You know, I do not envy you tomorrow. I don't blame you if you can't sleep. If the court renders a favorable decision, if the two men are held to answer for Sam's death, then it will not be necessary for us to seek reprisal. It's a big burden to have on your shoulders, but one thing I do know. Whatever the outcome, you will have given our people a chance to be heard. That's more than we have had up till now. So please do not put any more pressure on yourself by worrying."

Tom fidgeted, sighed and then cleared his throat. "That's only partially what's bothering me. I feel like a warrior going into his first battle.

I feel I'm capable, but I'm not positive. The waiting is what's killing me, sir. There are so many things that can defeat me. For one thing, the best criminal lawyer in town is defending the two accused. I'm such a green-horn, I know he'll rip me to pieces."

"You're right, Tom, tomorrow's decision hinges on so many things, but only one thing counts: Meng-Sui. From what I've seen of you, I wouldn't worry about your luck. Your Meng-Sui seems very strong. Just do your best. If Sam's Meng-Sui decrees that he will get justice, he'll get it. Remember this: Don't let things you can't control detract from your concentration. Just do your best."

Tom leaped up from his chair. "It's easier said than done, sir. Another thing, if the verdict favors us, perhaps my life will be put in jeopardy by the Fahn Gwai spectators and Trouble's friends. Already, the district attorney has warned me about the possible repercussions."

Professor put out a hand, detaining Tom. "Sit down, son, you'll wear yourself out. As I see it, there'll be many nights before cases. If you can't survive this night then it might be better if you find another profession."

Tom flopped back into the chair and silence ensued, both men caught in the web of their own thoughts. When he finally spoke, Professor's voice was gentle. "If I were you, I'd keep my mind riveted on the tenets of law. Do not be distracted by personalities; don't think of Sam Yin or Sui, or of Liah, or anybody. Focus on what you have learned and apply it."

Tom heaved a deep sigh. "You're right, sir. I guess I've got the last-minute jitters. Although for the past few weeks I've been espousing democracy and due process of law, part of me wants to quit and let Liah and the Council mete out our own brand of justice."

The scholar allowed Tom to dwell on his words for a moment, then gently said, "Yes, that would be the easy way out, but what do you have in mind to do for a living then? Dishwashing, sweeping floors or sorting laundry? Perhaps you could get a job doing clerical work in a Fahn Gwai's office."

Tom gaped at Professor. The scholar apologized. "I'm sorry to be so blunt, but you haven't given a realistic thought to your future. You do not have the luxury of being self-indulgent. Your life is not your own. Having committed yourself to the law, you need to think of what you can do for your clients and the people of Chinatown who look to you for legal guidance. Then there are the youths who look to you as an example. You can't let them down."

Tom knew Professor was right and didn't respond. Professor relit his pipe and said, "The temperature has dropped a bit. How about a bite at Wong's? Then you can try to get some sleep."

Tom nodded mutely, smiling weakly at Professor, his eyes reflecting his gratitude for the scholar's encouragement.

Just as Tom and Professor emerged from Pig Alley, Chon Woo hailed them. Before they knew it, Tom and Professor were inside the Dragon's Den bar. A drink for good luck, Chon said. One toast then led to another as Lim Tao and Wong Sam joined them. An hour later, Professor called a halt. "Tom must have a clear head tomorrow. We were on our way to Wong's for supper and while we thank you, Tom and I need to leave."

Tom, mellowed by the many drinks, accepted the hearty well-wishes he received from the patrons at Wong's Café. Wong Foon, proprietor of the café, led them proudly to a booth. The night's meal was his treat, he said. Professor chuckled. "All right, sir, but make it something light, for Tom has yet to sleep."

Toward the end of their meal, Tom sobered. If only he could be as philosophical as Professor, he thought. Life certainly would be much simpler if he could relegate success or failure to Meng-Sui. Tom was deep in thought when Professor startled him with a nudge. Madam Quock, her friends, and Yook Lan had entered the café. Tom moaned quietly. Professor hurriedly whispered, "Just keep your mouth shut and you'll be fine."

Madam Quock swept up to the booth and majestically cooed. "Tom, what a pleasant surprise. I thought you'd be in bed by now. I want to congratulate you on tomorrow's victory."

Tom sputtered. Professor shot him a warning glance as he turned to the ladies. "Yes, I'm sure Tom realizes he has not only your good wishes but the entire town's. Now, if you don't mind, I must get him back home."

Madam Quock was not to be put off by Professor's words. She went on cooing. "I was just telling Yook Lan the other day that we don't see you often enough. Why don't you come to our home for supper? You name the night and hour."

Tom shot a sympathetic glance at Yook Lan as her face reddened. Both knew Madam Quock was laying plans to match her daughter to Tom. Professor interceded again. "We really must be leaving. Thank you for the invitation. I'm sure Tom will call just as soon as he is free. Now, ladies, good night."

Outside the café, Tom breathed a sigh of relief. He turned a serious face to the scholar, "Well, once again I owe you a debt of gratitude. Madam Quock! I can't believe how obvious she is. I feel sorry for Yook Lan, sir."

Professor chuckled. "No need for gratitude, Tom. I hope now you'll be able to sleep. Thankfully the heat's abated a little."

At the entrance to Pig Alley Tom said good night to Professor and turned toward Mah Loo. Once home, Tom flopped onto his bed and breathed deeply. Eventually, sheer exhaustion overcame him and Tom began to snore.

—

The judge rapped his gavel on the lectern and Tom heard him announce his verdict: Guilty! Trouble and Stuckey had been found guilty! Elation swept through Tom's body, but the feeling quickly turned to terror as a sea of spectators descended upon him. He felt their fists pummeling him and heard their shouted invectives. The judge pounded his gavel, shouting for order, but the sound was drowned out by the angry voices of the spectators.

Tom screamed and opened his eyes. He was lying sideways on the bed and his bedding was strewn on the floor. His body sagged with relief and he silently thanked Kwan Koong that it had only been a dream.

He glanced at the alarm clock: six-thirty. Rising quickly, he showered and dressed. Looking at his reflection in the mirror, he muttered, "Well, today is the day, guy. Don't screw up." Before his emotions could well up, Tom grabbed his briefcase and went out the door, closing it firmly behind him.

The leisurely walk to the courthouse gave Tom time to gather his thoughts and his courage. Although it was a few minutes before eight, he saw the throng of people already pushing their way into the courthouse. When he actually stepped inside the courtroom, he was taken aback. The courtroom was filled to capacity. There were even spectators standing ten deep in the back of the large room. The din was almost deafening.

As he walked down the aisle to the prosecutor's table, cameras flashed and reporters swooped in on him. Did he feel he would win? Was he scared? How did he feel? One overbearing reporter pushed through the crowd and demanded, "Do you think your appearance in court today will set a precedent for other Chink kids to become lawyers?"

Tom held his anger in check and pushed the reporter roughly aside as he made his way to the table. Once seated, Tom was able to pick out a few voices amidst the babble. A woman's voice wished him luck, obvious friends of Trouble and Stuckey yelled obscenities at him, and more than one person hurled threats against him.

Tom silently cursed Elton Barkley, the district attorney, who had asked Tom for his assistance, for not being there. For something to do, he opened his briefcase, readied his papers, and reviewed some of the legal documents. All the while, he was aware of the mounting tension in the crowd.

As he waited, Tom told himself he must not fail today. He must prove to Barkley that the man's confidence in his abilities was well founded. Tom remembered when Barkley had first petitioned Judge Thompson for permission to use Tom on the case. Barkley had argued that although Tom had only just passed the bar exam, Tom's legal training and intimate knowledge of the Chinese community would be of benefit to the proceedings." Thankfully, the Judge had agreed.

A few minutes passed, which to Tom felt like hours. A sudden panic attack threatened to overwhelm him and Tom desperately fought the impulse to get as far away from the courthouse as possible. Suddenly, a voice boomed out above the general noise level, "Hey Chink! What makes you think you got a chance today? A Chink lawyer, what a laugh!" The man's jeer gave rise to other insults. "Them Chinks ought to stick to cleaning out the toilets and doing laundry!" "Next thing you know there'll be a Chink running for President!" The ensuing laughter ceased when the guards brought Trouble and Stuckey through a door at the back of the courtroom to the prisoner's box. The moment Trouble saw Tom he swore and shouted, "Hey Chink! Since when is killin' a Chink a crime? We'll get you too, Chink! You wait and see!" Most of the spectators responded with approval.

At nine o'clock sharp, the curtain behind the judge's lectern rustled and the room quieted. Tom was frantic. Where was Elton? Tom winced as Judge Thompson emerged through the curtains. Oh, God, prayed Tom, let Elton show up. There was no way he could try the case by himself. Just then the Prosecutor made his entrance into the courtroom. Tom slumped back in his chair and breathed a big sigh of relief. "God," he whispered, "am I glad to see you."

Elton eyed Tom coolly. Elton understood Tom's panic, for he had felt it too on his first day in court. He recalled those feelings of fright for a moment then impulsively put a hand on Tom's shoulder, smiled, and whispered, "Scared shitless, eh?"

Tom nodded. Elton grinned, "Good! A man's no good if he's got no sense when to be scared. Just keep your mind on winning and you'll be all right. Now, let's listen to the judge's spiel about justice."

Judge Thompson gazed at the jammed courtroom. He took in the carnival atmosphere and cursed silently. Hell, he thought, this certainly doesn't feel like a court of law; it's more like a three-ring circus. He was angered for a moment at the hot potato that had been thrust into his hands. This wasn't your usual murder case. This one would clearly pit a white man versus a yellow man. Shit! His gaze fell upon Tom and he felt compassion, for if it were him, he'd be scared out of his mind.

Impatiently, he picked up a sheaf of papers, adjusted his spectacles and stated, "Case of the People of Los Angeles County against Trouble and Stuckey!" Frowning, Judge Thompson demanded to know the defendants legal names. However, before the defense attorney Seymour Taylor could respond, Trouble shouted, "'Trouble's what I been called all me life." Judge Thompson struck his gavel on the lectern sharply and told Trouble to be quiet. Seymour Taylor scowled at his client and replied, "Your honor, the defendant's legal name is James McKinnon. Mr. Stuckey's legal name is Bert Stuhson."

Once the Prosecutor and Defense had both delivered their opening statements, the prosecution began to call their witnesses. The moment arrived for Tom to call Charlie, the Dragon's Den bartender and his legs felt like rubber as he approached the witness stand. Tom saw the fright on the little man's face and his nervousness instantly disappeared. He nodded slightly as if to tell Charlie not to be afraid, that things would be all right.

Charlie smiled nervously back at Tom. First, Tom asked Charlie his name in English, then repeated the question in Chinese. Charlie grinned

"Me Lim Fong and me Charlie. Me speakee Fahn Gwai."

Tom felt the tension subside and asked Charlie what he did for a living.

"Me vook at Dlagon Den bah. Me makum dlinks."

Laughter mingled with a few snorts went through the courtroom at Charlie's pidgin English.

Tom asked if Charlie had ever seen the two men in the prisoners' box.

Charlie nodded eagerly. "Me know!" Pointing at Trouble, Charlie said, "Dat one, Tlubble." He winced when he saw Trouble's scowl, then continued, pointing to the other man. "Dat one Stluckee. Both velly bad men."

Seymour immediately objected saying, "The Chink, er, witness, has no right to malign my clients, Your Honor." Judge Thompson sustained the objection and instructed Tom to inform his witness to keep his personal opinions to himself.

Tom then asked Charlie, "Did Trouble and Stuckey visit the Dragon's Den bar on the night of Sam Yin's death?" Charlie nodded and said, "Him, big man dere, Tlubble, come in velly mad, velly dlunk. Him glab Charlie, tell me bling whiskey. Him say he hit me I don' do it chop chop. Me bling two bottles, him velly, velly mad… likee he clazy!" Charlie's hand went over his mouth after his last remark and he waited for a reprimand, but Seymour just glowered silently. Charlie continued, "Him get clazy mad! Tlubble say he gonna kill Chink." Charlie described how Trouble had then punched Stuckey when his friend had tried to calm him down. "Him, Stluckee velly mad too, him try hit Tlubble, den change mind. Him say 'les go'. Den bof 'em go out."

Tom then asked Charlie if he was sure everything he'd said was true. Indignant, Charlie said forcefully "Me no tell lie. Evlybody in bah hear same as me, see same as me. You ask Muflee. Him tell Charlie to tell evlybody in Chinatown look out and lock doors"

Judge Thompson glanced over at Seymour, half-expecting the attorney to object, but there was no objection. As soon as Tom took his seat,

Judge Thompson asked if Seymour wished to cross-examine the witness. Seymour shook his head no and replied, "However, I reserve the right to recall the witness at a later time."

Tom motioned to Charlie that he could step down. The little man scrambled off his seat and an officer escorted him out through a side door. Hans was waiting there to drive the Chinese witnesses back to Chinatown to forestall any possible violence.

Tom almost fell into his chair, already exhausted and glad his first ordeal was over. Elton Barkley smiled and nodded his approval.

The courtroom quieted down when Michael Murphy was called next to the witness stand. He sat stiffly, his hands gripping the arms of the chair as Elton asked him questions. He acknowledged that he had known both Trouble and Stuckey way back in the days of laying the rails. Elton Barkley then asked, "Did you see both of the defendants at the Dragon's Den bar the night of the murder?"

"Yes, sir."

"Was it, as the bartender said, that both Trouble and Stuckey were drunk and disorderly?"

Murphy squirmed in his seat. "Yes, sir. Trouble was even more drunk and belligerent than usual."

Elton then asked if Trouble had indeed threatened to "kill himself a Chinaman." Murphy just nodded and was asked by the judge to answer aloud. "Yes."

Elton continued, "I see. What did you say to Trouble when he made that threat?"

"I told him to go ahead but be ready to be hanged for it. That's when Stuckey came over and tried to calm Trouble down. Trouble wouldn't have it and knocked Stuckey clear across the room. We thought those two would start going at it, but the two of them were so drunk, they could hardly stand up straight. "

"After they left, what did you do?"

Murphy sighed. "I told Charlie to warn people that I thought Trouble might really do what he'd threatened to do. I didn't want anyone hurt because of that maniac."

Elton thanked Murphy and then said to Seymour, "Your witness."

Seymour Taylor strode up to the witness box, leaned against the railing, and squinted at Murphy. Murphy waited apprehensively as the tall, spare man, a shock of white hair on his forehead, stood and eyed him. Murphy knew of the man's razor-sharp mind, his equally sharp tongue and, more than anything, his spotless record of defending known criminals. He tried to prepare himself for the grilling to come. Seymour became his enemy. Murphy observed the man's expensive gray double-breasted suit that hung perfectly on his slightly rotund figure, his creamy white silk shirt and green necktie, and thought to himself that it had all been bought with blood money.

Following the dramatic pause, Seymour suddenly spat out, "I heard you made quite a bundle making bets on the Chinese railroad workers during the laying of the Transcontinental Railroad. How much did you win?" Elton objected as to relevance but Seymour told the judge that it established bias toward the Chinese. The judge thought a moment and then allowed the testimony to stand and instructed Murphy to answer the question.

Murphy's face turned red and he leaned forward, his eyes blazing. "Nothing, I got nothing! The bets were between the bosses. I was paid to do a job and that's it. Don't you go insinuating that I'm a Chink lover!"

Seymour's face creased with a slight smile. True or not, he hoped he had given the judge something to ponder over. Seymour continued to hammer at Murphy, trying to establish that Murphy was prejudiced toward the Chinese because of his previous association with the coolies and now with the residents of Chinatown who washed out the train engines in the yard Murphy supervised. Seymour then suddenly switched topics and attacked Murphy's relationship with Trouble trying to establish that he and Trouble had had a long standing feud dating back to when they were both working on the railroad. Murphy had to admit that they had had more than a few fights but denied that he hated Trouble or wanted to see him punished.

Dismissed, Murphy abruptly left the witness box and walked angrily out of the courtroom. Although Tom didn't like the innuendos Seymour had made, he had to admit that the lawyer had effectively cast some doubt on Murphy's credibility.

Following Murphy's testimony the prosecution proceeded to present witnesses to establish the entire timeline, including graphic testimony from Dr. Sung concerning the extensive damage to Sam's body including having his throat slit.

The next witness was to be Sui Yin, Sam's wife, but the judge lifted the sleeve of his robe and consulted his watch, which read eleven-thirty. He then announced, "Court is recessed for lunch until two o'clock this afternoon."

—

Tom assembled his papers and shoved them into his briefcase. Elton nodded to him and walked over to speak with Seymour. Left alone, Tom felt somewhat ostracized and a little disappointed that Elton had made no move to join him for lunch. He was heading out to the luncheonette when he heard a familiar voice. "Hi, Tom," said Dr. Sung. "I thought we'd share a bit of lunch. How about it?"

"Sure," Tom replied. "I thought you'd returned to Mercy Hospital."

"I took the day off. I want to watch the trial. Boy, that Seymour is a nasty one."

"Yeah," muttered Tom as they went out the wide swinging doors of the courthouse.

Dr. Sung took Tom to a small restaurant owned by a widow named

Mrs. James. Mrs. James came from the kitchen, wiping her hands on an apron and gave Dr. Sung an affectionate hug. Stepping back, she beamed, "Is this the young man you told me about? The one who is defending the rights of the murdered man?"

Dr. Sung smiled, "The same. Tom, this is Mrs. James. Wait until you try her beef stew or her meat loaf. It's what I imagine they'd serve in heaven."

It occurred to Tom that Dr. Sung must take lunch there often, for there was a familiar conviviality between Dr. Sung and Mrs. James. Moreover, the waitresses all knew him and the hospital was only a few blocks away.

A Japanese doctor, Sahi Yamaguchi, came up to Tom and grinned. "Lots of luck, Tom! For all our sakes, I hope justice prevails today. Oh, I'm Sahi, by the way. Doc here has often spoken of you and I feel as if I already know you."

During lunch, Tom asked Dr. Sung about Sui's condition, afraid that she would be too unstable to be a credible witness. "Don't worry, Tom. I've given her something to keep her calm and I've asked Selah to accompany Sui to the courthouse. I'll be around just in case."

When court resumed, Elton called Sui to the stand and Selah led Sui Yin into the courtroom. Tom gasped in shock. He couldn't believe that anyone could've aged so quickly. Sui was so thin that her bones stood out sharply. Her eyes were dull, glazed, half-shut, almost unseeing. Selah had to help Sui hold up her right hand for the swearing-in and Tom had to ask her twice for her name before she whispered it. Sui Yin slumped in the witness chair and a woman's voice was heard to exclaim, "Poor thing! It's cruel to force her to testify."

Before starting the questioning, Tom whispered, "Sui, if you do not tell the Fahn Gwai all you know, we will not be able to punish the men who killed Sam Do you understand?" Sui stared at Tom half-comprehendingly for a second then nodded slowly. Tom knew Sui wouldn't last long on the stand, so he got straight to the point, "Sui, do you see the men who murdered Sam?"

Sui peered around the room and when she saw Trouble and Stuckey, her eyes widened in horror. She stood up shakily, clutched the railing, and shrieked. "There, there!" she screamed, pointing at the defendants. Suddenly she sagged back into the chair and screamed, "They killed my Sam! May the Gods send thunder and lightning to strike them dead!"

She continued to shriek and cry, filling the courtroom with her anguish. Although the spectators could not understand Chinese, Sui's message was clear.

Tom stood by helplessly. When Selah tried to comfort her, Sui pushed Selah away with surprising strength and screamed, "Those two devils. They broke down the door, started beating Sam and trying to cut his throat with a knife. Sam told me to run so I ran out the back with my baby. They are devils! They are murderers!" Sui then collapsed in a heap as Dr. Sung sprinted to the witness stand, placed his black bag on the floor, and prepared a syringe. Sui fought his efforts to help her like a tigress, pushing, shrieking and flailing her arms. Her screams rent the air, electrifying the silent courtroom.

Judge Thompson, his face stony, watched the proceedings for a few moments then whispered to the bailiff that the doctor could use his chambers. The bailiff, a large man, carried Sui to the judge's chambers accompanied by Selah and Dr. Sung. Everyone including Seymour Taylor was visibly upset by Sui's outburst. Trouble and Stuckey looked to their friends in the audience for support, but they were all looking down at their feet.

Judge Thompson pounded his gavel and when order had been restored declared, "Court will take a half hour recess."

During the break, Tom sat glumly in his chair. The sight of Sui Yin and her emotional outburst had completely drained him. He fought to focus on his resolve to avenge Sam Yin's death, not only for Sam but for Sui Yin's sake. In her disturbed state, Sui might as well be dead too.

When court resumed, Elton rested the prosecution's case and Seymour called a few of Trouble and Stuckey's friends as character witnesses. However, his case was soon concluded as well. As a last attack, Seymour raised an objection to Tom's translation of the witnesses' testimony saying, "After all, how can we trust that Mr. Soo has faithfully rendered what the witnesses have actually said?" Ready for this, Elton replied," I cannot say I blame Mr. Taylor for his misgivings; however, to address this issue, we have enlisted the services of the renown Dr. Albert White, professor of Asian Studies at Eastern Studies Academy of New York to record the testimony given here. At this time, I request that the judge allow Mr. White to read his own translations."

Judge Thompson nodded and Seymour Taylor glared angrily at Elton, who gazed straight ahead with a slight smile creasing his lips. By the time the tall, distinguished, goateed professor had finished translating Sui's testimony, several women in the audience were sobbing. Suddenly Stuckey screamed, "I didn't kill the Chink! I only kicked in the door. Trouble was the one who beat him up and kicked him and finally cut his throat. I tried to stop him, but I couldn't! He was like a crazy man! I couldn't stop him!"

Trouble turned to Stuckey and tried to attack him but his shackles prevented it. In a rage, Trouble began cursing Stuckey and calling him a traitor and a coward. The Judge pounded his gavel to no avail. Trouble continued to rant and extended his curses to include Tom, Elton, and the courthouse staff. Finally the Judge ordered the bailiff to remove the defendant.

Once order was restored, Elton Barkley and Seymour Taylor approached the bench at the command of Judge Thompson. Tom couldn't hear the judge's words, and looked quizzically at Elton when they returned to their seats.

Judge Thompson adjusted his spectacles, looked out over the courtroom, and announced, "The court has heard the testimony and will render a decision after considering all the facts. Until then, the two prisoners will be returned to their cells to await judgment."

The courtroom rose and Judge Thompson took his leave. Then the spectators spilled out into the aisles and made for the exit chattering excitedly. Without a word of praise or encouragement to Tom, Elton walked over to Seymour and began a discussion. Tom tossed his papers into his briefcase and tried to contain his anger at Elton's summary dismissal. Tom pushed his way down the aisle ignoring the crush of reporters and the glare of the flashbulbs.

Once more, as he stepped into the foyer, he heard Dr. Sung's voice. Rushing over Tom asked in a concerned voice, "Is Sui all right?" Dr. Sung smiled gently, "She's sleeping off the sedative I gave her. She'll should be fine when she wakes up. How about I give you a ride back to Chinatown." Tom heaved a sigh of relief and replied, "Thanks. I didn't relish the thought of walking through this crowd."

As they walked toward the elevators, Tom confessed his relief that the trial was over. Dr. Sung smiled and replied, "You did extremely well, Tom. I suggest we go see Madam Liah now. Although Madam Liah believes that Sam's and Sui's Meng Sui will dictate the outcome of the trial, she'll want to know all the details."

Seeing Dr. Sung's serious expression, Tom turned to him and asked, "Don't tell me that a doctor like you schooled in the science of medicine believes in Meng Sui too?" Dr. Sung smiled and explained, "Tom, I have learned that science alone cannot explain everything in life. Whether one calls it luck or Meng Sui, there is an element beyond scientific logic that governs our lives." When they turned off Alameda South onto Marchesson Street, Tom suddenly turned to Dr. Sung, and confessed that he wasn't up to meeting with Liah. "Perhaps later after I've calmed down."

"Very well, Tom, then let's go visit Selah. A drink will help settle your nerves. Besides that will give me a chance to check on Sui."

An hour and two drinks later, Dr. Sung tugged at Tom's arm. "I know you don't feel like being interrogated by Madam Liah, but you really should go. I promise you, we'll only stay a short while You owe her the privilege of hearing first hand what transpired."

When he saw the crowd of people near the entrance to Peacock Alley, Tom was shocked. Tom recognized some of the faces; others were unfamiliar but all seemed to be waiting there to congratulate him. A sudden sense of satisfaction came over him as he realized how much having one of their own participate in this trial meant to the citizens of Chinatown. Dr. Sung seemed to understand what Tom was feeling when he said, "I've forgotten how it is to be looked up to by so many." Then a thought popped into his head. "Just think, Tom. Now we've got a doctor and a lawyer in Chinatown. What say we jointly open up an office to serve our people? It's something I've always had in mind to do but never got the chance."

Tom was taken aback and replied, "I've been focusing so hard on passing the bar that I haven't really thought about what comes after." Dr. Sung nodded. "It's all right. Take your time and think it over. And don't worry about the logistics. I'll find a place and take care of all expenses until you're on your feet. How's that sound?" Tom nodded thoughtfully.

Their discussion ended when they entered Number Three. Liah met them in the front room and invited them back to the kitchen. "You're just in time for supper." She paused, "I know you're tired, Tom, but I simply must know what happened today. Perhaps you can brief me."

Cook greeted Tom and informed him that he had prepared all of his favorite dishes. Tom murmured that he wasn't really very hungry, but Dr. Sung shook his head. "Oh no you don't, Tom. We're having supper here tonight. I don't get to eat this kind of food very often. I think I smell spiced ribs. And, Cook, is that the aroma of eight-spice soup?"

Tom smiled and tired as he was nodded. His weariness diminished, however, as Liah lifted a pot cover revealing his favorite dish of steamed pork with dried squid. At the supper table, Tom recounted the day's events and told Liah that he was hopeful that Sam and Sui would get justice. "Of course we will have to wait until the judge has reached his verdict."

During the course of the meal, Liah chided Dr. Sung for having left Chinatown to work at the Fahn Gwai hospital. She smiled and said, "If you were here, you could enjoy Cook's delicacies more often." Dr. Sung smiled back and confided to Liah that he and Tom might just open up an office in Chinatown. Hearing this Liah grinned.

Eventually Liah brought up Aileen's perceived skinniness, her bad appetite and restless sleep habits. Dr. Sung pushed himself back from the table and reached for his black bag. "Come on, Aileen. Let's take a look and prove to your grandma that you're just fine." After his examination, Dr. Sung eyed Liah and suggested that although Aileen seemed fine physically, perhaps he would come by later and talk.

Seeing the dark circles under Tom's eyes and his nodding head, Dr. Sung told Liah, "I know it's bad manners to eat and run, but Tom has had a long grueling day in court and I prescribe a good night's sleep. Thank you for excellent supper."

On their way out, Liah confided to Dr. Sung that she believed her Eldest Daughter had been abusing Aileen, and wondered if that could be the reason the child slept so fitfully and was so thin. Dr. Sung shook his head. "Any harm she might have suffered, I'm certain your loving care will heal. As for you, Madam, how is *your* health? You aren't too far from also being called skinny. Will you be honest and tell me if there is anything bothering you?"

Liah chuckled. "I thank you, Doctor, for your concern, but I am fine. Incidentally, earlier you made mention of opening an office in Chinatown. I happen to know there is a vacancy on Marchesson Gai, right next door to Selah's. Why don't you look into it? Speak with Marchesson. If you tell him what you and Tom are doing and that I am all in favor of it, he will most likely offer you a discount on the rent."

Dr. Sung grinned. He recalled how his people would always claim to be the relative of someone whenever it would gain them a discount. "I shall certainly mention your name, Madam Liah, but Tom isn't ready to commit yet. When I am ready, I shall certainly speak to you and perhaps the two of us can persuade Tom to join me. For the time being, I thank you again for a wonderful supper and I promise to come see you soon."

—

On the sixth day of October Elton Barkley, Seymour Taylor, Tom Soo, and Sui Yin, accompanied by Dr. Sung met in the district attorney's office. Affidavits were signed as well as papers allowing Sui Yin to take Sam's body home to be buried in the family plot.

Three days later, on a crisp, calm morning, a truck drew up in front of Selah's place. Sui's brother and a distant cousin of Sam's would drive Sui Yin to the dock where she would embark on the boat for China. Selah came down the stairs carrying two small leather cases. She placed them on the floor next to the basket containing the baby's needs. "These two cases and the basket are to go aboard with Sui. Understand?"

Sui's brother nodded. Sui's steamer trunk and four large suitcases were to be checked in for loading into the hold. When all was ready, Selah went upstairs and returned with Sui Yin. Selah held Sui's infant close, lifting the blanket to gaze down at the sleeping child. Without a word, she handed the bundle to Sui Yin, embraced the widow and whispered a blessing for Kwan Yin's mercy. Then, impulsively, she took Sui Yin's face into her hands and said, "Find the strength to live for your son's sake, Sui Yin. Take good care of him and make a new life for yourself, dear. Try and forget the ugliness and sorrow you have encountered here."

Sui felt Selah's warmth and briefly emerged from her lethargy, tearfully returning the embrace. Selah assisted her into the truck and nodded to Sui's brother that he could go. However, just then, Professor came out of Peacock Alley and shouted for them to wait. Breathlessly, he came up to the side of the truck where Sui Yin sat and pressed a large envelope into her hands. "Madam Liah said this money is for you and your son to use on the way home. She has asked Kwan Yin to bless your footsteps. Above all, she wants you to find a new life, not only for your own sake but for your son's as well. Do not worry, Sui. Madam Liah said neither you nor your son will ever want for anything. She will send money from time to time to see to your needs. May Kwan Koong protect you. Good-bye."

Selah and Professor watched as the truck slowly made its way down Marchesson Street and turned left onto Alameda South. Tears coursed down Selah's cheeks as she shook her head, and said, "Damn! I can't believe how sad this is. I hope Sui and her son will find some happiness. Let's go in an have a drink, Professor."

A TIME FOR ANSWERS

Sallie Chang and her Fahn Gwai boyfriend Brad were in the Dragon's Den Bar dancing to a jazz combo. The Saturday night crowd watched as she nestled into him closely, her head brushing his cheek, his blond hair a sharp contrast against her jet-black hair. They were at first unaware of the snickering and the snide remarks of the Chinatown regulars. One young fellow sneered, "Might as well give up on her. Once she goes out with white meat, she's won't go out with us." Another laughed. "Well, maybe she'd come back more experienced." Others made even more ribald comments.

Chon walked up to the youths and told them to keep their voices down, that he didn't want anyone to start trouble in his place. "Anyway, so what if he is a Fahn Gwai? Is it any different from you going out with Fahn Gwai dames?"

One of the more outraged youths retorted, "Yeah it is! She's Chinese. She should know better than to date a Fahn Gwai."

Chon snarled back, "I told you I don't want any trouble so leave them alone or I'll have you thrown out."

Sallie caught the gist of the conversation as Chon and the youths argued, then whispered to Brad, "Come on. Let's get out of here. I don't like the atmosphere."

Brad drew back and looked at her, "How come, Sal? I like this joint, The band is great." Then it occurred to Brad that perhaps the heated argument they'd overheard had been about them. "Hey, are those guys saying something bad about us?"

"Of course not," whispered Sallie. "At least nothing out of the ordinary. You're a guy. You ought to know how men talk."

Brad murmured, "Okay, baby, we'll leave right after this dance. There's a snazzy place in Chinatown that I'd like to visit. Some of the guys at work say they serve the best French food around."

While Brad was at the cashier, Sallie picked up her coat and purse, making ready to leave. Chon sauntered up and said, "What's the matter, Sallie? Why are you leaving so early?"

Sallie retorted angrily, "You know damn well why. I don't like the way the guys are talking about me."

Chon sneered, "Well, if you insist on dating Fahn Gwai, you can't blame the guys."

Sallie's eyes blazed. "Why is it you men can take out white women but I can't date a white guy?"

Chon's eyes narrowed as Sallie marched out with Brad in tow. After they left, Chon went upstairs and made a telephone call. The conversation was brief as Chon said, "I'm warning you. I think she's too headstrong. But it's your neck, not mine, Sang. I'm giving you fair warning."

Although Chon had no love lost for Sang and he certainly thought Sang was a fool for involving himself with Lee Tzo, he thought it couldn't hurt to let Sang know about Sallie and the Fahn Gwai.

Sallie and Brad walked along Dragon's Den Road, then made a mad dash through Pig Alley to Marchesson Street. Brad led her toward Peacock Alley and stopped in front of Number One. Sallie gasped, "You're joking, Brad. We can't go in there."

"Why not?" argued Brad. "Some of the guys in Dad's office said this place had great atmosphere and wonderful food. Come on."

Sallie shook her head. "This place is owned by Madam Selah. Don't you have any idea what kind of place this is?"

"Madam who?" Brad demanded, "You Chinese have really have a lot of weird names."

Sallie bristled. "How come you think our names are weird? At least our names have meaning. That's more than I can say for Fahn Gwai names."

"Hey, hold on a minute, baby. I meant no disrespect."

In the middle of their argument, Lee Tzo sauntered out of the cobblestone alley with Mei-Tai a few feet behind. When he spied Sallie, his eyes widened and Sallie pursed her lips, pushed Brad forward, and pulled open the door.

"Now that's a quick change of mind, baby."

Sallie's pale face and wide eyes betrayed her fear. Her voice quavered as she bravely quipped, "It's a woman's prerogative, Brad."

They stood a moment in the foyer, then Brad led Sallie into the bar. Seeing them enter, Lalo came from behind the bar and guided them to a secluded booth. Brad whispered, "What a snazzy place. I never knew such a place existed in Chinatown." Brad saw Sallie's displeasure at his mention of Chinatown and held up his hands to forestall another argument.

A few minutes later, Selah came downstairs and saw Lalo motioning for her to come over. After she took her usual seat at the end of the bar,

Lalo whispered, "In de last booth, stranger Fahn Gwai and local gel."

Selah wandered amongst the customers in the bar and wound up at the booth occupied by Brad and Sallie. Sallie smiled and said, "Miss Selah, I do not think you recognize me, but I am Sally Chang, Uncle Fred's niece."

"Oh, yes. I recognize you now. You've grown. How are your mother and father? And what brings a nice girl like you to my place?"

Brad interjected, "I'm afraid, Miss Selah, that it's my fault. I'd heard that you serve great food here and I forced Sallie to come." Sallie laughed and said, "Brad didn't know this was a brothel."

Selah gazed at Brad, recognized a family resemblance, and thought what a spitting image of his father, Elton Barkley, he was. After some small talk, Sallie went to the ladies room and Brad quickly told Selah that his father was Elton Barkley, the district attorney, and that Sallie did not know it. "She'd drop me like a hot potato if she knew. I'd be grateful if you don't give me away." Selah reassured him smiling to herself.

When Sallie returned, Selah led them to the kitchen where she told them that she'd allow them to have dinner this one time. She told them, "A girl like Sallie cannot be seen in my place without unwanted repercussions." Brad and Sallie both nodded and thanked Selah.

All through their meal of Louisiana seafood and hush puppies, Brad kept staring at Selah. He finally apologized and said, "Forgive me for staring, but, except for Sallie here, you are the most beautiful woman I've ever seen."

"Oh, Brad, that's the nicest thing I've heard in a long time. What a sweet compliment." Selah turned to Sallie, "Is he always so gallant?" Sallie giggled self-consciously and shook her head.

"Well, Brad, I like compliments, at least honest ones." Selah glanced at Sallie and continued, "You know, Brad, honesty is truly a virtue. Without it, our lives are nothing but a sham. Don't you think so, Sallie?"

Under Selah's direct gaze, Sallie flushed and nodded. It seemed to

Selah that she'd touched upon a raw nerve. Perhaps the rumors were correct, that Sallie was somehow involved with Sang and Tzo.

Brad was unaware of the sudden tension between the two women. He was enraptured with the stuffed zucchini and the hot salad with its exotic dressing. "Selah, I don't suppose you'd consider giving me the recipe for this dressing. It's absolutely delicious."

Selah smiled but politely declined saying it was not hers to share. Sallie murmured nervously, "Auntie Selah, I didn't know you had such a gourmet chef." Selah remarked dryly, "My dear, when you reach my age, you'll discover men relish beautiful women, appreciate good food, and admire beautiful surroundings. That's one reason my girls get premium prices. You know, Sallie, you always get what you pay for." At that point Sallie became even more tense and remained silent for the remainder of their meal.

Once dessert had been served, a kumquat-pineapple parfait served with baked mint wafers, Sallie told Brad that she was really tired and would like to leave. They thanked Selah, who remarked as they left, "Don't forget. For both your sakes, the two of you shouldn't visit here again."

—

The next day Mert happened to drop in for a drink and Selah mentioned Sallie's visit. Not to her surprise Selah found out that Liah too had heard the rumors about Sallie and Tzo and had asked Tom to quietly check into Sallie's finances. On a hunch, he had checked both at the Chinese bank and the commercial bank in Fahn Gwai town where some of Chinatown's residents kept their monies and through which sent money back to their families in Hong Kong or Canton. "Well, in her account at the Chinese bank, Sallie had under a hundred dollars, but at the Fahn Gwai bank she had nearly a thousand dollars. On her salary, how could Sallie have saved so much in such a short time?"

Selah shook her head and commented, "Sallie doesn't know who her boyfriend Brad really is either. He begged me not to tell her. With Brad on the one hand and Tzo on the other, I think Sallie is heading for some big trouble. Mert was silent and a bit tense after Selah finished; then he turned to Selah and said, "I probably shouldn't spread rumors but the druggist told me a girl came in the other day to purchase ergot (a drug often used to induce abortion circa 1920). The girl wore dark glasses and a wide-brimmed hat, and he couldn't be certain who she was but the general description fit Sallie."

"My God, as if she isn't in enough trouble!" cried Selah. Mert nodded, knowing that unwed mothers in Chinatown were often shunned even by their own families. In addition who knew what Elton Barkley would do if he found out that his son had fathered an illegitimate child with a Chinese girl. Mert didn't tell Selah but he knew that Tom would be devastated if it were true because Tom secretly harbored feelings for Sallie.

—

Thanksgiving dinner at Number Three was, as usual, a noisy affair. Besides the members of the Council, Madam Quock, Yook Lan and Sen Fei, there was Eldest Daughter with her five children—Aileen, seven; Mary Marie, six; Elizabeth Sue, five; and Walter, Liah's first grandson, age three and her second grandson, John, who had just turned a year old. At one point, Cook winced at the clamor and bickering, fearing Liah would lose her temper. Amazingly, she raised her cane only once and then to tap Aileen gently on her back, with a glance warning her to behave.

When finally the meal was over, Toh gathered his family, thanked his mother-in-law and departed for home. Cook took a deep breath and savored the sudden silence. Then he set himself to the task of cleaning up.

Liah looked around for Aileen, also noticing that Amah was gone. She went to her bedroom and stood still and hard as a statue. Amah was gently applying Tiger Balm to wounds on Aileen's arms and back.

Liah suddenly screamed, "I'll kill that no good daughter of mind. I'll kill her I will!"

Amah shook her head, "I tried to comfort her, but Aileen won't stop crying. I cannot believe a mother would do these things to her own child." Liah's anger turned suddenly to gratitude toward Amah who clearly loved Aileen almost as much as she did. "The Gods have eyes, Amah, my loyal friend. Do not waste your tears."

Aileen eventually fell into a fitful sleep and Liah sighed. "Amah, I'm so ashamed of Eldest Daughter. I will tell you something I have not even told Cook because he worries too much. I have suspected for some time that she has been having shameful affairs behind Toh's back. Recently I forced the truth out of my son-in-law and he confirmed my suspicions. However, he says that no matter how bad a wife and mother she is, he will not divorce her and bring shame on the family. What could I do except agree? However, Toh's honor is endangering the lives of his children. I will give my daughter a little time to change her ways, but if she doesn't I will be forced to step in."

Amah gaped disbelievingly at Liah. "Does Toh know who the other man is?" Liah nodded and said, "Her lover is a member of his own family association, which is another reason he wants to keep the truth quiet. I'll bide my time but if my spies catch my daughter and that scoundrel together, I will deal with the both of them."

For a long time, Liah sat on the edge of the alcove bed gently stroking Aileen's back. The child whimpered in her sleep when Liah's hand accidentally touched one of the bruises but Liah whispered that it was all right, and Aileen sighed and went back to sleep. Suddenly Liah became concerned that should something happen to her, who would take care of her granddaughter? She turned to Amah and begged her to promise that no matter what happened she would be there to take care of Aileen. Amah took Liah's hands in hers and said, "Rest assured I will surely do so. However, do not speak about the possibility of your death. The Gods have and will continue to favor you. As for me, I do not know what I would do without you."

Liah smiled at Amah and replied, "My heart and mind are at peace now that I have your oath. Now, go out and help Cook. I wish to pray to Kwan Yin." Long afterward, Liah still knelt before Kwan Yin in silent prayer. Cook finally appeared at the doorway and for the first time was filled with anger against Eldest Daughter. The odor of Tiger Balm was pungent as he glanced at the now sleeping child. The ointment, manufactured in Singapore, was heady but effective as a healing agent. Afraid the overpowering odor would give Liah a headache, he stepped in and placed his hand on Liah's shoulder. Without a word, Liah rose and silently followed him out into the kitchen.

Cook told her, "I think what you need is a bracing cup of brandy broth. You must keep up your strength despite your sorrow. The child needs you in good health."

Liah smiled broadly. Cook, as usual, was using Aileen as a foil to coerce her into taking better care of herself. Despite her anger at Eldest Daughter and anxiety over Aileen's future, Liah felt hope returning. Cook was her staff of life.

The next day Liah felt the need for her bamboo pipe, but before she could ask, Cook told her that he would now prepare her pipe. A smile played on his face as he also murmured, "And whatever else you might need."

Liah felt a weakness come over her. She always did whenever she anticipated intimacy with Cook. It was one of the aspects of their relationship that was redemptive, that healed all pain, restored tranquility and reaffirmed her femininity. Despite her well of emotions, Liah could only nod and smile shyly.

A JUDGE RULES

On the twentieth of December, in the Fahn Gwai's year of nineteen hundred and twenty-two, Chinatown was tense, for this day would decide whether the Fahn Gwai's court would render justice for Sam Yin's murder. The townspeople shuddered; if there were no justice, then they knew the Council would render their own judgment.

In darkened alleyways, corridors and hallways, for days the people had been asking one another if there was any inkling as to what the verdict would be. Had anyone spoken to Tom? Did Tom say anything? There was a constant cluster of people waiting at the entrance of Peacock Alley and each time a member of Liah's family appeared, there was a hushed silence as if Eldest Son or Fifth Son would give them the word.

At seven-thirty, Tom went to Wong's Café for breakfast and ran into Professor, who'd already eaten. "I didn't know the Fahn Gwai courts opened so early, Tom."

"Not until nine o'clock, sir. However, I want to get there early to go over my notes and talk to Elton Barkley." He grinned slightly. "Besides, I couldn't sleep."

Tom arrived at Barkley's office to find the attorney had been there since dawn. Barkley noticed Tom's apprehensive expression and said, "Don't fret Tom. Pay no heed to the newspapers and certainly don't listen to all the pundits. A case is never decided by the media. Now, shall we go to court?"

Once inside the courtroom, Tom felt the same emotions he had felt the first time—fear, nervousness, inadequacy. He forced himself to focus. To take his mind off the impending verdict, he began to take in the courtroom. As usual, there was the heckling and derision from Trouble and Stuckey's friends, although it seemed to Tom that their catcalls were somewhat muted from before. Also as usual the reporters were jostling for position and yelling out questions to both Elton, Seymour, and himself. Flashbulbs seemed to pop off like a pack of firecrackers. What sickened Tom was the betting he heard going on. When Elton returned to the table, Tom said as much and to his surprise, Elton told him to lighten up. "Just look back at history. Rome had their gladiatorial arenas, the French revolutionaries had their guillotines, and even our own Wild West had their hangings. People always made light of the occasion even though for those involved it was life or death."

Tom protested, "But, sir, betting on the verdict?" Elton laughed, "Why not? Come on, Tom, you're Chinese. You of all people should know that gambling is part of human nature. It's found in every culture. If you want my advice, it's this. Keep your emotions out of your cases. It won't do you or your clients any good."

A sudden movement behind the curtain signaled that the judge was about to make his appearance and a hush came over the courtroom. Tom sat stiffly in his chair as the bailiff cried for order; and announced that court was now in session.

Judge Thompson took his seat and stared out over the crowded courtroom, then began to speak. "Ladies and gentlemen, I have spent considerable time and thought on the issues of this case. I've consulted both the law and my conscience in coming to my decision. However before I announce the verdict, I want to say a few things. From the outset this case has been sensationalized and cast in the context of a double standard, one for the whites and one for the Chinese. From what I have seen take place in this courtroom, this hearing could easily have occurred in the 1800s instead of the 1920s. However, I must remind you that in the United States today the law is the law regardless of skin color. The question before us is simply whether the two defendants killed the victim, Sam Yin."

As he listened to the Judge, Tom felt his hopes rising and he held his breath waiting for the verdict to be announced. The fact that the Defense Attorney was looking glum only accentuated his feeling. Everyone was now hanging on the Judge's next words, "I find that the defendants, James McKinnon and Bert Stuhson, did willfully and unjustly murder Sam Yin. They are to be bound over until the day of their sentencing. Court is dismissed."

The moment Judge Thompson disappeared through the curtains, the reporters and photographers surged toward Tom, Elton and Seymour. Tom was overwhelmed by the sheer volume of questions being shouted at him and the glare of the flashbulbs going off non-stop. In the pandemonium, Tom heard Hans' voice and saw the big man pushing his way towards him.

"Come on, Tom!" shouted Hans. "Let's get the hell outta here." He grabbed Tom's arm and dragged him toward the judge's chambers. "Hey Cat," Tom protested. "We can't go in there."

Hans laughed and said, "Well, it's either that or fight our way through that mob. Now come on. I've got the Judge's permission."

Safely in the police car, Tom slumped down in the seat and sighed, the adrenaline leaching out of his system. He thanked Hans And the officer mumbled something under his breath, Tom only catching the word "unnecessary." The rest of the trip passed in silence.

Upon arriving in Chinatown, Hans dropped Tom off and congratulated him on his victory. Tom saw from the faces of the residents that the news of the judge's verdict had already reached them. People stood on the street and hung out of their upper floor windows. As he passed, several people reached out to grab his hand. Some of the faces were familiar to him and some he vaguely recalled, but all were smiling proudly. He walked as if in a trance down Pig Alley and crossed from Dragon's Den Road onto Marchesson Street.

As he approached Peacock Alley, the first person to greet him was Professor. Holding his customary bag of sunflower seeds, the scholar fell in beside Tom and silently offered him some. They had walked a few yards when Professor turned and asked, "Well, Tom. Was it worth all the hard work? Did it meet your expectations?"

Tom nodded with a smile. "Well," drawled Professor, "I, for one, commend you. I know this trial has not been easy on you, especially with the fate of the Chinese community riding on the outcome. I want you to know that everyone, including myself, is extremely proud of you. I also want you to do me a favor. I know you are tired and the last thing you want to do is relive the trial, but I am asking you to let the people of Chinatown savor their hero and their victory. This may be the only bright spot in their otherwise drab existence for a long time. Now let's go see Liah."

Although the distance between the acacia tree and Number Three was short, it took the two men a long time to traverse it due to the throng of people wanting to congratulate Tom and pat him on the back. As they finally made their way to the front door, Aileen opened it wide and shouted that Tom had arrived. Once inside, Tom's fatigue slipped magically from his shoulders as he anticipated Liah's reaction when he told her the details.

Oddly the door to the kitchen at the end of the corridor was closed. As Tom reached out to push open the door, Professor suddenly propelled him forward and Tom almost staggered into the room. Looking around, Tom was dumbfounded. Dr. Sung, Selah, the entire Council, Liah and most of her family were all gathered there grinning. "Surprise!" they all shouted in unison and everyone began clapping.

Liah motioned for Cook to hand her a glass, which she filled with Ng Ga Pei and handed to Tom. "This is a special day for both you, Tom, and for Chinatown. Your joy is our joy; your pride is our pride. We all know how hard you've worked for this day."

Tom was touched knowing that Liah almost never demonstrated any kind of emotion publicly, except perhaps toward her grandchildren. Mert then raised his glass and offered a toast to Tom, "To Tom, our Champion!" This was followed by a toast from Dr. Sung who told everyone, "I'd like to make another toast. Almost no one from Chinatown save me was there to witness how hostile the people in the courtroom were toward Tom. Nor did they hear the multitude of Fahn Gwai curses and threats. Despite the terror he must have felt, Tom courageously faced up to the hostility and successfully fought to ensure Sam Yin's eternal peace. For your courage, your dedication and for the wonderful example you've set for the young people of Chinatown, I applaud you." The doctor paused a minute, then added in a quiet voice, "I am certain that your mother and father as well as your ancestors, if they were here today, would be as proud of you as we are."

As everyone raised their glasses to drink, tears suddenly clouded Tom's vision and he quickly blinked in an attempt to stem the rising tide of emotion he felt. He felt Cook's hand on his arm and looked up to see the tall man's understanding smile. Cook raised his glass in a silent toast with an approving nod of his head.

Liah broke the moment of ensuing silence by telling everyone, "I know Tom must be famished. Let's all go partake of the feast Cook has prepared in Tom's honor."

Upstairs, the Council members sat at one table, with Eldest Son and Selah as hosts. Tom was seated next to Liah at the family table. Aileen tugged at Tom's sleeve and said excitedly, "Uncle Tom, we're going to have cold cracked crab with Grandma's secret sauce!"

Indeed, it was a feast. Tom couldn't help grinning each time Cook placed another of his favorite dishes on the table: sautéed sweetbreads, steamed pork with salt fish, Peking duck with steamed buns, chicken filets with sea urchin and black mushrooms, and sweet-sour red snapper with pickled scallions.

Once all the food had been served, Liah raised her chopsticks, a signal for supper to begin. She alone waited until Cook was seated before she reached for her rice bowl. Cook nodded his thanks and Liah smiled. Tom chuckled, "I have a sneaking suspicion I'm going to make a pig of myself tonight."

Liah's mind strayed from the celebration of Tom's day in court when she glanced over at the second table and observed Lee Tzo. Unknown to her, Professor, too, was also spending time observing Lee Tzo. Both had come to the conclusion that the police must have been tipped off about Wong Sang's gambling parlor and about Liah's Apinyin business by some stool pigeon in Chinatown. The leading suspect was, of course,

Lee Tzo, but he couldn't speak English. Who then was his agent? The evidence seemed to be pointing at Sallie, who just happened to work at the telephone exchange and spoke excellent English. The girls' suspicious bank balance and love of expensive things did nothing to help prove her innocence.

Liah's thoughts were interrupted when Cook announced the evening's piece de resistance: cold, cracked crab with Liah's secret marinade. Tom groaned audibly, as he'd already eaten far too much, but he rationalized that he had enough room to at least have a taste. Besides, Tom knew Cook would give him the leftovers to take home.

Cook helped by Third and Fourth Sons cleared their table, and then spread several layers of newspaper on the table. "Now," Cook said, "eat up and just throw the shells on the table. When we're done, we'll wrap everything up in the newspapers and throw the whole lot out."

Aileen clapped her hands excitedly and demanded to have a crab all to herself, but Liah shook her head. "Don't you remember how you broke out in hives last year? You don't want to endure that again do you? I'll let you have some of mine. OK?" Aileen looked disappointed but nodded.

Soon, the empty crab shells formed a tall mound in the center of the table. Tom pushed his chair back and moaned that he couldn't eat another bite. Turning to Cook he said, "I thank you, sir, for all the work you've put in to make this exceptional feast. As usual, I always over indulge whenever I eat here."

Cook humbly accepted Tom's thanks, then took Aileen's hand. As he led her to the sink to wash her hands, she shouted, "Oh, goody, goody! It's time for presents now."

Once the tables had been cleared, Liah reached inside her tunic, withdrew a long, flat box adorned with ribbons, and handed it to Tom saying, "This is a token, Tom, of my affection and pride. For you are a thoughtful, compassionate person and it's a joy to know you. We are gathered here tonight to thank you for giving Sam Yin his eternal peace." Tom opened his mouth to deflect her praise, but Liah help up her hand to silence him. "Do not try to diminish your accomplishments. We have heard from the good Doctor a first hand account of the trial and verdict."

There was a round of applause and Aileen rushed up to Tom, urging him to open his present and asking if she could have the pretty paper and the ribbons. Liah laughingly pulled her away saying, "Forgive my granddaughter's poor manners."

Tom shook the box first in an effort to guess its contents. Finally giving up, he carefully unwrapped the box and grinned as he handed both paper and ribbons to a very happy Aileen. A moment later, he held up a luxurious brown leather wallet. "It even has my name on it!"

Liah smiled and suggested that Tom look inside and when he opened the billfold, he saw three crisp new one-hundred-dollar bills. "Madam Liah," he gasped, "I can't accept this. I don't deserve it."

Professor chided, "We all know better, Tom."

Liah then told Tom that the wallet also contained a secret compartment where he could hide things. Curious, Tom examined the wallet carefully, finally snapping open the coin pouch. Seeing another snap at the bottom of the pouch, Tom unsnapped that one too. Lifting the flap of leather revealed the secret compartment, which contained two small gold coins. Madam Liah had given him two fifty dollar gold pieces in addition to the $300! Dazed, he fell back into his seat. That was enough money to set up his practice!

Shaking his head, Tom looked at Liah and said, "I don't know what to say. Thanks just doesn't do justice to what I'm feeling right now."

Dr. Sung winked at Tom. "Meng Sui coupled with Liah's support make all things possible. And let me just say that you have absolutely earned everything. I think that after today, the Fahn Gwai will think twice before they attack any of us again."

Selah applauded, as did everyone else. "Now, darling," she cooed, "there's nothing that can make up for the stress you've endured, but here is another expression of the pride and affection we have for you. Put it to good use." Selah embraced Tom, kissed him on each cheek, and handed him a small red envelope adorned in gold Chinese characters. "This is from Professor and me."

Tom grinned and declared, "This is like having Christmas come early." He turned to Selah and the scholar and held up the packet of lucky money. "I thank you both from the bottom of my heart, not only for this but for always being there when I've needed you."

Professor, slightly tipsy from having imbibed a goodly amount of Ng Ga Pei, swayed to his feet. "Now listen, everyone. Tom, as you know, has been a junior member of the Council for the past few years. Well, no more. Today the Council charter was amended and Tom was accorded full membership with all privileges." Professor lurched forward and pressed another red envelope into Tom's hands saying, "Accept this as a token of the entire Council's esteem." Tom made eye contact with each of the Council members and murmured his thanks.

One by one the celebrants shook Tom's hand, thanked Cook and Liah, and departed. Chon Woo was among the last to leave. Chon grinned and told Tom that he never had any doubt that Tom would win justice for Sam and Sui. "Come in to the Dragon's Den and the drinks will be on me." He then offered to escort Sen Fei, Madam Quock and Yook Lan home. After a flurry of ostentatious congratulations from Madam Quock, an embarrassed nod from Yook Lan, and a shy handshake from Sen Fei, the room fell shockingly silent.

Tom sat idly fingering the wallet when a sudden thought occurred to him. Turning to Cook and Liah, he asked, "What if the verdict had been Not Guilty? You already had the wallet engraved with my name."

Cook chuckled and Liah grinned. "I'd have kept it until you finally won a case."

IN WITH THE NEW

The telephone exchange which serviced Chinatown was usually staffed by a bilingual operator since most Chinese callers almost never knew the number of the person they wanted to reach; rather they asked for the person they wanted to speak with by name or by the person's relationship with another person– for example, the cousin of Suey Sing or the mother of Ah Fat. Sallie was working the switchboard on New Year's Eve when Lee Tzo's call came through. The pimp demanded that Sallie hide a parcel at Selah's place. She wavered, but finally refused. "You said I didn't have to help you any more. Besides, Selah warned me to never visit her place again."

Sallie trembled as Tzo warned her that she had no choice and reminded her of all the money he had already given her. Sallie angrily replied, "No! I've done enough for you!" Her hands were shaking as Tzo then threatened her life and told her that he'd stop by later with the package. Sallie cried, "No! I won't do it! I'm done!" She then pulled the plug on his call, took off her earphones and rushed to the bathroom. Leaning over the sink, her heart pounding wildly, Sallie splashed water on her face and arms. After a moment of furious thinking, she dug in her purse, looking for her friend Tom Soo's card.

Returning to her switchboard Sallie rang Tom's number but got no answer. Then she tried Brad's number and also got no response. Panic was setting in as Sallie then started to call Selah for help, but stopped remembering their last meeting. Fearful, Sallie decided to finish her shift and try both Tom and Brad again later.

—

Emmi and Mert were perched atop ladders fastening a huge bag of confetti to a ceiling light fixture in the front room. Emmi clambered down and stood back to survey their work. "The streamers look great, Mert. They make the room look so festive. I think we're all set. I got the records out and put them on the table and Cook is almost done preparing the food. I'm going to bathe and dress now."

Aileen had sat watching her uncle and aunt decorate from her grandma's upholstered front room chair. "Can I stay up and see the old man leave and the baby come in too?"

"No!" scolded Emmi. "You're too young. Besides the old man isn't really an old man. It's just symbolism."

"What's 'sim-bo-lizm' or whatever you called it? Huh, Auntie Em?"

Instead of answering, Emmi told Aileen that she asked too many questions. Mert good-naturedly informed her that the word symbolism meant using familiar things to represent an idea. "Now go away. We're going to spike the punch. Sis, are you sure you put enough fruit and sugar in?"

"What's spiking, Fifth Uncle?"

Mert growled, "Sis is right, Aileen! You ask too many questions. Spiking means adding liquor, which is also called firewater."

Aileen decided grown-ups sure spoke funny. She still did not understand why adding liquor to punch was called spiking it and how water could be on fire. "Can I have a taste of the punch, Fifth Uncle?" Mert nodded and filled a cup, which he handed to his niece. "But after I put in the firewater, you are not to drink it, understand?"

At ten o'clock, Tom stopped by Professor's house to ask if he'd mind going with him to see Liah. He explained that Sallie had just telephoned him to say that Tzo had demanded she hide a package in Selah's place for him and she'd refused. Tzo then threatened her life. "I would really appreciate it if you would go with me to ask for Liah's help. Sallie sounded almost hysterical."

Professor nodded. When they arrived, the two had to weave their way through the crowd of dancers to get to the kitchen. "Oh, Tom," exclaimed Liah, "how nice to see you. I want to wish you a Happy New Year before I escape to bed. This din is deafening." She then noticed Tom's worried expression and asked what was the matter. After Tom had told Liah about Sallie's predicament, Professor suggested that they assign a bodyguard to protect Sallie and others to monitor Lee Tzo's movements with instructions to immediately report to Liah if he was seen near Selah's place.

Tom pleaded, "I would be most grateful if you would do this for me if not for Sallie, Madam Liah. Sallie sounded so frightened on the phone."

Liah nodded wearily, "All right, Tom, if it will relieve your anxiety. Where is the girl now?"

"She's working at the telephone exchange. When she gets off around midnight, I promised I'd meet her and walk her home."

Liah said, "Very well," and motioned to Cook to fill four thimble-sized cups with Ng Ga Pei. "Now that the young lady's problem has been taken care of, I'd like to drink a New Year's toast."

Tom's face was flushed when he left Number Three, thinking there was never a time when just one drink was sufficient. Although still worried, Tom felt somewhat relieved as he and Professor stepped onto the cobblestone walk. "I feel like a heavy weight has been lifted off my shoulders, sir. I thank you for assisting me in getting Madam Liah to watch over Sallie. You have my wishes for a very happy and auspicious New Year." Professor responded, "You're welcome Tom. Why don't you bring Sallie back to Number Three after you pick her up? I'm sure Liah will not mind if you attended the party. I hope I see you there later."

—

At eleven thirty Wong Sang and Lee Tzo entered The Dragon's Den Bar. Seeing them Chon Woo scowled, feeling it an ill omen as the men took a booth in the darker corner of the bar usually reserved for clandestine lovers. The men huddled together and spoke in whispered tones, stopping whenever someone walked past. "I'll bet those two are up to no good," Chon muttered to himself.

His curiosity eventually got the best of him and Chon sauntered up to the booth and greeted the pair. Wong Sang looked around uncomfortably and Lee Tzo's displeasure made it evident that Chon was not welcome. Nevertheless, Chon asked, "Why so serious tonight? It's New Year's Eve. You should be celebrating instead of talking business; and speaking of business, Wong Sang, I would have thought you'd be minding the crowd at your gambling house tonight."

Wong Sang retorted angrily, "It's none of your business what I do or don't do. We only came in for a drink to celebrate the New Year."

"Don't get sore, Sang, I was just asking. Take your time and have one on me."

Just before midnight, Wong Sang and Lee Tzo rose abruptly and hurried out. Seeing them leave, Chon thought to himself, "I just know those two are up to something. I wonder what they're up to."

—

The revelers were enjoying Cook's special fried chicken when Tom burst into Number Three some time after midnight. Mert waved a hello while chomping on a chicken drumstick, but Tom didn't seem notice as he blurted out, "Sallie's missing! I've got to talk to your mother!"

Mert took him upstairs to where Professor, Liah and Selah were chatting. They listened attentively as Tom tried to render a coherent account of Sallie's disappearance; how he had arrived at the telephone exchange a few minutes after midnight and waited. When she didn't come out, he went in and asked the guard if he could find Sallie and tell her that he was outside waiting. However, the guard had told him that Sallie had already left with two men friends. Out of breath Tom cried, "What are we going to do? I'm afraid that Sallie's been kidnapped by Tzo. Should we call the Fahn Gwai police?"

"No! We will handle our own affairs," Liah said forcefully. She then gently pushed Tom into a chair and offered him a thimbleful of Ng Ga Pei. "Drink this and calm down. We can't help Sallie unless we think." The four of them discussed the situation and decided they would spread the word and send people out to search for Sallie and Lee Tzo.

Selah returned to Number One to tell Amah, Lalo, and Chelo about Sallie's disappearance. As she opened the door, the raucous noise and tobacco smoke almost overwhelmed her. She wondered how men could get so drunk in such a short span of time. She'd only been gone long enough to walk over to see Liah. Shaking her head, she ran up the stairs to check on the girls. When she returned a few moments later, her blood pressure rose as she descended the stairs and saw Wong Sang in the foyer.

Wong Sang sauntered up and asked Selah if he might have Sophia for the duration of the evening. Selah's eyes blazed but she quoted him a price of one hundred dollars. As she stared down at Wong Sang, something in his eyes and his attitude felt slightly out of character. "Well, do you want her or don't you?"

Wong Sang's eyes betrayed his anger as he nodded. Selah rudely motioned for him to wait in the bar. She'd notify him when Sophia was ready.

As Sophia led Wong Sang up the stairs, some of the Caucasian patrons made obscene gestures and several shouted for Sophia to let them know if a Chink was any different from them. Selah's first reaction was to kick the snobs out, but Lalo's eyes counseled self-control. Selah nodded her understanding.

"Lalo," she whispered, "I've got a feeling that something bad is happening and it might have something to do with Wong Sang. He hasn't been in here since we opened and he didn't even blink when I charged him $100 for Sophia."

"Missy, no worry. Me watch good. Me tell Chelo too. We bof stay sober, no dlink!"

"Thank you Lalo but I also want the two of you to stay here tonight. I know it's New Year's Eve, but I'll make it up to you. Okay?"

Lalo's spirits fell. He and Chelo had planned a hot time out that night, but the loyalty he felt for his mistress took precedence, so he nodded.

"Good!" she sighed, "I'm going upstairs to rest a bit. Keep your eyes and ears open."

Selah fell onto her bed intending only to rest her eyes but fell asleep. Some time later a noise, like the sound of a door closing, awakened her. Her room was dark and there was no further sound. Though she had been dozing, Selah was almost certain she'd heard a door open. Awake now, her first thought was that Lalo and Chelo had gone out. A slight fear began to grip her and she reached for the tiny revolver she kept in her nightstand.

Then she heard a creaking noise, a characteristic of the rear door, and was galvanized into action. Crouching low, she crept down the stairs, her heart pounding. She paused halfway down and rested on the railing, cursing the darkness. There was a thud on the thickly carpeted floor below and Selah heard Chelo's voice and Lalo's excited response: "I tink we got 'im!"

Selah leaned weakly against the railing, thanking God for both her friends. Chelo grunted, "Hol 'im, we catchum other one!"

Their voices gave Selah courage and she continued down the stairs and snapped on the foyer lights. She blinked and gaped in disbelief. The dwarf was sitting atop Wong Sang, laughing and waving his arms excitedly.

"So! You had mischief on your mind, Wong Sang," Selah spat out as she fought for self-control. "Explain yourself or I'll blow your head off!"

The sound of a scuffle then erupted in the bar. A few seconds later Chelo and Lalo entered the foyer, dragging Lee Tzo between them. "Lookie, Missy, me and Chelo catchee 'nother fishee."

Selah glared and said, "Looks more like a rat to me." Wong Sang then began to whimper. "Selah, I didn't want to come here tonight, but Tzo threatened to tell Liah that he and I are partners in a new gambling house."

Lee Tzo lunged forward and spat on Wong Sang. Lalo and Chelo tightened their grip until Tzo winced. "Say nothing," Tzo hissed, "if you value your worthless life."

Wong Sang, now completely unnerved, babbled, "Somewhere here he has hidden some Apinyin pods and had Sallie call a tip into the police. When you're in jail, he plans to take over your place. He has Sallie hidden some place and means to kill her tonight. Please protect me, Selah. Protect me from him and his gang from Dai Faw."

Selah whirled about and whacked Lee Tzo on the head with the butt of her revolver. "Where's Sallie? Answer me! Speak up or I'll kill you right here and now!"

Tzo remained silent as Chelo trussed first Wong Sang then Lee Tzo.

Just then someone rapped on the front door and Professor and Mert could be heard calling out. Upon entering they gaped at the sight of Sang and Tzo tied up on the floor. Selah quickly told them what Wong Sang had said and Professor sprang forward, demanding that Tzo not add the crime of murder to the crime of having cooperated with the Fahn Gwai police. But the pimp began to laugh maniacally. "You think," he gasped, "you or the great Madam Liah can save Sallie? She is dying even as we speak!" His eyes glared at them evilly and his laughter resumed.

Expecting that they would not get any further information from Wong Sang or Lee Tzo, Selah suggested that Lalo and Chelo incarcerate the two of them in the ice plant, which was deserted over the holidays. "Meanwhile," she said, "everyone should keep searching for Sallie. I'll help once I find and dispose of the opium that Tzo hid here."

—

Lalo and Chelo hauled Wong Sang and Lee Tzo through the shadowy side streets, and finally along the dirt road to the icehouse. The junkyard and stockyards had none of their nondescript shabbiness as they were washed in the clean and pure starlight of the predawn. The half-breeds jimmied the lock on the side door of the icehouse and dragged the two prisoners through the icehouse door and deposited them on the cold damp floor. Looking around Lalo spied the overhead conveyer belt with hooks dangling down every few feet. Lalo laughed and said, "We hang dem on dose hooks like meat!"

The two men strung up Sang first, then Tzo, hanging each of them by a stout rope tied around their waists. When they were done, Chelo turned to Lalo and said, "Les go." They had turned off the lights and were about to exit when Chelo thought he heard a noise. He grabbed Lalo's arm. "Whoa, man, did you hear dat?"

Together they searched the open warehouse but found nothing. Before leaving, however, they decided to check the ice-storage locker. On entering the dim room, Lalo saw movement out of the corner of his eye and turned to look. As his eyes adjusted to the darkness, Lalo shouted, "It's the gel! Call tell Missee!"

—

Selah slammed down the telephone, then quickly picked it up again and dialed Dr. Sung. After a short conversation, she hung up and turned to Professor, Tom, and Mert. "Come with me, boys," she ordered them. "Amah and the dwarf can continue searching the house for the opium. Chelo and Lalo just found Sallie in the icehouse and she's almost dead."

At the icehouse, a wailing siren announced Dr. Sung's arrival. He jumped out of the ambulance even before it rolled to a stop and rushed into the icehouse. After what seemed like an eternity, Dr. Sung and an orderly wheeled Sallie out on a gurney. Covered with blankets to keep her as warm as possible, Sallie's eyelids fluttered and she made a weak attempt to speak. Selah hushed her whispering, "No darling, don't waste your energy now. We'll talk after you regain your strength."

Dr. Sung got into the ambulance after helping to load Sallie in the back and said to Selah, "I'll call you as soon as I know something, but I think she'll be all right. Lucky you found her when you did. A few minutes more and it would have been too late."

Suddenly Selah turned to Chelo and Lalo and asked, "What did you two do with Tzo and Sang? I didn't see them inside." Chelo grinned and took them back into the icehouse where he pointed upward at the far end of the conveyer belt. Selah glanced up, her mouth fell open, and she began to laugh hysterically. Her companions joined in as they too spotted the pair dangling from the hooks. When their laughter subsided, Selah suggested it was time to get back to the brothel to ensure the opium was found and disposed of before the police showed up.

Once back, Chelo and Lalo took over the search of the bar while Selah joined Amah in the dining room. Tom and Mert methodically searched the kitchen cupboards shelf-by-shelf, removing each jar, bottle and canister. Tom was perched on a ladder running his hand over the tops of some tall cabinets when Professor came in from the back porch holding a glass container and smiling. "I found them! They've been mixed in with some tasty looking chilies."

Before Selah could warn him, Professor had pulled out one of the chilies and had taken a bite. Within seconds the scholar began to sweat and his face had turned bright red. Selah quickly poured cold tea into a glass, squeezed some lemon juice into it, and gave it to Professor saying, "Drink this. It will quench the fire."

When Amah finished separating the opium pods from the chilies, Selah handed the bag of pods to Chelo and Lao and asked them to dispose of them. Then Selah instructed Amah to tidy up while she made coffee and cooked breakfast for all of them. As tired as they all were, the mention of food and especially coffee served to perk them up a bit.

They were on their third cup of coffee when at seven-fifteen there came a rude pounding on the front door. They all glanced at one another and Selah nodded. She slowly walked to the door, asked who it was, and recognized Hans' voice. She then opened the door and demanded to know why he was harassing her on New Year's Day. Without answering he rudely pushed a search warrant into her hands and began giving instructions to his uniformed officers. Selah warned the men assigned to search upstairs, "You'd damn well better knock before entering the girls' rooms. I'll not be responsible if some of you get hurt."

Selah returned to her breakfast followed by The Cat who stared when he saw the group sitting around the dining table. Selah invited The Cat to join them but was not surprised when The Cat declined.

An hour later, The Cat gruffly gathered his men together and ended the search, which had turned up nothing. He chomped down angrily on his unlit cigar and whirled to face Selah. His voice was slightly menacing as he spat out, "You were lucky this time, Selah, but you won't be so lucky the next time or the time after that. I'm going to catch you with the goods one of these times."

Acting puzzled, Selah asked The Cat, "What goods were you hoping to find? I run a brothel not a general store." The Cat retorted, "Don't play the innocent with me! I know you're good friends with Madam Liah and I know for sure that she's the main peddler of opium in Chinatown. I wouldn't put it past you to be helping to hide her stash." Without saying another word, he turned on his heel and led his men outside.

Selah returned to the dining room after locking the door and found both Mert and Tom asleep with their heads resting on the table. Professor smiled wanly and said, "They're both exhausted."

Selah nodded sympathetically and replied, "You don't look so chipper either, sir. Do you think you can get Fifth Son home? Tom's got too far to go, so I'll have the girls fix him a room upstairs. He can sleep here." Professor then walked over to Mert, nudged him awake, and told him he'd help him get home.

Liah had been anxiously waiting at her front door when the scholar arrived with an exhausted Fifth Son. Professor waited in the kitchen while Cook and Liah put Fifth Son to bed. When they returned, Liah said in a concerned voice, "You look absolutely exhausted as well, sir." Professor nodded and replied, "I am, Liah. We've been up all night and as soon as I've told you what has happened, I, too, will go home to bed."

There was a protracted silence after Professor finished his tale. Cook was clearly shocked as the story unfolded while Liah's face became hard as stone. Tired as he was, Professor spoke up on behalf of both Sallie and Wong Sang. "Although Sallie had been helping Tzo, she ultimately turned him down and has paid dearly for it. As for Wong Sang, he was blackmailed into helping Tzo."

"Blackmailed?" demanded Liah. "What do you mean?"

"Tzo threatened that he would tell you that he and Sang were going to be partners in a new gambling house on Dragon's Den Road."

"Is that all?" scoffed Liah, "Then Sang is not only greedy, but stupid. I've known of their impending partnership for a while."

Liah then urged Professor to return home and get some sleep. "We must act quickly. We cannot allow Tzo time to think up some excuse. We will call an emergency meeting of the Council for tonight and ask two representatives from each Tong to attend. Don't worry about notifying the attendees, Professor. Cook will do that. You must get all the rest you can."

After Professor had left, Cook eyed Liah sternly. "Now that we are alone, I suggest you go back to bed. Tonight's meeting will require all the strength you can muster." He paused then went on, "Do you need a little puff of your bamboo pipe?"

Liah smiled wanly and at first shook her head thinking that she needed to be clear-headed tonight. However, the stress made Liah change her mind and she nodded.

1923

YEAR OF THE BOAR

GATHERING OF THE ELDERS

That evening Liah entered the kitchen from her bedroom and Cook stared and shook his head. "If I live to be a hundred, I'll never tire of seeing you dressed in a cheongsam. And seeing how serene you appear, no one would ever guess the stress you're under or how little you've eaten or slept."

She blushed and smiled. "Kwan Yin's mercy and wisdom sustain me, sir. My lucidity, thankfully, has returned. I am ready."

Their eyes met for a fleeting moment and each told the other though words were not spoken that together they would weather the coming storm. Their unspoken conversation ended abruptly with the quiet opening and closing of the front door. Liah smiled. It was Professor and Tom; those two did not allow the door to slam as so many others would.

Liah's heart went out to Tom as she took in his tired countenance. Her voice was gentle as she told Tom, "I want you to know that I've decided to keep Sallie's identity a secret tonight." Tom's face showed the relief he felt and as he started to thank her, Liah held up her hand and shook her head, "There is no need to thank me, son. There is nothing to be gained by involving Sallie in tonight's proceedings."

Tom's eyes misted over as he informed Liah that Sallie's condition had stabilized and that Dr. Sung had said she'd recover fully in a few days. "If Lalo had not done what he did to keep her alive during those first few minutes, Dr. Sung said he didn't know but that Sallie wouldn't have pulled through."

Liah remarked, "Sallie is a most fortunate girl in more ways than she knows. Her Meng Sui has decreed that she live through this experience and I sincerely hope she learned her lesson."

Tom nodded and Professor urged him to finish his coffee, noting that the others would soon be there. It was on Tom's tongue to ask what punishment Liah meant to mete out to Sang and Tzo, but the Council members and the body of Elders began arriving. For several moments, the front door continually opened and slammed shut.

Chon Woo was last to arrive and he peevishly declared that the meeting better be important enough to warrant his getting out of bed so early on New Year's Day. Liah eyed him sternly and Chon had a flash of intuition that this must be about Wong Sang and Lee Tzo, who were nowhere to be seen. He lowered his gaze and quickly followed when Liah led the men upstairs to the Council chamber.

Liah began by apologizing to the Elders for having to inconvenience them on this, the Fahn Gwai's New Year, but indicated that an event had taken place, which required their presence. "A treacherous crime was perpetrated against Chinatown when one of ours stool-pigeoned to the police." She held up her hand for silence as the group erupted. "I will summarize the details of the event and we will then hear from various witnesses."

Her voice broke with emotion several times as Liah told the august gathering of Tzo's continual attempts to overthrow her and usurp the Council chairmanship and of Tzo's plot to incriminate Selah by hiding Apinyin pods in her brothel then notifying the police. Her eyes blazed as she further accused Tzo of kidnapping a young woman whom he'd forced to help him in his schemes. "Wong Sang, whom you all know, is also implicated. He was under obligation to Tzo for his support in opening a new gambling hall."

When she finished, Liah took a deep breath, then announced, "We will now bring in the prisoners so that we may confront them with their crimes. However, before we do, I must point out that as treachery was involved, it may be necessary for the Council to impose the death penalty. If any of you here is wary of your ability to keep secret these proceedings, I give you permission to leave." She waited a moment, but no one moved. She nodded and then turned to Professor who immediately left the room to get the prisoners.

While they waited, Elder Kwan inquired why Tzo had been allowed to join the Council in the first place with such a shady background. Liah sighed and recounted how several years earlier the balance in their treasury had been meager and that Tzo's donations had allowed the establishment of the children's school and the fund for the aged, sick and needy. "Moreover, we all agreed that it would be easier to keep an eye on the man inside our ranks rather than outside."

Just then the Council room door was flung open and Lalo entered, half-dragging, half-supporting Lee Tzo while Chelo followed, propping up Sang in his arms. Chon stared openmouthed as the pair were manhandled to a couple of straight back wooden chairs facing the assembled Council members and Elders.

Lee Tzo, unlike the cringing Sang, held his head high as he fell into his seat. Even with his gag and rumpled gown, his lips swollen from the hot chili Lalo had forced between his lips, arrogance still burned deep in his hate-filled eyes. Lee Wah, unable to meet the pimp's hard glare, averted his eyes.

Once the prisoners were seated, Professor introduced Selah as the first witness and the Elders gasped in surprise, for while they'd heard about the red-haired beauty, most of them had never seen her before. Their surprise quickly turned to admiration when she bowed and addressed them in impeccable Cantonese. She then recounted Wong Sang's visit to her brothel and the subsequent capture of both Wong

Sang and Lee Tzo as they were hiding Apinyin pods in her establishment for the Fahn Gwai police to find. Selah went on to state that Lee
Tzo had even admitted to having called the Fahn Gwai police as well
as to having kidnapped a young woman whom he had previously inveigled into helping him.

Tom Soo, who was next to testify, was ill-at-ease. He chose his words
very carefully, praying that he wouldn't slip and reveal Sallie's identity.
At the end of his testimony, he pleaded for leniency for Wong Sang.
"Honored Elders, members of the Council and Madam Liah, I hope you
will not consider me presumptuous, but Wong Sang was being coerced
and ought to be granted a degree of leniency. While his greed and stupidity got him ensnared by Lee Tzo, I do not believe he is deserving of
the death penalty." Tom paused, then continued, "It should be noted
that he, too, was betrayed when someone, most likely Lee Tzo, turned
him in to the police and his gambling hall was raided and destroyed."

Wong Cheung asked to be heard next. For the first time, Lee Tzo
seemed cowed and would not meet the big man's eyes. "As you know,
Apinyin is illegal in Chinatown for all except Madam Liah, who has
permission to keep a small quantity in her possession as a result of her
participation in the Fahn Gwai's rehabilitation program. This has made
it possible for others less fortunate to buy the needed opiate from Liah
at a nominal price. Lately, however, the illegal sale of Apinyin has been
growing. I am sure all of you remember the unfortunate death of the
young Apinyin peddler who was caught selling the opiate in our very
own temple."

Wong Cheung then paused, looked over the assembled group of
Elders and Council members, and decided that the time had come to
reveal his mission in Loo Sahng. In a strong voice he notified the Elders
and the Council how Elder Wong of the House of Wong in Dai Faw
had ordered him to protect Madam Liah and prevent Lee Tzo and his
dissident gang from overthrowing Liah and taking over the Loo Sahng

Chinatown. "I have a document in my possession which will give proof to what I tell you as well as the names and roles each dissident has played in Dai Faw's internal disruptions."

The Elders clamored for a look at the document, but Wong Cheung told them that it was in a safe place and that he would produce it for them at a subsequent meeting. Given Wong Cheung's stature, the Elders all agreed that that would be acceptable.

With his gag removed, it was then Wong Sang's turn to plead his case. In a shaky voice, he said, "As Tom has told you, Lee Tzo first threatened to reveal our partnership in a new gambling hall, which would directly compete with the one Madam Liah and I own. He then threatened my life should I not do exactly as he ordered. However, I had no part in actually hiding the Apinyin in Miss Selah's establishment. I only let Lee Tzo in. I also had no part in the attempted killing of the girl. I understand that I have acted dishonorably and I humbly beg your forgiveness." Suddenly Wong Sang's nerve collapsed and he started to cry, "Please don't kill me. I beg of you. Please don't kill me."

Finally, Professor walked up to Lee Tzo and removed his gag. For a moment, Lee Tzo worked his mouth, loosening his stiff jaw muscles. Then without warning, he spat. Professor and the other men closest to him all leapt back to avoid being hit by the spittle.

Elder Lee Ti faced the panel and shook his head. "Long have I warned and even longer have I pleaded with Tzo to use good judgment and quit his subversive activities, but he would not listen." The old man turned to face the pimp. "Now you have dishonored our good name and The House of Lee cannot help you. May Kwan Koong have mercy on you."

Lee Tzo glared at Elder Lee Ti and sneered, "You call yourselves Elders, but you're nothing but a bunch of weak old men. As for you on the Council, there isn't a man among you who wasn't bought by Liah in one way or another. Professor got his school; Tom got his education;

and as for the rest, they got prestige and Liah's support in their business endeavors. They're all Liah's toadies. Which brings us to you Liah. You can fool most of the people with your seeming concern for their welfare, but you can't fool me. I know you're just out to line your own pockets and keep everyone else from getting out of line. You're a fraud! As for giving me a death sentence, you wouldn't dare. You know full well such an act would likely set off a full-scale tong war."

The angry pimp continued to rant and couldn't be silenced until Liah had Lalo replace the gag. Once order had been restored, Elder Lee Ti turned to the panel and said, "I humbly apologize on behalf of the House of Lee and as much as it pains me to say it, I will not ask you for mercy for this man. For the future welfare of Loo Sahng Chinatown, you must weigh the facts and pronounce the appropriate sentence to fit your findings, however distasteful that sentence might be."

A heavy pall fell over the room as Elder Lee Ti's words sunk in and Liah ordered that the prisoners be returned to their place of confinement. Sensing that the group needed time to reflect, Liah suggested that they eat supper before holding further discussions.

Although Cook had as usual prepared a veritable feast, supper was largely a solemn, silent, and strained affair, each man wrestling with his conscience over the taking of another's life. Tom, being the youngest and least worldly of the group, found the thought of participating in the death of another human being, however evil, to be abhorrent.

After the meal was over, Liah offered Ng Ga Pei to the men, hoping that the potent rice wine would help dull the stress and pain each was surely feeling. The ensuing discussion was brief and after Professor advised the men of their duty to render a sentence in accordance with the Tenets of Law, the balloting began. In the end, Wong Sang was sentenced to be lashed, with each member of the Council administering two lashes. Although Tom felt a surge of relief that Sang would be allowed to live, he cringed at the thought that he, too, would have to wield the whip. Silently he rued the day he had joined the Council. Lee Tzo's sentence came even more rapidly, as if each man wanted the ugly decision to be done with. It was a unanimous vote for the death penalty.

The prisoners were then summoned to hear their sentences read. Upon hearing that he would live, Wong Sang began to sob uncontrollably, while Lee Tzo stood unflinchingly and glared at the men who had pronounced his sentence. Tzo's eyes burned with intense hatred but he remained silent.

All that remained was to set the date for the lashing and the execution. However, Liah sensed that the men were emotionally exhausted and recommended that the dates for the sentences to be carried out be determined at a subsequent meeting. All quickly agreed.

Turning to the Elders Liah told them, "Although it will be a most disagreeable task, all of you will be required to witness the execution. However, I request that you not speak of tonight's events until after the sentences are carried out. Once the execution has occurred, you may inform the people of how and why Lee Tzo was put to death. Now, if you are ready to leave, my Eldest Son will drive you. The Council and I thank you for your diligence on behalf of Chinatown."

The Council chamber quickly emptied with Tom and Professor remaining behind to support Liah as grief became etched on her face the moment everyone had left. For the first time, Tom could see the vivid age lines, which heretofore had escaped his notice. Liah, he thought, looked old.

Once everyone had left, Cook appeared upstairs. He looked at the half-eaten food and the faces of the three friends, then went to the credenza and removed a bottle and four glasses. He set them on the table, saying, "I think we can all use a drink." As he filled the glasses with special amber Ng Ga Pei, he remarked, "Remember, there is nothing we can do to alter the verdict. Meng-Sui and justice must be served. Let us not dwell on the necessity of taking a life."

After they had each downed the shot of liquor, Liah set down her glass. She looked gently at Tom and said, "I would not, if I were you, let this night's proceedings weigh on your mind. Tzo's guilt dictated his sentence. You are young, Tom, and the shock will wear off quickly. For this, I give thanks to Kwan Yin. Just remember that Tzo's passing will eliminate the evil that he has been perpetrating upon Chinatown."

Tom's vision blurred as he thought how like Liah to think of his well-being even as she herself was feeling anguish over having contributed to the impending death of another human being. After another drink, both Professor and Tom took their leave.

—

It had been Liah's wish that her granddaughter not be around during the Council meeting. Consequently, Fifth Son had taken the child to a wild animal show and subsequently to a movie. Shortly before one o'-clock in the morning, Aileen burst into the house shouting for her grandma. "Grandma, I saw a panther climb a ladder and jump through a fiery hoop! There were also a lot of elephants dressed in colored skirts and leis. I even got to feed some peanuts to the biggest elephant. I had so much fun!"

When finally Aileen fell asleep, Liah returned to the kitchen where Fifth Son was waiting. Liah seemed withdrawn as she seated herself and lit a cigarette. Mert winced at the pain he saw deep in her eyes and asked, "Mah-Mah, did they pass a death sentence?"

Liah nodded wordlessly, later adding that Wong Sang had been sentenced to a lashing by the Council. Mert touched his mother's arm. "Mah-Mah, do not blame yourself. The decision was that of the members. Besides, Lee Tzo is a traitor and deserves to die. Please do not make yourself ill over this. It would be bad for all of us who count on you, especially Aileen."

Liah smiled wanly. It seemed that everyone knew that by mentioning Aileen's welfare, Liah would do whatever was necessary. "Thank you Fifth Son, but it doesn't matter that it was the Council members who voted for the death penalty. Their vote is also mine. However, you need not worry, son. I will sleep now and be fine in the morning."

Despite her words, Liah could not fall asleep and finally succumbed to her bamboo pipe. Upstairs, Cook could not sleep either. He knew Liah would feel responsible for Lee Tzo's death and she would unconsciously punish herself.

THE DISCOVERY

The following morning was gray and gloomy, for the night mist had not yet burned off. At seven o'clock, a dilapidated old truck made its way alongside the train tracks on its route to collect the trash at the rear of Peacock Alley. The driver waved at the flagman, stopped his truck briefly to exchange a few words, then drove up to the overflowing rubbish cans.

The driver got out and hoisted each can into the air, allowing the side of the can to fall onto the raised side of the truck bed. He then tipped the can and let the trash fall into the bed. When a can was empty, he casually dropped it back on the ground. Some cans remained upright, but most landed on their dented sides, rolling every which way. As he reached for the can at the end of the line, the driver let out a scream and ran back to the flagman yelling, "Man o man! A daid man on top de trash. Somebody call fo' da pohlice! Quick, man!"

The old flagman eyed the driver to see if he was trying to pull a prank on him. Deciding that he might be telling the truth, he said, "OK, show me."

The driver shook his head and replied, "I ain't gonna go back dere. I sees him once. Thas enuff! Yo' all wants to see him, go yoself. He's dere, by de last can."

The flagman stuck his red flag in his back pocket, walked over to the refuse strewn area, and approached the lone upright trashcan cautiously. Suddenly, the old man stopped as he saw an arm hanging limply over the side of the can. He turned at once and hustled over to the train yard supervisor's office.

A half-hour later, Detective Lahr from homicide arrived to find Hans and Little John already questioning the driver and the flagman. Lahr nodded to Hans and told him that he was taking over the investigation. Hans shrugged and told Lahr that the two men knew nothing but that the dead Chink was a pimp by the name of Lee Tzo. "I'd check out whatever the dead guy has clenched in his fist if I were you."

Lahr grunted and walked over to the body where he pried a bag out of Lee Tzo's hand. Opening it he exclaimed, "Opium pods. You're the expert on the Chinks, Hans. Do you think this is a turf killing?" Hans shrugged and said, "Beats me. I'd have to do some digging."

Just then the coroner's wagon drove up and the two uniformed officers asked if they could remove the body. Officer Lahr nodded and said, "Let me have the autopsy report as soon as you have it done."

Leaving the scene, Hans and Little John swung by Wong's Café to see if the news of Lee Tzo's death had spread through Chinatown but everything seemed normal. They then went in search of Tom Soo and found him walking down Marchesson Street on his way to breakfast. When told of Lee Tzo's death, at first Tom could only stand there numbly with his mouth hanging open. However, his wits soon returned and he began to think furiously. He obviously needed to fashion some plausible story and it had to be as factually based as possible so that everything would check out when the police investigated. Tom told the two officers, "I can't believe it. I just saw him last night at Number Three. There was a big New Year's Day party at Liah's and the whole Council was there." Tom then answered Hans's questions about who else was there, when the party broke up, and especially when Lee Tzo left and with whom. As Hans and Little John drove off, Tom immediately set off for Professor's house.

—

By the time Hans and Little John returned to the station, they found a mob of reporters and photographers in the foyer. The journalists were swarming around Lt. Swanson, shouting out questions and snapping photographs.

Hans shouted over the din, "What the hell's going on here?"

Lt. Swanson smirked and asked sarcastically, "Why, I thought you could tell us. You do know that there's been a murder in Chinatown don't you?"

Just then a photographer snapped a picture of Hans and the exploding flashbulb caused him to involuntarily shield his eyes and a moment later to strike out at the offending newsman. "Do that again and I'll level you," he growled.

Lt. Swanson then ended the impromptu press conference by saying, "When I know something, you'll know it. Now, clear out of here. We've got work to do."

As soon as the officers were alone, Lt. Swanson asked gruffly, "Well, what have you found out?"

Hans replied testily, "We haven't found out a damned thing except that the news hasn't spread to Chinatown yet. However, after this circus, it won't take long now." He purposely neglected to tell the Lieutenant that he had told Tom Soo and that everyone in Chinatown would have found out by now.

Later that afternoon Lt. Swanson burst into Hans' office and flung a newspaper on the desk angrily asking, "How is it that you don't know anything, but Banyon apparently does? Have you seen his story in *The Daily News*? Was it you who told him that there's an opium war going on in Chinatown?"

"Hell no! He must have found out about the opium pods in the Chink's hand and stretched the truth like he always does."

Little John nodded in corroboration. "That's right, boss. When Banyon came to see us, we didn't tell him anything."

Clearly frustrated, Lt. Swanson growled, "Well, you two had better solve this one quick. I don't want the brass on my ass about some Chink opium war going on right under our noses and us not knowing anything about it."

—

Professor and Tom entered Number Three and went directly to the kitchen where Cook was filling a teapot with boiling water. Tom blurted out, "Lee Tzo's dead, Cook! We have to tell Liah right away." However, Cook shook his head and told them that Liah had been unable to sleep and had taken a strong draught of Apinyin. "She won't awaken until at least noon."

Professor slumped into a chair and shook his head, "I still can't believe it. Who could have done such a thing and how?" Tom replied, "I don't know but I do know that we had better make sure everyone who was here last night tells the police the same story I told them." Cook nodded his head and said, "You're right. We should start spreading the word before we do anything else."

Just then the telephone rang and Cook answered it with some trepidation. A call so early could only mean trouble. Cook listened for a moment then replied, "No Selah. It wasn't Liah's doing. She's been sleeping off a draught of Apinyin since one o'clock this morning and hasn't even heard the news yet. Professor and Tom will be over to tell you all we know as soon as we finish talking."

—

Liah awakened at two o'clock in the afternoon and groggily made her way into the kitchen where Cook, Professor, and Tom were waiting.

She took her seat, nodded to them as Cook lit a cigarette for her, and took a sip of hot tea. Reluctantly, Professor then broke the news to Liah.

Seeing the shock register on Liah's face, any nagging suspicion that Tom had that Liah might have been involved instantly vanished. When Liah had recovered, she asked, "How can this be? Didn't Selah's servants lock them up securely in the temple after the meeting?"

Cook nodded and replied, "All we know is what Hans told Tom: the body was discovered at seven o'clock this morning clutching a bag of Apinyin pods in his hand. Professor checked and Wong Sang is still tied up and locked in one of the storerooms in the temple. He claims to have been asleep all night and to have seen nothing."

Liah then told them, "We must hold an emergency Council meeting tonight. And be sure all the Elders are present, too. We'll start at seven thirty." Pausing, she continued, "Whoever did this deed spared us the necessity of doing it ourselves and I for one am grateful. Nevertheless, we must prepare everyone for the inevitable Fahn Gwai intrusion which is sure to descend on us now."

—

Hans and Little John were parked on Marchesson Street when, at a quarter to seven, a number of men began to arrive at Number Three. By seven thirty, over twenty people had filed in. Inside, the Council members and Elders sat by nervously waiting for the meeting to begin. To their great surprise and puzzlement, Professor indicated that the first order of business would be the punishment of Wong Sang. Somewhat oddly, it was Chon Woo who asked if Wong Sang's sentence couldn't be postponed or even cancelled in light of Tzo's death.

Liah sternly rejected the idea. "Council decrees must be carried out else they have no meaning and under the circumstances I believe we should carry out the sentence now. If we wait, the Fahn Gwai police investigation will only intensify and we might not be able to carry out our duty for a long time."

After a brief discussion, the Council reluctantly agreed with Liah and Wong Sang, disheveled and unshaven, was brought in. He sagged between Chelo and Lalo who led him to a hastily erected post at the end of the room. Once Wong Sang had been bound securely to the post, Liah reiterated that each Council member would administer two lashes and that Chon Woo would be the first to go.

Chon Woo bit his lip, irritated at Liah for picking him to be the first to draw blood. Gingerly, he accepted the lash from Professor, not quite certain what to do with the length of rawhide. After swinging the whip around a few times to get the feel of it, he swung it at Wong Sang's exposed back. When the whip made contact, everyone winced. A bright red bloody welt appeared and Wong Sang audibly gasped. Chon Woo hastily finished the second of his two lashes, handed the whip back to Professor, and shakily returned to his seat.

Tom became increasingly nauseated as the progression of lashes turned Sang's back into a mass of bloody stripes. When it was finally his turn, perspiration beaded his face and his palms were wet as he clumsily swung the whip. Steeling himself, Tom swung the whip and Sang once more cried out. Tom closed his eyes and swung again hearing the impact as leather met flesh.

Wong Cheung, last to administer punishment, gazed at the men in the room and saw the speculation in their eyes. As a former hatchet man, would he give Wong Sang two forceful blows or go easy on him? He sighed silently knowing that he would never escape his past no matter how hard he tried. He then raised his arm and deftly flailed the whip in such a way that it cracked loudly. Everyone gasped, but in reality, only the tip touched Sang's torn back. One final flick of the whip and Wong Sang's punishment was mercifully over.

Wong Cheung handed the whip back to Professor and accepted a small cup of Ng Ga Pei. He then walked over to Sang where he gently helped the injured man down the pain dulling liquor. Lalo and Chelo untied Sang and Liah declared, "Wong Sang, your debt has been paid and your honor has been restored. May the memory of this night deter you from straying from the correct path in the future. Wong Cheung will assist you back to your house and will apply a healing balm to your back. He will also give you an Apinyin potion, which will help you to sleep." Liah then instructed Wong Cheung to use the tunnels to avoid detection by the Fahn Gwai police.

Once Wong Sang had been helped from the room, Professor brought up the topic of Lee Tzo's death. Inasmuch as most everyone in the room harbored some suspicion that Liah had something to do with the killing, Professor did his best to establish her innocence and asked that anyone with any information should bring it to light. He then went over the story that everyone was supposed to tell the police if questioned.

When the meeting finally concluded. Liah thanked each attendee personally and inquired if they needed a ride back home. Liah instructed Mert to drive those who did.

After everyone had left, Cook sat and commiserated with Liah as best he could. He understood the fortitude it had taken for Liah to carry out Wong Sang's punishment and the penance she would impose on herself. He also understood that she would have to endure the doubt that some would still harbor concerning her involvement in Lee Tzo's death despite her plea of innocence.

—

On the eighth day of January, funeral services were held at the temple in Peacock Alley. Lee Tzo's body had been released to the Dai Faw Lee Family Association and the expenses for the funeral and the eventual shipment of his remains back to Hong Kong for permanent burial would be paid by the House of Lee.

Lee Tzo's funeral was attended by the girls in his brothel, the Council members and a handful of others. As Professor passed by the bier and stared at the pimp's face, he swore to himself that Tzo's countenance even in death held the trace of a sneer. Afterwards, Tom commented that it could have been his imagination but it seemed to him that Tzo looked like he was sneering. Most of the Council members agreed and Lim Tao declared, "That man would sneer in the face of Kwan Koong himself."

The traditional feast was held at Tzo's brothel and Professor was somewhat surprised at the genuine sorrow exhibited by Tzo's girls and especially by Mei Tai, who, rumor had it, had been tortured by Lee Tzo after Mei Lei had disappeared. Perhaps, thought Professor, Lee Tzo had not been entirely evil after all. In any case, Liah and Selah had already agreed that Selah would watch over the girls until they decided what they wanted to do.

Cook and Professor were just leaving the feast when they were surprised to find Wong Sang slowly making his way toward Number Ten. When they asked him why he was up and about so soon, he replied, "Though he led me astray, he was not a monster. I feel like I owe him the courtesy of paying him his final respects for those kindnesses he extended to me." Cook and Professor nodded and helped the injured man up the steps.

Afterwards, Cook and Professor offered to escort Sang home, but he said, "I must go and speak with Liah. I have had time to reflect on my situation and have come to understand that it would have been easy for Liah to arrange a sentence of death for me as well as for Lee Tzo. For that I owe her a debt of gratitude. As for my lashing, I understand that I had it coming under the Tenet of Laws. It was my doing, not hers. For that I owe her an apology."

When Cook brought Wong Sang into the kitchen, pity surged within Liah as her eyes took in the man. He appeared to be injured in spirit as well as the body. That conjecture was strengthened when he suddenly broke down and began crying. In between sobs, Sang reiterated his gratitude for Liah sparing his life and apologized for his greed getting in the way of his better judgment. He finished by saying, "I only wish there were some way I could make amends."

Liah replied gently, "My friend, I am deeply sorrowed by what has occurred to both you and Tzo. As for making amends, you are in a position to possibly be of great assistance to us. We must find Tzo's killer before the Dai Faw Lee Family Association accuses us of his murder. What can you tell us of his connection with the Dai Faw gang?"

Wong Sang lifted his head, gazed into Liah's eyes, and came to the conclusion that Liah really had not had anything to do with killing Tzo. He shook his head wearily and replied, "I'm afraid I can be of little help. Tzo never really trusted me. He told me next to nothing and wouldn't allow me to attend any of his private meetings with the people from Dai Faw." Liah nodded, thanked him for his honesty, and offered him some of Cook's brandy broth, which was thought to have restorative powers.

Fifth Son returned home from work and was shocked to see Sang sitting in the kitchen drinking soup. However, he kept quiet and at his mother's request, drove Sang home. Cook went along to help Sang into the house and to apply another application of the healing ointment to his back. Alone, Liah mouthed a silent prayer to Kwan Yin that Wong Sang would recover his health. Despite Sang's forgiveness, Liah bore the guilt of having arranged his punishment.

WAR IS DECLARED

Although the Fahn Gwai police investigated Lee Tzo's murder for several months, they were unable to solve the crime. Everyone they questioned in Chinatown told them the same story and no new leads were uncovered. It was the same in Chinatown. Despite the Council's urgent plea for information, no one came forward. It was as if a ghost had murdered Tzo. Finally in the middle of October, a full ten months following the mysterious death of Tzo, a letter arrived from the House of Lee in Dai Faw addressed to the head of the House of Lee in Loo Sahng. The author of the letter stated that the House of Lee of Loo Sahng was being held responsible for the ignoble death of Lee Tzo and demanded one thousand dollars as payment for their loss of face. The letter was signed not by Elder Lee Ting as expected but by a Lee Sam, whom no one knew.

After reading the letter, Professor frowned and turned to Lee Ti, the senior Elder of the House of Lee in Loo Sahng. "Do you not think this letter strange, as it is signed by someone other than the Eldest member of the Dai Faw Tong?"

Elder Lee Ti sighed and replied, "As soon as I read the letter, I sensed at once that my fears may have become reality. Ever since we started hearing rumors about the dissidents in the Dai Faw Tong and Lee Tzo's possible connection to them, I have feared that the dissidents might take over leadership of the Dai Faw Tong. I think this Lee Sam may have ousted Elder Lee Ting and seized power. At any rate, I would appreciate it if you would come with me to share the letter with Liah and get her opinion and advice."

After Professor had read the letter to Liah, Elder Lee Ti reiterated his fear that Elder Lee Ting may have been ousted and perhaps even killed by the dissidents. He shook his head and told them, "The Elders, myself included, are getting old and are ill equipped to deal with the younger headstrong youths who would bleed their own people rather than support them. I, for one, am grateful for the strong leadership of the Council in Loo Sahng for adhering to our traditions of respect and decency. As a consequence our youth here have not been lured into bad behavior like those in Dai Faw."

After thinking quietly for some minutes, Liah said, "I suggest that Professor write a letter in reply explaining the circumstances that led up to Tzo's death. The letter should document Tzo's numerous attempts to undermine the Council and my leadership as well as mention our suspicions that Tzo was involved in the sale of Apinyin in our very own temple, which led to the death of the young salesman The letter should then relate how Tzo tried to hide incriminating evidence in Selah's home and then told the Fahn Gwai police where to look. Professor should then state that for this treacherous act, the Council had voted to impose the death penalty and that before the sentence could be carried out, some unknown person or persons kidnapped Tzo and murdered him. Finally, we should say that although we have no proof, we believe Tzo may have been slain by one of his own gang as punishment for getting caught."

Liah then turned earnestly to Elder Lee Ti and said, "Sir, I truly hope that the House of Lee believes that I had nothing to do with Lee Tzo's death."

Elder Lee Ti gazed at Liah for a moment and then sighed, "I must admit that there are some who harbor the suspicion that you had something to do with Tzo's death; however, most believe that you did not. I am in the latter camp."

"Perhaps, sir," murmured Liah, "it might be a good idea if the Council were to meet with two members from each Tong in Chinatown. At that time, we could tell them about the letter and detail all the facts about Lee Tzo's death."

Elder Lee Ti nodded and replied, "That's a good idea, Liah. I would also suggest that we publish our account of what happened in the Dai Faw and Noo Yok Chinese newspapers. Everyone should know our side of the story."

—

On the fourteenth of October the Council met with the two invited members of each Tong. Although most of the men assembled had already known about some of the things that Lee Tzo had either done or been suspected of doing, many had not been privy to everything. Consequently, Professor begged their indulgence and went through the entire litany of Tzo's transgressions culminating with the episode for which he had been sentenced to death. All agreed that the Council had been justified in imposing such a punishment. Then Elder Lee Ti read the letter from the Dai Faw House of Lee demanding a payment of one thousand dollars as retribution for Lee Tzo's murder. The Council members and Elders alike were shocked and outraged.

Lim Tao declared that the House of Lee's position did not make sense. No one in Loo Sahng Chinatown had any reason to kill Tzo since the Council had already legitimately sentenced him to death. The only thing that made sense, he said, was that one of Tzo's gang killed him either as punishment or to keep him quiet or both.

Most of the Elders agreed with the Council that to pay the money would be tantamount to an admission of guilt and almost no one was willing to do so. Much to Professor's surprise, the majority were actually willing to go to war over the issue, perhaps believing that the Dai Faw House of Lee was just trying to extort whatever money they could and would back down if threatened with a real war.

Having personally suffered the effects of violence and death, Professor tried to caution the group about making a hasty decision. However, even Kam Fong, a normally timid person, spoke up, "I am not an aggressive man, but there are times in life when one must take a stand. Professor, I know the pain you suffered when you lost your family, but I see no other course in this matter. This time scholarly logic won't solve the problem. We must fight, sir!"

Just then Wong Cheung cleared his throat to get their attention and the men turned their gaze to the big man and waited for him to speak. "I am afraid Kam Fong is correct, Professor. These extortionists wouldn't be satisfied with just one payment of monies. It occurs to me and perhaps to some of you as well that it is highly likely that these hoodlums murdered Lee Tzo to give them an excuse to extort money from us. We must fight them or they will continue to make demands on us. In doing so, we would probably be doing the people of Dai Faw a favor. The papers I have from Elder Lee Ting indicate that this dissident gang has been threatening to turn over to the Fahn Gwai Immigration authorities as illegal immigrants those Chinese who do not pay them blackmail money. Although I now abhor violence, I believe there are times when it is called for and unfortunately for us this is one of those times."

Professor nodded his head wearily and replied, "I cannot dispute your logic, although my heart is heavy as I contemplate the possible consequences of this action. Nevertheless, if that is to be our decision, I recommend we depart from our tradition of waiting one year before replacing a departed Council Member. We will need all the help we can get."

As a chorus of assent went around the table, Wong Cheung again spoke, "If we are to elect a new Council member, we should consider adding someone who has experienced war. I believe Jui Jinn fought in what the Fahn Gwai call World War I and was thought to be a good soldier."

"That's a great idea," exclaimed Tom, "not only is Jinn proficient with weapons but he is also respected among the younger men in Chinatown. I think he would make an excellent addition to the Council."

After Jui Jinn was unanimously elected, the meeting was concluded and the record signed. As everyone was drained of energy by that time, Liah volunteered Fifth Son to drive the elderly among them back home.

Once everyone had left, Cook suggested to Liah that they share a late supper. As they started to descend the stairs, Cook took Liah's arm to support her. At Cook's touch Liah felt a pleasant warmth surge through her body. She giggled and murmured, "Do you think we'll ever put up a railing?"

Cook smiled and replied, "It doesn't matter. I'll always be here to assist you whenever you need me."

Liah's face shone with love and her eyes sparkled. Later, as Liah expressed her gratitude to Kwan Yin, she also thanked Kwan Koong, as she knew she would need Cook's support in the perilous time to come.

—

At the end of October, Elder Lee Ti sent word to Liah that a letter had just arrived from the House of Lee in Dai Faw refuting the claims made in Professor's letter and declaring that a state of war now existed between the Dai Faw Tong and the Loo Sahng Tong. Professor also brought word that the Six Companies Association was remaining neutral in the dispute. Hearing this, Liah cursed the Association for their cowardice, "With the resources and influence at their disposal, this war could be avoided without bloodshed."

The day following the start of the war, Professor posted notices around Chinatown notifying everyone and urging them to remain calm, to help themselves by setting in stores of foodstuffs, and to reinforce their doors and windows. The notices also recommended that they venture outdoors as little as possible during the hostilities as doing so would be taking a grave risk. Children were not to attend Fahn Gwai or Chinese school nor should they play outdoors. If there was time, the citizenry would be notified of impending violence by a red flag flown on the temple tower and by the tolling of the temple bell. Provisions were made for the outdoor people to stay inside an empty warehouse and Liah arranged for donated food and water to be distributed to them.

Inasmuch as it was likely that Liah would be a primary target, her sons banded together with seven of their male cousins and came up with a strategy to guard and protect her. However, detailing out the strategy generated much dissension amongst the sons. As the Eldest, Thomas tried to issue orders to each of the others who balked at both his leadership and their assignments. Shouting matches were frequent as they worked out who would do what, where they would do it, and when. Finally, however, a plan was made that everyone, however grudgingly, adopted.

At the same time, Tom was informing Jui Jinn that he had been elected to the Council. At first, Jinn was puzzled. "Why me?" he asked Tom, "There are a lot of other more qualified candidates. I don't understand." Tom then related that he had been selected for his war experience and his influence on the youth in Chinatown. Jinn nodded and told Tom, "That sort of makes sense, but I was only a corporal in the war not an officer. What do you expect me to do?" Tom shrugged and offered, "For one thing, I think we could use someone to teach us how to shoot a gun." Jinn laughed and replied, "Well, that I can do. I was considered an expert marksman in the Army."

Over the course of the next week, Jui Jinn taught Liah's sons, the Council members, and a few others how to shoot both the rifles and the handguns they had managed to procure. Although most of the men were just average shots, a few including Thomas and Shelly proved to be adept at hitting the target.

—

On the tenth of November, Professor hastily made his way to Number Three and informed Liah that six strangers had just registered at the Lotus Garden Hotel. "Shall we fly the red flag over the temple and ring the temple bell to warn everyone?"

Liah thought for a moment and replied, "No, not yet. I think we should start spreading the word quietly so that Lee Sam's men, if they are his men, do not become alarmed and begin the fight before we are ready. While you're out informing everyone, Cook will get the outdoor people to move into the warehouse immediately."

By nightfall almost everyone in Chinatown had gotten the word and the Council met to finalize their defensive strategy. A schedule was drawn up for daylight patrols and observation posts were designated for those who would keep watch at night when it would be too dangerous to patrol the dark streets. As an added precaution, the Council members and Liah's family would use the secret tunnels under Chinatown to get from one place to another.

They hoisted the red flag over the temple the following day and also rang the temple bell. It took only a half-hour for the streets of Chinatown to empty. Doors and windows were bolted and barred, shutters were secured, and while most businesses remained open, they, too, were prepared to barricade their doors at an moment's notice.

Behind the boarded-up and locked doors of Number Three, Cook was busily preparing bags of sandwiches and fruit and thermoses of hot coffee. Liah watched, huddled in her upholstered chair. Clearly worried but unable to do anything constructive herself, she reminded Cook to make a larger lunch for Third Son who was always hungry. She then complained that the war would mean they would have to cancel their Thanksgiving feast. Cook gazed at Liah for a moment and responded, "I know you feel frustrated Liah, but you must try to stop nagging and complaining. As for Thanksgiving, I will prepare our usual turkey and ham dinner with succotash and sweet potatoes. In fact, I have ordered several dozen extra wings, drumsticks, and gizzards because there are never enough to go around."

—

Although Lee Sam's men were frequently seen around Chinatown over the next few days, they initiated no overt attacks. It seemed as if they might be acquainting themselves with the area. One night Thomas was having a late supper before going on watch when he noticed how haggard Cook appeared. It suddenly occurred to him that over the years Cook had done so much for the family and taken such good care of their Mother and yet none of them had ever really expressed much gratitude towards him. While he thought he ought to say something, no words came to mind and he merely finished his supper and started to make his way to the trap door to the tunnel in the basement.

He was halfway down the corridor when he stopped, turned to face Cook, and told him, "Sir, before I go I want you to know that my brothers and sisters and I truly appreciate all the things you have done for us over the years and we are especially grateful for the way you have cared for our Mother. While we may not have thanked you in so many words, please do not think we are unmindful of your actions. In many ways, we have come to look upon you as we would a father." With that, Thomas lifted the trap door and disappeared into the basement.

Cook stared at the trap door long after Thomas had closed it from below. Despite his weariness, Cook felt re-energized. Eldest Son, who had clearly started assuming the position of Head of the Family in this time of crisis, had for the first time acknowledged that Cook was part of the family.

—

At two in the morning, Thomas and Mert were up on Selah's roof garden keeping watch over Peacock Alley. Mert peered over the high parapet shrouded by tall shrubberies and thought for a second that he'd seen movement down at the far end of Peacock Alley near the cluster of trash cans. He whispered to his brother, "Thomas, look at the area around the trash cans. I thought I saw something move?"

Thomas stared into the gloom for a few moments then suddenly saw a furtive movement. Something or someone seemed to be slowly edging their way toward the front of Number Three. Soon the glow from the gas lamp on the street cast two man shaped shadows on the cobblestones. Suddenly Thomas gasped as a match flared in the darkness and he saw what one of the men was holding. Taking careful aim, Thomas squeezed off a shot at the man holding the match. He was rewarded as the man staggered and fell, the match going out when it hit the ground.

Thomas told Mert to keep his rifle trained on the spot where the two men had been and rapidly made his way back to Number Three, telling Selah over his shoulder what had just happened. As he cautiously approached the front of the house revolver in one hand and flashlight in the other, he carefully looked around for the two men but saw no one. He waved at Mert and bent over to pick up the object he had seen when the one man had lit his wooden matchstick—three sticks of dynamite!

Fortunately, Liah had been in a deep Apinyin induced sleep and the gunfire had not wakened her. Cook, however, was awake and Thomas quickly filled him in. Afterward, Thomas traversed the underground tunnel beneath Marchesson Street coming up in the storage room of the herbalist's shop on Dragon's Den Alley. Another tunnel took him to the back room of the House of Kwan on Lion's Den Alley, where he made his way up to the roof and used a series of ladders connecting one building to another until he finally reached the roof of Man Fook Low Restaurant facing Alameda South. His cousin, Lee Wing and Shelley were so intent watching the street below that they didn't hear Thomas approach and were startled when Thomas announced himself. He quickly told them about the attempted dynamiting and asked if they had seen any of Lee Sam's gang. They shook their heads and Thomas then went about visiting all the other look out posts and warning them to stay sharp. However, nothing further happened that night.

—

Hans and Little John were patrolling Chinatown the following day and Hans took note of the relatively few people on the streets. He also noticed that most of the houses had their doors closed and their windows shuttered. Even the businesses, which usually were bustling with customers, were sparsely populated. Hans told Little John, "It's really quiet around here, too quiet. The last time I saw a Chinatown this quiet was in San Francisco when the Chinks had themselves a Tong war." Little

John replied, "Wouldn't we have heard something if there were a Tong war going on?" Hans shrugged and said, "Not necessarily. The Chinks don't like us butting into their affairs and won't tell us anything. They won't, but maybe Selah will, if we can convince her that they're better off with us knowing than not knowing. At least we won't blunder around like a bunch of ignoramuses and make things worse."

After Selah had reluctantly confirmed the Tong war but wouldn't reveal what it was about, Hans told Little John, "Well, now we know. The question is, what do we do now that we know. Until we come up with something, we should probably step up our patrols. I don't think they'll pull anything as long as we're around."

—

It was Thomas's habit to park his truck at the entrance to Peacock Alley when he returned from work each day. It was no different one Saturday morning a few days after the dynamite incident. Shelly was riding shot-gun as Thomas drove the truck up to the cobblestone entrance and turned off the ignition. Suddenly a volley of gunfire shattered the front windshield. Miraculously unhurt except for a few cuts from the flying glass, Thomas and Shelley both dove for the floor of the cab. Revolvers in hand, the two brothers cautiously peeked over the glass-strewn dash-board a few seconds later to see if the gunmen were coming to finish the job. However, there was no one around. Soon Cook, Selah, Profes-sor, and others had gathered around and worriedly asked if they were all right. Assuring them that they were, Thomas recommended that they all return to their homes.

Liah was livid when she heard what happened and swore to kill Lee Sam and all his gang members herself. Thomas smiled and said, "Mah, calm down. You don't even know how to shoot a gun, let alone kill someone. It was Shelly and me they were after and we'll take care of it." Both Liah and Cook got worried looks on their faces and told the pair not to take foolish chances. Thomas responded, "Don't worry about us. We know how to take care of ourselves."

—

A few nights later, Theo, Thomas, and Shelly were on watch on the roof of the Man Fook Low restaurant when they saw four of Lee Sam's men walking down Alameda South toward Macy Street. As they approached Jui Jinn's café, Professor happened to walk out the door. Immediately, one of the four men reached into his pocket and drew out a gun. Without hesitating, Thomas and Shelly both fired their rifles and two of the four men went down. Theo fired but missed and the two remaining gang members took off running.

Hans and Little John had been patrolling a few blocks away when they heard the sound of the shots. Turning on their patrol car siren and flashing lights, the two policemen rushed to the scene. When they arrived, they found a crowd surrounding two men lying on the ground bleeding from bullet wounds. Hans tried speaking to the pair but neither seemed to understand English. After trying to question the people in the crowd, Little John told Hans sarcastically, "As expected, no one saw or heard anything. They just happened to find these two lying on the ground."

—

The following day, Thomas and Shelly decided that enough was enough. So far they had been on the defensive, reacting to whatever Lee Sam's gang initiated. It was time to go on offense. The question was how to do it. They were having a drink at Selah's discussing the situation when Selah mentioned that Hans was anxious for the war to end but didn't want to make the situation worse by flooding Chinatown with police. He knew that would just make everyone mad and the violence would continue just as soon as they left. Suddenly Thomas knew exactly what they should do. It would be risky but it might end things at least for a while.

—

At seven o'clock on Monday morning, two Mexicans wearing serapes and floppy sombreros entered the front door of the Lotus Garden Hotel. One was toting a huge lug of vegetables, the other an oversized basket of fruit. The two peddlers looked around the foyer, then walked up to the clerk and asked if he'd like to buy their produce.

The manager, Sam Lui, was standing beside the clerk and did a double take, recognizing Liah's two oldest sons after a moment or two. Thomas whispered to Sam, "Quick, give us the master key and their room numbers." After Sam complied, one of Lee Sam's men who had been in the adjoining parlor walked into the lobby. Thinking quickly, Sam Lui quickly opened the till, grabbed three dollar bills, and stuck them into Shelly's hand. "Takee fruit to kitchen, OK?" As Shelley walked past, Lee Sam's man insolently stuck his hand in the basket and snagged an orange.

Once in the kitchen, Thomas and Shelly ditched the produce and told the old cook to keep quiet. They ducked inside the bathroom and pressed a button located behind the water closet. A panel swung open, revealing a hidden staircase. Closing the panel after them, Liah's two sons silently made their way up the staircase coming out inside the musty linen closet on the second floor.

Slowly opening the closet door a crack, Thomas peered into the corridor. Seeing no one, the brothers pulled out their revolvers and proceeded to the first of the rooms occupied by Lee Sam's men. Fortunately the lock was well oiled and they were able to enter the room quickly and quietly. Four men were asleep on the two double beds. Thomas and Shelly quickly and efficiently knocked them out and then tied and gagged them with the bed sheets. Afterwards they searched the room and found a number of rifles and handguns, which they left out in plain sight. Kwan Koong protected them as they entered two more rooms and incapacitated seven more gang members.

When they returned to the kitchen via the hidden staircase, they asked the old cook how many of Lee Sam's men were in the parlor. He told them that there were four and that they were having breakfast. Taking a deep breath, Thomas and Shelly rushed into the parlor and caught the remaining four men by total surprise. After relieving them of their weapons, they marched those four upstairs and trussed them up like their brethren. They then told Sam Lui to call the police and report a disturbance in the hotel.

—

A little while later, Hans and Little John parked their patrol car in front of the Lotus Garden Hotel. Seeing no one hanging around outside, the two officers entered the lobby and found Sam Lui behind the desk. Quickly Sam told them in broken English that it sounded as if some of his guests had been fighting in their rooms upstairs.

Drawing their weapons, Hans and Little John cautiously climbed the stairs to the second floor and listened for a moment. Hearing nothing, they proceeded to the first of three partially open doors. Quickly ducking their heads into the first room, they were astounded to find four men lying on the floor tied up and gagged with an assortment of weapons around them. The scene was repeated twice more after which Hans and Little John holstered their guns and called for a police van to haul the prisoners in.

As the van pulled away, Little John turned to Hans and said, "I don't know who served these guys up on a platter for us, but I'm not looking a gift horse in the mouth. Do you think this will end the war?" Hans thought for a moment and then replied, "I don't think so. The Chinks hold grudges and I'm guessing they'll just send in a bunch more just like these guys until someone finally surrenders."

INTERVENTION

The escalating hostilities finally persuaded the Six Companies Association to take action. Liah received a telephone call from the Six Companies headquarters on the third of December informing her that Elder Lew Yet Hai would arrive in Loo Sahng in two days to confer with the Council. Liah replaced the phone in its cradle and then called Professor and Elder Lee Ti to tell them the news.

On the afternoon of the fifth, Elder Lew Yet Hai arrived by taxi. The old man had taken note of the deserted streets as they drove through Chinatown. As he stepped out of the taxi in front of Number Three, the Elder took in a deep breath of the fragrant air, surveyed the lush foliage, and nodded to himself that his source had been correct about Peacock Alley.

Cook, alerted by the sound of the taxi, was standing at the door to escort the old man inside. Liah greeted him, bowing low to show respect, then motioning for him to be seated in her upholstered chair.

Cook then brought out a pot of tea and a plate of meat buns. Although Liah tried to engage the Elder in conversation about the situation, the Elder demurred and requested that any discussion be postponed until he had sufficient time to rest and gather his thoughts. However, the Elder did pass on Elder Lee Ting's greetings. Liah breathed a sigh of relief as she heard that Elder Lee Ting was still alive and well. Elder Lew Yet Hai then said to her, "Elder Ting has told me that the unification of Loo Sahng Chinatown was largely your doing and that you have made provisions for the sick, aged and needy. He also said you were instrumental in establishing the Chinese school here as well as the temple. If so, you are to be commended." Liah bowed at the old man's praise.

—

Elder Lew Yet Hai and Liah were sipping tea in the Council room around five thirty when the Council members started arriving. Once everyone was present, Elder Yet Hai told them that he had been instructed by the leaders of the Six Companies Association to ascertain all pertinent facts concerning the murder of Lee Tzo as well as the recent hostilities.

For the next two hours, Elder Yet Hai extensively questioned everyone connected with the case. Both Liah and Professor began to feel concerned as the Elder listened impassively to the many witnesses. Finally Liah sensed that the Elder was tiring and suggested that they postpone any further testimony until after supper.

Supper that evening was attended not only by the members of the Council and Elder Lew Yet Hai but also by all of Liah's children as well. The Elder nodded his approval upon noticing that all conversation was conducted in Chinese, chopsticks were used instead of forks and spoons, and the family seemed to genuinely respect their elders. Elder Yet Hai commended Liah for instilling traditional Chinese values in her offspring.

When supper was finished, Thomas and his siblings rose to leave. Thomas bowed to Elder Lew Yet Hai and said, "Sir, inasmuch as my brothers and I all work at night and, owing to the current hostilities, we also patrol Chinatown, we must excuse ourselves and get some sleep. We sincerely hope your mission to our town provides you with the information you need to help end this senseless fighting." As Number One Son was speaking, Liah could not help but feel proud of her eldest.

The questioning of witnesses resumed soon after and continued for almost three more hours. Finally the last witness was called. As usual,

Selah made quite an impression on the Elder, who could not hide his surprise at her appearance as well as her flawless command of the Chinese language.

When Selah had finished, Liah turned to Elder Lew Yet Hai and said, "Sir, I hope that after hearing the facts tonight, you will understand that we in Loo Sahng have done nothing wrong. Lee Tzo was tried under our Tenet of Laws, found guilty, and sentenced to death, even though many of us were loathe to do so. The allegation that we then murdered Tzo makes no sense. As Wong Cheung has testified, it is more likely that Lee Sam and his group of Dai Faw dissidents had Tzo killed for failing in his mission and is using his death as an excuse to extort monies from us."

A shocked silence engulfed the room after Liah had finished. While they had certainly expected her to defend the Council's actions and deny the allegation that they had murdered Tzo, they did not expect her to directly implicate the Dai Faw House of Lee in the crime. Since they had no proof, it would be impossible to prove. Wong Cheung was the only person in the room who seemed unaffected. His only reaction was to give Liah a half-smile as if to commend her for her courage.

—

Cook had been pacing nervously down in the kitchen as the session had dragged on and was contemplating going upstairs to see if they wanted food and drink brought in when the Council Room door opened and Elder Lew Yet Hai descended the stairs. Seeing Cook, the Elder said, "Sir, you are to be complimented for the wonderful meal you prepared tonight. I believe you would be a welcome addition to the staff of any of the best restaurants in Dai Faw." Cook acknowledged the compliment and bowed low.

After Elder Lew Yet Hai had retired, Professor and Liah shared the outcome with Cook. Liah recounted that Elder Lew Yet Hai had only promised that he would gather the facts from all parties as quickly as he could and would then present them to the Elders of the Six Companies Association. However, he did say that he would recommend a truce be imposed until the matter could be resolved. Cook shook his head and replied, "It is disappointing that he did not give any indication that he agreed with our position."

Professor nodded but said, "Perhaps when Tom takes the Elder to the Fahn Gwai jail tomorrow to interrogate the hatchet men that Thomas and Shelly captured, he will learn something that will support our case."

The next day, Tom escorted Elder Lew Yet Hai to the City Jail where he was met by Hans. After Tom explained that The Elder wanted to question the prisoners, Hans arranged for the Elder to meet alone with each of the prisoners individually. While he waited, Tom asked Hans for photographs of the prisoners that Elder Lew Yet Hai could take back to Dai Faw with him for identification purposes. Hans agreed saying, "Sure, anything to help bring an end to this mess."

—

The following day, as Elder Lew Yet Hai prepared to return to Dai Faw, he met with Professor and Liah. "Although I do not possess the power to decide who is in the right in this matter, I will inform the Elders of the Six Companies Association that I do not believe that Loo Sahng is to blame and that you did not instigate the violence. I learned much from the men I questioned yesterday. As I told you before, I will also recommend that a truce be imposed until the Six Companies Association resolves the matter."

After the Elder departed, Liah smiled for the first time since the war had begun. "I feel like a great weight has been lifted off my shoulders," she declared. Both Cook and Professor nodded, but Professor cautioned, "Although this may be the beginning of the end, I believe we will all remain in danger until the Six Companies Association manages to officially end the war and Lee Sam and his gang are dealt with. We should not let our guard down just yet."

—

Five days later Liah received word from Elder Lew Yet Hai that the Six Companies Association had determined that the Loo Sahng Tong was blameless and that the leaders of the Dai Faw Tong had acted recklessly. As a consequence, the deposed Elders of the Dai Faw House of Lee had been returned to power. Lee Sam and his two lieutenants, however, had managed to escape before they could be brought before the Elders of the Six Companies Association.

When the Council was told that the war was over, everyone was overjoyed. However, the news that Lee Sam and his men were still at large cast a pall over the group. "Does this mean we can't go about our business like normal yet?" asked Kam Fong. "Do we still have to patrol the town?" chimed in Lim Tao. Liah told them, "I for one shall not let Lee Sam intimidate me. The Six Companies Association has issued a notice to all the Chinese communities in Gem San that Lee Sam and his men are to be apprehended and returned to Dai Faw to face justice. I think he will be too busy running and hiding to try seeking revenge on us."

—

Over the course of the following week, life returned to normal in Chinatown. People appeared on the streets, merchants again put their wares on display outside of their stores, and children once again ran around and played. This all came to an abrupt halt when another body was discovered in Dead Man's Alley. Hans asked Tom to look at the dead man in case he recognized him, but it was no one Tom knew. Hearing that, Hans fixed Tom with a hard stare and spat out, "This damn war isn't starting up again is it, Tom?" Tom shook his head and replied, "Not as far as I know. Give me a picture of this guy and I'll see if anyone in Chinatown recognizes him."

When Liah heard the news, she was devastated. The weight of the world that had just been lifted from her came crashing back down and she felt as if she would buckle under the load. Cook tried to console her but to no avail. Just then, however, Professor entered Number Three accompanied by a slender youth, who was clearly emotionally distraught.

Professor wasted no time and said, "This is Lee Nom Quai. The dead man whose body was found near Dead Man's Alley was his older brother. They were both members of Lee Sam's gang and they were sent here along with a few others to exact revenge on you and the Council. He and his brother did not want to follow Lee Sam's orders since he was no longer the legitimate head of the Dai Faw House of Lee. They were on their way to warn you when the other gang members ambushed them. Nom Quai managed to escape but his brother did not. He has told me the names of the other gang members in Loo Sahng and, more importantly, he has told me where Lee Sam is. We must tell Elder Lew Yet Hai immediately!"

—

As Liah watched, Cook put the marinated beef into a heated wok and stir-fried it until the beef was pink. Then he transferred it into a bowl. He added more peanut oil into the wok, sprinkled in minced garlic and ginger, then poured sliced onions, bamboo shoots, black mushrooms and sea urchin into the bubbling, spicy oil. Quickly mixing the ingredients, Cook added the beef back in plus a bit of soup stock and then clamped the cover on the wok to let the ingredients cook. After a few minutes, he removed the lid and poured in a mixture of cornstarch and water, which served to thicken the dish. As he poured the steaming mixture into a serving dish, Cook said, "That's the last one. Now we can eat."

Cook carried the dish into the front room and placed it on the table while the family, Professor, Selah, and Tom made comments about how wonderful everything smelled. Everyone was trying to be cheerful for Christmas dinner but the specter of Lee Sam and his remaining gang members had them all looking over their shoulders and jumping at the slightest noise. While they all enjoyed the feast, once dinner was over and the dishes were cleaned, they all retired early.

Once again their traditional New Year's Eve party was cancelled. No one wanted to take the chance that Lee Sam might try to use the occasion to inflict mass casualties.

1924

Year of the Rat

On the afternoon of the fifth of January, the telephone rang in Number Three and Cook answered it, listened for a few moments, and then gave the handset to Liah, telling her that it was Elder Lew Yet Hai. With some trepidation Liah took the phone and listened intently for several minutes after which Cook heard her end the call by saying, "Doh jeh, Lao Bak, doh jeh." (Thank you, Elder, thank you) Liah then smiled at Cook and said, "Elder Lew Yet Hai just told me that justice has been served. Yesterday the Fahn Gwai police found the bodies of Lee Sam along with his two lieutenants in Bakafeh (Bakersfield). Moreover, the gang members who murdered Lee Nom Quai's brother have been apprehended by the Six Companies Association and will be tried in Dai Faw. It's over!"

The rest of the year was anticlimactic compared to the one they had just lived through. Life returned to normal and once again people focused on making a living and bettering the lives of their children if not their own. For Liah it was no different. She took care of Aileen, attempted without success to get her unmarried sons to find suitable Chinese brides, and continued to try to improve conditions in Chinatown.

1925

YEAR OF THE OX

L ate in October of 1925, Liah awoke with tears in her eyes. Her Fourth Son, William, would be leaving soon to attend university in China. Although she knew that he was a grown man, now twenty-five, she could not help but think of him as the child he once was. She arose and went into the kitchen to seek comfort and solace from Cook.

At a quarter to seven that night, Professor, the Council members, and Madam Quock, without Yook Lan in tow, arrived at Number Three for William's farewell dinner. Next came Selah followed shortly thereafter by Toh, First Daughter, and their family. Having had to work late, Thomas and Shelly arrived after dinner had started.

When the time arrived for the giving of gifts, Selah immediately noticed Liah's brimming eyes and sat beside her, tightly holding her hand. Aileen sensed her grandma's sorrow and felt sad herself until the excitement of opening presents caused her to forget that she was sad. She tried to guess what each gift was before William opened it. Feeling Professor's gift, Aileen declared that it was a book. "You are correct, Aileen," said William smiling. "It is a bilingual dictionary." William bowed and thanked the scholar.

Kam Fong grinned as Aileen guessed that his gift was some kind of coat. "You're right again, Aileen. It's a raincoat. William will need one since it rains quite frequently in the part of China that he'll be living in."

Selah's gift was a compact leather case containing an assortment of toiletries, while each of the Council members gave William the traditional small red packet containing various sums of money. Suddenly there was a thud as something heavy hit the floor in the front room and a few moments later, Thomas and Shelly hefted a large steamer trunk into the kitchen, saying, "Now you've got something to carry all your stuff in."

When finally all the presents had been opened, Selah called for everyone's glasses to be re-filled. Professor then offered up a toast, "You, Fourth Son, have lifted our spirits and given us hope for the future. Your success sets an example for our youth, that they too can achieve their goals and be accorded their rightful place in this world. We extend to you our best wishes for continued success and good health. May Kwan Koong guide your footsteps."

At eleven o'clock, after ice cream and cake, Toh took his family home and soon afterwards the other guests departed. As Liah listened to the final farewells, her eyes started to fill with tears and she struggled to keep from weeping opening. Only Selah's firm grip on her arm gave her the strength to maintain her composure.

—

After the rest of the family was asleep, Liah finally said farewell to Fourth Son herself. Mother and son, caught up in their own emotions, sat quietly together at the kitchen table. At last, Liah broke the silence and in a choked up voice suggested that it might be good if Fourth Son visited his father while in China. William fell to his knees and buried his head in his mother's lap. "Mah-Mah, I don't wish for you to be so sad. If you want, I won't go. I can continue my studies here."

Liah's heart ached. As much as she wanted Fourth Son to stay by her side, she knew his sojourn to Hong Kong would be good for him. She lifted Fourth Son's head from her lap and kissed the top of his head. Wiping the tears from her eyes, she told William to do the same. She then reached inside her tunic and withdrew a small jewelry box and extended it to her son. William heaved a sigh, accepted the box, and took his seat again. He held the box in his hands, but made no immediate effort to open it, looking quizzically at his Mother. Liah smiled wanly and said, "I have kept this for you for many years waiting for the right time to give it to you. I think that now is that time."

William undid the ribbons, opened the lid, and his eyes filled with tears again. Inside the box lay the deep green jade ring which he had admired since he was a child.

Liah gently lifted William's face and said, "If your eyes are filled with tears, Fourth Son, how will you be able to see where Kwan Koong leads you? She then removed the ring from the box and placed it on the third finger of his right hand. "You are now a man, my son. Wear this ring with pride and may you find happiness and contentment." With a mischievous little smile Liah continued, "Hopefully when you return, you will bring me a new daughter-in-law."

William grinned and quipped back, "Even at a time like this, you're still looking to get us married off!"

1927

YEAR OF THE RABBIT

The year of 1926 flew by and before anyone knew it, Thanksgiving had snuck up on them once again, followed inevitably by Christmas and New Year's Eve. Unlike the year of the Tong War, all three occasions were celebrated by Liah's family in their traditional fashion culminating in a grand feast served up by Cook. Although Liah enjoyed each holiday and the chance to have her family and friends around, Liah eagerly looked forward to the coming of Chinese New Year, which would be the Year of the Rabbit. The celebration this year would be special since for the first time the Council had decided to publicize the event and even encourage the Fahn Gwai to attend.

Tom applied for and received a permit from City Hall that allowed them to close the three main streets in Chinatown so that the parade including the lion dance, the gymnastic performances, and the children's dances could be held without having to deal with traffic problems. In anticipation of Fahn Gwai visitors, several large platforms and tiers of benches were erected along the parade route. As part of the cultural festivities, Selah had agreed to put on a fashion show for the Fahn Gwai ladies, displaying not only the latest cheongsams, mandarin jackets and exquisite slipper-wear, but, through the generosity of the Chinese Casting Company, historical dynasty costumes as well. As preparations proceeded, Liah anxiously scanned the skies, praying to Kwan Yin that rain would not spoil the weeklong celebration.

On the morning of the day the celebration was to begin, Liah stepped outside the cobblestone arbor and scanned the sky. Although it was overcast, the air did not feel like it was going to rain and Liah prayed silently to Kwan Yin that if it had to rain, it would do so late at night.

The colorful lanterns strung along the length of the parade route were nostalgic. At home, the entire village would have been swept clean and the houses, stores, temples and public buildings would all have a fresh coat of paint. In addition to the lanterns, a profusion of potted shrubs and flowers would have transformed the village into a heavenly garden. Laughter, smiles and anticipation would be filling the air, just as it was in Loo Sahng Chinatown seven thousand miles away. At eleven o'clock the sun began to peek through the clouds and Liah breathed a sigh of relief.

Throughout Chinatown the thin trickle of Fahn Gwai, who had been arriving all morning, became a river. Impatient adults fought for seats in the bleachers and the streets were crowded with people searching for a good vantage point from which to observe the lion dance at noon. Liah was in the temple giving thanks to the Gods when she heard the roll of the drums and knew that the lion troupe would soon perform. She hurried through the secret tunnel back to Number Three. Once the lion had finished its stage performance and the gymnasts, who had accompanied the lion down the parade route displaying feats of strength and agility, finished their routines, Number Three would be the Lion's first stop. She wanted to make certain the long, thick rope of monies she had secured to a pole outside her door were secure.

Before the Lion appeared, Professor entered Number Three slightly out of breath as he had hurried to avoid getting caught in the crowd, which would soon be making its way to Liah's house. "I very much enjoy the sounds of our New Year's celebration, Liah. However, more so at a distance than up close. Up close, the firecrackers and screams of the happy children are deafening. Even now the streets are beginning to take on a red hue from all the exploded firecrackers. I'll bet by this evening, the streets will be completely covered in red."

Liah nodded happily. "I think of all the lovely aspects of New Year's, the aroma of flowers, food and fruits mixed with the slightly acrid scent of gunpowder is the most pleasant. Even the outdoor people have decorated their area with huge pots and barrels of Chinese lilies, hyacinth and Taro blooms." A sudden thought occurred to Liah and she said, "I hope the influx of Fahn Gwai won't cause us trouble."

Professor replied, "Tom and I have men patrolling the streets, especially the out-of-the way areas, making certain that the Fahn Gwai do not wander where they should not go. Perhaps next year we can hire special uniformed men to patrol our town during the celebrations so that our people can all celebrate."

Cook, who had just brought in a serving platter laden with food, chimed in, "I know the store owners are pleased. Their business establishments are jammed with curious Fahn Gwai buying souvenirs and what is to them exotic foodstuffs, especially lychee nuts and candied ginger and melon. I'm guessing those merchants wouldn't mind paying a small fee to help defray the expense of the protection."

Liah's front-room table was laden with all kinds of hot pastries, fried rice, chicken, spiced ribs, roast duck, stuffed black mushrooms and meat buns filled with chicken or pork and delicately seasoned with spices, green onions, cilantro and slivers of black mushrooms.

Liah looked around approvingly and smiled at Cook, "Now we are ready to greet our friends and family and share with them the bounty the Gods have given us. I hope we have enough food, for today many will come to pay their respects." Cook gave Liah a slightly peeved look and replied, "Liah, when have I ever not made enough food?" Embarrassed by Cook's light rebuke, Liah nodded and issued an apology.

Just then Thomas entered carrying a large box and began to pull out a number of bottles of Ng Ga Pei, bourbon and scotch telling Liah, "I'll set out a bucket of ice for those who want it, Mah. I've also got two cases of beer and, for the kids, three cases of soda. Is there anything else you want me to do? I want to go out and do some celebrating myself."

Liah shook her head. "Just be sure all you children are here at seven o'clock sharp for our banquet each night. Other than that, you can do whatever you want."

—

The eight days of celebration were officially closed with a special program of Chinese music, Chinese opera and an extra lion dance at nine o'clock at night. A last long fusillade of exploding firecrackers rent the air and the Year of the Rabbit had been properly ushered in.

Afterward, the Council members, Liah's family, and friends took seats around two dinner tables in the front room of Number Three for one of Cook's ten course banquets. During the meal, Professor commented, "I don't know about anyone else, but I was delighted at the behavior of the Fahn Gwai. Except for a few rowdy youths and drunks, the Fahn Gwai seemed to respect our customs and our privacy. In fact, several of the residents were delighted because the Fahn Gwai gave them money to pose for pictures."

Chon Woo, whose Dragon's Den Bar had done record business, crowed, "Yes, this was an outstanding event, one that we should repeat again next year. Every merchant I spoke to said that their business tripled and that they are anxious for another public celebration." Liah smiled to herself as various Council members congratulated one another on their wisdom and foresight. They had obviously forgotten that it had been Liah who had initially proposed the idea. However, she kept her silence and let them share the glory.

—

On the twenty-ninth of September, the family gathered to celebrate Liah's birthday. Earlier that morning, Liah had lain in bed, aghast that she was fifty-six years old. However, what troubled her was not that she was old, for in the Chinese culture with increased age came increased respect. Rather it was Liah's fear that she would not live long enough to see her granddaughter, Aileen, grow up. She had quickly gotten up, walked over to her private altar where she lit an incense coil, kowtowed three times on bended knees, and murmured her plea for sufficient time to help Aileen mature into a confident and successful woman.

That night Liah was about to open her presents when she saw Aileen's pensive face and recognized that Aileen was probably still sad that her friend Willie, now a college student, had returned to the university a few weeks ago. To get her mind off Willie, Liah asked Aileen to help her with the presents. A sparkle came into Aileen's eyes and she immediately made her way to Liah and sat down beside her. "I'll give you the presents and tell you who they're from, OK, Grandma?" Liah smiled and nodded, saying, "You can even help me unwrap some of them."

Aileen stared at the many brilliantly wrapped boxes wondering where to start. There were large ones, small ones, round ones, oval ones, and square ones. Just then Selah caught her eye and Aileen smiled. "Let's start with Auntie Selah's present."

Liah smiled and reached for a large, long box with gold and red ribbons tied into the biggest bow Aileen had ever seen. Not wanting to cut the decorative strands, Aileen set to work trying to remove the ribbons without damaging them. Cook watched from the sidelines, ready to step forward and help, but in a few minutes Aileen held up the ribbons with the bow intact. "Isn't this beautiful, Grandma?" Liah nodded and replied, "Very. However, what about the present?" Aileen smiled and somewhat sheepishly responded, "Oh yeah!"

Aileen took the cover of the box off and broke the seal on the tissue paper nestled inside. Liah then lifted out a gorgeous green and gold cheongsam, the sight of which made everyone ooh and aah. "This is almost too beautiful to wear, Selah. I thank you!" At the bottom of the box was a smaller package also wrapped in tissue, which turned out to be a pair of matching gold slippers. "I think I will look like an empress when I wear this outfit."

Aileen next handed her a flat square box wrapped in red paper and gold ribbons. With a serious face, Aileen told Liah, "You'll have to open this one yourself, Grandma. It's from Willie and me." Liah reached out and drew her granddaughter close, "We shall open this special present together, how's that?"

Liah gently undid the ribbons, handing them to Aileen, and then opened the lid. "Oh, child, these silk pajamas are lovely. This was very thoughtful of you and Willie. I must thank him when he returns for Christmas." Liah then kissed Aileen and gently wiped away the girl's tears, which had formed when Willie's name came up. "Now, shall we see what other gifts there are?"

There was a lovely porcelain teapot and cups from Madam Quock and a box of lychee nuts and tea from Sen Fei. The Council presented her with a translucent jade pendant on an eighteen-karat gold chain. Amah, Cook and her children had gone in together and gave her a huge pearl ring set in gold, surrounded by eight perfectly matched diamonds. Thomas was quick to say that Cook had paid for the lion's share of the cost. Liah gazed a moment at Cook and her eyes expressed her heartfelt gratitude. Slightly flustered, Cook muttered that Thomas's remark was unnecessary. However, Thomas grinned and replied, "Cook, you always throw in the most money for whatever gifts we buy for Mah. It's about time you got some recognition."

—

A week after her birthday, Liah received a letter from Fourth Son and as usual she asked Professor to read it to her. Liah was pleased to hear about the progress Fourth Son was making when Professor suddenly stopped short. Liah stared at Professor and asked with a note of concern in her voice, "What is the matter, sir? Is something wrong?"

Professor shook his head and smiled broadly. "I've got surprising news, but good news. It seems Fourth Son has taken himself a wife!"

Liah's mouth flew open and for several moments she was speechless. When she had recovered enough to speak she said, "How can this be, sir? We haven't had so much as a word from Sen. Surely he would have consulted me before allowing Fourth Son to marry someone." A moment later, she continued in a louder voice, "I'll bet this is Sen's way of finally getting revenge on me. I'll bet the girl is totally unsuitable!"

As Liah's outrage started to mount, Cook was quick to cut Liah off. "There is no pleasing you, Liah. First, you lament and carry on because your sons will not wed and now that one of them has, you still carry on. I don't believe Fourth Son would marry a girl beneath him, so I suggest you let Professor finish reading the letter. Then we can discuss the matter." Surprised at Cook's outburst, Liah halted her tirade before it even got going and quietly asked Professor to continue.

Professor nodded his silent thanks to Cook, readjusted his spectacles, and read on:

Mother, you will no doubt be angry about not having a chance to speak your mind before I got married, but both Father and I believe I am doing the right thing. In his defense, he did suggest I write to you, but there was no time. If Mei Gem is to return with me when my studies are completed, we needed to marry right away so that the authorities would have time to process the paperwork. I hope you understand.

Of my wife, Mei Gem is next to the youngest in a family of seven children, four sons and three daughters. We met at a college dinner. Mei Gem's father is an exporter in Hong Kong and Mei Gem's family has already made me feel like a part of their family. I believe I am truly blessed by Kwan Yin to now have two such wonderful families.

Mei Gem is a sweet, quiet girl and very intelligent. Mah-Mah, I'm certain you will both love each other. I will send more details soon.
    Yours dutifully,
    Fourth Son

Liah seemed to have calmed down considerably when Professor finished the letter. "Mei Gem," she murmured, "Beautiful Gold. If she lives up to her name, she ought to be very lovely indeed. Moreover, if she is as intelligent as Fourth Son says, their children should be both beautiful and intelligent."

Cook shook his head and remarked to Professor, "Can you believe it, sir? This is the same woman who was outraged at the marriage a moment ago and now she's dreaming about more grandchildren." Professor chuckled but ceased immediately as Liah threw a scowl in their direction. Briskly she said, "We must post the marriage banns and begin preparations for the wedding celebration upon their return. Professor, I would appreciate it if you would to see to it that the notice of marriage is published in the newspapers and that a bulletin is posted in Peacock Alley."

Professor nodded as Cook said lightheartedly, "I don't suppose the other boys will be sorry to hear of Fourth Son's marriage. They'll probably be hoping that this will get them off the hook for awhile." Professor chuckled again then quickly took his leave when Liah frowned. Cook was left alone to face Liah's displeasure.

1928

YEAR OF THE DRAGON

As 1927 ended, Liah was still finding it difficult to forgive Sen and Fourth Son for the way they had cut her out of the decision making process when Fourth Son was contemplating marriage, even though she understood the logic. She had managed to keep her frustration in check through the holidays even though she had not heard from Fourth Son since receiving the news in October. The uncertainty about when Fourth Son and his wife would be returning to the United States, however, was beginning to stretch her patience thin.

The Year of the Dragon celebration followed the successful script of the preceding year with a big parade and cultural events attended by an even larger crowd of Fahn Gwai. This year's parade featured not only the usual Lion but also a Dragon, whose long, sinuous body undulated down the parade route manned by no less than a dozen men.

By the time the ten-day celebration came to its usual thunderous close, Liah, who had again supervised and worried over every detail of the event, had reached her breaking point. It only required a tiny spark to send her into a rage fueled by all her pent up emotions. After verbally giving vent to her feelings, fortunately witnessed only by Cook and Amah, Liah became silent and unapproachable by all except for her granddaughter. However, even Aileen had to tread carefully around her.

Two weeks had gone by, though it felt more like a year to Cook and the family, when Selah dropped by one afternoon and handed Liah a letter addressed to her from City Hall. Her curiosity piqued, Liah asked Selah to read it to her. The author of the letter was the Event Coordinator for the City of Los Angeles and concerned the upcoming dedication of the new City Hall. The City was planning a parade as part of the festivities and wanted to know if Chinatown would like to enter a float.

Hearing this, it was as if a magical incantation had been uttered and broke the evil spell gripping Liah. Her eyes once again sparkled as she saw in her mind's eye a beautiful float made of exotic flowers and plants with lovely Chinese girls in dazzling cheongsams. She told Selah and Cook, "This will be a wonderful opportunity to showcase the beauty of our Chinese girls and the float making skills of our artisans. We must assemble the Council to start making plans immediately."

Selah and Cook both breathed a silent sigh of relief at Liah's transformation. Liah stared a moment at her two friends, then broke into a broad grin. "I know, I know. I have been impossible to live with these past two weeks and I apologize."

—

The Council meeting held to discuss plans for the Fahn Gwai parade was surprisingly contentious. Fortunately for the Council members, Liah's equanimity had been restored and she was able to let them talk it over without bludgeoning anyone verbally or physically. Chon Woo, among others, wholeheartedly endorsed the idea of building a float while Lim Tao and Lee Wah rejected the idea. The latter were of the opinion that the money would be better spent on projects within Chinatown.

After the two camps had debated the idea for a while, Jui Jinn respectfully asked to be heard. He explained that if they adopted his plan, both sides would get what they wanted. "I suggest we use this occasion to raise money for our charities. We could announce that the float would carry the Queen of Chinatown and her court. The girls wanting to be Queen would sell tickets to their supporters and the girl who sells the most tickets will be chosen Queen and her court will be made up of the four girls who sell the second, third, fourth and fifth highest number of tickets."

Tom immediately endorsed Jinn's idea but offered a modification, "That's a great idea Jinn. However, we should have a Queen and seven ladies in waiting. Eight is a more auspicious number."

The Council unanimously approved the idea and plans were set in motion to arrange the Queen of Chinatown contest and the designing and building of the float.

—

Excitement swept Chinatown as each Tong vied to seat one of their own on the throne. Each girl privately dreamt that a movie producer or director amongst the Fahn Gwai crowd might discover her. As a consequence, throughout the remainder of February and March each girl and her supporters canvassed and re-canvassed the population of Chinatown seeking to sell the most tickets. Family members and friends were encouraged to buy whole books of tickets rather than just a few.

Finally, on the morning of April second, Professor posted the name of the Queen on the bulletin board in Peacock Alley. Kwan Mei Gem, the seventeen-year-old daughter of Kwan had won the coveted crown, the House of Kwan having sold over three thousand tickets. There was to be a dinner that night where Professor would crown the young lady. As an additional way to raise money for the Council's charities, they had decided to charge an admission fee to attend the dinner and to sell raffle tickets for items such as a radio, a set of Chinese dishes and several grocery certificates donated by various Chinatown merchants. All told the event had raised over $1,000!

—

At four PM on the 11th of April, Professor walked into the kitchen of Number Three, his face creased in a broad smile. He then proceeded to tell Liah and Cook all about their float and the parade, "You would have been very proud of the float that our artisans created. It incorporated a Phoenix and a Dragon and the gold throne the Queen sat on was a replica of the one used by the last Empress of China. At the front of the float they built a beautiful jade gate. That's where your granddaughter, Aileen and Kwan Hsa's grandson were seated."

When Professor mentioned Aileen, Liah suddenly asked why Second Daughter and Aileen weren't with him. "If the parade is over, surely they could have returned home with you."

The scholar shook his head. "All of the girls will return home on the bus. I saw reporters talking to them and cameramen snapping pictures of them. I think some of them might even have been from the movie studios." Liah scoffed at the last, "What foolishness. Have you ever heard of a Chinese movie star?"

Just then, Theo, Mert and several of their friends barged into the kitchen. Theo told Liah that the parade of floats had stretched for over two blocks and that he had heard More than one Fahn Gwai say that the Chinatown float was the most unusual and beautiful.

Liah smiled proudly. "Ah, that is good. By the way, did Aileen appear frightened? Did she smile? Tell me, how did she look?" Theo and Mert grinned and told her that Aileen looked very pretty and that she had tossed rose petals at the crowd along the parade route.

When Thomas and Shelly came home an hour later, they brought copies of the evening Herald and the family gathered around the kitchen table to read the account of the parade and look at the pictures. Emmi squealed as she turned a page, "Look! Here's a picture of Aileen sitting on the lion, one of me standing next to the queen, another one of Aileen with her basket of flowers, and another one of me with all the other girls."

A week later, Professor came to Number Three with copies of the *Dai Faw See Bo* and the *New York China*. Both newspapers had a story about the Loo Sahng float and assorted pictures, including one of Aileen. With a satisfied look on his face, Professor declared that the event had been a proud moment for their Chinatown. Liah smiled and nodded, "A very proud moment indeed."

FOURTH SON'S RETURN

Liah's anger at Fourth Son dissolved when a special delivery airmail letter arrived on the fourth of May. Professor as usual read the letter for Liah and informed her that Fourth Son and Mei Gem would arrive in Dai Faw on the tenth of May. Liah exclaimed, "But that's next week! Why didn't he give us more notice?"

Professor responded, "They did not themselves know if the Chinese authorities would allow Mei Gem to board the ship until the last moment. They wrote this letter just before they embarked and it appears its delivery was somehow delayed. Fourth Son said they would call once they reached Dai Faw and let you know when they would arrive in Loo Sahng."

After Professor had taken his leave, Liah immediately summoned Cook and Amah and ordered, "Please ready the large guest room upstairs, the one in which my three cousins slept when they visited a little while ago."

Amah asked timidly if perhaps Fourth Son might not be planning to set up his own household to which Liah retorted indignantly, "My daughter-in-law is from the old country and knows that she must live with her husband's family." Cook was about to suggest that Fourth Son might not want to adhere to that particular Chinese custom but he wisely kept the thought to himself.

—

The morning of the tenth of May, Liah was ready to welcome Fourth Son and his bride. The house had been thoroughly cleaned and fresh food and liquor filled the cupboards as well as the cellar. Liah had also placed a bowl of red roses in the center of the table in Fourth Son's room: a welcome home gift from Selah. Thomas watched as his mother nervously arranged and re-arranged various household objects and laughed, "Calm down, Mah. Why are you so nervous? You'd think you were the bride about to meet her mother-in-law instead of the other way around."

"Yeah," echoed Theo as he leaned forward to snag a peach from the fruit bowl. Liah instantly slapped his hand, admonishing him that the fruit arrangement was for Fourth Son and his bride. "If you want fruit, go downstairs and help yourself from the pantry. These are already washed and polished." Liah then frowned and continued, "And one more thing, Third Son, do not embarrass your brother by acting like a fool. I don't want my daughter-in-law to think she married into a family of idiots."

Early that evening, William finally telephoned to say that they had arrived safely and made it through Customs and Immigration. Liah was so overcome with emotion that she could hardly speak. She managed to tell him softly, "Mother has been waiting for this day since the day you left and I am overjoyed that you have finally returned. Please talk to Eldest Son now. I must rest."

In a daze, Liah handed the receiver to Eldest Son, walked over to her upholstered chair, and sank into its depths. When Cook inquired when Fourth Son planned to arrive in Loo Sahng, Liah replied, "I didn't think to ask, but he'll probably inform Eldest Son."

After Thomas had hung up, he told his Mother, "William said they would arrive about three in the afternoon tomorrow. Shelly and I will pick them up at the train depot."

Shelley shook his head and quickly countered, "No, I think Mert should drive his car too. We can haul their luggage in the truck, but it wouldn't do for William's bride to ride in our truck."

Then Theo chimed in, "I sure hope William's wife is not so hoity-toity that she'd object to riding in a truck." Liah instantly admonished him, "I'm sure Mei Gem is a lovely girl, otherwise Fourth Son wouldn't have married her."

Thomas shook his head. "I wouldn't be too sure of that, Mah. Good men like Fourth Brother more often than not seem to end up with nagging, aggressive females. Look at Toh. Of course, William wouldn't dare bring a shrew home to meet you, right Mah?"

Everyone laughed except Liah. Cook held his breath, certain that this time Eldest Son had gone too far. However, Liah just leaned forward and affectionately cuffed her eldest son on the ear. "Speaking of brides, I have a suspicion that Second Daughter may be thinking of getting married. What do you know of her boyfriend?"

"He's a good guy, Mah," said Thomas. "He has his own truck and makes a good living off of his steady customers. Sis will marry well if she marries Hubert."

Liah nodded and replied, "I'm not usually wrong about people and this boy seems like he has a good heart. He is also wellmannered. Back in our village, the old women would say that his physical features foretell a long and healthy life."

—

Liah was up bright and early the next morning, scurrying about the house making certain everything was dusted and in its place. Cook watched her for a while then ordered her to sit down and eat breakfast.

Time seemed to stretch out for Liah as she glanced at the clock every so often only to find that just a few minutes had passed since the last time she had looked. When Aileen came home from school, Liah ordered her to wash up and change her clothes so that she would make a good first impression on Mei Gem. Once she had changed, Aileen went outside to wait for Fourth Uncle. Soon the sound of Thomas' truck and Mert's car announced the arrival of Fourth Son and his wife.

Liah walked to the door in time to see Aileen leap into her uncle's arms, kissing him and shouting "Welcome home!" William hugged her then unclasped her hands from around his neck and put her down in order to help Mei Gem out of the car. When William tried to introduce Aileen to Mei Gem, Aileen got shy all of a sudden and ran back into the house. William shook his head and said, "I see she hasn't changed one bit."

As Thomas and Shelly struggled with two large steamer trunks, William picked up two suitcases and motioned to Mei Gem to follow him. As he approached the door, he saw his mother through the screen. Dropping the bags, he threw open the door and embraced her, Mother and son clinging to each other for a long time. Liah drew back as she finally noticed Mei Gem. William smiled broadly and put his arm around Mei Gem saying, "Mother, I'd like you to meet my wife, Mei Gem. Mei Gem this is my mother." Mei Gem immediately bowed low and kept her eyes averted. Liah scrutinized her new daughter-in-law for a few moments then reached out and took Mei Gem's hands telling her, "I welcome you into our home. May your heart be as content as mine is now."

Liah took them into the kitchen and seated Mei Gem at the table. To Mei Gem she said, "Now tell me all about how you fared on your voyage to Gem Sahn and how you like Gem Sahn so far. If you are anything like myself, you're probably more than a little homesick and disoriented."

Mei Gem's eyes misted over and she hesitated a moment before nodding. "I still feel the pain of leaving my family, my home, and my country but I'm sure I will soon overcome my sorrow. I am most appreciative of your kindness and I am looking forward to learning all about Gem Sahn and my husband's family."

After supper, William handed out the gifts he had brought. Aileen clutched her package and immediately began trying to undo the strong cords. Cook handed her a pair of scissors but as usual Aileen shook her head and patiently kept attacking the knots. Meanwhile one by one William gave each of his brothers and sisters their presents. Finally, William handed Mei Gem a small package and indicated that she should give it to his Mother. Liah accepted it with a smile, took the wrapping off a rectangular jewelry case, and gasped at the delicately wrought gold spray inlaid with five seed pearls and a floweret of matched jade inside. Her thank you was drowned out by Emmi's shriek of delight over a beautiful red and gold cheongsam.

Aileen let out a squeal as she had finally untied the cords and un-wrapped a stack of books, an ink well and a set of Chinese brushes. William cautioned her, "You must be very careful with the tips of the brushes. It's very easy to damage them. If you want, I'll show you how they should be used."

"Oh, Uncle William, I already know how to use them. I go to Chinese school on Saturdays and I practice with Professor. Thank you so much." Aileen then ran over and hugged William after which she hugged Mei Gem, forgetting all about her shyness.

—

After most of the family had gone to bed, William caught up with his two oldest brothers. He told them about his time in China and about their father and his new family. They in turn told him about what had been happening in Chinatown, what was going on with the family, and how successful their trucking business was becoming. As they were saying goodnight, Thomas suddenly pulled out a folded wad of bills and shoved it into William's pocket. Clearly puzzled, William asked, "What's this for?" Thomas and Shelly smiled and said, "It's our welcome home gift to you. Welcome home brother." William, his eyes bright with tears, murmured, "Thanks guys. It's great to be home."

—

A couple of days after William's return, Liah informed him that they would be hosting a feast at a restaurant in Chinatown to celebrate their wedding. Seeing the amazed expression on William's face, Liah laughed and told him that for him she would indeed venture out of Peacock Alley. "Besides," she said, "this will give the town gossips something to talk about. They've been saying for years that my health has seriously deteriorated from too much Apinyin use. I'll show them."

While making out the invitation list, Liah asked William for the names and addresses of any relatives Mei Gem wanted to invite. At first, Mei Gem said there was no one, but Liah persisted and said that surely Mei Gem had some relatives in Gem Sahn. Mei Gem finally admitted that she did indeed have relatives but that they could not afford to make the trip to Loo Sahng. Liah then told Mei Gem, "Number one Daughter-in-Law, we are also your family now. It will give us great pleasure to bring your relatives to Loo Sahng to celebrate with us. Do not give it another thought."

Whatever barriers existed in Mei Gem's mind and heart crumbled as love for her mother-in-law surged within her, for in truth Liah would now be the only mother she would have in Gem Sahn.

—

On the twelfth of June, Chinatown was treated to the sight of Liah and her family strolling down Marchesson Gai en route to the wedding feast. Thomas had offered to drive his mother to the restaurant, but Liah had refused. "I want all of Chinatown to see me and my whole family, especially my new Daughter-in-Law. We shall walk and take pride in doing so."

Eldest Son and Second Son escorted their mother, followed by Mei Gem's first uncle, his wife and two sons from Second Town and Mei Gem's fourth uncle, his wife and their three sons and daughter from Dai Faw. Behind them came Third Son, Fourth Son, Mei Gem, Fifth Son and Second Daughter, followed by Toh and Eldest Daughter with their six children.

As they passed, many residents rushed outdoors to congratulate Liah, wishing her health and many grandsons. William grinned as Mei Gem blushed profusely. Some of the women gawked at Liah's expensive rust-colored brocaded cheongsam with embossed gold chrysanthemums, eyeing her heavy gold chain, and speculating on the value of her flawless, large jade pendant and her gold and jade bracelets.

—

When Liah entered the restaurant, the owner, Jew Soo, who was stationed at the entrance, was effusive in welcoming her, thanking her for the honor she bestowed on his humble place and offering his hearty congratulations. William didn't miss the proud expression on Mei Gem's face. He squeezed her hand to convey that he, too, was very proud of his mother.

The instant Liah stepped into the private dining room, a round of applause greeted her. As she acknowledged the welcome, her eyes roved around the tables. Sadly, she faced the fact that none of Sen's family was present. While they had all sent a money gift for the bride and groom, they had also sent excuses regarding why they couldn't attend. Liah could understand why Cousin Quock couldn't come, for fishing this time of year up in northern California was at its peak. However, the various reasons given by Sen's other relatives seemed thin at best.

Mei Gem looked out on the two hundred people seated in the dining room and shyly clung to William's arm. As they passed Cook, standing among the well-wishers along one side of the room, Thomas pulled him into the center of the family as they made their way to the head table. Cook quietly protested. After all, he said, he had not walked to the restaurant with the family because he did not want to cause Liah any embarrassment. Nevertheless, Thomas seated Cook beside his mother, much to Liah's delight. "This will give the gossips something to talk about," she whispered to Cook.

Mr. Marchesson and the Dean of Languages at William's college were the only Fahn Gwai in attendance and they were seated beside each other. The landlord wasted no time giving Dean Weston a synopsis of William's entire family history. "That little woman is a phenomenal human being. She raised all seven children pretty much by herself, making sure they minded their manners and maintained respect for their cultural heritage. I can't think of a woman for whom I have greater respect and affection."

During supper, William couldn't help noticing his mother's happiness. He thought perhaps that it was partially because Cook was finally being given public recognition as part of the family. Guiltily, he recalled his earlier youthful resentment against Cook, blaming him for the break-up of his parents' marriage. Now his father was remarried and content, so why not his mother?

During the course of the banquet, one toast after another was offered up and William and Mei Gem acknowledged each with a tiny sip of wine. However, even a small amount when repeated multiple times can amount to a lot after time. Thus when it was William's turn to speak, he was somewhat tipsy as he got to his feet. He smiled broadly at the assembled guests and spoke slowly so as not to slur his words, "I am not accustomed to drinking, so if I do not make sense at times, I humbly ask you to blame the wine. My wife, Mei Gem, and I want to thank all of you for coming to help celebrate our wedding. It is an honor, which we will never forget. I also wish to thank my mother for her continued love, support, and generosity as well as my wonderful brothers and sisters who have always stood by me. A special thank you is due Cook, who has stood beside our family, tending to our needs, and always holding our interests foremost in his heart. I thank all of them from the bottom of my heart." He then raised his glass and said, "Thank you all."

The applause was long and thunderous as Liah sat there wide-eyed and speechless. It was one thing to have Cook sit with her at the family table, but it was an entirely different thing for Fourth Son to publicly acknowledge Cook as part of the family. Cook raised his glass in William's direction as Professor led a second round of applause.

During one of the breaks between the serving of one dish and the next, Mei Gem felt Liah's touch on her arm and looked up to see Liah motioning for her to accompany her. Shyly, she took Liah's hand as they began visiting each table. William felt a pride he'd never known as his mother escorted Mei Gem around the room, introducing her daughter-in-law to all of her family and friends.

At the end of the banquet, Liah proudly announced to her guests that her third son would follow in his brother's footsteps and shortly leave on a visit to China. Glancing at Theo, Liah grinned sheepishly and said, "I pray to Kwan Yin that he too will return from his sojourn with a bride and that she is as wonderful a woman as Fourth Son has found." Mei Gem blushed as Theo elbowed his two older brothers as they whispered something racy in his ear.

Professor made the final speech of the evening and William found himself blushing as he listened to the scholar praise his intelligence, dedication to learning, and hard work, which had resulted in his numerous academic degrees and honors and set such a good example for the youth of Chinatown. However, his face got even redder when Professor lifted his glass and offered his toast, "To William and Mei Gem.

May they live long and prosper and may they produce many grandchildren for Liah to spoil."

It was almost ten o'clock in the evening when Liah walked home proudly with her family including Cook this time.

—

That night after everyone in Number Three had gone to bed, Thomas, Shelley and Theo were ensconced in Thomas and Shelly's room having a serious discussion. Theo had just told them that he had made up his mind to join the army of Chiang Kai Shek in his fight to unify China just as soon as he got to China. Thomas and Shelly both knew that Theo had never forgiven himself when his best friend had enlisted to fight in World War I but he hadn't. He had also felt badly about not doing more during the Tong war. Thomas told him, "Theo, I know you feel like you need to prove something to yourself as well as to everyone else, but it's not necessary. No one thinks you're less of a man just because you didn't fight in World War I. Hell, lots of us didn't. Think about what this will do to Mah. She'll be worried sick and you know she'd die if anything were to happen to you."

Shelly then chimed in, "You know, Theo, Thomas and I were talking the other day after we let you drive our truck and make some deliveries. We think you've got the makings of a good truck driver. Why not stay and become a partner in our business."

Although his brothers' offer was something that he had been wanting for some time, he shook his head and replied, "Thanks guys, but I've made up my mind and I'm not going to change it. This is just something that I have to do. I'd never forgive myself if I chickened out a second time. I know this will really upset Mah, but she'll get over it. Maybe you can explain things to her for me after I'm gone."

Thomas and Shelley were silent for a long time trying to think of some other way to persuade their younger brother to give up his plan, but they came up with nothing. They knew deep down that his stubborn streak wouldn't let anything change his mind. In the end they reluctantly agreed to keep Theo's plan a secret from their mother but they made him promise to write to her often once he was in China. Though they feared for his safety, both of the brothers had absorbed some of their mother's beliefs and decided that Theo's Meng Sui would in the end determine his fate.

A few weeks later, the family held a farewell supper for Third Son and, as had been the case when Fourth Son had left, the meal was a mixture of happiness and sorrow. As Thomas and Shelly watched their mother fighting to hold back her tears, they were in agony that they had failed to convince Theo to give up his plan. Liah herself was fighting the urge to cancel her son's trip. Once again the Gods seemed to be trying to tell her something, but again she couldn't fathom their message. At the end of the evening, she told Cook in a concerned voice, "I do not know why, but I have a foreboding about Third Son's trip. When I embraced him tonight, I felt as if I were doing so for the last time. I wish there were some good reason for me to make him stay here, but I can't think of one and if I arbitrarily tell him that he can't go, he will never forgive me. All I can do is pray that Kwan Koong will protect him and bring him home safely."

Theo's ship sailed the following day and perhaps because William had left the same way and had not only returned but also had brought home a wonderful daughter-in-law, Liah soon put her uneasiness aside.

—

The holidays that year were even more festive than usual because it was the first time Mei Gem had ever celebrated either Thanksgiving or Christmas. When she got her first taste of turkey she told them that while the taste was not unpleasant she had to admit that she preferred chicken. To her turkey was coarse in texture and not as sweet as chicken. Liah smiled and told Mei Gem that that was exactly what she thought the first time she had eaten turkey as well.

At Christmas, Mei Gem's face was radiant as she stared with child-like fascination at the Christmas tree with its blinking multicolored lights and at the multitude of gift-wrapped packages under the tree. However, Mei Gem was reminded of home when Thomas and Shelly lit the long strings of firecrackers in front of the house on New Year's Eve. Even here in Gem Sahn, she thought, they set off firecrackers to scare away the evil spirits.

1929

YEAR OF THE SNAKE

One early February day, William came downstairs just after noon and saw his Mother sitting in her upholstered chair staring into space. He suspected that she was worrying about Theo since they hadn't heard from him other than the letter he had sent when he had first arrived in China and visited Father. William sat down at the table, smiled, and took one of his Mother's hands in his. He then proceeded to tell her that she was soon to be a grandmother again. Liah stared at him for a second then excitedly exclaimed, "Long have I waited for this day. Kwan Yin has finally answered my prayers." Liah's happiness over the impending birth of her new grandchild occupied her attention and for a while she ceased to worry about Third Son.

—

April arrived in a profusion of blossoms, turning Peacock Alley into a heavenly garden. Mei Gem, who had been somewhat lethargic during the winter months, seemed to revive in the sunshine and each morning and evening, she and William would walk twenty lengths of Peacock Alley. Mei Gem smiled self-consciously at the passersby who stopped to extend their congratulations to William and to ask when the baby was due.

Finally, April slipped away quietly to join the legions of Aprils past and May jauntily took over the cobblestone walk. Mei Gem delighted in the look and smell of the roses and gardenias. She told William, "The aromas of these flowers are foreign to me but pleasant."

As Mei Gem's birthing time approached, Liah became restless and somewhat apprehensive. Each evening, she spent time gazing at the night sky and praying to the Gods that her grandchild would be born at an auspicious moment. One night, Cook asked curiously, "Why do you stare at the sky every night?"

Liah replied seriously, "Don't laugh. I am looking for an omen."

Cook did not laugh as he recalled the various superstitions that women in his village had just as adamantly believed in.

Finally on the seventeenth of June, Liah sensed that Mei Gem was close to giving birth and told Cook, "I will forgo my Apinyin tonight. I want to be clear headed if Mei Gem goes into labor."

As Liah had predicted, around 11:30 that night Mei Gem woke from a deep sleep and shook her husband awake. "My husband, it is time. Quick, call Mother!"

The fear and excitement in his wife's voice jolted William from his stupor and he ran barefooted down the stairs to his mother's bedroom. When William burst in, Liah knew immediately what was happening and ordered, "Fourth Son, first wake Amah then boil some water. Stay downstairs until you're called." Liah then proceeded to put on a robe and climb the stairs to attend to the birth of her grandchild.

—

Seeing that William was in no condition to perform even simple tasks like boiling water, Cook urged him to sit down and try to relax. "I'll boil the water for your mother and make some coffee for us at the same time. William looked at Cook with a hint of fear and panic in his eyes and said, "I'm scared, Cook. What if something happens to the baby? What if something happens to Mei Gem? Should I call Dr. Sung?" Cook smiled and told him, "Fourth Son, do not worry. Your Mother successfully gave birth to seven children all by herself and knows what to do. You must not panic." William retorted, "That's easy for you to say." Instantly he regretted his outburst and apologized but Cook told him to forget it. "We all say things we don't really mean when we're stressed."

By six-thirty in the morning, William and Cook were mentally exhausted. Mei Gem's periodic screams of agony had worn on them and time seemed to crawl by. Suddenly, the bedroom door opened and Amah rushed downstairs. She grabbed the pot of hot water off the stove and rushed back up ignoring the two men entirely.

A few minutes later the wail of a newborn could be heard and William and Cook looked at each other. William was a father!

Twenty minutes later, Liah emerged from the bedroom, her hair straggly and her face slightly damp. Wearing a weary smile she announced, "Son, you are the father of a healthy baby boy. You have ensured the Lee lineage will continue for another generation." Mother and son hugged, then Liah told William that he could go up and see Mei Gem and the baby but only for a little while. "Mei Gem is exhausted and needs to rest."

After William had gone upstairs, Cook made Liah sit down telling her that she too needed to rest. He then went over to the calendar and circled June 18, 1929. Liah, ignorant of what would occur later that year, smiled to herself, "This Fahn Gwai year of 1929, our Year of the Snake, is a most auspicious year indeed." She then got up, went to her altar to light a coil of incense, and offered up a prayer of gratitude to Kwan Yin.

—

Number Three became a beehive of activity as family and friends came to pay their respects and to see the newborn infant. As was the custom, everyone brought the baby a small red packet of lucky money. In turn Liah ensured that all got to share the traditional dishes of pickled pigs' feet and brandy chicken with herbs. These were thought to aid in the renewal of the mother's blood and to help her regain her strength.

Meanwhile, Professor and William conferred on a Chinese name for the baby. Although William favored naming his son, Sen, after his father, Professor pointed out that he should be sensitive to how that would make Liah feel. In the end, William decided to use Cousin Quock's name. "He is, after all, my favorite relative on my father's side. Upon hearing William's selection, Liah was delighted, for Cousin Quock was also her favorite of all Sen's relatives. Liah said the name out loud, "Lee Sui Leong. That has a good ring to it, don't you think?"

—

It was not until the infant's Red Egg and Ginger party celebrating the infant's first month of life, that Liah noticed a change in her granddaughter. When asked, Cook and Amah both agreed that the child was not her usual self and neither of them could find out why. Aileen had become incommunicative.

That night as Liah helped Aileen get ready for bed, she asked, "Is everything all right, Aileen? It seems like something is bothering you. Tell Grandma." Aileen was silent for a moment then she burst into tears. "Mah Mah told me that now that you have baby Sui Leong, you won't love me so much any more!"

In shock, Liah tightened her arms around her granddaughter, silently cursing her own stupidity. Why hadn't she been more attentive? She should have known a child of Aileen's sensitivities would feel left out. As Aileen's sobs subsided, Liah whispered, "Now, no more tears. Your mother is wrong. Do you not know you are the first-born? Do you not know that no other can take your place, not your brothers nor your sisters, not even Sui Leong? Of that you should have no doubt. Now go to sleep. Grandma will rub your back until you fall asleep. Remember, Grandma will always love you best."

TRADGEDIES COME IN THREES

The joy Liah felt over the birth of her new grandson was overshadowed one late July day when Professor walked into the kitchen. Seeing his somber expression, Liah asked with concern in her voice, "What is it, sir?"

Professor, clutching a letter in his hand, said softly, "I have just learned that Elder Lee Ti of the House of Lee in Dai Faw has passed away." As his words sank in, he saw in Liah's eyes that her mind had turned inward and he knew that she was reliving the past, remembering Elder Lee Ti as he was then."

Through a fog, Liah heard Professor say, "We should not mourn for Elder Lee Ti, for he has now been released from his earthly burdens and has joined his ancestors in their eternal peace. He leaves behind a host of people he has assisted and whose lives have been bettered through his actions. His presence will be with us always."

Liah whispered softly, "I am not so much grieving over Elder Lee Ti's passing as he was over ninety years old and had lived a long rich life. Rather, I grieve for all of us who remain. We will miss his wise guidance and counsel. I pray to the Gods that they allow me the time to accomplish all that remains to be done. If I achieve half of what Elder Lee Ti has, I shall count myself fortunate."

Professor nodded and assured Liah that it was his belief that the Gods looked favorably on her as evidenced by all she had accomplished thus far and by the wonderful family she had. Trying to get Liah to focus outwardly again, Professor then asked if Liah wanted him to write a letter to inform Sen. Liah heaved a sigh and seemed to come out of her reverie and nodded wearily, "Yes, please. Sen will want to light a taper to honor the Elder."

—

Liah was still grieving over the death of Elder Lee Ti when a second shock hit. On the thirty-first of July, Dr. Sung dropped by Number Three to deliver the news that Liah's friend Sen Fei was dying. Liah had been half expecting the news as she had watched her good friend rapidly age over the past few months. Nodding she declared, "I will not allow Sen Fei to die in a strange place amongst strangers. We shall move her in here and nurse her until her time comes She will enjoy the remainder of her days with those who love her." Without another word, she rose, went into her bedroom and closed the door Once she was alone, Liah fell on her knees before the altar, and beseeched Kwan Yin to have mercy on Sen Fei and make her final days comfortable.

Sen Fei was soon moved to Number Three and ensconced in First and Second Sons' downstairs bedroom, where it was easier for Sen Fei to move about. For the next several weeks, the family catered to the aged and ill actress. However, Sen Fei enjoyed just being with Liah's family. She delighted in holding Fourth Son's baby boy and took pride in Aileen's accomplishments both in Fahn Gwai school and Chinese school. Sen Fei even taught Aileen several songs that she had sung as a youngster.

Dr. Sung stopped by each day to administer to Sen Fei, pleased to see her smiling despite her failing condition. As he was leaving one day, he turned to Liah and commended her for what she was doing for Sen Fei. Liah replied, "I am only doing what the Gods have enabled me to do. Is that not what friends do for one another?" Dr. Sung nodded and told her, "You are indeed a true friend."

In the early hours of September the fourth, Sen Fei fell into a coma. Only after Dr. Sung determined that she would not regain consciousness did Liah allow Sen Fei to be taken to Mercy Hospital. As the orderlies wheeled the gurney bearing Sen Fei out the door, Liah felt a twinge of guilt. While she had originally planned to let Sen Fei pass on at Number Three, she had changed her mind. She did not want to chance that Sen Fei's spirit would refuse to leave and would continue to hover over the household. Dr. Sung came by two days later to tell them that Sen Fei had passed away quietly without ever having regained consciousness.

—

Liah's sadness over the passing of both Elder Lee Ti and Sen Fei lingered through September and in to October. Being somewhat superstitious, Cook was mildly concerned that another traumatic event was yet to come as the old adage, "Bad things always come in threes" predicted. Finally at the end of October it did, only no one in the household realized it at the time. On the 27th of October Thomas was reading the paper and casually told Liah and Cook about the stock market crash. No one in the family was overly concerned, since they did not own any stocks or bonds. Surely what happened to the Fahn Gwai stock market would not impact them.

—

At Thanksgiving dinner that year, Thomas and Shelley nudged their sister Emmi and whispered to her, "Go ahead, Sis, tell Mah about you and Hubert. Maybe it will lift her out of her doldrums."

Emmi glanced at Hubert, who was nervously sitting beside her at the dinner table, then took a deep breath and announced that they had decided to get married. Liah was silent at first and everyone began to get worried. However, she soon smiled and responded, "It's about time, Second Daughter. I was beginning to wonder if you would ever get married." Everyone laughed and began chattering about the wedding details.

When asked when they wanted to have the ceremony, Emmi looked at her Mother and replied, "If it's all right with you, Mah Mah, we'd like to be married in June—just a small wedding with a few friends and family, nothing elaborate. We'd rather save the money we'd spend on a fancy wedding so that Hubert can buy a new truck for his business."

Liah chuckled and patted her youngest daughter's arm. "We shall not be as lavish as for Eldest Daughter, but the townspeople will not be denied wedding cake and wine. Once you select a date, we will ask Professor to determine if it is an auspicious one."

Between preparing for the holiday celebrations and starting to plan for Emmi's wedding, Liah soon emerged from her self-imposed isolation and began to tackle life again with much of her old zest. Only once in a while did a cloud pass over her as she was reminded of those she had lost.

1930

Year of the Horse

An air of happiness returned to Number Three when Liah put her grief aside, and everyone looked forward with hope for the new year after the sadness of the last.

One morning, Liah was outside inspecting her pots of Chinese lilies and taro roots when she spied her peacock approaching. "Ah, my lonely friend, it has been a long time since we last spoke. Has time managed to blunt your grief over the loss of your mate? How would you like some lettuce leaves?"

She opened the screen door, hoping the peacock would follow her inside and to her great joy, the peacock shrieked raucously then daintily stepped through the doorway. While Liah was feeding the peacock, Professor entered the kitchen and grinned at the sight. "The Gods favor you Liah. The peacock is a potent symbol of good joss and he has entered your home. That is a truly a good omen."

Mei Gem smiled shyly as Professor related the story of how he and Liah had met and how he had told Liah that the peacocks could not be trained. Laughing he said, "That shows you how much I know. Look at him now."

Turning serious, Liah asked the scholar if the date Second Daughter had picked for her wedding was destined to be an auspicious one. Professor nodded and said that he had performed the appropriate calculations and it should indeed be a most auspicious date.

Cook laughed and told Professor, "Second Daughter told her mother they wanted a small wedding. Wait until she learns there are now about two hundred people invited to the wedding feast!"

Liah smiled and replied, "The wedding ceremony itself will only involve the family and close friends just as I promised. However, I said nothing about the size of the wedding banquet. I will not insult people by limiting the attendees."

"By the way, where is Second Daughter?" asked Professor. "I wanted to get her comments on the wedding announcement."

Liah looked up at the clock and replied, "I think she and her husband-to-be went to see Marchesson about a place to live, hopefully some where in Chinatown. Vacancies are scarce these days, I fear they may have to take up residence in another part of town."

Liah was pleased with the roominess of the storefront Second Daughter had managed to rent, even though it was located several blocks from Peacock Alley. She immediately began to tell Emmi exactly how it should be decorated. However, Emmi skillfully negotiated the exact details so that both Liah and she felt like they were getting what they each wanted.

The first half of the year flew by as the wedding preparations intensified. Deluged with the details of the ceremony itself as well as the wedding banquet, Emmi found herself questioning whether things had grown far beyond what she and Hubert had envisioned. Liah smiled and replied, "I only get to marry off my Second Daughter once. Allow me the pleasure of making sure your nuptials are memorable."

"But Mah-Mah," argued Emmi, "I thought perhaps some of the money we'd save with a small wedding feast could be used to help furnish our home." Liah countered, "Don't worry, child, Mah Mah will provide whatever you need." Emmi then shook her head and said, "Hubert takes his responsibilities seriously. He may not want to let you buy everything for us."

Liah smiled again. "Daughter, I do not know of a man who cannot be swayed by the wishes of his wife. You should be able to convince him to accept my gifts to the two of you."

—

On the nineteenth of June, nineteen hundred and thirty, the Chinese Year of the Horse, Emmi and Hubert were finally married. Although Liah had tried her best to persuade the couple to have a Chinese ceremony in the temple, Emmi and Hubert held out for a simple Fahn Gwai civil ceremony. Liah hoped fervently that the Gods would understand the Fahn Gwai tradition of a white wedding dress, white being the color that Chinese usually associated with death and funerals. In an attempt to appease the Gods, Liah had donated fifty dollars to the temple for purchasing tapers and incense for the altars, making sure the priest made it known to the Gods that the gift was in the name of Second Daughter and her husband.

The ensuing banquet lasted five hours and much to Liah's satisfaction was attended by almost all of those who had been invited. Once again, however, Sen's relatives had sent their regrets although they did send generous wedding gifts.

THE DEPRESSION TAKES ITS TOLL

The latter half of the Fahn Gwai year of nineteen hundred and thirty found a good many of Chinatown's residents out of work. Many of them had been laid off from Fahn Gwai businesses that were starting to suffer from the severe economic downturn. Those who still had jobs saw their wages cut sharply. As a consequence, the buildings housing most of the Family Associations as well as the outdoor shelters were overflowing.

At the Council meeting in July, the members learned that Lee Wah was leaving Loo Sahng for Dai Faw. "It is not my desire to move, but one of economic necessity. I am consolidating my business with that of my cousin in the hope that together we can weather these horrible economic times. Moreover, since my merchandise comes through the port of Dai Faw, I will avoid having to pay the extra freight costs to bring the goods to Loo Sahng. Perhaps some good can come of my situation, however. I suggest you contact Marchesson and see if he would be willing to rent my large warehouse to the Council. It can hold many people and has both bathroom and kitchen facilities." Liah and the rest of the Council members expressed their sorrow at his departure and wished him well.

Tom then told the Council that he had heard that the Fahn Gwai government was instituting a program for the needy and wondered out loud if perhaps some of their people should apply for aid. Lim Tao was firmly against the idea. "Tom, I am not demeaning your attempts to help our people, but we have never accepted charity, and certainly not from the Fahn Gwai. Our people will never do that. If the Council sets up quarters in Lee Wah's store and all the families and Tongs take in their own, we will not need outside help. The Council can tap our adversity fund to help provide rent and utility relief and the merchants in Chinatown can contribute food and staples. By banding together and helping each other we can weather this storm."

Several of the other members concurred but Chon Woo asked if perhaps all the talk of a Depression wasn't overblown. He pointed out that he had seen several homes and businesses being repainted and repaired. If times were so difficult, why were people spending money on non-essentials.

Professor responded to Chon Woo's question immediately. "It is true that the House of Wong and the House of Chan are repairing and repainting their buildings. It is also true that the butcher's shop and the laundry are as well. However, the real reason they are doing so is to aid our young men who are without work. While these young men would balk at taking charity, they are more than willing to work. It was

Liah's idea to start these projects to keep our young people from mischief and it's working. Have you also noticed that the eucalyptus trees along Mah Loo are being trimmed and some of our streets are being cleaned up and repaired? Well, Liah herself is paying those men."

Wong Cheung then spoke up suggesting that Liah should not bear the entire burden alone. He recommended that all of the Council members contribute to a fund to sponsor various public works. The idea garnered unanimous support, even Chon Woo agreeing to help out. The ensuing supper was a somber affair as they all realized that it would probably be the last time they would share a meal with Lee Wah.

—

As nineteen hundred and thirty continued to unfold, the Depression hit its stride. Liah's Apinyin trade brought in less than a third of normal, and most of her customers were now buying on credit. Chon Woo's bar fared no better, with business down by half. Liah frowned when her partner bemoaned the drop off in profits. "Chon, it is unseemly for you to be complaining. You've done better than most. People drink in good times and in bad. I only hope you had the brains to save a portion of your monies for times such as these." Chon Woo smiled wanly and Liah knew that he hadn't.

Professor also mentioned to Liah that Tom Soo had considered closing his law office in Chinatown, but didn't want to leave Dr. Sung with the entire expense of their suite of offices. Instead he had found work with a Fahn Gwai law firm and was spending his evenings doing pro bono work in Chinatown.

Liah's family did not escape the hard times either. At first, she noticed that Eldest Son and Second Son were not going out at night nearly as much as they used to. Then Thomas confided to his mother that they had closed down their trucking firm due to the lack of business. Fortunately, they had found jobs working for a Fahn Gwai trucking company, although the work was sporadic. Mert, too, was suffering. His fledgling electrical repair business went under and his hours and wages at the garage where he worked as an auto mechanic had been slashed.

CHRISTMAS

Christmas that year reminded Liah a lot of their first Christmas in Loo Sahng. The tree was small, the gifts were few, but the Christmas spirit was present in abundance. Despite a severe lack of ingredients, Cook managed to put together a dinner that rivaled all of his previous ones.

That night, Liah gave thanks to the Gods that even in this time of hardship they had continued to bless her with the necessities of life and the health and love of her family and friends. Liah was also grateful that she had enough to share with the outdoor people: a small gift for each of them, with a slab of roast pig, and a bottle of Ng Ga Pei.

When December 31st arrived, for the first time in years Thomas and Shelley joined their younger brothers and sisters to usher in the new year. As midnight approached, Cook prepared a draught of Apinyin for Liah and told the crowd of revelers, "Once Liah is asleep, you can play your records as loudly as you want and make all the racket you want. She won't hear a thing."

1932

YEAR OF THE MONKEY

Despite their prayers, the Depression continued unabated through 1931 and most of 1932. In his idle time, Thomas closely followed the hotly contested race for President between President Herbert Hoover and Governor Franklin D. Roosevelt. Roosevelt's confidence and his proposed New Deal program appealed to Thomas and gave him renewed hope that Roosevelt's election might finally signal a turnaround.

When Roosevelt won by an overwhelming margin, Thomas was hopeful that an economic recovery would soon ensue. However, the damage to the economy and the fabric of American society was too severe to overcome in a mere year or two. It would be some time before Thomas and Shelly would reestablish their trucking business. Meanwhile Liah and her family continued to eke out a living and help those that they could.

1933

YEAR OF THE ROOSTER

Liah was somber as nineteen hundred and thirty-three arrived. The swift passage of time dismayed her and the seemingly endless Depression had finally worn away some of her armor.

"I'm tired of being so frugal," she declared to Cook one day late in December. This coming year, we will lavishly celebrate our New Year of the Rooster. We will distribute moon cakes, side pork and Ng Ga Pei to all the outdoor people as well as to the infirm and needy in Chinatown. I shall also light coils of incense on their behalf, begging Kwan Yin to improve their lot in life."

Cook wryly suggested that Liah ought to at least wait until the Fahn Gwai New Year was over before making plans for the Chinese New Year. "I hear your sons are again planning on spending their New Year's Eve at home." He paused then went on, "I have it in mind to speak with Eldest Son and Second Son about reopening their trucking business. They will not take monies from you, but perhaps they will accept my help. Do you have any objection if I ask?"

Tears of gratitude formed in Liah's eyes. So great a love she felt for Cook, she almost cried. "Indeed not, sir. I thank you for offering and, of course, I shall reimburse you, should my sons accept."

Cook scowled. "You'll do no such thing, Liah! They are as much my sons as yours. We are a family."

When the celebration of Chinese New Year was over, Cook finally spoke with Thomas. For almost the first time in his life, Thomas sat dumbfounded as he listened to Cook's generous offer. That Cook should rob his savings in times such as these to help him deeply touched Thomas and his overwhelming emotions robbed him of speech. He thought to himself yet again that his mother was indeed fortunate to have such a man.

When words would at last come, Thomas softly thanked Cook, but explained that the time was not yet right to venture out on his own again. He and Shelley planned to remain at their jobs for at least another year. "Perhaps at that time we might inquire if your most generous offer is still open. For now, however, my brother and I are most grateful for your concern and generosity."

Cook nodded and replied, "There is no need for gratitude, Eldest Son. You must understand that I think of you as my family. Rest assured the money will be available to you whenever you need it."

—

On the fourth day of March in the Fahn Gwai year of nineteen hundred and thirty-three, Franklin Delano Roosevelt was inaugurated as the thirty-second president of the United States. When Thomas told his mother about the President's New Deal and the plan for a farm and business relief act, Liah shook her head and commented that the Fahn Gwai could learn much from the Chinese. "Isn't that the way we've survived all these years in Gem Sahn? Those who have help those who have not. At this very moment, are not our Family Associations and public houses filled to capacity with the needy? Don't we ourselves care for the outdoor people?" Thomas listened stoically to his mother but for once found nothing to say. What she said was the truth.

SHOCK WAVES

A few days later, Liah was seated at the supper table with her family when suddenly she heard a sharp cracking noise and the whole house started to shake. For a moment, Liah was sure the house was going to collapse. The cupboards flew open and dishes, pots and pans as well as jars of food and condiments rained down on the floor.

No sooner had the first temblor dissipated, than another violent shudder shook the house and Liah was again afraid they would be killed when the structure collapsed on top of them. Mei Gem screamed and dropped her chopsticks, grabbing her young son and clutching him to her bosom. It was all William could do to calm his wife.

As soon as the second shock wave died out, Thomas sprang to his feet and told everyone to get outside immediately. When Liah wanted to remain behind to telephone Eldest Daughter, Thomas ordered his mother out telling her that he would call instead. "You should lead them outside and help to calm Mei Gem and Aileen."

Against her will, Cook and Mert escorted Liah and the others outside. As they passed the outdoor shelter, Liah saw an old man scrambling to gather his few meager belongings. Liah cried out, "Old one, leave those things. Your life is worth more than they are. Come with us to safety."

Once out in the rail yard, Liah looked back at Number Three and prayed to Kwan Koong to protect their home. In her heart was stark terror. It was the same fear that had gripped her each time she had to flee from the Fahn Gwai. Praying also to Kwan Yin, Liah silently cried, "Please spare our home, beneficent Kwan Yin! I am too old to start over again."

Just then Thomas sprinted up to his mother and informed her that nobody answered the phone at his sister's house. Fearing the worst, Emmi began sobbing as did Aileen and Mei Gem. Thomas looked at them sternly and told them to be quiet. "They are probably fine and on their way here now." Thomas then said he was going to return to Number Three to listen to the news on the radio. "I'll come back when I find something out."

An hour later, Thomas appeared at their rear door and gestured for the family to return. He shouted, "The radio says the immediate danger is over. The center of the earthquake was in Long Beach where there is extensive destruction. But we're safe. Come on back."

The next day, Thomas informed his mother of the many deaths in Long Beach. Liah blanched and lit several coils of incense to Kwan Koong and Kwan Yin, beseeching mercy for their departed souls. She also humbly thanked the God and Goddess for her family's safe passage through the earthquake. Once again she sadly contemplated the whimsy of the Gods, that they could be so benevolent one day and so wrathful the next.

Fifth Son made a check of Chinatown for his mother and reported no major damage. He also said that he had visited Selah and that she and her girls were shaken but was all right. Later Professor came by and described the various damage suffered by the merchants, "Most were sweeping up the messes made when their wares fell on the floor and broke. I pity the fishmonger who had to pick up all the seafood that littered his floor. Some of the lobsters and crabs had even managed to escape outside."

Professor then shook his head and sighed, "This is certainly an inauspicious beginning to this year." Suddenly he noticed the rows of ceremonial papers sitting on one of the kitchen shelves and inquired what event they were for. Liah smiled, "Fourth Son's son will be four years old in a few months. We shall celebrate on the twelfth day of May and also thank the Gods for sparing our lives during the quake. Moreover, it appears that I'm to be a grandmother again. Mei Gem is with child again."

"Well!" exclaimed Professor, "That is more like it—some good news for a change. I'm so happy for you, Liah. When will the infant be birthed?" Liah replied, "In October, sir. As usual I would request that you prepare the child's horoscope."

Liah's face then took on a worried expression. "I've been meaning to ask you to write a letter to Sen for me, if you would. I've felt uneasy about Third Son ever since his departure. To date, I have been unable to decipher the Gods' message and frankly I am worried. I have done nothing but berate myself for ever allowing Third Son to leave. Please ask Sen if he has any news."

Professor had just agreed, when Aileen threw open the front door and bolted into the house, shouting that The Cat was coming. Soon Hans' bulk filled the kitchen doorway. "Mama!" grinned Hans, "How you? Savvy me, Apinyin?"

Liah's seriousness gave way to a mischievous smile as she screwed up her face and mimicked a cat, "Miaow! You no catchee me! Savvy? You no can see!"

Little John appeared behind Hans and listened to their banter. Once again it seemed impossible that the tiny woman before him could have done all the things that his partner claimed she had done, but then his partner knew the Chinese so much better than he ever would. Seeing Aileen, Little John walked over and asked how she was doing in school. "I hear from Sim that you're a very smart girl and hard-working. Is that so?"

Aileen gulped, stared a moment at Little John, then a slight smile spread across her face and she replied, "Yes, sir, I'm doing fine. Sim is now going to high school so I don't see him much any more. He also works very hard."

A sharp stab of conscience struck Little John. It had always been on his mind to ask Sim if he wanted to live with him, but somehow he'd never gotten around to it. He begrudgingly admitted to himself that the reason why he hadn't was that he feared the raised eyebrows and worse of his neighbors and friends. Suddenly, Little John felt a nudge and Hans told him it was time to leave. "Well, the next time you see Sim, please tell him to call me. We haven't talked in a while and I want to hear what he's been up to." Aileen said she would and the two policemen left.

SHOCK AND GRIEF

On a particularly hot late September day, Professor brought Liah a letter from Sen. Professor tore open the envelope, put on his spectacles and scanned the first page. His eyes widened and he hurriedly read the second page, finally raising his eyes to meet Liah's.

"What is it, sir?"

Professor took off his spectacles and wiped his face, then in a soft flat voice told Liah that her Third Son was dead. "Dead? How? When?" she cried as she fell back in her chair.

For a long moment, Professor stared at Liah. It seemed that she had suddenly aged before his very eyes. Cook hurried over to comfort her but Liah seemed oblivious to Cook's touch as well as to the presence of the scholar. All at once Liah rose from her chair, shuffled into her bedroom, and shut the door.

Inside her room, Liah fell upon the bed, sobs wracking her body. Why, oh, why, had she allowed Third Son to leave? She should have suspected his plan was to join in the fight against the Japanese. She realized now that the unease she had been feeling was The Gods warning her and she had failed to understand. She had failed in her parental duties, and for that, now Third Son was dead.

Later in the day Liah's family and friends including Professor, Tom, and Selah huddled together in the kitchen, grieving, and waiting for Liah to come out of her bedroom. Finally at ten o'clock that night, Cook entered her darkened room and, after some time, led a frail and hollow cheeked Liah into the kitchen.

Upon seeing her grandma, Aileen threw herself into her arms, sobbing hysterically as the rest of the group gathered around wiping at their own tears. Ten minutes later, Dr. Sung, summoned by Fourth Son, entered the kitchen and gazed with concern at Liah. Meeting her dull reddened eyes he tried to silently convey that he understood her pain, then slowly led her into her bedroom and shut the door.

A half-hour later, Dr. Sung reappeared, looking worried. He faced Liah's family and friends and told them, "Liah is, as you know, suffering terribly and while her heart is strong, her respiratory system is not. Her years of Apinyin use have weakened her lungs. She will likely survive the night, however, her longer-term prognosis is difficult to calculate. I want her watched continuously and, if she seems to have difficulty breathing, please notify me at once."

Reaching into his black bag, Dr. Sung then withdrew a small bottle of pills, which he handed to Fourth Son. "See to it that you all take one of these sedatives tonight. Time and rest will do the most to help ease the pain and sorrow I know you are all feeling. Although it does nothing to help you or Liah right now, Liah herself would acknowledge that Third Son's death was destined by his Meng Sui; so while it is appropriate to grieve for him now, do not let his passing prevent you from living your own lives in accordance with your own Meng Sui."

Dr. Sung then turned to Cook and whispered, "Yours is the unenviable task of tending to their sorrows, sir. May Kwan Koong grant you the strength. I'll be back tomorrow morning to check on Liah."

—

The next day Liah had recovered enough to declare that the family would observe a mourning period of thirty days, a common Chinese bereavement custom. "During this time you must be prepared to receive the spirit of your brother should he return to bid a last farewell to his home and family. As his mother, I will mourn for a year."

Throughout the period of mourning, the doorway to Number Three was draped in white, and everyone wore white clothing. The family abstained from drinking liquor and partaking of all pleasure. In the morning, at noon and again at night the burning of incense was accompanied by a prayer to the Gods to show mercy toward Third Son and grant him eternal peace. Three times a day, Liah prepared a tray containing Third Son's favorite dishes and set it on Kwan Koong's altar.

Liah refused almost all visitors, speaking only with Professor on matters of importance and with Selah, with whom she shared a few words each day. Most of the time she just sat silently in thought.

During that month of mourning, Aileen found herself shut out of her grandma's life and turned tearfully to Selah for comfort. Not only had Aileen lost her favorite brother, but it seemed as if she had lost her grandma too. Thomas became the de facto head of the house, although Cook and Amah continued to perform their normal tasks.

In the middle of October, Amah assisted Mei Gem in the birthing of her second child, another son. Despite William's pleas, Liah refused to go near Mei Gem or the infant, saying that the aura of death still surrounded her and she did not want to endanger either of them. The fact that she now had nine grandchildren, Eldest Daughter's six children, Fourth Son's two sons and Second Daughter's infant son, brought some comfort to Liah. However, thoughts of all her grandchildren could not erase the grief for the one son she had lost and Liah was soon overwhelmed by sorrow again.

As the holidays approached, Liah gave no indication whether the family would be celebrating this year or not. Finally, Thomas turned to Cook to ask his advice. However, Cook, who had noticeably aged as Liah remained in her self-imposed dungeon, merely shrugged his shoulders saying, "It is your decision, Eldest Son. The family will abide by your decision."

In the end they had a quiet Thanksgiving dinner with only Professor, Tom, and Selah present in addition to the family. Throughout the meal, Selah made light banter, shying away from any topic that might open any wounds for Liah. When dinner was over, Liah smiled sadly and thanked Selah, Tom, and Professor for coming. Softly she said, "I also thank my children who have tried to make my bereavement period as painless as they can. In the end, however, time is the only effective healing agent. I have been praying day and night to Kwan Koong and Kwan Yin for solace and for Third Son's eternal peace. If you will just bear with me a bit longer, I shall try my best to put aside my grief." Liah's voice then dropped to almost a whisper and she gazed at them with weary eyes. "However, it is so difficult. It seems like I am trying to climb a tall black mountain at night never knowing if I will ever reach the top."

1934

YEAR OF THE DOG

With no discernable improvement in Liah's condition, Christmas was celebrated much as Thanksgiving had been and the family agreed not to usher in the New Year with their traditional party. While Liah slept on New Year's Eve, the family ate a quiet supper with Willie who had just graduated from college and was home for good. His presence perked Aileen up and for the first time she discussed accepting the scholarship she'd been offered to attend the Los Angeles College of Creative Arts. Wistfully, Aileen said, "If only Grandma would talk to me. I so much want to share my happiness with her."

Emmi nodded and, clasping her two-month-old son tight, cried, "It's as if Mah-Mah isn't with us any more. Like she's spending all her time and energy holding on to Theo and won't let him go." Cook, who had become increasingly silent and morose as time passed, suddenly looked up and his face took on a determined look, "You are absolutely correct, Second Daughter! It is time that Third Son be allowed to seek his eternal peace. Your mother must let him be. We all must let him be."

They all stared at Cook, amazed by his transformation. Finally, Mert sighed and glanced at Cook, "You are right, sir. Theo would be mad at us for not letting him go."

"Good!" Cook's voice rang out authoritatively. "Now, I must speak of your mother who, I fear, is gravely ill. The combination of too much Apinyin and no food is killing her. It's almost as if she wants to join her son in death. We must find a way to lure her back to the land of the living. We must, or else we'll lose her."

Aileen's voice quavered, "I don't want Grandma to die, Cook! I need her! Grandma can't die!"

Thomas growled tenderly, "Yeah, we all need her; but I don't know what we can do. I'll talk with Dr. Sung tomorrow. Perhaps he'll have some suggestions."

—

Liah was abed when Dr. Sung arrived the next night. When he entered her bedroom, he was instantly assailed by the heady scent of incense, the acrid smell of burnt tapers and the faint sweet odor of Apinyin. "How can you stand this, Liah? I can't even breathe."

Liah stared at the Doctor dully, not quite recognizing him. When her eyes finally did focus, she moaned, "Do not waste your time on me Doctor. You should tend to those who still want to live."

"So!" accused Dr. Sung, "Because Third Son was killed, you believe that you should follow him? Third Son's Meng Sui dictated his path, not yours."

Sitting down on the edge of her bed he reached for her bony wrist and took her pulse. Then he cleaned his thermometer and placed it under her tongue. While waiting for the thermometer to register her temperature, he said, "It's such a shame about your granddaughter. Have you noticed her lately? For that matter, have you noticed your Fifth Son?"

Liah's eyes suddenly opened wide with concern. Had something happened to them? Dr. Sung said matter-of-factly, "For the past several months those two have shared your grief. They have lost weight and have become hollowed-eyed and listless. Aileen in particular has been grieving not only for her third uncle, but for you as well. She's afraid that you're going to die too and leave her alone with no one to love her."

All the time he administered to Liah, Dr. Sung kept up a running commentary on the effect she was having on each member of the family, and even hinted that Chinatown was not the same. Liah tried to sit up only to fall weakly back on her pillows. In a tiny voice, she begged the doctor to help her granddaughter and son.

"I'm sorry, Liah, there is nothing I can do for you, your granddaughter or your son. Only you can cure their ills. So it comes down to this. If you want to die, they will suffer as well. If you want to help them, you must let Theo go and return to the family that still lives and still needs you. It's your choice. May Kwan Yin guide your decision."

Dr. Sung shook his head as he emerged from Liah's bedroom. "I've done and said all I can. The rest is up to Liah. I'm sorry, kids. I will stop by tomorrow, unless something comes up and you need me sooner."

The next night, the entire family was eating dinner when the bedroom door opened and Liah walked shakily into the kitchen. Cook leaped to his feet and ran over to steady her.

"Well?" she said. "Why didn't someone tell me supper was ready?"

There was a moment of shocked silence, then the room erupted in laughter. The family took turns hugging her and Liah spoke softly to each in turn. Finally Liah turned to Aileen, smiled, and said, "Child, you look too thin. Dr. Sung told me you and Fifth Son have not been eating properly." Aileen cried tears of joy as she hugged her Grandma tightly.

Thomas chuckled. "Look who's talking about not eating properly!"

Amah tearfully embraced Liah and Cook slumped happily in his chair, feeling the block of ice that had formed in his soul start to melt. The woman he loved had returned to him.

—

The year of bereavement crept by slowly as the sun rose each day and set each night. Liah did her penance before the altar, praying for her son's eternal peace before Kwan Yin and Kwan Koong and offered up daily and nightly coils of incense and lighted tapers. While still weighed down with grief, Liah made superhuman efforts to spend time with her children. Even Eldest Daughter was solicitous to her mother, making certain nothing riled her. Finally, the year of bereavement had passed and a traditional feast for the family concluded their time of sorrow. Selah, Tom, and Professor were the only outsiders invited; however, Liah considered them an integral part of her family.

After dinner, Selah took Liah's hand in hers and said quietly, "Little lady, today you bid your final farewell to Third Son and he is now forever with his ancestors. It is time to focus on taking care of the living, which includes yourself. You must put the flesh back on your bones and stop abusing the lovely body the Gods gave you."

Long after the family was abed, Cook and Liah sat at the table in the kitchen with Cook holding Liah's hand. "You do not know how relieved I am that you have chosen to return to us. While you have been suffering with your own demons, I have endured my own purgatory, wanting to somehow ease your burden but knowing there was nothing I could do."

Liah's eyes misted and a sad little smile flitted across her face at the thought of the pain she had inflicted on those around her. "Ah, my true and good friend, I know I have been terribly selfish. Now that Third Son has begun his eternal rest, there is no more I can do for him. However, there is much I can still do for all of you. I will make amends. I promise."

Liah saw Cook's unshed tears and reached out to comfort him. The pent-up sorrow he had not expressed all during the bereavement period because the family needed him to remain strong now poured out as he sobbed in Liah's arms. "Weep," whispered Liah, "let the tears fall that you've held in for so long. Then we both must learn to laugh and love again."

Quietly they went upstairs and in the stillness and darkness of night, Liah and Cook renewed their bond. Afterward, Liah whispered, her

voice filled with love, "I had forgotten how good it feels to love you."
Cook, wordlessly, drew her close, later to murmur that it was time she
returned to her own bed.

—

Although she had not yet fully recovered her strength, the family insisted on celebrating her birthday. Thus on the twenty-ninth day of September, Liah gave in to family pressure and celebrated her sixtieth
birthday. While the party was a festive affair, Liah confided to Selah
that the years were starting to weigh on her and that she feared that the
Gods would not allow her the time to complete all the tasks she had set
for herself. Selah gently scolded her saying, "Push those thoughts from
your mind, Liah. The Gods have always favored you and your endeavors. It is your Meng Sui. If you take care of yourself, you might outlive
us all." Liah smiled and nodded, "Perhaps you are right. The Gods
favor those who help themselves rather than those who wait for help."

PEACOCK ALLEY

Early the next morning, Liah gazed out her front door at her beloved
Alley. The curtain of mist had not yet burned off, giving the cobblestones a mysterious, unfathomable depth. She had awakened early and,
unable to sleep, had gotten up. The house was quiet. She stepped outside and her eyes took in the acacia tree now faintly visible through the
shroud of mist. She then scanned the long garden at the rear of Peacock
Alley where the once decrepit fig tree still braved the elements.

It was incredible she thought—thirty years had passed since she first
came to Loo Sahng. So much had changed during that time, some for
the good and admittedly some for the bad; so much laughter had been
shared and so many tears as well. A kaleidoscope of images flashed be-

fore her eyes. Her mind came to rest on one particularly vivid memory, her first meeting with Professor. Without him, she would not have realized her dream, a permanent home, safe and without fear. Her eyes roved to Professor's blue door and silently gave him thanks.

She pulled her padded kimono closer as she walked toward the rear of the Alley. The fig tree was now symmetrically shaped and Liah thought fondly of Hoh Chan. It had been humid and hot when the wizen-faced old man appeared at Number Three one September morning in his oversized, pointed straw hat, thongs, pantaloons and jacket, the brown color of the rice farmers. With his long, flowing beard and beady bright eyes shining through the creases in his sunburned face, he was indeed the image of the God of Wisdom. He had used that wisdom to transform the drab alley into a paradise of color and fragrant aromas. She smiled as she recalled that Hoh Chan had volunteered to restore the foliage without even asking for a stipend. However, she had insisted he accept a token ten dollars a month and her invitation to take some of his meals with her. He had accepted reluctantly. Later Liah would come to find out that the old man had an abundance of pride and would not accept anything that looked like charity.

Liah inspected the roses, now heavy with buds. How that old man had labored. Not only did he cultivate the soil, fertilize, and prune, but also he took the excess plants to Mah Loo, in an attempt to beautify that pungent drab dirt road. Even the old fig tree now gave abundant fruit.

Liah thoughts then wandered to her children. Although it seemed impossible, Eldest Son was now forty-two. Second Son was forty-one, and, alas, still unwed. Liah frowned as she thought of her eldest daughter, now the mother of six and forty years of age. Tears came as Liah thought of Third Son. He would be thirty-eight years old if the Gods had not plucked him from the earth. Lest she fall into a morbid mood, she quickly moved on to Fourth Son, now a 36 year old professor and father of two sons. Fifth Son, so like her in nature, was now thirty-five, and also unwed. Liah shook her head sadly. Despite her many accomplishments, she had not achieved the goal of finding suitable wives for all her sons. She then smiled as she thought of her youngest child, Second Daughter, the 31-year-old mother of three sons, including the recent pair of twins.

Thinking of her eleven grandchildren brought a smile to Liah's face. The Gods had indeed been generous, despite the sadness they'd thrust on her. She glanced at her wristwatch and saw it was seven o'clock. Cook would be rising soon. She took in a deep breath of the fragrant air and made her way back to Number Three.

1939

YEAR OF THE RABBIT

The ensuing years were kind to Liah. She finally got to see her remaining sons marry, even though Thomas wed a Fahn Gwai woman over her strenuous objections. While she would have much preferred he take a Chinese bride, she thanked the Gods that he was at least married. Liah also felt great pride when Aileen graduated from the Los Angeles College of Creative Arts and began a career as an author of children's books. Chinatown itself continued to grow and, while Liah still participated in Council affairs, she relinquished the Chairmanship as younger more energetic Council Members were elected.

—

Liah awakened on September twenty-ninth, in the Fahn Gwai Year of nineteen hundred and thirty-nine, her sixty-fifth year on earth. A smile played on her face as she thought about the weeks of birthday preparations put in by her family, naively thinking that they could keep it secret from her. Poor Cook. When she had asked what he was going to cook for her birthday supper, he had not the skill to deceive her and had reluctantly admitted that the children were planning to take her to dinner at a nice restaurant. The Gods had truly been generous when they sent Cook into her life. She glanced up at the clock and saw it was almost noon, time to rise. As she threw the minhois back, she grinned to herself; she'd have make enough noise to warn the family that she was awake, just in case they were doing something they didn't want her to see.

When she finally walked into the kitchen, the entire family was seated around the table waiting. Gifts were heaped on a tray beside her upholstered chair. Each of her children embraced her and gave her a kiss as they wished her a happy birthday. Liah laughed as Mei Gem's son and Emmi's twins surged forward to give their grandmother kisses. "Stop, you're strangling me. Grandma will kiss each of you, one at a time."

As soon as lunch was over, Liah began opening her gifts. Her first present was from Fourth Son and Mei Gem and she gasped when her eyes took in the beautiful jade and pearl necklace with a clasp adorned with gold peaches. Mei Gem bowed low, shyly murmuring, "Honored Mother, may this day of felicitations follow you throughout your life."

Next came a padded satin robe with matching slippers from Emmi and Hubert. One by one she opened the many gifts and praised the thoughtfulness of the donors. Cook was pleased as Liah smiled broadly when she saw the seven-inch ivory cigarette holder and jeweled cigarette case he had given her. The final gift brought a gasp from Liah as she unwrapped a necklace made of gold coins. Thomas indicated it was from everyone in the family. Just then the front door slammed and they heard the sound of someone in flip-flops making their way to the kitchen. Liah grinned, "It's the old one."

Hoh Chan burst into the kitchen lugging a large heavy tub. "Much happiness on this, your birthday, Madam. I thought you'd enjoy having this kumquat tree in your front room. I personally grafted it from a tree that bears large, luscious fruit." He then plunked the tub onto the floor and grinned broadly. Liah's eyes sparkled with joy. Of all the gifts she'd received this day, Hoh Chan's was most special. The old man, having no worldly wealth, had nevertheless given her a gift from his heart and the sweat of his brow. She could almost envision him each morning and night, watering, nurturing, and pruning with loving care, the healthy three-foot-tall fruit tree. Tears of gratitude formed in her eyes, as Liah thanked him.

Cook then offered up a toast. "No birthday is complete without a toast. We drink to Liah's health and happiness. Wealth, she already has in the form of her loving family and friends. Happy Birthday!"

Liah lifted her cup and replied, "It is true. Mother shall never be poor while I have all of you around me. Mother is today the happiest woman in the world."

Thomas then grinned and said, "We have one more gift for you Mah-Mah. We have made reservations for supper at the Lotus House." Feigning surprise, Liah smiled with a sidelong glance at Cook and told them that would indeed be a special treat.

—

Liah spurned Thomas's offer to drive her to the restaurant. Instead, Aileen took her grandmother's hand and led her to the door. "Come on, Grandma, let's give the town a treat. It's been a long time since we've walked together in Chinatown. Liah smiled and nodded, motioning for the rest of the family to follow.

Once outside in Peacock Alley, she turned her head to look back and smiled happily, murmuring, "My, but the family has grown." She motioned for William to pick up his almost six-year-old son saying, "I don't want him dusty and dirty by the time we get to the restaurant."

As Liah and her entourage entered Marchesson Street, Liah chuckled. "This will quiet the gossips that believe I am either ill or crippled."

It took almost an hour for Liah and her family to traverse the remaining six blocks to the restaurant. Mei Gem smiled rather proudly and whispered to her husband that her mother-in-law was certainly well respected, "It seems we stop every few feet to speak with people who wish to pay their respects. They also seem to genuinely love her, don't you think?"

Jew Soo, owner of the restaurant was waiting at the entrance to welcome Liah. He congratulated her on her birthday, pressed the traditional small red envelope into her hands as he bowed, and then led them upstairs to the large private dining room.

Liah walked slowly up the stairs to the landing leading to the private room and as she crossed the threshold, the room erupted with an almost deafening, "Surprise!" Liah smiled at Selah and Professor, then tears misted Liah's eyes as she caught sight of Cousin Quock, Cousin Shah with his wife and sons, and Fatt On. Even Sen's second, third and fourth cousins were present.

Thomas shouted, "Look, everyone! For the first time in my mother's life, she is without words!" Everyone laughed and Liah started going around the room greeting everyone.

"Cousin Quock," inquired Liah, "are you yet fishing? I shall never forget the taste of those delicious crabs and shrimps you used to bring us. I am indeed honored by your presence."

The tall, yet husky bald-headed fisherman flushed pleasurably as his booming voice carried across the room. "Nonsense. It is I who am honored to be here. I am amazed by how well you look and by how much your family has grown!"

Liah's face was filled with love as she next greeted Fatt On. "Ah, my old friend. I cannot count the times I have thanked the Gods for bringing you into our lives. The generosity and kindness you have shown us over the years can never be repaid. I thank you now from the bottom of my heart."

Fatt On blushed as they exchanged a glance acknowledging their long history. He then reached for his cup and said, "A toast to Liah, whose vision and perseverance has brought sustenance, safety, and comfort to many. May health, wealth and happiness be your constant companions."

The ensuing ten-course banquet lasted a full five hours. Selah and Thomas, acting as hostess and host, kept the liquor flowing and Liah visited each table to mingle with all the attendees. When she came to Cousin Shah's table, Liah was unsure how he would greet her. It seemed ages ago that they had quarreled over Lee Tzo joining the Council. Would he still harbor resentment? Her trepidation was forgotten, however, as Cousin Shah warmly congratulated her on her birthday and introduced his wife and children.

As she listened to the speeches after dinner, Liah reflected on all the people she had interacted with in Chinatown over the long years: Professor, without whom she could not have established and maintained the Council; Selah, whose loyalty and intelligence provided Liah with another woman to share her problems with; Dr. Sung, Sallie, Tom Soo, Chon Woo, even Wong Sang; all had been an integral part of her life. To Wong Cheung she felt especially grateful, as it was his silent strength and loyalty that had protected her during the stormy years when Lee Tzo was trying to oust her and take over the Council. Liah was saddened as her thoughts settled for a moment on the murdered Sam Yin. She hoped that Sui Yin and her son had been able to start a new life in China. She also said a silent prayer to the Gods for her departed friend Sen Fei and Elder Lee Ti of Dai Faw. Then Liah's mind turned to the Dobneys on whose estate her children had received their early education. Liah wondered briefly what had happened to her mistress from whom she had received the incomparable gift of her koong jeks. Hopefully, Kwan Yin had answered Liah's prayers and her mistress was now happy and content.

The faces she saw in her mind's eye blurred into the sea of smiling faces before her as Liah heard Selah's voice praising her for her undaunted efforts to forge Chinatown into a safe place for her people to thrive. "Through Liah's heroic efforts, we now go about our lives without the fear of Fahn Gwai persecution, our children are taught to honor our Chinese heritage and culture in our own school, and we worship in our temple. Let us drink a toast to the most courageous and dedicated woman in Chinatown."

Liah raised her glass to acknowledge the applause and her eyes met Selah's for a second, both feeling the unspoken love and unbreakable bond between them. Next it was Cook's turn. He had not wanted to speak, but Liah's children had insisted. It was Eldest Son who had persuaded him saying, "Cook, we all know that you love Mother and that she loves you as well. It is only right that you sit beside her at dinner and speak your heart. You should know that we children think of you as we would a father." Liah would have cried had she known how much her children thought of Cook. Nevertheless, Cook was somewhat embarrassed and merely toasted Liah quickly saying, "To the woman we all love and admire." His eyes betrayed the full extent of the love he felt.

Professor concluded the speeches with accolades for Liah's unwavering efforts to unify Chinatown; for her generosity made without public fanfare; and for her unselfish devotion to the cause of advancing the lot of all Chinese. Professor then went on, "Today is an auspicious day, not only because it is Liah's feast day, but because it is also the anniversary of the day Liah first set foot in Chinatown. Our lives today are much improved because of her foresight and courage and few know the agonies she has endured and the sacrifices she has made to achieve her goals. So with sincere and humble gratitude, I offer up a toast. May the Gods continue to favor her, may they bestow upon her peace of mind and may they allow her to age with dignity. May her clan increase and may succeeding generations remember and appreciate what Liah has done for them. A toast every one!"

Liah's vision blurred as she acknowledged the tumultuous applause. Her glass held high, she stood beside Cook and her eldest son, smiling through her tears.

When everyone had been reseated, Liah fondled the necklace of gold coins her children had just given her, and began to speak in a soft voice, "Many years ago, I dreamt of a town for our people, a place where we could safely live, birth our children, and prosper. Today that dream is a reality. However, it was not me alone who made this dream come true. None of this could have been achieved if it were not for the dedication and tenacity of the Council." Liah then raised her glass. "I want to personally thank each and every Council member for their loyalty, their efforts, and, most of all, for their belief in my dream. I also want to thank the one man who stands out from all these without whose assistance and wisdom, my dream would have remained only a dream. He is surely the Golden Warrior in this Golden Land. I propose a toast to On Wei, otherwise known as Professor, and all the members of the Council."

The scholar was stunned and his vision clouded as he rose to acknowledge the applause. When the noise died down, he asked everyone to raise their glasses for a final toast, "I propose a toast to all of us; may Kwan Koong and Kwan Yin in their infinite wisdom and mercy guide our steps so that we fulfill our Meng Sui and honor our ancestors."

The farewells were lengthy, especially for those who lived out of town, for Liah sensed it might also be good-bye. With each handshake and smile, Liah felt a pang of sadness, for at their age, would they ever see each other again?

On the walk back to Number Three Liah continued to bask in the glow of the celebration. Moreover, she felt content. "Who would have ever thought that we would have achieved so much?" She smiled as she thought, "I wonder what Sen would say now?"

Alone in her bedroom that night, Liah reflected on her sixty-five years on earth. The memories were still fresh in her mind and it seemed incredible that so much time had passed. As she unconsciously fingered the necklace of coins still around her neck, her thoughts turned again to her children and grandchildren and she whispered a prayer to Kwan Yin to keep them safe. Then she felt a catch in her throat and wiped away a tear as she thought of Third Son. In the darkness, Liah whispered, "Mother is not forgetting you, Third Son. You will always be in my thoughts and prayers. Someday we shall be reunited but until then I must continue to allow my Meng Sui to unfold."

Soon afterwards, Liah fell asleep, vaguely aware that the constriction around her heart since Theo's death had finally eased. Dimly, she felt a sense of well-being steal over her. In her dreams that night, Liah walked the cobblestones of her beloved Peacock Alley with her peacock and his mate, omens of good joss and happiness.

About the author

Dorothy Hom grew up during the first half of the 20th century in Los Angeles Chinatown, a motley, dusty, smelly area along Alameda Street near the Union Pacific and Southern Pacific train yards. Two unpaved roads crossed a three-block-long stretch that ended at a dusty dirt road that housed a stable and a slaughterhouse. These were known to the inhabitants as the "stinky perfume makers."

The only beautiful spot in this otherwise bleak neighborhood that ran along the chain-link fence separating it from the train yards was an alley, a cobblestone walk just a block-and-a-half long with a jumble of lilies, geraniums, and thorny bushes lining the fence. A trellis covered one part of the walkway and there a profusion of honeysuckle vines gave off a welcome aroma.

At the entrance to the alley, a brave acacia tree offered some protection against the hot summer sun and chilling winter winds. An ancient, tired fig tree at the other end of the alley kept company with the trash bins and garbage cans. A peacock and his hen stood guard; they seemed to be able to distinguish between residents and outsiders and noisily prevented strangers from entering.

Everyone knew Dorothy and she knew everyone. She also knew that she was her grandma's favorite grandchild.

It is said that little children have big ears, and Dorothy certainly had them, with big eyes to boot. Otherwise, how could she have known about the many intrigues and passions that played out in the alley, which gives life to the many composite characters she so adroitly brings to this novel?

Although Dorothy is a published poet, this is her first novel. She continues to live in Los Angeles, enjoying her books, her garden, her friends, and her family.

ABOOKS

ALIVE Book Publishing and ALIVE Publishing Group
are imprints of Advanced Publishing LLC,
3200 A Danville Blvd., Suite 204, Alamo, California 94507

Telephone: 925.837.7303 Fax: 925.837.6951
www.alivebookpublishing.com

CPSIA information can be obtained at www.ICGtesting.com
Printed in the USA
BVOW03*0746140314

347377BV00002B/2/P